Mountain Top

DEEPER WATER

ROBERT WHITLOW

THOMAS NELSON
Since 1798

NASHVILLE DALLAS MEXICO CITY RIO DE JANEIRO BEIJING

Published in Nashville, Tennessee, by Thomas Nelson. Thomas Nelson is a registered trademark of Thomas Nelson, Inc.

Thomas Nelson, Inc., titles may be purchased in bulk for educational, business, fund-raising, or sales promotional use. For information, please e-mail SpecialMarkets@ThomasNelson.com.

Publisher's Note: This novel is a work of fiction. Names, characters, places, and incidents are either products of the author's imagination or used fictitiously. All characters are fictional, and any similarity to people living or dead is purely coincidental.

ISBN: 978-1-59554-584-8

Printed in the United States of America

09 10 11 12 13 BTY 6 5 4 3 2 1

Mountain Top

To people who dream.
You work in the dark,
but your insight helps others live in the light.

When a prophet of the L*ORD* *is among you,*
I reveal myself to him in visions,
I speak to him in dreams.

Numbers 12:6 NIV

One

"WHAT ARE YOU GOING TO DO ABOUT THE LETTER?" THE VOICE on the phone demanded. "If it fell into the wrong hands, it could cost us millions!"

"I shredded it," the man sitting behind the expensive desk replied without emotion.

"Did anyone on your staff see it?"

"No. I open my own mail."

"But he could still talk."

"Of course, or send a letter to someone else. But I have a plan, and when I'm finished, no one will believe anything he says. It's not going to be an issue."

"You'd better be right. That's why you're in this deal—to make sure everything goes smoothly on the local front. How is our friend in Raleigh doing?"

"Ahead of schedule. But he's low on cash."

"Again? That was quick."

"It doesn't take long when you have his habits. He wants to see you."

"Okay, buy him a plane ticket, but I'm going to lower his limit."

"Not too much, or I'll have to give him a raise on this end."

SAM MILLER DID SOME OF HIS BEST WORK WHILE ASLEEP. SEVERAL nights each week, he had night visions more vivid than movies and spiritual dreams so real he could smell the fragrance of heaven. Muriel never stirred. She had to get her rest so she could fix his breakfast. Sam's lawncare equipment ran on gasoline; he needed eggs, sausage, and biscuits with gravy before facing another day.

Sam rolled over and opened his blue eyes. He ran his hand over his closely cropped white hair and reached for the tattered notebook on the nightstand beside the bed. Some of the pages listed information about customers: the Smiths wanted their grass cut and patio edged before a party on Friday night, the Blevinses had decided to plant day lilies along the back of their property line. Other sheets recorded what Sam had seen and heard during the night: faces of people who lived in Shelton with diverse needs that ranged from salvation for a wayward child to money for an overdue car payment. Several pages contained crude drawings of strange images without easy interpretation. Notes, questions, and Bible verses filled the margins.

Beside the notebook was a picture of Sam and Muriel taken forty-three years earlier. It was their second wedding anniversary. Sam, wearing his Marine Corps dress uniform, stood unsmiling and stern next to his short, curly-haired wife. The soldier in the photo didn't have the large, round belly of the man in the bed nor the twinkle that lit his blue eyes. Those changes came later. Muriel's light brown hair remained curly and her figure trim, but her tanned face was now lined with wrinkles that were the road map to a hundred different ways to smile.

Sam sat up and rested his feet on the threadbare rug that covered part of the bedroom floor. He opened the notebook to a blank page. At the top he wrote the date and the words *Within three months you'll see your son.* He shuffled into the living room. Family photos on the walls recorded the life of Matthew Miller from cradle to manhood.

Tragedy was no stranger to the Miller family. Matthew, an Army medic, had died in Somalia. His pictures stopped with a grainy photo taken at dusk in front of a field hospital. Mountains without trees rose in the background.

Sam went into the kitchen and looked out the window above the sink. Muriel could wash a fifty-cent plastic plate and enjoy a million-dollar view. Their small house rested atop a knoll positioned like a step stool before the Blue Ridge Mountains. In the early light, Sam could see heavy frost on the grass and wispy ice on the trees in the distance. He leaned over and smelled the crisp morning air through a narrow gap at the bottom of the window. Weather ruled his business, and winter's schedule was less rigorous. When spring arrived, daffodils would jump out of the ground in clumps of yellow celebration all across the backyard, and Sam would be out the door to greet them with the first rays of the sun.

Sam always made the morning coffee. He could drink it strong and black, but Muriel liked it so diluted with milk and sugar that it could be served to a child. Sam made the coffee weak. Later, he'd get a strong cup at the Minute Market. The coffee started dripping into the pot, and he returned to the bedroom. Muriel was out of bed and wrapped in her housecoat. Sam leaned over and kissed the top of her head. She responded by patting him on his fuzzy right cheek.

"It's time for my bear to come out of hibernation," she said. "Are you going to shave this morning?"

"Yep, then take tomorrow off before church on Sunday."

SAM SHOWERED AND SCRAPED HIS CHIN FREE OF STUBBLE. Buttoning his shirt, he could smell the sausage in the skillet. Muriel rarely bought sausage at the store; she canned it fresh each fall like her mother and grandmother before her. Sam didn't raise pigs, but he knew a man who did. Homemade sausage seasoned with the perfect blend of sage and pepper couldn't be compared to meat from a factory wrapped in a plastic tube. The smoky smell of sausage in the skillet reminded Sam of boyhood breakfasts cooked on an open fire in the woods. His stomach rumbled in anticipation.

The cupboard at the Miller house didn't look like a grocery store shelf. Mason jars of green beans, tomatoes, okra, squash, and yellow corn cut from the cob filled the narrow space. Sam's garden was legendary. Two acres on the flat spot at the bottom of the driveway produced more than enough to feed the Millers and provided extra income through the sale of fresh produce to Sam's customers. Mrs. Sellers loved to eat Sam's sun-ripened tomatoes like apples.

Sam came into the kitchen, gave Muriel a hug, and rubbed his cheek against hers.

"How's that?" he asked.

"Much better. The biscuits are in the oven."

"I want to take a sausage biscuit to Barry Porter," Sam said. "He's going to deliver two loads of pine bark mulch to a job this morning."

Sam sat at the small kitchen table and watched Muriel's morning routine. Every movement had meaning. She didn't waste energy or ingredients. Sam picked up a jar of molasses and tipped it so the amber liquid rolled to one side.

"How is Barry's boy doing?" Muriel asked.

Sam returned the molasses to its place on the vinyl tablecloth.

"He ran off with a married woman to Florida. He's eating slop and calling it steak, but I saw him turning toward home the other night. I'm going to remind Barry to keep looking down the road and welcome him back when he repents."

Muriel opened the oven door and took out four golden biscuits. When Matthew was a teenager, she baked six to eight biscuits that always disappeared before the male members of the family went out the front door.

"Why don't you take Barry two biscuits?" she suggested. "You eat one, and I'll nibble on the other."

Sam scratched his head. "Only one for me? I don't want to pass out while spreading the mulch around Mrs. Smith's patio. I need all my strength to lift that shovel."

Muriel turned her back to him as she put the sausage on a clean serving plate and sprinkled flour and pepper into the skillet for the gravy.

"I'm thinking about the extra weight these biscuits and sausage are causing around that stomach of yours," she said. "You know your cholesterol is inching up, and Dr. Murray told you to watch your diet."

Sam's mouth dropped open, and he stared at her back for a moment. "Are you serious?"

Muriel turned around with a serious look on her face. "I love babying you, but sometimes I feel guilty fixing what you want all the time."

Sam grinned. "Don't worry. The gravy cuts the calories in half."

"We won't argue about it this morning, but I'm not fixing fried chicken tonight. I found a recipe for broiled chicken that sounds real tasty. It uses some of the herbs I dried last summer."

"Sounds great. The touch of your loving hands is the key to a good meal."

Muriel shook her head. "For a country boy, you're a smooth talker."

After all the food was on the table, she sat down across from him. They bowed their heads.

Sam prayed for Barry's son, moved into his usual blessing over the meal, and concluded with, "And Master, please take all the cholesterol out of this fine breakfast. Amen."

"Your health is not a joke," Muriel said when he finished. "I want to keep you with me as long as possible."

Sam reached across and put his weathered hand on top of hers. "And I don't want either of us to leave a moment before Papa's perfect time."

AFTER BREAKFAST, SAM PUT ON A HEAVY COAT AND WENT OUTSIDE while Muriel washed the dishes. The sun was a large yellow ball in the east, and the frost was in full retreat across the yard, exposing the dead grass. Without any wind blowing, the mountain air would warm up rapidly. The coat, hat, and gloves would keep Sam comfortable until he started working. He filled an orange cooler with water from a back porch sink supplied by pipes prevented from freezing by thick insulation wrapped around them.

Sam kept the utility trailer he used to haul his equipment in a small storage shed. Parked in front of the shed was a dented red pickup truck with the words "Sam Miller – Lawn Maintenance" written on both doors in white paint. Underneath was Sam's phone number. The boy who painted the advertisement on the truck did a neat job. Three years later, the letters and numbers were only chipped in a few places.

Sam unlocked the door of the shed and went inside. The familiar odors of gasoline and dry grass greeted him. Sam owned a large commercial mower, a regular push mower for trimming, and an edger. He did all the maintenance on the equipment himself. The past week, he'd rebuilt the engine in the commercial mower so it would be ready for the spring season. He placed a rake, shovel, mattock, and other hand tools in a rack toward the front of the trailer and secured everything with a strap. He reached into his pocket for the keys to the truck so he could back it up to the trailer. As he stepped away from the building, movement at the bottom of the driveway caught his eye. A Barlow County sheriff's car turned into his driveway. Sam walked around the side of the house. The car pulled up to his front door and stopped. Two deputies got out.

"Morning, Sam," the older of the two men called out. "Cold enough for you?"

It was Lamar Cochran, the chief deputy. Sam and Muriel had known the Cochran family for years. Lamar, a large man with reddish-brown hair, looked almost exactly like his father.

"Howdy, Lamar," Sam said. "Not too bad. Who's your running mate?"

"This is Vic Morris," Cochran replied. "He grew up in Hendersonville and joined us a few months ago."

Sam wiped his right hand on his pants and extended it to Morris.

"Good to meet you," Sam said.

Morris hesitated a moment before shaking Sam's hand.

"Don't have any biscuits to offer you," Sam said to the two men. "Muriel won't make any extras because she knows where they'll end up." Sam patted his stomach.

"Uh, that's all right, Sam," Cochran replied. "I need to talk serious with you."

"Come inside. I'm always here to help."

Sam turned away and climbed the three steps to the front stoop.

Cochran glanced at Morris and sighed. "Okay. I guess it won't hurt. Where is Muriel?"

"Cleaning up after me, of course," Sam replied, opening the door.

The three men entered the small living room. Sam stuck his head in the kitchen.

"Lamar Cochran and a young deputy named Vic Morris are here," he said.

Muriel wrapped her housecoat more tightly around herself and came to the doorway. Cochran nodded to her. Muriel gave him a big smile.

"Hey, Lamar," she said. "How's your mama? I haven't seen her in quite a while."

"Not doing so well. Her sugar is messing her up big-time, and my brother and I had to put her in the nursing home. That way, there is someone to watch her diet and give her the right medicine."

"I'll have to get down to see her—"

"Don't, Muriel," Cochran interrupted, looking at the floor. "This isn't a social call."

Sam tilted his head to the side. "What do you mean?"

Cochran nodded toward Morris, who pulled a sheet of paper from his back pocket.

"Mr. Miller, this is a warrant for your arrest," Morris said. "We're here to take you to jail."

Two

Reverend Michael James Andrews didn't take Mondays off.

"Why would you need a day to relax?" asked Bobby Lambert, one of Mike's former law partners and an elder at the Little Creek Church. "You only work one hour a week. Every day but Sunday you can tell folks that you're going to pray then slip out the back door to the golf course."

"I can't ignore the eternal peril of my current clients," Mike replied. "Keeping them out of trouble is a twenty-four-hour-a-day job. Take you, for example. Convincing the Almighty to have mercy on your wretched soul is harder than getting Judge Coberg to grant a temporary restraining order in a covenant not to compete lawsuit. Every time I come up with an argument in your favor, you find new and creative ways to sin."

Mike's regular day away from the office was Friday. After almost ten years as a trial lawyer, the brown-haired, broad-shouldered minister continued to view Monday as a normal workday. Not going to the church on Friday, however, created the illusion of a long weekend. By Thursday morning, he'd written and practiced his sermon several times, so there wasn't much to do but wait for Sunday morning at 11:25 a.m. to deliver it.

Mike never felt guilty walking down a broad fairway on Friday afternoons. However, gone were the days when he could lose a dozen balls a round in water hazards without giving it a second thought. Golf was an expensive pastime, and on a minister's salary Mike didn't have the money to pay greens fees and rent a cart whenever he had the urge to play a round of golf. So, while in seminary he took up mountain biking. When his wife, Peg, questioned the change, he told her he'd rather elevate his heart rate pedaling up a steep hill than in frustration over a five-foot putt that rimmed out of the cup.

Little Creek Church was located fifty yards from the small, rocky stream that gave the church its name. For more than 140 years, the congregation of independent Presbyterians averaged 50 to 100 members with the graveyard behind the church being the only part of the church that steadily grew.

During the past ten years, everything had changed. Development of Barlow County's beautiful mountain property had resulted in the construction of hundreds of vacation and retirement homes in the hills surrounding the church. The influx of people caused the church to experience rapid growth.

When Mike decided to leave law practice in Shelton and become a minister, the Little Creek elders followed his progress through seminary in Virginia and issued a call as soon as he graduated. Questions about his lack of experience vanished after doubters heard him preach. In his booming, baritone voice, Mike transferred his oratorical skills as a successful lawyer to the pulpit.

The small white sanctuary couldn't handle the crowds. Some of the older members, not wanting to vacate the well-worn pews occupied by their ancestors, fought the building program, but their efforts proved as futile as a skirmish by Confederate soldiers against advancing Yankee troops in 1865. Within a year and a half, a new sanctuary stood like a big brother next to the old one. The old sanctuary became a wedding chapel and funeral parlor.

Mike's office was at the back corner of an administration wing connected to the new sanctuary. He sold the leather-inlaid, walnut desk from his law office and let Peg decorate his new work space. She selected an effeminate worktable with Queen Anne legs and expensive antique furnishings. Typically, Peg ran over budget, but Mike bit his tongue and didn't complain. He secretly paid the extra expense and viewed it as an investment in convincing Peg to accept the transition from lawyer's spouse to minister's wife.

Mike put down a book about how to be an effective minister in a changing community and looked at the large clock on the wall. It was 11:15 a.m., and he'd only had two phone calls all morning. Compared to the stress of a law office, the pace of church leadership was like floating down a slow-moving eastern North Carolina river. At semiannual ministerial meetings, Mike heard other pastors complain about the hassle and pressure of their jobs, but he kept his mouth shut. Dealing with a church member's concern about the condition of the flower beds in front of the old sanctuary or complaints about the choir director's hymn selections was a lot easier than a four-hour deposition in which the opposing lawyer continuously raised spurious objections and a duplicitous witness refused to tell the truth. There was a light knock on his door.

"Come in," he said.

Delores Killian, the sixty-year-old church secretary, stuck her head into the office. A widow and holdover from the old guard, one of Mike's early triumphs had been winning her support. His strategy was simple. He never asked her to do anything except what she'd always done, and she praised him to all her friends as an excellent administrator.

"Someone is here to see you who didn't have an appointment," Delores whispered in a husky voice that revealed a forty-year love affair with cigarettes.

"Who is it? I'm having lunch in Shelton with Dick Saxby, a man who visited the church on Sunday, and need to leave in a few minutes."

"Muriel Miller. She's not a member of the church. Her husband is in jail, and she wants you to go see him."

"What are the charges?"

Delores raised her eyebrows. "She didn't tell me, and I didn't ask."

Mike waved his hand. "Don't bother. I'll talk to her on my way out."

During his legal career, Mike handled criminal cases and interacted with scores of men wearing orange jumpsuits, handcuffs, and leg irons. Since becoming a minister, he'd not visited the jail and had, in fact, ignored the squat gray building a couple of blocks from the courthouse. He returned to his book. It was an interesting chapter. The author offered several creative suggestions for bringing rural and cosmopolitan church members together. After several minutes, Mike dictated a memo of his findings for the elders. Mike was a hunt-and-peck typist, but Delores was even worse at transcribing dictation.

After checking his hair in a small mirror beside the door, he walked into the reception area where he was startled by the sight of a small, gray-haired woman with a wrinkled face. She sat on the edge of a small sofa and wrung a tissue in her hands. The woman's dress, a plain yellow cotton print, revealed her country roots. She looked up at him anxiously.

"Oh," Mike began. "You're Mrs., uh . . ."

"Miller," Delores said. "Her husband—"

"Is in jail," Mike finished, regaining his bearings. "I'm sorry to hear that."

Muriel stood, and Mike shook her hand. Her fingers were small but her grip firm.

"Reverend Andrews, would you visit my husband? He's been in jail for almost three months."

"Do I know him?"

"His name is Sam Miller. We live off McAfee Road. He has a lawncare business."

Mike thought for a moment but couldn't connect the name with a face. McAfee Road was ten miles on the west side of Shelton, almost twenty miles from the church. No one that far away came to Little Creek Church.

Muriel continued, "He told me you were a good lawyer."

"Not for over six years. I represented a lot of people when I practiced law, but I don't remember your husband."

"Oh, he's never gone to see a lawyer in his life."

"Then why contact me?"

Muriel lowered her eyes and spoke in a soft voice. "He had a dream Saturday night and saw you coming to see him at the jail. When I visited him on Sunday, he told me to get in touch with you here at the church."

Mike's jaw dropped open slightly. Delores leaned forward in her chair.

"Excuse me," Mike said. "Could you explain what you just said?"

Muriel sighed. "Sam has a lot of dreams. The Lord shows him things that are going to happen and stuff about people he's supposed to pray for." Her voice grew stronger. "It's nothing that doesn't happen in the Bible. Jacob had a dream and saw angels on a ladder; Joseph had dreams about himself and interpreted dreams for others—"

"I know the Bible," Mike interrupted.

"Of course you do," Muriel responded quietly. "I just didn't want you to think Sam was a nut."

Mike caught Delores rolling her eyes out of the corner of his vision.

"I'll walk out with you," Mike said to Muriel. "I have a luncheon meeting in Shelton."

They entered a short hall. Mountain landscapes painted by Peg hung on the walls. Mike opened the door for Muriel. It was a warm but pleasant spring day. They walked down a brick sidewalk to the new parking lot. The asphalt sparkled in the sun. Mike had a reserved parking space marked "Senior Pastor."

"Why is your husband in jail?"

"He didn't do anything wrong."

It had been years since Mike heard that familiar line.

"I understand, but he must have been charged with something."

"They claim he took money from the church. But it's either a lie or a big mistake."

"Embezzlement?"

"Yes, that's the word."

"Which church?"

"Craig Valley. It's a little place not far from the house. Sam was filling in as their preacher for a few months while they looked for a new man to take over."

"Is that your home church?"

"Not really. We move from church to church as the Lord directs."

Mike glanced sideways at the strange remark. They reached his car, a Lexus holdover from his days as a lawyer that now had more than 250,000 miles on the odometer. Beside his car sat a red pickup truck with Miller's name on the side. At least that part of this odd woman's story was true. Mike faced her.

"My sympathies are with you, and I'll pray for your husband, but I'm not the man you need. You should hire a practicing lawyer who can request bail. Three months is a long time to sit in jail. If your husband hasn't given a statement to the police, tell him to keep his mouth shut until he talks to an attorney. Confession is good at the church altar, not during a jailhouse interrogation."

Satisfied with his succinct and accurate counsel, Mike opened the door of his car. Muriel didn't move.

"Good luck," Mike said.

"Don't forget the dream," Muriel responded.

Mike slid into the car seat and looked up at her.

"Believe me. I won't."

Three

THE ROAD FROM LITTLE CREEK CHURCH TO SHELTON FOLLOWED the winding course of a valley nestled between two wooded ridges. Three times the road crossed a bold-flowing stream before climbing over one of the ridges and dipping into town. Mike and Peg's house was on a street near the top of a ridge. When the leaves fell from the trees, they could see into the center of town, a picturesque view at Christmas when colored lights along the downtown streets twinkled and large angels with trumpets to their lips perched atop every other lamp pole. Mike liked to bundle up in a blanket, sit outside in a lounge chair, and enjoy the show.

Mike and Peg bought their house when he first started practicing law and were on the verge of purchasing a much larger home when he decided to go to seminary in Virginia. So, instead of moving into a showcase home in the best area of town, they lived in a modest condominium for three years and rented out the house in Shelton. After completing seminary, Mike accepted the call to the Little Creek Church, and they returned home.

Childless, their only house guest was Judge, an eight-year-old Hungarian vizsla. The short-haired, gold-colored hunter/retriever acquired his name the day Mike and Peg picked him out from the litter of a breeder in Highlands.

"Look how that one barks at all the other pups," Peg remarked as they watched the dogs tumbling around in the pen. "I think he's the one."

"He reminds me of Judge Lancaster in Morganton," Mike said.

"Why?"

"He spends all his time barking at the other lawyers."

"Then that's what we'll call him," Peg replied.

"Lancaster?"

"No, silly. Judge."

Recently, Mike had suggested they might sell their home and look for a house closer to the church, but Peg cut him off. Her social orbit had the town, not the church, at its center. So, they stayed put. Mike's salary from the church was barely enough to pay the mortgage and their other bills. Mike kept reassuring Peg that the growth of the church would soon justify a significant increase in salary. Her response was a slight twist of her lips that communicated skepticism more effectively than words.

Mike drove down the hill into town. Shelton had twelve traffic lights. Each light had a number on a tiny sign above it that provided a convenient way to give directions—turn left at number six and right at four. The courthouse square was flanked by numbers one through four.

Mike parked on the west side of the courthouse square, across the street from the law firm formerly known as Forrest, Andrews, and Lambert, the most respected law firm in Barlow County. The gold letters over the front door now read Forrest, Lambert, Park, and Arnold. Mr. Forrest claimed it had taken two lawyers to replace Mike.

Mike entered the Ashe Street Café, a long, rectangular room with booths along two sides and tables down the middle. Waitresses brought plates of hot food from the kitchen at the rear of the room. Several men were waiting for a place to sit. He nodded in the direction of Butch Niles, the manager of the trust department for the Bank of Barlow County and a popular young representative in the General Assembly. Standing beside Niles was Jim Postell, the longtime county clerk of court and a savvy local politician.

"Hello, Preacher," said Niles, slapping Mike on the back. "I've been hearing good things about you. What are you going to do next? Run against me for the legislature?"

"The only election I need to win is a majority vote of the church elders," Mike responded. "And there's no way a lawyer turned minister could ever be elected to anything. Half the people in Barlow County are mad because I sued them, and the other half wouldn't vote for me because I'm not part of their denomination."

Niles chuckled. "What if I didn't run and could get Jim to endorse you?"

"Then I could be governor."

A table opened for Postell and Niles.

"Why don't you join us?" the clerk of court asked. "The regulars will be here in a few minutes. We'll argue politics, but it won't amount to anything."

"No, thanks, I have an appointment."

Other members of the legal and business community drifted into the café. There was no sign of Saxby. Mike looked at his watch and inwardly kicked himself for not confirming the appointment. He checked his PDA but hadn't entered a contact number. He then called the church, but Delores had left and turned on the answering machine. He looked at the table where Niles and his cronies were sitting. There weren't any empty seats. Everyone else in the café was preoccupied with lunch and conversation.

Laughter came from the direction of the rear of the restaurant. Mike suddenly wanted to get out of there. After one more glance at his watch, he turned to the blond-haired woman behind the cash register.

"Sue, if a man named Dick Saxby comes in looking for me, tell him I waited as long as I could but had to leave for another appointment."

"Sure thing, Mike. Do you want anything to go?"

"No, thanks."

Mike breathed a sigh of relief. Walking down the sidewalk toward his car, he muttered, "I don't have another appointment."

Blurting out a false excuse as a way to get out of the restaurant didn't make sense. Bogus meetings had never been part of Mike's strategy for managing his day, and he considered a lie an act of cowardice. He stopped at light number four and waited for it to turn green. No one was harmed by his misstatement, but it still made him feel uneasy. It would be awkward to return to the café, but—he stopped.

He could visit the jail and make his statement true.

The light turned green, but Mike didn't cross the street. He glanced in the direction of the jail. Not visible, he knew it stood two blocks away, set back from the street with a small parking lot in front and an exercise yard surrounded by a high fence and razor wire in the rear. He looked again at his watch. He'd set aside more than an hour for lunch and didn't have any reason to return to the church. He began walking slowly down the street toward the jail. Muriel Miller might not deliver his advice to her husband about keeping his mouth shut. It wouldn't hurt to do it himself.

THE VISITORS' WAITING AREA HADN'T CHANGED IN SIX YEARS. Same plastic furniture and light green paint on the walls. Except for the presence of a thick metal door, it looked like the reception room for a cheap insurance agency. Mike knocked on a small glass partition in the wall. A young female deputy slid it open.

"May I help you?" she asked pleasantly.

"I'm Mike Andrews. I'd like to talk with a prisoner named Sam Miller."

The woman pointed to a sign on the wall next to the opening. "Visiting hours are Wednesday evening from 6:00 p.m. to 8:00 p.m., Saturday morning from 9:00 a.m. to noon, and Sunday afternoon from 1:00 p.m. to 4:00 p.m."

"Oh, I'm a minister," Mike said. "Mr. Miller's wife asked me to visit him."

"That doesn't change the rules."

Mike hesitated. "I'm also a lawyer."

The woman's eyes narrowed. "Do you have a picture ID and your attorney card?"

Mike took out his wallet and handed over his driver's license and state bar association card. He'd maintained his law license by paying a small annual fee and attending a yearly seminar at the coast where he took enough classes to satisfy his continuing legal education requirement. Peg liked the beach, and in the afternoons Mike played golf.

The woman disappeared with the items. Mike waited, tapping his finger on the counter. When she didn't return, Mike began to wonder if she was calling Raleigh to find out if anyone had reported a suspicious man traveling across the state impersonating an attorney. Finally, she reappeared, joined by a familiar face.

"Mike Andrews!" bellowed Chief Deputy Lamar Cochran. "What brings you down here?"

"Hey, Lamar, nothing different, still pretending to be a lawyer."

"It's okay," Cochran said to the woman deputy. "Mr. Andrews practiced law before he went to preaching. Let him in."

An electric buzzer sounded, and Mike pulled open the metal door. Cochran waited for him on the other side. The two men shook hands.

"You've kept your law license?" Cochran asked.

"Yeah, once you pass the bar exam, it's hard to give it up. There's not much required to maintain good standing, but I may go inactive in a few years."

Mike followed Cochran into the booking area. A wire-mesh screen on one side of the room overlooked a broad hallway, the holding cell for drunks, and two interview rooms. The cell block lay behind another solid metal door.

"How do you know Sam Miller?" Cochran asked.

"I don't. His wife stopped by the church and asked me to visit him. Is anyone representing him?"

"I don't think so." Cochran shook his head. "I've known Sam and Muriel since I was a kid. He's a bit odd, but I always thought he was harmless."

"Embezzlement?"

"Yeah," Cochran said, lowering his voice. "But I hope it ain't true. Sam is getting up in years and ought to be rocking on the back porch enjoying the mountains, not sitting in a cell block with a bunch of reprobates who broke the law while high on dope."

"What about bond?"

"Too high for him to meet. I gave him the number for a bondsman but don't know if he ever called him."

"Well, let me have a look at him," Mike said. "I'll try to steer him in the right direction."

"I'll get him myself."

Cochran entered the cell block. Mike stepped from the booking area into the hallway. He'd forgotten the smell and feel of the jail. The odor changed depending on the day of the week. Mike had visited the lockup on Saturday nights when there was no escaping the stench of stale sweat and human waste. By Monday afternoon, the foul odors of the weekend had been replaced by lemony disinfectant. Today, the floors were clean, the drunk tank empty. The feel of the jail, however, never changed. Despair clung to its walls. Hopelessness hovered in the air. When he left the correctional center, Mike always celebrated his freedom with a deep breath.

He opened the door to one of the interview rooms. It was empty. Glancing down at the table and chairs, he realized he hadn't brought a legal pad. He thought about asking a booking officer for a sheet of paper but decided not to. He didn't need to take notes. He wasn't even sure why he'd come.

The door to the cell block opened. Cochran returned, followed by a white-haired, rotund man wearing an orange jumpsuit. The older man stepped from behind the chief deputy, saw Mike, and smiled.

"Hello, son," he said, holding out his hand. "I'm Sam Miller. Thanks for coming."

"You can use either room," Cochran said.

"We'll park in number one," Mike replied. "I won't be too long. I need to get back to the church."

Mike held the door open for Sam, who lowered himself into a plastic chair. Mike sat on the opposite side of the table. He got right to the point.

"Why did you want to see me?"

"So we can help each other."

"Help each other?" Mike asked in surprise.

"Yep."

"You're the one in jail, Mr. Miller. How are you going to help me?"

"There are all kinds of jail. One of the worst is the prison of wrong thinking. I spent many years locked up there before I found the key and opened the door."

"Excuse me?"

"Sorry, I'm jumping ahead. We have so much to talk about."

"Don't you want to talk about the reason you're here?"

"Of course," Sam answered, patting his stomach. "You're one reason. But first you can ask me anything you want. I don't want to rush anything."

Mike decided to humor him for a few minutes, then make a quick exit. He could call one of the judicial assistants at the courthouse and find out why an attorney hadn't been appointed to represent the old man. Even if Miller didn't qualify for an appointed lawyer, someone should arrange an evaluation of the older man's mental competency.

"Has a detective asked you questions about the embezzlement charge?" Mike asked.

"Yep. Several times."

"Did you talk to him?"

"Yep, but there wasn't much to say."

"What did you tell him?"

"The truth."

"Did you sign a statement?"

"The last time he came by, he wrote down what I said, and I signed it."

Mike winced. A signed statement never helped the defense.

"What did he ask you?"

"About me and the church. Who took up the offerings? Who counted it? Why so much money turned up in my checking account. Stuff like that."

"How much money turned up in your checking account?"

"Around $100,000. I told him it must have been a bank mistake. I don't keep very much in my personal or business account, and I've never had that kind of money at one time in my life. Cash goes out as soon as it comes in around my house. The detective said he would double-check with the bank and let me know what he found out. He was a nice young fellow, but he never got back with me."

"Do you remember his name?"

"Perkins."

The name wasn't familiar to Mike.

"Are they claiming you stole $100,000 from the church you were serving as a fill-in preacher?"

"I guess so."

"What's the name of the church?"

"Craig Valley Gospel Tabernacle."

"How many people attend?"

"It's been growing. There are about fifty adults and the same number of young-uns."

"How did the church get that much money in the first place?"

Sam shrugged. "I don't know. They've been saving up for a new building. The concrete for the foundation was poured last fall, but I don't know how much they've collected altogether."

Mike sat back in his seat. The old man seemed capable of carrying on a normal conversation when he wanted to.

"Has a magistrate set bail?"

"Yep, it's $100,000, too. That number keeps coming up. I'm not sure what it means."

"It means a felony charge," Mike replied grimly. "Have you tried to post a property bond or called a bondsman?"

"Muriel showed the magistrate the deed for our property, but it wasn't worth enough, so I had to stay put. It's not been easy, but there's been fruit."

"I'm glad they've improved the menu."

"What menu?"

"The food. I'm glad the food is decent."

"I wouldn't say that, especially compared to what my wife puts on the table."

Mike leaned back in his seat. "Mr. Miller, I haven't had lunch today, and I didn't come here to talk about food. Explain in simple terms, with as few words as possible, why you sent your wife to the church to see me."

"Papa told me."

"Your father is alive?"

Sam pointed at the ceiling. "My Papa will never die. He's the Ancient of Days."

Mike stared at the tip of the old man's index finger. "You're telling me God is your father?"

"Yep. Isn't he your father, too?"

"Uh, of course. I thought you meant an earthly father."

"Nope. He's been dead over twenty years. I was just answering your question as simply as I could."

Mike put his hands together beneath his chin. "So, God told you to contact me."

"Yep, so you can be my lawyer."

"Mr. Miller, I used to practice law, but it's been six years since I stepped into a courtroom."

"You could still do it if you wanted to."

"Technically, yes, but as a practical matter, no."

Sam hesitated. "If it's the money, I'm sure we can make arrangements. I don't have much, and Muriel had to dip into our savings to keep the lights on, but I can scrape enough—"

Mike leaned forward and looked directly into the old man's face. "It's not the money. I stopped practicing law because I wanted to obey God, and I'm not going back into the courtroom for any amount of money. You're a minister. You should understand what I'm talking about."

Sam nodded. "You had to count the cost, didn't you?"

"Yes, and I'm making less now in a year than I used to in three months. But I don't believe the size of a person's bank account is the true measure of success."

"That's a good answer. I wouldn't want anyone representing me who believed anything different."

"I'm not going to represent you."

Sam smiled. "Papa knows how to make the most of every situation. I spent a few nights in the brig for fighting years ago, but it was a lot different coming here now. Do you feel the hopelessness in this place?"

Mike tilted his head to the side. "Yes."

"It tried to jump on me, but I sent it packing. The boys in here need help in the worst way, and Papa has let me do some good. There was a young man in the cell block who gave his life to the Master a couple of weeks ago. He'll be a preacher someday. He's not as smart as you, but he'll gather in his share of the harvest."

Mike stared at Sam for a second. "Mr. Miller, I'm glad we've had this talk, but I need to leave. I sympathize with your predicament, but as I told your wife, I'm not the man to help you."

Sam sat silently for a moment. "Then why did you come see me?"

"I was just standing on the sidewalk after a guy stood me up for lunch and decided it wouldn't hurt to come by the jail and meet you."

"Who put that thought in your head?"

"I have no idea, but that's not the sort of thing I'm talking about." Mike stood to his feet. "I hope things work out for you."

Sam didn't budge.

"You were a man of integrity as a lawyer before you became a minister," Sam said. "And I know Papa loves you. Pray about helping me, and see what He tells you."

"Okay, but I'm also going to call the courthouse and ask someone in the judge's office to appoint a lawyer to represent you so you can get out of jail."

"I'd like that a lot. This Saturday, Muriel and I will celebrate our forty-fifth wedding anniversary. She's a jewel of a woman."

"And you should be with her."

"You're right about that."

Mike opened the interview room door and held it as the old man stepped into the hallway. Sam stopped and turned around so he faced Mike.

"Oh, and tell your wife that Isaac is on the way," he said.

Mike didn't respond. Nobody named Isaac was in Mike and Peg's circle of family, friends, or acquaintances; however, Mike had already figured out that Sam Miller was the type of person who could keep a conversation going indefinitely with off-the-wall comments.

Lamar Cochran came forward and gently touched the white-haired man on the arm.

"Sam, you have to return to the cell block," he said.

"You know what I'd like for supper?" Sam asked the chief deputy.

"Some of Muriel's fried chicken."

"Yep."

"If that was on the chow line," Cochran replied, "we'd have people breaking into this jail."

Cochran looked at Mike and shook his head sadly.

"The guard will push the release for the door," the chief deputy said. "See you around town."

Mike let the metal door close slowly behind him. The female deputy ignored him as he left the building. He didn't look back. Outside, the air was fresh and clean. Mike took a deep breath. He walked away from the jail, as always, glad to be free.

Four

BACK AT THE CHURCH, MIKE HUNG UP THE PHONE. THE WOMAN who handled the assignment of criminal cases to younger lawyers in the circuit told him Sam hadn't requested that an attorney be appointed, but she would send one to the jail. Mike suspected a competent lawyer could quickly get to the bottom of the embezzlement charge and clear it up if it was a clerical error at the bank or arrange a plea bargain if it wasn't. Mike dropped a message from Muriel Miller asking him to call her after he met with Sam into the trash can. He'd fulfilled his civic and religious duty.

Mike returned to studying the book on church growth and didn't take a break for three hours. Several times he caught himself humming a song that had nothing to do with the words on the page. When he finished studying, he decided to take a short walk around the church property and make sure everything was neat and tidy.

"I'll be back in a few minutes," he said to Delores as he passed her desk.

The secretary was working the crossword puzzle that appeared in the local paper and didn't look up.

"Don't forget, I need to leave early for my appointment at the beauty shop," she said.

The grass in front of the new sanctuary had been freshly mowed, but the flower beds looked ragged. He walked behind the old sanctuary. To his right was the church cemetery. Small, weathered headstones streaked with gray filled most of the older section. The newer plots, with larger, more impressive monuments, were over a slight rise in the ground. The old cemetery needed major work.

Just beyond the cemetery lay Little Creek, swollen to springtime levels, but still not much more than a steady stream. During dry spells in summer, the creek dwindled to a trickle, prompting the Baptists down the road to remark that a few drops of water was enough to keep the Little Creek congregation going. That, and the support of a handful of stalwart families, had sustained the church through the generations since its founding shortly after the Civil War.

Trees lined the water, but on the church side, a short path led to an opening that had served as a watering hole for horses and mules when the members of the congregation came to church in wagons. A small spring nourished the creek at the spot, and Mike enjoyed watching the bubbles rise to the surface as the water forced its way past the smooth rocks on the bottom. He dipped his hand into the cold water and rubbed it on his face. He felt doubly refreshed—the water on his cheeks, a tangible sense of blessing in his soul.

Mike stepped away from the creek and looked at the church. It was a beautiful setting with the wooded hills in the background. Joy, like the water below the ground, rose to the surface of his consciousness. Mike's call to ministry had survived the cross-examination of those who doubted. Now, after the upheaval of leaving his law practice and three years of seminary training, it had brought him to a pleasant place.

"Thank You, Lord," he said, then paused before saying, "Thank You, Papa."

Mike smiled and shook his head at Sam Miller's method of addressing the Almighty. Casual familiarity with God might work for an old man who ran a lawncare business, but not for him.

DELORES LEFT THE CHURCH FOR HER HAIR APPOINTMENT AT 3:00 p.m. Shortly after she left, Nathan Goode stuck his head into Mike's office. The unmarried twenty-five-year-old, part-time choir director and youth minister often stopped by the church on Monday afternoons to see Mike after finishing his regular job as music teacher at the local high school. The young man's black hair crept down his neck, and he had a closely trimmed goatee. Close up, the holes that had once housed multiple earrings could still be seen; however, he'd transitioned from nonconformist to upwardly mobile professional, using his salary from the church to make the payments on a silver BMW.

"Any complaints come in today?" Nathan asked.

"All quiet."

"I wasn't sure about using the alternate tune for the Doxology. It was a pretty big gamble. I watched Mrs. Harcourt. She kept sticking her finger in her ear. I'm not sure if she was trying to clean it out or stop it up."

"The Harcourts left town for Florida after the service and didn't give any feedback. They'll be gone three weeks and won't remember what happened by the time they return. Are you going to try out something new this Sunday?"

"No, I'm going to use a high school flute player for the offertory. That should be tame enough."

"Okay."

"And I have an anthem that dates back a few hundred years. Can you recruit Peg for choir practice this week? This piece has an alto solo made for her voice."

"It might work if I give her a choice between the choir and nursery duty."

In addition to painting classes, Peg had received classical voice training in college and could sing along with the opera CDs she listened to in the car. Mike's taste in music ran more toward Bruce Springsteen.

"Oh, and I enjoyed your sermon," Nathan said.

"You don't have to say that." Mike smiled. "Your job is secure, at least until Mrs. Harcourt gets back into town."

"No, seriously. I'm learning a lot. Your explanation of God's sovereignty put a different spin on some things for me."

"He's the conductor. Our job is to follow."

"Yeah, I appreciated the analogy. I trained under conductors who mixed two doses of terror with three scoops of fear. They were motivated by ego and pride, not love and compassion. I've been thinking about what you said off and on all day."

MIKE ENJOYED THE DRIVE HOME AT THE END OF THE DAY. HE lowered the window of the car and let the breeze blow across his face. He glanced at the ridges running alongside the road. With the arrival of spring, the hills no longer looked like gray-backed porcupines. Budding trees raised green fingers toward the sky. Soon, the gently rising slopes would be thick with summer foliage.

Mike and Peg lived at the end of a dead-end street. He parked on the street in front of the house. For the past hour, his stomach had been growling in protest at the decision to skip lunch. When he got out of the car, he could hear Judge barking inside the house.

A side door opened into the kitchen, a sunny room with a breakfast nook where Mike and Peg ate unless they were entertaining guests. Peg kept the house spotless. Her efforts to train Mike in perpetual neatness had been less successful.

Throughout the house were paintings by Peg. Like many artists, Peg's creativity had gone through phases. The first years after their marriage were filled with Appalachian mountain scenes, perhaps a response to the dramatic change from the upper-class suburb of Philadelphia where Peg grew up. She then entered a long stretch devoted to children. Mike particularly liked a series of watercolors depicting boys playing baseball. The slightly blurred images captured the idyllic world of summer much better than a crisp photograph. Peg then began painting older people sitting in chairs or in front of windows with their eyes closed as the world's activity passed by. This past winter, she'd returned to landscapes and completed several oils of barren trees shaped like giant candelabras. Mike never criticized Peg's work. Unless crafting questions on cross-examination or organizing a sermon could be considered an art form, the creative world wasn't a place he visited.

No smells of supper greeted Mike when he entered the kitchen. The cooktop was bare and the oven cold. A few leftover hors d'oeuvres not eaten by Peg's monthly book club were on the counter. Peg wasn't in sight. Judge wagged his tail, and Mike reached over to rub the dog's slightly wrinkled forehead.

"Did the ladies in the book club tell you how cute you looked?" he asked then raised his voice. "Peg! I'm home and hungry!"

Eating a carrot stick, he went through the great room with its large picture windows and looked up the stairs. Judge pattered after him.

"What's for supper?" he called out.

Peg, fit and trim, appeared at the top of the stairs. Dressed in jeans and a cotton shirt, she had a tissue in her right hand and something Mike couldn't see in the left. Her short blond hair bobbed up and down as she rapidly descended the stairs. Her blue eyes were rimmed in red, but there was a smile on her face, revealing the dimple in her left cheek.

"What's wrong?" Mike asked.

Peg reached the bottom of the stairs and threw herself into his arms. She sniffled then burst out laughing. Mike held her. After fifteen years of marriage, he knew it was wise to let a woman unpack her feelings on her own terms. Peg pulled away and wiped her eyes with the tissue. Mike waited. She held up a thin strip of paper in her right hand. It contained a blue circle.

"Don't you think this would make a beautiful painting?" she asked.

"It's a bit abstract."

"Wrong. It's the most real thing I could ever do."

Mike gave her a perplexed look.

"Do you know what this filled-in circle means?" she asked in a giddy voice.

"Uh, no."

"I'm pregnant!" Peg screamed.

Judge barked. Mike took a step backward.

"Are you sure?"

Peg reached into her pocket and pulled out the instructions from a pregnancy test and held the slip of paper next to a photo on the sheet.

"What does that tell you?"

Mike stared at the images. There was no question about the similarity between the test results and the guidelines provided by the manufacturer.

"Yeah, it looks the same. But don't you think you should go to the doctor?"

"Of course." Peg grabbed him again. "But I know I'm pregnant! I can feel it!"

"You can't feel a baby this early."

"I know that," she said, grabbing his hand and placing it over her heart. "It's a knowing inside here. That's why I bought the test. I'd been feeling odd and wondering if something was wrong. This afternoon while I was out running with Judge it hit me that I should pick up a pregnancy test at the drugstore." She held up the slip in triumph. "And it was positive!"

Peg sat down on the steps and began to laugh. Still in shock, Mike didn't move. Judge nuzzled Peg's leg. Peg reached out, took Mike's hand, and looked up into his face.

"After all these years of doctors, exams, procedures, and giving up, I can't tell you how happy this makes me."

"A baby," Mike murmured. "We're going to have a baby."

THEY CELEBRATED AT THE MOUNTAIN VIEW, THE NICEST restaurant in town. Peg picked at her salad. Famished, Mike didn't leave a crumb of a crouton on his plate.

"I wonder if I'm going to have any strange food cravings," Peg said.

"Right now, nothing would seem strange to me," Mike replied, looking over his shoulder toward the kitchen area.

"You ordered the biggest steak on the menu."

"But it's not here yet. Missing lunch and finding out that I'm going to be a father has increased my appetite."

"Why didn't you eat lunch?"

"I had a glitch in my schedule."

"What happened?"

Mike told her about Muriel Miller's visit to the church, and his encounter with Sam at the jail.

"How did it feel being a lawyer again?" Peg asked, leaning forward.

"It's not my world anymore."

"Are you sure?"

"Of course," Mike scoffed. "The law and the prophets don't mix."

Their meal arrived. Mike savored the thick, juicy steak. On the third bite, he thought about Sam Miller and hoped the old man would get out of jail in time to enjoy fried chicken on his wedding anniversary.

MIKE AND PEG AGREED TO KEEP THEIR NEWS SECRET UNTIL confirmed by the doctor. That night, Peg fell asleep in Mike's arms. In the morning, she didn't lie in bed with her face to the wall but fixed coffee while he shaved and showered.

"Call me as soon as you know anything," Mike said as he kissed her on the cheek.

Peg wrapped her arms around him and placed her head against his chest. Mike didn't know what to think. It had been years since she'd displayed this type of affection before he left for work. He held her for a long time then kissed the top of her head.

"I love you," he said.

"I love you, too." She lifted her head and gave him a lingering kiss on the lips. "Have a good day. I'll call you from the doctor's office."

Mike drove to the church in a daze. If pregnancy could awaken this level of passion and tenderness in a woman, it must be the happiest state known to man.

"GOOD MORNING, DELORES," HE SAID, STOPPING AT THE SECretary's desk.

Delores coughed and cleared her throat. "I took a message off the answering machine from Mrs. Miller, the woman who came to see you yesterday."

Delores handed Mike a pink slip of paper. He suspected the lawyer sent to interview Sam Miller hadn't made it to the jail yet.

"If Mrs. Miller would be patient and her husband would exercise common sense, everything could be handled in proper order," Mike replied, crumpling up the slip of paper and dropping it into Delores's trash can. "But I'll call the court administrator to make sure everything is on track."

He went into his office and called the courthouse.

"I talked to Greg Freeman and mentioned your concern about the prisoner's competency," the court administrator said. "He promised to go by the jail yesterday afternoon."

Mike didn't know Greg Freeman, who had come to town after Mike left for seminary. He looked up the young lawyer's office number. A male voice answered the phone.

"Greg Freeman, please," Mike said. "Tell him Reverend Mike Andrews is calling."

"This is Greg."

Freeman's voice sounded more like a member of the church youth group than an attorney.

"Welcome to Shelton," Mike replied.

"Thanks, I grew up in Wilmington, but I'm enjoying the mountains."

"Great. Listen, I'm calling about a defendant in a criminal case named Sam Miller. Have you been to the jail—"

"I'm sorry about that," Freeman interrupted. "I met with him yesterday without realizing that you're representing him."

Mike sat up straighter in his chair. "I'm not representing him. When we talked at the jail, I made it clear that I wouldn't get involved."

"He claims you're his lawyer. Based on the financial disclosure sheet, he isn't going to qualify for an appointed lawyer, and I thought he might want to hire me as a paying client."

"I wish he had," Mike said, looking out a window at the trees along the creek. "He needs help."

"No doubt, but there wasn't any use talking to him. He's convinced that you're on the case."

"He's wrong. That's why someone should be appointed to represent him. He may be delusional, and the fact that he thinks I'm his lawyer proves it. I haven't been in a courtroom in over six years."

"I heard you were pretty good."

"Who told you that?" Mike asked in surprise.

"Your name came up last week when I was having lunch with Judge Coberg. He told me about a case in which you cross-examined a witness who confessed on the witness stand. It sounded like something from a TV show."

"Warren Ridley," Mike answered. "It was a white lightning case. A real throwback."

"Yeah, the judge said that's what convinced him you should be a minister. He claimed anyone who could get this Ridley guy to admit his guilt when another man was about to be convicted ought to be in a pulpit urging people to confess their sins. It was hilarious the way the judge told it."

Mike smiled at the memory of the mountain man sputtering and fuming on the witness stand until finally throwing up his hands and acknowledging that he'd secretly built a moonshine still on a neighbor's property.

"That story has been overblown, but if I'm so good, I should have been able to convince Sam Miller that I'm not going to be his lawyer."

"Maybe you should put it in writing."

"Yeah, that's my next step. Sorry to inconvenience you."

"No problem, it's a pleasure meeting you over the phone. Let me know if I can help."

"Thanks, and I'll suggest to Miller that he consider hiring you."

Mike hung up the phone and added Greg Freeman to his list of church prospects. He turned on his computer and quickly typed a letter of nonrepresentation that included a place for Sam Miller to sign.

"Back to the jail," he said to Delores.

"Why?"

"I have to set Mr. Miller straight that I won't be representing him. I don't think the elders or members of this congregation would want me practicing criminal law on the side."

THIS TIME, THE FEMALE DEPUTY ON DUTY DIDN'T OBJECT TO Mike's request for access to the cell block. Lamar Cochran wasn't on duty, and an unfamiliar officer brought out Sam Miller. The older man greeted Mike when he entered the hallway. Mike didn't respond. They went into the same interview room. Mike spoke without sitting down.

"Mr. Miller, I thought I made it clear that I wouldn't be representing you. You don't qualify for an appointed lawyer and need to hire a private attorney. Mr. Freeman is willing to help, but whether you hire him or someone else, you need to act as soon as possible."

Sam looked up at Mike. The old man didn't seem upset at the news.

"Have a seat," Sam said. "I understand."

Mike placed the letter he'd typed on the table.

"This is a letter stating that I'm not your lawyer. Sign it. I have an extra copy for you."

Sam picked up the sheet of paper, looked at it for a few seconds then placed it on the table. Mike held out a pen.

"Do you have any questions?" Mike asked.

"Yep."

"Go ahead."

"Did she laugh?" Sam asked.

"Who?" Mike asked in surprise.

"Your wife."

"Why would she laugh?"

"I told you yesterday that Isaac was on the way."

Mike stared at the old man for several seconds.

"What are you talking about?"

"Your baby. Did your wife laugh when she gave you the news that you're going to be a daddy?"

"Yes," Mike answered slowly. "And cried, too."

Sam patted his stomach. "That's understandable. It's been a long wait. But she's a new woman. A fresh wind from heaven is going to refresh her soul."

Mike sat down in the chair opposite Sam. "How did you know my wife was pregnant? I didn't know it myself until I got home yesterday afternoon."

"I told you Isaac was coming. I figured she'd be laughing since that's what his name means."

Mike's eyes widened in disbelief. "You believe I'm going to have a son?"

"Yep. But I have a fifty-fifty chance of guessing right anyway."

"How did you know my wife was pregnant?" Mike insisted.

Sam grinned. "Papa showed me. It's a sign and a wonder."

"Well, it makes me wonder all right, but you didn't answer my question."

"It was part of the dream," Sam answered patiently. "The one that sent Muriel to the church to fetch you."

"What dream?"

Sam sat back in his chair. "You told me to get right to the point yesterday, so I didn't mention it. Do you want the whole explanation?"

"Yes."

"Okay. Here's what happened. In the dream, my truck broke down on the side of the road in front of your church. A lawyer I know came out of the sanctuary to help me. His wife was with him, and she was laughing and pointing at her stomach. It was obvious that she was pregnant, but she put her finger to her lips, so I knew it was a secret. The lawyer started working on my truck and fixed whatever was wrong with it, then I left." Sam stopped.

"That's it?" Mike asked.

"Yep."

"How do you know it was my church?"

"I don't get over that way much, but I've been by it on the road. Little white building beside a stream that dries up to a trickle in the summer."

"Yeah, but we have a bigger sanctuary now." Mike furrowed his brow. "Who was the lawyer?"

"Jim Somers."

"He's been dead for years!"

"Yep."

"And his wife is close to eighty."

"Yep. That let me know it had been a long wait for you and your wife, like Abraham and Sarah. When the lawyer from the church fixed my truck, it told me that you were the one who was going to help me get out of here and down the road of life."

Mike tapped the letter on the table with his right index finger but didn't look at it.

"But why was Jim Somers in your dream? Neither he nor his wife ever attended Little Creek Church."

"Because I knew him. I used to cut his grass. It's a way Papa uses to speak to me. He shows me a person I know to tell me about someone I don't. You'll learn."

Mike thought for a moment. The unusual man's logic was filled with holes.

"But we have other lawyers in our church," Mike said. "Maybe one of them is supposed to represent you. Do you know Jack Smith? He's a fine lawyer."

"No. You're the one."

Mike shook his head. "Mr. Miller, that is an interesting story, and I can't deny that my wife is pregnant, but your interpretation—"

"Is often the hardest part, I admit," Sam said. "And I've made mistakes. Papa is never wrong, but when things get in my old brain, they can get tangled up and confused."

"Maybe that's what's happened this time, or you were working through a psychological problem you have with lawyers."

"I don't have anything against lawyers. We're all sinners in the hand of the Enemy until the Master sets us free. Papa doesn't pay attention to labels."

Mike digested the unorthodox terminology used by the old man.

"Okay, but you didn't see me in your dream, did you?"

"No, but before I was arrested I knew you were coming in three months, and when I put the two dreams together it all seemed to fit. Where we go from here is around the bend and out of sight, but the first step is for us to get together so you can help me get out of this mess, and I can teach you what I know."

"You had another dream?" Mike asked in dismay.

"Yep. I've had thousands of them. Some are dreams, others are visions."

Mike placed his pen on the letter. He'd heard enough for one day.

"Sign this letter. I know you want to spend time with me, but I don't need to be your attorney for that to happen. Maybe we can talk about your dreams and visions after you make bond and get out of here."

"What's your wife's name?" Sam asked.

Mike was irritated. "You don't know?" he responded with a hint of sarcasm.

"Nope."

"Margaret, but I call her Peg."

"Muriel wants to meet your wife, but I told her to call and check with you first."

"Does your wife have dreams, too?"

"Not like I do."

Mike hesitated. He didn't want to drag Peg into interaction with the Miller family.

"I'll see."

Sam stood. "Thanks for coming."

"What about the letter?" Mike asked, remaining in his chair.

"You and Peg pray about it and let me know."

"And you're going to stay in jail until I get back to you?"

"Yep. I don't want to, but you're not giving me much of a choice."

Mike stiffened and his eyes narrowed. Miller's attempt to manipulate him through guilt was not going to be successful.

"Mr. Miller, I have one piece of advice for you. Hire a lawyer."

Mike left the room without shaking the old man's hand.

Five

MIKE KNEW WHAT TO DO. THERE WAS NO LEGAL REQUIREMENT that he obtain Sam Miller's signature on a piece of paper, and based on their second meeting, it would be easier to ignore the situation than try to address it directly.

When he arrived at the church, Mike saw Peg's SUV parked in front of the administration wing. Beside it was the same red pickup he'd seen the previous day. His irritation returned. He walked quickly through the administration wing. No one was sitting in the waiting area. Delores tilted her head toward his office.

"They're in there," she whispered.

"Peg and the Miller woman?" Mike barked.

"Yes."

Mike burst into the room. Peg was sitting on a small love seat with her shoes off and her legs tucked beneath her. Muriel Miller sat beside her.

"Honey, I think you know Mrs. Miller. She was waiting to see you when I stopped by. Do you remember the painting I did of the woman at the pond?"

"Uh, yes."

"Based on the person you saw in your dream, doesn't Muriel look just like her? When I saw her, it made me wish I'd brought my pencils so I could do a quick sketch."

"Maybe," Mike grunted. "I thought you were going to the doctor."

"I did. Everything is fine. I'm in great shape for a thirty-nine-year-old woman about to have her first baby."

Mike frowned. "We weren't going to say anything to anyone."

"Muriel already knew about it. Her husband had a dream about the baby. It's the most amazing thing—"

"I know all about the dream," Mike interrupted. "I've been to the jail and heard the whole story."

"How is Sam?" Muriel asked anxiously. "His heart isn't in the best shape."

"He's okay under the circumstances. He didn't mention any physical problems."

"I hope he's taking his blood pressure medicine."

Mike turned one of the chairs in front of his desk so that it faced the love seat. He sat down and leaned forward.

"Mrs. Miller, I can't get your husband to listen to reason. I keep telling him that I'm a minister, not a lawyer, but he changes the subject. He insists that I'm going to represent him. I know you want him out of jail, and he should have had a bond reduction hearing a couple of months ago, but there's nothing I can do about it."

Muriel reached for her purse and pulled out a tissue. "I'm worried something bad is going to happen to him."

"My sympathies are with you," Mike said. "But talking to me about it is a waste of time for both of you."

Muriel blew her nose. When she began to speak, the words tumbled out. "Sam can be hard to understand when you first meet him, especially when he's talking about the things the Lord shows him. Over the years, we've been asked to leave more than one church, but he has a heart of gold and wouldn't hurt anyone or take anything that didn't belong to him. I know he's not guilty of any crime. After he got over the shock of the arrest, he started looking for what the Lord wanted to do in the situation. He's been witnessing to the men in the jail, but he's convinced one reason this has happened is so he can meet you."

Out of the corner of his eye, Mike saw Peg bite her lower lip.

"I don't have to be his lawyer to talk to him," Mike said.

"That's not the way he sees it."

"But I've turned him down."

"I know, and I'm not trying to make you feel bad for not helping us or talk you into doing something you don't want to do."

"Then why did you come?"

Muriel put her hand on Peg's shoulder.

"For her. Sam says you're going to become more like him, and I wanted to help your wife get ready for it. There wasn't anyone to guide me, and I had it rough, especially in the early years."

Mike could imagine that forty years of marriage to someone like Sam Miller could be stressful. He spoke gently but firmly.

"That's kind of you, Mrs. Miller, but Sam doesn't have the right to decide the path God has for me."

"I know how it sounds to you. Believe me, I do. The revelation about the baby was to help you accept him, but if that doesn't work, I guess I'll have to wait and see where my help comes from."

"Your help comes from the Lord," Mike said.

Muriel managed a slight smile. "Yes, that's always true."

Mike stood to signal the end of the conversation. Muriel rose to her feet, and Mike escorted her to the door.

"Good-bye," she said to both Mike and Peg.

"Bye," Peg responded.

Mike shut the door and leaned against it.

"I'm glad that's over," he said. "Sorry you were dragged into it."

"Sorry?" Peg responded, her voice rising. "You're right about that!"

"What do you mean?"

"I wish I'd had a tape recorder running. Is that the way you used to talk down to your clients?"

"When did you start taking up for uneducated mountain women and their husbands?" Mike shot back.

"Didn't you hear her? She wants to help us. To help *me.* How often does that happen around this church?"

"That's an exaggeration."

"Any examples?"

Mike thought a moment but couldn't quickly retrieve a recent instance.

"Uh, the gifts for the house we received when I took the job."

"That was almost three years ago!"

"That's not the point. Don't tell me you believe that nonsense about me becoming like Mrs. Miller's husband?"

"You have dreams all the time."

"But they don't mean anything."

"Maybe not, but she seemed like a nice old lady, and you treated her like a first-grade child."

"If you thought I was out of line, why didn't you say anything?"

"Would it have done any good?"

Mike hesitated. It was time to cool the rhetoric.

"Probably not."

"That's the most honest, sincere thing you've said in the past fifteen minutes! What a parting platitude—'Your help comes from the Lord,'" Peg mimicked his voice.

"She agreed with me!" Mike protested, his voice getting louder again.

"But God uses people," Peg said, pointing at his chest. "I've heard you say it many times from the pulpit. God initiates—"

"We respond," Mike completed the sentence. "But do you really think I should represent this guy?"

Peg held up her hands. "That's not for me to decide. But the way you cut her off was coldhearted. At supper last night, you made her husband sound like a nut. Why didn't you mention that he told you about the baby? You're still enough of a lawyer to recognize relevant information, aren't you?"

"It didn't cross my mind. As I was leaving the interview room, he made an off-the-wall comment about Isaac coming to visit us. I didn't make the connection."

"Maybe you should have paid more attention."

Mike responded in a softer voice, "There's no easy way to explain some of the things Sam Miller said to me, but the real issue is whether I want to represent him. If I did, there could be consequences. I'd need to get approval from the session."

Peg shrugged. "Tell them it's a pro bono project for an old man who may be mentally unstable but needs guidance through the court system. What are they going to do? Cut your salary?"

Mike couldn't suppress a slight smile.

"Don't you have a meeting with the elders tonight?"

"Yes."

"You can put together a persuasive argument by then. How much time would you spend on a case like this? Didn't you think it might be just an error at the bank?"

"Maybe, but you never know. And every conversation with Sam Miller will be twice as long as necessary."

Peg relaxed against the love seat. "I'm fine with any decision you make so long as you apologize to Muriel Miller the next time you talk to her."

Mike shook his head. "I always knew you would have been a better lawyer than me."

Peg leaned forward and patted him on the cheek. "Don't flatter me. Any woman could do what I do."

THE ELDERS OF LITTLE CREEK CHURCH MET ON THE SECOND Tuesday of each month. Mike always prepared a written report on the state of the church and the items for discussion and action. He'd learned not to include specific recommendations in his report because a few members of the eight-person group opposed any new ideas merely for the sake of argument. So, Mike adopted a simple strategy. He didn't offer an opinion on matters under consideration until after the elders tossed out ideas and criticized one another. Then, when someone made a suggestion close to Mike's opinion, he threw his support behind it and subtly tried to maneuver the final outcome to a desired result. Occasionally, when a better idea came forth, he quickly jettisoned his own idea and praised the person who suggested the better alternative.

Mike usually didn't go home for supper before the 7:00 p.m. meeting. He kept frozen pizzas in the church refrigerator and put one in the oven shortly after Delores left for the day. While he waited for the pizza to cook, Nathan Goode came into the church kitchen.

"What's for supper?" Nathan asked. "Pepperoni or meat lover's?"

"Hawaiian."

"When did you go Polynesian?"

"It's the pineapple. I have fresh pieces to put on when it comes out of the oven."

"Big enough for two? I'll eat fast and help clean the kitchen before anyone gets here."

"Sure."

Nathan rarely came to the session meetings. The music director had a basketful of hassles with the bureaucracy at the high school, and Mike didn't want to add another layer of officialdom to the young man's life.

Mike took the pizza from the oven, sprinkled the pineapple on top, and cut the pizza into large slices.

"Anything you want me to mention to the elders?" he asked as he nibbled a hot bite.

"A twenty-five percent raise and four weeks paid vacation."

"What else?"

Nathan grinned. "Nothing, sir. Working with you is worth more than any amount of money."

"Save that for the school principal."

They ate in silence for a few minutes.

Nathan poured a soft drink into a glass. "There are a couple of kids who told me they're going to visit the youth group."

Not many teenagers attended the church. It was a problem Mike hadn't been able to solve.

"Who are they?"

"One plays electric guitar, the other is a drummer."

Mike reached for another slice of pizza. "You're starting a rock band on Sunday night?"

"Alternative praise music would be more accurate. Nothing too extreme, but different enough to be interesting to the kids. Aren't you the one who told me I would have to take risks in ministry if I wanted to help the people who really need it?"

"Did I say that?"

"Once when you hired me and another time in a staff meeting."

"I'm not sure this plan is going to fly under the radar."

"The drummer is Chaz Gaston, the younger son of Mitchell Gaston. He's a kid on the brink of trouble who could go bad if no one steps in to help him."

Mitchell Gaston had moved to the mountains from Atlanta after selling an Internet start-up at the height of the dot-com boom. All his children except Chaz were grown and out of the impressive house on the crest of a nearby hill. Luring the Gastons to the congregation would appeal to the elders.

"That might work," Mike replied. "Do his parents like the fact that their son plays the drums? I don't want to encourage something the parents don't support."

"They invested five grand in his set."

"I'll bring it up tonight."

MIKE RETURNED TO HIS OFFICE AND INCLUDED "CREATIVE WAYS for increasing interest in the youth group" to the night's agenda. At the end of the list he added "Unique opportunity for outreach to the community." On his own copy he penciled in "Taking risks in ministry to help people on the edge." In Sam Miller's case, that meant the edge of reason.

The session met in a conference room that contained a long wooden table surrounded by twelve burgundy chairs. More chairs lined the walls. On Sunday mornings, the room was used by an adult class known for its coffee. Mike often wandered in before the class started and grabbed a cup.

On session nights, Mike prepared two pitchers of ice water and brewed a pot of decaf coffee. It wasn't unusual for the meetings to last two or three hours, and he didn't want to prolong the time by pumping caffeine into the elders' veins.

There were six men and two women on the session. Used to persuading juries that included all kinds of people, Mike's emphasis was on building consensus regardless of gender.

By 7:00 p.m., the room was ready. Mike placed neat stacks of papers for each elder at the end of the table. With Barbara Harcourt's absence there would be seven in attendance. Bobby Lambert arrived. Bobby spent most of his time poring over contracts and business documents. He researched legal issues for Mr. Forrest but never appeared in court independently. Normally an impeccable dresser, his former law partner's tie was loosened and his hair disheveled.

"What's going on with you?" Mike asked.

"Wishing your name was still over the front door," Bobby replied. "Mr. Forrest has been impossible to deal with for the past couple of weeks."

"Is it his blood pressure?"

"I asked him about his health the other day, and he told me to mind my own business. He's been huddled in meetings and dumped several files on my desk that have taken tons of time to sort through and figure out. I can't double-bill the client for file review, and I have to work overtime to keep my own receipts on track."

"What kind of files?"

"Transactional stuff that Mr. Forrest can do in his sleep. That's what makes it so strange. You know how efficient he is at putting deals together. I've pirated his form books, but each situation requires customization."

His first three years at the firm, Mike served as Maxwell Forrest's associate and learned to appreciate the challenges and rewards of a corporate practice. Creating the right legal framework for each business arrangement could be interesting and the interaction with clients stimulating. Mike shifted into trial work when the firm's litigation partner retired but remained available as a backup for Mr. Forrest.

"What about the other guys?"

Bobby lowered his voice. "Park is moving to Charlotte to work for an insurance defense firm. This is his last week. All his work has been shifted to Arnold, who is working longer hours than I am."

As the other members of the session arrived, Mike greeted them. When they were seated, he asked Milton Chesterfield, the oldest member of the group and the richest man in the church, to pray. Milton's prayer was as predictable as the opening lines of Genesis. Mike had never heard him utter a modified version.

"Sovereign God, help us to do Thy will in this meeting. Amen."

The elders followed the written agenda. Mike sat back and listened. First, the financial report. Offerings exceeded the level needed to keep pace with the budget, but two elders urged fiscal caution and curtailing expenditures. Mike didn't fret. After thirty minutes of discussion, nothing changed.

The facilities report included a presentation by Libby Gorman on the condition of the church cemetery. Some of the older monuments and markers needed repair, and she believed family members should bear the expense of work on their plots, with the church paying for those with no known living descendants. One of the largest plots in the cemetery was devoted to deceased members of the Chesterfield family.

"I think the church should take care of the maintenance for everyone," Milton said. "I shouldn't be punished because my family stayed loyal to the church and didn't move away."

"I think it would be a privilege to tidy up our family plots." Libby sniffed.

"What efforts did you make to find relatives?" Milton asked.

"My daughter-in-law spent hours on her computer trying to track folks down," Libby answered. She held up a sheet of paper. "And I sent out forty letters."

"This issue is covered by the Equal Protection Clause of the Constitution," Bobby said, winking at Mike mischievously. "Everyone who is dead should be treated the same, especially if the body was transported in interstate commerce. Anything less would be a denial of their due process rights—"

"Thanks for sending the letters, Libby," Mike interrupted. "Did you receive any responses?"

Libby glanced down at a pad she'd placed on the table. "Uh, eight so far, including four from people willing to pay something if the amount is reasonable."

The discussion continued for another half hour. In the end, Bobby was the one who suggested an acceptable compromise. Payment for repairs by descendants was voluntary, but if they did so, the church would place a small marker on the plot indicating that it had been restored through a generous gift from the family.

Most of the argumentative steam in the group had been vented by the time they reached the youth group item. However, Mike didn't try to water down Nathan's proposal. "He wants to allow students to play electric guitars and drums," Mike said.

"In the sanctuary?" Libby asked in dismay.

"No, of course not; I would have stopped that myself. The music will be confined to the youth room and only on Sunday nights."

"It's important to maintain decorum at *all* times," Milton added with emphasis. "Including the Sunday sermon. Mike, you have a lot of good things to say, but at times you get carried away—"

"Let's stay on the issue," Bobby interjected.

"The boy who plays drums is Mitchell Gaston's son," Mike added calmly. "It's a great opportunity to connect the Gaston family with the church."

Milton's eyes opened wide. "Why didn't you say so in the first place?"

After a few minutes of discussion, permission was granted, provided the volume wasn't too loud and no parents complained. Mike didn't push. An open door was all Nathan could ask for. It would be up to him to sell it to the parents.

"The last item on the agenda doesn't require discussion, only your approval," Mike said, straightening his papers in preparation for the end of the meeting. "It involves a fellow minister who needs legal assistance that I'll provide without charge. I wanted to let you know about it before I did anything. Milton, will you pray?"

Before Milton began, Bobby Lambert put down his coffee cup and spoke. "What kind of assistance?" the lawyer asked.

"A misunderstanding about church finances," Mike replied nonchalantly.

"How serious a misunderstanding?" Bobby persisted.

Mike looked at Bobby and tried to send an unspoken signal to leave the issue alone.

"Yeah, give us the details," Rick Weston, another elder, said.

Mike shrugged. "It resulted in a criminal charge but may be the result of a bank error."

"Is it a felony charge?" Bobby asked.

Mike nodded. "Class C."

"Then it involves at least a hundred thousand dollars," the lawyer said, sitting up in his chair. "That's a big error for a bank to make."

"It's just zeros to them," Mike replied. "I haven't investigated anything in detail. His wife contacted the church and asked for help. I met with him at the jail."

"You went to the jail?" Libby asked. "That's not an appropriate place for our minister to be seen."

"The apostle Paul spent a lot of time in jail," Bobby said. "How much time did he build behind bars, Mike? Three or four years?"

"At least," Mike said. "But this man is not the apostle Paul."

"What's his name?" Libby asked.

"Sam Miller."

"The yardman?" Milton asked.

"Yes," Mike said.

"He's no minister," Milton grunted. "He used to cut my neighbor's grass."

"He's a lay preacher," Mike answered. "I doubt he has any theological education or recognized ordination."

"Wouldn't he qualify for an appointed lawyer?" Bobby asked.

"No, he owns a home and runs a small business."

"Then he should hire his own lawyer!" Milton said sharply. "This is a church, not a legal aid society! If you don't have enough to keep you busy, we need to discuss modification of your job description."

Mike started to respond then stopped.

"What's really going on?" Bobby asked. "Why do you want to do this?"

Mike paused before answering. If he wanted to retreat, now would be the time to do so gracefully.

"Because I believe God wants me to help him," he said with more conviction than he felt. "I'm working very hard to be a faithful pastor for this church, and this is not some kind of professional identity crisis. I'm more confident of my call to the ministry than ever and have no interest in returning to the law. This church is where I want to be, and I intend to stay here as long as you'll have me. I'm simply asking you to allow me to help someone in need, and trust me to do it in a way that honors God." There was silence for several seconds. The elders glanced at one another.

"Mike, would you please step out of the room for a few minutes while we talk?" Bobby asked.

Mike hesitated. "Let me make one thing clear," he said. "I want to do this, but if you tell me no, I'll accept your decision and won't mention it again."

Mike stepped into the hallway. The sounds of muffled voices came from the room. He resisted the childish impulse to put his ear to the door and listen. He began pacing up and down the hall, convincing himself that whether or not he helped Sam Miller was an insignificant matter, no more important than how to pay for gravestone maintenance.

By his fifth turn on the carpet, he'd lost the internal debate. He was vulnerable. If his request was approved, there would be whisperings around the church about his actions. If he lost, he would have needlessly expended valuable capital and diminished his stature before the session. He inwardly kicked himself for having a knee-jerk response to Peg's pressure. Time passed. The door opened, and Libby came out.

"Just going to the restroom," she said with a wave of her hand.

Mike didn't walk past the open door. In a few minutes, Libby returned to the conference room without looking at him. He felt as though he were waiting for a jury—only he was the one on trial. He kept pacing up and down the hallway. He thought about Sam Miller. The old man was probably snoring in his bunk, dreaming about gumdrop fairies and cupids. The conference room door opened.

"Come in," Bobby said. "We're ready."

Mike took his seat, but his sense of authority was gone. He quickly scanned the faces around the table. They were inscrutable. Bobby cleared his throat.

"We voted and decided that you can represent Sam Miller."

"It wasn't unanimous," Milton interjected.

"Until he finds another lawyer," Libby added. "Bobby is going to see what he can do to help on that part of it."

"Fair enough," Mike said, trying to regain control. "If any of you have any questions, please feel free to contact me."

"Let's pray and go home," Bobby said, stifling a yawn.

"Before we adjourn," Mike said, "I have one other bit of news and wanted you to be the first in the church to hear it." He paused for dramatic effect. "Peg is pregnant. It was confirmed at the doctor's office this morning. She's fine, and we're looking forward to the arrival of a new member of the Andrews family in about nine months."

Congratulations echoed in Mike's ears as he locked up the church. He'd wanted to announce the news of the baby from the pulpit on Sunday before the entire congregation, but it was necessary to knock the Miller case off the minds of the elders. Nothing worked better than the announcement of a long-awaited baby.

Six

MIKE STIRRED THE CUP OF COFFEE PEG PLACED ON THE BREAKfast table in front of him, took a sip, and nibbled a toasted English muffin covered in melted butter and homemade jam given to them by a woman in the church.

"Mrs. Ayers gave us this jam," he said.

"I know," Peg answered as she joined him at the table.

"So someone from the church helped us a few months ago."

Peg smiled. "I think the jury has already left the courtroom following yesterday's closing arguments at the church office."

Mike took another bite of muffin. "And you won, but when I tried to enforce the judgment with the session, I didn't do very well. I could have used a co-counsel."

Peg sipped her coffee. "I'm supporting you from here."

"Which I appreciate," Mike answered truthfully. "And you don't have to get up and fix breakfast to prove it. You need more rest, not less."

Peg reached across the table and tapped his wedding ring with her index finger.

"I want us to practice being a family. For years we've been passing each other in the process of living separate lives."

"That's an extreme way of putting it."

"It started when you went to work at the law office, and since then we've never placed a high priority on being together. I had my friends and painting; you had your career and golf. It was easier for both of us not to interact. Am I right?"

"Yes," Mike admitted.

"Do you want to change or keep the status quo?"

"Change sounds good, but what does it mean to you?"

Peg removed her hand from his. "Didn't you take a counseling course in seminary? What do most women want from their husbands?"

"Quality time."

"To do what?"

"Talk."

"Correct."

Mike looked at his watch. "I need to get going in a minute. When do you want to start having quality time?"

"While you eat your muffin. Ask me a question."

"What kind of question?"

Peg smiled. "You're so smart. That's the perfect question because it lets me tell you what's on my heart. While you were at the session meeting last night, I sat in my reading chair in the bedroom and prayed in a way I've never done before. I put my hand on my stomach and talked to God about our baby, about me, about us. Then I tried to listen. One of the things I realized is that if I want a family in nine months, I'd better start acting like I have one now. And that means being serious about my faith and more committed to loving you."

Mike was speechless. Peg continued.

"I know you've got a soft spot deep down inside, and I promise not to tell anyone about it. You've put up walls of protection because I've been so prickly, but I want to love you enough to convince you to tear down the barriers between us."

"That's great."

"Any other response?"

"I'm not sure what to say."

Peg stood up. "Don't try. An admission of inadequacy is nice from a self-confident male who is always trying to fix everything."

She walked over to the kitchen sink.

"I do have another question," Mike added.

"Go ahead."

"What prompted you to pray last night?"

"Muriel Miller encouraged me to do it. She even wrote some Bible verses on a sheet of paper and suggested I read them. Will you see Sam today?"

"Yes, I'll go to the jail, file a notice of representation at the courthouse, and try to talk to someone at the district attorney's office."

"Is Ken West still the DA?"

"He is, but he's probably assigned something like this to an assistant."

"Who will do your typing?"

"I'll swing by the old office and get Juanita to do it. It won't take her five minutes."

"And don't forget to call Muriel Miller and apologize."

MIKE PHONED THE CHURCH AS HE DROVE DOWN THE HILL TOWARD Shelton. The familiar raspy voice answered the phone.

"Good morning, Delores," Mike said. "I won't be coming in this morning. I have several things to do in town."

"Like buying a baby bed?"

"News travels fast."

"There were twelve messages on the answering machine when I arrived this morning, and someone phoned me before I woke up to make sure it wasn't a false rumor."

"It's true. Peg saw the doctor yesterday. But I'm not picking out pacifiers. I discussed the Sam Miller situation with the session, and I'm going to help him until another lawyer can be hired. I have several stops to make and won't be at the church until this afternoon."

"What should I tell all the callers?"

"Take messages. I'll get back to them before the end of the day. Oh, and I need Muriel Miller's number."

"I put it on a slip and gave it to you."

"Remember, I dropped it in the trash. Check your records."

Mike waited.

"Here it is," she said.

Mike wrote down the number on a pad he kept in the car.

"You're not going to ask me to type any legal papers, are you?" Delores asked.

"No, but I can't think of anyone better able to keep the church running when I have to be away for a few hours."

Delores hung up without responding.

Muriel Miller didn't answer the phone. Mike listened to a brief message about Sam's lawncare business and asked her to call his cell phone number as soon as possible. He hung up as he turned into an empty parking space in front of his old law firm.

None of the law firms in a small town like Shelton had reception rooms filled with expensive antiques and fancy Oriental rugs, but Forrest, Lambert, Park, and Arnold had the nicest waiting area in town. Two leather couches and a pair of leather armchairs gave it an old-club feel. A tightly woven tan carpet covered the floor. In the center of the room rested a low coffee table covered with an assortment of magazines bearing Mr. Forrest's address. Rustic paintings of primitive mountain homesteads by a local artist decorated the walls. The receptionist sat behind a shiny wooden desk at the far end of the room in front of the door leading to the offices. The firm kept the reception room refrigerator cool on even the hottest days. When Mike entered, a new female face greeted him behind the desk. He introduced himself.

"I used to be a partner in the firm," he said. "I need to see Bobby's secretary for a minute."

"Yes, sir. I know who you are. I'll let her know you're here."

The receptionist answered a call and waved him through. Beyond the door, a long hallway extended to the rear of the building. Every room, library, conference area, secretarial suite, law office, and the kitchen opened onto the hall. The first door to the left was the conference room. It was empty. Next, he passed Mr. Forrest's office. The door was closed, and Mike didn't knock. The senior partner only shut his door for a good reason and didn't want to be disturbed except for a matter of life, death, or a visit from Jack Hatcher, the president of the Bank of Barlow County.

Mike's former office was now used by Jeff Park, the lawyer moving to Charlotte. Jeff was on the phone with his back to the door. Juanita Jones, the secretary Mike hired and later shared with Bobby Lambert, worked in the next office.

Despite her first name, the dark-haired, middle-aged secretary had no connection to any Spanish-speaking area of the world. Her family had lived in Barlow County for more than seventy-five years, and she only knew enough Spanish to pronounce the items on the menu at the local Mexican restaurant.

"Are you on break?" Mike asked.

Juanita glanced up at the sound of his voice. "Hey, Mike, I'm so sorry."

"About what?" Mike asked in surprise.

Juanita put her hand over her mouth. "Didn't you hear about Danny Brewster?"

"No."

"He was murdered in prison. Stabbed by another inmate with a homemade knife. It happened a couple of weeks ago."

Mike's face fell. Early in his career he'd represented the mentally limited young man who was charged with multiple counts of burglary. Mike didn't believe Danny knew the difference between being invited into someone's home and breaking and entering, but Judge Lancaster denied an incompetency motion. Ken West offered a plea bargain, but Mike went to trial, confident he could pin responsibility for the crimes on Danny's older brother, the person who sent Danny into the houses. The jury didn't buy Mike's theory and the judge sentenced Danny to ten years in prison. Mike spent two years appealing the conviction but lost.

"He was supposed to get out in a couple of months," Juanita said.

"I thought he was in a special unit," Mike said numbly. "Not with the general prison population."

"I don't know. After you moved to Virginia, nobody kept tabs on him."

"I thought about him the other day but didn't follow up," Mike said, shaking his head. "Is his mother still in the area?"

"Yes, she contacted me looking for you after it happened. I gave her your number at the church and urged her to call you."

"I haven't heard a word."

"Do you know how to reach her?"

"No. She didn't have a phone the last time we talked."

"I'll track her down and let you know. What else can I do for you?"

Mike turned around and shut the door.

"I can't believe I'm doing it, but I've agreed to help an old man who is in some trouble. He runs a lawncare business and preaches on the side. He's a strange person, but I think he's as innocent as Danny and—"

"Sam Miller," Juanita interrupted.

"Do you know him?"

"Oh yeah." The tone of Juanita's voice changed. "But I don't know why you'd want to help him. I think he's either a fraud or a fortune-teller. He told my cousin Lou some things and claimed he was speaking for God, but it was all bogus. I think Lou even gave him some money."

"Did he ask for the money?"

"I don't know the details. Lou is a trusting person who is vulnerable to manipulation. What kind of trouble is Miller having?"

"Criminal charges. He's accused of embezzling money from a church."

Juanita pursed her lips. "That figures. I know the law says the accused is innocent until proven guilty, but I'd be careful. You're wrong about one thing. Sam Miller isn't another Danny Brewster. Danny was a sweet boy abused by that sorry older brother of his. This is different, and I'd hate to see your name linked to Miller in a way that damages your reputation. It's one thing for an ordinary lawyer to represent someone in a criminal case, but you're in another world now. People will assume you believe Miller is innocent, and if he's not, the taint of his guilt will spill onto you."

"You feel that strongly about him?"

"Yes. I've always told you the truth. You could have fired me when I did it before." Juanita smiled slightly. "Now, I'm immune from a pink slip signed by you, but that doesn't change who I am. My cousin's experience with Sam Miller was bad, and I don't want you to get hurt."

Mike was silent for a few seconds. "I appreciate your concern. My main job is to get Miller out on bond so he can hire another lawyer. Bobby is going to work on that part. Is he here?"

"No, he had to leave early this morning for a meeting in Asheville. He's doing a lot of work for Mr. Forrest."

"Yeah, he mentioned that last night at the church."

Juanita lowered her voice. "Did he tell you about Jeff?"

Mike nodded.

"A whole lot of new work is getting dumped on me, too," Juanita continued. "I was here until seven o'clock last night."

Mike made a quick decision. "And I'm not going to add to your load by asking you to type any paperwork for the Miller case."

"Are you sure?" Juanita replied hurriedly. "I wasn't trying to avoid helping you."

"I know, but what you've told me is more valuable than a few pecks on the keyboard. Tell Bobby I'll call him later."

"Okay."

"And thanks for letting me know about Danny." Mike opened the door to leave. "One other thing. What is your cousin's full name?"

"Lou Jasper."

STILL THINKING ABOUT DANNY BREWSTER, MIKE WALKED ACROSS the street to the courthouse. He would track down Danny's mother and offer condolences, but he wasn't sure what else to do. He walked up the familiar steps to the courthouse. The first floor of the building had high ceilings that helped keep the courthouse cool in summer, but, more importantly, communicated to those who entered the gravity of the business conducted there.

The district attorney's office was on the ground floor next to the main courtroom. Emblazoned in gold paint over the entrance were the words *Ken West, District Attorney.* At the rear of the office suite was a door that opened directly into the courtroom. On trial and arraignment days, the prosecutors would make a grand entrance beside the bench where the judge sat. It always looked a little too cozy to Mike, but there was no legal reason to seal the door. The government lawyers argued that proximity to the courtroom resulted in increased efficiency.

No one was in the reception area. Mike looked down the hall. He knew the rotund district attorney's office was the last one on the left. He edged down the hall.

"Anyone here?" he asked.

When no one appeared, Mike retreated to the reception area. Photographs of West posing with well-known political figures hung on the wall.

"May I help you?" a female voice asked.

Mike turned and faced a lanky young woman with sandy hair who looked like a high school intern spending part of her senior year at the courthouse.

"Is Ken West in?" Mike asked.

"No, the rest of the staff is at a training session in Raleigh," she said with an accent that revealed mountain roots. "I'm Melissa Hall, one of the assistant district attorneys. Would you like to leave a message?"

Mike introduced himself.

"Maybe you can help me. Are you familiar with the Sam Miller case?"

"Do you have a case number?"

"No, but I know it's an embezzlement charge."

"I'll check his name on the computer."

Hall leaned over the computer at the receptionist's desk.

"Here it is," she said, raising her eyebrows. "The case has been assigned to me."

"Have you done any investigation?" Mike asked.

Hall looked up. "We don't charge someone with a crime unless there has been an investigation."

Mike managed a smile. "I meant subsequent to any reports from the police."

"Why do you want to know?"

"He's asked me to help him."

"Have you filed a notice of representation?"

"No."

Hall closed the computer screen. "Then I can't give you any information."

Mike kept his voice calm. "I thought Ken might give me an off-the-record perspective on the case. If you don't feel comfortable pulling the file and talking to me, it can wait until he gets back."

"I've only been here six months and would prefer that Mr. West make that decision."

Mike handed her his card. "I understand. This is my number at the church. Ask Ken to give me a call."

Hall took the card and looked at it. "You're a minister?"

"Yes, but I practiced law for ten years. Maxwell Forrest and Bobby Lambert were my partners."

"I'll give Mr. West your card."

Mike left the courthouse satisfied. Hall had given him important information about the case without meaning to. The fact that Ken West had assigned Sam's case to a neophyte lawyer was positive. The weakest and least serious cases flowed downhill to the junior prosecutors.

Mike drove to the jail. He waited in the hallway while an officer brought Sam from the cell block. The older man wasn't smiling. When he came closer, Mike could see a splotchy red mark on the side of Sam's face. They went into an interview room.

"What happened to your face?"

"I turned my back on a new cell mate, and he knocked me down."

"Why?"

"He found something missing from his personal stuff and started swinging. Everyone scattered, but I moved too slow, and he caught me square in the head. I hit the floor and everything went fuzzy. When I came around, some of the other fellows in the cell had grabbed him. The guards got there and dragged him out. He was kicking, screaming, and biting. I didn't think about trying to help him until he was gone."

"What could you have done to help him?"

"I'm not sure, but the Master can still calm a storm."

"Listen, jail is a dangerous place," Mike said, thinking of Danny Brewster. "Don't have some idealistic notion that you're going to save everyone in your cell block. Keep your eyes open, and watch your back. How does your face feel?"

"About like it looks," Sam said with a grimace. "Don't say anything to Muriel. She's worried enough as it is."

"Did you see a doctor?"

"Nope, but it hurts to chew."

"Your jaw could be fractured."

"I don't think so."

"Well, you need to get it checked out. They should take you to the emergency room for an X-ray. I'll speak to the officer on duty before I leave."

"Does that mean you're going to be my lawyer?"

"For now."

Mike placed a blank legal pad on the table and told about his meeting with the elders and their decision.

"Thanks for going to all that trouble," Sam replied. "I know how tough it can be getting Papa's family to agree."

"And you understand this is a temporary situation?"

"Yep. Everything this side of glory is temporary."

Mike stared at Sam for a moment. "Do you believe the Lord has shown you anything about the criminal charge?"

"Nope. Everything has been about helping the men in here and getting to know you. The rest is like the guy who hit me yesterday, a blow out of the blue."

"Do you want me to request a protective transfer to a solitary confinement cell?"

"Nope. I think everything is going to be all right. Most of the guys back there are decent enough. They get into trouble on the outside when they start drinking or drugging."

"Okay, but be on guard against the ones who are crazy all the time."

"Yep."

"And don't try to force religion down anyone's throat. It can be offensive and might be taken the wrong way." Mike shifted the legal pad on the table. "I stopped by the district attorney's office and met the prosecutor assigned to your case."

"What did you find out?"

While Mike related his brief conversation with Melissa Hall, Sam listened closely, nodding several times and patting his stomach twice.

"Make sure she meets the choir director at your church," he said when Mike finished. "That girl is a good singer, and her voice is going to be a key to unlocking his heart to Papa's love and healing her heart from the pain of the past."

"What?" Mike asked in surprise.

"While you talked about her, I could hear a woman singing. Then a big key came down from Glory—"

"And unlocked your jail cell," Mike interrupted. "Are all our conversations going to be like this?"

Sam smiled then winced in pain. "Yep, so long as Papa turns on the spigot. When that's happening, it would be foolish not to drink."

"I'm not thirsty."

"Maybe not, but you have a sharp mind, and you'll remember everything I'm telling you. Papa can't use folks who are lazy. You're a hard worker."

"And I'm going to work my way out of this situation as soon as possible. I'll check the real estate records on your property, then file papers with the court to get your bail reduced to an amount that will let you post a property bond. How much is your mortgage?"

"Nothing. It's paid for. The Bible says to let no debt remain outstanding except continuing debt to love one another. Muriel and I haven't carried any debts for years."

"If the people at the bank find out that's what you believe, they'll never cooperate with me." Mike sat back in his chair. "One last item. Do you know a man named Lou Jasper?"

"Yep. Nice fellow who lives in the western part of the county. I met him a few years ago."

"My former secretary says you took some money from him and lied to him."

"I'm sorry to hear that's what she thinks. Papa has a great call on that boy's life. He's a dreamer, too. I interpreted a few for him, but he was curious, not serious. When he had a dream that meant he had to forgive some people he didn't like, he quit calling me."

"Do you remember the dream?"

"Yep, but it wouldn't be right for me to tell you."

"Okay. Did he give you money?"

"He was real excited at first, and I think he wrote out a check for $150. I used the money to buy a secondhand washing machine for a widow woman who didn't have one."

"Why would his cousin say you're a liar?"

"Maybe I made the mistake of telling him too much, too soon. The call on a person's life may be great, but the path getting there is never smooth. There are lots of tests. It's not automatic. Then, if a true word doesn't happen, folks will blame the messenger when the fault lies closer to home."

"Careful," Mike said. "I believe in predestination."

"I can't argue that stuff. I just know what I've seen. You'll have to figure out if it agrees with what you learned in preacher school. I don't claim to be unfoolable."

"You mean infallible."

"That's what I get for trying to use a fancy word. I've made mistakes."

"But not with your bank account?"

"No. I'm sure about that one."

Seven

Mike left the tax appraiser's office with proof that Sam Miller's hillside property was worth $65,000. He knew the actual market value was much more. If the eight-acre piece was combined with the parcel next door, it would create a nice tract for a developer who would tear down Sam's house and plant at least a dozen larger homes in its place.

It was too early for lunch so Mike drove home. Peg and Judge were gone, but when he went upstairs he found Peg's Bible open on her chair in the bedroom. A notebook lay facedown beside the Bible. Mike reached over to pick it up then stopped. It would be more fun letting Peg tell him what she discovered than to find out by snooping.

The household computer was in a small downstairs bedroom they'd turned into a study. Mike clicked open the word processing program. It took him fifteen minutes to properly format a one-page pleading notifying the court of his representation in the *State of North Carolina v. Sam Miller*. A Motion to Reduce Bond followed next. As he labored to make everything look professional, he hoped he wouldn't have to type a brief or requests to charge the jury. By the time he'd added a certificate of service upon Melissa Hall and a fill-in-the-blank notice of hearing on the motion to reduce bond, it was almost noon. He printed out several copies of the pleadings.

Bobby's car wasn't in sight at the law firm when Mike returned to town. The trip to Asheville would probably consume most of his friend's day. Mike filed his notice of representation in *State v. Miller* at the clerk's office. He was now officially on the case. He walked upstairs to the office suite used by the superior court judge currently serving Barlow County. Judges rotated across western North Carolina on a circuit designed to lessen the likelihood of favoritism to local lawyers and citizens; however, judges like Harris Coberg still held court in their home districts.

A young man Mike didn't recognize sat behind the clerk's desk in the waiting area for the judge's chambers. Mike introduced himself.

"Who'll be on the bench this week to hear a bond motion in a criminal case?" Mike asked.

"Judge Coberg has started a six-month rotation," the man responded.

"Great. When can you give me a fifteen-minute slot?"

The man glanced at his computer screen. "Tomorrow at nine-thirty."

"Tomorrow?"

"Unless you want to move it to next week."

"No, that's fine. I'll take it. Is the judge in his chambers?"

"No, he's at lunch."

Mike filled in the date and time on the notice and dropped off a copy at the district attorney's office. As he left Shelton and drove to the church, Juanita Jones called him on his cell phone. "Are you on your way to the golf course?" she asked.

"I haven't thought about a golf ball all day," Mike replied. "Did you locate the number for Danny Brewster's mother? I really want to extend my condolences."

"Got it right here."

Mike flipped open his PDA and entered the number while driving with his knees.

"Thanks for letting me know," he said. "And I won't forget your comments about Sam Miller. I want to do the right thing."

"I know. That's the reason I always considered you the best. You had both the will to fight and the desire for truth. I'll be praying for you."

When he reached the church, he phoned Danny's mother. A shaky voice answered the phone.

"Mrs. Brewster, it's Mike Andrews. I just found out about Danny and want you to know how sorry I am."

"I didn't have the money to get him brought home, and they buried him in the prison graveyard," Mrs. Brewster replied. "He didn't have a proper funeral or anything."

"I wish I'd known sooner."

"It's my fault for not calling you."

"No, you've had too much on your mind." Mike paused. "Would you like to have a memorial service here in Shelton?"

"It's been almost two weeks since he died. I guess it's not too late to do something."

"No, it's not. Danny was a fine young man, and those who loved him ought to have a chance to get together to share their sorrow and remember the happier times."

"I've been working on Sundays and haven't been regular at the church down the road. They have a new preacher who doesn't know our family at all—"

"I'd be honored to serve as the minister. I could look for a place on your side of the county to have the service."

"Danny sure did think a lot of you. He saved every one of your letters and read them over and over. They were in his things they sent to me from down yonder."

Mike felt a knot in his throat. He'd corresponded regularly with Danny for several years but slacked off during his time in seminary and had only written twice since returning to Shelton. Danny faithfully replied to every communication. His letters always listed what he'd eaten that day and a Bible verse written with a red pencil. On the back of each letter, he included a crude drawing of something at the prison—his cot, a basketball goal, the guard tower, even the toilet in the corner of his cell. The drawings made Mike both sad and angry.

"I didn't write him enough, Mrs. Brewster," Mike said. "I'd like to do this for him if you'll let me."

"Danny would be glad about that. He was awful proud of you becoming a preacher."

Mike looked at his calendar. "What day of the week is best for you?"

"Wednesday is my day off. We've got kinfolks and neighbors who would come."

"Then we'll do it next Wednesday afternoon. I'll get back to you tomorrow. Do you have an answering machine on your phone?"

"Yes, sir."

MIKE WAS EMOTIONALLY DRAINED WHEN HE WALKED THROUGH the door of the house and plopped down in his chair in the breakfast nook. Peg was cutting up tomatoes for a salad.

"What happened today?" she asked.

"Danny Brewster was murdered in prison two weeks ago," Mike answered in a flat tone of voice.

Peg stopped preparing the salad and gave him a hug. "I'm sorry. Who told you about it?"

"Juanita." Mike shook his head. "He was stabbed by another inmate with a homemade knife. I don't know any details, and I'm not sure I want to find out."

"I know that hurt."

"I called Mrs. Brewster and arranged to have a memorial service on Wednesday."

They sat down to eat. Halfway through the meal, Mike spoke. "You know, Danny was innocent because he didn't know the definition of wrong. I've always blamed the system for failing him because my ego wouldn't let me admit my mistake. It's time to be honest about my responsibility."

"No, Mike. His conviction and death weren't your fault."

"Indirectly they were. My stubbornness forced him to go to trial when he could have received a lesser sentence in a plea bargain and spent less time in jail. It hit me almost as soon as Juanita told me. Back then, all I could think about was winning. It's easier to recognize selfishness and stubbornness with the benefit of hindsight."

Peg turned away.

"What is it?" Mike asked.

"Nothing. Just thinking about the past."

WITHIN MINUTES OF THE TIME MIKE'S HEAD TOUCHED THE pillow, he fell asleep. He rarely woke up until the alarm clock blared in the morning. His nights, however, were filled with unconscious activity. Since childhood, Mike's sleep had been populated by dreams. Most he forgot before dawn, but occasionally one survived the leap from night to day. He had a couple of recurring dreams but never submitted them to an expert for interpretation.

At 3:00 a.m., Mike came roaring out of slumber and sat up in bed. Breathing heavily, he stared into the dark room.

"What is it?" Peg asked sleepily.

"A nightmare," Mike replied. "So bad it woke me up."

Peg leaned on her elbow. "Are you okay?"

"Yes, but I wasn't in the dream."

"Do you want to tell me about it?"

Mike rubbed the side of his face, which was scratchy from an almost twenty-four-hour growth of beard.

"I dreamed Danny, Sam Miller, and I were sitting in an interview room at the jail. Sam was talking his usual nonsense, but Danny seemed to enjoy listening to him. I was frustrated with both of them. Suddenly, the door burst open, and four large men without faces rushed into the room and grabbed Danny and Sam. I was paralyzed. I tried to protest but couldn't think of anything to say. I felt completely helpless. Two of the men dragged Danny away. The other two picked up Sam's chair and started walking out of the room. Sam looked at me and waved good-bye. I had the sense he could easily get away by jumping out of the chair to the floor. I tried to scream a warning, but nothing came out of my mouth. That's when I woke up."

Peg turned on the light on the nightstand.

"I think you're just trying to work through stress," she said. "You had a lot dumped on you yesterday. You were calm at the time but needed to process the tension out of your system."

"Maybe, although it was like watching TV."

Peg reached over and turned off the light. "Ask Sam about it. He's the expert on dreams."

THE FOLLOWING MORNING, MIKE SPENT EXTRA TIME IN FRONT of the mirror adjusting his tie. Peg came up behind him and peeked over his shoulder.

"How are you feeling?" she asked.

"Still tired. I stayed awake for a while because I didn't want to go through the dream again."

"Did it come back?"

"No, but I did wake up with Danny Brewster's face in my mind. Do you remember how toothy he looked when he grinned?"

"Yes. File that in your mental photo album as a happier thought."

Peg smoothed his collar and stroked his hair. "You know, if you really want to create a good impression in the courtroom, you need more gray hair."

Mike shook his head. "I'm going to be a father, not a grandfather."

"We'll probably get those questions anyway."

Mike turned around. Peg looked great in workout clothes from the University of Virginia, their college alma mater and the place they met and fell in love. She leaned up and kissed him.

"I might, but you won't," Mike said. "Visitors to the church often ask if you're my daughter."

Peg shook her head and frowned. "It's a sin to lie."

DOWNSTAIRS, MIKE DRANK A CUP OF COFFEE AND HALFHEARTEDLY nibbled a slice of wheat toast. Judge sat beside his chair, hoping for a crumb from the table.

"Time to ride into battle," Mike said, looking at the clock on the wall.

"I'll be in the castle with your noble beast when you return."

Mike patted Judge on the head and gave him a sliver of crust. "I wish a human judge would do what I ask in return for a piece of bread."

IT WASN'T A BUSY CRIMINAL ARRAIGNMENT DAY. WHEN THAT happened, the influx of family and friends anxious about the fate of loved ones made it hard to find a parking place near the courthouse. Only a few people were on the sidewalk.

Butterflies fluttered in Mike's stomach. A bond hearing was a perfunctory affair that wouldn't create much tension, but Mike's long absence from the legal arena made him nervous. Sitting in the car, he phoned the jail to confirm that Sam would be present. As he walked up the courthouse steps with a thin folder in his hand, Mike replayed in his mind the legal standard for reducing a bond.

The main courtroom in the Barlow County Courthouse was painted a light cream color. The dark wooden benches had been recently restained, and the faint odor of finishing compound lingered in the air. Half a dozen lawyers were milling around the front of the courtroom. When Mike approached, conversation stopped. Earl Coulter, a veteran criminal defense lawyer, came over and shook his hand.

"Welcome, Preacher. Glad you're here. I could use a character witness in a sentencing hearing for one of the Vinson boys. How much would it cost to get you to vouch for him?"

"It says *Not for hire* on the back of my new business card," Mike replied. "And I don't think you want me giving my opinion of whether your client is a threat to society."

"You know Zane, don't you?"

"Yeah, I got him a deal for two years in and two years on probation when he was about twenty."

"He ran through that and has built more time in prison since. Two years at a work camp would be a blessing from heaven if I could get it today."

Mike pointed up. "You and Zane had better talk to my new boss if you want that kind of help."

Mike stepped through the opening in the wooden railing that ran across the courtroom. Passing into familiar territory, the butterflies in his stomach left. A short young lawyer with dark hair and angular features came over to him.

"I'm Greg Freeman. How is Mr. Miller doing?"

"That's why I'm here," Mike replied. "I filed a motion to reduce his bond, but I'd still like to see him hire an attorney. I'll keep working that angle with him."

Several chairs along the wall opposite the jury box were reserved for the attorneys. Mike sat in the second chair from the end and scribbled a few notes on a legal pad. People began to drift into the courtroom. Bobby Lambert and Maxwell Forrest walked down the aisle and through the gate. Mike stood up.

"Good morning, Mr. Forrest," he said.

Mike never called the gray-haired, distinguished-looking senior partner by his first name and knew few people under fifty who did.

"Good to see you, Mike," Forrest replied with a smile. "Are you testifying as a character witness?"

"No, sir."

"I forgot to tell you," Bobby said to his senior partner. "Mike is representing a man pro bono. When he asked permission from the elders to do it, you'd have thought he wanted to bring a basket of snakes to the Sunday morning service."

"I'm saving the snake request for next month," Mike said.

"That should be easy compared to the other night. Convincing the other members of the session to let you help this man was one of the most difficult jobs of persuasion I've had all year."

"Sorry I missed the argument," Mike said. "I could have learned something, but you kicked me out of the room for the debate."

"I didn't want you to learn all my manipulative tricks. You might use them against me."

Forrest smiled. "If you boys had spent as much time thinking up ways to help our clients as you did upstaging each other, all of us would have made a lot more money."

The back door of the courtroom opened, and a sheriff's deputy brought in a line of four prisoners from the jail. Bringing up the rear and looking around the courtroom with a quizzical look on his face was Sam Miller. There was a visible bruise on his jaw where he'd been struck. The prisoners went into the jury box and sat on the front row. Mike walked toward Sam, but before he reached him, Judge Coberg came into the courtroom.

"All rise!" an elderly bailiff ordered.

Mike gave Sam an encouraging look before returning to the lawyers' side of the courtroom.

"Be seated," the judge said as soon as he positioned himself behind the bench.

It had been many years since Harris Coberg practiced law. His shoulders had started to droop, and his right hand had a slight quiver, but his piercing dark eyes retained the intensity that had made him a successful prosecutor long before Ken West arrived on the scene.

"We'll take up the criminal matters first," the judge said in his deep voice.

The judge glared at the table where the State's attorneys sat. There was no sign of Ken West or anyone else from the district attorney's office.

"What time is it?" the judge barked at no one in particular.

Mr. Forrest was immediately on his feet. "Five minutes after nine, Your Honor."

"Thank you, Mr. Forrest."

The side door leading to the DA's office opened, and Melissa Hall entered with several files crookedly held beneath her arm.

"Glad you could join us," the judge growled. "When I'm presiding, court begins promptly at nine. Is that a problem for you?"

"My apologies, Your Honor," Hall replied. Mike could see the young lawyer's face flush from across the room. "Mr. West was scheduled to handle this morning's docket, but he called in sick."

"Are you ready to proceed?" the judge asked in a voice that dared her to request a postponement.

"Yes, sir."

"Let's have it."

"*State v. Hughes.* Defendant's Motion for Independent Testing of Alleged Controlled Substance," Hall replied.

Partway through the hearing, Judge Coberg glanced over at the lawyers' section and nodded slightly at Mike.

Mike settled into his chair and listened. Assistant DA Hall didn't put up much of a fight to a defense request for independent testing of alleged cocaine found at the defendant's mobile home.

Greg Freeman handled the second hearing, a motion to suppress evidence of stolen merchandise found in the trunk of his client's car. The key issue was the reasonableness of the initial stop of the vehicle. The deputy hadn't figured out the nuances of the Fourth Amendment prohibition against unreasonable searches and seizures, and Freeman roasted him on cross-examination. Hall's attempt to rehabilitate the deputy's testimony only reemphasized his lack of probable cause to stop and search the car. The judge cut into Hall's questioning.

"Deputy, you can't stop a car in Barlow County and pry open the trunk with a crowbar because you heard at a bar the defendant was involved in a burglary."

"But everyone knows he's guilty," the deputy protested. "And I found the stuff to prove it!"

"Not in my courtroom!" The judge's right hand shook as he extended his finger toward the witness. "Next time, do your job right!"

The deputy silently appealed for help to Hall, who looked down at the paperwork on the table.

"Do you understand?" the judge continued.

"Uh, yes, sir."

"I'm not sure you do, Deputy, but by the next time you appear before me, I hope the sheriff's office will have corrected the flaws in your criminal justice education." The judge looked at Hall. "Tell Mr. West that I expect him to do a better job screening searches so the court's time isn't wasted with this kind of sloppy law enforcement."

"Yes, sir."

"Mr. Freeman," the judge continued. "Draw up an appropriate order granting the motion to suppress."

Freeman returned to the lawyers' section and whispered to Mike, "I don't think the judge has granted two defense motions in a row this year."

"I'm next. I hope it's three."

"'*State v. Miller,* Motion to Reduce Bond,'" the judge read from the sheet before him, then glanced up at Mike. "Mr. Andrews, are you representing Mr. Miller?"

"Yes, sir."

Mike moved to the defense table where Sam, still dressed in a jailhouse orange jumpsuit, joined him. The bruise on Sam's cheek had turned from red to purple. The old man smiled at Mike.

"Papa and I say 'Good morning,'" Sam said.

"Keep Papa out of this," Mike replied.

"Proceed," the judge said.

"Yes, sir," Mike answered loudly. He handed certified copies of the real estate records to the judge and Hall. "I tender these records into evidence."

"No objection," Hall responded.

Mike continued. "Judge, this is an embezzlement charge with bond currently set at $100,000. Mr. Miller and his wife own property free and clear in Barlow County, and his residence and the surrounding land have a tax value of $65,000. We'd ask that the bond be reduced to that amount. Mr. Miller has lived in the Shelton area for more than thirty years and operates his own lawncare business. He has no prior criminal record and doesn't pose a serious risk of flight. He's been in jail three months since his arrest."

The judge silently read the documents.

"How is your jaw?" Mike whispered to Sam.

"They sent me to the hospital for an X-ray. It's not broke, but it hurts to chew."

The judge spoke. "Are you going to present testimonial evidence from the defendant?"

"If you think it necessary," Mike answered. "I didn't want to take up too much of the Court's time, and given Mr. Miller's stable background, the records admitted are sufficient to support reduction of the bond."

"That's an issue I'll decide," the judge responded wryly. "Before I do, I have a few questions for Mr. Miller. Ms. Hall may also want to inquire."

Mike turned to Sam. "Go to the witness chair."

Sam ambled to the elevated seat on the right-hand side of the bench. With his rotund belly and white hair, he certainly didn't look like a threat to society.

Mike's concern was that Sam's words would sabotage the motion. The judge administered the oath. Sam looked at Mike.

"I'm ready when you are," he said.

Out of the corner of his eye, Mike saw Bobby Lambert suppress a laugh. Mr. Forrest sat stone-faced beside him.

"Judge, do you want me to go first?" Mike asked.

"Proceed."

"Yes, sir."

Mike faced the witness stand.

"What is your name?" he asked.

"Sam Miller."

"Tell the judge about your background."

"Which part?"

"Your business."

"I cut grass, plant trees and shrubs, fertilize, trim, and do whatever needs to be done to a yard. I've cut the judge's grass a few times when he was out of town and couldn't do it himself."

Mike quickly checked Judge Coberg's expression. His countenance remained inscrutable.

"Do you have a criminal record?" Mike asked.

"Nope."

Mike approached the witness stand and handed Sam a copy of the real estate records.

"Do you and your wife own this property?"

"Yep."

"Any mortgage?"

"Not in a long time."

"If you're released on bond, will you stay in Barlow County until the charges against you have been resolved?"

"Unless the Master sends me elsewhere."

Mike's jaw tightened. "But you'll obey an order by the court instructing you to stay close to home if it's a condition of your bond, won't you?"

Sam shifted in his chair. "I render unto Caesar, but Papa is my boss."

Mike tried to ignore the murmurings that rippled across the courtroom but quickly decided not to dissect Sam's answer in an effort to explain it. The more Sam spoke, the more unstable he would appear.

"Will you be present for all scheduled court dates?"

"Yep, so long as I know about it."

"Subject to any redirect examination, that's all from the defendant."

Mike turned over a fresh sheet on his legal pad and hoped for the best.

"Ms. Hall, you may ask," the judge said.

"No questions."

Mike barely concealed his shock. Even an inexperienced prosecutor could make Sam look ridiculous and perhaps even delusional. The judge stared at Hall for a moment then turned toward Sam.

"Mr. Miller, when was the last time you traveled outside Barlow County?" the judge asked.

"Let's see, Muriel and I drove over to Lake James about a month before I was locked up."

"Did you catch anything?"

"No keepers. I spent most of the time sitting on a stump enjoying the view."

"If you get out on bond, will you have time to plant your garden?"

"Muriel got everything started in the cold frame, but I need to transplant my lettuce, broccoli, and cauliflower."

The judge wrote something on the legal pad in front of him. For all Mike knew, it could have been a reminder to contact Sam Miller for fresh vegetables.

"What happened to your face?" the judge asked.

"A boy at the jail lost his temper and started swinging. I didn't see it coming."

"Who was it?"

"Brinson."

"Was he mad at you?"

"Nope. I think he was mad at you. He mentioned your name along with some other words I heard all the time in the Marine Corps but don't want to repeat today."

"And I've heard enough today," the judge replied. "Motion granted. I find the defendant's real property is sufficient collateral. Mr. Andrews, do you have an Order prepared?"

"No, sir. Will you be in your chambers later today?"

"Until three o'clock."

Mike accompanied Sam back to the jury box.

"You did a good job," Sam said.

Mike spoke in a low voice. "I didn't do anything. He was upset that you got hit." Mike paused. "And probably wants to make sure you get out of jail in time to plant your garden."

The judge called out, "*State v. Garfield.* Mr. Lambert for the defendant."

"He's partial to cauliflower," Sam replied. "But I could tell he respects you."

"I'm not sure *respect* is in his vocabulary when he's thinking about lawyers." Mike pointed across the courtroom. "But did you see Greg Freeman in action? He's a sharp young attorney."

"Yep, but you're the one for me."

"You're harder to convince than Judge Coberg," Mike replied softly. "After the judge signs the Order, I'll come by the jail. You should be home for supper. I'm sure your wife can fix something easy to chew."

Mike left the courtroom. He was halfway down the hall when he heard his name.

"Mike, just a minute!"

It was Mr. Forrest. He was leaning against the wall and breathing heavily. Mike returned to him.

"I'm sorry, I didn't know you wanted to talk to me," Mike said.

The old man caught his breath. "It's about Miller. I don't think it's wise for you to be representing him."

Mike's jaw tightened. Anyone but Maxwell Forrest would have received a curt response. Mike took a deep breath.

"It's temporary, until he can find another attorney," Mike said. "Maybe Greg Freeman could help him. I thought Greg did a good job this morning."

"A much better choice," Forrest said, clearing his throat. "A young lawyer with no reputation to protect."

Mike narrowed his gaze. Forrest continued, "Jack Hatcher at the bank is concerned about this situation. There was a lot of money involved."

"I planned on contacting someone at the bank about the account. If the charges are the result of a data entry error, I wouldn't do anything to cause public embarrassment for the bank."

"There's no mistake, Mike," Forrest said soberly. "I've seen the documentation. It's embezzlement, although not a very artful attempt."

Mike shrugged. "If that's the case, it will probably be a matter of working out a guilty plea. Could you call Mr. Hatcher and arrange access for me to the bank's records?"

"I'd rather not."

"Why?"

"Your involvement creates an awkward situation."

"How?"

"You're no longer with the firm, of course, but our names remain linked in the minds of many people, and a possible conflict with the bank would be an undesirable scenario. As a minister, you hold a position of respect in the community that is above the unpleasantness of involvement in a criminal case. Trust me. I'm only trying to protect you."

Mike was puzzled. "Is there more to this than I know?"

"Not really, except recognizing the wisdom of disengaging yourself from this matter so you can return to what the good Lord called you to do."

Mike spoke slowly, "Mr. Forrest, I really appreciate your concern. It gives me a new perspective."

Forrest patted Mike on the shoulder. "Good. You were always a quick learner."

"WHY WOULD ANDREWS GET INVOLVED IN THE FIRST PLACE?" Jack Hatcher asked.

Maxwell Forrest shifted the phone receiver against his ear and made a note about the call on his time and billing slip.

"He's always had a touch of crusader in him, but it doesn't matter who handles the case. The evidence is ironclad."

"Could Andrews delay the case?"

"Of course. No defendant wants speedy justice."

"The board of the bank wants a conviction, the sooner the better."

"I can encourage the process to move along."

"Do it."

MIKE WENT HOME AND PREPARED THE ORDER REDUCING SAM'S bond then returned to the courthouse. Two lawyers were vigorously arguing a motion for summary judgment in a civil case. With no spectators present, the attorneys were like gladiators fighting in an empty arena. Mike sat in the front row and listened.

After the attorneys packed up their briefcases, Judge Coberg spoke to Mike. "Mr. Andrews, you may approach."

Mike came forward and stood in front of the judge.

"I prepared the Order in the Miller case. Do you have time to review it before lunch?"

"So long as you didn't write it in Hebrew or Greek."

"Your Honor, my familiarity with ancient languages proved as fleeting as my understanding of the Rule against Perpetuities."

"Let me see what you have," the judge said.

Mike handed a single sheet of paper to the judge, who quickly scanned and signed it. The judge sat back in his chair.

"I've missed seeing you in my courtroom. How's the four-legged Judge doing?"

"Still barking at anyone who doesn't agree with him."

"I ought to name my new pointer Preacher," the judge responded.

"Only if he points in the right direction."

Judge Coberg rewarded Mike with a rare smile.

"Are you enjoying the ministry?"

"Yes, sir."

"Still have an itch to practice law?"

"No, sir. My involvement in this case is not the sign of a trend."

The judge nodded. "Nonetheless, I'm glad you're helping Sam Miller. He's a unique individual. I've known him a long time and was surprised to see him on the criminal calendar. Do you think I should recuse myself?"

Mike stepped back in surprise. "Why?"

"Because I like his cauliflower."

"He mentioned that to me, but I don't have any objection to you sitting on the case."

"The DA might. I'm going to send you and Ken West a disclosure memo about my prior contact with Mr. Miller."

"You've rubbed shoulders with a significant percentage of the people who live in Barlow County," Mike protested.

"How many of them are like Sam Miller?"

Mike studied the judge's face. The dark eyes revealed nothing.

"We're all different," Mike replied slowly. "How is Mr. Miller unique?"

A slight smile again lifted the corners of the judge's mouth. "You don't have me on the witness stand or kneeling at the altar, Reverend Andrews. If you have to ask that question, you don't know your client."

MIKE MADE SEVERAL COPIES OF THE ORDER, FILED THE ORIGINAL in the clerk's office, and dropped a copy by the DA's office. He left the courthouse and walked to the jail. Mike took off his jacket and threw it over his shoulder. At the jail, he handed the Order to the officer on duty.

"I'll send word around to the back," the deputy said. "They'll bring him up."

While he waited, Mike called Muriel Miller and gave her the good news. Her voice cracked with emotion as she thanked him, and he could imagine the tears rolling down her wrinkled cheeks.

"How long will it take you to get here?" Mike asked her.

"I don't know. I left the truck's lights on last night, and it has a dead battery. I'm still waiting for someone to come by and give me a jump start."

"Don't worry about it," Mike said. "I can bring Sam to your house."

"But that's out of your way."

"It's not a problem. I don't have to be anywhere else, and I only have one client."

In a few minutes, Sam came out wearing blue jeans and a denim shirt.

"I'm taking you home," Mike said. "Muriel knows you're coming but couldn't pick you up because the battery in your truck is dead."

"That's happened before. She doesn't like walking up to a dark house."

Outside, Sam looked up at the sky.

"The grass has been growing, and so have I," he said. "Ninety-six days in jail is a long time. It was tough, but I can see why so many of Papa's children have been locked up. It forced me to think seriously about some things."

Mike didn't take the bait. "I'm parked at the courthouse," he said. "Can you walk that far?"

"My legs are fine," Sam replied. "It's my jaw that hurts."

Sam set a surprisingly brisk pace. Mike fell in beside him.

"You're a fast walker," Mike said.

"When you make your living walking behind a lawn mower, you can't be a slowpoke. Muriel is worried about my heart, but I get more exercise than most men half my age."

"I didn't say anything to her about your jaw."

"Thanks. They took away the boy who hit me, and he didn't come back. I was sorry to see him go."

"Why?"

"After someone hurts you is often the best time to help them. They're invulnerable."

"You mean vulnerable."

"That, too." Sam shook his head. "I'm going to have to stop trying to impress you with my vocabulary."

They passed the local drugstore where Mike enjoyed ice cream cones when he was a boy. No longer dressed in jailhouse garb, Sam looked even less like a criminal. The old man glanced around as they walked and seemed to study each person they encountered on the sidewalk.

"Tell me about Judge Coberg," Mike said. "He seemed to know more about you than just the fact that you cut grass and grow vegetables."

"I never worked for him regular, but when I did, he always paid me on time."

"There must be more to it than that. He's going to notify the DA's office that his relationship with you may justify his removal from the case. He didn't give me any details, but I suspect you've had conversations with him similar to what you've told me."

"He's not one of my sons. We never talked too much, and he was always at the courthouse or out of town when I worked at his house."

"He said you were a different type of person."

Sam smiled. "That could be said about him, too."

They reached Mike's car and got in. Sam settled in the leather seat and sighed.

"This sure is comfortable. I've missed my recliner at home."

Sam gave directions to his house then immediately closed his eyes. Mike wasn't sure if his client was awake or asleep.

After they passed the west edge of commercial development for Shelton, fewer and fewer houses dotted the countryside. There weren't many farms in the rocky soil of Barlow County. Most of the people who lived outside the city limits did so because land was cheaper and neighbors more distant. Like Sam, they drove into the more populated areas to work. When they came to a stop sign, Sam opened his eyes and looked at Mike.

"You know one thing I learned in jail?" Sam asked.

"I guess you're going to tell me whether I want to hear it or not."

"It's something you'll agree with. You bringing up Lou Jasper the other day got me thinking. Papa showed me that sometimes I run my mouth when I ought to keep quiet. Even after all these years, I get excited when He shows me something and look for the first chance to tell it."

"If the Lord really reveals something to you, it's understandable that you would be excited."

"But it's not an excuse for loose lips. The right word in the wrong time is as bad as the wrong word in the right time. I need to call Lou and apologize."

Mike, temporarily caught in the convoluted web of Sam's logic, didn't immediately respond.

"Uh, I'm not sure I follow you, but I don't see why an apology is necessary. You said Lou Jasper didn't follow through on what you shared with him."

"That's his problem. I have to deal with mine."

They turned onto McAfee Road.

"Which house is yours?" Mike asked.

"A half mile on the left," Sam said. "It's yellow with blue shutters and sits on top of a little hill. You can't miss it."

They passed a mailbox resting on a car tire painted white and partially buried in the ground. A few stodgy Angus cattle glanced up from a field on the right-hand side of the road. They drove up a steep driveway to a small frame dwelling.

"Could you park in front of my truck so you can give me a jump before you leave?" Sam asked.

They got out of the car. Muriel came onto the small front stoop. Mike held back while Sam walked quickly across the grass and climbed three concrete steps to greet her. They embraced. Mike could tell that Muriel was crying. He looked away. When Sam turned around, his eyes were red, too.

"Toss me the keys to your truck, and I'll hook up the jumper cables," Mike said, backing away. "You need to spend time together without me interfering."

"Don't be silly," Muriel said with a wave of her hand. "Come in the house. You can mess with that old truck later."

"She's right," Sam added. "We won't keep you long."

The interior of the small house looked surprisingly normal. Mike wasn't sure what he'd expected, but Sam Miller didn't live in a cave. He glanced around the modestly furnished yet meticulously clean room. Muriel went into the kitchen and returned to the living room with two glasses of iced tea. Sam, sitting in a fat recliner, squeezed a thick slice of lemon in his glass and took a deep drink.

"Thank you, sweetheart," he said. "This is delicious."

Mike positioned himself on a plaid sofa and took a sip.

"Yes, ma'am. It's very good."

Muriel, a glass of water in her hand, looked at Sam. Mike saw her expression change to one of alarm and concern.

"What happened to your face?"

She kept her lips pressed tightly together while Sam related the story of the attack.

"It wasn't near as bad as some of the licks I took when we first got married," Sam said. "Getting hit by four drunk sailors who thought they could whip two Marines was a lot worse."

"And you were a lot younger," Muriel said. "I'm just glad you're out of that jail." She turned to Mike. "Thanks again for helping us."

"You're welcome."

Mike relaxed on the sofa and listened while Muriel brought Sam up to date on their household news. Sam had lightbulbs at the edge of the roof to change and a leaky faucet to fix. Hearing the couple talk about everyday issues made

Sam seem more normal. Mike drained his tea glass of the last drop. Muriel took it to the kitchen for a refill.

"Preacher," Sam said, "I have a question."

"What?"

"Will there be sweet tea in heaven?"

"Only in the Southern part."

Sam laughed. "That's where I want my mansion."

Muriel returned to the room.

"You should have seen Mike in court," Sam said to her. "He was smooth as your egg custard. Judge Coberg thinks highly of him."

"And he thinks highly of you," Mike responded. "Especially your vegetables. However, everyone doesn't agree with the judge. My former boss was in the courtroom this morning. He caught me in the hallway after the hearing and told me it would be an embarrassment to both of us if I continued to represent you."

"What's his name?" Sam asked.

"Maxwell Forrest."

"Oh, yeah, I've heard of him."

"He also mentioned that Jack Hatcher, the president of the bank, was very interested in your case."

"Is he the man you wrote the letter to?" Muriel asked Sam.

Sam put his fingers to his lips and shook his head.

"What letter?" Mike asked sharply.

"Mike, I told you I can't go running my mouth about everything."

"And you can't expect me to represent you if I don't know the facts." Mike placed his glass on a coaster. "Mr. Forrest told me the bank records clearly show how you embezzled the money. Why shouldn't I believe him?"

"I passed the money test many years ago. It doesn't have a hold on me."

Mike looked at Muriel. "Why is he making this so hard for me? Ever since we met he's been dumping a lot of stuff on me that I don't understand or want to hear. Now, he won't answer a simple question."

"Sam, you've got to tell your lawyer what he needs to know so he can represent you. I'm glad you're home, but this isn't over. The thought that you might be sent off for a much longer time—" Muriel stopped.

Sam went to her chair and kissed the top of her head. "I'm here now, and we're going to start praying about the future."

"What about the letter?" Mike persisted.

Sam returned to his recliner. "I don't have a copy and can't see how it could have anything to do with what's happening now."

"You should let me make that decision. Do you have any notes?"

"Check in one of your notebooks," Muriel suggested.

"Yeah, a written notation may refresh your memory," Mike said.

Sam sighed. "Okay. You seem determined to find out one way or the other."

Sam left the room. Muriel spoke. "He writes things down in a notebook that he keeps beside the bed. He has stacks of them in boxes on the floor of our closet, so it may take him a while to fetch it."

"How long ago did he write the letter to Mr. Hatcher?"

"Maybe six months ago."

"Did he show it to you?"

"No, but I remember he thought it was unusual."

"If he thought it was unusual, I'm sure it was different," Mike said. "Does he know Mr. Hatcher?"

"I don't think so, but he's written lots of notes and letters to people he doesn't know. He writes the president a couple of times a year."

"President?"

"Of the United States. He sends it directly to the White House. He never hears back, but that doesn't seem to discourage him."

Mike guessed the FBI couldn't check out every eccentric individual who regularly wrote the president.

"What about Judge Coberg? Does he write him?"

"Not that I know of, but it could have happened."

"Has he ever had any dreams about the judge?"

"Not so fast," Sam said as he entered the room. "Don't use your lawyer tricks on Muriel." He held up a tattered notebook. "I think what you want to see is in here."

Sam sat in his recliner and began turning the pages. Mike leaned forward on the couch so he could get a better view. It was impossible to decipher the meaning of the words, numbers, and drawings scrawled on the pages.

"Here are the verses Papa gave me to share with Myra Cordell," Sam said to Muriel. "She was thinking about killing herself. How is she doing?"

"Better. Her daughter has moved back from St. Louis to stay with her for a while."

"Get back to your notebook," Mike said.

While Mike sipped his tea, Sam kept turning the pages.

"Tell me about the photos on the wall," Mike asked Muriel.

Muriel gave him a brief family history.

"Matthew dying overseas was a hard blow," she said. "Losing a young-un is one of those things you never get over. Now we're praying for Anne Marie, one of my great-nieces. She's battling leukemia."

"I'll put her on the prayer list at my church."

Mike entered her name in his PDA.

"Ah, take a look at this," Sam said. "Down at the bottom of the page."

He handed the notebook to Mike, who examined the heavily stained and wrinkled sheet of paper for a few seconds.

"I can't read it. What's that brown stuff?"

"Coffee, I guess. I must have spilled a cup on it while I was writing the letter at the kitchen table."

"Can you make it out?" Mike asked.

Sam squinted at the paper. "Some of it. What I do in the night is write down a few words that remind me of other things in the morning. Have you started keeping a notebook by your bed?"

"No."

"You should."

"Let's see," Sam said. "I remember it was nighttime in the dream. There was a hatchet, a box of finishing nails, a baseball bat, and a tree. They were all standing up and talking like men. I could see Cohulla Creek behind them. The baseball bat gave a man I know named Larry Pasley a string of glass beads. They were pretty, but I knew they were worthless. Larry seemed happy, but I knew he was being duped. They didn't know I was watching because they didn't believe I could see in the dark. But day and night are the same to Papa. And here in the margin are the verses I sent, Ephesians 5:11–14."

Sam looked up at Muriel. "What does that passage say?"

"It's about the deeds of darkness. I'll get the Bible."

Muriel left the room and returned with a black Bible that showed signs of heavy use. She touched her index finger to her tongue as she flipped through the pages.

"Here it is," she said. She read slowly and deliberately. " '*Have nothing to do with the fruitless deeds of darkness, but rather expose them. For it is shameful even to mention what the disobedient do in secret. But everything exposed by the light becomes visible, for it is the light that makes everything visible."*

"Yep," Sam said. "That's it."

"What does that mean?" Mike asked.

"Exactly what it says. Papa always tells it like it is."

"I know, but why would you send those verses to Jack Hatcher at the bank?"

"'Cause he was in the dream. Papa often uses pictures to speak to me."

Mike stared at the sheet of paper.

"Jack Hatcher was the hatchet."

"Yep."

"Who are the other people?"

"I'm not sure."

Mike continued to stare. "Maxwell Forrest."

"Yep, that might be right, but there was only one tree. A forest has a bunch of trees."

"I'm doing the best I can," Mike answered. "Who is a box of nails and a baseball bat?"

"I don't have a clue."

"How did you know it was Cohulla Creek?"

"They were standing near a spot along the creek where I like to pray when the weather is nice. There is a rock that sits out in the stream. I can sit on the rock and enjoy the view in both directions. Praying by a creek, listening to the voice of the Lord in the waters—it restores my soul."

"Did you put all the symbolism in the letter?"

"What?"

"The pictures. Did you tell Jack Hatcher that you saw him as a hatchet in a dream?"

"No, he would have thought I was crazy. That part was for me, not him."

"The crazy part makes sense. How can you interpret this stuff and claim God is communicating to you?"

"After you eat a lot of peaches, you know what a good one tastes like."

Mike gave Sam a puzzled look.

"Check the fruit—the change in a person's life or things turning out exactly like Papa showed you. Have you counted how many dreams are in the Bible?"

"No."

"Me either. But there are hundreds of them."

Mike's face remained skeptical. "So what did you write?"

"I don't remember exactly, but I think I warned him not to take advantage of Larry, who owns property along the creek. It looked like Larry was getting the bad end of a land deal."

"How did you know that?"

"Because they were meeting at night, handing him some worthless beads. And it fit with the verses about the deeds of darkness. Do you understand?"

"Land deeds."

Sam smiled in satisfaction. "Yep. You're going to do just fine. And I told Mr. Hatcher that the Lord saw what he was doing and would bring it into the light."

"It's a far-fetched theory. Did you mention other people being involved?"

"Not by name, since it wasn't clear, but I told him I saw a group of people. It's not as important that I understand what I see as the person receiving it. They're the ones who have to ignore it or act on it. Since they were all together, I figured he could tell them himself."

"What about Larry Pasley? Did you contact him?"

"Yep. I went by his place. He lives in an old shack that his grandpa built, and his family has owned property up that valley for a long time. Larry dropped out of school when he was a boy and can't read and write very well. He said he'd been paid enough money to buy a new hot water heater and a color TV and in a few months might get enough to buy a trailer for his son and daughter-in-law. I told him it might not be a good deal, but he told me I didn't know what I was talking about. He'd had a lawyer check everything out for him."

"Who was the lawyer?"

"I didn't ask, and he didn't say."

"Was he selling his home place?"

"I doubt it, because he bought a new hot water heater."

"Is that all?"

"No, there was something else. I remember ending the letter with a little poem. I've never done that before."

Sam turned the page in his notebook. "Here it is. I put it on the next page."

"Let's hear it."

"Don't laugh at me. I barely graduated from high school, and I'm not much of a poet."

"Go ahead."

Sam cleared his throat like a schoolboy about to recite before the class.

Deeds of darkness produce only tares.
Those who sow for gold will reap despair.

He looked up at Mike. "It's not much, but at least it rhymes."

Nine

Mike and Sam went outside to jump-start Sam's truck.

"I had a troubling dream last night about you and Danny Brewster," Mike said as they walked across the yard. "I didn't want to bring it up in front of Muriel."

"I'm listening."

Mike told him the dream about the interview room at the jail and dark figures who carried Danny and Sam from the room. Sam leaned against the side of the truck and listened.

"I woke up in a sweat," Mike concluded. "What do you think?"

"We're in a fight, and it's not just against flesh and blood. You helped Danny in his case and now you're helping me. Some of our enemies have faces; others are in the spiritual world. I've seen the faceless ones myself. They are pure evil."

Mike shuddered slightly. "Why didn't you get out of the chair?"

"Because I was at rest in the battle."

"You were in danger."

"I know. And with your help, I won't mess up."

"I was paralyzed and couldn't think of anything to say."

"Words with power come from your spirit, not your mind," Sam replied with a smile. "Keep loving Papa, walking with the Master, leaning on the Helper, and eating the Word. After a while, you'll learn how to fight the Enemy in the right way."

Sam attached the cables to the dead battery. Mike raised the hood of his car.

"Hook up your end of the cables," Sam said. "Make sure the ground is on black."

Mike attached the cables to the battery of his car and turned on the engine. He joined Sam while they waited for the dead battery to build up a charge. Sam got in the truck and turned the key. The truck engine sputtered to life. Mike unhooked the jumper cables from both batteries and coiled them up.

"I'll let it run awhile," Sam said. "It'd better start tomorrow because I need to be out of here at the crack of dawn. There's no telling how much business I've lost."

"Was there anything in the paper about your arrest?"

"Just one line, but you know how people are. That could really hurt me."

Mike thought a moment. "Would you be willing to put in a bid to cut the grass at Little Creek Church? It's a long way across the county, but it might be worth the drive. The cemetery alone would take a full day."

"That's mighty nice of you," Sam said appreciatively. "I'll try to get over there and take a look at it."

IT WAS ALMOST 1:30 P.M. BY THE TIME MIKE RETURNED TO Shelton. He pulled into a parking space near traffic light seven and made notes on a legal pad about his conversation with Sam Miller. The information in Sam's notebook was too speculative to serve as a cogent defense in the case. Mike's stomach growled. He'd missed lunch, and the sweet tea provided by Muriel Miller wasn't a substitute for a meal. Mike called the church. Delores answered.

"Any problems?" he asked.

"No, it's been real quiet. I've been reading one of my magazines."

Delores loved gossip magazines and kept close tabs on the real and imagined scandals of movie and soap opera stars.

"Anything I need to know that's going on in Hollywood?"

"Not really, but if I see a good sermon illustration, I'll mark it."

A CONCRETE-BLOCK BUILDING ON THE OUTSKIRTS OF TOWN WAS home to the world's greatest hamburger. Owned by identical twin brothers, the Brooks Brothers Sandwich House had been serving up hamburgers topped with homemade chili and sweet onions since Mike attended high school. He pulled into the gravel parking lot.

Next to a pale yellow building was a long wooden table under a tin roof that provided open-air eating. The building itself was too small for a dining room, so all the brothers' business was either take-out or eaten by customers alfresco style at the communal table. Between noon and one o'clock, the line of construction workers and businesspeople stretched out the door.

The kitchen was open to public view, and one of the brothers was busy flattening round balls of fresh meat on a grill top. In a pan on a single-coil electric unit rested a smoking pot of chili. Orders were written on the white bags used to hold each order. The Brooks brother at the grill looked up when Mike entered the restaurant.

"Hey, Mike! How you doing?"

"Pretty good."

Mike had known the Brooks brothers for more than twenty years. He'd watched their hair turn gray and their waistlines grow, but he'd never been able to tell them apart. In middle age, they remained carbon copies of each other. While one brother cooked, the other filled Styrofoam cups with tea and lined up orders of thick-cut french fries.

A rough-looking man named Dusty with the sleeves cut out of a biker T-shirt took the orders. Scowling, and with a pen in his hand, he stood behind the counter and waited for Mike.

"I recommend the fried liver mush," Dusty said. "It's fresh and crisp."

Mike would occasionally eat the square patties of liver, but if Peg found out, she made him brush his teeth twice and gargle with mouthwash before getting close to him.

"No, my wife has been extra nice to me the past few days, and I don't want to ruin it. I'll have two cheeseburgers all the way."

He moved down the counter toward the cash register. Hamburgers sizzled on the black grill. Above the cash register hung a small bell that Dusty rang every time a first-time customer came into the shop.

"Been on any cruises lately?" Mike asked Dusty.

The counterman saved his money so he could book a cheap three- or four-day cruise every year.

"It's coming up in a month."

"Where are you going?"

"Aruba, Grand Cayman, and St. Thomas."

The brother pouring tea laughed. "Don't believe him, Mike. It's the same thing he always does. They fly him to Miami, drop him in a dingy, and tow him to the Bahamas where he drinks beer for forty-eight hours before coming home."

Dusty patted his belly with a grin. "I know what they mean by all-inclusive—it's all the boiled shrimp and beer I can put down from the time the boat leaves Miami until it gets back to the dock."

The door opened and Braxton Hodges, a reporter with the Shelton paper, entered. Braxton, a balding man with glasses and rumpled white shirt, reported on everything from livestock winners at the county fair to the annual black-tie fund-raiser for the local hospital.

"Heard you were in court this morning," the reporter said to Mike after he ordered.

"That's not news."

"It is in Shelton. Getting bored with the pulpit?"

"No, just trying to help someone out of a jam."

Dusty handed Mike his sack of food. "The liver mush makes a tasty dessert."

"Talk Braxton into it," Mike said. "He can write an article about what it does to his digestive tract."

Mike went outside with his food. He bowed his head for a silent blessing, then pulled out a burger and took a bite. Like the Brooks brothers' physical appearances, the hamburgers were always the same and uniformly excellent. Braxton Hodges joined him.

"Admit it," Hodges said. "You wanted a thick slab of liver mush between two pieces of white bread."

"If a loaf of mush had been hanging on the forbidden tree in the Garden of Eden, I don't think Adam and Eve would have sinned."

Hodges smiled. "Years ago I started to write a story about the history of liver mush. I didn't go back to Genesis, but like many regional dishes, I discovered it was created by poor folks who couldn't afford to get rid of anything remotely edible. I finished the prep work but couldn't get past the third paragraph of the article. I dreamed about pig livers for weeks."

Mike took a large bite from his burger. The combination of onions and chili with the slightly crispy meat was superb.

"Have you had any dreams worth reporting lately?" Hodges asked.

Mike looked sideways as he chewed his food. "What kind of newspaper reporter question is that?"

"If you're hanging around Sam Miller, I figure you've been talking to him about dreams."

Mike wiped his mouth with a thin napkin. "Until I started representing him, I didn't realize how famous the old guy is around here."

"Who else mentioned him to you?"

"Can't say. It's an ongoing case."

Hodges shrugged. "You probably couldn't tell me much I haven't heard. He's been writing letters to the paper for years. Most of them land on my desk then transition to the round metal file I keep on the floor."

"What does he write about?"

"Nothing for the editorial page. Mostly about his dreams mixed in with Bible verses. For a man who cuts grass for a living, he has a very vivid imagination. I guess that's what happens when you walk behind a lawn mower for thirty years. If I could come up with some of the stuff he writes, I'd quit reporting the facts and start writing the world's greatest science fiction novel. In the meantime, I'm waiting on his prediction for the end of the world. Once that's in, I'm running a full story on him."

"Do you always throw away the letters?"

"All except one."

"Why?"

Hodges turned toward Mike. "Because he wrote it to me."

"Tell me."

Hodges dipped a french fry in ketchup. "Now you're the one in confidential territory. The only thing I'll say is, whether from looking in a crystal ball or reading his Bible, Sam Miller knew a few things about me that no one else knows. It got my attention."

"It wouldn't be hard to guess your sins," Mike said.

"It wasn't like that," Hodges answered seriously. "It was encouraging—in a religious sort of way. And ever since, I've always had a soft spot for him. I was sorry when he got into trouble."

"He's worried the report of his arrest in the paper is going to hurt his business."

"I buried the crime blotter for that issue at the bottom of the fourth page. As a felony, I couldn't keep it out; however, the negative publicity could have been worse. The publisher in Asheville got a call from Jack Hatcher asking us to write an investigative piece. I put him off and haven't heard anything since."

Mike stopped unwrapping his second burger and put it down.

"Jack Hatcher called the owner of the paper?"

"Yes, which I found strange. Hatcher should want to keep the situation quiet, not publicize it. The bank wasn't at fault, but no one likes to think their money is going to end up in the wrong account."

"How do you know the bank wasn't in the wrong?" Mike asked. "That was the first possibility I considered when I met with Sam."

"A bank error that made it all the way to a criminal prosecution? That's a stretch. Even a sloppy investigation would uncover that type of problem."

"You've got more faith in the criminal justice system than I do." Mike shrugged. "A few wrong keystrokes, and anyone could be a millionaire. The more I've talked with Sam, the less I think he would embezzle a hundred thousand dollars."

Hodges shrugged. "I've seen him around town but never met him. He could be a wife-beater who grows marijuana in an abandoned chicken house."

"I've been to his place and met his wife a couple of times. That's not happening. Do you know if he writes letters to anyone else?"

"No one has ever mentioned it to me, but I wouldn't be surprised."

Mike paused and decided to make a calculated gamble.

"Last year he wrote a letter to Jack Hatcher."

Hodges looked up. "Really? What did it say?"

"I haven't seen it, but I believe it was inflammatory and would like to find out more about it. It could definitely shed light on Hatcher's personal interest in the case." Mike took another bite of hamburger and chewed it thoughtfully. "Could you revisit the idea of an investigative article about Sam and see if you could uncover anything?"

"If a one-liner hurt Miller's business, what do you think an article is going to do? He'd starve or leave town."

"Liver mush," Mike responded simply.

"Sam Miller likes liver mush?"

"Probably eats it three times a week for breakfast, but that's not what I had in mind. Just because you research an article doesn't mean you have to print it."

Hodges grinned. "I see, but I couldn't spend a lot of time working on something that wasn't going to run."

"It might be a quick dead end, but then again—it might be the piece of journalism that wins you a Pulitzer prize."

MIKE FELT ENERGIZED DURING HIS DRIVE TO THE CHURCH. Appearing in court was stimulating, but the investigative part of the law, whether researching a legal issue or uncovering a factual matter, had always been his favorite part of the practice. He could happily sit for hours in front of a computer screen, analyzing a tricky point of the law and enjoyed tracking down and interviewing hard-to-locate witnesses in out-of-the-way places.

Most clients he'd represented in criminal matters had been so obviously guilty that a jury trial wasn't the prudent path to follow. In those cases, he usually worked out a plea bargain. The Danny Brewster burglary and Ridley moonshine cases were different. Because there was doubt in his own mind, the desire to find the truth about the charges against his clients motivated him to work harder. In the Ridley matter, the result was a stunning victory. Danny Brewster's story had a tragic conclusion. Mike wasn't sure where Sam Miller's future lay.

When he entered the administration wing of the church, Delores put down her magazine and stifled a yawn.

"You have a big stack of congratulatory phone messages on your desk."

"Congratulating me for what?"

"The baby, of course. Have you forgotten that you're going to be a father?"

"No, I'll get right on it."

Mike settled in behind his desk and began returning phone calls. The wholesale excitement about the baby was touching. Several wanted to talk at length, offering advice about everything from safely designed nursery room furniture to the wisdom of using a pacifier. It was almost five o'clock before he reached the bottom of the stack. He stood up, stretched, and stuck his head out the door.

"That's it," he told Delores. "I'm up to date."

"Not quite," she replied, holding up a thinner stack. "These came in while you were on the phone."

"Should I return them now or tomorrow?" Mike asked.

Delores flipped through the names. "I'll pull out the ones who will be upset if they don't hear from you today."

AN HOUR LATER, MIKE LEFT THE CHURCH. WHEN HE ARRIVED home, Peg was in the kitchen stirring a pot of soup. He came over to the stove and sniffed. She greeted him with a kiss. Judge, who lay in his bed in the corner, raised his head and gave a short woof.

"What did you have for lunch?" Peg asked.

"Brooks Brothers."

"I thought I tasted a hint of onion. Something light would be good for supper. Will you stir while I put together the salad?"

Mike took the spoon. Peg opened the refrigerator.

"What happened in court?" she asked.

Mike told her about his day. She listened without comment until he reached the part about his encounter in the hallway with Mr. Forrest.

"Maxwell Forrest squeezed all he could from you when you worked for him," Peg said matter-of-factly. "Now that you're no longer under his control, he'll treat you differently."

"I thought you loved it when I was part of the firm."

Peg placed two large salad bowls on the table. "I did. But you're in a different place now. If Mr. Forrest thinks you're going to hurt his business, he'll cause problems for you."

As they ate, Mike related the private courtroom conversation with Judge Coberg about Sam.

"I know what happened," Peg said, pouring more dressing on her salad. "Sam has told him things about court cases."

Mike put down his fork. The idea that the judge may have received information about a legal dispute from a totally independent source like Sam Miller was unnerving. Peg continued, "I don't know, of course, but it fits what we know about him. He could have had a dream or something."

"I tried to talk to Sam about it, but he wouldn't open up. He has notebooks filled with information about dreams and visions he's had. Some of them are symbolic and so vague it's impossible to figure out. I went behind his back to Muriel about the judge, but—Sam cut me off."

"I could ask her."

"When are you going to see her again?" Mike asked in surprise.

"I don't know, but it wouldn't hurt me to take on a new friend."

"I doubt Muriel Miller owns a tennis racket or a pair of running shoes."

"Are you telling me not to see her?"

"Of course not. It just seems odd."

"No more than you taking Sam's case."

"But—" Mike stopped. "Anyway, I ran into Braxton Hodges at Brooks and asked him to see what he can find out about some of the issues."

"His wife was at the country club this morning. She has a regular doubles game on Thursday."

"It's Thursday?" Mike asked.

"All day."

Mike let out a groan. "And I haven't started my sermon. The Miller case has thrown off my whole routine."

"That's not supposed to happen until after the baby is born."

"Well, I'm practicing. I wanted to relax tonight, but I'd better get to work after supper. I'm not even sure what I want to talk about."

"You'll think of something." Peg carried her empty soup and salad bowls to the sink. "That's the most I've eaten all day. My food choices are already changing. You know how much I love apples? I had to force myself to eat one for lunch."

"I've had an unusual food craving, too," Mike said. "It's probably a sympathetic reaction."

"What did you want to eat?"

"Liver mush. I talked about it with Braxton. If you really loved me, you'd fry a couple of patties to go with my grits in the morning."

Peg threw a wet dishrag at him. Mike caught it with his right hand.

"That's not a preference; it's a perversion. But it gives me an idea for your sermon. Preach about the clean and unclean animals."

Mike shook his head. "No way. That might split the church. We have too many barbecue lovers who would revolt if I condemned them for eating pork."

Ten

MIKE AWOKE EARLY ON SUNDAY MORNING AND SLIPPED OUT OF bed. Peg was sound asleep and didn't stir. Putting on a pair of old shoes, he took Judge into the backyard and walked across the wet grass. There was a light fog in the air.

Mike enjoyed early mornings, especially Sunday. He spent time praying while most members of his congregation were still in bed. The ritual helped him feel like the shepherd of his flock, watching over them from a hillside as he asked God to bless them.

He sat on a small cast-iron and wood bench near the edge of the hardwood trees that bordered their lot. In a few weeks, the bench would be surrounded by flowers. Judge left his side and explored the smells in the nearby woods. Mike closed his eyes and ran through the main points of the sermon he'd written on Thursday night. The words had flowed rapidly through his fingers onto the computer screen. He couldn't deny Sam Miller's subtle influence on his thinking. Phrases the old man used stuck stubbornly in his mind until he was forced to extract and examine them.

A robin flew to the ground near his feet and plunged its beak into the soil to capture a wiggling worm. The truth, like the worm, didn't always come in a pretty package, but that didn't make it any less vital for life.

"YOU LOOK NICE," MIKE SAID TO PEG AS THEY PULLED OUT OF the driveway. "*Glowing* might even be a more accurate word. The blue in your dress really sets off your eyes and hair."

"Thank you," she said. "I'd kiss your cheek, but that would mess up my lipstick and raise questions at church."

They saw few cars on the valley road until they neared the church.

"Are you ready for the onslaught of people?" Mike asked. "If the number of phone calls I received is any indication, this pregnancy is being viewed as a church-wide event."

"I'll smile sweetly and keep my mouth shut."

"I'm not trying to squelch you," Mike began, "It's just—"

Peg reached over and patted his hand. "Don't worry. I'll be good."

THEY PULLED INTO THE CHURCH PARKING LOT. SUNDAY SCHOOL attendance lagged behind the growth in the main worship service. Persuading the congregation to get out of bed and come early to church, even with the temptation of good coffee and fresh donuts, was a challenge.

"I'm going to Nathan Goode's class this morning," Peg announced when Mike turned off the car engine.

"Why? What do you have in common with teenagers?"

"Our child will be a teenager someday. If it's as bad as some people say, I'd better start early."

"Take notes. Oh, and I forgot to tell you. Nathan has an alto part he really wants you to sing."

"A solo?"

"I'm not sure. There's also going to be a flute solo by a high school student."

Mike saw Peg receive three congratulatory hugs before she crossed the parking lot. As an expectant mother, her acceptance by the church was bound to go up. Mike retreated to his office where, for the next forty-five minutes, he alternately reviewed his notes and paced back and forth across the room practicing his delivery. As time drew near to go to the sanctuary, he stopped and looked out a window that gave a partial view of the parking lot. He spotted several first-time visitors, the best sign of a healthy church and a radical departure from the norm prior to Mike's arrival at Little Creek. He slipped on his black robe and checked his appearance in the mirror.

Mike and the choir crowded into an anteroom adjacent to the front of the sanctuary for a brief prayer. Peg was lovely in a burgundy choir robe trimmed in gold. The same robe made Nathan Goode look like a fugitive from *Alice in*

Wonderland. For the minister and choir members, wearing robes was a non-negotiable tradition. They all entered the sanctuary to the stately sound of an organ prelude. Mike stepped into the pulpit area.

From the first time he sat in the high-backed chair behind the pulpit, it felt right. During the ensuing three years, he'd never tired of steering the service like the captain of a ship.

It was close to a full house, more than three hundred and fifty people. Mike scanned the crowd until his gaze fastened on an older couple sitting on the far left side of the sanctuary in the second pew from the front. The man turned his head from side to side then looked up at the ceiling for several seconds as if closely inspecting the rafters. Mike looked up, too, but saw nothing except wood. The woman beside the man stared straight ahead with a slight smile on her wrinkled face.

It was Sam and Muriel Miller.

After the opening prayer and a congregational hymn, the flutist played her song. Mike tried to interpret his client's expressions as the service progressed. The first time their eyes met, Sam smiled broadly. Mike nodded in greeting but remembered Muriel's comment that she and Sam moved from church to church "as the Lord" led them. It was one thing to spend time with Sam Miller at the jail or in the privacy of his living room. Having him in the Little Creek congregation where he might say something bizarre to one of the members of the church made Mike's stomach tighten in a knot.

The choir performed a baroque anthem that sounded familiar. Peg sang a brief solo. Her clear, mellow voice moved perfectly from note to note. Mike listened with pride.

Mike delivered a pastoral prayer that followed an outline familiar to the congregation. He requested divine help for the world, the nation, the state, Barlow County, the church, and anyone who had been sick enough during the week to require a night in the hospital. When he said "Amen" and opened his eyes, he saw that Sam still had his head bowed.

The announcements for the week were printed in the bulletin; however, Mike had learned not to trust the congregation's ability to take note of them and dutifully read the list. He reached the end and paused to allow silent consideration of the money contributed the previous Sunday. To read aloud the numbers would be in bad taste.

"The last announcement isn't in the bulletin," he said. "Peg and I are thrilled to announce that she is expecting our first child. She's been to the doctor and everything looks fine."

There was a splattering of applause. Mike looked at Peg, who was beaming. Out of the corner of his eye, he saw Sam Miller with his left hand raised in the air like a schoolchild wanting to attract the teacher's attention. Mike quickly looked away as the clapping died down. An impromptu speech by Sam definitely wasn't in the morning bulletin. "Thank you very much," Mike said. "You can't imagine how grateful Peg and I are for the love and support of this congregation."

During the offering, Mike avoided looking in Sam's direction. As the offering plates left the sanctuary, Mike stood up and stepped forward to the pulpit. He kept his notes folded in his Bible and slipped them out to preach. His mouth suddenly dry, he took a quick sip of water from a glass he kept on a shelf in the pulpit.

"Our scripture lesson this morning is a single verse from the words of Jesus in John 10:27. *My sheep listen to my voice; I know them, and they follow me.* Recently, these words have come to have a new meaning for me."

Mike paused and distinctly heard Sam say, "Yep."

Mike hurriedly continued, "We're God's sheep if we've submitted to Him as the shepherd of our souls, and personal communication with Jesus is the birthright of every Christian. This morning, I'm going to discuss ways to recognize the voice of God and how to respond to what He says.

"Some of you may wonder how God can carry on multiple conversations at once. We become easily confused in a four-way conference call; however, God can talk with everyone on earth at the same time. It's one of the great advantages of being omniscient and omnipresent. And the reason I'm in this pulpit is because I heard the voice of God calling me to leave my happy life as a lawyer and become a minister."

There were a few laughs from the congregation. Mike noticed that Bobby Lambert's expression didn't change.

"As many of you know, I like to go mountain biking," Mike said. "Often, my dog, Judge, goes with me. About six years ago, Judge and I took off one Saturday morning and went to the base of Jefferson's Ridge so I could ride the abandoned logging roads. I took a small backpack containing snacks for me, dog treats for Judge, and extra water bottles for both of us. I also had a copy of the New Testament. We left the car at Hank's Grocery and started up the road that begins behind the store. It switches back and forth as it climbs the ridge and is washed out in a lot of places. Judge is built for rugged terrain, but even with the bike in low gear, it's a strenuous workout for me. It took almost an hour to reach Stratton Bald, the highest point on the ridge. It's one of my favorite places in Barlow County because I can see all the way from Shelton to the Blue Ridge Mountains."

Mike, a faraway look in his eyes, could see the ridge in his mind's eye and hoped the congregation was joining him.

"I love mountain tops because they are places of perspective. The higher I go, the more connected I am to the vantage point of God. When Judge and I reached the highest point, we sat down to enjoy the sun and the light breeze that always blows across the crest of the ridge. I'd been thinking and praying about going into the ministry for over a year but couldn't decide what to do. I'd asked people for advice and received so many opinions that it would take a pack of index cards to keep them straight. Opening my New Testament, I started reading in Galatians. The first verse got my attention."

Mike turned the pages of his Bible. "'*Paul, an apostle—sent not from men nor by man, but by Jesus Christ.*' My heart began beating a little faster, not from the ride on the bike, but in anticipation that something important was about to happen. I read verses 15 through 17: '*But when God, who set me apart from birth and called me by his grace, was pleased to reveal his Son in me so that I might preach him among the Gentiles, I did not consult any man, nor did I go up to Jerusalem to see those who were apostles before I was, but I went immediately into Arabia and later returned to Damascus.*'"

Mike looked up at the congregation. "At that moment, those verses became the voice of Jesus to my life. I knew without a doubt that I should preach the gospel. I no longer needed the opinions of others, even people I respected. I knew what to do. I didn't go to Arabia, but to seminary in Virginia, and ended up at the Little Creek Church, not Damascus. However, the application of those verses to me as the guidance of the Lord couldn't have been clearer. The term 'called to preach' has been used so often that we accept stories like mine as orthodox Christianity. Ministers are expected to hear from God. It should be part of their spiritual résumé."

Mike stepped from behind the pulpit and made sure he had everyone's attention before he continued. He raised his voice.

"But what about you? Do you have the same right to receive guidance from the Lord as a person considering a career-altering switch into full-time ministry? Is there a distinction between God's children that gives access to some but not to others? Can all the followers of Jesus have the hope of hearing His voice? Was my experience on the mountain top six years ago a once-in-a-lifetime event? After that, did God become mute and abandon me to my own devices? I think not. As one of God's sheep, I want to continue to hear His voice, and I believe with all my heart that each of us has the same opportunity. Let me tell you why."

Mike launched into the main body of his sermon with enthusiasm. Time passed quickly as he gave the congregation examples of the ways in which God communicates, using several biblical stories to make his points. When he glanced at his watch, he realized that he'd run almost ten minutes over the normal time limit. He quickly jumped to his conclusion.

"Don't you think it would be worthwhile to calm down the frantic activity of our minds and listen? Perhaps we'll revisit this topic in a future sermon. Amen."

Mike gave Nathan the sign to sing a single verse of the final hymn. After announcing the benediction, Mike took his place at the main front door in the narthex and shook hands with the people as they left. He braced for negative comments about the length of the message but, except for a few references that he was really fired up that morning, none came. Milton Chesterfield wasn't present. Bobby Lambert approached.

"Mr. Forrest said he talked with you after the hearing," Bobby said.

"Yes."

"Good. He appreciates your altruistic motives toward the downtrodden but cares more about your reputation in the community. Listen to him."

Bobby moved past Mike and out the door before he could respond. The crowd thinned; Peg joined him.

"You were awesome this morning," she whispered in his ear. "Your sermon was a lot better than the one I suggested."

Mike shook the last person's hand, and they were left alone in the narthex. He realized he'd not seen Sam and Muriel Miller leave the sanctuary.

"Did you talk to the Millers?" he asked Peg.

"No, I came around the side of the church after leaving the choir room."

He stepped back into the sanctuary. Sam was still sitting in the pew with Muriel beside him.

"Come on," Mike said to Peg.

They walked down the aisle and approached the couple from the side.

"Good morning," Mike said.

"Yep, it is," Sam said.

"Is everything okay?" Mike asked.

"It will be."

"The service is over," Mike said.

Sam tilted his head to the side. "Not for me. I've been sitting here doing what you told us to do—calm down and listen to Papa. You were so right. The cares of the world have dulled my senses. I need to be more like the boy Samuel. When you read those verses about the Lord speaking to him at Shiloh, it made tears come to my eyes. None of his words fell to the ground, but so many of mine have ended up in the dust."

Mike reached over and put his hand on Sam's shoulder.

"Don't be too hard on yourself," he said. "It was your influence that inspired the sermon."

Sam smiled. "That's good, but it doesn't change what I need to do. Like you on the mountain top, I can't let man interfere with what Papa wants to do with me. You may have stopped preaching, but there are still words bouncing all around this room. If it's okay, I'd like to stay a while and listen."

Mike paused for a moment but heard nothing except the sound of his own breathing.

"Okay. Peg and I will wait for you at the door."

"How long do you think Sam will stay in there?" Peg asked as they walked back up the aisle.

"I don't have a clue. But I can't complain. He's the only person who took my message seriously enough to do something about it."

They waited in silence for several minutes in the narthex. Peg sat in a chair for a while, then stood and stretched.

"Ever since I found out about the pregnancy, I've enjoyed sitting quietly in the chair in our bedroom and reading my Bible. I'm trying to listen to God."

"I know. I thought about you and Sam when I was preparing the sermon."

Mike stepped toward the sanctuary to check on the Millers. When he reached the open door, an invisible presence suddenly rested on him. It was much stronger than the pleasant sensation he experienced beside the creek. He leaned his hand against the wall.

"Are you okay?" Peg asked.

Mike stepped back, and the weight lifted. He stepped forward. The invisible weight returned. He retreated, and it left. He repeated the sequence a few times with the same result.

"What in the world are you doing?" Peg asked. "It looks like a new dance step."

"I felt something when I crossed the threshold into the sanctuary," Mike responded. "It left when I stepped back."

Before Peg could ask another question, Sam and Muriel came from the sanctuary.

"Thanks for waiting," Sam said. "It's been a good day in church."

They went outside. Peg and Muriel walked ahead; Mike and Sam lagged behind. Mike mentioned what he'd felt.

"Papa is letting you know that He's in the house. The weight you felt is the glory. Look it up in your concordance. I had to search that one out myself."

"Did you feel it?" Mike asked.

"No, but it happens to me a lot."

"I wanted to go back into the sanctuary and stay there," Mike said.

Sam smiled. "Yep. What did King David say? 'Better is one day in the house of the Lord than a thousand in the tents of the wicked.'"

They reached Sam's red pickup at the far end of the parking lot.

"Are you still interested in giving the church a quote on cutting the grass?" Mike asked.

"Yep, but before I name a price, I'd like to cut it once and see how long it takes."

"Okay."

"Would you like to have lunch with us?" Peg asked.

"No, thanks," Sam replied. "I'm still chewing on what your husband said this morning. I think that's all I'll be eating for the rest of the day."

Muriel stepped forward and gave Peg a hug. "You look lovely."

"I've been doing what you suggested," Peg replied.

Muriel rewarded her with a wrinkled smile. "I can see it in your face. It's showing a lot quicker than the baby."

Sam and Muriel drove out of the parking lot. Mike took Peg's hand as they turned toward their car.

"What do you think about the Millers?" Mike asked.

Peg was silent for few steps. "They're simple, yet complicated. Harmless, but a little scary."

Eleven

MIKE WAS AT HIS DESK MID-MORNING ON MONDAY WHEN Delores brought in the mail.

"I hope you're not in trouble," she said. "You have a letter from Judge Coberg."

She'd placed the envelope from the superior court judge on top of the stack. Mike picked it up.

"No, it's something I expected."

Delores stood in front of his desk while Mike opened the envelope. He stopped and looked at her.

"Is there anything else?" he asked.

"Where do you want me to file the things you get from the court?"

"Uh, since we're not running a law firm here, I'll keep the correspondence and letters at home. I have to protect the attorney-client privilege with Sam Miller."

Delores sniffed as she turned to leave the room.

"Unless it's something that's part of the public record," Mike called after her.

Delores closed the door without further comment. Mike realized she'd been somewhat aloof all morning, but the reason for her coolness would have to wait. He turned his attention to the letter addressed to him and Ken West with a copy to Melissa Hall. Referencing the *State v. Miller* case, the judge briefly wrote:

> *Counsel for the State and the defense are hereby notified that on several occasions the defendant, Sam Miller, has provided information to the Court about pending cases. Should the State or the defense desire to schedule a hearing regarding specific information, please notify me.*

Mike put the letter in his briefcase. He picked up the phone, not to dial the judge's office, which would be an improper ex parte communication, but to contact the district attorney.

"Ken West, please," he said. "It's Mike Andrews."

Mike waited. In a few seconds the familiar, booming voice of the veteran prosecutor came on the line.

"Mike, why would the minister of the church beat up my newest assistant in court on Thursday?"

"You've mixed me up with Greg Freeman. Have you read your mail this morning?"

"No, I'm still working on last Thursday."

"Pull out a thin envelope that came today from Judge Coberg and open it."

Ken West weighed almost three hundred pounds, and Mike could hear the prosecutor's chair squeak in protest as he swiveled it.

"That's not it," the veteran prosecutor muttered. "Okay, here it is. I assume you mean the one regarding the Miller case."

"It's the only case I have."

"Humph," West grunted after a minute. "What is this supposed to mean?"

"That's why I called you. I wanted to find out your position."

"I don't know enough to have one. You're not going to waive your client's right to a jury trial and let the judge decide the case, are you?"

"No."

"Then the jury will determine the facts, assuming we don't work out a plea bargain."

"Correct. Do you want to meet with the judge?"

"Probably, but let me talk with Ms. Hall so she can be involved in the decision. I'm not going to jerk this case away from her. It will be good experience for her to respond to the different strategies you'll use in an effort to manipulate her."

Mike ignored the dig. "Did your office perform any independent investigation of the factual basis for the charges against Miller? Ms. Hall wouldn't let me manipulate that information out of her."

"Good for her. I've been knee-deep in the Anson murder case and trying to rework our budget proposal for the next fiscal year. I don't recall much about this file except that it involved a church and met the $100,000 felony threshold."

"Could you take a look at it and get back to me? The judge is going to expect a response from us."

"I have a case review meeting with my assistants later this week. I'll put it on the agenda and get back with you."

SEVERAL VISITORS HAD ATTENDED THE CHURCH ON SUNDAY. Part of Mike's Monday morning routine was to work through the visitor cards and thank the people for coming. Sometimes routine calls uncovered immediate needs in the lives of people desperate for someone to talk to. Today, one woman spoke with him for thirty minutes about her teenage daughter. Mike promised to ask Nathan to make a special effort to reach out to the young woman. When he crossed off the last name, Mike stood up, stretched, and went to Delores's desk.

"I had quite a few calls to visitors this morning," he said.

"I've been getting a lot of calls, too," Delores replied.

"What kind of calls?"

"About your sermon on Sunday."

"I know I went longer than usual, but I didn't get any negative feedback from folks as they left the church."

"Well, my phone rang quite a bit Sunday afternoon."

"Who called?"

"Different people."

Mike didn't pressure Delores for names. Eventually, she always revealed her sources of information.

"What was the complaint?" he asked.

"That you didn't sound like yourself, and the stories you told were weird."

"Anything else?"

"One person was upset when she found out that Mr. and Mrs. Miller were in the sanctuary."

"Why do you think it's called a sanctuary?" Mike asked testily.

"Don't get mad at me. If you don't want to know—"

"Was it a member of the session?"

Delores didn't respond, but Mike easily interpreted her expression as a yes.

"Well, Libby Gorman made her wishes known at the meeting," he said. "And Sam Miller had a business reason to be here. I asked him to look at our property and submit a bid to cut the grass. Our current service does a sloppy job, especially in the cemetery."

"But they don't have any criminals working for them."

Mike stared at her for a moment, decided not to remind her of the presumption of innocence until proven guilty, and returned to his office. He didn't come out until Delores left for lunch.

After she had gone, Mike fielded a phone call from a church member wanting to know the charge for a nonmember to rent the old sanctuary for a wedding. A few minutes later, the phone rang again.

"Little Creek Church," Mike said.

"I didn't know the pope answered his own phone," Braxton Hodges responded.

"I don't think I'm qualified for the job."

"You don't seem afraid to multitask," the newspaperman replied. "Preacher on Sunday, lawyer for the people on Monday. Do you have a few minutes to talk?"

"Sure. The answering machine will pick up the calls."

"I'm working on an article about your client, Sam Miller."

"Good. What have you found out?"

"That when I left a message for Jack Hatcher this morning, he didn't immediately return my call."

"He's a busy bank president. Even if he wants you to write an article, he's not going to drop everything to talk to a reporter."

"But Maxwell Forrest did. He phoned me ten minutes after I told Hatcher's assistant that I wanted to ask a few questions about the Miller embezzlement case."

"That makes sense. After all, it is a legal matter. What did Mr. Forrest say?"

"Nothing worth printing. He rolled out a nebulous comment or two that the pertinent information had been turned over to the proper authorities. I could tell he was processing me toward a quick end to the conversation until I asked him if there had been any correspondence between Miller and Jack Hatcher."

"What did he say?"

"Do you want to listen?"

"You recorded the conversation?"

"Yes."

"Did you tell him?"

"Do I have to?"

"No, so long as you're a party to the conversation."

"I already knew that, so don't send me a bill for your opinion."

"Are you recording this conversation?"

"Not unless you change your mind about running for pope."

"No chance. Turn on the tape of Mr. Forrest."

"Actually, it's digital, which makes it a lot clearer. I'll start at the beginning."

Mike pressed the receiver close to his ear, but it wasn't necessary. The voices were clear. He could easily recognize Hodges's nasal tone and Forrest's carefully modulated Southern drawl. In every conversation, Maxwell Forrest chose his words with skill.

"I think you're doing the community a service," Forrest said. "Many people don't follow the results of the criminal docket, and an article might deter someone thinking about mismanaging church money in the future."

"Let's hope so," Hodges replied. "One other thing. Did Mr. Hatcher receive any correspondence from Miller prior to the filing of the embezzlement charge?"

"I'd have to check with Mr. Hatcher about that."

"Could you do that and let me know?"

"Mr. Hatcher gets a lot of correspondence."

"People who get a letter from Sam Miller usually remember it."

There was a long silence on the phone.

"Mr. Forrest? Are you still there?"

"Yes. Any newspaper article should focus on the circumstances surrounding the criminal charges, not the bank."

"Which it will. But are you aware that Mr. Miller writes letters to people he doesn't know? I received a note from him myself a few years ago and still keep it in my desk."

"Are you going to include your note in this article?"

"No."

"Have you met Mr. Miller?" Forrest asked.

"No."

"Does Mr. Miller contend that he wrote a letter to Mr. Hatcher?"

"You're asking a lot of questions, Mr. Forrest. Could we go back a few steps? Would you check with Mr. Hatcher and find out if he received a letter from Sam Miller?"

"I'll run it by him, but I still don't see what it has to do with your article."

"Embezzling money from a local church is a serious charge. That alone is newsworthy. When combined with Miller's odd personality, I think I have a story a lot of people will be interested in reading. When should I expect to hear from you?"

"In due time. I'm late for an appointment. Good-bye."

Mike heard a click.

"You know Maxwell Forrest," Hodges said. "What did you think?"

"He'll vigorously protect the bank's reputation. It's the firm's biggest client."

"Do you think a letter exists?"

"If it hasn't ended up in the landfill with the ones Sam sent the newspaper."

"Did Forrest know more than he told me?"

"Maybe, but he'd be naturally cautious. When faced with an unexpected problem, he slows down and reconnoiters before moving forward."

"I'm not going to write an article, but from what I've seen from Sam Miller over the years, trying to interpret one of his weird, Bible-verse-filled letters wouldn't qualify as serious journalism."

"It depends on what it says. Let me know if Mr. Forrest gets back in touch with you."

"I'll record every word."

MIKE SPENT PART OF THE AFTERNOON TYPING STANDARD MOTIONS to file in the Miller case: a request for a list of potential witnesses, a copy of the statement given by Sam to interrogating officers, and the disclosure of any exculpatory evidence that might assist in establishing Sam's innocence. Mike felt especially uneasy about the signed statement taken by Detective Perkins. Few items of evidence were more damaging to a defendant than a written confession the prosecutor could wave in front of a jury during closing arguments. Mike hoped Sam's persistent obfuscation of reality flowed over into the statement.

There was a knock on the door. Nathan Goode entered.

"Good job on the anthem," Mike said. "And thanks for cutting the final hymn short. I ran way over."

"I check my watch as you come in for landing."

"What about the youth group last night? Nobody called complaining, so I assume there weren't any problems."

"Not a hitch. The Gaston boy showed up with his buddy who plays guitar. The kids liked it. I enjoyed it, too."

"What are you planning for this week's Sunday morning service?"

Nathan outlined his idea. "The anthem has a soprano solo. I thought I'd invite a guest soloist."

"A high school student would be fine. The girl on the flute did a beautiful job."

"I've been spending time with someone recently who could be for the soprano section what Peg is to the altos."

"What does *spending time* mean? Are you giving her voice lessons?"

"She's way beyond me. She was a voice major in college then decided to go to law school."

"Who is it?" Mike asked, sitting up straighter in his chair.

"Melissa Hall. She works for the district attorney's office. She grew up way back in the mountains just over the line in Tennessee. You'd never guess her interest in classical music by talking to her, but she can sight-read like a pro and hit the high notes without a problem."

Mike visualized the young prosecutor with a microphone in her hand serenading a crowd. It was a radically different venue from the Barlow County Courthouse.

"Where did you meet her?"

"At the Shelton community theater tryouts. We're going to perform *Oklahoma!* at the end of the summer. Nobody could touch Melissa's voice for the female lead."

"Hmm," Mike responded. "Does she know I'm the pastor of the church?"

"No."

"You should let her know. She's prosecuting a man I'm representing pro bono in a criminal case, and she might feel uncomfortable at the church."

"If she's willing to sing, do you have a problem with her coming?"

"Me? Of course not. The church is open to everyone."

PEG, DRESSED IN HER RUNNING GEAR, ENTERED THE GARAGE with Judge on a retractable leash as Mike pulled into the driveway.

"Are you going to keep running?" he asked when he stopped the car and got out.

Peg brushed a few stray strands of blond hair from her eyes. "Until the day before delivery. Judge and I both need regular exercise, and I can't imagine taking a total break from running for nine months."

"Did you ask the doctor about it?"

"Yes, she told me it would be fine for the first two trimesters so long as I felt okay. After that, we'll have to discuss it, but Jodie Wheeler ran five miles less than a week before her daughter was born."

"Jodie Wheeler ran the Boston Marathon a few years ago. Be careful."

Peg kissed him on the cheek and patted her abdomen. "Our baby is going to be in shape from day one."

They entered the house. The mail was jumbled on the counter in the kitchen.

"There's a small roast with potatoes and carrots in the Crock-Pot," she said.

Mike stood at the counter and began sorting. The bill pile was disturbingly high. Peg picked up the lid. Judge, who was standing beside her, barked.

"Yes, it smells good," she said to the dog.

Mike reached the bottom of the stack. The last item was an envelope from Forrest, Lambert, Park, and Arnold.

"Something from the old firm," Mike said.

Peg glanced at him. "I saw, but since it was addressed to you, I didn't open it."

Mike tore off the end of the envelope. Inside was a letter from Maxwell Forrest. Mike read it, furrowed his brow, and then examined it more slowly. Peg came over to him.

"What is it?" she asked.

"Mr. Forrest is ordering me not to come to the office or discuss the Miller case with anyone at the firm. I talked with Juanita last week, and she must have mentioned it to him."

"Can he do that?"

"Partly. I don't have the right to go beyond the reception area. That would be trespassing. But a private gag order as to firm personnel is way out of bounds. I wouldn't expect anyone to violate the attorney-client relationship with the bank, but my duty to Sam involves investigating the facts, no matter who has the information."

Twelve

MIKE'S PREOCCUPATION WITH THE MILLER CASE DIDN'T KEEP him from eating the fork-tender roast. While they ate, Judge lay underneath the table, occasionally giving a slight groan that communicated his deep desire to lick a plate or gulp down a less-than-perfect piece of meat. Mike responded to Peg's attempts at conversation with grunts that were first cousins to Judge's groans.

"Are you enjoying your food or just filling up your stomach?" Peg asked as Mike speared the last carrot on his plate.

"Oh, it's great. The meat almost melted in my mouth. And the carrots are just right."

"Still thinking about the letter?"

"Yes."

"Have you figured out what's going on?"

"No, but my focus for the case has been off. I've been thinking about the end, not the beginning. I need to interview the leaders of the church where Sam was preaching. It's their money that was allegedly embezzled."

"What's the name of the church?"

"Craig Valley something. I'll call Sam and find out who to talk to."

Mike took their plates to the sink. Judge followed him and looked up with such longing that Mike put one of the plates on the floor so he could lick it.

"When are you going to talk to him?" Peg asked.

"Tonight. He works during the day."

"Before or after you eat a bowl of the apple cobbler I bought from the little lady who sells them from the back of her car at light number nine?"

"Do we have ice cream?"

"Of course. But you shouldn't have more than one scoop. If you keep eating like you did tonight, you're going to get big around the middle faster than I am."

Mike's stomach had always been solid from daily sit-ups. He touched his shirt and felt a slight pudginess.

"Skipping a meal then gorging isn't the best," he admitted. "But tomorrow would be a better day to begin cutting back than tonight."

After dessert, Mike helped clean the kitchen. Peg went upstairs, and Mike phoned Sam Miller. "Do you have time to talk business?" he asked.

"Did you buy a notebook yet to put beside your bed?" Sam responded. "You're going to need it."

"No."

"Don't put it off."

"If I promise to get one, will you agree to answer a few questions without getting off track?"

"Go ahead."

Mike told Sam about the conversation between Braxton Hodges and Mr. Forrest.

"If it still exists, getting a copy of the letter you sent Jack Hatcher is going to be difficult," Mike concluded.

"Why do you need a copy?"

"Your testimony about the letter wouldn't prove that it existed or was delivered to Jack Hatcher. He could deny any written communication from you, and there wouldn't be anything I could do about it. Without verification, your story about hatchets, baseball bats, and glass beads would sound ridiculous. And there may be something in the letter you've forgotten. You've had lots of dreams and visions since that night."

"True," Sam agreed. "Can't you file one of those subpoena things?"

"Yes. There is a procedure to request documents held by a third party in criminal cases. I'll do that at the proper time and see what turns up. But first I need to interview some folks from the Craig Valley church. What's it called?"

"Craig Valley Gospel Tabernacle."

"Have you had any contact with them since the charges were filed?"

"Nope. The young detective who met with me at the jail told me not to talk to anyone from the church. He said it would look like I was trying to harass them, and they might charge me with something else."

Mike felt a spurt of anger at the detective's intimidation tactic. He would like to teach Perkins a lesson, but nothing allowed by the law or his faith immediately came to mind.

"That's not true. You'd have to actually threaten someone to cross the line. Do you think any of the church leaders would talk to me about the case?"

"Yep."

"Who would be the one most likely to cooperate?"

"Larry Fletchall is the head deacon. His daddy was a preacher and a friend of mine."

"Do you have his phone number?"

"Yep, but I think it would be best to meet with the other deacons, too."

"How many are there?"

"Four."

"That's a manageable group. Set it up for any evening this week except Wednesday. I have a memorial service for Danny Brewster, the former client I told you about who died in prison. The service is in the afternoon but might run late."

"I know some Brewsters who live on the west side, but I don't recall Danny."

"Same family. Call me after you contact the folks at Craig Valley."

"Okay. And I'll come to your church before the end of the week to cut the grass so everything will look nice on Sunday. I could really use the business. Several folks have called and canceled on me. This should be one of my busiest times of the year, but I didn't have anything to do this afternoon except work on my equipment."

"Are people giving you a reason?"

"Nope, but you know there's been talk. People are nervous about having someone who's been in trouble with the law on their property."

AFTER MIKE HUNG UP THE PHONE, HE TURNED ON A BASEBALL game, but his thoughts returned to Danny Brewster. Mike's memories of most clients he'd represented had faded, replaced by people who needed his help in the present. But his memories of Danny endured. Mike could still recall details of his investigation, conversations with Danny, questions to the witnesses at the trial, even a few lines from his closing argument to the jury. Anger without an outlet rose up in him. He could try to convince Braxton Hodges to write an article for the paper about Danny, but he doubted the prison death of a young man convicted of multiple counts of burglary would warrant public interest.

Mike continued to stew until another vivid memory of Danny, an antidote for anger, rose to the surface and forced him to smile. While in the local jail, Danny made a large cross from toothpicks in a craft class, painted it with bright colors, and gave it to him. Mike still had the cross in his desk drawer at the church. The colors had faded, but the love behind the gift remained.

Judge pattered into the room and sat beside the chair with his head on the armrest so Mike could rub the area of wrinkled skin on the dog's forehead. Mike put his hand on the dog's head and started scratching. A few minutes later, Peg, wearing her pajamas and a painting in her hand, joined them.

"Remember this?" she said, turning the painting so he could see it. "Don't you think she looks like Muriel?"

It was an oil painting of an older woman wearing the type of plain dress worn by Muriel Miller and standing in a field of wildflowers. The area where the woman stood was filled with light, but she teetered at the edge of total darkness that covered a third of the painting. Peg portrayed the woman in profile with hair the same length and color as Sam's wife's.

"It could be her."

"But in your dream she doesn't stay in the sunlight."

"No." Mike involuntarily shuddered.

Several times since he'd married Peg, Mike had watched the old woman leave the light and walk into the darkness until it enveloped her. Each time he witnessed the sequence of events, he tried to force the woman back to shore by the strength of his will but without success. When she failed to reappear, he always woke to a deep sense of sadness and regret, as if the loss was as great for him as for her.

The phone rang. It was Sam. Mike shook his head to clear the troubling images prompted by the painting and dream.

"Thursday night at seven o'clock at the church," Sam said. "All the deacons will be there. Come by my house about six-thirty, and we'll ride together."

"I'll be there."

"What's going on?" Peg asked when Mike hung up.

"I want to interview the leaders of the church where Sam was preaching and find out what they know about the embezzlement charge. I'll need to leave here about six o'clock on Thursday so I can pick up Sam."

Peg yawned. "Anything else going on that you can tell me about?"

Mike pointed at the television. "Unless Cincinnati gets more than four innings a game from their starting pitchers, it's going to be a long season along the Ohio River."

Peg was asleep before the Reds came to bat in the seventh. Judge lay on the floor in front of the couch. Judge liked Mike, but he loved Peg. The dog had spent many miles in tandem with her as they jogged Peg's favorite routes.

Peg's nose twitched. Mike enjoyed watching her sleep. He reached over and turned the painting so he couldn't see it. Watching Peg was much more pleasant. At rest, she reminded him of a picture on the wall of her old bedroom at her parents' home. In the photo, Peg, a little blond-haired girl wearing pajamas, lay with her head on a pillow while holding a stuffed rabbit wrapped tightly in her arms. Mike muted the volume on the TV for the remainder of the game. After the last out, he picked Peg up in his arms. She awoke but pretended to remain asleep as she rested her head against his shoulder.

Carrying Peg to bed had been one of Mike's favorite rituals during the first year of their marriage. The top sheet and comforter had already been pulled down. Mike smiled, kissed the top of her head, and covered her up.

"DID YOU FLOAT UP TO BED LAST NIGHT?" HE ASKED WHEN PEG came into the kitchen in the morning.

"No, I dreamed Prince Charming picked me up in a golden carriage drawn by rust-colored horses and took me to his castle on a hill above the town."

Mike smiled. "At least the hill-above-town part is real."

Peg ground some coffee beans and brewed a pot while Mike released Judge to run around in the backyard. Mike returned to the smell of dark liquid in the pot. He poured a cup and took a sip. Peg knew how to unlock the secret of the coffee bean.

"This is the best," he said.

Peg sat across from him.

"Aren't you going to have a cup?" he asked.

"I'm cutting back on caffeine."

Mike studied her face as he raised the cup to his lips.

"You're a beautiful woman," he said.

Peg gave him a puzzled look. "Without makeup or doing more than running a brush twice through my hair?"

"Yes."

MIKE PARKED IN THE GRAVEL DRIVEWAY OF THE BREWSTER HOUSE and walked across the yard that was more weeds than grass. Rose Brewster came onto the front porch that was flanked by two cracked and discolored concrete fountains with no water in them. She'd aged more than the years since he'd seen her. She was in her late fifties but looked closer to seventy.

"Come on in," she beckoned. "Everyone should be here in a little while."

Mike shook her hand, weathered from contact with chemicals at the metal processing plant where she worked. She opened the screen door, and they stepped into a living room filled with about twenty folding metal chairs.

"We moved out all the furniture and borrowed chairs from the church my sister attends. They have to be back for Wednesday night family supper."

"This will be fine. Who's coming?"

Mike braced himself for her answer. All day long, he'd been trying to get ready to face Danny's older brother Quentin, the one who duped Danny into breaking into the houses.

"I'm not exactly sure. Some folks are working. Others are sick. My mother and her sisters are riding over together from Boomer."

"What about Quentin?"

Rose shook her head. "Didn't you know? He's got the HIV and moved to Asheville so he could get free treatment. He don't come around too much."

Mike winced. "I'm sorry, Rose. You've had more dumped on you than a human being could be expected to stand."

"Sometimes I feel like that man in the Bible who had so much trouble."

"Job."

"Yeah. And I'm still a-waiting for things to get better. Do you want to see the letters you sent Danny? I put them in a box so you could take them with you."

Mike followed Rose into the kitchen. Dishes of food wrapped in aluminum foil rested on the table.

"The neighbors have chipped in nice," she said, pointing at the table. "A few of them are going to come."

"That's good."

"Danny was my baby," Rose said as she opened the drawer of a small plastic filing cabinet. "And he thought the world of you."

She handed Mike a cardboard shoe box. He lifted the lid. A stack of letters was bound together by a thick rubber band. The box also contained copies of pleadings Mike had filed in Danny's case along with the brief to the Court of Appeals and the Court's decision denying a new trial.

"As far as I know, he saved everything you ever sent him, even the legal stuff that he couldn't read or understand."

There was a loud knock at the front door.

"I'd better get that," Rose said. "Make yourself at home."

Mike flipped through the papers, not sure what to do with them. With the box under his arm, he walked down the short hall to the living room. Passing a bedroom, he saw Danny's picture in a frame beside Rose's bed. It was a high school photo featuring Danny's unique grin. The service was scheduled to start at 4:00 p.m., but people straggled in for another twenty minutes. Mike waited.

At 4:30 p.m., Rose looked at him and announced, "I guess that's about it."

Mike stood before the group. Even with the front door open it was stuffy in the little house. He left the notes he'd prepared in the pocket of his jacket beside the toothpick cross.

"One of the things we like to do at memorial services is remember the person who has passed on. I remember Danny as a young man with a big smile, simple faith, and generous spirit. When he found out I was a Christian he always wanted to pray after we had a meeting about his case. No one I represented left a deeper impression on me than Danny. In fact, knowing him influenced me to go into the ministry so I could focus on people's spiritual, not just legal, needs."

Mike took out the cross and showed it to the group then handed it to Rose.

"It was a privilege serving as Danny's lawyer, and losing his case was the worst experience of my career. I'll never forget the moment of the verdict." Mike paused and let a wave of emotion pass. "After the jury foreman spoke, Danny turned to me and asked me what had happened. When I told him the bad news, he patted me on the back and told me it would be okay."

Mike lowered his head for a moment before continuing with more intensity. "But it wasn't okay. Our court system failed, I failed, and the prison system failed. And now Danny is gone. There's a part of me that wants to scream at the injustice of it all. But Danny never cursed the darkness that exists in this world. His answer was to let his light shine."

Mike looked at Rose. "Do you remember how much he liked the little song many of us learned as kids about letting our light shine all over the neighborhood?"

Rose nodded. "He loved that song."

"That song has kept me from anger and despair over Danny's death. His light never went out, and I guarantee you, at this moment, it's blazing like a bonfire. Danny won't be coming home to us, but as King David said after one of his sons died, *'I will go to him, but he will not return to me.'* If we're one of God's children, we'll one day join him in a place where no evil dwells. Grieve. It's healthy. But also remember the goodness that came through knowing a wonderful young man."

Mike scanned the faces of the mourners. "Now it's your turn. Like Danny, we're not in a hurry. Let's hear from you. It's time for you to remember."

Mike sat down. There was a long, awkward silence, and Mike wondered if anyone would speak. Then, one of Danny's aunts stood up.

"I got a story," she said. "When Danny was about twelve years old, he and his mama came over to our house to eat one Friday night. I'd worked all day and was beat, but I knew how much Danny liked potatoes fried in a skillet with onions, so I was in the kitchen peeling potatoes. He came in to see me, stood right beside me at the sink, and watched for the longest time without saying a word. Finally, he spoke up. 'Aunt Betty, you make the best potatoes in the world. I love to put ketchup on them and eat a whole plate. When I eat one of your potatoes, it makes me feel good all over my insides, not just in my stomach.'"

Betty looked at Rose. "You raised that boy right, and don't you ever believe anything else."

Several others spoke. One story made Mike laugh; another brought him to the edge of tears.

Finally, Rose wiped her eyes with a tissue and spoke.

"Thank you for coming." She turned to Mike. "I appreciate you telling me to do this. I hadn't seen Danny for several months before he got killed, and listening to y'all makes him seem more alive to me."

Later, Mike and Rose were standing beside each other in the kitchen.

"You know," Rose said, "Danny didn't believe me at first when I told him you was going to school to be a preacher. He said Mr. Andrews didn't have to go to school to be a good preacher. He already was one."

"And I want to be a better one."

"You did a good job today."

"It's not hard when it's about someone like Danny."

Mike lingered until everyone except Rose's sisters had left. He gave Rose a hug, took the shoe box from her, and put it in the passenger seat of the car.

"Can I give you the cross?" he asked.

"No, but thanks for showing it to me. He meant it for you."

Rose put the cross in the top of the box.

When Mike arrived home Peg met him in the kitchen.

"How was it?" she asked.

"I hope Rose felt loved and comforted. For me, it was like stepping back in time."

"What did you find when you went back?"

Mike set the shoe box on the kitchen counter. "This."

While Peg leafed through the letters and legal paperwork, Mike spoke.

"As a lawyer I met people from all across Barlow County. That doesn't happen anymore. Our church congregation is a lot more homogeneous than I'd realized."

"Do you miss it?"

"A little," Mike admitted, "but not enough to go back." He smiled slightly. "Maybe that's the reason I'm representing Sam Miller. He should be different enough to satisfy my itch for the peculiar for a long time."

That night Mike didn't know what time it was when he awoke. He glanced at the clock. The numbers were blurred, and he blinked his eyes several times. It was 3:18 a.m. There was no notebook or PDA on the nightstand, but the dream was so vivid that he could easily remember it until morning. He yawned and closed his eyes before waking up again. It was 3:38 a.m. Trying to make it through the rest of the night in twenty-minute intervals wasn't going to work. Mike rolled out of bed and walked barefoot downstairs. Judge rose from his bed in the kitchen and greeted him with a loud woof.

"Quiet!" Mike said. "Don't you know what time it is?"

Mike opened the back door so Judge could go outside then retrieved his PDA from its place in the kitchen beneath where he hung his car keys. Returning to his chair in the living room, Mike opened a blank screen and entered the date. Judge scratched at the door, and Mike let him in. The dog always received a treat when he went out in the morning.

"Remember this in a few hours," Mike said as he deposited a large dog biscuit between Judge's teeth. "If I only get one scoop of ice cream, you only get one dog biscuit."

Finally settling down in the chair, Mike started to record what he'd heard and seen, but the sequence of events and words spoken in the dream was hazy. It had been as vivid as the dream about Danny, but he couldn't recall it as clearly. He could remember talking to a group of men. He didn't recognize any of them, but knew they were affiliated with the Craig Valley Gospel Tabernacle. Sam Miller was also present.

"What was it?" Mike muttered.

It had something to do with finding out information about Sam's case. Everyone was sitting in a dimly lit room. The atmosphere was very tense and no one spoke. Then something happened that changed everything, and the light in the room increased. However, in the midst of waking up, dozing a few minutes, going downstairs, and taking care of Judge, the details of the dream now escaped him. Mike furrowed his brow until it wrinkled like Judge's forehead, but all he could muster was a general sense of the scene. Closing the PDA, he returned to bed.

And slept the rest of the night.

Thirteen

"I HAD A DREAM," HE TOLD PEG IN THE MORNING. "BUT I LOST the details before I could write it down."

"What do you remember?"

Mike told her what he could recall. Peg poured him a cup of coffee.

"Maybe it will come back to you later in the day," she said.

"If anything can help, it's this coffee," Mike replied, taking a sip. "It should wake up my lazy brain cells."

SEVERAL TIMES DURING THE DAY, MIKE TRIED TO REMEMBER additional details of his dream, but nothing came. He arrived home to a message from Peg that she'd gone shopping with a friend and wouldn't be back before he left for his meeting at the Craig Valley church. Mike fixed a salad before leaving to pick up Sam. He put on a coat and silk tie so he would look like a lawyer.

The sun was barely above the tree line when Mike turned onto the driveway to the Miller house. Sam stepped onto the front stoop and waved as he approached.

"Did Papa send you a letter last night?" the old man asked as soon as he sat down in the passenger seat of the car.

Mike had heard so many of Sam's off-the-wall comments that he responded without thinking the old man was crazy.

"Is that what you saw?" Mike asked.

"Yep. It had your name on it in big print."

"Did you open it?"

"Nope. It wasn't addressed to me, but the return address was *Craig Valley Gospel Tabernacle.*"

Mike told about his dream in the night as he drove down McAfee Road.

"It was so vivid, I didn't think there was a chance I would forget any part of it."

"You're like a little baby that has to be told the same thing over and over before it understands. Papa is teaching you a lesson. You should have listened to me about the notebook. As you get more mature, you'll get better at remembering. Then the hard part is interpreting what Papa shows you."

"I'll use my PDA."

"What's that?" Sam asked.

Mike took the device from his pocket and showed it to Sam.

"Oh, yeah, but that thing is no good if your batteries are dead. My notebooks don't need batteries."

"I keep it charged. If I start having dreams with meanings, they are going to be high-tech."

Mike told Sam about Danny Brewster's memorial service.

"That's good," Sam said when he finished. "It makes me look forward to meeting Danny myself." Sam paused. "And it makes me feel better about you being my lawyer."

"Why? I lost Danny's case, and he went to prison where he was murdered."

"Yep, but there's no condemnation from Papa. That's the important thing."

They rode in silence for several miles.

"What kind of reception are we going to get from the deacons?" Mike asked.

"Larry is one of my sons, so everything should be fine. He was in a hurry when I called him, and we didn't have a long conversation."

"I didn't know members of your family attended the church."

"Yep. Including you, I have ten sons," Sam answered. "Papa has bunches of sons, and sometimes He lets me help raise them."

"Spiritual sons."

"Yep, isn't that the most important part of being an earthly papa?"

They made several turns. The Craig Valley area contained several clusters of houses.

"Is the church near the Rea home place?" Mike asked, referring to the oldest house in Barlow County.

"Yep. Less than a mile past it on a side road."

They passed the Rea home, a weathered log cabin built in 1758. A marker along the road gave a brief history of the site where Scottish immigrants first settled in the county.

"Turn at the next right," Sam said.

It was a paved road. The church, a small, rectangular, concrete-block building painted lime green, was a short distance on the left. A wooden sign with black letters on a white background proclaimed the name of the church. Underneath the name was a place to identify the pastor. It was painted over with new white paint. Two pickup trucks and an older-model car were parked out front. To the side of the building, a large flat place had been cleared and trenches for concrete footings had been dug. Wooden stakes with strings surrounded the work area.

"That's where they're going to build," Sam said.

Mike parked beside one of the pickup trucks. They went to the front door of the church, a double brown door that looked too flimsy to withstand a hard kick.

"You take the lead and introduce me," Mike said.

Sam pushed open the door. The inside of the church was as plain as the outside. Rows of wooden pews rested on a floor covered with thin, cheap carpet. A raised platform with two steps leading to it contained a single chair and a wooden pulpit. There was a piano to the left of the platform, but no area for a choir.

"They use one of the adult Sunday school rooms for deacon meetings," Sam said. "It's behind the sanctuary."

They walked down the aisle, through a door to the right of the platform, and entered a short hall. No one was in sight. Sam opened a door. Mike followed. Inside, he saw four African-American men on their knees around a table. They stopped praying and stood. The tallest of the men stepped forward and extended his hand to Mike.

"I'm Larry Fletchall," he said.

After he shook Mike's hand, Larry turned to Sam.

"We got here early so we could pray for you."

Mike couldn't help staring. The room was similar to the one in his dream, but the men he saw in the night were white, not black.

"Are you okay?" Sam asked him.

"Huh? Yeah."

Sam spoke to the other men. "Jesse Lavare, Bob Gordon, John Franklin. Good to see you again."

"Don't, Sam," Larry said. "We've been trying to pray through on this situation for over an hour. We agreed to meet with you and your lawyer, but you betrayed our trust. We can't pretend nothing happened."

"But I didn't do anything," Sam started, then stopped. "I'd better let Mike speak for me."

The men rose from their knees, their faces serious. They were working-class men dressed in clean pants and open-collared shirts.

"Could we all sit down?" Mike asked.

They sat around the table. As in Mike's dream, the lights in the room were dim. One of the bulbs in the overhead fixture must have burned out.

"Thank you for agreeing to meet with me," Mike began. "Part of my job is to find out what happened."

He put a legal pad on the table.

"No notes," the oldest of the men said. "We don't want you trying to twist our words if this thing goes to court."

Mike placed his pen on the pad. "All right. I won't write down anything unless you give me permission; however, it might be helpful to record a name or phone number if that comes up."

Larry nodded. "We'll see."

Mike continued. "First, I'm a minister who used to be a lawyer. I don't want to do anything that would embarrass you or hurt your church. My job is simply to investigate the charges against Sam. To do that, I need to ask you some questions. I'm not going to try to trick you, and if you don't want to answer, that's fine."

Mike gave a reassuring smile, but no one reciprocated. He suspected his natural charm wasn't going to create an atmosphere of trust.

"I'll get right to the point. How many bank accounts does the church have?"

"Two," Larry answered. "An operating account and a building fund."

"Who has access to the accounts? Who can sign checks?"

"All the deacons are on the operating account," Larry answered. "Jesse, Bob, and I signed the card for the building fund account."

"What about former deacons?"

"They're removed from all accounts when they stop serving on the board."

"How long have you been without a pastor?"

"About a year."

"Was your former pastor on either bank account?"

Larry looked at the older man. "Bob, was Brother Mark able to sign checks?"

"No," Bob replied. "It hasn't been that way since Brother Tyner was here."

"How long ago was that?" Mike asked.

"Over twenty years," Bob answered.

"Was Sam given authority to sign checks?"

"No," Larry replied. "But when we went to the bank, the man showed us the checks Sam filled out and put in his account."

"Who did you talk to at the bank?"

Larry reached into his pocket and took out a business card.

"Brian Dressler and another man who didn't give us his card."

Mike knew Dressler, a vice president at the bank.

"How many checks were there and for what amounts?" Mike asked.

"Two, one for $10,000 and another for $95,000."

"Who signed the checks?"

"They had Jesse's signature on the bottom, but they went into Sam's account."

Mike turned toward Jesse. "Did you sign checks in those amounts?"

Jesse, a large man with powerful arms and a deep voice, jumped up from his seat. "No! And don't you come in here accusing me—"

"Wait, calm down," Mike interrupted. "I only meant, did you sign checks in that amount for a legitimate building fund purpose? Did you have construction bills to pay?"

Jesse continued to glare at Mike.

"No," Larry responded. "There weren't any bills to pay."

"Do you recall the dates on the checks?"

Larry looked at Jesse. "Do you remember?"

Jesse sat down, but there was still anger in his voice. "They were two days apart. It was during the time Sam was preaching for us. He forged my signature on the first one, and when it went through decided to do another one. It was most of the money we'd saved over the past five years for our building fund."

Mike saw Sam out of the corner of his eye. The old man was sitting with his eyes closed, patting his stomach.

"Did you pay Sam when he was preaching here?" Mike asked.

"Yes," Larry said. "A hundred dollars a Sunday."

"Did you pay him by check?"

"Yes."

"From the operating account?"

"Yes."

"Did he know about the building fund?"

"Yes," Larry said, shaking his head with obvious regret. "He told us five years ago that a greater harvest was coming, and we needed to build a bigger barn to hold it."

"Was he right? Has the church grown?"

"Yes. Sam knows what has happened."

Jesse grunted. "Don't come in here with that soothsayer stuff."

"No, Jesse," Larry said. "We agreed that I would do the talking."

Jesse stood and stretched out a meaty hand clenched in a fist at Sam. Raising his voice, he thundered, "He came in here like a fortune-teller and fooled everybody! I warned them, but they wouldn't listen to me! Then he tried to make it look like I was the one who done wrong!"

Jesse took a step toward Sam. Larry jumped to his feet and reached out, but Jesse pushed him aside. Mike stood and stepped between Jesse and Sam, who pushed his chair against the wall.

"Don't! You'll be sorry!" Mike yelled.

Jesse came directly into Mike's face. "And have to hire some dirty lawyer turned preacher!"

Mike felt a hand on his back.

"Now," Sam said softly.

Mike stared into Jesse's face and knew the threat of harm wasn't a bluff. Suddenly, involuntary tears filled Mike's eyes. The room blurred, and if Mike had wanted to block a blow from Jesse, he couldn't have seen clearly enough to do so.

No blow came.

Mike rubbed his eyes with his hands, but the tears continued. He couldn't remember the last time he'd cried in public or private. The emotion he felt at Danny Brewster's memorial service was the closest he'd come to tears in public since he was a teenager. Mike groaned. The tears continued to flow. He sobbed with an agonizing groan that embarrassed him even more. He heard Larry's voice.

"Sit down, Jesse."

Mike held his sleeve against his eyes. After several moments, he took a deep breath.

Sam spoke. "Papa's heart breaks when His children hate. Those were His tears for us."

Mike looked up. Jesse had returned to his chair. The large man sat with his head down, staring at the floor.

"It's the Spirit of the Lord," Bob said simply.

Mike could feel the tears drying on his cheeks. Larry turned to Bob.

"What are we supposed to do?"

"Quit talking and go back to praying," Bob replied.

Larry motioned toward Mike and Sam. "With them?"

"Yes."

Jesse stood up and quickly moved toward the door. "I don't want any part of this! A lying spirit has come on all of you!"

Larry reached toward Jesse.

"Let him go," Bob said.

Jesse left the room, leaving the door open behind him. Without another word, Bob slipped to his knees in front of his chair. The other men and Sam did the same. Mike hadn't prayed in a kneeling position for years, but he joined them. The room was silent for several minutes. Then, Mike felt the heaviness he'd experienced the previous Sunday in the Little Creek sanctuary.

"Oh, God; oh, God," Larry began.

For the next hour, Mike listened as the men cried out to the Lord in a way he'd only imagined. Mike didn't believe emotion moved God's heart, but he suspected the three deacons didn't agree with him. They acted as if the future of the Almighty's will for Sam Miller and the Craig Valley Gospel Tabernacle depended upon their zeal. Sam didn't speak, and Mike wondered if the old man prayed the same way. The deacons' words built to a zenith and ebbed several times before Larry said, "Amen and amen."

Mike opened his eyes. Everyone rose from the floor.

"Thanks for meeting with us," Sam said. "The time will come when we will break bread together."

"The light will come; the truth will be known," Larry said. "My heart is clear."

"Amen," the other two men echoed.

"Who should I contact if I have other questions?" Mike asked.

"Me," Larry replied.

MIKE AND SAM WALKED THROUGH THE SANCTUARY. SAM TURNED and faced the pulpit.

"I'll be back," he said then turned to Mike. "You, too."

When they sat down in the car, Mike took a deep breath and exhaled.

"I didn't know what to expect, but that was different," he said.

"Yep."

"Were you surprised by Jesse's reaction to you?"

"He's shaken my hand many times, and I've prayed for him and his family. I don't know all that lives in a man's heart. Sometimes, a good heart lets a bad guest come for a visit. I hope that's the situation with Jesse."

Mike put the car in reverse and drove away from the church. They passed the Rea homestead.

"I have a theory about what happened at the bank," Mike said. "And Jesse is at the heart of it."

"How?"

"It's not complicated and eliminates the existence of proving a bank error. Jesse wrote the checks from the building fund and put them in your account to discredit you and eliminate your influence in the church. He'd be taking a tremendous risk, but it would explain the financial transactions. Finding out the number of your bank account wouldn't be too difficult. He then simply presented the checks for deposit to your account."

"But he said his name was forged on the checks."

"He could have modified his normal signature so it would look like a forgery. We can have the checks examined by an expert. It might not turn up anything, but it would be worth a try. Getting Jesse to admit a criminal act would be next to impossible; however, there are three credible witnesses who will testify about Jesse's attitude toward you this evening. It might be enough to create a reasonable doubt."

"What would happen to Jesse?"

"Nothing, unless the DA decided to prosecute him. If the charges against you are dropped or a jury finds you not guilty, I suspect the whole matter would all go away. It's not the kind of case Ken West, the district attorney, likes to take all the way."

They rode in silence. Mike turned onto another road.

"But do you think Jesse wrote those two checks?" Sam asked.

"It was a stupid thing to do, but if he's as mad at you as he showed at the church, anything is possible. Now, he's probably scared that he'll get caught."

"Did you see anything about Jesse in your dream?"

Mike shook his head and smiled. "I'm not sure about my dream. All the men in my dream were white. Why didn't you tell me it was a black church?"

"Would it have made a difference?"

"Of course not, but it makes me question my dream."

"Does Papa see in color?" Sam asked with a grin.

"Don't mess with me," Mike responded.

"It doesn't make me doubt your dream," Sam continued. "Papa likes variety. All creation shows it."

"Well, whatever happened at my house around 3:18 a.m. didn't seem to have much relevance to that meeting."

"Is that when you woke up?"

"Yes, it's one of the few things I remember."

"Do you have a Bible in the car?" Sam asked.

"Check the backseat."

Sam reached behind him. While Mike drove, Sam flipped through the pages.

"What are you looking for?" Mike asked.

"A clue to understanding your dream."

Sam turned several more pages. "Here's something. Listen to this. '*As I have often told you before and now say again even with tears, many live as enemies of the cross of Christ.*' That's Philippians 3:18. Your tears came when you looked at Jesse. The time of a dream is often important."

Mike didn't look at Sam. "You can believe there is a connection if you want to, but I think plugging a verse into an alarm clock and concluding it's a message from God is speculation."

"Just consider it. I'm trying to help you get smarter about the things you're moving into."

Mike turned onto McAfee Road.

"I'm not sure about the tears or the time of night," he said. "My goal is to move you safely through the criminal justice system and out the other side without any more tears for Muriel or jail time for you."

Fourteen

The following day, Mike filed a flurry of motions in Sam's case, including a request for scientific evaluation of the checks deposited to Sam's bank account. Late in the afternoon, he received a call from Melissa Hall.

"I went over your motions with Ken," the assistant DA said. "There isn't much in the file, but we'll let you copy what you want."

"Is there a statement from Miller?"

"Signed after receiving his Miranda rights."

"And the checks?"

"Yes, copies along with other bank records."

"Okay. When will the file be available?"

"Whenever you want to review it. The secretary knows you have permission. Also, Ken wants to have an informal meeting with Judge Coberg about the letter the judge sent. Would you have any objection to meeting with the judge in chambers before bringing in an outside judge for a hearing?"

"That's fine."

"What is your availability?"

"Any time except Sunday morning."

Mike waited for an acknowledgment of his attempt at humor but none came. He looked at the calendar on his computer. "Actually, I would prefer to do it next week, either Tuesday or Wednesday afternoon."

"Both of those times work for Ken. I'll check with the judge's clerk and confirm via e-mail."

That evening Mike took Peg out to eat. On the way home, they passed a road that led away from town and deeper into the mountains.

"How is your energy level?" Mike asked.

"Mostly good."

"Do you have any plans on Friday?" Mike asked.

"Just my usual date with Judge for a run. I might call Elizabeth Lambert for lunch."

"Would you like to climb Jefferson's Ridge? I've been thinking about it since my sermon."

"I thought you and Bobby were going to play eighteen holes."

"I'd rather spend time with you."

Peg turned sideways in her seat. Mike stared straight ahead and fought off a guilty smile.

"Bobby canceled on you," she said.

Mike nodded. "Yes. Sam Miller thinks he sees the past and the future, but he's no match for you. Bobby is still swamped at work and can't break away for a few hours. But I'd still rather be with you than playing golf with Bobby."

"Are you going to ride your bike while Judge and I run along beside you?"

"No. We'll all be on foot."

Peg was silent for a moment then sighed. "Okay. It's time."

"For what?"

"To go with you to the top of the mountain."

Thursday morning, Delores buzzed Mike.

"The lawn man is here," she said curtly.

Mike made a final note for a finance committee meeting and came out of his office. Sam, dressed in blue overalls and wearing a cap from a local feed and seed store on his head, stood in the waiting area. Delores had scooted her chair as far away from her desk as possible and eyed the older man suspiciously.

"Glad the church is still standing," Sam said.

"What do you mean?" Mike asked.

"In a dream last night, you and I were sitting in the sanctuary of your church when Bud Putnam came running in."

"The fire chief?"

"Yep. The building was on fire. We had to leave and went outside to the parking lot. When I looked up, the roof of the church was covered in flames. At first, I wasn't sure about the meaning. Papa often uses fire to represent good things, like His presence in a place, but the more I watched, the more I knew this was not a good fire. It was a fire from hell."

Out of the corner of his eye, Mike could see a shocked expression on Delores's face.

"Let's go outside," he suggested. "I'll show you what to cut."

The two men walked down the hallway.

"It wasn't an actual fire, was it?" Mike asked.

"I don't think so."

"Why would you see a church on fire?"

"Fighting. When I see a church on fire in a bad way, it's usually because there has been a lot of friction caused by fussing. Have you ever started a fire with a flint rock?"

"No, and friction isn't a problem here. We have a unified, growing congregation."

The two men walked out of the building. Mike helped Sam lift his push mower from the back of his truck and unload a couple of old metal gas cans. Sam quickly set a ramp and rolled off his riding mower.

"Make sure you have plenty of smoke detectors," Sam said.

"We do. The insurance policy requires it. The custodian checks the batteries the first of every month."

"I'm talking about the kind that can detect a foul spirit from the pit."

Mike rolled his eyes. "The cemetery is the only tricky part of the property to cut. Everywhere else is clear enough that you should be able to use your big mower; however, the cemetery has some very old, partially missing markers. Be careful not to break a mower blade on a piece of marble or cause any damage. Families take the resting place of their ancestors seriously."

Sam leaned over and checked the oil in his riding mower.

"I'll be careful. It's the hidden dangers that can cause the biggest problems."

Mike returned to the administration wing.

"I can't believe you invited that man to cut our grass," Delores sniffed when he reached her desk. "He's a criminal—"

"Wait a minute," Mike interrupted. "He may have been tried in the court of public opinion, but in the eyes of the law, he's innocent until proven guilty."

"You know what I mean," Delores retorted. "Coming in here talking about setting fire to the church!"

"It was a dream, not a literal event. And he didn't mention anything about burning down the church. God speaks to men and women like him through pictures and symbols. Don't let it bother you. I'll be here until he finishes working."

The phone rang, and Delores picked it up. Mike went into his office. Over the next few hours, he occasionally glanced out a window to check on Sam's progress. The old man was a steady worker, but once, Mike saw him kneeling at the water hole where the spring bubbled up through the rocks. At noon, Mike let Delores leave for lunch and went outside. Sam was finishing up the far side of the cemetery. Mike waved him over. Sam turned off the push mower and walked across the graveyard.

"Do you want anything to eat or drink?" Mike asked.

Sam mopped his forehead with a yellow bandanna he took from the front of his overalls.

"I brought a plate of cold fried chicken, green beans, and black-eyed peas left over from supper last night."

"Want to heat it up in the microwave?"

"It's good cold, but better hot. What are you going to eat?"

"A cup of yogurt."

Sam scoffed. "Not unless you have a chicken leg first."

Sam retrieved a small cooler from the front seat of his truck and followed Mike into the church kitchen. After a couple of minutes in the microwave, the fragrance of the chicken seeped into the room. Mike sniffed.

"You should have tasted it last night," Sam said, patting his stomach. "Since I got out of jail, Muriel has been spoiling me rotten."

When the beeper sounded, Mike opened the door of the microwave. It was an impressive amount of food.

"Get yourself a plate," Sam said. "I'm going to share Papa's bounty with you. It's the least I can do, seeing that you're not charging me to be my lawyer."

Mike handed the old man a plate, and before he could protest, Sam scraped half the meal onto the second plate.

"Pray and eat up," Sam said, handing it to him. "If you're still hungry, you can eat all the yogurt you want."

They sat on folding metal chairs at a rectangular table. Mike prayed and took a bite of chicken.

"What did she put in this batter?" he asked.

Sam held up a drumstick. "A secret recipe Colonel Sanders didn't know about."

The meal reminded Mike of dinners at his aunt Sue's house. Twice a year, Christmas and the Fourth of July, his family gathered at the large white home of his father's sister in an older section of Raleigh to visit and eat, not necessarily in that order.

"What will I tell Peg when she asks me about lunch?" Mike asked as he collected the final bite of black-eyed peas. "I've been trying to cut back."

"Pray she doesn't ask," Sam replied. "If she does, tell her you ate organic."

"Organic?"

"That's a word, isn't it?" Sam replied. "For food that's homegrown without using bag fertilizer."

"Yes. I can believe that about the vegetables, but did you raise this chicken?"

"No, but I know the man who did. Muriel likes him because he kills and cleans them, too."

"Tell Muriel it was good. Sorry I can't offer you dessert."

"I skip the sweets if I can have the rest."

Mike rinsed the empty plates in the sink and put them in the dishwasher. "How is the work progressing?"

"You were right about the cemetery. It's slow going, but once I finish I should move faster with the big mower. Do you know about the spring at the edge of the creek?"

"Yes, I like to go there. It used to be a watering hole for horses."

Sam nodded. "I splashed some of the water on my face and got refreshed. There have been some praying people in this church. It would be good if a few new ones came to the surface to put out the fire."

Mike didn't respond. He liked it better when Sam talked about Muriel's fried chicken.

FRIDAY MORNING, MIKE LIFTED HIS DAY PACK FROM ITS HOOK on the wall of the garage and brought it into the house. Judge saw the pack and began barking.

"Settle down. You're included," Mike reassured him.

He loaded the pack with water, snacks, a jacket for Peg, and an old quilt.

He was lacing up his boots when Peg entered the kitchen. She was dressed in jeans and a yellow T-shirt with her hair in a ponytail sticking out the back of a ball cap.

"How do I look?"

"Perfect," Mike answered. "I saw your hiking boots in the corner of the garage. Do they still fit?"

Peg propped her left foot on his leg. "Are my feet swelling yet?"

Mike tickled the bottom of her foot. Peg didn't flinch.

"No, and I see you haven't lost your willpower. Don't fix the coffee. I thought we would stop for breakfast on the way."

They went outside. It was a cool morning but without any clouds in the sky. "Do I need a jacket?" Peg asked.

"Probably not, but I put one in the pack."

"And my pillow in case I want to lie down in the grass and take a nap?"

Mike pointed to his chest. "This is your pillow."

They took Mike's car. Peg didn't like to get her car dusty, and the parking lot behind Hank's Grocery wasn't paved. Judge jumped into the backseat and lay down peacefully. Mike drove to the bottom of the ridge and through Shelton to the west side of town. He and Peg didn't have to debate where to eat breakfast. He pulled into the parking lot for Traci's Restaurant, a low-slung brown building with plate-glass windows along the front and one side. Calico curtains hung in at the edges of the windows. Mike cracked the back window for Judge, who sat up and sniffed the morning air.

"I'll bring you a bite of sausage biscuit," Peg promised the dog as they left the car.

A single door opened to a small waiting area beside the cash register. The restaurant was an L shape with bench seating along the walls and a row of tables down the middle. Within a few seconds of entering, Mike heard a female voice call his name.

"Mike! Get over here!"

Across the room, a skinny waitress in her late fifties motioned with her hand and pointed to an empty table. Mike and Peg came over to her.

"How are you, Judy?" Mike asked.

"Better now that you're here."

Judy turned to Peg and patted her on the arm. "I used to see him all the time when he was practicing law. Now that he's a preacher, he's quit eating breakfast."

Judy had raised three children with no help from their father. For many years, she reported to work at 5:00 a.m. and worked through the lunch shift, arriving home in time to greet the school bus and begin her second job as a mother.

"Don't tell me what you want," Judy said to Mike. "Let me take care of you."

Peg gave her order. The waitress returned with coffee: black for Mike, sugar and extra cream for Peg.

"Fill me in on the family," Mike said.

"I have a new grandbaby, a little boy who is already sleeping through the night. But the funny thing is my younger daughter Margie. She's been working out at the gym and is almost as buff as I used to be."

When in her twenties, Judy had been a serious weight lifter. She still retained enough wiry strength to beat unsuspecting bus boys in arm wrestling.

"Peg and I are going to have a baby," Mike said. "We just found out."

Judy lifted her hands in the air. "Hallelujah. You get all that lawyer pressure off and get pregnant."

"I thought that applied to women," Mike replied.

"No, honey. It's always the man."

Judy hustled away to take care of another table.

"What did she mean?" Peg asked.

Mike shook his head. "I'm not sure. Until I met Sam Miller, Judy was the most difficult person to understand I knew."

The waitress returned with two eggs over easy for Mike, crisp bacon, and dry toast. Peg's plate held two scrambled eggs with a sausage biscuit along with a large glass of orange juice.

"I looked out the window and saw that dog of yours in the car," Judy said.

"We're going for a hike up Jefferson's Ridge."

"That's good. Your baby will be an early walker. I did a lot of walking when I was pregnant. It paid off until I had to start chasing them around the house."

Judy moved on at a rapid clip. Peg sipped her orange juice.

"In her mind, everything is connected," Peg said. "If I like orange juice, our child will want me to buy bags of oranges."

"Are you going to swim this summer?" Mike asked.

"Probably."

"Good. When you combine swimming with your running and my bike riding, we're going to produce a future triathlon champion."

When they finished, Mike left a generous tip on the table. Peg offered part of her sausage biscuit to Judge in her open palm. The dog scooped it up with a swift flick of his tongue.

Mike drove away from town. Within a half mile, the number of older houses along the road dropped off, and they began to climb higher. New asphalt roads to the side signaled points of access to housing developments in the hill. Land that farmers once considered less desirable because it was rocky and hilly now commanded good prices.

After driving almost ten miles, they reached Hank's Grocery, a seventy-year-old country store and center of the local economy. The fourth-generation owners of the store stocked general merchandise even though most people now treated it like a convenience mart. Hunters and fishermen appreciated the availability of shotgun shells and fish hooks, and it was also possible to buy a connector hose for a clothes washer. A large graveled area behind the store had once served as a feed lot for cattle. Mike parked the car.

"I'll be right back," he said to Peg. "I'm going to let someone in the store know we're here."

Mike walked past a Mercedes and opened the screen door. The store was dark and the layout chaotic. A well-dressed woman placed a head of lettuce, several tomatoes, a cucumber, and a jar of salad dressing on the counter.

"Good morning, Mike!" called out Buzz Carrier, the thirty-five-year-old owner of the store.

"Good morning. I have Peg and Judge with me. We'll be gone till early afternoon."

"Have a good time."

Mike held the door open for the woman as she left with her purchases. He turned back to the man at the cash register.

"Do you have a set of small Allen wrenches?" he asked. "I need to work on my bike."

Buzz motioned toward the rear of the store, a close-packed array of shelves and boxes. "I'll find them before you get back."

Mike walked past a large propane tank to the parking lot. Peg was holding the end of Judge's leash as the dog sniffed the woods at the edge of the lot. When he saw Mike, Judge barked and strained in his direction.

"Ready?" he called out to Peg.

"Or not," Peg replied. "Judge is about to jerk my arm off. I need to let him go or start running myself."

"Turn him loose."

Peg pulled the dog in and unhooked the leash. Judge took off toward the opening in the woods that served as the entryway to the old roadbed and disappeared from sight. Mike didn't worry. He'd trained the dog to come on a whistle. He and Peg passed into the splattered shade cast by the young leaves on the trees beside the trail. He took Peg's hand in his.

"That feels much better than a pitching wedge," Mike said, squeezing her hand.

Peg squeezed back. "You're so romantic, comparing my hand to a golf grip. Did you read that in one of your marriage counseling books?"

Mike laughed. "No."

He whistled, and in a few seconds, Judge tumbled down the bank to their right. Mike scratched the dog's neck and released him to continue exploring.

They climbed gradually yet steadily. The woods had encroached on the old roadbed, but it remained a gently sloping, broad trail. Mike marveled at the ingenuity of the men who had determined the path up a mountain. Contours that could be seen from the air were much more difficult to gauge on the ground. The loggers who constructed the roadway didn't punish those who climbed but rather wooed them. The switchbacks were interspersed with flat runs across the face of the hill to places where the climb resumed at the best gradient available. After his initial burst of explosive energy, Judge returned and stayed closer to them.

"Don't try to race your pregnant wife to the top of a mountain," Peg said, catching her breath.

"Sorry."

Peg sat on a large rock to the side of the trail. Mike opened his backpack and handed her a water bottle. Before drinking from his own, he poured water in a plastic dish he'd brought for Judge. Mike held the dish steady so the dog wouldn't tip it over with his vigorous lapping.

"How do you keep Judge from going too fast on your runs?" Mike asked.

"After we get started, he understands the leash a lot better than most men do. A quick jerk and he heels."

"Is that what you want from me?"

Peg stood up and patted Mike's cheek. "No. That would be boring."

They continued up the trail and turned a corner onto a flatter section.

"You surprised me the other day when you told me you had no regrets about my leaving the law firm."

"I'm not sure that's what I said, but I'm full of surprises. My nesting urge is getting stronger, and for the past few days, I've been studying the home furnishing catalogs we get in the mail. Don't you think it's time to make some major changes in the house?"

"How much is this going to cost?"

"I don't have a clue, but don't worry." Peg paused. "Yet."

As they trudged onward, Mike thought about the hit to their savings a major overhaul of the house would cause.

"I told you not to worry," Peg said, cutting into his reverie, "but there is something I want to tell you when we reach the top of the hill."

"Why wait until the top?"

"Because I can't climb, breathe, talk, and grow our baby at the same time."

They could see clear sky above the trees that marched up the hillside, but several switchbacks remained before they broke into the open. Mike enjoyed watching Judge. Vizslas could be trained as both trackers and pointers. The dog moved from side to side as his sensitive nose appreciated the entire palate of scents on display in the wild.

The top of the hill was crowned with a canopy of trees. The trail ran beneath the trees along the ridgeline for a hundred yards before ending at the edge of a small mountain meadow. It was still early spring at this altitude, and only a few green strands of grass were beginning to sprout from the brown stalks of the previous year. Mike dropped the backpack on the ground and served water all around. Peg rubbed her forehead with a red kerchief she took from a hip pocket of her jeans. A slight breeze stirred the warm air.

"Didn't need my jacket," she said.

"I know, but I brought it anyway."

"And I felt cherished and cared for."

"Are you going to tell me now?"

Peg smiled. "Show me your holy spot."

"What holy spot?"

"The place where God spoke to you from the burning bush and ordered you to ignore your wife's advice, leave the successful practice of law, and lead His people out of bondage."

Mike pointed to the west side of the meadow.

"Over there."

Judge was rolling back and forth on his back in the grass. He jumped up when Mike and Peg moved away. The meadow was small, about three hundred feet across and five hundred feet long, but from its exposed position on top of the hill it seemed larger. The dead grass crunched beneath their feet as they walked. Judge joined them. On the west edge of the meadow, a row of exposed rocks had broken free into the sunlight. One jutted from the ground about three feet.

Mike pointed. "There. That's where I was sitting when I read the verses in Galatians."

Peg took Mike by the hand and led him over to the rock.

"Sit," she said.

A puzzled look on his face, Mike sat on the rock. Peg knelt down in the grass at his feet and stared away in the distance for several seconds before looking up at him.

"I need to ask your forgiveness," she said.

"Why?" Mike shifted his weight on the rock. "I'm the one who forgot our anniversary two years ago."

"No, I'm serious. Please listen."

Mike grew still.

"I've put you through a lot the past six years," she said. "A few times I kicked and screamed out loud and did it a lot more than that on the inside. I wasn't with you in the transition to the ministry, and when you continued in that direction, I decided you didn't care about me. Our marriage wasn't as important as your lofty notions of saving the world. Last November, I came close to leaving you."

Mike's eyes widened in shock. He'd known there was tension, but chalked it up to the stress of major changes, not a potential end to the marriage.

"I never—," he began.

"Let me finish," Peg interrupted. "I paid a deposit on an apartment in Asheville and talked with a divorce lawyer." She looked down at the ground. "I even signed the verification page on a divorce petition."

Mike felt as if he'd been punched in the stomach. A spark of hurt and anger flared up inside him. Peg looked at his face.

"You have a right to be upset," she continued. "I was wrong, and not telling you about this has eaten at me. I thought it would go away, but after listening to your sermon last week, I knew I had to be honest and ask you to forgive me."

"Was there anyone else?"

"No, just selfish me."

Mike's mind was spinning.

"Why did you stay?"

Peg reached into the front pocket of her jeans and pulled out a well-creased sheet of notebook paper and held it up in her hand.

"In part because of this. The day after I met with the lawyer, I received a letter in the mail that described exactly how I felt. It got behind my defenses then warned me that a decision I was considering would not bring the joy and happiness I wanted. I threw the letter in the trash but couldn't get it out of my mind. I pulled it out, and, during the next few days, read it over and over. It was just enough to make me reconsider. I called the lawyer, stopped the divorce, and forfeited the deposit on the apartment."

"Who sent the letter?"

"It wasn't signed, so I never knew." Peg paused. "Until you met Sam Miller."

Mike's jaw dropped. "Sam Miller wrote you a letter?"

"Yes. After you told me about the letter he sent Jack Hatcher, I remembered what happened with me. I called Muriel and went over to their house. Sam looked at the letter and said, 'Yep. I wrote it. But only Papa knew our paths would cross someday.'"

Mike smiled slightly. "That sounds like Sam."

"He'd forgotten about it. Muriel says he writes lots of letters, but doesn't keep any copies."

"So I've learned."

Peg touched Mike's knee. "But this isn't about Sam Miller. It's about us. I'm the one who walled off my heart, who abandoned you, who forgot something a lot more important than our anniversary—the vows we made on our wedding day. I put out the fire of my love, and I've been wrong, terribly wrong."

Mike saw tears in Peg's eyes as she continued, "We agreed to walk together through life no matter what. Now, I want to remove everything that would be a wedge between us and build the right kind of marriage for us and our child. Will you forgive me?"

"Of course."

"No." Peg shook her head. "That's too quick. I want you to know how deeply, terribly sorry I am for being so selfish. I haven't supported you in the way I promised when we married or the way God wanted me to. I said I loved you, but I've been rotten."

Mike slid off the rock onto the grass beside her. He took her in his arms, brought her close, and kissed the top of her head.

"I don't feel worthy to say I forgive you," he said.

"But do you?"

Mike took a deep breath. "Yes."

"Think about it. Are you sure?"

Mike held her tightly and spoke softly into her ear.

"With all my heart."

Fifteen

STARING AT THE BLUE SKY, MIKE LAY STILL SO HE WOULDN'T wake Peg. Her secret burden lifted, she'd rested her head on Mike's chest and dozed. The old quilt cushioned them from the scratchy grass. There wasn't a cloud in the sky. Mike could hear Judge crashing through the grass off to the left.

Reeling from Peg's revelation, Mike couldn't take a nap. He couldn't believe he'd been so oblivious to the mortal danger threatening his marriage. He'd always considered himself an astute judge of people but failed miserably at discerning what his own wife was considering.

God, using Sam Miller, intervened.

Before falling asleep, Peg let him read the letter from Sam. It was a simple message of warning and encouragement but had done the job. Peg could be tough to convince, and the power of a few words scrawled on a sheet of notebook paper was stunning. That the lawncare man took the time to write a letter to a total stranger was unfathomable. Mike cared about people, but Sam Miller took the concept of loving your neighbor to another stratosphere.

Peg's nose twitched. Mike kept his breathing regular so his chest rose and fell in rhythm. Peg moved her head slightly and snuggled closer to his chin.

"I love you," she said.

Mike stroked her hair. "I love you, too," he managed.

"How long have I been dozing?"

"Not long."

Judge suddenly appeared over Mike's face and licked his nose.

"That's a wet alarm clock," Mike said, pushing the dog away.

Peg looked up. "Remind me not to kiss that spot until you wash your face."

They sat up. The breeze across the top of the mountain had picked up while they rested. It felt clean and fresh. Peg stretched her hands in the air then threw her arms around Mike's neck and gave him a long kiss on the lips.

"You were holding back," she said when their lips parted. "Do I need to ask you to forgive me again? I'll do it five times a day until you're convinced I mean it."

"I know you meant it. It's just going to take time for me to adjust to how close I came to losing you."

Peg took his hand and placed it on her abdomen. "Any time doubts come to your mind, think about the child inside me, and remember that I'm committed to you—completely."

Mike looked into her eyes. There was an honest clarity present that gave no room for deceit.

"Even if I'm not perfect?" he asked.

"You're perfect for me."

Peg stood and brushed a few pieces of dried grass from her shirt.

"I'm ready to go," she announced. "We have lots to talk about on the way down."

"What else?" Mike asked apprehensively.

"Redecorating the house. We need to get a nursery ready and make the whole house safe for a baby. Now, I can really put my heart into it."

They held opposite ends of the blanket and shook it before folding it up. Judge came running over, and Mike poured water into the plastic dish for the dog to drink.

"That's amazing about Sam Miller," he said to Peg as Judge lapped up the water. "Every town doesn't have a yardman who writes letters to save marriages."

"It should."

Peg was filled with carefree chatter on the return trip down the mountain. Mike tried to match her mood but couldn't. Peg carried the knowledge about how close they'd come to divorce to the top of the mountain. He bore it down. Several times, he started to say something, but Peg's reminder of the child growing within her stopped him. Never had such a tiny person exerted such great influence over him.

"How did you manage to keep your secret?" he asked finally. "Except for confidential information in my cases, I've never been able to keep anything important from you for more than a few days."

Peg slowed her steps. "After I changed my mind, I was ashamed but still angry with you. If I'd said anything, it might have caused a huge fight that would have driven us farther apart."

"What's different now?"

"Sam and Muriel told me what I needed to do."

Mike stopped. "That's amazing."

"Am I that hardheaded? Can't you tell that I'm changing?"

"Yes," Mike replied and started walking again.

"Do you like it?"

"Yes. But it's—"

Peg glanced sideways as they rounded a bend in the trail.

"A challenge relating to the new me?"

"Just different. I'm a minister who is supposed to believe God transforms people for the better, but when my own wife tells me it's happening to her, I wonder if I can handle it."

"At least you won't be bored."

Peg took a few quick steps ahead down the trail. Judge ran along beside her. Mike plodded along in the rear.

They reached the parking lot. Mike went into the store. The Allen wrenches were waiting for him on the counter.

"Beautiful day, isn't it?" the store owner said as he rang up the purchase. "How was your hike?"

"Not what I expected. You can always see farther from the top of the ridge." Mike paused. "Today, I saw the past."

Buzz tilted his head to the side. "Don't mess with me, Mike. I have enough strange people from other parts of the country coming in here. I don't need any of the local folks getting squirrelly."

THAT NIGHT AFTER PEG WENT TO SLEEP, MIKE LAY IN BED WITH his eyes open. During the drive home, he'd decided his ignorance had been a disguised blessing. He'd not known his marriage was stalled on the train tracks until it moved out of danger. As his eyes adjusted to the darkness, he turned on his side so he could see Peg. A pale sliver of moonlight crept into the room and faintly illuminated her golden hair. He hadn't admitted it to Peg, but his pride was deeply wounded by her secret rejection. He tossed and turned for a long time. He hoped the hurt would soon find healing in the hospital of his soul. Instead, he revisited the dream of the old woman who passed into darkness. She looked familiar, like Muriel, but distinctly different. He woke up wishing Peg hadn't brought out the painting.

THE FOLLOWING DAY, HE SPENT SEVERAL HOURS WORKING OUTside. Late morning, Peg joined him and together they planted flowers. Peg had a knack for landscape design, and their yard moved with grace from one season of the year to the next. Daffodils and tulips in later winter, day lilies in the spring, and mums in the fall. Kneeling beside each other, their hands frequently touched as they worked the soil. Once, Mike glanced up and saw Peg wipe her sleeve across her eyes.

"Why are you crying?" he asked.

"I'm happy. I know we're dirty, but I've never felt so clean on the inside. Is this what it means to be forgiven?"

"Yes."

Peg sat sideways on the grass. "And doing this with you is special. Do I need to ask you to forgive me today?"

Mike smoothed the soil around the flower he'd deposited into the ground and sat with his legs stretched out in front of him.

"No. I'm not going to be petty, but it may take a while for me to be healed. When I counsel people, I tell them forgiveness forgets."

"That's impossible."

"I know," Mike admitted. "And I won't be so glib to toss it out in the future until I've done it myself and can explain it better."

"What would you say?"

Mike thought while they continued working. He put down the bulb planter.

"That the memory of a wrong isn't stronger than the grace to forgive and go on."

Peg smiled. "That would make a good sermon."

SUNDAY MORNING ARRIVED. MIKE ENTERED THE PULPIT AREA. To his delight, Sam and Muriel Miller had returned.

The topic of forgiveness wasn't in Mike's notes, but he mentioned it a few times with Peg in his line of sight. The radiant look on her face caused him to smile. The power of forgiveness he expressed to the congregation welled up in his own heart.

After the service, the last two people in the narthex were Sam and Muriel.

"Peg showed me the letter you sent her," Mike said as he shook Sam's hand. "Thanks."

Sam smiled. "Papa holds the whole world in His hands, doesn't He?"

"And I'm going to stick by you," Mike replied. "Don't worry any more about it."

"Yep. I knew you would help." Sam patted Muriel's hand. "She wasn't so sure until Peg came by the house. Then all the pieces of the puzzle fell into place."

Mike followed Sam and Muriel out the front door of the church. Peg and Bobby Lambert were talking in the parking lot near Bobby's car.

Mike went over to them.

"Do you have a minute?" Bobby asked.

"Sure."

"It's about the Miller case," Bobby added then stopped.

"Is that my cue to find something appropriate for the minister's wife to do?" Peg asked. "I'll look for someone who needs a tuna casserole this week and set up a time to deliver it."

"Go easy on me, Peg," Bobby said. "Why don't you catch up with Elizabeth? She's getting the kids from the nursery. I think she brought you a card congratulating you on your pregnancy."

Peg departed with a smile. Bobby shook his head and turned to Mike.

"How do you handle her tongue? It's sharper than a razor."

"She reserves her soft side for me. What did you want to tell me?"

"Have you found anyone to take the Miller case?"

"No one has come forward."

"Your client saw Greg Freeman in court the other day. For a young lawyer, he handled himself well. Miller should be glad Freeman is interested in taking him on."

"That's not going to happen," Mike said bluntly. "Sam has made up his mind that I'm going to be his lawyer, and I'm on board. I've begun my investigation."

"But Mr. Forrest—"

"Is a man I greatly respect, but he isn't my boss. According to him, I shouldn't even talk about the case with you."

"What?" Bobby replied with a surprised look on his face.

Mike told him about the letter. Bobby swore softly then immediately apologized.

"He's been bugging me about your involvement in the deal all week," Bobby said, "but I had no idea he'd ordered you to stay off the premises."

"Or talk to anyone from the firm."

"He can't do that."

Mike shrugged. "It removed any question I might have about how strongly he disagrees with what I'm doing, and any hope of cooperation from the bank went out the window, too."

"What have you found out on your own?"

Mike placed his hand on the top of Bobby's new car. "I'm sorry, but I don't think I should discuss details of the case with you. We're not law partners anymore."

Bobby looked away for a second before responding. "From now on, my interest will be as an elder of this church, not a lawyer."

"That's right."

Bobby looked Mike directly in the eyes. "And as an elder, I urge you to find someone else to help Mr. Miller. I went to bat for you before the session, but our approval was contingent on you taking steps to disengage from representation as soon as possible. If you don't get out soon, we'll have to bring it up for discussion."

"I understand. All I ask is notice. Ecclesiastical due process, you know."

"Mike, this isn't a joke. Consider this conversation your notice."

Mike set his jaw. "Okay, but I think I can explain to the satisfaction of a majority of the session why I believe I should remain involved."

TUESDAY AFTERNOON, MIKE ARRIVED A FEW MINUTES EARLY TO Judge Coberg's chambers. The judge's secretary, a middle-aged woman Mike didn't recognize, phoned the DA's office.

"Tell Mr. West and Ms. Hall that Mr. Andrews is here," she said. "The judge wants to get started as soon as possible."

Mike waited for the prosecutors to arrive. When Ken West walked in, he shook Mike's hand as vigorously as he had at election time. They went into the judge's office. Melissa Hall followed her boss but didn't come out from his shadow. Mike stepped to the side and greeted her.

Judge Coberg's chambers contained personal items collected during his long career. Along with the usual pictures of politicians and other judges, a corner was devoted to baseball memorabilia. The judge only collected items from before the 1960s. It had been several years since Mike had seen the baseball collection, and he noticed a number 9 Boston Red Sox jersey hanging behind a glass frame.

"Who wore it?" he asked the judge, pointing to the frame.

"Ted Williams. My wife bought it for me a couple of years ago."

On the front corner of the judge's desk, Mike saw one of the judge's trial notebooks containing his personal analyses of the decisions by the appellate courts. Many times during a trial or a motion hearing, Mike had seen the judge reach for one of his notebooks, flip to a handwritten notation, and issue a ruling from which he wouldn't retreat.

There were three chairs positioned in front of the judge's desk.

"Ken," the judge said, "do you remember the Debary case? You tried it."

"How long ago and what was the charge?"

"Eighteen years ago, an assault and battery by a stepfather against his six-year-old daughter."

"Yes, sir. The little girl suffered a broken arm when the man hit her. A lawyer came all the way from Charlotte to defend it and went back with his tail between his legs."

"As he should have. During a pretrial hearing, I asked if any neighbors were going to testify."

"I don't recall that coming up."

"Well, it did. And I suggested that someone should interview a man named Hopkins who had moved to Missouri after the charges were filed. I even mentioned the town where Mr. Hopkins lived. The defense lawyer wanted to object but didn't know what to say. After all, it's the duty of the Court to determine the truth. When the case came to trial, the little girl was unable to testify, but the Hopkins fellow saw exactly what happened."

"Yes, sir. It's coming back to me."

The judge sat back in his chair. "Sam Miller wrote me a letter about the Debary case. He'd read about the charges in the paper, told me the name and address of Mr. Hopkins, and claimed Hopkins was an eyewitness."

"What was Miller's connection?" West asked.

Mike wasn't surprised by the judge's answer.

"None. He didn't know anyone. He claimed he got the information in a dream and wrote it down."

West was silent for a moment before he spoke. Mike was almost surprised Ken West hadn't received a letter from Sam. The DA's ego would have been wounded if he realized he'd not been included in the group with the president of the United States, Judge Coberg, Jack Hatcher, and Peg Andrews. West spoke.

"That's odd, but it could have been a way for Miller to tell what he knew without admitting personal knowledge."

"I would agree, except that it's happened more than once. On three other occasions, Miller has either written or called me with information about a case. What he passes along is sometimes hard to interpret, but in every instance, it's proven reliable."

"Did he give you any information about the charges against him in this case?" West asked sharply.

"No," the judge responded dryly. "If that had happened, I would already have recused myself, and we wouldn't be having this conversation. He's cut my grass a few times, and I buy vegetables from him in the summer, but I have no personal relationship with him. However, I believe the unique aspect of some of our previous interaction should be disclosed."

West glanced at Melissa Hall. "What do you think? You're the one who is going to try this case."

Hall turned toward Mike. "Are you going to waive a jury trial?"

"I'm considering all options," he replied.

Hall faced the judge. "Your Honor, if Mr. Andrews requests a bench trial, I would ask you to recuse yourself; however, if a jury will determine the facts and credibility of the witnesses, I have no objection to your continued involvement."

"How about you, Mr. West?" the judge asked. "I'd like to hear from you, too."

West grunted. "Miller's crystal ball must have gotten a bit cloudy if he thought he could get away with embezzling a hundred thousand dollars from a church. However, just because he claims to be psychic doesn't mean you can't preside in the case. I agree with Ms. Hall, and as a safeguard, I would ask Mr. Andrews to instruct his client not to attempt to contact the Court about his case or any other matter while the charges are pending."

"That's appropriate," Mike responded.

"Does your client object to me presiding in the case?" the judge asked Mike.

"I haven't asked him," Mike answered.

"Do so. Then decide whether you want a jury trial and notify Ms. Hall and me."

"Yes, sir."

The judge shuffled through the papers on his desk. "Mr. Andrews has filed several motions. Any need to have a court reporter present to record testimony for or against his requests?"

"No, sir," Hall said. "We have no objection to the standard pretrial disclosure motions and have agreed to open our file to Mr. Andrews so he can copy any documents he wants an expert to examine."

"When is that going to happen?" the judge asked.

"Today, if possible," Mike replied.

Hall nodded. "That's agreeable. We'll provide everything else he wants by tomorrow. The case will be on the trial calendar in a few weeks."

"That's rushing it, don't you think?" Mike responded quickly.

"Delay for the sake of delay isn't an option."

"But I won't know what else I need until you furnish answers to my requests."

"That's enough, counselors," the judge barked. "Mr. Andrews, if you want a continuance, file a motion."

THE LAWYERS LEFT THE JUDGE'S CHAMBERS, AND MIKE FOLlowed the prosecuting attorneys downstairs to their office. The DA's office controlled the appearance of cases on the criminal docket, and there wasn't much Mike could do to delay the Miller case.

"I'll have the file pulled, and you can review it in our conference room," Hall said.

Mike went into the small, plainly furnished room and sat at the old conference table. The prosecutors had no clients to impress with fancy surroundings. Mike tapped his fingers against the scratched wooden surface of the table. On several occasions, he'd been ushered into the room and seen it covered with evidence: sawed-off shotguns, burglary tools, and stacks of documents needed to prove larceny.

A secretary brought him the file. Mike quickly flipped past copies of the checks signed by Jesse, the bank records for Sam's account, and the bill of indictment charging Sam with the crime. Mike wanted to see the signed statement taken from Sam by Detective Perkins. It was the last item in the file.

I, Sam Miller, make this statement of my own free will after having been told of my right to remain silent and have an attorney present to represent me. During the time I served as temporary pastor of the Craig Valley Gospel Tabernacle, money was illegally taken from the church building fund and put in my bank account. I did not have the right to sign checks for the church or transfer church money into my account.

—Sam Miller

Mike frowned. Perkins was a crafty interrogator who had transformed a nonincriminating statement into a document that could be used against Sam at trial. On its face, Sam's statement admitted nothing criminal, but it could still be valuable to the prosecution. Sam accepted as true the detective's conclusion that money had been taken illegally from the church building fund. That mistake allowed Perkins to construct a statement removing every legitimate reason Sam might have for church money ending up in his bank account.

At trial, the detective would read the statement and make it sound like a wholesale admission of guilt obtained after a grueling interrogation. Mike could point out the precise language of the statement, but that would result in courtroom sparring with the detective, which always had a negative impact on one or two jurors who believed law enforcement officers were exempt from original sin. It was a thin file, a simple charge, the perfect case for Melissa Hall to cut her prosecutorial teeth.

Mike took the file to the front desk and asked for copies. Hall came to the door of the reception area.

"Finished?" she asked.

"Yes, waiting for copies. Why the rush?"

"This case has been pending for three months. Ken wants it on the docket, and I have no reason to argue with him."

"Is the bank pushing for a speedy trial?"

"I have work to do."

"Do you have a few minutes to talk?"

Hall looked at her watch. "A few. I'll be in my office."

The secretary handed Mike the documents. He cross-checked them with the ones in the file to make sure everything was included. As he did, he compared Sam's signature at the bottom of the statement with the endorsement on the reverse of the two checks. It looked the same. There was an unusual extra loop at the bottom of the *S* that appeared in all three signatures. Mike put the copies in his briefcase.

The door to Hall's office was open, and she was on the phone. Mike knocked on the door frame. She motioned for him to come in and sit down.

"That's not going to be a problem," she said into the receiver. "Get back to me on Monday."

She hung up the phone.

"Any surprises?" she asked Mike.

"Not really."

"What did you think of the statement taken by Detective Perkins?"

"It is what it is."

Hall smiled slightly. "Mr. Andrews, I'm new at the legal business, but I made it through law school and passed the bar exam. There's no criminal admission in your client's statement; however, we believe the bank records are enough to convict Mr. Miller under the embezzlement statute. Ken talked to me about the case while you were reviewing the file, and I'd like to make an offer."

"What is it?"

"Because all the money was recovered, I can offer six months probation on the lesser included misdemeanor of illegally lending the money of a charitable organization without its consent. No jail time. No fine."

It was a good offer. If Sam had admitted committing the crime, Mike would have recommended it without reservation. Even so, an opportunity to spare Sam the dangers of prison was tempting.

"I'll discuss it with him."

"We'll leave it open for ten days. After that, it's withdrawn, and we go to trial."

Mike studied the young DA's face for a moment.

"What did you think of the judge's revelation regarding his prior contact with Miller?"

"It was the appropriate thing to do, so we can decide whether to file a motion for recusal."

"No, I mean the information my client has given the judge over the years. What do you think about that?"

"I have a personal opinion."

"What is it? Do you believe that sort of thing is real?"

Hall hesitated. "My grandmother had dreams in which she saw things before they happened."

"And you believed in her gift?"

"Yes."

Hall turned in her chair, picked up a photograph on a small table behind her desk, and handed it to Mike. A large number of people that included little children, teenagers, and adults surrounded an old woman sitting in a chair. A small white church building, not unlike the old sanctuary at Little Creek, could be seen in the background.

"My grandmother is in the center of the picture, and I'm standing beside her," Hall continued. "It was her ninetieth birthday. She lived two more years. Now, she's in heaven."

All the people in the photo were plainly dressed. Hall's grandmother wore a print dress and old-fashioned black shoes. She had a bouquet of flowers in her hand and a sweet smile on her face. A younger, gangly version of Melissa Hall stood behind the old woman's right shoulder. Mike returned the snapshot.

Hall stared at the picture that remained in her hand for a few seconds before looking up. "I'm no saint, either, but listening to your client talk about the Lord and call Him 'Papa' made me think about my grandmother. She didn't use that term, but it was the same kind of familiarity. I asked Mr. West to let me offer you a favorable plea bargain."

"And I appreciate it. Sam is odd, but all he wants to do is help other people. The more I've been around him, the less I believe he tried to steal money from the Craig Valley church."

"I disagree. My grandmother said spiritual people don't always have the character to match the gift."

"But what if Miller isn't guilty?"

Hall's face hardened. "Then you'd better convince Ken and me within the next ten days. After that, it's up to a judge or jury."

Sixteen

MIKE LEFT THE COURTHOUSE AND CALLED THE MILLER HOME. Muriel answered.

"Where is Sam this afternoon?" he asked.

"At the Bowen house."

"On Polk Street?"

"Yes. He's worked for them since before Mr. Bowen died."

Polk Street was a block from traffic light eleven. Mr. Bowen, an insurance broker, was a client of Forrest, Andrews, and Lambert for many years, and Mike had encountered him at the office several times. He didn't know his widow.

The houses on Polk Street were built in the 1920s. Most had been remodeled and updated. Mrs. Bowen lived at the end of a street in a brick home with broad holly bushes and a small, neatly manicured front yard. Large shade trees stood along the edges of the lot. Mike pulled in behind Sam's truck, which was parked beside Mrs. Bowen's older-model Cadillac. Sam wasn't in sight.

Mike walked up a driveway made of cobblestones covered by bits of moss. The backyard was enclosed in a fence. He could hear a small dog barking as he approached the white wooden gate. Mike looked into the yard, which was surprisingly large and sunny, with islands of flower beds in several places and two outdoor fountains. Near the house was an artificial pond surrounded by vines and exotic-looking plants. Mike could see why Sam would need to spend a lot of time in the yard. The yardman and a small, slender woman were standing at the rear of the lot.

"Sam!" Mike called out.

Sam and the woman turned around.

"Come in!" Sam yelled.

Mike unlatched the gate. The little brown dog nervously sniffed his ankles for a few seconds before running across the yard toward the woman. Mrs. Bowen faced him. Her gray hair was pulled back tightly in a bun, and she was wearing a dark skirt, blouse, and sweater. Sam stepped forward as Mike approached.

"Mike, do you know Mrs. Bowen?"

Mike extended his hand. Mrs. Bowen must have been at least eighty. Her fingers were slightly gnarled by arthritis, but she gripped his hand firmly. Diamonds glistened on several fingers.

"No, but I met your husband several times when I worked with Maxwell Forrest."

"Humph," Mrs. Bowen sniffed. "I still get letters from him wanting me to come in for a chat. Why should I do that? If I do, he'll ask a few questions about my bulbs then send me a bill for estate planning!"

"It's good to have your will reviewed from time to time," Mike offered.

Mrs. Bowen narrowed her eyes. "Did Maxwell Forrest send you here? I'd better not get a bill in the mail for a house call!"

"No, ma'am. I'm a minister now, not a lawyer."

Mrs. Bowen turned toward Sam. "Is that right?"

"Yep. He's one of my boys."

Mike started to protest but stopped when he saw Mrs. Bowen relax.

"Then the Lord surely is in the miracle business!" the old woman exclaimed. "A lawyer turned minister must make the angels scratch their wings in amazement!"

"Yes, ma'am," Mike agreed and turned toward Sam. "Will you have time to talk before you go home?"

"Yep. I'm finished here. Mrs. Bowen and I were visiting for a few minutes."

Sam reached into his pocket and handed the old woman a piece of paper. "Here's my bill and a word of encouragement about one of your grandsons."

"Billy?" the old woman asked.

"Yep."

Mrs. Bowen blinked her eyelids behind her glasses. They walked toward the gate.

"You have a beautiful yard," Mike said.

"I couldn't do it without Sam. We're growing old together, but I'm ahead on the race to the finish line."

"I'll be back toward the end of next week," Sam said. "The grass is beginning its spring growth spurt but won't need to be cut until then."

The old woman went into the house. Mike and Sam stepped onto the driveway.

"So, I'm one of your boys," Mike said.

"Which puts you on her prayer list," Sam replied. "It's a good place to be."

"She ought to put Maxwell Forrest on it."

Sam chuckled. "Do you think she's bitter toward him?"

"Maybe. Or mad at lawyers in general."

"I have no complaints about my lawyer. Papa picked him."

"We had our meeting with Judge Coberg this afternoon," Mike said.

Sam leaned against the side of the truck while Mike told him about the conference in the judge's chambers.

"Yep," Sam said when he finished. "The judge and I have also had a few talks when he gets his cauliflower. Did you know he's studied all the verses in the Bible about being a judge?"

"No. I need to tell the judge and DA if you want a jury trial."

"What do you think?"

"In almost all criminal cases, I recommend a jury trial."

"Okay, that's what I want."

Sam moved toward the front of the truck.

"That's not all," Mike said. "The case will be on the trial calendar in a few weeks."

The news of an impending court date stopped Sam in his tracks. He turned toward Mike.

"Then we'd better get ready. I'll try to do my part and leave the lawyering up to you."

"That's what I'm doing. I went to the DA's office and reviewed your file. I have copies of everything in my car."

After retrieving his briefcase, Mike laid out the documents on the hood of Sam's truck. "Here's the statement you gave to Detective Perkins."

Mike waited while Sam read it.

"Do you remember signing this?" Mike asked, pointing to the signature.

"Yep."

"Didn't you realize how the words could be twisted to make it look like you knew about misappropriation of funds from the checking account?"

"What?"

"That money was wrongfully transferred."

"The detective told me what happened. He wasn't lying."

"But—," Mike began then decided not to argue. "Anyway, the statement could give us trouble at trial."

He took out the checks.

"What about the signature endorsement on the back of these checks?" he asked. "It looks the same as the one at the bottom of your statement."

Sam held up the checks and squinted at them. "Yep. It looks like my handwriting."

"Is that your account number?"

"I don't have the whole thing memorized, but the last four numbers are right."

Mike waited. Sam put down the check copies but didn't say anything else.

"Well?" Mike asked.

"What?"

"How are we going to explain your apparent signature on the checks?"

"I didn't do it."

"Okay, I hope the handwriting expert agrees." Mike put the papers in his briefcase, clicked it shut, and put his hands on top of it. He spoke in measured tones. "After I reviewed the file, I talked with Melissa Hall. If you agree to plead guilty to a misdemeanor charge of illegally borrowing money from a nonprofit organization, you would receive six months on probation with no jail time or monetary fine. The offer will remain open for ten days then it will be withdrawn, and we go to trial."

"Say again?"

Mike repeated the basis and terms of the plea bargain.

"Do people do that?" Sam asked.

"What?"

"Plead guilty when they didn't do anything wrong?"

"It happens, and there are court cases that allow it. The fear of going to jail is a strong motivator. Sometimes it's easier to take something certain and avoid the possibility of a harsh sentence." Mike paused. "There is also the danger of prison. You saw what happened to you at the local jail. A state facility can be a hundred times worse."

"What are you trying to tell me? I hear fear in your voice."

"Aren't you afraid?"

Sam managed a weak smile. "I've been in tight spots in the past and always saw Papa come through in the end. Sometimes I suffered before help arrived; other times I escaped from the mouth of the lion. I'm not sure which kind of situation I'm facing. Have you ever told an innocent client to plead guilty?"

"I've had a few who told me they were innocent, but when the DA put an offer on the table they jumped on it. They were probably guilty but wouldn't admit it." Mike continued more slowly, "I've never advised an innocent client to plead guilty, but I wish I'd encouraged Danny Brewster to do so. He trusted me and would have done anything I suggested. There was an offer on the table prior to trial that would have given him twelve months in jail and the rest of his time on probation. If he'd taken a deal, he might be alive today."

"Papa kept that boy in His hand and—"

"I know," Mike interrupted. "But I can't ignore what happened when he went to prison."

Sam reached out and put his hand on Mike's shoulder. "And you wouldn't be a true pastor if you did."

Mike looked into Sam's eyes. "Do you want to consider the offer and talk it over with Muriel?"

"I'd best not mention it to Muriel. She's so worried about me going to jail, she can't rest at night. Most nights I wake up several times, but she's always been able to sleep through anything. Now, she's often awake when I come out of a dream."

"So what should I tell Melissa Hall?"

Sam looked past Mike's shoulder for a moment before answering. "Tell her Papa is going to turn her mourning into dancing and restore the song she thought she'd lost."

"And after I deliver that message, do I turn down the plea deal?"

"I don't see the apostles telling lies to get out of jail, and I don't intend to start either. How could I lose in court? I've got the best lawyer in the world."

"Don't say that about me," Mike replied.

Sam shook his head "If you think I meant you, think again."

IT WAS TOO LATE IN THE AFTERNOON TO RETURN TO THE church, so Mike drove home. Peg and Judge weren't there. Mike leafed through the mail then noticed the blinking light on the answering machine in the kitchen. He pressed the Play button.

"I know you're recording this message, which is fine with me," a voice said. "I like to record conversations, too. I'll be at the office until six o'clock. Give me a call to set up a meeting."

Mike dialed the direct number for Braxton Hodges's desk. The reporter answered on the second ring.

"Where are you?" the reporter asked.

"At home."

"What were you doing at the courthouse this afternoon?"

"Meeting with the judge on the Miller case. I didn't see you."

"I was driving by and saw you come out the front door. Are you in the mood for a hamburger tomorrow?"

"I don't have to be in the mood."

"Meet me at Brooks at noon."

"Can't you talk to me now?" Mike asked.

"No."

The phone clicked before Mike could ask another question.

THAT NIGHT, MIKE LAY AWAKE WHILE PEG SLEPT PEACEFULLY beside him. He'd been able to get his mind off Sam's case during supper and a quiet evening, but once he turned off the lights, various courtroom scenarios began flashing across his mind. He wasn't sure of the best approach to take in defending the case, and trial strategy without focus was the grist of nightmares. So, he stayed awake, not wanting to process in an unconscious state what he couldn't sort out while alert. It had been so many years since a criminal case kept him up at night that he'd forgotten the churning feeling produced by responsibility for the freedom of another human being.

And he'd never represented someone like Sam Miller. He and Muriel shared one primary goal—they didn't want Sam to go to prison.

MIKE SPENT A BUSY MORNING AT THE CHURCH. TIME WORKING on the Miller case required more efficient performance of his duties as pastor.

"Delores, write the announcements for the bulletin after contacting the chairpersons for the finance, worship, and building and grounds committees."

"I've never done that in the past," she protested.

"You're smart enough to handle it. I'll proofread the text before we send it to the printer." Mike checked his watch. "I'm late for a meeting in town at noon. Don't forget to include notice of the session meeting on Tuesday."

Mike heard Delores grumbling under her breath as he passed her desk but didn't take time to slow down and unruffle her feathers.

BRAXTON HODGES WAS STANDING AT THE OUTDOOR TABLE unwrapping his food when Mike pulled into the parking lot.

"I'll be there in a minute," Mike called out.

"Take your time. I don't like to talk with my mouth full of hamburger and onions."

Mike entered the restaurant. It was packed with customers. He waited at the counter behind a large bearded man with "Paul" embroidered on his blue work shirt.

"Three hamburgers all the way, an order of fries, and tea," Paul said.

"Not hungry today?" asked Dusty.

Paul pulled at his beard. "I had a snack a couple of hours ago."

Mike placed his order and waited. One of the twins was manning the grill while the other cooked fries and poured tea. After paying for his food, Mike went outside. Hodges was on the last bite of his hamburger. Several other men, including Paul, stood along the long wooden table. Eating rather than talking was the priority, and the table was quiet.

"Eat," Hodges said. "We'll sit in my car for a few minutes after you finish."

Hodges tossed his empty bag into a fifty-five-gallon metal drum. Mike ate as fast as he could and still enjoy his food. Hodges gave him a status report about the high school baseball team.

"They have two strong pitchers," the reporter said, "but no middle relief, and once they get into the play-offs and need a third starter, there isn't much there. The shortstop, a scrawny kid named Charlie Martin, will be the leadoff batter. I wouldn't be surprised if he bats over .400. He's impossible to strike out. The younger Hinshaw boy will get his share of home runs. His older brother was a brute, and he's about the same size."

"Who have you been talking to?"

"Coach Gott. I'm going to do a big feature on him since he's retiring after this season."

Mike ate his last french fry and took a sip of tea.

"I'm ready," Mike said.

Hodges pointed toward his car.

"This is kind of a reverse of Woodward and Bernstein, isn't it?" Mike asked as they walked across the gravel parking lot. "You're the source; I'm the one needing information."

"If you want to play that game, my code name is 'Hamburger Chili.'"

Mike opened the passenger door of the plain-looking Pontiac and pushed aside a stack of old newspapers so he could sit down. The backseat was cluttered with notepads, envelopes, empty coffee cups, and individual scraps of paper.

"Sorry about the mess," Hodges said. "In my world, deadlines come before either cleanliness or godliness."

The reporter reached into the backseat and retrieved a brown envelope.

"What do you know about the Cohulla Creek watershed?" he asked.

"Uh, it's one of the most beautiful areas this side of the Blue Ridge and a good place to catch trout on Thursday if the State Game and Fish warden stocks it on Wednesday."

"Who owns it?"

"Part utility company, part state, with a little in the hands of private investors."

"Did you know that in the 1930s there was a plan to dam the creek and create a lake at Horseshoe Bottoms to generate hydroelectric power?"

"No, I wasn't born then."

"Me either. But all those plans were scrapped when it became cheaper and easier to make electricity by burning coal than by harnessing water."

"Which is good for fishing but doesn't do a lot for the economy in general."

"You're ahead of me. Over the past three years, there has been a huge change in the percentage of ownership between utility, private, and state."

"What kind of change?"

"Utility company ownership is down to a couple hundred acres on the south side. Private owners now hold options on two thousand acres, and the state controls about six thousand acres, including Horseshoe Bottoms. There has been discussion in the legislature about selling the state's remaining share of the watershed to open the entire area for private companies that could create a deepwater lake surrounded by residential development."

Mike opened his eyes wider. "That would be one of the biggest things that ever hit this county."

"Yes. And a lot of money could be made by people in the right place at the right time. The options controlling access to Horseshoe Bottoms are already in place."

"Who holds the options?"

Hodges held up the envelope. "Companies in Nevada and New York."

"Who are the local contacts?"

"That's where it gets fuzzy, but I have an opinion. I believe the initiative for this whole project came from within Barlow County." Hodges paused. "Have you seen the new house Representative Niles is building?"

"No."

"It's a monster. Some would say a monstrosity. I've heard rumors of Italian marble, gold-plated fixtures in the bathrooms, and a bunch of other stuff a man who works in the trust department of a bank couldn't afford. He's telling everyone he hit a home run on an investment, some new stock offering he bought for pennies and sold a year later for dollars. But I'm skeptical."

"Butch Niles is getting a cut for getting this through the legislature?"

"If I printed that, it would fall in the category of unsubstantiated allegations and would result in a lawsuit putting our puny newspaper out of business. However, if my guess is true, there has been a high level of coordination between people wanting to make a lot of money, those holding political influence, and politicians with enough inside information to let the group get ahead of the curve."

"What about environmental concerns? I always thought Cohulla Creek would end up as a state park, not a huge subdivision."

"You're behind on that one. The developers' plan includes dedication of a tract for public use, a nice little picnic and camping area, but without boat access for the unwashed masses. Only landowners get to ski on the pristine waters."

"How do you know about this?"

"Through the inadvertent help of a former bank employee who now heads the accounting department at the paper. His cubicle is near mine, and I didn't want him to hear me talking to you the other night."

"He told you about this?"

Hodges shook his head. "Not exactly. I have my sources."

"Braxton, are you rummaging through the trash again?" Mike asked with a smile. "I hope you washed your hands before you ate your hamburger."

"Trash? You're in the dark ages before computers."

"You snooped on someone's computer?"

"Are you my lawyer?" the reporter asked. "This has to be confidential."

"Yes, I can handle two clients."

"His laptop. He'd brought one from home until we got him up and running on our system. Last week, he left it on when he went to the restroom, and I couldn't help but see what was on his screen. I sent the information in the file to my computer and printed it out after he left." Hodges held up the envelope. "It's in here."

"Who are you talking about?"

"Brian Dressler."

"From the Bank of Barlow County? He's one of Jack Hatcher's chief assistants."

"Not anymore."

"Why did he leave the bank?"

"I'm not sure, but it wasn't a friendly divorce. I didn't participate in his interview at the paper, but he needed a job as soon as possible and took a huge pay cut. His wife has cancer, and he needed health insurance. That's about the only employee benefit we have that's first rate."

Mike remembered Sam's dream about the hatchet, deeds of darkness, and Cohulla Creek.

"This is all juicy local gossip that I wouldn't hear sitting in my office at the church," Mike replied lightly, "but what does it have to do with Sam Miller?"

"Miller is mentioned in a memo in the file."

Mike sat up straighter in the seat. "Let me see the memo."

Hodges opened the envelope and handed a single sheet of paper to Mike, who quickly read it. It was a memo from Dressler to Hatcher about the meeting with the deacons from the Craig Valley church. It listed the check numbers, the amount of the checks, and the deposits to Sam's account. It contained no new information.

"I met with the leaders of the Craig Valley church and already know all this," Mike said.

"That doesn't surprise me, but why would that memo be in this file? Everything else has to do with the Cohulla Creek project: companies holding the options, the acreage involved, and preliminary plans for development of the property."

Mike shook his head.

Hodges leaned closer to him. "Read the last line of the memo."

Mike held up the sheet of paper and read, "'*This should take care of the Miller problem. Will keep you advised.*'"

"Doesn't that sound strange?" Hodges asked.

Mike shrugged. "Yes, but it's ambiguous and subject to various interpretations. Just like the statement Sam gave Detective Perkins. What expands this case beyond a routine embezzlement charge is the degree of interest Maxwell Forrest and Jack Hatcher have in what's going on, including my involvement."

"Admit it. They know you're one of the best investigative attorneys in this circuit. Ken West once told me you drove him nuts with all the time and energy you put into even little cases."

Mike grinned. "If God hadn't taken away my ego, that sort of compliment would make my head swell."

"Then use what's left of your brain. Sam Miller wrote one of his crazy letters to the president of the bank and made Hatcher think he knew there was something shady about the acquisition of the Cohulla Creek property. Hatcher tells Dressler to frame Sam on an embezzlement charge so anything the old man says, especially about the bank, will be automatically discredited."

Mike was impressed by the reporter's deductive abilities but knew that without Sam's consent he had to keep his own information private.

"If you print that story it will definitely be libelous," he said.

"I know, but you're a defense lawyer. You can say anything you want in court and get away with it. Isn't your strategy in a criminal case to put everyone on trial you can think of except your client?"

"Yes, it can be an effective way to go on the attack."

"Which is what I want to do. If you stir this thing up enough, something may break for me. A little light can dispel a lot of darkness, and a story like this would be the opportunity of a lifetime."

"Have you considered going directly to Dressler?"

Hodges shook his head. "I thought I'd leave that to you."

Seventeen

Mike left Brooks Sandwich House with a full stomach and a computer disc containing the information Braxton Hodges had obtained from Brian Dressler's computer. While driving back to the church, he debated when to call Dressler and how to bring up the subject of the memo. He decided the best approach would be to set up a face-to-face meeting as soon as possible. Delores didn't speak when he greeted her as he passed her desk.

Mike went into his office and shut the door. There were two stacks of phone messages on top of the announcements for the bulletin. Delores's work on the bulletin was accurate but without the embellishments Mike normally added to make the upcoming events more appealing. He took out his red pen to make changes then stopped. Better to leave it alone than to raise her ire. He went to the door.

"Delores, the wording of the announcements was fine. No corrections needed. However, next week I'll make sure I allocate the time to take care of it myself."

"That's better," she replied. "You've been acting more like a lawyer than a minister. Ordering me around like a twenty-year-old clerical worker, staying out of the office half the time, thinking more about one man who committed a crime than the three hundred law-abiding people depending on you here."

Mike withdrew before his face revealed his irritation at the secretary's attitude. He didn't want to see her the rest of the day, but a sudden idea drew him back to the office door.

"How is your sister?" he asked.

"Not good. We had a long talk this morning. Her husband filed for divorce and hired a sleazy lawyer who got a crooked judge to sign an order kicking her out of the house. She's checking into a motel this afternoon but has no place to go."

"Could she come up here and stay with you?"

"That wouldn't work. She's allergic to cigarette smoke."

"What about Jo Ellen Caldwell? Doesn't she have extra space?"

"Do you know her?"

"Not well. She visited the church about a year ago."

"I hadn't thought about her," Delores said thoughtfully. "That's a great idea. She has an extra room available since her granddaughter moved out. I'll call her right now."

Delores had the receiver in her hand before Mike closed the door. Impressed with his insightful suggestion, Mike began returning phone messages and included an appropriate apology for his tardiness in returning the call. After he finished the last one, he called the paper and asked for Brian Dressler.

"He left a few minutes ago," the receptionist said. "Would you like to leave a voice mail?"

"No, I don't want to leave a message," Mike said. "I'll check back tomorrow."

Mike pushed aside an unfinished financial report and inserted the Dressler disc into the computer. He scrolled through the file. Except for the memo about Sam, the data looked like benign corporate records. Mike felt slightly uneasy reading what was obviously considered confidential information by the companies furnishing it to the bank. The bank's exact role wasn't clear. Nothing in the records indicated the source for funding.

High dollar options to purchase land along the Cohulla Creek watershed had been in place for several years. Real estate options held a high degree of risk since all the earnest money, which amounted to several hundred thousand dollars, would be forfeited by the prospective buyers if the sale wasn't completed. The option contracts didn't make finalization of the sale contingent on legislative action authorizing the sale of Horseshoe Bottoms. In fact, they contained no contingencies. Thus, the original owners probably thought they were getting a great deal from out-of-town speculators. Even if Braxton Hodges didn't write a massive exposé of local corruption, the current owners' anger when they realized what the developers intended would be newsworthy.

The more recent documents confirmed the project was as big as Mike imagined. The pro forma financial data had eye-popping projections for revenue in the tens of millions. Mike didn't recognize the names of any of the people connected with the business entities; however, the last folder he opened caught his attention. It contained a letter from his old law firm as local counsel for Delvie, LLC, a Nevada limited liability company. The letter was signed by Bobby Lambert. In the letter, Bobby provided Dressler information about the credit worthiness of Delvie, LLC. However, the supporting documents mentioned in his former partner's letter weren't included on the disc. Mike shut down his computer without printing anything. The information in the files didn't span the canyon between the charges against Sam and the bank's involvement in the Cohulla Creek project.

THE FOLLOWING DAY, MIKE PHONED THE NEWSPAPER SEVERAL times but never caught Dressler at the office. He began to wonder how the new head of accounting at the paper could hold a job when he didn't show up. Finally, he called Braxton Hodges.

"Where is Dressler? He's never there, or he's avoiding my phone calls."

"It's his wife. She's taken a turn for the worse and is at the hospital receiving treatment. He won't be back in the office until next week. I should have let you know."

"Any other news on your end?"

"Plenty. It's going to be a late spring, so you'd better not plant your Silver Queen corn for another week or two. I interviewed the county extension agent, and we'll have a suggested schedule for planting all your garden vegetables in this week's paper. Don't miss it."

Mike chuckled. "I'll take that as a negative about matters of interest to me."

"Imagine the world without Silver Queen corn. Oh, Maxwell Forrest never called me back about any correspondence from Miller and Hatcher."

"Which doesn't mean much."

"Except that he doesn't want to talk to me, a sure sign of something to hide."

"Talk about media bias. Have you considered that some people are afraid to talk to reporters?"

"And lawyers. But does that apply to your old boss?"

"No," Mike admitted. "Mr. Forrest isn't intimidated by anyone."

MIKE DELAYED LETTING MELISSA HALL KNOW ABOUT SAM'S decision rejecting the plea bargain and desire for a jury trial. It was a week before the deal would expire, and in spite of Sam's clear instructions to nix any offer, Mike didn't want to eliminate any option prematurely.

The following morning, he woke up later than usual. He'd stayed up working on his sermon, and while it wasn't yet up to his usual standards, he was satisfied that all the main points were properly organized. Peg wasn't in bed when he opened his eyes. He went downstairs in his pajamas and bare feet and found Peg in the kitchen with a coffee cup and an open notebook on the table in front of her. She put down her pen when he entered the room.

"What are you working on?" he asked.

"Writing down a dream I had last night."

"You never remember your dreams except bits and pieces that don't make sense."

"I remembered this one. It was so vivid."

"Tell me."

Peg hesitated. "Not until I have time to think about what it might mean. It may be important in a religious way."

"I'm a minister. I've been dreaming for years. Trust my experience and training."

Peg smiled. "How many classes in dream interpretation did you take in seminary?"

"None."

"That's what I thought. If you had, I'm sure you would have made an A, but I may call Sam Miller and ask him about it. He has a lot of experience."

"Wait a minute. I'm Sam's protégé, and he didn't say anything about God giving you dreams."

"Jealous?"

Mike poured a cup of coffee and took a sip.

"I'm not in danger of violating the tenth-commandment prohibition against jealousy when it comes to my wife," he teased, "but don't make me wait six months before you let me know what you really think."

As soon as he said the words, Mike wished he could take them back. Peg's face fell. She closed her notebook.

"Were the words in your sermon the other day about forgiveness just a minister talking down to his congregation?" she asked.

"No, it came straight from wrestling with our situation. I meant every word."

"It's a new day. Do I need to ask you to forgive me?"

"No. I'm sorry," Mike responded quickly. "I shouldn't have said that. I know what you said on the mountain was from your heart, and I received it that way. Seeing the glow on your face Sunday was worth the pain."

"Is that what you really think?" Peg asked.

"Yes, and I respect your right to keep the dreams to yourself until you feel comfortable sharing them. Call Sam Miller if you like. I'm sure he'll be glad to help if he can."

Judge, as if knowing Peg needed to be comforted, came over to her. She patted the dog on the head.

"I was thinking about going over to Cohulla Creek today," Mike said. "Would you like to go with me?"

"No. My energy level isn't very high this morning. I'd better stay here and take it easy."

"You're not sick, are you?"

"No, pregnant. Are you going to park and ride your bike?"

"Yes."

"Then take Judge with you; he'll enjoy it."

PEG WASN'T IN SIGHT WHEN MIKE PREPARED TO LEAVE. JUDGE, sensing an outing, paced back and forth across the kitchen floor.

"Peg!" Mike yelled up the staircase.

"Bye!" she called back.

Mike climbed several steps of the stairs. He wanted to clear the air between them. Judge barked and scratched at the door. Not sure what to say, Mike retreated down the stairs.

WITH JUDGE ON THE SEAT BEHIND HIM AND HIS BIKE IN A RACK on the roof, Mike drove west of Shelton. The main access road to Cohulla Creek was about a mile from Sam Miller's house. Mike turned onto a gravel road. Within a few hundred yards, he began to notice red and orange survey ribbons tied to the lower limbs of trees. The color had faded from some of the ribbons, but others appeared fresh. Survey ribbons marked more than boundaries; they were the first sign of permanent change coming to the woods.

The road crossed the creek on a one-lane bridge. A fisherman wearing hip waders stood at the edge of the water below the bridge. Focused on his line, he didn't look up when Mike drove by. The emerging leaves shaded the road as it skirted a small hill then emptied into a parking area where fishermen left their vehicles. Mike parked beside a white pickup truck. From this point forward, the road remained passable for vehicles but received less maintenance and became more dirt than gravel.

Judge bounded out the door and immediately put his nose to the ground. Mike unhooked his bike and lifted it from the roof rack. He slipped on a small backpack and whistled for Judge, who had ventured down the road.

To Mike, a mountain bike earned its name if used to climb hills and mountains. Hopping curbs in Shelton didn't count. The red paint on his bike was nicked from contact with rocks and trees. Only once had he hurtled over the handlebars. During a ride in Virginia, his wheel had slipped into a deep rut, causing him to become airborne. His helmet slammed against an exposed tree root. Stunned for a few seconds, Mike recovered and continued.

He'd ridden along Cohulla Creek shortly after they moved back to Shelton, but because it was relatively flat, and he wasn't a fisherman, the route dropped off his list. Mike enjoyed the physical workout required in a climb followed by the exhilaration of reaching a high place of perspective above the world below. The Cohulla Creek watershed didn't offer any thigh-burning challenges.

He pedaled upstream. The dirt road stayed close to the creek for several hundred yards then rose slightly until the stream lay thirty or forty feet below on the right. Mike pedaled at an easy rate. Judge loped alongside him. The dog could maintain his pace as long as Mike's legs could pedal the bike. More survey ribbons appeared at various intervals then stopped when they passed onto land owned by the state. Two vehicles containing fishermen passed them on the road. The ground rose sharply on the opposite side of the creek, but on the roadside, Mike could easily envision areas for housing development. The road dipped down and rejoined the creek, which slowed and broadened in a flat, wooded area. They'd reached Horseshoe Bottoms.

Mike stopped and looked behind him. He wondered how far upstream the lake would extend. Without a doubt, it would be a magnificent setting—a mountain finger-lake filled with clear, cool water surrounded by gentle hills. Mike would enjoy stepping onto the front porch of a home on one of the hills to inhale a view.

Mike remounted his bike. The road split in two, climbing into the hills to the left and continuing near the stream on the right. He'd not remembered the fork in the road.

"Which way, boy?" he asked Judge, who was sniffing the air.

The dog padded onto the road into the hills. It looked like a newer cut.

"That's the way I wanted to go," Mike said, slipping his feet into his toe clips and shifting into a lower gear.

Sure enough, it was a new track that ascended the hill in a series of short switchbacks. Large rock gravel spread on the road made the ride bumpy. Mike had to hold the handlebars tightly. He came around the corner into a cleared area. A new silver SUV was parked beneath a large oak tree. Mike slowed to a stop beside a large poplar tree. The front doors of the SUV opened.

Maxwell Forrest and Jack Hatcher got out.

Even on a Saturday far back in the woods, Mr. Forrest was wearing a starched shirt and silk tie. Hatcher, his brown hair closely cropped in military fashion, was dressed casually. The back doors of the SUV opened, and two men Mike didn't recognize stepped onto the ground. Mr. Forrest raised his hand in greeting. Mike resisted the urge to jump on his bike and ride down the hill. His flight response was immediately replaced by anger at the thought of the letter Mr. Forrest had written him. Mike leaned the bike against a tree. Judge, his tongue hanging out as he panted, stood beside him.

"You've come a long way to see me," Forrest said. "It would be a lot easier to catch me in town."

"I thought I was banned from the office," Mike replied.

Hatcher cut in. "Good to see you, Mike. What are you doing out here?"

"Just going for a ride in the woods with my dog. Sorry to disturb you."

"You're not disturbing anything," Hatcher replied. "Meet Dick Bunt and Troy Linden."

Two men in their fifties, one bald and the other with a thick head of salt-and-pepper hair, stepped closer and shook his hand. Mike tried to remember if he'd seen their names while reviewing the information supplied by Braxton Hodges. Linden sounded familiar, but he couldn't be sure.

"Nice dog," said Bunt, the bald man. "I have a friend in San Bernardino who has a vizsla. What's your dog's name?"

"Judge," Mike replied.

Bunt laughed. "I've seen a few judges I considered dogs. Does he have a last name?"

"No, that might get me into trouble."

"Mike is a lawyer who used to work with Maxwell," Hatcher said. "Now he's gone into the ministry."

"Except for one case," Forrest grunted.

"How long have you been the pastor at the church?" Hatcher continued.

"Almost three years."

"The bank financed their new sanctuary," Hatcher said to the other men. "As soon as Mike came on the scene, the congregation began to grow by leaps and bounds."

"What brings you gentlemen so far into the woods?" Mike asked.

"Showing Dick and Troy around."

"Beautiful area," Bunt added.

"Yes," Mike said, nodding. "But it looks as though things are about to change. Someone used several rolls of survey ribbons along the road. If I had to guess, I'd say these hills are about to be carved for residential development."

Hatcher spoke. "That's happening all over this part of the country."

"Yes, it's one of the reasons we've had so much growth at the church," Mike said as he turned toward the two strangers. "Are you gentlemen real estate developers?"

"I've dabbled in it," Bunt replied. "Troy and I are always looking for business opportunities, but most of our work has been in the commercial real estate area."

"What part of the country?" Mike asked.

"All over. We're not limited."

"Anything in Las Vegas?" Mike asked.

"Why do you ask about Las Vegas?"

"Maybe it's your accent," Mike replied. "It sounds western, but not Texas."

Bunt stared at Mike. Forrest cut in, "Mike, could we have a private chat?"

"So long as we don't go to your office."

Forrest walked away from the vehicle toward the edge of the clearing. The other three men moved in the opposite direction. Judge, his breathing returned to normal, sniffed the ground around the SUV.

"Don't lose your salvation over the letter I sent you," Forrest said. "Look at the situation from my side. The bank has an interest in the successful prosecution of an individual who embezzled money from one of its customers. I can't give you access to our building where bank files are kept until this matter is dealt with, one way or another."

"Is there anything in your files that would impact my client's case?"

"I don't see how there could be, but that isn't the point. I can't compromise the confidentiality of the firm's attorney-client relationship with the bank." Forrest paused. "Even for one of the best lawyers I've known since opening my office in this county forty years ago."

"A phone call before you sent the letter would have been nice."

"I probably should have done that, but I've been very busy. Too busy. The firm is undergoing changes. Park is leaving. Arnold is smart and has a great future, but he's not ready to assume primary responsibility for major clients."

"Any replacements on the horizon?"

"Not yet, and until that happens, Bobby and I will be spending most of our time chained to our desks."

"Except Saturdays along Cohulla Creek."

"With businessmen who have a right to keep their plans private," Forrest responded. "Where were you going with your cross-examination of Mr. Bunt?"

"Who knows? You stopped me."

"Don't play that game. I trained you to know the answers to questions before you asked them. You're right about the survey ribbons. It's no secret. There are options on record at the courthouse, although I have no idea why you would care. You're not a trout fisherman or an environmentalist."

"Just a bike-riding preacher who still doesn't understand why a busy, important lawyer like you is so interested in Sam Miller."

"I told you. I'm looking out for the bank's reputation."

"I hear you, Mr. Forrest, but that's not enough. My client has been offered a sweet deal to plead guilty, but I can't advise him what to do without access to the bank's records. That's the only way I can properly evaluate the charges against him."

"If he's guilty, let him plead. I'm sure the district attorney's office has the pertinent information. Have you filed a motion—"

"They've allowed me to copy the entire file."

"What was in it?"

"Not much. Copies of two checks along with records for the accounts involved."

"What else do you want? That's all the bank would have in its records."

"There must have been an internal investigation before the matter was referred to the sheriff's office. And I'd also like to know about any communication between the bank and my client."

"Your client should have copies of anything the bank sent him, and he'd be aware of anything coming from his end."

"Miller cuts grass for a living. His filing system is a shoe box in the bottom of a closet."

"His lack of organization isn't the bank's problem."

"I know, but it will become the bank's problem when I file a subpoena dragging a bank officer into court so I can take a look at what they have. I don't want to do that, and it shouldn't be necessary."

Forrest glanced over at the other men. "I'll talk to Hatcher about it," he replied. "But not today. This meeting doesn't have anything to do with your client. And my advice to you the other day still stands. You have no business practicing law as a hobby."

"When will I hear from you?" Mike asked.

"Don't give me a deadline," Forrest replied, his jaw set. "I'll get to it. You can count on it."

They started walking toward the other men. Bunt and Linden got into the SUV.

"Good to see you, Mike," Hatcher said as he opened the driver's-side door. "We need to be on our way. Be careful on your ride. I bet the gravel on this road makes it hard to maneuver on a bicycle."

"I'm used to it," Mike answered. "Maneuvering in tough places is part of the fun."

Hatcher backed out of the parking area and started down the hill. Mike didn't want to inhale a cloud of dust by following too closely behind them and waited several minutes. He poured some water into a plastic bowl and set it on the ground in front of Judge, who greedily lapped it up.

"What did you think about those men?" Mike asked the dog.

Judge didn't respond. His focus in life didn't extend beyond the liquid at the end of his nose.

MIKE CAREFULLY COASTED DOWN THE HILL TO HORSESHOE Bottoms. By the time he reached the main road, there wasn't any dust in the air caused by the departure of the SUV. Mike retraced his route along the creek road.

Just before the road began to climb to its vantage point above the stream, he veered toward the water and stopped at a creek-side campsite. A well-used fire ring made from rocks taken from the streambed lay in the middle of the clearing. Judge began a circular reconnaissance and quickly unearthed a candy wrapper. While the dog investigated the smells left by campers, Mike walked down to the creek. The water rushed along at a rapid clip. Mike sat on a large rock, watched the water swirl by, and listened to the sounds of the stream. He wondered if this was the spot Sam Miller liked to visit.

Taking off his shoes, Mike dipped his feet into the water. Spring might be in the air, but the water in Cohulla Creek hadn't received the news. It felt ice cold. Mike left his feet in the water until they became slightly numb, then put on his socks and shoes. He returned to the campsite. In search of fresh scents, Judge had ventured farther into the woods. Mike unzipped his backpack to get a snack bar and saw the message light flashing on his phone. Maintaining an adequate service signal in the woods was difficult, but he had a single bar. Mike pressed the button to retrieve his message and waited. It was Peg.

"Please call me! I'm at the emergency room. I'm bleeding, and the doctor is going to order an ultrasound!"

Eighteen

PEG DIDN'T ANSWER WHEN HE HIT THE SPEED-DIAL NUMBER for her cell phone. Mike left a voice mail that he was on the way then mounted his bike. Pedaling furiously, he tore along the road. Mike had read in a pregnancy brochure that prenatal bleeding often occurred during the first trimester of a pregnancy. But that didn't lessen his concern. Peg wouldn't have gone to the doctor unless she thought the situation might be serious. Judge gamely tried to keep up but began to lag behind. Mike came around a corner and waited for the dog to rejoin him and continued at a pace the dog could manage. There was no use sprinting ahead; he'd have to wait for Judge at the end of the ride anyway.

Mike rounded a corner and skidded into the parking area. He quickly locked his bike onto the rack. Judge hopped into the car and lay down in the backseat. Skidding around corners, Mike didn't encounter any other vehicles on the way out of the wilderness area. He reached the main highway and tried Peg's number again, but there was no answer.

The Barlow County Hospital was outside the Shelton city limits on the south side of town. Mike reached the parking lot for the emergency room and saw Peg's car. He dashed through the sliding doors, rushed up to the desk, and introduced himself.

"Your wife is in zone three," the attendant told him. "I'll have someone take you to her."

Mike waited impatiently until a nurse's aide appeared and led him into the treatment area. Peg lay in a bed in a room divided by a white curtain. Her eyes were closed. Mike leaned over her.

"Peg," he whispered intensely. "It's me."

She opened her eyes. They looked listless.

"The pain," she said, touching her abdomen. "It was horrible."

"What's wrong?"

"I don't know. They did an ultrasound, but Dr. Hester hasn't talked to me."

"Do you still hurt?"

"Not as much. They gave me something to stop the pain. I didn't want anything, but they said it wouldn't hurt the baby."

"Is the baby okay?"

"I don't know. The technician who did the test wouldn't tell me anything."

Mike pulled a chair to the edge of the bed and held Peg's hand. It was shocking how quickly she'd gone from vibrant energy to lethargy. He heard footsteps. A short, dark-haired man entered and introduced himself as Dr. Hester. A female nurse accompanied him.

"The baby appears fine on the ultrasound," the doctor began.

Mike exhaled in relief. Peg nodded slightly.

"Thank God," she said.

"How are your cramps?" the doctor asked.

"Better, but I'm afraid it's because of the medication."

"It's safe. That's why we gave it to you."

"What's causing this?" Mike asked.

"Bleeding and cramps this severe can be the precursor to a miscarriage, but fortunately the placenta appears intact. I want her to stay in the ER until we're sure the bleeding has stopped, then I'll let her go home to bed rest."

"Total bed rest?"

"Until she sees her obstetrician. I called Dr. Crawford, and she concurs. Make an appointment with her the first of the week."

"Can she walk up steps?"

"Do you have a downstairs bedroom?"

"Yes."

"Put her there. The next few days are about avoiding unnecessary strain of any type."

The doctor left, and Peg closed her eyes. Seconds later they popped open.

"Where's Judge?" she asked.

"In the car with the windows cracked. He's passed out in the backseat, as worn out as you are."

"Take him home, then come back for me."

"I'm not going anywhere."

Peg didn't argue. She closed her eyes. Two hours later, an orderly rolled her to the curb. Mike held the door open so she could get in the car. Judge, his tail wagging, watched.

"What about my car?" she asked.

"Why did you drive in the first place? You could have called Marla or Elizabeth."

"Marla wasn't home, and I thought it would be quicker to come myself."

"We'll figure out how to get your car later. First, I want to get you home and into bed."

Peg was more alert during the ride home.

"I don't need to ask Sam Miller about my dream," she said as they reached traffic light six.

"Why not?"

"Because I think I know what it meant."

"Do you want to tell me?"

Peg paused before responding. "Yes. I was sitting in a lounge chair on the top deck of a huge cruise ship. I was alone, which was odd because you know how they're always jammed with people. If I wanted something, all I had to do was ring a little bell, and a waiter would bring it to me. I ate the best fruit you can imagine. I thought about getting up but decided there was no better place to be on the boat than resting in the chair."

"Were you pregnant?"

"Not that I remember."

"Why did you think it was a religious dream?"

"Because in addition to the crew assigned to take care of me, there were angels present."

"How did you know they were angels? Did they have wings?"

"No."

"Then how did you know?"

"I'm not sure. I just did. That's one of the things I still want to ask Sam."

Mike's face was troubled. A dream about angels, especially before a trip to the hospital, worried him.

They arrived home. Judge, revived by his long nap in the car, ran around the corner of the house. Mike tried to help steady Peg as she got out of the car, but she shooed him away.

"I'm not an invalid. I can walk to the downstairs bedroom. Just get me into bed so I can dream about my cruise ship."

Mike opened the door of the house for her.

"Was I on the cruise?"

Peg stepped up into the kitchen. "I'm not sure. If you put on a waiter's uniform it might come back to me."

Mike managed a slight smile. The return of Peg's wit was a sign of health.

THE DOWNSTAIRS BEDROOM WAS AT THE REAR OF THE HOUSE next to the computer room. For years, Peg had used it as her art studio and emergency dumping ground for items that needed to be quickly removed from sight when guests arrived. Mike opened the door. To his surprise, it was as neat and tidy as a photograph in a home decorating magazine.

"What happened in here?" he asked.

"Nesting urge. I cleaned it out last week without any idea I'd be using it myself."

Mike pulled back the covers. Peg slipped off her shoes and climbed into bed.

"I'll put on my pajamas later," she said. "The medication is making me tired."

Mike tucked her in and kissed her on the forehead.

"I'll put on my ship waiter's uniform while you sleep," he said, trying to be more lighthearted than he felt. "I want to be a part of both your conscious and unconscious lives. Should I close the door?"

"Open is fine. Judge might want to lie on the floor beside the bed."

An hour later, Peg woke up hungry. Mike opened a can of soup. While it was heating up on the stove, he called Sam Miller. Muriel answered the phone, and Mike told her what had happened.

"Is her mother coming?" Muriel asked.

"She lives in Philadelphia and has severe arthritis. She needs daily assistance herself."

"Then I'd like to come over and help out."

"Uh, let me check with Peg."

When Mike turned around, Peg was standing in the doorway.

"What are you doing out of bed?"

"I had to go to the bathroom. Who are you talking to?"

Mike kept his hand over the receiver. "Muriel Miller. She wants to come over and help. I wasn't sure if you wanted one of your friends or someone from the church—"

"Tell her yes," Peg said, turning toward the bedroom.

Mike lifted the receiver. "We don't want to impose on you, but that would be great."

"Sam should be home in a few minutes. I'll get him to bring me."

MIKE WAS IN THE COMPUTER ROOM REVISING HIS SERMON when the doorbell rang. Sam and Muriel Miller stood on the front landing. Muriel stepped into the front hall. Mike led the way.

"Peg is in a bedroom behind the stairs."

Peg was sitting up in bed reading a book. Her face lit up when she saw the older woman.

"Thanks for coming," she said.

Muriel came to the side of the bed and took Peg's hand in hers.

"Tell me what happened."

Mike left the bedroom and returned to the front door. Sam remained outside, staring up at the edge of the roof. Mike joined him and looked up as well.

"Is there a problem?" Mike asked.

"Nope, this is a Passover house. The angel of death isn't going to stop here."

"How can you tell?"

"By the blood."

"You see blood on my house?"

"Yep."

"Sam, that's gross."

"You wouldn't think so if you knew it meant your firstborn son is going to live and not die."

Mike stared hard at Sam. "And Peg will be all right, too?"

"She's going to have the boy. Beyond that, I can't say. The two of you may have to go through Pharaoh's testing."

"Pharaoh's testing?"

"To prove what is in your heart."

"You're mixing your metaphors. The plagues were for the Egyptians, not the Israelites, and the Passover came after the plagues, not before."

"It did, but Papa works in circles, not lines. He'll give the promise then let our circumstances take us around the back side of the mountain before fulfilling it. The blood on your house will work, but its power isn't proven until your faith and obedience overcome the challenges against it."

"I'm not sure what that means, but you must have been reading in Exodus this week."

"Nope. I'm in Lamentations."

Mike hesitated a moment then told him about Peg's dream. "The angels worried me. That's why I asked you if she was going to be all right."

"There are plenty of messengers around here, not just in heaven. I'll think on it, but don't be too quick to believe it's bad. Even a dream with warning often has a way of escape."

"What should I do?"

"Take care of her. Your part is easy."

"Okay," Mike said. "Come inside. We also need to talk about your case."

The two men went into the kitchen.

"Do you know what I see in here?" Sam asked.

"No idea."

Sam pointed at a fruit bowl on the counter next to the refrigerator. "A bunch of perfectly ripe bananas."

"Would you like one?"

"Yep."

Mike handed Sam a banana.

"Make sure Peg eats one tonight," Sam said. "She needs plenty of potassium."

"Yes, Doc," Mike replied.

Sam peeled the banana. They sat at the kitchen table while Mike told him about the information obtained from Dressler's computer.

"Do you know Dressler?" Mike asked.

"Nope."

"I want to talk to him, but he hasn't returned my phone calls. His wife is—" Mike stopped.

"What?" Sam asked.

"Dressler's wife is in the hospital receiving treatment for cancer. Peg's car is in the parking lot at the emergency room, and I need to pick it up. Could you give me a ride over there? Maybe we can talk to Dressler."

During the drive to the hospital, Mike told Sam about his bike ride along Cohulla Creek and the encounter with Mr. Forrest and Jack Hatcher near Horseshoe Bottoms. Sam listened without interrupting.

"What do you think?" Mike asked when he finished. "If this was a movie, it would be a good place for the Lord to tell you something specific that will help me defend you."

Sam shrugged. "Believe me, I'd like more light myself. Cohulla Creek is a pretty spot. Years ago, I would go for long walks far back into those woods. I'd hate to see it ruined."

They parked beside Peg's car and walked around to the hospital's main entrance. Babies were born in Shelton, broken bones set, and minor surgery performed, but serious cases were whisked to Asheville or beyond. It puzzled Mike that Dressler's wife was receiving care at the local hospital. There were only two floors to the facility. They approached the information desk.

"Mrs. Dressler's room, please," Mike said.

An older woman serving as the volunteer on duty punched a few keys and looked at her computer screen.

"Room 237."

They walked down a spotless hallway to the elevator area. Mike pushed the Up button. The elevators at the Barlow County Hospital were nursing-home slow. It took an incredibly long time to travel up one floor. Mike fidgeted while they waited for the elevator door to open.

"If Dressler is here, let me do the talking," Mike said.

"Are you going to tell me that every time we go somewhere?"

"Yes, until further notice. Keep all your blood-on-the-doorpost comments to yourself."

The elevator door opened, and an orderly rolled out an old woman on a gurney so Mike and Sam could enter. At the second level, Mike impatiently waited for the door to open then walked quickly down the hall. Sam lagged behind.

"Come on," Mike called over his shoulder.

Sam didn't respond. Mike reached room 237 as a nurse exited.

"Is Mr. Dressler here?" Mike asked.

"No, I think he left to get something to eat."

"Did he say when he'd be back?"

"No, but he's never gone for long."

Mike turned to Sam.

"We could wait in the lobby and catch him on the way in. I don't want to intrude into his time with his wife—"

While Mike talked, Sam pushed open the door to the room.

"Where are you going?" Mike asked sharply. "We don't know these people."

Sam didn't respond but continued into the room. Mike looked up and down the hallway. No one seemed to be paying attention. He followed Sam into the room.

The woman in the bed was a bony silhouette beneath the sheets with a single IV tube attached to her left hand. She looked old, but after a closer look, Mike suspected she was in her mid-fifties.

It didn't take medical training to see she was near death. Four times since becoming a minister, Mike had been present when someone died, and on two occasions he'd heard the telltale breathing pattern that signaled the end. He stopped just inside the door. Sam walked directly up to the bed, held the woman's hand for a second, and gently touched her on the cheek.

"Marie," Sam said. "Papa sent me to you."

"No," Mike began, then stopped.

The ragged breathing continued. Mike stepped to the end of the bed and watched.

Sam leaned over and began speaking into the dying woman's ear. Mike couldn't hear what he said. Mike nervously glanced at the door. There could be an ugly scene if Brian Dressler walked in while two strange men hovered around his helpless wife. Sam touched two of his fingers to his tongue and placed them on the woman's forehead. He sighed loudly several times and blew into the woman's face. He seemed to be watching something closely then straightened up and turned to Mike.

"We can go now."

Relieved, Mike moved toward the door. In a few seconds, they would be in the hallway where they could either leave or wait for Dressler. He glanced back to make sure Sam was in tow. When he stepped forward, he collided with the wooden door as it opened into the room. Stunned, Mike staggered backward.

"What the—," Dressler said.

Mike put out his hand and touched the wall.

"Sorry," he said as his head cleared. "We were stepping out of the room to wait for you."

Dressler stared at Mike but didn't move out of the way.

"Andrews, isn't it?" he asked.

"That's right, Mike Andrews."

Dressler extended his hand. "I remember you from Maxwell Forrest's office. I heard you went into the ministry. Thanks for coming. Marie and I don't have a pastor to help us and haven't attended church in years."

"That's okay," Mike managed. "And this is my friend, Sam."

Dressler shook Sam's hand.

"We should have waited in the hall," Mike began.

"No problem. You just startled me. I've been here by myself for a couple of days. No one has visited." Dressler paused. "You may not have heard, but I'm no longer with the bank."

"I know," Mike replied. "Braxton Hodges is the one who told me about your wife."

"I see. Please, sit down."

There were two wooden chairs in front of the air-conditioning unit and a comfortable chair that could be converted into a nighttime couch. Mike and Sam sat in the wooden chairs.

"Hospice nurses were coming to the house," Dressler continued, "but she reached the point that I couldn't handle the in-between times."

"Braxton told me she was receiving treatment for the cancer," Mike said.

"No, we're finished with all that." Dressler looked at the floor. "There's nothing to do but wait. She's been unconscious for three days. The doctor said she might go anytime."

"Her eyes are open," Sam said.

Sure enough, Marie Dressler's eyes were open, and she was staring at the ceiling.

"Marie!" Dressler said.

When Dressler spoke, his wife's eyes moved in the direction of his voice. The dying woman began moving her lips and making sounds, but Mike couldn't distinguish the words. Dressler immediately leaned over with his ear close to her mouth. Mike caught a few words but had no idea what she was saying. He glanced at Sam, who was sitting with his eyes closed, a slight smile on his face, and his hands clasped in front of his stomach. Mike looked back at Dressler. As his wife continued whispering to him, the former banker's left cheek revealed the trail of a tear. Dressler remained riveted in front of his wife's face.

In a few moments, he kissed his wife on the forehead near the spot Sam had touched with his fingers. Then, he leaned over and spoke into her right ear. The woman's eyes remained open but revealed no emotion. When Dressler withdrew, she closed her eyes and continued breathing with a steady pace that didn't sound like the harbinger of death. Dressler sat down with a thud and closed his eyes.

The three men sat in silence for several minutes. In most circumstances, the enforced quiet would have felt awkward, but at the time it seemed the natural thing to do. Finally, Dressler looked up.

"I shouldn't have ignored you—," he began.

"Is everything okay now?" Sam asked.

Dressler nodded.

"Including what happened in Mobile?"

"She was speaking so softly, how could you hear?" Dressler responded in surprise. "Did you read her lips?"

"That's not important. What matters is that she can run free into the arms of the Master. She needed His forgiveness and yours."

"But she was more in the right than I was." Dressler shook his head. "It made me mad at God when she became sick. I should have been the one to suffer."

"But Papa is good enough to let both of you make amends."

Sam turned to Mike. "I'm finished here. Why don't you pray together while I step into the hallway?"

Before Mike could respond, Sam rose from his seat and left the room. Mike watched the door shut behind him then turned to Dressler, who had a puzzled look on his face. Mike wasn't prepared to explain Sam's actions and didn't want any questions.

"May I pray for you?" he asked quickly.

Dressler nodded.

Mike bowed his head and closed his eyes. He spoke hesitantly at first but in a few moments gained confidence. Words started coming easily. As soon as he finished one sentence, the next one stood ready to take its place. Several times, words of familiar Bible verses prompted his requests for Brian and Marie Dressler. He didn't rush, but let the pace of the prayer form as his inward impressions set the tempo. He continued until nothing remained to say except "Amen."

He glanced up into Brian Dressler's face. Marie's eyes remained closed, but the banker's eyes were at peace. He reached across and shook Mike's hand.

"Thank you, thank you," he said warmly. "While you were praying, it seemed the weight of the world rolled off my shoulders. The past few months have been unbelievably difficult."

"You're welcome."

Mike stood.

"Tell the other man from your church how much I appreciate you coming," Dressler said.

Mike tried to think of a smooth segue into legal matters, but when he saw Marie Dressler's serene face over her husband's shoulder, he didn't have the heart to bring it up. He took a step backward toward the door.

"I will. Call if I can help you."

MIKE RETURNED TO THE HALLWAY; SAM WASN'T IN SIGHT. MIKE approached the nurses' station and handed his card to the woman behind the counter.

"I'm a minister helping the Dressler family. Can I be placed on the list to obtain information about her condition?"

The woman took the card. "I'll clear it with her husband."

"Of course." Mike glanced down the hall, but there was still no sight of Sam. "Did you see a heavyset, white-haired man come out of Mrs. Dressler's room?" he asked the nurse.

"No, but I just returned from break."

Mike walked slowly down the hallway, peering into rooms with open doors, half expecting to see Sam leaning over someone he'd never met. But there was no sign of him. Mike returned to the elevator and downstairs to the main lobby. Sam was sitting in a chair reading the newspaper.

"What are you doing?" Mike asked.

"Not what we thought when we came here tonight."

"Yes, that's true," Mike admitted. "After I prayed, I couldn't bring myself to ask Dressler any questions about your case. I'll have to find another time to bring it up."

"That's okay. Have you noticed how most people thought the Master should be doing one thing, but He was often interested in doing something else?"

"Yes."

"Why is that?"

Mike thought a moment. "Because He only did what He saw His Father doing."

"Yep. And living that way is what this life is all about. Tonight did more for my case than a bunch of those motions you filed at the courthouse."

They walked out into the night air. With the setting of the sun, air from the mountains drifted down on Shelton. Even in the middle of summer, evenings were often cool. Mike shivered slightly.

"Where did you meet Marie Dressler?" he asked Sam as they stepped from the sidewalk to the parking lot.

"In that hospital room."

"I mean before tonight."

"Never."

"Then how did you know her name?"

Sam grinned. "It's on the plastic bracelet they wrap around your wrist when you come into the hospital."

Mike chuckled. "Okay. But it didn't say anything about Mobile on the bracelet, did it?"

"No, Papa shared that with me."

"Are you going to tell me about it?"

"Nope. That stuff is washed from the record books of heaven."

They neared the cars.

"Is she going to live?" Mike asked.

"Yep. I believe she'll live forever. I threw her a lifeline, and she grabbed hold of it with all her might. Her flesh is weak, but her spirit is willing."

"But what about here on earth? Is she going to get well? I've never seen a miraculous recovery from terminal cancer."

"Oh, it can happen. But I don't want to be presumable."

"You mean, presumptuous."

"That, too."

Nineteen

MONDAY MORNING, PEG WAS EXAMINED BY DR. CRAWFORD, HER obstetrician, who kept her homebound and on bed rest until her next appointment. Peg tried to protest, but the doctor wouldn't entertain debate.

"Peg, at your age it's not the time to take chances. We'll monitor the baby with monthly ultrasounds during the rest of the pregnancy. If everything looks fine, I'll let you get up during the third trimester. Maybe earlier, but no promises."

Peg was glum when Mike opened the car door for her.

"Do you feel like stopping by the hospital for a few minutes?" he asked as they left the doctor's office. "I'd like to check on Marie Dressler, the woman Sam and I visited on Friday evening."

"I don't see how I can protest. According to Dr. Crawford, I'm at your mercy for the next eight months."

"No, according to your cruise ship dream, it's the other way around."

Mike drove to the hospital and parked in a clergy spot.

"I'll be right back," he said. "I won't be long."

"Don't rush. I'm not going to run away."

There was more activity on the ward than there had been Friday evening. Several people joined him in the slow-motion ride to the second floor. Mike walked past the nurses' station to Marie Dressler's room. The door was shut. Mike knocked and waited, but there was no answer. He pushed open the door and looked inside.

The room was empty, the bed neatly made.

Mike's heart skipped at the possibility the sick woman had gone home. He opened the closet. No personal belongings remained in the room.

He returned to the nurses' station and introduced himself.

"Did Marie Dressler go home?" he asked.

"No, she expired Saturday morning."

"Expired?"

"Yes, she died at 5:46 a.m."

Mike deflated. "Where was the body taken?"

"It was picked up by Lingerhalter's Funeral Home."

Mike returned to the car.

"How is she?" Peg asked.

"Dead," Mike answered flatly.

"Oh."

Mike phoned Braxton Hodges at the newspaper.

"I met with Dressler at the hospital on Friday, but we didn't talk about the case," Mike said. "When I came back this morning, I found out his wife died on Saturday. Do you know anything about the arrangements?"

"We received a group e-mail this morning that the funeral service and burial will be in Mobile."

"Any idea when Dressler will return?"

"I'm not sure. I'd be surprised if he hangs around the newspaper. A guy like him can relocate and find a higher paying job at a bank."

"Let me know when he shows up."

"Sure. I want to get to the bottom of this as much as you do."

"I thought she might recover," Mike said to Peg when he hung up the phone. "I've never had a hospital visit like the one Friday night."

"Tell me about it."

Mike gave her the details. Peg listened without comment until the end.

"How old was she?"

"I'm guessing in her mid-fifties, but she looked older."

"Did they have children?"

"I don't know. It didn't come up."

Judge bounded past them and around to the backyard when they opened the garage door.

"With me out of commission, how is he going to get his exercise?" Peg asked. "He needs a good run every day."

"That will fall on me."

The next morning, Mike rolled out of the smaller bed he shared with Peg in the downstairs bedroom and stumbled into a jogging suit. He disdained skintight cycling gear and forbade Peg from buying him formfitting black shorts or aerodynamic nylon shirts for Christmas. "Don't be too hard on him," Peg mumbled as Mike tied his shoelaces.

"Are you talking to me or Judge?"

Peg rolled over and snuggled deeper into her pillow.

It was still dark when Mike and Judge went down the street to the entrance of a nature trail that skirted their neighborhood. The trail ran along the back of the subdivision and descended to the bottom of the hill not far from traffic light eight. It was a quick five minutes to reach the bottom and a strenuous ten-minute climb to the top of the ridge beyond Mike and Peg's house. Mike listened with satisfaction as Judge panted when they strained toward the crest of the hill and turned around for another descent. Two circuits were enough to give both man and dog a vigorous morning workout. When Mike returned to the house, Peg was in the kitchen with the coffee dripping into the pot.

"What are you doing out of bed?" he asked sharply.

"Making a slight detour from the bathroom to fix your coffee."

"Don't make me handcuff you to the bedpost."

Peg poured a cup of coffee and started toward the downstairs bedroom. "Surveillance cameras would be more humane. Or you could ask Judge to keep a log of my activities."

"Judge would be cheaper. We'll give him a try first, but I'm warning you in advance that I might make a surprise visit home to check on you."

"Visit any time."

Mike sat on the edge of the bed. "Are we okay with each other?"

"Yes."

Mike took a breath and exhaled. "Good."

After Mike cleaned up in the master bathroom and dressed for work, he went to the downstairs bedroom. Peg was sitting up in bed with her Bible open.

"Did you know Sam and Muriel pray together every morning at the kitchen table?" she asked.

"She also fixes homemade biscuits and gravy."

"Which explains the size of Sam's belly. We don't have to do everything like the Millers; however, praying together would be a low-fat thing to do before you leave for work." Peg stretched out her hands. "They hold hands."

Mike joined his hands with hers. "Anything else?"

"Not that I remember."

"Does Muriel pray?"

"I'm not sure, but since she prayed for me the other night, I haven't felt any pain. That's another reason I wanted to argue with Dr. Crawford about the need for bed rest, but I guess that wouldn't have made any difference in her recommendations."

"No, but we can still pray."

Mike closed his eyes. He started to speak, but the same inner nudge that had prompted him to pray at the hospital now restrained him. Other than blessing a meal, he and Peg hadn't prayed together more than a handful of times in their marriage. Finally, Peg spoke.

"Jesus," she said in a soft voice, "we love You this morning."

Mike pressed his lips together. The Name, spoken by his wife, touched a tender spot in his heart. Peg continued, and Mike listened in amazement as she talked to God with a familiarity that made him slightly jealous. His wife, who for years had been resistant to his brand of faith, had leaped over him into the arms of Jesus.

"Thank you for being close to us today," she said. "Amen."

Mike looked within his heart for something to add, but everything that came to mind seemed petty. He squeezed her hand.

"Amen," he said.

Peg opened her eyes.

"Why didn't you pray?" she asked.

Mike stood, came over, and kissed her on the cheek.

"Because there wasn't anything to add."

He kissed her again.

"Call me if you need anything. I'll be home before the session meeting to check on you."

"I'll be good. I promise."

WHEN MIKE ARRIVED AT THE CHURCH, DELORES WAS TYPING the weekly report of church statistics. Mike documented every change in attendance at church meetings, Sunday school classes, and the size of offerings. Having the data at his fingertips had been handy at session meetings, and so far, all the important numbers since his arrival at the church had been up.

"Giving has been down the past three weeks," Delores quipped as he came by her desk. "I don't recall that happening in quite a while."

"But attendance has been up. Don't fret the weekly numbers. Monthly totals are more significant."

"Then why do you want me to keep a weekly record?"

"Because it helps me stay more current," Mike responded patiently.

Delores sniffed. "I just don't want to be doing busywork."

"It's helpful. You know there are elders who love to see the latest data. Any calls this morning?"

"No complaints, if that's what you mean."

MIKE WENT INTO HIS OFFICE. THE FIRST ITEM ON HIS TO-DO list was to locate a handwriting expert. In normal circumstances, he would have called Bobby Lambert for a referral. He tapped a finger against his desk and considered his options. An Internet search would yield results but no guarantee of competency. Experts for hire could be nothing more than pretenders with bogus diplomas and spurious pedigrees. He dialed Greg Freeman. This time a secretary answered the phone and put him through.

"Good morning," Mike said. "Is this the number to call for free legal advice?"

Freeman laughed. "A lot of people believe so. What can I do for you?"

"I need a handwriting expert. Any recommendations?"

Freeman was silent for a moment. "About a year ago, I deposed a handwriting expert in a will contest case. He testified against my client's position, so I tried to discredit him. The more questions I asked, the more convincing he became. I couldn't shake his research and opinion."

"Sounds like my man. Can you locate his contact info?"

"Just a minute."

Mike waited. Freeman came back on the line.

"Darius York. He doesn't have a PhD, but that's not how they learn the craft. York is a former FBI agent who retired to the mountains near Blowing Rock. He supplements his income by providing handwriting analysis. The first ten minutes of the deposition were a recitation of his qualifications and experience. I thought he would never stop talking about how much he knew."

"Is he expensive?"

"Yes, but he's close by."

Mike frowned. "I need something fast. West has put the Miller case on a fast track."

"Why?"

"I suspect it's political, but that doesn't do me any good. I've got to get ready."

"Here's the number for York, and you can mention me as a referral. It will flatter his ego."

"Is he arrogant?"

"A little, but he can back it up."

Mike jotted down the number.

"Thanks."

"Sure. If you need anything else, let me know."

Mike hung up the phone and immediately punched in the numbers for York. An answering machine picked up the call, and he left a detailed message.

Mike made copies of the checks, Sam's written statement, and the estimate for cutting the grass at the church. He hoped the documents would provide enough comparison samples of Sam's handwriting for York to render an opinion.

MID-AFTERNOON, MIKE WENT HOME TO CHECK ON PEG AND found her napping on the couch in the great room with an open notebook turned upside down on the floor beside her. She woke up, stretched up her arms, and held him tightly around the neck when he leaned over to kiss her.

"How are you surviving?" he asked.

"Wishing I really was on the deck of a cruise ship. One day of inactivity is not too bad, but when I think about months with nothing to do except travel between the bed and the couch, it gets depressing. Both Judge and I started getting restless when it was time for our run."

"Are you feeling okay?"

"Yes, but it would have been nice if you'd come home for lunch."

"I worked on the Miller case part of the morning and spent lunch in a counseling session. I've been putting people off who want to come see me, but there was a husband and wife who really needed emergency help."

"Did you help them?"

"I don't know. The husband is hardheaded and resistant to my suggestions.

Sometimes I think my opinion carried more weight as a lawyer than it does as a minister. If he files for divorce, he'll find out that no one gets his way one hundred percent of the time."

Peg scooted away from the edge of the couch and patted it with her hand. Mike sat down.

"I'm glad we didn't go that route."

"Me, too."

"Are you ready for the session meeting?"

"Mostly. I have to print copies of the agenda and get the room ready."

"Can't Delores do it?"

Mike put his hand on Peg's forehead. "Do you have a fever? You sound delusional. I made the mistake the other day of asking her to do something new, and she went into a funk."

"Can I ask you to do something?" Peg asked.

Mike withdrew his hand. "I'm open to reasonable negotiation."

"Where's the trust?"

Mike saluted. "I'm wearing my waiter's uniform, and your every wish is my command."

"Pick up my notebook."

Mike leaned over and retrieved the notebook.

"Go into the office, find a blank page, and write me a short letter. Make it something you'd like me to read while you're gone tonight."

"What kind of letter?"

"A friendly one," Peg answered.

"That shouldn't be too hard."

"Okay."

"And when you finish, put a load of white clothes in the washer, pick up and vacuum the upstairs bedroom, and clean the master bathroom."

"Dr. Crawford told you to stay off the steps," Mike responded sharply. "Have you been upstairs?"

"No, but you have, and I have a mental image of our bedroom and bath that needs to be erased. After you finish, we'll plan an early supper so you can get back to the church."

Mike took the notebook into the office and sat at the desk. Handwritten personal notes had never been a big part of his relationship with Peg, but he was smart enough to realize she wanted to include them in their future. He started to write something sentimental, but his ideas, though nice, didn't feel right. He leaned back in the chair.

And remembered the letter Sam wrote Peg.

That letter needed a bookend, a written resolution for any doubts lingering in Peg's mind that he was ready to forgive the past and go on. Turning to a blank page in the notebook, he began to write.

He intended to fill, at most, a single page, but it quickly stretched to four sheets. Thoughts and emotions he hadn't expressed in person flowed out. And he also discovered his need to ask Peg's forgiveness. She was his wife, but he'd been selfish, too—hiding behind a few Bible verses in Galatians as justification for unilateral action that fundamentally altered their lives. In part, he'd used the Bible as an excuse to impose his will, not as guidance for a future to be shared with the one God joined to walk with him.

Having acknowledged his failings and asked for forgiveness, he concluded with words of hope for what lay ahead. At the bottom of the page, he wrote in large letters "All my love, Mike."

"I'm done!" he called out from the office when he finished.

"Was it that hard finding something nice to write?" Peg responded from the couch. "You've been in there forever!"

Mike returned to the great room and handed her the folded letter.

"No, I just wanted to put off starting my chores."

Twenty

MIKE FINISHED HIS PREPARATIONS FOR THE SESSION MEETING with plenty of time to spare. He'd put on a fresh shirt and tie before returning to the church. He wanted to look his best for the meeting.

After every agenda was neatly in place and the decaf coffee was dripping into the pot, he walked around the room, praying silently as he placed his hand on each chair. While making his second circuit, a voice interrupted him.

"What are you doing?" Bobby asked.

Mike turned quickly toward the door. His former partner's shirt might have been starched twelve hours before, but it was thoroughly wrinkled now. His yellow tie was loosened.

"Waiting for you," Mike said. "How's it going?"

Bobby plopped down in the nearest chair. "Have you ever felt like you have too many irons in the fire?"

"A thousand times."

"That's the way I feel, and I'm worried that a couple of them are about to be taken out to brand me."

"Avoid that if possible."

"How's Peg?"

"On bed rest."

"I wish the doctor would tell me to lie around the house and do nothing except press the remote control for a few weeks. Park cleaned out his office and left yesterday. At least eighty percent of his remaining caseload has landed in my office."

Mike poured Bobby a cup of coffee.

"I'll try not to keep you here too late tonight," he said. "We have a light agenda."

Bobby took a sip of coffee. "How's business?"

"What do you mean?"

"Your caseload. Since I haven't heard from you, I assume you're still handling the Miller case."

"Yes, but it's moving along at a fast clip. Ken West is bumping it up on the trial calendar."

Mike studied Bobby's face for any response, but his former partner stared past him across the room. Bobby picked up the agenda and took a sip of coffee.

"I'm glad to see you have the Miller case on the agenda for discussion. If the case is jumping up the calendar, I look forward to hearing about your exit strategy."

Mike glanced down at the packet in front of him. "That's not about the criminal case. Miller cut the grass this week. If you come out in the daytime, you can see what a neat job he did."

Before Bobby responded, Libby Gorman and Barbara Harcourt came in together and were immediately followed by Milton Chesterfield, along with the other four members of the session.

"Did you ride together?" Mike asked in surprise.

"Everyone but Libby and Bobby had supper with Barbara," Milton responded.

"Did you show them any new photos of the Florida grandkids?" Mike asked Barbara.

"Only a few," the older woman responded crisply.

"Let's get started," Mike said to the group. "I've promised Bobby that I'll get him home at a decent hour."

When everyone was seated, Mike continued. "The first item on the agenda is the quarterly report of the finance committee."

Rick Weston, the credit manager at a local car dealership, served as the chairperson of the committee. A quiet man, Rick rarely expressed an opinion. He read the report in a monotone voice. Mike was relieved when no one pointed out the slight downturn in giving.

"On the other side of Rick's report are the attendance figures," Mike said. "We continue to attract new visitors almost every Sunday."

They plodded through the remaining committee reports. It had all the marks of a lethargic meeting. Mike had placed Sam's bid to cut the grass as the last item and labeled it "Grounds Maintenance Bid from Miller Lawn Care." As the elders moved through the agenda with no more than minor discussion, Mike inwardly debated whether to present Sam's bid or table it until another meeting. Bobby had yawned several times, but they were ahead of schedule.

"The last item is a bid from a new company to cut the grass and maintain the shrubs and flower beds. Does anyone have an opinion about our current service?"

"It's not good," Libby responded immediately. "A few weeks ago, I noticed that the grass on one side of the church had been cut, but the other side looked ragged. It reminded me of my grandson's hair after his older sister gave him a haircut."

Milton coughed. "Is this a bid from Sam Miller, the man you're representing in the criminal case?"

"Yes, but this doesn't have anything to do with that," Mike answered. "Miller's bid is fifteen percent cheaper than our current service, and I believe he'll do a better job."

"Does he need the money to pay your fee?" Milton asked.

"No, I'm handling the case pro bono. I thought I made that clear when I asked permission to help him."

"And it doesn't concern you that he's charged with stealing money from a church?" Milton persisted.

"Yes, but he won't have access to our bank accounts or records."

"The church would pay him with a check," Rick said softly. "Then he would have our account information."

At Rick's comment, Mike quickly examined the faces around the table. Everyone except Libby Gorman looked grim. Libby appeared perplexed.

"You haven't found another attorney to represent Miller?" Milton asked.

"No, he wants me to help him, and I'm willing to see it through. The case will come up for trial in a couple of weeks. After that, my involvement will end."

Bobby pulled the knot in his tie closer to his neck. "Unless it isn't called for trial, or you request a continuance, or Miller is convicted and you file an appeal."

"Of course, those are possibilities. Trial work is always unpredictable."

Barbara Harcourt spoke, her voice strained and imperious. "I wasn't here when the session discussed this matter, but in my opinion, it is totally improper for our minister to represent a criminal. There are plenty of lawyers around, and this man should have hired one of them."

"I understand," Mike answered, keeping his voice calm. "But this is a unique—"

"There's only one thing to consider," Milton interrupted, pointing his finger at Mike. "We've gone over this matter in detail on two occasions, and we want a commitment from you to withdraw immediately from the case. We didn't get a chance to talk to Libby before the meeting, but the rest of us are unanimous in our decision."

"And I voted against it in the first place," Libby said.

"Was that the reason for your joint supper before this meeting?" Mike asked, his voice hardening. "Don't you think it would have been appropriate to allow me to offer my perspective before ambushing me at this meeting?"

Milton cleared his throat.

"We're aware of your position. It would have been pointless to rehash it."

Mike turned to Bobby. "Are you part of this?"

"I made my position clear two weeks ago," Bobby answered. "None of us enjoy putting this kind of pressure on you, but it's the only way to make you wake up and realize that what you're doing is inconsistent with your calling as the senior minister of this church."

"Really? Doesn't the Bible say that God is interested in justice? What do the prophets say about acquitting the guilty and convicting the innocent?"

"We're not here to debate," Milton responded. "We need your answer."

Mike waited until everyone in the room looked at him then slowly scanned the room. Only Rick and another elder didn't hold his gaze.

"And if I decide to honor my commitment to Sam Miller," Mike said slowly, "what then?"

"Get out of the case or leave the church. Is that clear enough?" Milton shot back.

Mike hesitated. Political prudence would dictate a request for time to consider his options, but he didn't feel either political or prudent. He wanted to call the elders' bluff. The church had grown and become much stronger since his arrival. Many of the new members were linked to him as leader. Any harsh action taken against him would split the congregation. He turned to Bobby.

"I need to know your position," he said.

Bobby looked at Milton and nodded his head. The exchange between the two men pierced Mike's heart. He'd hoped Bobby was a reluctant, not willing, participant in the assault against him.

Milton took a sheet of paper from his pocket. "We've made arrangements for an interim pastor to fill the pulpit."

"You've already lined up someone to replace me?"

"On a temporary basis. He's a retired minister from Shelby. You would be given a sabbatical."

"Sounds more like a permanent suspension than a sabbatical."

Bobby spoke. "That's not what we would tell the congregation. In fact, our hope is that we could present this action in a positive light. Peg is experiencing a high-risk pregnancy and needs your help at home. We would announce the sabbatical as a gesture from the session to accommodate your family situation. Then, if things work out, you could return to the pulpit without any stigma of disciplinary action."

Mike couldn't believe what he was hearing.

"The sabbatical would be with full pay and benefits for three months," Rick added. "One month for each year of service."

"Thanks, that's generous," Mike replied with thinly veiled sarcasm.

Milton Chesterfield's eyes flashed. "You better believe it is! And if you want to lose it, keep talking! Just because you used to be a hotshot lawyer in Shelton doesn't mean you can come out here and run over those of us who have been in this church longer than you've been alive!"

"If I recall, you were on the committee that interviewed me and voted unanimously for me to come," Mike responded coldly.

"Stop it!" Bobby held up his hands. "This isn't easy for any of us, and we don't need to end up in an argument. I move we ask for a written response from Mike by the end of the week. If he withdraws from the Miller case, this discussion will have served its purpose. If not, we have a plan to move the church forward and allow Mike to do what he wants to do."

"Second," Barbara responded quickly.

"All in favor," Milton said.

Mike watched seven hands rise into the air, and with a sinking feeling in his heart, knew his days as pastor of the Little Creek Church had come to an end.

Normally, Mike stayed after a meeting until everyone departed the premises. Tonight, he couldn't wait to get away. Abandoning all pretense of civility, he left the conference room and walked directly to his car. He heard Bobby call his name, but he didn't turn around. Bobby had been right about one thing—any additional words would only fuel a fight.

During the drive home, Mike's mind raced in a hundred directions. He'd never been threatened with firing in his life. The thought of posting his résumé on the seminary Web site in an effort to locate another pastorate made him feel slightly nauseous. Returning to law practice in Shelton in the face of open animosity from his former firm was not an option. He pulled into his driveway. Ever loyal, Judge greeted him at the kitchen door.

"Peg!" Mike called out. "Where are you?"

"Lifting weights in the bedroom!" she responded. "Please bring me a glass of ice water."

Mike took longer than necessary to fix the glass of water. He stopped to let Judge go out to the backyard.

"You sure are a slow waiter!" Peg yelled. "In my dream you were always at my elbow!"

Mike took the glass of water into the bedroom. Peg was leaning against a couple of pillows with a sketch pad in her lap.

"What are you drawing?"

"A concept. I'd like to paint some watercolors for the baby's room."

"Maybe you can do a few extras to sell."

Peg laughed. "Don't be silly. I'm not interested in going commercial."

"In a few months we could use the money."

"What do you mean?"

"It's serious."

Peg's face fell. Mike sat on the edge of the bed.

"The elders told me to get out of Sam's case or leave the church."

"What? That's crazy!"

Mike told her what had happened at the meeting. When he reached the part about the sabbatical and the reason for it, she began to cry. He handed her a box of tissue.

"Do you want me to stop?" he asked.

Peg blew her nose. "No, it just hurts so badly. I'm more mad than sad. To use my pregnancy as an excuse to the congregation is so dishonest and unfair."

"Yeah, it's cowardly."

His voice growing more despondent as the adrenaline released during the meeting drained from his system, Mike finished his account of the night's events.

"I've prided myself on staying ahead of the curve on the political activity taking place at the church, but this caught me off guard. Bobby should have tipped me off to a mutiny of this magnitude, but he may have been the one who came up with the sabbatical idea in the first place."

"Elizabeth Lambert hasn't returned my calls for almost two weeks."

Mike grunted. "She didn't have the courage to face you, knowing what was in the works."

Peg shook her head. "It doesn't make any sense. Such a mean attitude. If they knew more about Sam—"

"It wouldn't make any difference. He's already a convicted felon in the minds of some members of the session. And Milton was just looking for an excuse to vent his animosity toward me. To him, Sam is irrelevant."

"Who agrees with Milton?"

Mike shrugged. "I'm not sure how many people believe the church would be better off going backward than forward. I've worked hard for three years to communicate a vision for the future—tonight it came crashing down in a few minutes. The support I thought I had among the leadership of the church was an illusion."

"That may not be true."

"I have to assume the worst. Part of my failure has been in believing what people said to my face and trusting it as their true opinion."

"Mike, that's awful. It makes the church sound like a charade."

"It's made up of imperfect people."

"Who are supposed to be getting better."

Mike smiled slightly. "Like you are. I'd like to think you're the result of my ministry, but Sam Miller has had more to do with what God is doing in your life than I have."

"That's not true. You've been so steady and faithful. Even when I was angry with you or wanted to ignore you, it wasn't possible. And you've helped a lot of people."

Mike kissed her forehead. "That's sweet, but can't you let me wallow in self-pity and doubt for a few minutes?"

"We'll schedule your pity party later. When are you going to tell Sam about this?"

"I'm not sure I should. He's facing enough pressure without taking on my problems. I don't like being coerced into doing—"

"What you don't want to do," Peg said, finishing his sentence. "That's your pride and ego talking."

"So? It's still about doing the right thing."

"And when you're upset isn't the best time to make an important decision. You've told me that plenty of times when I was in an emotional upheaval. Sam needs to be brought into the loop. He'll find out anyway if he and Muriel visit the church."

"It'll be all over town," Mike added gloomily. "There's no way the spin Bobby wants to put on this is going to stand up to the scrutiny of the rumor mill. One of the elders will crack, and the real reason will leak out. The fight within the church will begin, and the whole community can enjoy the latest gossip about the big blowup at Little Creek Church."

"Don't make your final decision until you talk to Sam. I've supported you on this from the beginning, but you should talk to him and give it some time. You don't have to respond until the end of the week. When you figure out the right decision, you'll make it."

"Are you worried about what will happen to us?"

Peg pointed to Mike's letter that lay open on the nightstand. It seemed a week since he'd penned it, and he'd forgotten all about it.

"Of course, but a woman can trust her future to a man who would write a letter like that."

Twenty-one

MIKE SPENT A RESTLESS NIGHT TOSSING AND TURNING IN BED. Shortly before dawn, he gave up on sleep and went downstairs to the kitchen. He tried to pray and read the Bible, but couldn't concentrate. He looked at the clock. It was early, but he suspected Sam Miller didn't linger in bed. He picked up the phone.

"Did I wake you up?" he asked when Sam answered the phone.

"Nope. I've been listening to you all night."

"What?"

"In my dreams."

"I hope I made sense. Can you meet me for breakfast?"

"Sure. Muriel will enjoy sleeping in."

"How about Traci's in thirty minutes?"

"Yep."

Mike put on a pair of sweatpants and a T-shirt. When he arrived at the restaurant, the sun had turned the sky a dull gray. In a few minutes, it would rise above the clouds to dispel the remaining darkness. The restaurant did a brisk morning business from customers anxious to get a two-cups-of-coffee start on the day. Sam's truck was parked at the side of the building. Mike entered and saw Sam sitting alone in a booth. Judy brought over coffee. Sam hadn't shaved for a couple of days, and Mike rubbed his own bristly chin.

"Judy, do you know Sam Miller?" Mike asked after the waitress greeted him.

Judy smiled. "Yeah, Sam and Muriel have been there a few times when I needed them."

Judy took their order.

Mike glanced around the restaurant. He wished he didn't have any worries greater than whether to order his eggs scrambled or over easy.

"Do you know why I wanted to talk to you?" he asked.

Sam didn't hesitate. "The fire started."

"Yes. I got out of an elders' meeting last night without being fired on the spot, but I didn't hear the sound of any sirens coming to the rescue."

Mike told Sam about the meeting. In the middle, Judy brought the food. Mike managed a few bites between sentences. Sam's remained untouched.

"Aren't you going to eat?" he asked. "There's nothing worse than cold grits."

Mike saw a deep sadness in the older man's eyes that made them look more gray than blue.

"How can I eat when I hear about Papa's children devouring one of their own? Go ahead."

Mike continued his story.

"It was rough," he concluded. "I didn't want to burden you with this, but Peg insisted I talk it over with you."

"She was right. And it helps me understand a dream I had last night."

"About the church?"

"Nope. You and I were in the courtroom. Judge Coberg was there along with the young woman district attorney, Miss Hall. Four people who have been my longtime enemies were in the jury box."

"Who? I want to make sure I strike them if they turn up in the jury pool."

Sam shook his head. "You don't need to know. Not yet. One is dead and another moved away a long time ago. The other two are still in the area. Anyway, when I saw the jurors, I knew I didn't have a chance in court. I went into the hallway. Muriel was there, and when I told her about the four people in the jury box, she got scared. I hugged her, and we went back into the courtroom. The judge banged his gavel, and we left."

"What happened next?"

"That's it."

"Did you go to jail?"

"No."

Mike poked his eggs with his fork. His breakfast had also grown cold.

"Do you think you accepted the plea bargain?"

"Is that how it would work?"

"Maybe. Although, the judge would want to talk to you, so you could explain that you were taking the DA's offer because you didn't want to go to jail, not because you committed the crime."

"If I did that, what would happen at your church?"

"The reason given for suspending me would go away, but I'd still have to deal with the opposition of one or more of the elders." Mike leaned forward and spoke with all the earnestness he could muster. "But I want to make one thing clear—you're not going to plead guilty to a crime so I can keep my position at the church."

"That's what I have to decide, isn't it?"

MIKE LEFT THE RESTAURANT, NOT SURE WHETHER TO GO HOME or to the church. Driving through town, he concluded hiding out at home would be an act of retreat. Even if his days at the church were numbered, he was determined to hold his head up high until the end. He called Peg on his cell phone and told her about his breakfast with Sam.

"At this point, I don't believe I could trust his decision to take the plea bargain," Mike said.

"But he's the client. He can decide for himself."

"That's how the conversation ended. When I first met him, I questioned Sam's competency. If he pleads guilty just to help me, I'll know he's crazy."

"It's not right for an innocent man to plead guilty, but Muriel may not want to risk him going to jail. Are you on your way home?"

"No, I'm going to the church."

"Why?"

"To take your advice and carry on as normally as possible."

Mike felt a surge of confidence as he turned into the church parking lot. It reminded him of the calm before the start of a big jury trial. The challenge was at hand; the preparation complete; ignoring the battle ahead not an option; he was going to war. In those moments, he'd experienced the euphoria reserved for happy warriors. He marched through the front door of the administration building.

"Good morning, Delores," he said cheerily. "I've been up early and ready for the day."

"I hope it gets better," she responded. "How was the session meeting?"

Mike quickly studied the church secretary's face. Delores couldn't conceal knowledge of information as inflammatory as the previous night's action by the elders. Her countenance was clear. Libby Gorman had kept her mouth shut—at least for the first twelve hours.

"Brisk and businesslike," Mike answered. "Any calls?"

"Uh, yes, I put a note on your desk from a man named York. He said he was a former FBI agent."

"Good. Hold my calls for a few minutes."

Mike phoned the number for Darius York. A man with a Midwestern accent answered the phone.

"York, here."

Mike introduced himself and the reason for the contact.

"How many documents do you have?" York asked.

"Two checks and an interrogation statement that can serve as a sample of my client's handwriting."

"Do you have the documents in front of you?"

"Yes."

"Did he sign the statement?"

"Yes."

"Are the checks originals?"

"No, everything is a copy."

"Does the signature on the two checks look the same to you?"

Mike studied the checks for a moment. "Yes."

"How similar?"

Mike looked more carefully. The shape of every letter, the location of the dot on the *i* in Miller, the curve in the *S* in Sam all matched exactly.

"Identical."

"Can you make the original checks available for analysis?"

"Maybe. The case has been fast-tracked, and I'm not sure who has custody of the original checks. They weren't in the DA's file, so I assume they're at the bank."

"Without the originals, I'm not sure I can help you."

"Why not?"

"Technology. It's not hard to electronically collect a signature and imprint it on a check so that it looks genuine. A copy of the original check masks the transfer process. If the signature appears legit on the copy and that's all I have to work with, I'll have to testify it's a match. I can offer an explanation of the process for lifting a signature and transferring it onto the checks, but you'll have to decide if that type of information helps you or hurts you."

Mike stared at the checks. His theory about Jesse Lavare as the instigator of the charges against Sam was evaporating. "What would the originals show?" he asked.

"I could examine the signatures under a microscope and identify the transfer process, if any."

"And if I can't get the originals?"

"I could still microscopically examine the signatures. If they are identical at the microscopic level, it would give you an argument that the checks are forged, because no one can exactly duplicate a signature. They would be too perfect. I've testified that way in other cases."

"Successfully or unsuccessfully?"

"Both. Juries don't always trust expert witnesses, even former FBI agents."

"You're not trying very hard to market your services."

"I do what I do because I enjoy it. The government sends me three checks every month whether I go outside the door or not."

"Will you examine my copies while I try to locate the originals?"

"Yes. Did the lawyer who referred you have a copy of my fee schedule?"

"No."

"And I can give you the open dates on my calendar."

Mike made notes on a sheet of paper. York was expensive but available.

"Agreed," he said when York finished. "I'll overnight everything to you today."

Mike hung up and wrote down the amount of money he'd need from Sam Miller. With his own job in jeopardy, Mike couldn't finance the case. That check would need Sam's original signature. There was a knock on the door.

"Come in!"

Delores stuck her head inside. "Bobby Lambert called twice while you were on the phone, and you received a fax from your old law firm."

"Did Bobby leave a message?"

"No, I asked if it was an emergency, and he wouldn't tell me."

"Let me see the fax."

Delores handed him several sheets of paper. The cover sheet was from Maxwell Forrest's office. Delores remained standing in front of his desk.

"Anything else?" Mike asked.

"I'm not sure what to say," the secretary said. "I had no idea."

The knowledge absent from her eyes when Mike arrived at the church was now present.

"Libby called you?"

"I got so mad at her that I almost hung up the phone. You've been out of the office a lot, but you do more in half a day than the last two pastors did in half a week. I know what's going on at the church better than any member of the session!"

"Did she tell you about the sabbatical?"

"Yes, and nobody is going to buy that story." Delores's eyes flashed. "I'm going to war on this. In two hours, I can get a phone campaign started that will make the elders wish they'd—"

Mike held up his hand. "Don't. Please. Not yet. Maybe never."

"You can't leave us," Delores shot back. "This church has a chance to be something more than a place where people are married and buried."

Mike couldn't hide his shock at her perspective.

"Don't look so surprised," she continued. "I've seen the good you're doing."

She quickly listed five individuals and three families significantly helped by Mike's ministry.

"There's no way to avoid a big church split if you leave now. The feuding and fussing will be ten times worse than the fight over whether or not to build the new sanctuary."

"Which is why I'm asking you to take it easy. What happens now is more important than my—"

"Don't even start with that stuff," Delores interrupted with a snort. "Giving up and leaving would be the worst thing that you could do for this church. There are plenty of weak preachers who would run at the first sign of trouble, but you've got the backbone to fight. Milton Chesterfield and his family have tried to run this place forever. I thought those days were over, but I guess I was wrong."

"Did Libby tell you they've already contacted an interim pastor who would serve if I'm kicked out on sabbatical?"

"No. Who is it?"

"I'm not sure. Someone from Shelby."

"I'll call Libby and find out more information. I was too mad to listen before."

"Leave her alone. I don't want either one of us to react in a wrong way."

"I can't just sit here and do nothing!"

"Yes, you can. Do you remember Sam Miller and me talking about the church being on fire?"

"Yes. I don't think he should be hanging around here. The man is dangerous and is a threat to—"

"Don't take his words literally. The fire he saw in a dream represented conflict. I didn't see it coming, but now that it's here, I don't want either one of us to pour gas on it. That's not the way this is going to be worked out."

"What do you mean? I've never believed you were a quitter."

"I'm not. Peg and I will pray until we get direction."

Delores sniffed and shook her head. "Prayer is fine, but I'm going outside to smoke a cigarette."

Delores left the office. Mike stood at the window and watched her walk resolutely to the edge of the old cemetery. In a few seconds, she blew out a billow of smoke that showed the vigor she brought to her habit.

Mike returned to his desk and picked up the fax from Mr. Forrest. The cover sheet stated that the attached records constituted the complete Bank of Barlow County investigation into the misappropriation of funds from the Craig Valley Gospel Tabernacle construction account. The papers contained no new information, and Mike knew without a doubt the records were incomplete—the memo from Brian Dressler to Jack Hatcher wasn't included.

He glanced at the two slips indicating the times of Bobby's calls. Still mad at Bobby, Mike dialed the number for Braxton Hodges.

"Any word from Dressler?" he asked.

"No. He's still in Alabama with his family."

"Do you know when he'll get back?"

"No. What have you found out?"

Mike read from the sheets forwarded by Maxwell Forrest.

"At least he responded to you," Hodges said. "He's never returned my calls. I've had my finger on the Record button so long that it's starting to cramp."

"Ken West has his finger on the trigger of the Miller case. It'll appear on the next term of criminal court."

"Whew, you just got involved. Can they do that?"

"Probably. It would be hard for me to argue that my caseload is so heavy I can't be ready for trial. Dressler needs to be questioned and available to testify if needed."

"I'll let you know as soon as he shows up. Any other leads?"

Mike debated whether to mention the encounter with Hatcher, Forrest, and the developers at Cohulla Creek.

"That's a newspaper term," Mike answered, dodging the question. "What have you found out?"

"Not much, unless you consider it important that one of the men mentioned in Dressler's file has a criminal record."

Mike sat up straighter in his seat. "Which one?"

"A guy named Troy Linden from New Jersey. He entered a no contest plea in state court in New Jersey about ten years ago. Got a slap on the wrist and paid a fine of a few thousand dollars."

"What was the charge?" Mike asked, making notes on a legal pad.

"Improper lobbying."

"Bribing a public official?"

"That's what I would guess."

"How did you find this?"

"We're a tiny paper, but we're part of one of the best proprietary databases in the country. It's a great equalizer. When it comes to background information, I can find out as much as a reporter in New York or Los Angeles. Give me a name, and I can give you a history. I punched in everyone mentioned in the files. The info on Troy Linden was a one-paragraph blurb in a local rag that included a quote from his lawyer that his client didn't admit any wrongdoing."

"What did Linden do?"

"No details given."

"Anything interesting on anyone else?"

"No."

"Are you going to follow up on Linden?"

"As soon as I finish an article about the good health benefits of herbs and spices. Did you know a teaspoon of cinnamon a day is great for your heart?"

"I should be chewing a stick right now."

"Me, too. It's a lot better than the cigarettes I used to smoke. Amid all the crazy claims out there, at least no one still believes inhaling the burning residue produced by the leaves of a dried tobacco plant is good for you."

"My secretary at the church might disagree with you."

Mike hung up the phone and called his old law office. Waiting on hold, Mike's anger at his former partner's betrayal began to grow. Until the past twenty-four hours, their friendship had transcended every competing influence. When Bobby answered the phone, Mike spit out his opening comment.

"How did it feel stabbing me in the back last night? It hurt on my end."

Bobby didn't immediately answer.

"Did you hear me?" Mike repeated.

"Yes, but I'm not going to talk to you now."

"Then why did you call?"

"Meet me in the deed room at the courthouse at one-thirty."

"Why do you want to do that?" Mike asked, then listened to the silence of a dead phone.

Mike glared at the receiver for a few seconds before slamming it down. He checked his calendar. He had an appointment at 1:30 p.m. and couldn't go to town in the early afternoon. He didn't call Bobby back to let him know.

A few minutes later, Delores knocked on the doorjamb. Mike glanced up.

"Did you call Bobby Lambert?" she asked. "Libby claimed he was the one who came up with the idea for the sabbatical."

"We talked briefly. He wants to meet me in town after lunch, but I have an appointment."

"Not anymore. It's rescheduled for tomorrow morning at ten."

Mike grunted. "It doesn't matter. I'm still not ready to talk to Bobby. I couldn't keep from getting angry in a one-minute phone conversation."

"Maybe that's what he needs to hear from you. It might make him think."

Mike shook his head. "He's never listened to me, and I doubt he's going to start now."

MIKE WENT HOME TO CHECK ON PEG. THE CHURCH HAD ALWAYS been a place of peace for Mike. Now, his home felt more like a refuge. Peg was lying on the couch in the great room. Mike kissed her on the forehead.

"Can't you do better than that?" Peg responded. "I'm not sick."

Mike kissed her on the lips.

"Thanks," Peg replied. "I didn't have much to look forward to all morning."

Mike sat on the couch beside her feet. "You're one person I can please and be glad doing it," he said. "Did Muriel come by to see you?"

"Yes, she brought supper. It's in the refrigerator. All I have to do is put it in the oven about five o'clock."

"Chitlins?"

"No, but you guessed the right animal. It's a pork loin basted in a special sauce she came up with. There are also lima beans, creamed corn, homemade biscuits, and a pecan pie for dessert."

"I hope Sam won't go hungry."

"And Muriel already knew about the DA's offer to Sam. She brought it up and asked me what I thought about it."

"What did you say?"

"That I don't know the ins and outs of criminal law and never liked criminal cases because you became so focused on your clients that you forgot about me."

"But you think Sam's case is different?"

"You're still one hundred percent focused on it. However, I think he deserves the attention. Did anything happen at the church?"

Mike told her about Delores's strong negative reaction to the session's actions and willingness to heed his advice.

"Can you trust her?" Peg asked when he finished.

"She seemed with me one hundred percent."

"You've tiptoed around her feelings for three years. Why would she suddenly have a less-self-centered attitude?"

Mike thought for a moment. "She considers herself the mother hen of the church. By delivering an ultimatum to me, the elders invaded her turf without asking her permission. And you know that she and Milton have been in competition for years."

"Just be careful. You can be too quick to trust someone who claims to be doing the right thing when in fact they have a secondary agenda."

"What would be Delores's agenda? She was ready to go on the warpath for me and burn her bridges."

"I'm not sure. I've always thought she was the type of person who could be friendly one day and turn into an enemy the next."

"I already have one of those."

He told her about the call from Bobby Lambert. Peg sat up and listened, her eyes wide.

"Eat a snack for lunch and meet Bobby at the courthouse," she said when he finished.

"What? And punch him in the nose?"

"He called you twice and tried to set up a meeting. Didn't he try to pull you aside after the session meeting last night?"

"Yes."

"He's reaching out to you for a reason."

"If he wants me to grant absolution and relieve his guilt, he's looking to the wrong person."

"Why? You're the one he wronged."

Mike stared at Peg. "Are you serious?"

Peg picked up her Bible from the low table beside the couch.

"Muriel and I talked about what we're going through. She suggested I read a verse in Colossians."

Mike's jaw dropped open. Peg, turning the pages, didn't notice.

"Here it is. *'Bear with each other and forgive whatever grievances you may have against one another. Forgive as the Lord forgave you.'* Muriel and Sam have been attacked in a bunch of different churches, and she said the only way to survive is to forgive. I've been thinking about the last sentence of that verse ever since she left."

Mike shook his head. "I hate it when a layperson like you gets spiritual."

Peg grinned. "Don't give me too much credit. I'm not ready to invite the Chesterfields and Harcourts over for supper, but give Bobby a chance. He's been your friend almost as long as we've been married."

"You have too much time to lie around and think," Mike answered.

Peg handed her Bible to him. "It's your decision. You know a lot more about the Bible than I do. And Muriel may have been wrong or taken the verse out of context."

Mike went into the kitchen and fixed a large sandwich for himself and a smaller one for Peg. He left the Bible on the counter unopened. He didn't have to read it. He knew what it said. He put the food on two plastic plates, cut up some fresh fruit, and returned to the great room where he arranged everything on a pair of TV trays.

"I'm going into town for a few minutes after lunch," he said as he speared a piece of cantaloupe with his fork. "It's been a while since I went by the deed room at the courthouse to make sure no one has tried to sell the house out from under us."

"Wouldn't selling it without our permission be hard to do?" Peg asked with a smile.

"Impossible. Just like forgiving people who've wronged me in the same way Jesus forgave me."

Twenty-two

AT 1:45 P.M., MIKE WALKED UP THE SIDEWALK AND INTO THE courthouse. If Bobby Lambert wanted to show remorse, there was no harm in letting him stew in his guilt a few extra minutes. The deed room was in the windowless basement of the building. Mike had searched a few real estate titles in his career but pitied the lawyers and paralegals who spent the majority of their time, mole-like, on the lowest level of the courthouse.

Bound in large, leather-covered folios, some of the older deeds were beautifully handwritten documents dating back to the 1830s. More recent records were kept in computer files that could be accessed in seconds. Mike walked down a flight of stairs to an opaque glass door marked "Register of Deeds" and opened it. A few men and women glanced up in curiosity when he entered. Mike nodded to an elderly lawyer named Rex Bumgardner, who had spent his entire career in the deed room and achieved status as a living oracle of the history of land ownership in Barlow County. Written recitals of real estate transfers would survive his death, but his stories describing how and why the land changed hands would be buried in the ground with him.

There was no sign of Bobby. Perhaps he'd not bothered to wait when Mike didn't show up on time. Mike approached Mr. Bumgardner.

"How are you, Mr. Bumgardner?" he asked in the soft voice that deed room etiquette required.

"Fine, except for my arthritis. Don't get old, Mike. It's no fun."

"I don't plan on it. Has Bobby Lambert been down here today?"

Mr. Bumgardner glanced over his shoulder. "He was here a few minutes ago."

Mike walked past the shelves of deed books and looked down the aisles. He didn't spot Bobby until he reached the far corner of the room. His former partner was standing with his back to him and held a leather deed book in his hand. He turned as Mike approached and closed the deed book.

"What do you want?" Mike asked.

"Did you ever read the old handwritten deeds?"

"Not unless I had to. What is this all—"

"Take a look in here," Bobby said, handing the book to Mike. "There is something in it you might find helpful. Read it, then forget you saw me here."

Bobby stepped past Mike, who grabbed him by the arm.

"Why are you doing this to me?" Mike asked sharply.

Bobby jerked his arm free. "Because whether you believe it or not, I'm your friend."

"That's not much of an apology."

Bobby turned his back on Mike and left the aisle. Mike glared after him. He turned the heavy book over in his hand. It was one of the oldest volumes, the red leather cracked and worn. Mike placed the book on a nearby stand and opened it. It covered a nine-month period of land transfers in the 1850s. He flipped through the pages without seeing any mention of Cohulla Creek and wondering why such an old book would have any current relevance. He was about to close it and return it to its place when a loose sheet of paper, folded in half and placed between the sheets, caught his attention. Mike opened it. The script was barely legible. His eyes went to the bottom of the page where in a familiar scrawl Maxwell Forrest had written "Minutes from JH."

It was from Jack Hatcher.

Mike spread open the paper and examined it more closely. Dated the previous year, it appeared to be informal notes Hatcher had made at a meeting. Hatcher mentioned the "CCP," which Mike interpreted as the Cohulla Creek project, as well as references to "TG, DB, and BN"—Troy Linden, Dick Bunt, and Butch Niles. Linden and Bunt participated in the conference via speaker phone. Halfway down the sheet, Mike's eyes stopped when he saw the name "Miller." Beside the name Hatcher had written "How?" and underlined it twice. On the next line, he'd written "BD will handle." Brian Dressler. The remainder of the memo contained action steps related to the CCP and the dates by which they were to be completed. A circle was drawn around a day in May only a few weeks away. Mike tried to figure out the significance of the May date, but there wasn't enough information to do so. There was no reference to anyone else.

Except for the handwritten notation at the bottom of the sheet, nothing linked the document to Maxwell Forrest.

Mike folded the sheet and stuck it in his pocket then returned the volume to the stacks. He reentered the open area of the deed room and approached Mr. Bumgardner.

"Did you find Bobby?" Bumgardner asked.

"Yes, sir."

"I don't see him down here too much. Did you hear that Park is moving to Charlotte?"

"Yes." Mike paused. "Mr. Bumgardner, are you aware of the activity associated with the Cohulla Creek watershed?"

"Sure. Some of the local landowners have called me with questions, but I've not done any work for the companies buying the options. That's being handled by outsiders probably charging three times as much as I would."

"What's going on?"

"The usual. It's one of the prettiest stretches in the area, and developers would understandably be interested."

"But what about the tracts owned by the state?"

"That will probably end up in a state park. It's a great little trout stream."

"No rumors otherwise?"

Bumgardner shook his head and looked at Mike more closely. "If you know one, I'm listening. The folks seeking my advice wanted my opinion about the fair market value of the options. I gave it based on the available land and how it could be developed."

"If the options are already sold, my information wouldn't make any difference."

"Except that a few of the options expire soon, including the main ingress and egress route to the area. A key parcel is tied up in the estate of a man who died last summer. If that option isn't exercised, it will be tough for the developers to get all the heirs to agree on anything."

ON THE WAY OUT OF THE COURTHOUSE, MIKE MET MELISSA HALL near the district attorney's office.

"Did you get my fax?" Hall asked. "I sent it to the church before lunch."

"No, I've been away from the church for a few hours."

"Ken instructed me to withdraw the plea offer in the Miller case and notify you in writing."

Mike's eyes narrowed. "The ten days aren't up."

"I know, but you didn't accept the deal while it was still on the table."

"Why renege on the offer?" he asked testily. "That's not very professional. The integrity of the system depends on lawyers keeping their word to one another."

Mike saw Hall's face flush.

"I'm following orders."

"Is Ken still pushing the case up the calendar?"

"Yes, and I'll be the one handling it."

"Good." Mike paused. "By the way, how many cases have you tried?"

"Two misdemeanors. This will be my first felony. Have you tried a lot of criminal cases?"

"Plenty, but this will be my last."

MIKE LEFT THE COURTHOUSE. HIS PHONE BEEPED, INDICATING that he had a voice message. It was from Sam.

"Tell Miss Hall I'll accept the plea deal. I believe my dream was a warning that my enemies will be in the jury box, and if I go to trial, I'll be convicted. Papa was looking out for me, and even though it doesn't make sense, I'd be foolish to ignore the message."

Mike hit the Redial button. The phone at the Miller house rang, but no one answered. He was about to click off when Muriel answered.

"Is Sam there?"

"No, he's on a job."

"Did you know he called me?"

"Yes. He doesn't want to have a trial. He's going to tell the judge that he didn't do anything wrong but will plead guilty to the charge you mentioned, so he won't have to go to jail."

"Where can I reach him?"

"Let me check his work schedule."

Mike waited.

"He has several places to go on the east side."

Muriel gave Mike the addresses. Mike made notes on a legal pad.

"I have got to talk to him," Mike said. "There have been some new developments."

MIKE DROVE TO THREE PLACES BEFORE HE SAW THE FAMILIAR TRUCK and trailer parked alongside the street. Sam was on his riding mower, cutting a large flat yard that had a single maple tree in the middle. The tree was covered in young leaves that would turn brilliant yellow and orange in autumn. Mike parked behind the truck and stood beside his car while Sam made another loop around the yard before cutting off the mower's engine.

"Did you get my message?" Sam asked as he approached and wiped his hands on his overalls. "My decision doesn't have anything to do with your situation at the church, and I know what I said the other day about the apostles, but there are times when I have to do things that seem wrong at the time. Later, it turns out right because Papa had another plan in—"

"The DA's office withdrew the offer a few hours ago," Mike interrupted. "Taking a deal to end the case is no longer an option."

For the first time since he'd known Sam, the older man looked shocked.

"But why? I thought we had ten days to decide."

"It should have been left open. Usually, the DA's office honors its commitments to make sure the system runs smoothly. But with me, there's no incentive. They can renege without worrying that I'll do something to them in another case."

Sam wiped his forehead with a red bandanna he took from his back pocket.

"What is Papa up to?"

"I don't know, but I've been busy. As of now, we need to assume that we're going to trial."

Mike told Sam about his conversation with Darius York. Sam didn't seem encouraged by the strong likelihood that his signature was lifted from a real check and imprinted on two forged ones. When Mike reached the part about York's fee, the look on the old man's face stopped Mike from asking him for money.

"The handwriting evidence will give the jury a scientific reason to believe in your innocence. But that's not all I have to show them."

Mike reached into his pocket and pulled out the paper Bobby had left in the deed book.

"I have a copy of the minutes of a meeting Jack Hatcher had a year ago with some of the people involved in the Cohulla Creek land development. Your name is mentioned along with Brian Dressler's."

Mike placed the sheet on the hood of his car.

"It looks like something from one of your notebooks, but with what I already know, I can make some sense of it." He went over the minutes in detail and concluded by saying, "This should give you hope. I can drag all these people into court and sequester them. They won't know what hit them until I start my questions."

He waited for Sam's response.

"I appreciate what you're doing," Sam said slowly. "If this trial was about who has the best lawyer, I'm sure we'd win. But the important thing for me to figure out is Papa's plan. Without that, all the lawyer skill in the world won't help me in the way I need it most."

"Sam, this isn't a religious game; it's real. You're charged with a criminal felony, and if you're convicted, you could go to prison for a long time. I believe God will help us if we ask Him, but that doesn't mean He's going to tell us everything in advance. We may have to walk blind and trust Him to keep us from falling in the ditch."

Sam's face softened. "I see what you're saying. We're all little children who don't see everything perfectly, and Papa looks out for us in a million ways we never realize. There are many times I've had to trust Him with the future when I didn't understand the past." Sam paused and continued with more intensity. "But doing what the Master wants is all I care about. In something as big as this, I have to know His will so I can obey it."

"I'll leave that up to you. But I'm clear about my obligation. I'm going to represent you in this case and do everything in my power to prove your innocence. I will not abandon you."

Mike knew it was the only decision his conscience would allow, and speaking the words with conviction empowered him. He might end up as lonely as the solitary maple tree, but at least he'd stand up for what was right without yielding to intimidation.

Sam put his hand on Mike's shoulder and looked him in the eye.

"Thank you. What happens next?"

"I'm going to track down Brian Dressler. He could be the key to the whole case."

WHEN MIKE LEFT SAM, HE PHONED BRAXTON HODGES.

"Any word on Dressler?"

"No, what about your end?"

"Just pursuing leads," Mike answered noncommittally.

"You're holding back on me," Hodges said. "I can hear you sniffing like a bloodhound on the scent."

"A legitimate defense for the case is coming together, but there's nothing I can reveal—yet. Mr. Forrest claimed Sam was an inept criminal. I could say the same thing about the people trying to frame him."

"At least tell me if you've gotten a copy of Miller's letter to Hatcher. You don't have to read it to me, just tell me it exists. I want to print a facsimile in the paper when I break my story."

"I wish I had the letter, but I don't."

"But I can hear it in your voice. You've found something good."

"Maybe better. Talking to Dressler is my number one priority."

"I'm staring into his empty cubicle as we speak. Nothing has been touched since the day he left for Alabama."

"Let me know as soon as he shows up."

"Will do. You'll owe me a hamburger when this is over."

MIKE RETURNED TO THE CHURCH. DELORES WASN'T AT HER DESK. The fax from Melissa Hall had been slipped into Mike's in-box. Even if Delores could be trusted, it disturbed him that she knew an offer had been extended then withdrawn in the Miller case. Mike checked his phone messages. None of the other elders had phoned. No cracks appeared in the unity of those seeking to bring disunity to the congregation.

An hour later, Nathan Goode came in and sat down while Mike finished a phone conversation about vacation Bible school with the children's ministries coordinator.

"Have you heard the rumors?" Mike asked when he hung up the phone.

"It's not true," Nathan replied. "I admit to four earrings in my right ear, but I never broke the law except for a few traffic tickets when I owned an old car that was unsafe at any speed."

"No, I'm serious," Mike answered. "I need to tell you about last night's session meeting. If I continue to represent Sam Miller in the criminal case I mentioned to you, I'm going to have to leave the church."

Nathan's jaw dropped open. "If you're kidding, this is the worst joke of the year."

"It's not a joke. I'm sticking with Miller, which means I'm out by the end of the week. They're calling it a three-month sabbatical, but there's no guarantee that I'll return."

"Are you sure about this? Can't someone else help this guy?"

"They could, but I'm going to do it. If you knew the whole story, you'd understand. I can't tell because much of it is confidential."

"And the elders won't cut you any slack?"

"No, there are a few who would like to kill my career and another who stabbed me in the back."

"Wow. When this comes out in the open, the congregation will revolt and vote out the elders. This is worse than some of the lamebrained stuff the school board does."

"We're an independent church, but it's not that easy under our bylaws. And I'm not sure a new session would solve the problems."

Nathan shook his head. "They're crazy."

"You still have a job," Mike continued. "Your name didn't come up."

"But it will. You don't have to name the assassins, but if Milton Chesterfield and Barbara Harcourt are mad at you, there's no telling what they think about me."

"Miller had a dream about this situation before it happened. He saw the church on fire, only I didn't know about it."

"Then I'd better get out, too. Don't shut the door. I'll be right behind you."

"Don't rush it," Mike responded. "Living on a teacher's salary is going to put a crimp in your car payment, and I think you're doing a super job with the teenagers. Give it a chance."

Nathan gestured over his shoulder toward the door. "What was Delores's take?"

"Was she at her desk when you came in?"

"No."

"She seems supportive, but I'll have to see where she ends up. Delores is an independent thinker."

Nathan looked at Mike for a few seconds. "If I hang around for a while, what should I plan to do on Sunday?"

"Select something subject to the approval of the interim minister. I think 'Blest Be the Tie That Binds' would be a nice hymn selection."

"No," Nathan replied, shaking his head. "Since you can't tell me what to do anymore, we'll sing the 'Battle Hymn of the Republic'—with special emphasis on the grapes of wrath."

Twenty-three

DURING THE DRIVE HOME, MIKE DEBATED WHETHER TO CALL each elder individually or send a letter to the group. He decided a letter would be better. That way, no one could misinterpret his words or misquote him.

The smells of the supper left by Muriel Miller wafted through the kitchen. Mike took a couple of quick sniffs on his way to the downstairs bedroom. Peg was sitting in front of her easel, putting the finishing touches on a beach scene watercolor with a small boy scooping sand into a red plastic bucket.

"What do you think?" she asked.

"Very peaceful. If we have a girl, he can be her beach buddy."

Peg cleaned her brush and laid it on the stand. "Did you see Bobby?"

"Yes."

Mike told her what had happened in the deed room.

"I was right," Peg said. "There is good in him."

"But he wouldn't talk to me—"

"Because he's scared. That's been obvious since all this started. He likes to cut up and joke, but he's not a risk-taker like you. To Bobby and Elizabeth Lambert security is everything. Believe me, she commiserated with me when you made your decision to leave the law firm and told me she'd never let Bobby leave his job."

"Did she know you were considering a divorce?" Mike asked.

"No, I kept quiet because she would have told Bobby, and he would have blabbed to you." Peg paused. "But her comments fed into my selfishness. Bobby stepped on thin ice when he helped you."

"I'll keep that in mind, but if I use the minutes of Hatcher's meeting in court, it will undoubtedly cause Mr. Forrest to question Bobby."

"Then he's trusting you to protect him."

"Which he didn't do for me at the church."

Peg tilted her head to the side. "I've been thinking about that this afternoon. I think Milton Chesterfield wanted to kick you out, but Bobby came up with the sabbatical idea to stall him and sold it to the rest of the elders because everyone didn't fully support Milton. The sabbatical is designed to give you time to work things out."

Peg's theory stopped Mike in his tracks. He mulled it over for a few seconds.

"Did you talk to Bobby?" he asked.

Peg smiled slightly. "I cannot tell a lie. He called me this morning after you wouldn't talk to him at the church. He didn't mention the paper he passed along to you at the deed room, but he explained what happened with the elders. Bobby and two other elders opposed Milton's motion. Libby wasn't there, and the session was split down the middle. Bobby didn't believe he could count on Libby and suggested the sabbatical as a compromise."

"His instincts were right about Libby. She gets mad at Milton, but she would ultimately side with him, especially if that's where Barbara landed. But I don't know why Milton and the others staged a sudden revolt. Serious problems usually simmer before they boil. The desire to oust me came like a tornado out of nowhere. I still don't see why representing Sam was used as the litmus test by Milton and the others. Bobby was the only elder who seemed irritated by my continued involvement. The others seemed indifferent; no one else mentioned it to me as a problem."

"Bobby didn't offer an explanation. He just wanted us to know what happened."

"There's more to it than that. In Sam's dream, the church burned to the ground, which wouldn't happen unless something at the church was going to be totally destroyed."

"I just hope the dream is figurative, not real."

"It's not literal." Mike sniffed the air in the room. "But if we don't eat soon, our supper may be in flames."

After they finished supper, Mike pushed away his empty plate.

"No wonder Sam Miller is round enough to play Santa Claus," he said. "It would take a lot of miles behind a lawn mower to work off a meal like that."

"If you ate like this every night, you could play Santa Claus by Christmas."

"And you could be a pregnant Mrs. Claus."

Peg started toward the sink.

"Stop," Mike said. "I'll take care of the cleanup."

Peg returned to her chair. "Make sure you save the leftovers," she said. "We'll need them."

Mike cleared the table.

"After I finish in here, I'm going to write an e-mail to every member of the session, notifying them of my decision to continue defending Sam and thanking them for the sabbatical to help take care of you."

"And that's it?"

"Don't you agree?"

Peg sighed. "Yes, I just wonder how we'll feel in four months when there's no more salary."

"Maybe I can work for Sam. I cut several lawns in our neighborhood when I was growing up."

Peg stared down at the table. Mike came over and put his arm around her.

"I know this is a serious decision. But it isn't just about Sam Miller. In the back of my mind, I think God is moving us to the next stage of our journey. We didn't anticipate finding a position at Little Creek when I finished seminary in Virginia. I didn't foresee Sam Miller coming into our lives, but it's opened our eyes to spiritual things and caused us to be more honest with each other. I can't predict the outcome of our current situation; however, I believe we have no choice but to trust the Lord. During the next three months, one of my jobs is to recognize the next opportunity He's preparing for us."

"Not bad for an impromptu sermon. But don't try to stop me from complaining."

Mike picked up her left hand and kissed it. "Complain all you want, as long as you stick with me."

It only took Mike a few minutes to compose the first draft of a letter to the elders, but he spent more than half an hour revising it. The final result was more conciliatory than he'd anticipated and sounded more like a thank-you note than the defiant rejection of an unreasonable ultimatum. He promised to support the session's decision to the congregation and offered to facilitate the transition to the interim minister. He took the letter to Peg, who was lying on the couch in the great room watching TV and scratching Judge's neck.

"What do you think?" he asked when she finished.

"You write like a man who doesn't easily give in to road rage."

"I don't have a problem with road rage."

"I know, and that makes you different from a lot of people. The elders who have a conscience should feel ashamed of their duplicity when they read this. The ones who don't care about character will consider it a sign of weakness."

"Weak?" Mike asked. "I don't want to look weak."

"Anyone who interprets your letter as weakness doesn't know the true definition of strength." Peg reached up and patted Mike's chest. "You have a strong heart. And not because you can pedal a bike up a mountain."

MIKE RETURNED TO THE OFFICE. HE STARED AT THE E-MAIL before pressing the Send button. A step this significant justified a last-second opportunity to abort if a final warning surfaced in his mind. None came, and he launched his missive into cyberspace. He spent the rest of the evening watching the Cincinnati bull pen barely hold on to a five-run lead.

THE FOLLOWING MORNING, MIKE RECEIVED A CALL FROM Braxton Hodges.

"Dressler is back in town," Braxton said.

"Is he in the office?"

"Not yet and won't be for long. According to the managing editor, Dressler has resigned his position at the paper and is moving back to Mobile."

"Do you have his home number?"

"I can get it, but you don't have to track him down. He'll be in a meeting here at eleven o'clock, and you should be able to catch him after it's over."

"How long will the meeting last?"

"Not more than thirty minutes. I'll be in it and will make sure to stall him if you're not here."

"Don't worry. I'll be there."

Mike turned left at traffic light number four and arrived at the offices of the Barlow County newspaper. The paper was printed in Asheville and shipped to Shelton for twice-a-week delivery. The newspaper office was in a drab brown building on a side street a block from the courthouse. He parked beside Braxton Hodges's car. Glancing in the front seat of the reporter's car, Mike saw the familiar collection of fast-food bags and sandwich wrappers. Inside the building, Mike approached a young woman sitting behind a cheap wooden desk and asked for Hodges.

While he waited, Mike examined the framed front pages that covered two walls from floor to ceiling. The newspaper had been in business for more than seventy years. Headlines of major world events—news of wars, assassinations, presidential elections, and two state football championships for the local high school—were included in the historical gallery. Braxton Hodges opened a door leading to the newsroom.

"The meeting is over, and Dressler is waiting to speak with you."

Mike entered a newsroom that bore little similarity to the bustling hive of a big-city publication. No phones were ringing; the workers in view didn't seem in a hurry. News in Shelton happened at a slower pace.

"Where can I meet with him?" Mike asked.

"In the conference room. Everyone else has cleared out, but I asked him to stay. When I mentioned your name, he immediately agreed to hang around."

"Does he know why I'm here?"

"Of course not. This is an investigation. In those situations, the best information comes out when people don't know what's important."

They came around a corner to a door marked "Conference Room A." Hodges opened the door for Mike.

"I'll leave you in private," Hodges said.

Dressler stood and shook Mike's hand. The former bank officer looked tired. The conference room was only large enough for a small table surrounded by six chairs. Dressler motioned for Mike to have a seat.

"Thanks for waiting," Mike began as he sat down.

Dressler sat down across from him.

"No, thank you for coming to the hospital. Your visit enabled Marie to go in peace. It also helped me face the funeral"—Dressler paused—"and the future. You don't know the details of our problems, but losing my wife would have been a thousand times worse if we hadn't been able to come to terms with some very hurtful events in our past."

"I'm glad we could help."

"And please tell the man who came with you how much I appreciated him as well."

"I will. His name is Sam Miller."

Dressler didn't hide his surprise. "The man who embezzled money from the church?"

"Did he?" Mike responded.

"Well, I know—" Dressler stopped.

"That he didn't do anything wrong?"

Dressler leaned away from the table. "Since leaving the bank, I don't know anything about the investigation. That's in the past."

"But it occurred while you were still employed at the bank. I'm defending Mr. Miller against the criminal charges. Your name came up during the course of my investigation, and I'd like to ask you some questions."

Dressler stared at Mike for a few seconds. "Is that why you came to the hospital? To ask me questions about Sam Miller?"

"Yes," Mike admitted, "but once we arrived it became obvious God had something else in mind that was more important than my questions. Without Sam's unselfishness, none of what you thanked me for a few minutes ago would have happened. Just because an event is in the past doesn't mean it's not affecting the present and the future. Isn't that what you said?"

Dressler looked around the room.

"Are you recording this conversation?"

"No."

Dressler glanced over his shoulder at the closed door then leaned forward and lowered his voice. "I met with the representatives of the church to verify that Miller didn't have authorization to transfer funds into his account."

"Who asked you to meet with them?"

"Jack Hatcher."

"What else did Mr. Hatcher ask you to do?"

"Answering that question is not going to help Mr. Miller or me."

"Why will it hurt you?"

"I want to work in the banking business in south Alabama. I already have a black mark against me because of my termination. If I end up testifying adversely to the bank in a criminal case, it would make it more difficult for me to move on with my life. I have two grandchildren who are depending on me as the primary means of their financial support, and I need to get back to work as soon as possible."

"Why couldn't you help Sam Miller? He helped you."

Dressler looked down at the table and sighed.

"Because all I have are suspicions. If you're looking for hard evidence of improper activity by the bank, I'm not the person to give it to you."

"What are your suspicions?"

Dressler hesitated. "What have you found out in your investigation?"

"That the signature on the two checks was imprinted. Sam didn't sign them."

Dressler nodded. Mike waited.

"Your response?" Mike pressed him.

"I think you're on the right track."

"Why?"

Dressler pressed his lips tightly together. Unlike most bankers, he didn't have a face that hid its struggles. Mike watched the conflict until Dressler leaned back in his chair and spoke.

"Part of my job at the bank was to stay abreast of technological developments that could affect bank security. Hatcher approached me with questions about forgery techniques, and, at the time, I assumed someone had presented false signatures on checks negotiated at the bank. I made my own inquiry about recent irregularities and nothing turned up. A few days later, Hatcher asked me to research legitimate companies with the capability to make a printed signature appear original. He said he might want to hire an outside consultant. I gave him a few names, then authorized payment for an invoice that came across my desk a month or so later. Within a few days, I was assigned to oversee the internal investigation of the Miller transactions. When I examined the signatures on the checks, I saw they were not just similar, but identical. It was a very stupid attempt to embezzle money, but there was also the presence of sophisticated technology that didn't serve the embezzler's purpose. It didn't make sense. A smart forger would have lifted two different signatures from the same person and used them. Then, my meeting with the men from the church confirmed that Miller was an uneducated man who might have tried to steal money but wouldn't have done so in the way presented to me. I brought it up with Hatcher, and he told me not to worry about it because Miller was a 'troublemaker.'"

"What happened next?"

"Nothing. Hatcher accepted my report and instructed me to close the file."

Mike wasn't sure he was getting all the truth. He took a copy of the minutes from his briefcase and laid it on the table.

"Please read this."

Dressler put on a pair of reading glasses. The banker pressed his lips together. Mike had to force himself to breathe normally.

"How did you get this?" Dressler asked when he finished.

"Lawfully in my investigation. Were you present at this meeting?"

"No."

"Why did Hatcher assign you the task of 'handling' Miller?"

"He didn't. All I handled was the brief investigation I mentioned."

"That's not the way I read it."

"I can't explain it either unless that's what led to our initial conversation. Cohulla Creek is another matter."

"What do you know about it?"

"It's under consideration for residential development."

"How big?"

"Very big, but not yet public. Do you know what's going on there?"

"I know about the options on file at the courthouse, and the plans to obtain property from the state to build a man-made lake."

"How did you find out about the lake?" Dressler asked with raised eyebrows.

"It's hard to keep something this big quiet in Barlow County."

Dressler shrugged. "It will all come out eventually, but until that happens, my knowledge of the deal is the leverage I have against a negative reference from the bank. Hatcher and the other developers want to keep the scope of the project secret until every piece is in place."

"Is it an honest deal?"

"What do you mean?"

"How is Butch Niles involved?"

Mike watched Dressler's face closely while asking the question. He saw the banker's jaw tighten.

"Niles is the one responsible for my termination at the bank," Dressler responded through clenched teeth.

"But you were senior to him in the bank's hierarchy."

"Not at the end. He assumed control for my area of responsibility and wanted someone else in the position. Hatcher backed him, and I didn't have a chance."

Dressler hadn't answered Mike's question but continued talking.

"So I really can't give you any information that you don't already have. I'm not a lawyer, but I don't think my conversation with Hatcher about printing signatures on checks is going to help Mr. Miller."

"Probably not," Mike responded. "It's nonspecific and remote."

Dressler stood up to signal an end to the meeting. "And thanks again to you and Mr. Miller for coming to the hospital."

Not willing to retreat, Mike placed his pen on the table.

"One other question. What was the name of the company retained by Hatcher—the one that sent an invoice?"

"I don't remember."

"If you saw the name, would it come back to you?"

"Maybe."

"Where is your research?"

"It could be anywhere. I didn't open a file. I just handed the list of companies to Hatcher."

"Will you let me know if you remember the company?"

"Sure."

Mike pulled out a subpoena and handed it Dressler.

"Sorry, but I have to give this to you before you leave town," Mike said. "Otherwise, I'd have to serve you in Alabama."

Dressler glanced at the subpoena then dropped it on the table. "This will be a tremendous inconvenience, and I don't think I can help Mr. Miller."

Mike resisted the urge to point out that praying for Marie Dressler had been inconvenient, too.

"It's part of a bigger picture," he said, as casually as he could muster. "I'll let you know if the scheduling of the case changes."

"Leaving the subpoena on the table isn't an option?" Dressler asked.

"No, sir. I'll notify the court it was personally served while you were in Barlow County."

Mike obtained Dressler's contact information in Alabama and remained in the conference room after the banker left. In less than a minute, Braxton Hodges joined him.

"Well?" Hodges asked.

"*Well* is a good word to use," Mike replied with a shrug. "I have to keep digging to find any fresh water. I didn't get much from Dressler except the water I poured in to prime the pump."

"Huh?"

"He asked me what I knew, then fed it back to me with a few minor embellishments. I subpoenaed him to the trial, but I may not use him."

"What about Butch Niles and Cohulla Creek?"

Mike related the few tidbits of information. "But all that shows is the scope of the project was known within the upper echelons at the bank. That's not a big revelation. He didn't respond to my specific question about Butch Niles."

"Why would he try to protect Niles? He's the one who fired him."

"I don't know. The degree of appreciation Dressler had for our visit to the hospital only took me so far. It unlocked his wife's heart to God but wasn't a master key to the Miller case."

"What are you talking about?"

Mike smiled. "Nothing you would print in the paper, although it would be at least as interesting as the articles about alternative health remedies."

"Did you read them?"

"Absolutely, and I'm anxiously waiting for the next installment. I'm hoping you can locate a herbal truth serum that I can slip into Jack Hatcher's sweet tea at the Ashe Café. Are you hungry?"

"Sure. Let's go."

It was a short walk from the paper to the restaurant. When Mike and Hodges entered, Mike saw Bobby Lambert, Maxwell Forrest, and two other men he didn't know already seated at a back table. Bobby looked up at Mike and immediately turned away. Forrest had his back to the door.

"Sarah Ann," Mike said to the hostess on duty. "Braxton and I would like to sit in the smoking section."

"You don't smoke," Hodges said as they crossed to the far side of the restaurant. "And I quit."

"Yeah, but I don't want to be next to my former law partners."

Mike sat so he could see the rest of the room.

"What's going on with you?" Hodges observed. "You're not the one on trial."

"If you only knew," Mike responded.

The two men ordered their food.

"Tell me," Hodges asked when the waitress left.

"Off the record?"

"Sure."

Mike shook his head. "Church politics have given me a serious bite wound."

"How bad?"

"Next week I start a three-month sabbatical from Little Creek that may prove permanent."

Hodges whistled. "What did you do?"

"Other than agreeing to help Sam Miller, I'm not sure."

Hodges picked up the knife from the table and held it out like a teacher lecturing with a pointer. "I know the routine. A dynamic young minister comes to a church that then starts to grow. People get excited, and the minister believes the church is moving toward the new millennium. Behind the scenes, the old power brokers get upset and run him off."

"How do you know so much about church politics? I didn't think you went to church."

"I don't."

The waitress returned with their sweet tea.

"My father was a preacher," the reporter said after she left. "Growing up, I attended two elementary schools, one middle school, and two high schools, the last one for my senior year only—all courtesy of church politics. Can you imagine what it would be like to move to a new town for your senior year of high school?"

"No."

"But flexibility and the ability to interact with new people have helped me in the newspaper business."

"Why don't you write the religion articles? The woman who does—" Mike stopped.

"Isn't much of a writer?" Hodges replied with a shrug. "Agreed. But I can't do it and maintain journalistic objectivity. I'm still mad about some of the garbage my family had to wade through when I was growing up. Venting my personal feelings on the religion page wouldn't help us sell papers or attract advertisers."

"Where is your father now?"

"If what he preached was true, he's in heaven."

"Do you believe in his truth?"

Hodges looked at Mike and laughed.

"I believe a lot of things, but I'm not sure how many of them are true."

Mike looked up as Bobby, Forrest, and the two men with them walked to the cash register. Hodges turned in his seat.

"There go your friends."

"Do you know the other two men?" Mike asked.

"No, but that doesn't mean they're not locals."

Mike relaxed as the group left the restaurant.

"I'm beginning to feel like a conspiracy theorist," he said.

Hodges leaned forward. "The masses love a good conspiracy. I'd get a kick out of writing a series of articles about some of the conspiracies that have popped up in our nation's history. It would be interesting reading, and even though I made it clear the stories weren't true, plenty of folks would believe they were real."

"Is that how you view Christian faith?"

Hodges shook his head. "Very slick, Preacher. You turned our conversation to religion smoother than a politician about to make a promise."

Mike grinned. "It's a fair question."

"Which I'm afraid to answer."

"Afraid?"

"Because the answer could change my life here and in the hereafter if it exists."

The waitress brought their food. Without asking Hodges's permission, Mike bowed his head to pray.

"God, help Braxton fear You enough to believe in Your love. Bless this food. Amen."

He looked up. Hodges had a quizzical expression on his face.

"What did that mean?" the reporter asked.

"I'm not sure, but it covered a lot of theological ground in a few words."

Hodges took a bite of steaming mashed potatoes and gravy. "What prompted you to make the leap of faith?"

Mike returned a fried chicken drumstick to his plate. "Which one? The most recent jump into the unknown was the decision to help Sam Miller."

"The first one. For my father, that was the only one that mattered."

"It happened during my junior year in high school. I attended a weekend retreat with a buddy who went to a different church. There was an evangelistic speaker, and when he gave the invitation on Saturday night, I left my seat and walked to the front. A counselor prayed with me."

Hodges swallowed a bite of chicken. "I did that at least a dozen times from age five to fifteen, but it never worked for me. After my first trip to the altar, my father insisted every subsequent visit was simply a rededication of my life to God. I kept trying, but after a while, my rededicator wore out, and I gave up." Hodges leaned forward. "Did things really change in your life after you prayed at the retreat?"

Mike looked directly into Hodges's eyes and spoke with all the earnestness he could muster. "I haven't had a sinful thought since."

Hodges burst out laughing and didn't stop. While Mike watched, the reporter's humor caught a second wind, and he sat back in his seat, continuing to guffaw until he wiped tears from his eyes.

"I didn't know I was that funny," Mike said when the reporter calmed down.

"You're not," Hodges replied. "It was so unexpected. I thought you were going to move to the next step of your evangelistic outline. When you didn't, it caught me totally off guard."

"You don't need an outline. Given your childhood, I'm sure you know the message of the gospel."

"Yeah, when I was a kid, I had to memorize questions to ask people and the correct answers to suggest in case they didn't get the point. I never did very well with it."

"Those approaches can work, but just because it didn't connect with you doesn't mean you're a hopeless reprobate."

"My first wife might disagree."

"And she may be right except for the hopeless part. People change because God's grace is a fact, not a concept."

Hodges ate several more bites of food before he spoke. "I might come hear you preach on Sunday, especially if you promise to make me laugh."

"You're welcome to visit, but I won't be there. My sabbatical begins at sundown Friday."

"Oh yeah, sorry."

"Don't let the way the church has treated your father or me stop you from having an open mind. The longer I believe, the more convinced I am about the truth that God wants to be involved in our lives."

"I've never been able to make that connection."

Mike thought for a moment. "What did Sam Miller write in the letter he sent you?"

Hodges put down a forkful of green beans without eating it.

"He claimed my attitude toward my father had warped my view of God and that I'd violated the verse about honoring parents."

"The fifth commandment."

"Yeah, it made me mad at first until I realized he was right."

"Did he know your father?"

"No. I grew up in Tennessee. Miller is a total stranger to our family. He could have researched my history, but I doubt it."

"I'm sure you're right about that. Sam relies on what he sees in a dream or his impression of the moment. Did he offer a solution for your problem?"

"He said if I spent more time with my son, I would better understand God's love for me."

"Did you do it?"

"No. I didn't want to hassle with my ex-wife. She always throws up objections to regular visitation, and my work schedule makes it hard to stick to specific times."

"How old is your son now?"

"Sixteen. He and his mother live in Hickory. A few years ago, she married a furniture company executive who makes five times what I do."

"It might not be too late to test out Sam's theory."

The door of the restaurant opened, and Butch Niles entered. Hodges raised his hand in greeting, and the legislator headed toward their table.

"What are you going to say to him?" Mike asked.

"Just watch. Niles cultivates a good rapport with the local press."

Mike and Hodges stood up as Niles approached to shake their hands.

"Mike has been trying to convert me," Hodges said as he released Niles's hand. "He almost had me convinced, but one thing stopped me."

"What?"

"That verse in the Bible about not trusting lawyers."

Niles shook his head. "Dr. Garrison at our church says that meant some kind of religious lawyer."

"That's true," Hodges replied. "But Mike is one of those, too. Want to join us?"

Niles looked around the room. "No thanks, I'm meeting someone. Bank business."

The door opened and Troy Linden, carrying a navy blue leather briefcase, entered.

"Got to go," Niles said.

"Call me if you hear any tidbits from Raleigh," Hodges replied.

"Sure thing."

When Niles left, Mike turned to Hodges. "That's Troy Linden."

"I know. I recognize him from his mug shot from New Jersey. If I ever write a story, it will be fun showing a photo with a number beneath the picture on the front page."

"I wonder which one of them will pay for lunch."

"Troy is the one with the deep pockets. He'll make sure Butch Niles has all the mashed potatoes and gravy he can cram in his mouth."

Twenty-four

DELORES CONFRONTED MIKE AS SOON AS HE APPROACHED HER desk. "I thought you were going to wait!" she snapped. "You should have taken the advice you gave me."

"You read the e-mail to the elders?"

"Yes, and it sounded like someone else wrote it." Delores held up her hand. "And don't tell me to pray about it. I have to do something."

Mike leaned against the front of her desk. "You're a key person. If you don't react, others will follow your lead."

"I can't promise that."

"As soon as the word gets out that I'm going on sabbatical, callers with questions are going to start phoning. That will be your chance to set the tone for the whole church. If you vent your frustration, it will spread like wildfire. If you don't act upset, it may help things work out down the road."

"That's hard to do when I don't know what's going to happen." Delores eyed him suspiciously. "Have you already decided not to come back after this so-called sabbatical is over?"

Mike answered carefully. "No door is closed in my mind."

"Are you going to fight for your job?"

"I don't think that will be necessary. God is going to take care of this battle without my help."

"Please." Delores snorted. "Leave Him out of it. You'd almost convinced me."

"I'm not ordering you to keep your mouth shut. That wouldn't work anyway. Just think it over. Do you have a copy of my e-mail to the elders?"

Delores picked up a sheet of paper from her desk. "Yes."

"Except for the part about Sam Miller, you can use it to answer people's questions."

Delores didn't respond.

Mike went into his office but left the door cracked open. He waited until he saw the light on his phone blink as a call came into the church then stepped quietly to the door and listened.

"Good morning, Little Creek," Delores answered crisply.

After a few moments of silence, she asked, "Who told you that, Emma? Mike hasn't been fired. He's taking a sabbatical to be with Peg during her pregnancy. The session voted Tuesday night, and Mike accepted their offer. Here's what he said about it—" Mike returned to his desk. He didn't have confidence of total victory with Delores. Working with her was a war of many battles.

In a few minutes, she paged him.

"Braxton Hodges from the paper is on the phone."

Mike picked up the receiver. "What did I do to deserve so much attention from the press? Are you secretly working on a feature article about me?"

"That's on my list as soon as I finish a series about Confederate soldiers buried in Barlow County. Listen, do you remember the briefcase Linden brought to the restaurant?"

"No."

"My journalistic eye noticed it. It was different, kind of a dark blue color."

"Okay."

"Linden didn't leave with it. He gave it to Niles."

"I thought you weren't going to stay at the restaurant."

"I didn't, but I saw Niles walking on the sidewalk toward the bank when I went out a few minutes ago. He was carrying the briefcase, and Linden wasn't with him."

"And you think the briefcase was stuffed with money?"

"Maybe."

"Did you follow Niles into the bank and watch the teller count it?"

"Preachers aren't supposed to be sarcastic," Hodges replied. "Do you want to hear me out?"

"Yeah, go ahead."

"While Niles is walking happily down the street, someone comes up and stops him for a few moments of private conversation. I pull into a parking space and watch. Niles is nervous, looking around, glancing over his shoulder, and putting both hands on the briefcase while the man is talking to him. Even from across the street, I could see that Niles was upset. Finally, he says something I can't hear and storms off toward the bank."

"Who was he talking to?"

"Sam Miller."

"Oh no!"

Mike quickly tried to remember whether Sam had mentioned anything to him about Butch Niles. He couldn't remember anything.

"I'll check with Sam when I give him an update on the case."

"And get back to me, so I can include the exchange between them in the article I'm writing."

"Forget it. Keep researching the broken-down tombstones of Confederate soldiers."

Mike called the Miller house, but no one answered. Upon arriving home, he knew why. The familiar red pickup truck was parked in his driveway. Mike went inside. The kitchen was empty, and he didn't hear any sounds in the house. He went into the great room and found Sam sleeping in his recliner. Mike cleared his throat. Sam didn't stir. He stepped back into the kitchen.

"Peg!" he called out. "I'm home!"

"I'm in the art room!" Peg responded.

Mike returned to the great room; however, his client was still fast asleep. Mike quickly stepped over to the chair, concerned the older man might be unconscious, not merely asleep.

"Sam," he said in a normal tone of voice.

No response. He looked closer and couldn't see any sign that Sam was breathing.

"Sam!" he said louder as he shook the older man's shoulder.

Sam stirred to life. He blinked his eyes and looked up at Mike.

"Are you okay?" Mike asked.

Sam rubbed his eyes and shook his head. "This is an awesome chair. I bet you have some incredible visions while you're sitting in it."

"Not really. I use it to watch TV."

Sam leaned forward and patted the leather arms of the chair. "Well, I think it's a rocket ship to Glory. I went up so fast I could have used a seat belt. Do you want to know what I saw?"

"Not now. What did you say to Butch Niles today?"

"How do you know about that?"

"A friend saw you talking to him but didn't hear the conversation."

"Wasn't much of a conversation. Last night, I figured out he was the box of finishing nails in my dream and told him to stop doing wrong at Cohulla Creek."

"Why did you say anything to him? It's just going to antagonize the people who want to see you sent to prison."

"Do you know why they were finishing nails?"

"Are you listening to me?"

"Yep, but I'm also trying to help you understand. Finishing nails mean that Representative Niles is the one who's going to finish the deal. There is a double meaning with the nails. It sounds like his name, and he's also going to nail down the deal."

"Okay, but why talk to Niles in the first place? He's not going to change his mind."

Sam cocked his head to the side. "Are you listening to yourself?"

"Yes."

"Do you believe the Master can change people for the better?"

Mike rolled his eyes. "Yes."

"What do they have to do?"

"Repent and believe."

"How will a person know to repent if no one tells them about their sin?"

"Are you cross-examining me?"

"Only to help you understand Papa's ways better."

"Mike!" Peg called. "Are you coming?"

"Yes!" he responded.

"Go on," Sam said with a wave of his hand. "I'd like to catch another quick nap before supper."

By the time Mike left the room, Sam's eyes were closed. Peg and Muriel were in the art room.

"Sue Cavanaugh stopped by for a few minutes to check on me," Peg said. "The interim minister at the church is a retired medical missionary named Vaughn Mixon. He'll be there tomorrow."

"A courtesy call from one of the elders would have been nice," Mike replied.

"She found out about it from Libby Gorman. There won't be a general announcement until Sunday morning."

"How are you feeling?" Mike asked.

"Less bored now that Muriel is here."

Returning to the great room, they found Sam asleep in the recliner.

"Should I wake him up?" Mike asked. "He claims the chair is the seat of heavenly revelation, but I need to give him an update on the case."

"Can it wait?" Muriel responded. "When this happens, it's better not to chain him to earth."

"How long will he sleep?" Peg asked.

Muriel looked at her watch. "I'll rouse him in an hour or so and take him home for supper. After that, he'll probably be up for a while writing in his notebook and reading the Bible."

It was an odd evening. Mike, Peg, and Muriel carried on a conversation in a normal tone of voice, and Sam slept through it all. After an hour passed, Muriel rose from her seat, went over to Sam, shook his shoulder, and spoke loudly in his ear. He blinked and opened his eyes.

"You're not very good company tonight," she said. "Let's go home."

As he came fully awake, Sam turned to Mike. "If you ever decide to sell this chair, let me know."

"Is the chair that special?"

Sam smiled. "Don't fight me. Let me build your faith."

EARLY SUNDAY MORNING, MIKE'S FEET WERE ON THE FLOOR before he remembered that he didn't need to go to church. He started to lie down again, but the pain of rejection brought him awake. He looked over his shoulder at Peg, who was sleeping peacefully. With each day, his confidence in the sincerity of her desire to remain committed to the marriage grew. He couldn't imagine the pain he'd be going through if she'd decided to leave simultaneously with the trauma at the church.

Quietly leaving the room, he opened the door for Judge to go outside. It was a fine morning, and the grays of night were giving way to streaks of color in the trees and bushes that signaled the new day. Mike watched Judge trot happily around the yard in his familiar morning ritual and wished his own Sunday morning routine hadn't been so cruelly disrupted. The dog returned, and Mike directed him back to the kitchen.

"No, she's not awake," he said when the dog headed toward the art room.

Mike went into the great room and sat in his chair. He reached for his Bible, but instead of opening it, placed it in his lap and closed his eyes.

Instantly, he was in another place.

It was a barren landscape with trees so broken and disfigured they looked like old men about to topple over. The ground was various shades of sickly brown, none of which indicated any hope of future fertility. The sky was gray, the sun hidden. A few puddles of polluted water collected in what looked like shallow bomb craters that pockmarked the earth as far as he could see. An oily slime on top of the water glistened with a sickly rainbow of color. To his right rested a simple table with a spotless white tablecloth thrown over it. A plain wooden chair was pulled up to the table.

Mike sat down in the chair. Although the table was bare, he bowed his head in a silent blessing. When he opened his eyes, there was a bowl of soup before him. Mike quickly glanced around but saw no one. He dipped a spoon into the soup and tasted it. It was not easy to identify. He ate another spoonful and decided it had to be a type of bisque containing complex flavors. As the soup encountered different parts of his tongue, it interacted with each category of taste buds. It was delicious. Mike continued eating, savoring each bite until he reluctantly scooped up the last of the soup and raised it to his lips.

He woke up.

The sun was streaming in shafts into the backyard. He looked at the clock and realized it had been almost an hour since he sat down in the chair.

"What was that all about?" he spoke out loud.

Mike opened his Bible and flipped through the pages, looking for a verse in the Psalms. He heard footsteps as Peg came into the room. She sat on the edge of the chair and squeezed close to him.

"I know it's hard for you to stay home instead of going to the church," she said.

"I was depressed when I woke up, but then I came out here and had a dream."

"Tell me."

When Mike reached the part about the delicious soup, Peg interrupted.

"You could taste it? I've never had a dream involving taste."

"Yeah, it was so real I can still remember the flavors. When you're back on your feet and in the kitchen, I want you to fix it for us."

Peg smiled. "You'll have to take me with you to Dreamland so I can get the recipe."

"When I finished the soup, I woke up. Then I thought about this verse." He picked up his Bible. "Psalm 78:19: *'Can God spread a table in the desert?'* It describes exactly what I saw and experienced—a wonderful meal in a desolate place."

Shortly before 11:00 a.m. the doorbell rang. Judge barked and followed Mike to the door.

Sam and Muriel Miller stood on the front steps. Sam spoke. "Since you're a preacher without a congregation, I thought we might have church here this morning."

Mike held the door open. "Come in."

They went into the great room.

"Can I sit in your chair?" Sam asked.

"Only if you promise not to go to sleep during the sermon."

Peg joined them. She and Muriel sat on the couch. Mike brought in a chair from the dining room and placed it so that he faced the other three.

"What's going to happen during this church service?" he asked.

"You're the preacher. What's on your heart?" Sam replied.

Mike glanced at the clock.

"I want to pray for the service at Little Creek."

Sam nodded. "They can take the sheep away from the shepherd, but the shepherd's heart remains with the flock."

Mike told them the little he knew about Vaughn Mixon.

"He's a good man," Sam said.

"Do you know him?" Mike asked in surprise.

"Nope, but Papa does."

Mike looked at Peg. "I step into that hole just about every time Sam digs it."

"Let's pray," Sam said.

Peg started speaking before Mike could organize his thoughts. Her direct, commonsense approach to life came through in practical requests. Sam or Muriel interjected an occasional "Amen."

When Peg grew silent, Sam took up where she left off. He prayed in spurts, as if listening for a few moments then speaking what he heard. Mike had grown used to Sam's use of "Papa" and "Master," but was startled by the old man's knowledge of the Bible. He effortlessly quoted long passages from memory. And his knowledge wasn't limited to the New Testament. He used verses from the Old Testament, too. Apparently, Sam did more than walk mindlessly behind a mower all day. Mike felt slightly jealous; a response he knew would make Sam happy.

When Sam grew silent, Mike waited for Muriel, but she didn't say a word. After a minute or so, Mike cleared his throat to speak, but an inner restraint held him in check. Three times, he prepared to break the silence but couldn't do so. Finally, the old woman spoke. And when she did, Mike was grateful he'd waited.

"Father, let the sweetness of Your love flow over the people of the Little Creek Church. Many of them are taking the baby steps of faith. Bring them along the path with gentleness and wisdom." Her voice increased in intensity. "Protect them. Do not let the Enemy trip them up. Let the people remember the love Mike and Peg have for them and how they showed that love to them day by day."

As Muriel continued, emotion welled up in Mike. The old woman understood the heart of the Father for His children and the concern of a pastor for his flock.

The prayers of the others so beautifully communicated the need of the moment that when it was finally Mike's turn, he searched for something to add but did nothing more than provide the final "Amen."

He looked up into the eyes of the other three people in the room.

"If there was regular prayer like this for every church in America, our nation would change."

"Yep," Sam replied. "It doesn't make the evening news, but there are more praying people than you might think. I've seen the lights in the night, and they cover the whole country."

Mike looked at the clock. "I didn't prepare a sermon."

"Tell your dream," Peg said. "Sam will like it."

Mike pointed to the chair. "I took a ride on the rocket ship."

While Mike talked, Sam smiled and nodded knowingly. Mike tried to wipe the grin from the old man's face by describing in greater detail the devastation of the landscape, but nothing changed Sam's countenance. When he reached the part about the soup, Sam's face lit up. Mike stopped.

"Do you want to say something?" he asked.

"Nope."

Mike finished by reading the verse from Psalms.

"That's better than a bunch of sermons I've heard," Sam said, patting his stomach. "It's something I can carry with me when we go home. It also reminds me of a vision I had many years ago." He turned to Muriel. "Remember when we were helping that church on Mackey Road?"

"Yeah, a lot of people got saved before things turned rough."

Sam spoke to Mike and Peg. "It was during the time I met Larry Fletchall's father. His name was Victor. Back then, blacks and whites working together in the ministry didn't happen very often, but Papa showed Vic and me that we were supposed to do some meetings together. Neither of us knew much about the ministry, but Papa showed up, which is all it takes to have good church. It was a great time until a bunch of preachers, some white, some black, started telling lies about us and stirring up trouble. Some of the people working with us got sick, including Vic, who ended up in the hospital."

"Our son Matthew was little," Muriel added. "And he started having nightmares."

"Anyway, one night I had a vision. I was standing on a battlefield that looked a lot like your wilderness except there were people lying around wounded. When I saw their faces, I recognized Vic, our son, and several others. Nearby was a table, and I sat down. An angel appeared and asked me if I wanted to order soup or a salad. I thought it was a stupid question and pointed to the people who were hurt. How could I consider eating when I was in the middle of such a horrible battle? The angel repeated the question several times then I woke up. Do you know what it means?"

Mike shook his head.

"I wasn't sure either," Sam continued. "But like you, Papa reminded me of a verse. It's in Psalm 23."

Mike thought for a moment. "He prepares 'a table before me in the presence of my enemies.'"

"Yep. We may think the world is coming to an end, but Papa isn't upset. He let me know that He's in control and could offer one of His children a quiet meal even if things in life are rough. Soon after the vision, Vic got better, and Matthew was able to sleep at night. A lot of the folks who founded the Craig Valley church were saved in those meetings." Sam paused. "You know, I need to remember that one. It will help me face what's up ahead for both of us."

Peg invited Sam and Muriel to stay for lunch.

"We're eating your leftovers," she said.

"No thanks," Muriel replied. "We're going to visit a woman who lives not far from our house. I have to pick up something to take to her."

Mike walked them to the front door.

"What exactly did you say to Butch Niles when you saw him on the side-walk the other day?" he asked Sam.

"Nothing except the interpretation of the dream."

"Did you quote the poem?"

"Nope."

"Did he understand what you told him?"

"Yep. But understanding isn't the same as obeying. He got upset, but it doesn't mean he won't think about it later and do the right thing. I've seen that happen many times. Remember how long it took you to agree to help me?"

"Yeah."

"But now you know it was the right thing to do." Sam put his hand on Mike's shoulder. "And hearing what Papa is doing in your life gives me hope for what lies ahead."

After Sam and Muriel left, the phone started ringing, and Mike fielded calls from members of the congregation. He quickly learned that Bobby Lambert spoke on behalf of the elders, and Vaughn Mixon made it clear that his stay at the church was temporary. He didn't want Mike's job. Many of the people who called said they would be praying for Peg and looked forward to Mike's return. When the calls slowed, Mike went into the downstairs bedroom.

"Did you hear my side of the conversations?" he asked.

"In part. A lot of the people support you."

Mike sat on the edge of the bed. "At the session meeting, I thought my time at Little Creek was over. Now, I'm not so sure."

"We'll have to wait and see. One thing I've realized in the past weeks is that a lot of big changes can happen in a short period of time."

MIKE WOKE UP MONDAY MORNING AND FIXED BREAKFAST FOR Peg. He brought it to her in bed with a short love note placed beside her toast. Peg opened the note and read it while he waited.

"Thank you," she said.

"How are the eggs?" Mike asked. "I know you like them over easy."

Peg took a bite. "Perfect. When did you learn to do that?"

"It took six eggs to get two right. In the process, I discovered a lot about how eggs react to heat."

Peg sipped the coffee. "Where's your breakfast?"

"I ate the mistakes."

Mike sat on the bed and watched her eat. "The elders told me to care for you. Since they're the ones in charge of my life, I'd better do what they say."

Peg laughed. "That sounds interesting, but who's going to take care of you?"

"I'm self-sufficient."

"You've not been self-sufficient since you lived like a pig in college."

"We didn't live like pigs."

"I saw the kitchen at the fraternity house. But you're much more domesticated now."

"A domesticated pig instead of a wild pig?"

"That's not a fair comparison, considering how beautifully you fixed my breakfast."

"What else am I going to do today?"

Peg nibbled a bite of toast. "Keep me company."

"That will be pleasant. Anything else?"

"Work on Sam's case."

LATE IN THE AFTERNOON, MIKE TOOK A SHORT NAP IN HIS CHAIR in the great room. He'd not had any dreams as dramatic as the table in the desert, but several times he'd awakened with a thought or a phrase that he entered in his PDA. The phone rang as he rested with his eyes closed. It was Darius York.

"I called the church, and the secretary gave me your home number," York began.

"This will be the place to reach me for the time being," Mike said. "What can you tell me?"

"I've reviewed the writing sample you sent and ran a comparison on the checks. It's your man's signature on the bottom of the checks, but it's not a sophisticated imprint job."

Mike felt a sudden knot in his stomach. "What do you mean?"

"The name on the checks was stamped with a signature stamp. There isn't any smearing of the ink, but there's no doubt an old-fashioned stamp was used. Did your client use a signature stamp in his work?"

"I don't know. I'll have to ask him."

"If he had one, find out who had access to it."

"Okay. But that doesn't jive with the information obtained from a former bank officer involved in the investigation."

Mike summarized his conversation with Brian Dressler. "I was hoping for a high-tech imprint of the signature," Mike concluded. "That would have given me a better defense than the unauthorized use of a signature stamp."

"If your client is innocent, the people wanting to make him look guilty adopted a simple yet clever strategy to do so."

"Did you discover anything else?"

"The payee name and date were typed on an old IBM Selectric typewriter."

"I doubt my client owns a typewriter. He writes in notebooks."

"What does he do for a living?"

"He has a small lawncare business. No employees."

"The typewriter used to produce the checks was a business model, heavy-duty and state-of-the-art when introduced, but a dinosaur today."

"Could you identify the specific unit?"

"If I had a proper sample. The print produced by each typewriter is unique, especially after the passage of time increases eccentricities in the typeface."

"Would it be the type of machine used at a bank?"

"Absolutely."

"Do you still want to see the originals of the checks?"

"Yes. The copying process masks details that would be easier to locate if I had access to the originals."

"Could you come to Shelton to review them? The judge wouldn't let them leave the custody of the bank or the State."

"Yes."

Mike thought a moment. "Do your qualifications as an expert witness include analysis of typewriters?"

"I've performed less work with machines, but they're easier to identify. Unlike handwriting, their peculiarities are reproduced repeatedly."

"Can you send a report of your findings thus far?"

"Why?"

"So I can be sure about your opinion."

"I won't back off my assessment."

Mike felt uneasy. "I don't like to go to court without something in my hand to guide my questions."

"What more do you need?"

Mike listed several items.

"I can give that information."

"Okay."

"Do you want me to return the documents you sent me?"

"Not yet. I'll let you know as soon as possible if I find out anything about the original checks or the location of a typewriter."

MIKE HUNG UP AND CALLED MELISSA HALL. THE RECEPTIONIST paged the assistant DA, who answered the phone.

"How is your wife?" Hall asked before Mike could speak. "I heard you've taken a leave of absence from the church to take care of her."

"She's off her feet and taking it easy. It's hard because she was an everyday runner and very active."

"Are you going to ask for a continuance of the case to take care of her?"

Mike didn't answer. Judge Coberg might grant a postponement, but Mike wouldn't be completely honest in asking for one.

"That remains to be seen. When will the Miller case be on the trial calendar? I haven't received notice of trial."

"It's being worked up, but Ken has it penciled in as a backup in a week and a half. After that, there won't be a criminal court trial week for at least two months."

A two-month postponement looked very attractive. Mike made a note on his legal pad.

"If you're still pushing the case up the ladder," he said, "I need to see the original checks. I won't stipulate to the use of copies."

"I haven't received them yet."

"My expert wants to examine them prior to trial."

"That shouldn't be a problem. I'll call the bank and let you know. He can look at them here at our office. Any preliminary idea what your expert is going to say?"

Mike was so surprised by Hall's request that it caught him off guard. Modern rules of disclosure had limited the opportunity for trial by ambush in most areas of the law, but in a criminal case it was still possible to blindside the prosecution in the heat of battle.

"Uh, he's not finished his report and wants to have access to the original checks before doing so."

"I'd like to know if there are any irregularities."

Mike didn't answer. "Call me as soon as you have the checks."

Mike phoned Muriel Miller, who told him Sam never used a signature stamp or owned a typewriter. Sam's invoices, like the dreams and visions recorded in his notebooks, were all handwritten.

FRIDAY MORNING, MIKE TOOK PEG TO THE HOSPITAL FOR another ultrasound. Dr. Crawford came in shortly after the technician left.

"Everything looks good," the doctor said. "Have you had any problems?"

"The sudden shift to a sedentary lifestyle has been a shock to my system, but no bleeding or cramping pain since I came to the ER."

"What are you doing during the day?"

Peg described her routine. "And Mike's been with me all this week. The church gave him a three-month sabbatical to look after me."

"Really?" The doctor raised her eyebrows. "I didn't know churches offered family-leave time for husbands."

"It's not a FMLA request," Mike replied. "It was a decision by the church leadership."

"And I commend them for it," the doctor replied. "What's the name of your church?"

"Little Creek."

"Sounds like a good place to be." Dr. Crawford turned to Peg. "Increase the amount of walking around the house and the yard so you won't lose too much muscle tone. We want to strike a balance between avoiding stress on the baby and maintaining your own health. Your weight is good. The baby is growing fine, and the heart rate is within normal limits. Things look stable."

"Can you determine gender?" Mike asked.

"Too early for that. We may be able to tell at the next examination."

Peg patted her stomach. "Keep growing."

"How are you doing emotionally?" the doctor asked Peg. "Any depression or unusual mood swings?"

"Not too bad. Having Mike around has helped a lot."

"Bring more variety into your activities, but stop physical activity at the first sign of trouble and let me know."

"I have a case on the trial calendar in about ten days," Mike said. "Should I request a continuance to stay with Peg?"

"You're still working as a lawyer?"

"It's a pro bono case."

"How long will the trial last?"

"Could be several days depending on jury deliberation."

"That shouldn't be a problem so long as Peg has someone available on call. I'm sure you have friends who could fill in, or you could use a sitting service. Contact my office if you need a recommendation for outside help."

As they drove home from the doctor's office, Mike spoke to Peg. "I guess I can't use Dr. Crawford's recommendation as an excuse for a continuance in Sam's case."

"Do you need one?"

"There are still a lot of loose ends. Every time I pull out one string another takes its place."

They arrived home. Peg got out of the car, but Mike stayed in the driver's seat.

"Aren't you coming in?" she asked, leaning back into the car.

"I want to go to the church," he replied.

"Go," she said. "I've been impressed you haven't called or gone over there before now."

"You'll be okay?"

"Yes. I'm going to walk Judge around the yard a few times to celebrate my release from house arrest."

Twenty-five

Mike parked but didn't go directly to the church office. Leaning against his car, he let his eyes roam across the property. Every season in the hills of North Carolina offered unique beauty, but spring and fall were his favorites. Once started, spring came quickly to the mountains. The ancient trees beside the old sanctuary were in full foliage; the barren spots in the grass filled in. He listened. The explosion of birdcalls that had surrounded him a few weeks earlier during mating season had settled down to the less-ardent conversations of routine life. The creek now ambled rather than rushed, but Mike knew fresh water still bubbled to the surface of the spring.

Mike realized how much he'd tightly wound his expectations for the future around his work at the church. To end it would be painful. He'd seen the stress etched across the faces of other ministers and secretly looked down on their weakness, thinking his background as a trial lawyer inoculated him against the pressures of the pastoral ministry. The past few weeks had blown apart his confidence. He'd privately vacillated between unleashing Delores as the opening salvo of an all-out war to save his ministry and immediately resigning to avoid prolonging the pain.

He walked into the administration wing. Delores glanced up as he approached her desk.

"It's about time!" she exclaimed. "You've already cost me a steak dinner bet with Nathan."

"What do you mean?"

"I told him you would call on Monday. When that didn't happen, we did a double-or-nothing bet that you would come to the office by Wednesday.

You totally let me down, so I have to buy him a gift certificate for two to the Mountain View."

"I pretended to be on vacation," Mike replied.

"And how often did you call in the last time you went on vacation?"

"Every day. You could have picked up the phone and called me."

"That would have nixed the bet." Delores paused. "And I wanted you to have a break if you really wanted one."

"Thanks. How are you holding up?"

Delores touched a pack of cigarettes in plain view on her desk. "I've upped my nicotine intake. And don't be too hard on me," she added hurriedly. "I haven't cussed out Milton, and I've kept my mouth shut about how bad the elders treated you."

"How about Dr. Mixon?"

"He's a nice man but not near the preacher you are."

Mike stifled secret pleasure at her words. Delores continued, "But I saved you a CD of the sermon. Do you want to hear it?"

"Uh, sure." Mike took the CD. "Thanks. Any mail or phone calls I need to take care of?"

"There is a huge stack of stuff on your desk, but Bobby told me to leave it alone. The elders are meeting Saturday morning to sort through everything. I think it would be better for them to deal with it and realize how much you do."

"Any emergencies?"

"I'm taking names and numbers for people who need counseling. I think the session is going to authorize payment by the church if an individual or couple wants to go to a private counselor."

"That could cost a lot of money!"

Delores lowered her voice. "Milton put a big check in the offering plate to make everything look good."

The church treasurer and one of the deacons were the only people who knew who and how much was contributed each week. Mike purposely kept himself ignorant of the information.

"Delores, you know better than to snoop—"

"It was on top of the stack of checks, and I couldn't help seeing it. I didn't look at anything else."

"I ought to suspend you without pay for a week."

"Then I couldn't pay for Nathan's dinner. I think he's going to take Melissa Hall. She was with him again at church on Sunday."

"I'll be seeing quite a bit of her myself. The Miller case is on the trial calendar for a week from Monday. She'll be handling the prosecution."

"Good!" Delores exclaimed. "Once that's over, maybe we can get back to normal around here."

"I'm beginning to wonder if I know what normal looks like." Mike turned to leave. "Oh, one other thing. Don't you have a friend who works at the Bank of Barlow County?"

"Gloria Stinson. She's been a secretary there for years."

"Which department?"

"Different ones. She used to have her own little office, but now she's part of a clerical pool. Only the big shots have their own secretary. If she weren't so close to retirement, she'd probably quit."

"Could you ask her if the bank has any old IBM Selectric typewriters?"

"Do you want to buy one?"

Mike nodded. "Yeah, if it's the right one. Don't mention my name when you call. Because of the Miller case, I'm not the most popular person at the bank."

"Gloria can tell me. She keeps up with everything."

DELORES PHONED MIKE ON HIS CELL BEFORE HE WAS HALFWAY home.

"I talked to Gloria. She tells me they still use a couple of IBM typewriters to fill out forms that don't have templates in the computers."

"Any for sale?"

"She didn't think so, even though they rarely use them. She has one near her desk, and a lady who works in her area has the other one. She said you could find a used one at an office supply company a lot easier than trying to purchase one from the bank."

Mike slowed the car as he came to a bridge across the creek.

"Could you ask her to type a few words on each one and give it to you? I want to make sure about the font before I decide what to do."

"Sure."

Mike took a slip of paper from his pocket and slowly read a sentence provided by Darius York. "Tell her to type 'More liberty is needed in the USA for all those who love the truth.'"

"Why that?"

"Did you write down the sentence?" Mike asked without answering.

"Yes."

"And ask her to do it as soon as possible and let me know. Thanks."

Mike hung up the phone before Delores could launch another question. If Gloria properly capitalized the sentence, Mike would have the letters Darius York needed to evaluate the type on the checks.

THAT NIGHT AFTER SUPPER, MIKE AND PEG SAT IN THE GREAT room and listened to the CD of the church service at Little Creek.

"What did you think?" Mike asked after the closing hymn.

"Do you want me to compare his style to yours and tell you how much better you are in the pulpit?"

"It sounds petty when you put it that way."

Peg reached over and patted him on the hand. "You're my favorite speaker, even if you reject my sermon suggestions, but I'd like to meet Dr. Mixon and hear more stories about Africa. I think he can inspire the congregation to be less provincial and self-focused. And his prayer for us seemed sincere."

"Yeah. He came across that way when I talked to him."

"Look at it this way. We prayed with Sam and Muriel that God would bless the service at Little Creek, and He did."

"I don't want to be narrow-minded myself. I need to see Mixon more as an ally than a threat to my little kingdom."

"That sounds more mature."

Mike chuckled. "I want to be a big boy, but the little boy is still running around inside me wanting attention."

"Sometimes he's cute."

"Other times he's a selfish brat."

Peg smiled. "Don't be too hard on yourself. Many times, your little boy has been a lot less selfish than my little girl."

DELORES CAME BY THE HOUSE MONDAY MORNING AND HANDED Mike two sheets of paper. Gloria had done her job well.

"Perfect," he said. "There's nothing like the crispness of an IBM Selectric with a standard ball in place."

"What's this about?" Delores responded as she stood in the middle of the kitchen. "You're not in the market for a typewriter."

Mike looked up. "Yes, I am, but not for personal use. It has to do with the Miller case, and I can't tell you the details."

"You tricked me."

"I didn't tell you everything because I can't. I'd love to buy the typewriter if it's connected to the case. You and your friend have helped an innocent man."

"Will Gloria get into trouble?"

"Her name won't come up unless you mention it. No one will know how I got this information."

"But you might make her come to court. I know how you are when you get your mind set on something. You forget the effect it may have on other people."

"No. You trusted me, and she trusted you. I won't violate that. There is a legal way to avoid identifying her. If this works out for the case, I'll pay for both of you to go to the Mountain View."

"Okay," Delores replied in a way that didn't imply confidence. "But if something bad happens to Gloria, I'll never forgive you."

Mike drove into town and sent the sample sheets to Darius York via next-day delivery. He stopped by the district attorney's office to find out about the status of the original checks, but Melissa Hall wasn't in.

Mike phoned Braxton Hodges at the paper.

"We need to talk," the reporter said when he picked up the phone. "Are you available?"

"Yes."

"Come to my office."

Mike turned left at traffic light six and arrived at the newspaper building. Hodges took him into the same conference room where Mike had met with Brian Dressler.

"Investigative reporting is what makes my juices flow," the reporter said, leaning across the table. "Butch Niles recently went to Atlantic City where he dropped a lot of money in a weekend."

"How did you confirm it?"

"From one of the women who cleans his house. She heard Butch's wife complaining about it and mentioned it to the lady who cleans my duplex once a month. She passed the info on to me."

"That's triple hearsay," Mike replied.

"But it fits the corrupt politician model." Hodges paused. "And I have written proof."

The reporter reached into his pocket and pulled out several crumpled slips of paper.

Mike could see faint numbers printed on them.

"Receipts for chips at two different casinos," Hodges said. "The cleaning lady took them out of the trash. The total is close to $300,000."

Mike didn't touch the papers.

"Why did she take them?"

"Butch and his wife don't pay very well. I'm supplementing her income to be on the lookout for interesting information."

"You'd better be careful—"

"Don't worry," Hodges interrupted. "She knows not to take anything that hasn't been discarded."

"But still no relevance to my case."

"Maybe in a court of law, but not in the court of public opinion."

When he returned home, Mike had a voice mail from Darius York.

"I'm eighty-five percent sure we have a match on the typewriter," the former FBI agent said.

"Eighty-five percent?"

"Yes."

"I'm not sure that's high enough to help. Why can't you be more certain?"

"I'd need to see both machines and check all the letters, numbers, symbols, etc. Because it's an electric typewriter the pressure on the letters is uniform, so I have a good sample to compare with the letters on the checks. The sentence I gave you included those letters, but it takes more than a couple of significant similarities to increase the probability for a particular machine into the ninety-five-percentile range."

"I'm not sure I can obtain access to the machines."

"If you want a higher probability, that's the only way to get it. What is the status of the original checks?"

"Still waiting on the DA's office, but they have to furnish them this week. We're on the trial calendar next Monday."

"How much notice can you give me about the trial date?"

"The judge will hold a calendar call on Friday and set the preliminary schedule; however, that often changes because last-minute deals are struck over the weekend. Are there any days that don't work for you next week?"

"I'm clear but need as much notice as possible. The balance of my fee will have to be paid before I come."

Mike winced. "I'll give it to you when you review the original checks."

"Examining the checks will be helpful. It's all cumulative, and I don't want to speculate without the data to support my testimony."

"Of course not." Mike paused. "Sometimes, less is more. We may not introduce evidence about the typewriters if it lessens the impact of your opinion about the signature stamp."

Mike's confidence in the benefit he might achieve from Darius York was slipping. Jurors were skittish of experts, and if the members of the jury believed Mike was trying to hoodwink them with York's testimony, it wouldn't matter what the witness said. Mike, York, and Sam would all be considered guilty.

"That's your call," York said.

When he hung up the phone, Mike wished he could walk down the hall and ask Bobby Lambert or Maxwell Forrest what to do. One of the benefits of practicing with other lawyers was the availability of advice from peers, especially an attorney like Mr. Forrest, who had seen so much during the course of his career. Judge came into the study.

"You're a judge," Mike said as he scratched the dog's wrinkled head behind his left ear. "What do you think?"

Judge moaned slightly in appreciation for the attention.

"My sentiments exactly," Mike replied.

MIKE TURNED THE HOME OFFICE INTO A WAR ROOM. He devoted two legal pads to each witness and jotted down ideas for direct and cross-examination. On another pad, he listed possible exhibits and the pros and cons of their use at trial. His evidence professor in law school preached one maxim that Mike totally believed—"Never do anything in a case that will hurt you more than it helps you." Lawyers had a tendency to become myopic and view all evidence in the light most favorable to their client's position. To combat this, Mike liked to mock-try cases with surrogate jurors brought in to hear the evidence and offer detailed feedback. Paying

Darius York was already stressing Mike's bank account. He couldn't afford the expense of a mock trial.

Instead, he relied on Peg.

Once he finished a series of direct examination questions, he walked from the office to the art room and read them to Peg. She listened and told him what else she would like the witness to say. Toward the end of their third session, Peg yawned several times.

"Am I boring you?" Mike asked anxiously. "A bored jury is dangerous."

"No, but I need a baby nap."

Mike looked at his watch. It was 4:00 p.m.

"I'll call the DA's office."

Melissa Hall came on the line.

"Do you have the checks?" he asked.

"No, but a courier is bringing them over from the bank early Wednesday morning."

"Where can my expert examine them?"

"At our office with a member of the staff present. Early afternoon will be fine."

"Set it at one-thirty. If that changes, I'll let you know."

Mike confirmed the appointment time with Darius York then prepared a subpoena for production of the bank's IBM typewriters at the same time and place. He'd already sent out subpoenas for Dick Bunt and Troy Linden to the states where they resided to be signed by a local clerk and served by a deputy sheriff. Their presence wasn't essential at the trial, but he hoped to tag at least one of the men. Mike filled in a number of witness subpoenas. At the law firm, he'd used a private process server to deliver local subpoenas. Without that luxury, he drove to the bank himself.

The Bank of Barlow County had an imposing gray marble facing on the front with the name of the bank chiseled in large letters across the top of the building. However, marble covered only the front. The sides and back of the block-long structure were plain red brick. Prosperity in Barlow County was often only surface-deep.

Mike entered the lobby, a large open space with a two-story ceiling. Internet banking hadn't yet dented the market in Shelton, and a row of teller stations stretched across one end of the lobby. On busy Fridays, all eight tellers would be in place ready to receive payroll checks. Late afternoon on a Monday, only two teller spots were open.

To the left of the lobby was a bull-pen area for customer service representatives and junior loan officers who handled car financing, small personal loans, and applications for residential mortgages. A vice president in a glass-walled corner office supervised the floor operations. More significant business was always sent "upstairs."

The second-floor business area could be reached by a broad staircase or an elevator. Mike took the stairs. He and Peg didn't have an account at the bank, and he'd not been to the second floor since he and the church treasurer arranged the financing for the new sanctuary at Little Creek. At the top of the stairs, there was a reception area with leather chairs and several sofas. Two women routed people to the appropriate individual or department. Mike could serve the subpoena on any bank officer. He approached the younger of the receptionists and introduced himself.

"My mother visited your church," the receptionist replied in a chipper voice. "She liked it, but she moved to Nashville to help my sister who had triplets."

"I'm glad she enjoyed the service. Is one of the bank officers available? I have something to deliver, and it won't take long."

The woman glanced down at a sheet of paper.

"Actually, Mr. Hatcher finished a meeting a few minutes ago."

Mike smiled. "That will be fine."

He watched the woman dial Jack Hatcher's office and tried to read the reaction to the news that Mike was in the building. She hung up the phone.

"He'll see you," she said. "Do I need to take you to his office?"

"No thanks. I know the way."

Jack Hatcher's office suite covered an entire corner of the building. From his desk, the president of the bank could look out large, floor-to-ceiling windows and keep an eye on Shelton. Mike opened the door to the outer office where Hatcher's personal assistant worked. The carpet in his outer office was noticeably nicer than the floor covering. The same woman had worked for the bank president for many years. She nodded in greeting to Mike.

"Good afternoon, Reverend Andrews. You can see Mr. Hatcher now."

Mike stepped into the banker's office. Hatcher rose from behind his desk and came around and shook Mike's hand.

"Good to see you. Been on any more bike rides?"

"No, I've been staying close to home."

"Have a seat," the banker said, gesturing. "What can I do for you?"

Mike opened his briefcase. "I have two subpoenas to give you."

He handed the documents to Hatcher, whose genial expression evaporated at the first glance.

"You want me to appear at Miller's trial?" he blurted out.

"Yes, sir. Along with the bank's IBM typewriters. The machines have to be delivered to the district attorney's office before one-thirty on Wednesday. Your subpoena is day-to-day next week depending on when the case is called for trial. If you provide a local contact number, I won't object to the judge allowing you to be on telephone standby."

Mike watched the muscles in Hatcher's face twitch as the banker tried to formulate a response.

"Of course, the bank wants to cooperate with the legal process, but I'm a busy man. Can't a more junior officer provide the information you need?"

"No, sir. You have unique knowledge about the facts and circumstances that makes you the only witness competent to testify."

"What are you talking about?" Hatcher's attempt to maintain his composure cracked.

"Sam Miller. That's why I'm here."

"I don't know Miller! The man embezzled money from one of our depositors. What can you ask me about beyond the records turned over to the district attorney's office? I don't know what your client told you, but if you intend on putting the bank on trial in this case, you're making a serious mistake."

Mike hesitated. "Mr. Hatcher, I appreciate your willingness to discuss this with me, but you might want to consult your lawyer."

"Don't patronize me!" Hatcher's eyes flashed.

Mike narrowed his eyes. "Would you let me finish?"

Hatcher nodded.

"I asked for access to documents generated by your internal investigation, but the information Mr. Forrest provided didn't even include what I'd already uncovered on my own. That let me know there hasn't been full disclosure, and I intend to use every legal avenue available to get to the truth. My job is to represent my client. This case has already caused me considerable personal and professional hardship, and I don't intend on backing down now."

Hatcher waved his hand to signal the end of the interview. "Then you'd better talk to Maxwell Forrest if you want anything from us."

Mike stood. "He knows my number."

Mike returned to the waiting area and thanked the young receptionist for her help.

"Is Butch Niles in the bank?" he asked.

"No."

"When do you expect him back?"

The woman looked at her computer screen. "He'll be in the office all day Wednesday."

MIKE RETURNED HOME TO A BLINKING LIGHT ON HIS ANSWERING machine. He pushed the button and listened to the familiar voice of Maxwell Forrest. The older lawyer sounded calm, but Mike knew anger boiled beneath the surface.

"Jack Hatcher notified me about the subpoenas served on him. I'll file appropriate responses with the court. Copy me on anything else you deliver to the bank or its officers." There was brief pause. "And I expect you to comply with my instructions not to have contact with anyone at the firm about this matter."

Mike made several quick notes on one of his legal pads. Powerful businessmen like Jack Hatcher were often surprisingly easy targets on the witness stand. Used to dominating meetings and browbeating underlings, they didn't adapt well to the controlled environment of the courtroom where the judge reigned supreme, and the rules of engagement allowed an attorney to dictate the topic to be discussed.

He nodded in satisfaction. Whether Hatcher was in a church pew or on a witness stand, he would be in Mike's domain. And Mike would know what to do with him.

Twenty-six

After supper, he phoned Sam Miller. "I need to go over your testimony," Mike said. "Can you come to my house tomorrow afternoon?"

"Yep," Sam replied. "But I've given my testimony so many times that I don't need to practice it. I can tell you quick what happened. I was in darkness and sin until the Master set me free and brought me into the light. I've got a longer story that I use sometimes in a church meeting—"

"I'm talking about the questions and answers in court," Mike interrupted, with a silent plea for help directed toward the ceiling. "As a criminal defendant, you don't have to testify in court, but with the evidence against you, I don't see any way around it. We need to rehearse what you'll say so you won't get sidetracked or confused in front of the jury. I'm going to write out every question and answer. We'll go over them, then Muriel can help you memorize the responses. I'm also going to write out questions I think the district attorney is going to ask and ways to answer that won't make you look guilty."

"What time? I have a couple of yards that need cutting."

"Three o'clock?"

"That should work."

Peg had taken Judge outside for a brief walk in the evening air. Mike joined her. They skirted the edge of the woods and around the side of the house.

"Do you want me to pretend that I'm Butch Niles when we go inside?" Peg asked.

"Maybe later. I've been going hard all day and need a break."

"You didn't say two sentences during supper."

Mike took her hand. "Sorry, my mind is crunching all the possibilities. With all the subpoenas going out, it's impossible to completely hide what I intend to do, and I'm still working it out myself."

"Did you serve subpoenas on the men who live out of state?"

"Hatcher didn't mention it today, so I'll need to check tomorrow."

Peg stopped while Judge sniffed the edge of an azalea bush.

"Are you concerned the bad guys might have organized-crime connections?" she asked.

"The thought crossed my mind when I found out Linden bribed a public official in New Jersey," Mike admitted. "But that happened ten years ago. I think the current deal is probably simple greed."

"Should I be worried?"

Mike looked in Peg's eyes and saw anxiety.

"It's probably the baby," she continued. "My body is telling me to be careful and protect the life I carry. I know it's nonsense, but my imagination has gone down a few scary paths while I've been lying in bed."

Mike squeezed her hand. "Try not to worry. I'm just a lawyer doing his job. We're not living in a third-world country."

"I know, and I want you to defend Sam, but don't turn this into a big crusade. Some of the questions you read to me today sounded more like a U.S. Senate hearing than the defense of a small-town criminal case."

"You should have told me."

"I am."

"That's a hard line to draw. At first glance, the evidence against Sam looks so convincing that it will take a big target to cover it up."

THE FOLLOWING DAY, MIKE DEVOTED THE ENTIRE MORNING TO Sam's testimony. He cut it up into bite-sized pieces he hoped his client could digest. During a mid-morning break, he confirmed that both Bunt and Linden had been served with subpoenas. If Mike used all the witnesses on his roster, his estimate that the case would last a day and a half would be a gross underestimate. He could already envision keeping Jack Hatcher on the stand for most of a day.

Shortly before lunch, the front doorbell chimed. Mike opened the door to a young man in a suit.

"I'm from Forrest, Lambert, and Arnold," he said. "Are you Mr. Andrews?"

"Yes."

The man handed him a thick envelope. "This is from Mr. Forrest."

Mike took the packet and closed the door. He weighed it in his hand, already suspecting what it contained.

"Who was at the door?" Peg called out from the great room.

"Someone with a present from Mr. Forrest. Do you want to open it?"

"Not unless it's addressed to me."

Mike went into the office. The envelope contained motions to quash the subpoenas for all the people he'd served except Brian Dressler, and objections to delivering any written or tangible evidence. A second batch of paperwork included motions for protective orders designed to prevent the type of broad-range fishing expedition Mike considered essential to defense of the case. A hearing on the motions was set for Thursday after the calendar call. Mike walked into the great room.

"Mr. Forrest wants me to call Sam and Brian Dressler as my only witnesses without any information from the bank or anyplace else."

"What are you going to do?"

"Keep serving subpoenas."

When he resumed work on questions and answers, Mike started humming. Returning to the battlefield, he was like a warhorse that snorts in excitement at the smell of gunpowder. He worked steadily until Sam and Muriel arrived. They went into the kitchen.

"I don't want you sitting in my recliner and leaving the planet," Mike said. "We'll set up the kitchen like a courtroom and work in there."

Peg and Judge joined them.

"The judge is here," Peg said.

Mike smiled.

"You know, animals see things people miss," Sam continued. "We had a dog named Blue that knew when angels were in the room. Sometimes, he'd stare at the corner where Muriel sat to pray and read her Bible. I asked Papa about it, and He reminded me of a verse—"

"Okay," Mike interrupted as he moved a chair to the side. "This will be the witness chair. Muriel, you'll be the jury. I want Sam to look at you while he testifies. Eye contact with the jury is very important."

"The eye is the lamp of the body," Sam replied.

"That's right. And I want the jury to see that there isn't anything criminal in you."

Peg joined Muriel in the jury box. Mike sat in a chair across from Sam.

"This isn't like TV," Mike said. "In North Carolina, the attorneys sit while asking questions unless showing evidence to the witness or the judge. As soon as you are in the witness chair, make eye contact with the jury."

Sam looked at Muriel and Peg and smiled.

"Don't smile," Mike corrected. "This isn't a time for levity."

"What?"

"Look sincere and serious."

Sam looked at the women again.

"That's good," Mike said. "The jury will be very curious about you and will pay close attention to the first minute or so you're on the witness stand."

"I'm still concerned about my dream that my enemies will be on the jury," Sam said.

"We'll be together during jury selection, and you can let me know if you spot any unfriendly faces."

"It's going to take more than man's wisdom to know what to do."

"Then ask God to give it to us so we can make the right decisions. All it takes is a couple of strong jurors in our favor to influence the whole panel. There may be twelve people on the jury, but most cases are decided by a few strong-willed individuals. You pray while I ask them questions."

"Yep."

"Raise your right hand."

Sam complied. Mike administered the oath.

"The judge will do that when we're in court."

"Like he did the other day."

"Exactly. Then I'll ask you a lot of easy questions about who you are and what you do. Let's get started."

As they worked through the background questions, Mike was pleased with the relaxed way Sam projected his responses to the pretend jury, setting a tone of truthfulness that Mike hoped would carry over to issues central to the case.

"Tell the jury about the origins of your relationship with the Craig Valley Gospel Tabernacle," Mike said.

Sam looked at Muriel and Peg. "I was involved in the beginning of the church, and although the color of our skin is different, many of the members are like sons and daughters in the faith. Over the years, I've ministered to the people on Sunday and cut the grass during the week."

"What was your relationship with the deacons?"

"Mostly good, although there have been a few who didn't agree with me about Papa's ways. That's never a happy situation, but—"

"Hold it," Mike said. "Can you stop using the words 'Papa' and 'Master' when referring to God and Jesus?"

Sam gave Mike a rueful expression. "I figured that might come up."

"I know it makes people think about God as a person who loves us and Jesus as the One who is in charge of our lives, but it's a distraction. Without an explanation, I believe it will hurt your credibility with the jury. They'll be scratching their heads trying to figure out if you're sacrilegious instead of paying attention to what's important."

"I'm not sure what that big word means, but why can't one of us give an explanation? I like the way you put it. You've got a way of speaking that would make me jealous if it wasn't a sin."

"Because you're not the apostle Paul defending his faith before King Agrippa in the book of Acts. This is an embezzlement trial in an American courtroom."

Sam looked at Muriel. "What do you think?"

"Do what Mike suggests. That's why he's helping you."

"I'll try," Sam said to Mike. "But it's such a habit with me that I might slip up."

"If you do, I'll ask a follow-up question that will let you explain."

"I'm thirsty," Sam said. "Can we stop for a drink of water?"

Peg fixed Sam and Muriel glasses of ice water then motioned for Mike to leave the kitchen. They stepped into the great room.

"What is it?" Mike asked.

"Isn't your goal to make Sam look truthful and genuine?"

"Yes, but using those words could really backfire."

"Maybe if you or I used them, but coming from Sam, it sounds as natural as can be—a man so close in his relationship with God that he calls Him by a familial name."

"It could rub someone the wrong way."

"Yes, but it might convince someone that Sam is a good-hearted man who wouldn't embezzle money from Papa's people."

Mike smiled. "That's a good phrase. I'll consider it, but let's try it my way first."

They returned to the kitchen, and Mike resumed questioning. He was pleasantly surprised by Sam's ability to provide the right information even though Mike avoided leading questions.

"How did you learn about the extra money in your bank account?"

"When I received my bank statement. I opened the envelope and almost dropped it. I showed it to my wife and called the bank that afternoon to let them know there had been a mistake. The lady I talked to was real nice and said she would look into—"

"Can't go there," Mike interrupted. "It's hearsay. Do you remember her name?"

"Nope."

"Did anyone from the bank contact you and accuse you of embezzling money?"

"Nope. I hadn't done anything wrong."

Mike looked through his notes before he continued.

"At some point, maybe here, I'll ask you about the dream and letter to Jack Hatcher. You'll probably be the last witness, so Hatcher will have testified and, based on my questions, the jury will know about the letter. I haven't written out that portion of your testimony because it will be influenced by the information received from Hatcher, Dressler, Bunt, Linden, and Niles. Add in the expert testimony of Darius York, and we may have a circus on our hands with me as chief juggler. You won't be able to explain all the balls in the air, so we'll keep it simple. You've been kept in the dark as much as anyone in the courtroom about what is really going on."

Sam nodded. "That's true, except for what Papa shows me."

Mike nodded. "You've given me a new appreciation for that truth. Anyway, you should have the same approach to the cross-examination questions from Ms. Hall."

"What do you mean?"

Mike held up the copies of the two checks. "Mr. Miller, is your bank account number printed on the bottom of these two checks?"

"Yep."

"Sam, pretend I'm Ms. Hall. You have to say 'Yes' or 'Yes, ma'am.'"

Sam smiled. "My mama would be proud of you for that one."

Mike repeated the question.

"Yes, ma'am."

"Did you have authorization to transfer $100,000 from the Craig Valley Gospel Tabernacle building fund to your account?"

"No, ma'am, and I didn't do it."

"Isn't your signature on the bottom of the checks?"

"It looks like my name, but I didn't sign the checks. Someone else did, or they used an ink stamp without asking me."

Mike glanced at Peg, who nodded. Mike raised his voice.

"Do you expect this jury to believe that Mr. Jack Hatcher, one of the most respected men in this community, is behind a conspiracy trying to frame you on this embezzlement charge?"

Sam tilted his head to the side and looked at Muriel and Peg. "Mr. Hatcher, like the rest of us, will have to answer for what he's done in this life. All I can speak about is my actions, and I didn't try to take any money from my friends at the Craig Valley church. That's been the truth from day one."

"Not bad," Mike replied. "Not bad at all. Ms. Hall may not ask that exact question, but she'll come after you at some point in the questioning. I'm impressed with your ability to think on your feet."

"I've had plenty of practice."

"When?" Mike asked in surprise.

"Walking behind that mower."

WEDNESDAY MORNING, MIKE CONFIRMED WITH THE BANK THAT Butch Niles was in the building then drove down the hill into town. When he approached the young receptionist and started to introduce himself, she cut him off.

"I know who you are."

"Good. I'd like to see Mr. Niles, please. I called a few minutes ago to make sure he was in the building."

The young woman checked her computer screen.

"He'll be in meetings all day and won't be available," she replied curtly.

Mike leaned closer to her desk. "I know you're following orders, but tell Mr. Niles that if he tries to avoid service of this subpoena, I will notify the newspaper, and a reporter will be here within the hour to find out why."

The woman's eyes grew bigger. "I'll check again."

Mike sat on the sofa while she picked up the phone and talked for a few moments. When she hung up, she motioned for Mike to return.

"Can you come back at two o'clock?"

Mike started to protest because the time would interfere with Darius York's examination of the original checks.

"That will be fine."

He left the bank and drove to the jail. The same female deputy who had questioned his status as a bona fide lawyer was on duty.

"Is Lamar Cochran in?" Mike asked.

"He's in the back. I'll see if he's available."

The chief deputy pushed open the metal door, and the two men shook hands.

"Got another case?" Cochran asked.

"No, helping Sam has become a full-time job," Mike replied. "Would you be willing to serve a couple of subpoenas at two o'clock? I'll be in a meeting at the district attorney's office and can't do it."

"I'm on duty at the jail."

Mike took out the subpoena and handed it to Cochran. "It won't take long. I need to serve Butch Niles. He's supposed to be at the bank at that time."

"What does Niles have to do with Sam's case?"

"I can't tell you details, but Sam tossed a rock into a larger pond than he imagined and disturbed the water. Some big snakes are upset."

Cochran took the subpoena. "I'll take a late lunch break and do it."

Mike handed him a second subpoena for additional records. "Give him this one for documents, too. He can be served as an officer of the bank."

MIKE WENT TO THE COURTHOUSE. HE'D CHECKED WITH THE court administrator the previous day to make sure Judge Coberg would be in his chambers in case a dispute arose about the expert's examination of the evidence. Mike walked upstairs. Two lawyers were arguing a motion in the judge's office, but the secretary reassured Mike that the judge would be back from lunch before 1:30. His preparation complete, Mike returned home. Peg's car wasn't in the driveway. Mike immediately called her cell phone.

"Are you okay?" he asked anxiously.

"Yes, but I guess you forgot my doctor's appointment this morning, so I drove myself."

"Did you remind me?"

"Last night before we went to sleep, but I'm not sure your brain had any storage space available."

"I'll be right there."

"No need. I've already seen her. Everything looks good, and she's going to let me increase my activity to include driving short distances."

"That's great, but I'm sorry I forgot."

"I look forward to getting you back after next week."

Mike hung up the phone and called Darius York, who was on his way to Shelton.

"There will be some legal sparring about the typewriters," Mike said. "The judge will be available to sort things out."

"Will the checks be available?"

"Yes."

THE ADRENALINE PUMPING THROUGH MIKE'S VEINS WOULD HAVE allowed him to skip lunch, but he forced himself to eat. Peg came in while he washed an apple.

"Can I fix you something?" he asked.

"Part of that apple would be nice."

Mike cut it in two and handed half to her. They sat at the kitchen table.

"Libby Gorman's niece was at the doctor's office," Peg said after she took a bite. "Her baby should be here in about a month."

"Did you talk to her?"

"She saw me and looked the other way when I came into the waiting room. And she and her husband don't even go to the church!"

Mike sighed. "I'm sorry."

"I didn't have anything to be ashamed about, so I sat down beside her and asked how she was doing. She mumbled something then went to the restroom. When she came out, she sat on the opposite side of the room. It was bizarre. What could Libby have told her?"

"I can imagine a few things, but it appears the sabbatical spin isn't the only message out there."

Peg ate another bite of apple.

"People didn't like you when you were an attorney, but it was usually someone you sued."

"And some of them later hired me when they wanted to file a lawsuit. A minister is a different kind of target. Lawyers are expected to be mean. Ministers are supposed to be perfect, so any arrow of criticism can find a place to stick. I think it boils down to people feeling better about themselves if they can find something wrong with someone who is supposed to be righteous."

"That's sick."

Mike tossed his apple core across the room into the disposal side of the sink. Judge, who was lying on the floor, turned his head and watched the trajectory of the fruit.

"That's where you need to send what happened this morning. Don't carry it around. Grind it in the disposal and flush it out of your system. Otherwise, it will rot."

"Is that what you're going to do?"

Mike leaned back in his chair and laughed. "Take my own advice? That's tough to do."

MIKE WAITED FOR DARIUS YORK AT THE FRONT OF THE COURThouse. The former FBI agent was easy to spot as he walked up the sidewalk. York walked erect with his gray hair neatly trimmed, a small mustache the only departure from the TV stereotype of a government law enforcement officer. He carried a large black catalog case.

"Is everything you need in there?" Mike asked.

"Yes, so long as I have a power source."

They sat at a scarred wooden table in the courthouse library while York explained what he hoped to do with the checks and typewriters. Mike was pleased with the understandable way York described the evaluation process. Some scientifically minded people could only communicate with their peers. Mike looked at his watch. It was time to go.

They walked down the hall to the district attorney's office. Mike approached the receptionist and asked to see Melissa Hall.

"They're in the conference room," the receptionist replied.

Mike quickly tried to decide who else had decided to join them as they walked down the hall. Opening the door, his question was answered. Sitting on the opposite side of the table from Hall was Maxwell Forrest as counsel for the bank. The older lawyer nodded in Mike's direction without smiling. Mike introduced York.

"The original checks are in the file," Hall said.

Mike looked at Mr. Forrest. "And the typewriters?"

The older lawyer spoke in a measured tone. "Without conceding that any typewriters described in the subpoena are in the bank's possession, the subpoena is subject to a motion to quash."

Mike pressed his lips together. "I'm going to Judge Coberg's chambers to ask for immediate relief. You're welcome to join me."

"The hearing on the motion is set tomorrow," Forrest replied.

"But my expert is here today."

Mike turned to Hall. "Mr. York would like to review the checks while I talk to the judge."

"Okay," Hall replied, her eyes switching back and forth between Mike and Forrest.

"Are you going to approach him ex parte?" Mr. Forrest asked Mike.

"Only if you don't show up."

Mike left the room. Once in the hallway, he slowed and listened for the sound of footsteps behind him. He cleared his throat and glanced over his shoulder. The older lawyer was closing the door of the conference room.

"I'm coming," Forrest grumbled. "But you're only going to embarrass yourself if you continue with this foolishness."

"I'm already embarrassed."

The two men walked in silence up the stairs to the judge's chambers.

"Is the judge available?" Mike asked the secretary.

The woman picked up the phone and then motioned for them to go back. Judge Coberg was sitting behind his desk. Mike took a copy of the subpoena for the typewriters and Mr. Forrest's response from his briefcase and handed them to the judge.

"The Miller case is set for trial next week, and my expert is in town to examine tangible evidence. Mr. Forrest doesn't want the bank to produce the typewriters—"

"I see," the judge interrupted. "Mr. Forrest, your response."

"There's no showing of relevance sufficient to justify the burden upon the bank to locate and produce these machines, if in fact, they exist. This case is rife with attempts to abuse the subpoena power. Mr. Andrews is using multiple subpoenas as a club to threaten and harass various officers at the bank as well as demand extensive documentation without any justification of relevancy."

"Today, we're only here about the typewriters," Mike responded. "I wouldn't be troubling the Court except for the limited opportunity between now and the time of trial for my expert witness to examine this equipment."

"What is the relevance of the machines?" the judge asked.

"I want my expert to run comparison testing."

"Comparison to what? You're going to have to give me more than generalities."

"Checks," Mike replied. "I want to determine if one of these machines was used to type the name and amount on the checks listed in the indictment."

The judge nodded. "Very well. Motion to quash is denied. Mr. Andrews, how long will your expert be in town?"

"This afternoon."

The judge turned to Forrest. "Instruct the bank to locate and deliver the items identified in the subpoena to the district attorney's office before four o'clock."

Mike and Forrest left the office in silence. They walked down the stairs together. Upon reaching the bottom, Mike expected the older lawyer to turn left and exit the courthouse in the direction of his office. Instead, he stayed beside Mike as he approached the district attorney's office.

"Aren't you going to call the bank?" Mike asked.

"Take care of your own business; I'll handle mine," Forrest answered curtly.

York and Hall were in the conference room. York had set up a scanner and microscope on the table. When they entered, he was examining one of the checks under the microscope. A legal pad beside him contained a list of notes. Forrest stepped forward and looked over York's shoulder at the notes. Mike joined him and was about to slide the pad out of the way when he saw that the writing, if not in code, was so illegible that it would have taken an archaeologist to decipher.

"What are your findings?" Forrest asked.

"Don't answer," Mike responded quickly.

York looked up from the microscope at the two men hovering behind him. "Counsel, please allow me to do my job."

Forrest backed up. "Just curious."

Mike and Forrest sat across the table from each other, with Melissa Hall at one end and York at the other. The expert examined the checks and continued to make notes. The tension was palpable, and after a few minutes, Mike bowed his head and closed his eyes. Maxwell Forrest, like York, was doing his job, but Mike couldn't decide if the older lawyer was merely being an obstructionist or waging an all-out war. It was still impossible for him to imagine his former boss engaging in conscious criminal conduct.

"What did the judge do?" Hall's voice took Mike out of his reverie.

"Denied the motion to quash," Mike replied. "The typewriters are to be here by four o'clock."

Forrest spoke. "Mike thinks the checks were typed at the bank."

Hall's eyes opened wide in surprise. "You do?"

"I'm investigating any possible connections."

"What is the bank's position?" Hall asked.

"That this is a diversion designed to frustrate justice," Forrest replied. "Mike is an excellent lawyer, Ms. Hall, and you'd best be prepared for the unexpected when you go to court next week. Based solely on the subpoenas and potential witnesses I know about, this case could take most of the week to try."

"Is that right?" Hall asked Mike.

"Maybe." Mike shrugged.

Hall stood up. "I need to talk to Ken."

In a few minutes, the district attorney entered the room. York didn't look up from his microscope.

"Mike, can we meet with you in private?" West asked.

"Yes, as soon as we take a break to wait for delivery of some typewriters from the bank."

York looked up. "I'll be finished with the checks in about five or ten minutes."

Forrest looked at his watch. "I sent a text message to the bank. They will deliver three typewriters."

"I'll be in my office," West said, turning around. "I'll leave the door open."

Everyone resumed their positions around the table and waited. Mike opened his briefcase and began making notes on a legal pad. Fifteen minutes later, York pushed his chair away from the table.

"I'm done."

"Can he wait here for the typewriters?" Mike asked Hall.

"Yes, there's nothing scheduled for this room the rest of the afternoon."

Mike stood up and looked at Forrest.

"No communication with my witness, please."

Forrest waved his hand. "I'm just an observer on behalf of a client."

Mike followed Hall to Ken West's office. The district attorney swiveled his chair when they entered. Hall closed the door.

"What's going on with this case?" West asked.

"I'm representing my client with all the zeal I can muster," Mike replied. "You know I can't divulge my trial strategy."

"But taking up an entire week of court!" West raised his voice. "We have other business to attend to, including two aggravated assault cases against repeat felons."

Mike didn't respond.

"What if we put our plea offer back on the table?" West asked.

"Why did you withdraw it prematurely?" Mike shot back.

West rubbed his hands together. "As you can see from the other lawyer in the conference room, there is interest in Mr. Miller's case beyond the ordinary citizens of Barlow County."

"Then that should tell you something about my trial strategy. Perhaps officials at the bank know something about this case and the defendant that isn't in the skinny file in your office."

"If so, they haven't brought our office into the loop." West picked up a sheet of paper from his desk. "I have a list of the people you've subpoenaed. Most of the names are familiar to me, but who are Richard Bunt and Troy Linden?"

"Real estate developers—and that's all I'll tell you."

"Out of state?"

"That's obvious from the addresses on the subpoenas."

"Did you obtain service?"

"Yes."

West dropped the paper on his desk.

"And Ms. Hall tells me you believe the checks were typed at the bank."

"I'm exploring all options."

West sat up so quickly his chair groaned loudly in protest.

"Mike! Don't be so obtuse! If there is a fatal flaw in our case, I don't want to waste a week finding out!"

Mike kept calm. "Given the political pressure already brought to bear, it's hard for me to believe that opening my file to you is going to make these charges go away."

"Suit yourself. Ms. Hall needs trial experience, and as a preacher and lawyer you could give her a baptism of fire, but I've never been interested in prosecuting an innocent man."

Mike's eyes flashed. "Tell that to Danny Brewster's mother!"

West stared hard at Mike for a few seconds then turned to Hall.

"*State v. Miller* will definitely be the first case out of the gate on Monday morning."

Twenty-seven

WHEN MIKE RETURNED TO THE CONFERENCE ROOM, DARIUS York was alone. The expert had taken out a calculator.

"The other lawyer left right after you did."

Mike checked his watch. "Don't expect the typewriters a minute early. Let's go back to the library."

When they returned to the library, Mike checked to make sure they were alone. He sat at the table.

"What did you find?" he asked.

"The checks were signed with a stamp. Very carefully done to make it hard to spot at first glance, but once I put them under the scope, the ink pattern was obvious. If I could take a scraping of the ink, I could identify the type of pad used."

"And the stamp could have been manufactured from Miller's signature on another check?"

"Or more likely his signature card on file with the bank. If that matches the stamp, there will be no question in my mind what happened."

"Would there be collusion by the bank with the company making the stamp?"

"Not necessarily. Usually a signature on a blank sheet of paper is used, but the bank could have sent the signature card and told the company it was acting with the customer's consent."

Mike nodded. "I'll send Sam to the bank to get his signature card. Will you need to examine it under the microscope to see if it's a match?"

"That will help, although the loop on the *S* and the way he leans back the *e* in Miller are so distinctive, it should show up without magnification. When can you get the card?"

"I'll try to reach him now, and send him to the bank."

York touched his catalog case. "I scanned the checks, so they can be blown up and projected as part of a PowerPoint presentation to the jury. I've already worked up fourteen points of similarity on the checks. That puts use of the same stamp on both checks at over ninety-eight percent, but it would be helpful to create a few slides incorporating the signature card as well."

Mike flipped open his phone and dialed Sam's number. Muriel answered.

"This is Mike. Where is he?"

"In the storage shed working on one of his mowers."

"Please get him."

Mike waited, visualizing York's display. If the signature card matched the stamp, it would make it harder for Hall to argue that Sam had ordered a signature stamp. Linking the bank's typewriters to the checks would tighten the noose.

"Hello," Sam said.

Mike told him what to do.

"What if they won't give me a copy of my signature card?"

"Get the name of the person who refuses and let me know."

"Okay, I'll give it a try," Sam said with reluctance in his voice.

"Are you nervous about going to the bank?" Mike asked.

"Yep, I guess so. It's been hard not worrying even though I've tried to keep my mind on Papa and kept busy tinkering with my stuff."

"I can meet you at the bank if that helps."

"Nope, I'll head right over there."

"Then come to the courthouse. We'll be in the library. It's on the first floor."

While they waited, Mike and York worked through items to include in the presentation. The former FBI agent was what Mike called an automatic witness—swear him in and turn him on.

A few minutes before the typewriters were to be delivered, Sam came into the library. The old man looked out of place surrounded by legal books.

"Any problems at the bank?" Mike asked quickly.

"Nope." Sam handed a card to Mike. "I signed a new one, so they gave me the old one."

Mike and York ignored Sam as they leaned over the card.

"That's it!" Mike exclaimed. "It's identical to the stamp!"

York didn't immediately respond but took a magnifying glass from his case. Mike watched as York turned the card in several directions before looking up.

"You're right. I'll put it under the scope, but I think it's a match."

Mike glanced up at Sam. "Do you realize what this means?"

Sam shook his head.

Mike rapidly summarized the information York had developed, then held up the card in triumph.

"We're one step away from breaking the back of the prosecution's case. Once this comes into evidence, it opens the door for the other allegations connected with the bank to come in as relevant motivation to destroy you and your credibility."

York looked up at Sam, who was still standing near the door.

"You're an innocent man, Mr. Miller."

Sam didn't look pleased. "But you're not an innocent man, are you?"

"What do you mean?" York replied.

Sam touched his belly. "I saw bags of gold behind your eyes with writing on them in another language. The gold didn't belong to you, but you took it anyway."

Mike held out his hand. "Sam, don't be ridiculous. Mr. York is a former FBI agent. I've paid him to help us. He's doing an honest job."

"I'm not talking about this," Sam said, pointing to the information on the table.

Mike looked at York, who was staring at Sam as if the old man had grown two heads.

"Please, don't take offense," Mike said to York. "It's just part of what I've gone through representing him. Sam has dreams and sees things that aren't there."

"You didn't talk like that when I told you about Jack Hatcher and Butch Niles," Sam responded.

Mike stood up. "Sam, let's go into the hallway."

Mike grabbed Sam's arm and steered him out of the room.

"Why are you trying to sabotage our relationship with a man who is here to help you?" Mike asked furiously.

Sam tilted his head to the side. "If you'd seen those bags of gold, you wouldn't be getting mad at me. That man had better repent and make it right."

"That's not our job," Mike shot back.

"Why not?" Sam raised his voice. "Is Mr. York more important as a witness in my case or as a soul who will live forever in heaven or hell? What if he dies without meeting the Master in this life? What answer will he give when Papa looks in his face? What answer will you give for not caring enough to help him?"

Mike's head was spinning. "He doesn't want our help."

"How do you know? You hustled me out of there before we could find out."

Mike spoke in a softer tone. "I know you mean well, but you brought me into this case to defend you against a criminal charge of embezzlement. That includes finding and hiring an expert witness to testify to the truth. I've found one who is very competent and believable. Now, you're trying to take over defense of your case and destroy my hard work. If you do, there's no need for me to hang around."

"Why don't we let Mr. York decide? If he doesn't want to talk to me, I'll leave him alone. I can reveal the deeds of darkness, but conviction of sin isn't part of the job description Papa gave me. That's up to the Helper."

Mike didn't know what to do. In a few minutes, York would need to examine the typewriters.

"Okay," he said. "Let me go in alone. Wait here."

Sam folded his arms across his chest. "That's a good idea. You need to learn."

Mike felt his face flush but suppressed his anger. He reentered the library. York was sitting in his chair staring across the room.

"Does your client claim to be a psychic?" York asked when Mike shut the door behind him.

"No, I'm not sure what label he places on himself, but I've learned that I can't control what he says. This latest outburst is causing me to rethink my whole trial strategy. I'd planned on calling him as a witness, but if he suddenly starts accusing someone on the jury—"

"Can I speak to you confidentially?" York interrupted.

"Uh, yeah."

"At first, I didn't know what he was talking about, but there was an incident in my past that fits what he saw. It happened so long ago that I'd pushed it out of my mind, but it's not the sort of thing I could ever totally forget. Of course, the military statute of limitations has run out and it seems pointless—"

The door opened and Melissa Hall stuck her head inside. Mike could see Sam standing behind her.

"The typewriters are here," she said. "We're closing the office in thirty minutes."

"We'll be right there," Mike replied.

When Hall left, Mike shut the door in Sam's face and turned to York.

"Are you still willing to help?"

"Yes."

Mike breathed a sigh of relief. "Thanks for being a professional and overlooking my client's behavior."

"Don't worry about it. Let's get to the machines."

They left the library. Sam was waiting for them.

"Keep your mouth shut," Mike whispered to Sam as they walked down the hallway. "I'm smoothing things over with York."

There were three typewriters on the conference room table. Maxwell Forrest was present and accompanied by a man Mike didn't recognize but assumed worked for the bank. Melissa Hall stood off to the side. Mike watched Forrest closely eye Sam as the old man entered the room.

"Sit here," Mike motioned to Sam.

York opened his catalog case, took out a sheet of paper, and rolled it into the carriage of one of the machines. The conference room only contained a single outlet, and the cord attached to the machine wouldn't reach from the table to the outlet in the corner.

"Do you have an extension cord?" he asked Hall.

"No," she replied without hesitation.

York picked up the machine and placed it on the floor near the outlet. Plugging it in, he turned it on and methodically hit all the keys, both lowercase and uppercase, along with all the symbols. After repeating the process, he typed the exact information contained on each of the checks and repeated it as well. Finally, he typed the serial number for each machine on the bottom of the paper. While he worked, everyone in the room watched as intently as if the former FBI agent were performing brain surgery. Forrest made notes on a legal pad. Mike realized the bank was possibly retaining its own expert. The idea sent Mike quickly down the path of deciding how to respond to a battle of expert witnesses if the bank's expert was made available to the prosecution. York continued working until he finished and looked at his watch.

"That should do it with five minutes to spare," he said.

Mike turned to the man accompanying Forrest. "Your name, please?"

"Rick Post," Forrest replied.

"And his position?"

"At the moment, custodian of these typewriters."

Mike left the sarcastic remark alone. Post put the typewriters in boxes, placed them on a set of hand trucks, and rolled them out of the office. Forrest motioned for Mike to come into the hall.

"Do you have a minute?" Forrest asked.

"Yes." Mike turned to York and Sam. "Wait for me in the library. The courthouse doesn't close until five-thirty, so we have a little bit of time."

Mike and Forrest stepped into the hallway.

"Let's go into the courtroom," Forrest suggested.

The main courtroom was empty yet expectant, an arena waiting for arrival of the gladiators and the roar of the crowd. Forrest spoke.

"Mike, I've always held you in high regard as a person and a lawyer, and your move into the ministry was a great act of self-sacrifice that served as an inspiration to me. However, I know you're bound and determined to embarrass the bank and try to drag as many reputable businesspeople through the mud as you can. Whatever I have to do to defend my clients isn't meant to attack you personally. It's strictly business. I'm sorry you let yourself be lured back into the fight, but now you're here, and we're all going to get a little bloody before this is over."

"I'll stay within the rules."

"As will I, but mercy is limited to the walls of your church. When you come into this courtroom on Monday, mercy won't be a word in the dictionary."

Mike looked at the wooden floor for a few seconds before looking up and responding.

"And I sincerely hope you're not involved in what may have happened in this case."

Forrest looked Mike in the eye. "Have you ever known me to cross any ethical or moral line?"

"No, sir."

"Then we go into this with an understanding of the past, which I hope won't be violated in the future."

Forrest extended his hand, and Mike shook it. The firm grip that had greeted Mike's arrival in Shelton when he graduated from law school was noticeably weaker. They returned to the hallway and went in opposite directions.

Mike found Sam and York sitting across from each other.

"It won't be easy," York was saying.

"What now?" Mike asked.

"Nothing," York replied with a wave of his hand. "Let me set up and quickly check the typed samples. I'll do a more extensive review at home, but I can give you a preliminary opinion before I leave."

He placed enlarged copies of the two checks on the table and set up his microscope.

"Computers can do the same kind of analysis that I'm performing," York said as he prepared his equipment.

"But they can't testify under oath and give an opinion," Mike responded.

"True, but I may run them through a program on my computer to bolster the credibility of my opinion."

York placed one of the sheets of paper under the microscope and began moving it from letter to letter. In a few minutes, he removed it.

"It's not this one," he said. "The *r* and capital *M* are totally different."

He picked up another sheet and examined it, taking much longer. Mike looked at his watch. The courthouse would close in a few minutes. He really wanted an opinion before York left town.

"I think this is it," York said without raising his eye from the viewer. "I've found identifiable marks on five of the letters and two of the numbers with several more letters to analyze."

"Where would that put the percentages?"

York sat up straight. "Not sure, but by the time I finish, I should be able to convince a reasonable person that the checks were typed at the bank."

Mike broke out a smile. "It only takes one reasonable juror to stop a conviction, and a few strong ones for acquittal can usually carry the day. The signature stamp could have been explained away, but access to this typewriter is completely outside Sam's control. This is huge."

York began packing up his gear. "I'll do a thorough evaluation of the other typewriter as well and give you a call tomorrow."

"Good."

When he was finished, York stood and looked at Sam.

"Thank you, Mr. Miller."

"You're welcome, but mercy comes from Papa's heart."

After York left, Mike turned to Sam. "Mercy? What's that all about? I thought you were going to leave him alone."

Sam held up his hands in surrender. "He brought it up, and I answered him."

"What did you say?"

Sam rubbed his stomach. "I didn't think you liked the water in my well, and now you're asking for a drink the Master provided another man. What am I supposed to do with you?"

Mike shook his head. "Okay, keep it to yourself. But it's good to know there is still mercy at the courthouse."

MIKE DIDN'T REALIZE HOW TIRED HE WAS UNTIL HE'D LOOSENED his tie and deposited his briefcase in the downstairs office. Peg was in the kitchen sitting on a stool and preparing a large salad for supper.

"We're eating healthy for supper," she said. "I want our baby to like everything I'm throwing into this salad."

"Fine with me; I'll sleep soundly tonight whether my stomach is empty or full."

While they ate, Mike told her some of the events of the day. He left out Sam's warning to Darius York. He suspected Peg would be upset with him for the way he handled the situation. When he described his conversation with Forrest in the courtroom, she spoke.

"What was he trying to do? Get you to quit?"

"No, I don't think so. At first, I thought he was playing a mind game with me—a one-man good cop/bad cop routine, but now, I believe he was sincere."

"In his desire to spill your blood on the courtroom floor," Peg responded sharply.

"That part was just lawyer talk. It was the sentiment behind the words that came through in the midst of the blustering."

Peg shook her head. "Maybe I'd agree if I'd been there, but to me, he was just trying every angle to exert his will."

After supper, Mike sat in his recliner and closed his eyes. Within seconds he was in a large room without windows. The room was dark at first, but as his eyes became accustomed to the light, he could make out human shapes along the walls. Mike stood still and waited for one of the people to move or speak. Nothing happened. He waited a few more seconds then cautiously stepped toward the nearest figure. The closer he came, the more he expected a voice to challenge him, or perhaps an even more violent reaction. Two feet from the form, he slowly reached out his hand and touched it.

It was made of wax.

As Mike's eyes continued to adjust to the hazy, unnatural light, he could tell that life-size wax figures lined the walls of the room. Mike recognized the familiar forms of Maxwell Forrest, Milton Chesterfield, Braxton Hodges, along with people he'd known in the past but not seen in years. Other figures were total strangers. Some of the pedestals were empty, and he wondered whether someone had stolen the statues. Sensing a presence behind him, he quickly turned around.

And woke up.

THE FOLLOWING DAY, MIKE ARRIVED AT THE COURTHOUSE THIRTY minutes early. The fact that Judge Coberg had denied the motion about the typewriters gave him confidence that Sam's constitutional right to face his accusers would trump any privacy rights or arguments of inconvenience presented by Maxwell Forrest on behalf of the bank.

Mike entered an empty courtroom. Bowing his head, he dispatched a silent prayer thanking God for how well the case was going. When he opened his eyes, two other lawyers were entering the courtroom. In addition to motions and the call of the criminal calendar for the following week, the judge would receive guilty pleas for cases in which plea agreements had been reached. By the time Mike's watch showed nine-thirty, approximately twenty-five people and seven other lawyers, including Greg Freeman, were in the room. Maxwell Forrest wasn't one of them.

Melissa Hall was handling duties for the DA's office. She placed a large stack of files on the table without looking in Mike's direction. Several lawyers came up to her for quick discussions.

"All rise!" the deputy sheriff on duty announced.

Mike stood up as the door behind the bench opened. Judge Lancaster entered the courtroom.

"Be seated!" the deputy called out when the judge had taken his place on the bench.

Mike's heart was pounding and his mouth felt dry. William Lancaster was a rogue judge—unpredictable and, at times, capricious. Mike had experienced uneven success before him. The fiasco with Danny Brewster obliterated any positive memories.

"Court will come to order," the judge said in his slightly pinched voice.

"Judge Coberg was called out of town on a family emergency. I will be receiving pleas as well as presiding over next week's criminal trial calendar."

"Proceed," the judge said to Ms. Hall.

The young DA began calling cases. Individuals stepped forward, some with attorneys, others unrepresented. As the judge began receiving guilty pleas, Mike listened closely, not because he had any interest in the cases, but to determine if the judge was going along with the deals or rejecting them. Out of the first three cases, only one plea agreement survived intact.

Several attorneys sitting near Mike began to whisper. Mike couldn't hear their conversations but knew they were discussing whether to seek a continuance in an effort to avoid facing Judge Lancaster. The same thought crossed Mike's mind.

The requests for continuance began to flow, and Lancaster didn't seem to mind. The judge wasn't lazy, but his mood of the moment made him receptive to postponement of justice to another day. A few guilty pleas slipped through intact. When only a few people were left in the courtroom, the back door opened, and Maxwell Forrest entered. Bobby Lambert was with him. Forrest was a formidable foe, but Mike would rather face him than contend with his friend. The judge finished the first part of the calendar.

"Ms. Hall, how many cases are you placing on next week's trial calendar?"

"Seven," she responded. "First out will be *State v. Miller*."

"I'm representing Mr. Miller," Mike said as he stood to his feet.

The judge looked at him as if noticing him for the first time. "What are you doing here?"

"I've maintained my license, Your Honor," Mike replied, "and I'm defending Mr. Miller."

"What's the charge?" the judge asked Hall.

"Felony embezzlement from a nonprofit organization. The indictment charges the defendant with embezzling in excess of $100,000 from a church."

The judge turned to Mike. "It wasn't your church, was it?"

"No, sir."

The judge grunted. "How long do you anticipate it will take to try the case?"

"One day for the State's case," Hall responded.

"Two to three days for the defense," Mike said.

The judge leaned forward. "That's virtually the whole week! Isn't there a way to get this pared down so the court can handle more than one case?"

Maxwell Forrest spoke. "Your Honor, if I could interject?"

"Go ahead."

"The primary reason for the excessive length of trial is a plethora of subpoenas issued by Mr. Andrews to people across the entire country and his demand for voluminous records from the Bank of Barlow County. Mr. Lambert and I are here to argue several motions to quash the subpoenas."

The judge turned to Mike. "Explain what you're doing."

"We were going to argue the motions after the calendar call," Mike began.

"But I want to hear the matter now," the judge snapped, "since it may affect what I tell the rest of the lawyers on standby."

Mike cleared his throat. "Yes, sir."

Mike repeated his argument of the previous day. Every time he tried to speak in generalities, the judge interrupted with a specific question. As Mike talked about Troy Linden and Dick Bunt, he realized that Maxwell Forrest was smart enough to deduce Mike's trial strategy.

"Is Representative Niles going to claim governmental privilege?" the judge asked Forrest when the legislator's name came up.

"No, sir. The legislature is not in session next week. However, I think my client and the Court have a right to know why he's being summoned. Representative Niles was not involved in the investigation into the embezzlement and had no contact with the defendant."

The judge looked at Mike.

"That's not true, Your Honor. Mr. Niles and Mr. Miller had a conversation within the past two weeks."

"About the charges?"

"Not specifically. But there is a collateral connection that will be developed through the entire testimony I will present."

"What type of collateral connection?"

Mike felt his face flush. "With all due respect, to answer that question, I would have to reveal my trial strategy."

"Then you'd better decide what will convince me not to grant Mr. Forrest's motions."

Mike quickly gathered his thoughts. "The defendant possesses knowledge that may jeopardize business interests connected to Mr. Niles."

The judge narrowed his eyes. "Are you contending these witnesses engaged in a conspiracy against your client?"

"That is an issue the jury should have a right to decide."

The judge turned to Hall. Mike saw Bobby lean over to Forrest and begin whispering.

"Does the State have a position on these subpoenas?" the judge asked the assistant DA.

"Abuse of the subpoena power of the court is not constitutionally protected activity. Therefore, we concur with Mr. Forrest's arguments and hope the Court will not empower Mr. Andrews to engage in a spurious witch hunt."

"That's an interesting characterization," the judge responded dryly. "Does the term *witch hunt* apply to men as well as women?"

Everyone in the courtroom stared at Hall to see how she would respond to the overtly sexist remark. Mike saw a red tinge travel from her neck to her cheeks.

"Yes, sir," she managed.

"Court will be in a five-minute recess until I announce my decision," the judge said.

Judge Lancaster left the bench. Maxwell Forrest and Bobby came forward to talk to Melissa Hall. Greg Freeman approached Mike.

"Any predictions?" Mike asked.

"This is my first look at Judge Lancaster," the younger lawyer said, "and it's not pretty. You saw what he did to my plea bargain."

The judge had rejected the plea, forcing Freeman's client to choose between letting the judge sentence him without any guaranteed result or going to trial.

"If my case takes all week, you can bring the plea deal before Judge Coberg when he returns to the bench."

"That's what I'm counting on. Are you sure your case will take four days?"

"Yes. It always takes longer than you think." Mike motioned toward Hall, Forrest, and Bobby, who continued to talk in earnest. "They're trying to sell something to Ms. Hall right now, but I'm not sure what it is."

Mike tried to stay calm, but inside he was wrapped tight in the turmoil of suspense. The next words from the judge's mouth would dictate the scope of events for the next week and a half. A favorable ruling would allow Mike to proceed as planned; an adverse decision would force him to greatly restrict the scope of his defense. The judge returned. Instead of speaking, he wrote something on a sheet of paper in front of him.

"Motion denied," he said without glancing up. "Mr. Forrest, tell the subpoenaed witnesses you represent to be here Monday morning along with the tangible items requested by the defendant."

"Yes, sir."

"Thank you, Your Honor," Mike added.

The judge ignored him and turned to Hall. "What is the call list for the remaining cases on the trial calendar? I want everyone involved in the number two and three cases here on Monday in case there is an unforeseen delay in the Miller case."

"One other matter on the Miller case," Hall replied. "Mr. Forrest has been talking to me, and, uh . . ."

Maxwell Forrest stepped forward and continued, "Mr. Lambert and I will be filing a request to serve as special prosecutors in this case."

"That's up to the district attorney," the judge grunted. "But I'm warning all of you. Nobody is going to undermine the efficient administration of justice in my courtroom." The judge looked at Mike. "That goes double for you, Mr. Andrews."

"Yes, sir."

"I'll notify you as soon as Mr. West makes his decision," Hall said to the judge.

The judge waved his hand. "Go on. Give me the rest of your calendar."

Mike didn't hear Hall's response. His heart rate slowed as he closed his briefcase. Forrest's desire to be directly involved made sense. Never common, use of a special prosecutor occurred when the wealthy victim of a crime wanted to make sure the responsible person was convicted and hired the best trial lawyer in town to assist the State's prosecutor. Jack Hatcher and those connected to him were scared—scared enough to spend a lot of money to guarantee a guilty verdict.

WHEN MIKE TURNED ON HIS PHONE AFTER LEAVING THE COURTroom, he had a voice mail from Darius York. Mike punched in the expert's number.

"I spent the morning running comparisons on the typewriters and the checks," York said. "I'm going to blow up the individual letters on the checks and place them beside the ones from the sample sheet of the typewriter used. To emphasize the uniqueness of each unit, I'll also include the letters and numbers from the other two machines. Several letters stand out strong."

"Sounds good."

"It is. The machine used is by far the most distinctive of the units. Your client is lucky."

"I'm not sure he believes in luck."

"Whatever he believes is different from anything I've ever encountered."

"You don't have to tell that to me."

"He has a strong defense. I've rarely seen this type of exculpatory evidence. I know anything can happen in court, but Mr. Miller should walk away from this with a lawsuit against someone for causing him to suffer through this ordeal."

"When can I preview your presentation?"

"I'll have it ready by the end of the day on Sunday. I'll send it to you via e-mail as a PDF attachment so you can give feedback before I drive down on Monday."

"Great. You won't testify the first day of trial. It will take all morning to pick the jury, and the State's case will fill the rest of the day. I suspect most of the evidence on behalf of the bank will take place during rebuttal. The bank president and his business partners want to use a special prosecutor to make sure their interests are protected."

"I can't blame them," York responded. "The district attorney looked younger than my granddaughter."

"This is her first felony trial. She may deliver the opening statement and handle the direct examination of the detective who interviewed Sam, but you'll be cross-examined by an experienced trial lawyer."

"It's been done before. I can hold my own. Any word on their expert?"

"No, but the State has to serve me with an amended list of witnesses if they intend to use one."

AS HE DROVE UP THE HILL TO HIS NEIGHBORHOOD, MIKE thought about the Little Creek Church. He'd been so occupied with the upcoming trial that he'd not dwelt on the shadow lands beyond the jury's verdict. Several possibilities passed through his mind in quick succession, but he squelched them. For the moment, *State v. Miller* was his past, present, and future.

Peg was in the art room working on a sketch that would be the basis for another watercolor.

"Take a look," she said.

Mike stood beside her. It was a bird's-eye view of a 1950s-era beach house with a family on the sand between the house and the ocean. Several children splashed in the surf. Mike quickly counted.

"Five kids. Whose house is it?"

"A happy family's."

Mike pointed at the scene. "The father had better get off the beach towel and back to the office."

"No. There won't be a cloud in the sky."

"I wish I could say that."

"What happened?"

Mike told her about the specter of Judge Lancaster and Maxwell Forrest's intervention.

"Was Sam there?" she asked.

"No, defendants aren't required to be there. I hope he was cutting grass somewhere."

"But wouldn't it be a good idea for him to listen, so he can tell you what God is saying about the situation and the people?"

"That's something I haven't considered. Except for yesterday, I've kept Sam isolated so he wouldn't say the wrong thing in the wrong place at the wrong time. One crazy slipup from him, and I can forget all my careful planning."

"I still think it would be a good idea."

"There won't be another opportunity. Next time up is jury selection on Monday morning." Mike paused. "I've never selected a jury for a client who believed he could uncover the secrets of another person's heart. It should be an interesting process."

MIKE SPENT THE AFTERNOON WORKING IN THE DOWNSTAIRS OFFICE. After several hours, mental fatigue began to crack his capacity to analyze and organize. He pushed away from the desk and rubbed his eyes. He stepped out of the room and found Peg lying on the couch in the great room reading a novel.

"My brain is fading, but my body needs a workout," he said. "Would you feel abandoned if I took Judge out for a romp?"

The dog, lying on the floor beside Peg, raised his head at the sound of his name.

"Go," Peg said. "Both of you need the exercise."

"Let's go," Mike said to him.

"How long will you be gone?" Peg asked.

Mike looked at the clock. "A couple of hours at the most."

Peg stretched. "Okay. I'm cooking something special for supper."

"Liver mush?"

"If that's what you want, darling."

"Surprise me."

Mike put his bike on top of his car, and Judge jumped into the backseat. He drove along a rarely used country road that ran along the valley, climbed a few ridges owned by a pulpwood company, and then became a dirt road that disappeared into the woods. The only time Mike avoided the area was during deer season. He didn't want a trigger-happy hunter mistaking the handlebars on his bike for a rack of antlers on a buck.

Parking the car at an abandoned farmhouse, Mike unloaded the bike and set a leisurely pace that wouldn't tire Judge. The dog loped along beside him with his ears gently flopping up and down and his mouth slightly open. There were a few wispy clouds in the sky, and the mountain air refreshed Mike's cheeks as it crossed his face. Within a few minutes, he'd left the stress of the day behind and settled into enjoying the world in which God had placed him.

The track turned west and he climbed the first ridge. Stopping at the top, he took a small drink of water and poured a larger serving into a plastic bowl for Judge. They'd only seen two cars and three pickups since starting the ride. Unlike drivers in town, those in the country didn't seem to resent Mike's presence and gave him a wide berth when they passed him.

He coasted down the dip between the ridges before climbing a longer, steeper ridge. Leaving the bike in a lower gear, he worked hard enough that his thighs began to burn. The harder the climb, the farther Judge's tongue began to hang out of his mouth. They reached the top and turned off the road. A hundred yards from the road was a small burned-out area caused by a fire sparked by a lightning strike. With the arrival of spring, new growth had sprouted forth since the last time Mike had been to the spot. He sat on a felled tree and shared another drink with Judge.

The clearing faced east toward Shelton. He couldn't see the town, but several roads and a few scattered houses were visible in the distance. From his vantage point, it was possible to make out the outline of the eastern edge of the paper company's property. The privately held land was a hodgepodge of fences and mixed-use fields. The tree farm had order and symmetry. Some sections were filled with bushy young saplings peeking through the soil; others contained adolescent trees bunched close together as they fought for air and light; the remaining acres had already been harvested once, but the woodsmen left some of the best trees standing so they could grow even larger. It was quiet. Tree farming was a patient endeavor, measured in decades not years. It was a good illustration for the Christian life.

"But where will I preach it?" Mike spoke into the silent air.

No answer came. Mike continued to soak in the scene. Then a thought slipped softly into his mind.

Don't preach it; live it.

Puzzled, Mike turned the words over in his mind. Before teaching others, he knew he needed to understand the truth himself. But understanding alone wasn't sufficient if inconsistent with behavior. He sensed the words went beyond to something else. He mulled them over for several minutes. Nothing satisfactory surfaced. He whistled for Judge, who was crashing through the underbrush. The dog circled around and returned to the clearing from the rear.

"Let's go," Mike said. "Supper is waiting."

Twenty-eight

PEG HAD FIXED A STEW, NOT LIVER MUSH. BOTH MIKE AND Judge licked their lips when they came into the kitchen. Mike lifted the lid of the pot on the stove.

"How did you do it so fast?"

"I cooked it yesterday. It always tastes better the second day, so I decided to make that the first day and this the second day."

"I'm not sure Judge understands you."

"All he cares about is licking the plates."

Mike and Peg sat together in the kitchen with Judge on the floor between them. The words Mike heard during his bike ride stayed with him.

"I'll clean up," Mike said when they finished eating.

He was scrubbing the pot when the phone rang. He dried his hands and answered it. It was Brian Dressler.

"I have a conflict on Monday and won't be able to make it to the trial," Dressler said.

Mike kept his voice level but firm. "You're under subpoena. It's not an optional appearance."

"I have serious personal business involving one of my grandchildren. I'll be tied up all day Monday."

Mike leaned against the kitchen counter. He didn't relish the thought of seeking a criminal contempt order against the former banker.

"Could you catch a flight and be here on Tuesday?"

"I thought the trial was on Monday."

"The first day, but the case will probably last the whole week. I didn't intend on calling you until Tuesday afternoon or Wednesday morning."

"Why is the case going to take so long? It's not that complicated."

"Your part is foundational for what follows," Mike answered cryptically. "I know you can't tie everything together, but after listening to you, the rest of my evidence will make sense to the jury."

"I haven't made my arrangements."

Mike decided to probe for another reason for Dressler's reluctance.

"Has someone from Forrest, Lambert, and Arnold contacted you?"

"No."

"How about the bank?"

There was a moment of silence. Mike knew he'd touched something.

"I spoke briefly with Hatcher."

"What did he want?"

"He was trying to find out why I'd been subpoenaed."

"What did you tell him?"

"I answered his questions but nothing more."

Mike glanced up at the ceiling. "Mr. Dressler, this could take a while if you make me drag it out of you."

"Okay, I'll get to the bottom line. They know what you're trying to do."

"That doesn't tell me much. Based on our conversation at the newspaper, I'm not sure you know what I'm doing."

"I know more than I told you in Shelton."

"How much more?"

"I'm not saying, but if you press me in court, I'm going to invoke the Fifth Amendment. I've already consulted a lawyer in Mobile."

Mike had been confident in his theory of the case, but to have it so dramatically validated by Dressler was still a shock.

"What is Hatcher saying?" he managed after a brief pause.

"I don't know. But he's scared. I could tell it over the phone. I've never heard him so nervous."

"Did he mention anything about Linden, Bunt, or Niles?"

"No, and I didn't ask. This could get ugly, and everyone is looking out for himself. I wasn't sure if he was recording the conversation, so I let him do most of the talking. With all the publicity about high-level corporate misconduct the past few years, a scandal in a place as small as Shelton could still blow up higher than the surrounding mountains."

Mike's mental wheels were turning.

"It's not my intention to make you look like a criminal. Your credibility is important to my case. What else can you tell me about the meeting with Hatcher when Sam Miller's name came up?"

"Not much. He didn't call me in until it was almost over."

Mike had caught him in a lie.

"I thought you weren't there at all."

"Oh yeah, I guess that's what I told you."

Mike waited. Once a witness started talking, it was often easier to obtain more information without prompting. Dressler spoke slowly.

"I'll verify that a meeting took place but obviously can't relate what happened before I arrived. When I came into Hatcher's office, he told me there was going to be an investigation into an embezzlement scheme by a man named Sam Miller and instructed me to meet with the victims at the appropriate time."

"Are you sure about that?"

"Yes."

"Just a minute."

Mike walked quickly into the office and found the copy of the minutes Bobby gave him in the deed room. He returned to the kitchen.

"Do you remember when this meeting took place?"

"Not the exact date."

"When did you meet with the deacons from the Craig Valley church?"

"Not long after. Maybe two or three weeks."

Mike placed the sheet of paper on the counter and stared at it while he asked his next question.

"Would it surprise you to find out that the meeting in Hatcher's office was four days prior to the date of the first check Sam allegedly wrote on the Craig Valley church account?"

"Uh-oh, I'd better back up and talk to my lawyer about this."

Mike could hear the tension in Dressler's voice.

"But you didn't have anything to do with the forging of the checks," Mike said.

"Absolutely not."

"Then you don't have anything to worry about. The wrongdoing occurred before you entered the room. Did Hatcher talk to you about the meeting?"

"No."

"Did you attend other meetings in which Miller's name came up?"

"I won't answer that. Like I said, I need to talk to my lawyer."

Dressler's refusal to respond to the last question told Mike what he needed to know. At some point, Dressler had known the charges against Sam were false.

"I should talk to your lawyer," Mike said. "Can you give me your contact information?"

Dressler had hired a female attorney from a firm with five names in it.

"Let Ms. Dortch know that I'm going to call on Monday during a break in the proceedings," Mike said.

"Okay, I'll try to find out if there is a direct number to reach her."

"Will you have your cell phone with you, so I can notify you about the court schedule?"

"Yes."

Knowing Dressler was still hiding information, Mike didn't want to hang up the phone.

"One other thing," Dressler said.

"Go ahead," Mike said, listening closely.

"I'll always appreciate what you and Mr. Miller did for Marie at the hospital. I'll go as far in my testimony as my attorney will allow."

Mike hung up the phone, went into the great room, and sat down in his chair.

"Don't go to sleep," Peg said.

"I'm not sleepy. Did you overhear my conversation with Dressler?"

"Enough to know that he hadn't told you the whole truth and nothing but the truth."

"You're right, and the truth looks more and more like the picture I'd imagined."

THE FOLLOWING DAY, MIKE WAITED ANXIOUSLY FOR MELISSA Hall to provide the names of additional witnesses who would be called by the prosecution. The State wouldn't be content to rely solely upon Detective Perkins and Jesse Lavare, the Craig Valley church deacon. As the clock ticked closer to 5:00 p.m., Mike resisted the urge to call Hall, but at 4:55 the suspense became too great. He dialed the number for the district attorney's office. He didn't want to run the risk of finding out about supplemental witnesses on Monday morning and suffer an unwarranted verbal beating from Judge Lancaster when he objected to their right to testify.

"Ms. Hall has left for the day," the receptionist replied.

"How about Ken? Is he still in the office?"

"Yes."

Mike gave his name and waited. And waited. He was about to hang up when West picked up the phone.

"Are you going to let Mr. Forrest and Bobby Lambert serve as special prosecutors in the Miller case?" he asked.

"Can't see a reason not to. It will increase the educational value of the case for Ms. Hall. Puts a bit more pressure on you, doesn't it?"

Mike ignored the dig. "I haven't received a supplemental list of witnesses."

"Ms. Hall would be the one to give that to you."

"She's not in."

"I guess she's confident enough about the case to go home early."

It was pointless talking to West.

"Do you have her home number?"

"I'll send you back to the receptionist."

Mike endured another long wait before the woman picked up the phone and gave him the number. He dialed it and a man answered. Certain he'd dialed a wrong number, Mike immediately hung up then carefully entered the correct numbers. The same male voice answered. This time it sounded familiar.

"Nathan?" Mike asked.

"Hey, Mike."

"What are you doing there?"

"Helping Melissa fix an Italian dinner. How did you track me down here?"

"I was calling her. Is she available?"

"She went to the store to pick up a couple of ingredients we needed and should be back shortly. Are you at home?"

"Yes."

"I'll let her know."

A few minutes later, Hall returned the call.

"Sorry to bother you at home," Mike began, "but I didn't receive a supplemental list of witnesses."

"I'm set, but Mr. Forrest is making the decisions about anyone else," she responded crisply. "You'll have to talk to him."

"Okay. Have a good time with Nathan. He's a fine young man."

"Don't worry. I'm not going to hurt him."

"I didn't mean to imply—," Mike began then stopped. "I'll see you Monday morning."

The phone clicked off, leaving Mike with a dead receiver. He would enjoy destroying the State's case. Melissa Hall carried a chip on her shoulder that needed to be removed. He phoned Maxwell Forrest's direct number at the office. He knew from past experience that Forrest used voice mail to screen his calls. No one answered.

MIKE SPENT SATURDAY ORGANIZING HIS OPENING STATEMENT. He knew the broad brushstrokes of the picture he wanted to paint for the jury, but it was also important to provide enough details to show he could complete his painting. Dressler's phone call made Mike less concerned about concealing information from the prosecution. If Hatcher already knew Mike had unraveled the bank's deception, it would be more important to clue the jury into what lay ahead than try to conceal it from Forrest and Hall as trial strategy. Late in the afternoon, Peg knocked on the door of the office.

"Is your brain running out of oxygen?" she asked.

"Yes, I need to come up for air." Mike rubbed his temples and leaned back in his chair. "I worked hard on my sermons, but this is ten times more intense. Trying to anticipate every possible twist of the evidence in a case like this is impossible."

Peg stepped over and kissed him on top of the head. "Won't part of it have to wait until you see what happens in court next week?"

"Yes, but I'm developing contingency plans."

"Our supper isn't subject to a contingency. Muriel and Sam are bringing it. What time should they be here?"

Mike looked at his watch. "I need at least another hour. Did you feed Judge?"

"A long time ago. His powers of concentration are focused on his food bowl."

AN HOUR LATER, MURIEL MILLER STEPPED ACROSS THE THRESHOLD and held up a large plastic bag filled with fish.

"Do you like panfried trout?" she asked. "One of Sam's customers caught a mess of fish and gave us way more than we can eat."

"I'll get the cornmeal," Peg replied.

While Muriel and Peg fixed the fish, Mike took Sam into the office.

"Would you like to hear the current version of my opening statement?" Mike asked.

"Yep, although don't expect me to criticize it."

"You mean critique?"

"That, too."

"This is an opening statement, not a closing argument," Mike said while he straightened his papers. "I have to save the yelling and armwaving for the end of the case. The judge will call me down if I get too excited."

Sam closed his eyes while Mike talked. The lack of eye contact was disconcerting, but Mike assumed it helped the older man concentrate. Mike concluded with one of the proverbs most familiar to trial lawyers.

"The prosecution has the opportunity to call its witnesses first, but keep an open mind until all the evidence is presented. Proverbs 18:17 states, *'The first to present his case seems right, till another comes forward and questions him.'* The more you hear from this witness stand, the more confident I am that, at the conclusion of the case, you will find Mr. Miller not guilty of the charge against him."

Mike waited for Sam to respond. The old man's eyes remained closed.

"Are you awake?" Mike asked after a few more silent seconds passed.

"Yep," Sam replied as his eyes blinked open. "I was trying to go ahead of you but had trouble finding the way."

"Go ahead? What do you mean?"

"Feel the spiritual air that will be in the courtroom on Monday. It's one thing to sit here in your office; it's something else when our enemies are surrounding us. What you said sounded fine for now, but I wanted to see what your words would face on Monday. Your job is to talk. Mine is to pray that your speech won't fall on ears that can't hear. I like to be ready in advance. The Master often knew what lay ahead along the road."

"Okay, but did the opening statement make sense?"

"Yep."

Mike waited. "Anything else?"

"Nope."

"I mean, how did it make you feel?"

Sam shook his head with sorrowful eyes. "Sad, very sad. But not because it isn't good. You're a fighter, and when you see something wrong, you go after it with a sword. Listening to your speech, I felt anger rising up inside me, but it wasn't wearing the Master's face."

"The injustice of it all motivates me. I don't feel bad about getting upset," Mike said.

"The Master got mad, too. But if I get angry, it will open a door for worry about Muriel that will drag me down into a pit. Papa knows how to deal with the men who have done this to me. The older I get, the more wickedness makes me cry."

"Supper's ready!" Muriel called out.

Sam managed a slight smile. "Doesn't she have the sweetest voice on earth?"

They ate in the dining room. The sight of the food on the table reminded Mike of meals his family enjoyed at his great-aunt's house when he was a child.

"Say a quick blessing, Preacher," Sam said to Mike when they were seated. "The trout is sizzling and the creamed corn hot."

The fish was delicious, and Mike had never eaten better creamed corn and cornbread muffins. But the food was flavored with the upcoming trial—the slightly bitter apprehension of an impending fear. There wasn't much table talk. When they finished, Mike helped Muriel clear the table while Sam and Peg went into the great room.

"What is Sam telling you about the case?" Mike asked when they were alone.

"Always the same thing. He's trusting in you and the Lord."

"But what does he think is going to happen?"

Muriel dipped the skillet used to cook the fish into soapy water and began washing it. "Having lived with him all these years, I've come to expect the unexpected. Predicting the future isn't my job. That's his department. Right now, I'm trying to keep my mind on my three main prayer burdens: healing for our grandniece with leukemia, health for Peg's baby, and protection for Sam."

Mike didn't ask any other questions. Trying to force Muriel Miller to analyze everything Sam dreamed, spoke, or believed wasn't fair. Her simplicity was both a protection and a strength. Instead, she focused on prayer—the most important activity of any Christian.

Twenty-nine

Monday morning Mike awoke early, grabbed his bike gear, and slipped quietly downstairs. He'd finalized his trial preparation before going to bed Sunday night, and a brisk ride with Judge would do more to clear his mind than staring again at his notes. It was a slightly muggy morning with low mist rising from the ground. He completed two quick circuits on the hill that left Judge panting. Returning to the house, Mike greeted Peg, who was in the kitchen with fresh coffee in the pot.

"How are you?" he asked.

"A little queasy, but I have an excuse with the baby. What about you?"

"Queasy, but without a baby in my belly. I woke up this morning thinking about Danny Brewster."

"Any dreams?"

"No, just bad memories."

"This is a different case."

"I know, but there's the same pressure of representing an innocent man."

Peg came over, stood behind him, and rubbed his shoulders.

"And you've worked as hard getting ready as for any trial in your career. If preparation is the key to success, you couldn't have done more." Peg lifted her hands from his shoulders. "All you need is a cup of coffee, a shower, a prayer, and a kiss."

Mike looked up at her. "Could I have two kisses?"

Peg gave him a peck on the lips. "And you know I'll be here rooting for you. I thought about coming to the courthouse—"

"No," Mike said quickly. "I need to focus."

Peg rubbed his shoulder a little harder. "And I would be a distraction?"

"Yes. And seriously, Sam told me on Saturday that Muriel is going to stay at home because the arguing in the courtroom would just upset her. She'll come when it's time for the jury to deliberate. That won't happen until the end of the week."

"Maybe that's when I'll come, too."

Mike finished his coffee and went upstairs. After he shaved and showered, he stood in the doorway to their clothes closet. Peg sat on the edge of the bed.

"What are you going to wear?" she asked.

"You pick."

"The dark blue suit with a white shirt and gold tie. You never go wrong with that one. The tie complements the brown in your eyes."

Mike dressed and patted his stomach. "I bought this suit when I tried the Cramerton case. It still fits."

"It was always big."

Mike finished knotting his tie. Peg joined him, adjusted the knot, and stepped back to examine him.

"You'll be the most handsome lawyer in the courtroom," she said.

Mike smiled. "Bobby got all the girls in college. I'll settle for most persuasive lawyer."

Peg patted him on the cheek. "Before you go, I want to pray for you."

Mike bowed his head. They'd never prayed together before he left to go to court. Peg quietly expressed many of the desires of his own heart.

"And show Mike anyone in the jury pool who might be prejudiced against Sam because of his faith. Give them peace in the midst of the battle, and I ask you to comfort Muriel while she waits alone at home. Amen."

Mike opened his eyes. Peg gave him a long kiss on the lips.

"Okay," she said. "You're ready for anything."

Mike loaded his briefcase with the items needed for jury selection, his opening statement, and cross-examination of the witnesses identified by Melissa Hall, along with rough outlines of questions for the unknown witnesses he believed Maxwell Forrest would parade into the courtroom.

HE DROVE INTO TOWN AND PARKED ON THE OPPOSITE SIDE OF the courthouse from his former law firm. He didn't want to engage in any small talk with Mr. Forrest or Bobby. Sam, looking uncomfortable in a white shirt, dark pants, and blue tie, waited for him near the rear of the courtroom. Prospective jurors were finding places to sit on the benches. Mike shook Sam's hand.

"This is it," Mike said. "Are you ready?"

"I reckon," Sam replied, "but it still looks fuzzy to me."

Mike glanced toward the district attorney's table. There was no sign of Ken West or Melissa Hall.

"Did you look over the jury list?" Mike asked.

"Yep." Sam handed him two sheets of paper. "Muriel and I wrote down stuff about the people we know."

Mike glanced at the sheets in surprise. "You know all these people?"

"Several of them, but as I read the names, Papa showed me things about others I've never met."

Mike quickly read the notations beside a few of the names.

"'Cut his brother's grass for years. Problems with daughter and blames Papa. Mulched flower beds last fall. Doctor told him without surgery his heart may not last another three years. Can't forgive uncle who took over family business and didn't pay fair price.'" He looked up at Sam. "What am I supposed to do with this personal information?"

"Eat the meat and spit out the bones," Sam answered.

"But you're not going to try to talk to anyone—"

"Not during the trial," Sam replied. "I'm not going to make it hard for you to do your job."

Mike searched the courtroom. There was no sign of Bobby, Forrest, or any of the witnesses Mike had subpoenaed. He suspected they were congregating at Forrest, Lambert, and Arnold.

"Sit in the spectators' section until they call the case," Mike said to Sam.

Mike joined Greg Freeman and several other lawyers. As the clock moved closer to 9:00 a.m., the courtroom filled up. But without any sign of Maxwell Forrest or Bobby. Mike leaned over to Freeman.

"Have you been in the DA's office this morning?"

"Yes, I had to drop off some pleadings I filed this morning."

"Did you see Mr. Forrest or Bobby Lambert?"

"No, but they could have been in the conference room."

The side door to the prosecutor's office opened, and Melissa Hall entered.

No one joined her. Immediately thereafter, Judge Lancaster strode into the courtroom.

"All rise," the bailiff sounded out.

The judge took his seat and looked at Hall.

"Call your trial calendar," he barked.

Hall stood. Mike rose to make his response.

"*State v. Turner*," Hall said.

Mike's jaw dropped open. Greg Freeman hurriedly stood to his feet.

"Ready for the defense," the younger lawyer said.

Mike stepped toward the bench. "Your Honor, I'm here to try *State v. Miller*. I've subpoenaed multiple witnesses locally and from several other states. Last Thursday, I was assured by the district attorney's office that this would be the first case called for trial. The Court ruled on several motions to quash—"

"The indictment has been dismissed," Hall answered with a side glance at Mike. "It was a late development that wasn't confirmed until a few minutes ago."

For a moment, Mike was speechless. "Uh, was it a dismissal with prejudice?"

"This is a criminal case, Mr. Andrews," the judge answered wryly. "Voluntary dismissal prior to call of the case would allow reindictment without violating the constitutional prohibition against double jeopardy."

Mike glanced over his shoulder at Sam, who was sitting with a puzzled look on his face in the second row. Mike turned to Hall.

"But why was the indictment dismissed? There has to be a reason, and my client has the right—"

"You and Ms. Hall can chat later," the judge interjected. "The Court has business to take care of. Ms. Hall, proceed for the State."

Mike walked over to the lawyers' section and sat down. Greg Freeman and his client were already setting up shop at the defense table in preparation for jury selection. Mike motioned to Sam, who approached.

"The indictment has been dismissed," he said numbly. "We're not going to trial."

They walked up the aisle and exited the courtroom as the clerk of court began calling the names in the jury pool. No one paid any attention to Mike and Sam. When they were outside the courtroom, Mike stopped.

"What happens now?" Sam asked.

"I'm not sure. You heard my discussion with the judge. You could be reindicted, or the charges could simply go away. Maybe Mr. Forrest and Jack Hatcher told the district attorney's office to dismiss the indictment because they knew about the damaging evidence I was going to bring out in court, but that doesn't make sense. Whatever the reason, all the witnesses I subpoenaed will be free to leave, and I'm not sure if I can find and serve subpoenas on them in the future. If it turns out you're reindicted next week, this was a dirty move."

"Did you think the charges might be dropped?" Sam asked.

Mike shook his head. "No, it caught me completely off guard."

"What do I do?"

"Go home and hug Muriel, but call me if you get another visit from the sheriff's office. I'll talk to Lamar Cochran and ask him to tip me off if a warrant is issued for your arrest. I'll also notify Darius York and Brian Dressler that they won't be needed in court."

"Thanks for all you've done."

Mike shrugged. "All I did was show up."

"You know what I mean. Without all your hard work, they wouldn't have run away."

"But you could still be charged."

Sam rubbed his stomach. "I don't think so. Something inside tells me this forged check thing is over and done with."

"I hope you're right."

Sam turned to leave, then stopped and faced Mike.

"When will I see you again?" he asked.

Mike put his hand on the old man's shoulder. "Anytime you want. I might ask you for a job helping take care of Mrs. Bowen's backyard."

"Now, I can get started on the irrigation system she wants for the flower beds farthest from her house. I could use a strong back like yours to do some digging."

Sam left the courthouse. Mike lingered, still wound tight in anticipation of the trial but with no place to release his energy. He didn't share Sam's optimism about the future.

He went to his car but didn't start the engine. He could go home, but watching TV game shows on Monday morning didn't appeal to him. He had to find out what had happened to the case. Getting out of his car, he returned to the courthouse and marched into the district attorney's office.

"Is Ken available?" he asked the receptionist.

"I'll see if he's in," she replied.

Mike glanced down the hallway and saw the large form of the district attorney lumbering into his office. Mike didn't wait for clearance from the receptionist. He walked down the hall and knocked on the door.

"It's open!" West responded.

Mike stuck his head in the door. "Do you have a minute?"

West waved his hand. "Mike! Come in and have a seat. Sorry I was so short with you the other day. You did a great job for your crystal-ball-reading client. The way you hassled the bank forced them to find out what really happened."

Mystified, Mike sat across from the district attorney. "Can you give me additional details?"

"Not much, beyond the evidence implicating Brian Dressler."

"Dressler?" Mike didn't hide his shock.

West leaned forward. "Don't act surprised. You tracked him down and subpoenaed him after he was fired by the bank."

"Yes. But I also intended to question several other people."

"I know, and cast doubt on your client's guilt from as many angles as possible. Whether you use a shotgun or a rifle doesn't matter so long as you kill what you're after."

Mike sat with a blank look on his face.

West continued, "But don't look to me for an apology. With the information in our file, there's no way we could have figured out what really went down. It took the bank to unravel Dressler's modus operandi."

"What exactly was he doing?" Mike asked slowly. "I want to explain it correctly to Mr. Miller."

"You'll have to ask Maxwell Forrest for the details, but he described it as a form of internal check kiting. Dressler created a personal slush fund by shifting money between noninterest-bearing accounts that had little activity. The money didn't stay out of an account for a full business day, so it never appeared as a debit; however, Dressler could use the funds to bankroll his day-trading habit."

"The Craig Valley church building account was one of his sources?"

"Correct, and as chief of internal security at the bank, he covered his tracks. I asked Forrest if Dressler made a bad stock trade that he couldn't cover, but apparently a problem with Dressler's wife led to his downfall."

"She's dead."

"I know. Dressler was chained to his desk while running his scam. One day he left in a hurry because his wife had an emergency and didn't put all the pieces back in place. A $100,000 withdrawal showed up on the church account. Dressler had to come up with a scapegoat and targeted your client to explain the money flowing out of the account."

"How did he know my client and his connection with the church?"

"Not sure, although it was a subtle touch accusing a white man of embezzling money from a black church. Played nice on the race card in a backhanded kind of way."

"Have you seen the bank records documenting any of this?"

"No, and the bank may not do anything to Dressler because he never actually stole the money. It's all computer entries. Hatcher is considering his options, but at this point, I believe his major concern is avoiding negative publicity."

"I'd suspect as much from him," Mike answered wryly.

"Did your expert confirm that the checks allegedly signed by your client were typed at the bank?"

"Yes."

"That was a very smart move on your part. I don't think Dressler anticipated someone making the connection."

Mike stared past West's left shoulder at a street scene on the north side of the courthouse. A woman was pushing a stroller with twins along the sidewalk. Life moved on.

West continued, "You wanted to tear into Dressler, didn't you?"

Mike returned his focus to the DA. "I wanted to bring out the truth."

West chuckled. "Don't we all? There's nothing more fearsome than a capable lawyer cloaked in the zeal of a righteous cause."

"Do you know if the other witnesses I subpoenaed are in town?"

"No."

"So, can I tell Sam Miller not to worry about a reindictment?"

West waved his arms. "Absolutely. He's in the clear. The next time he'll be in front of a jury should be to prove his punitive damage claim against Dressler."

West stood to his feet. Mike joined him.

"Someone else will need to handle that case," Mike said.

West shook Mike's hand.

"I agree. Go back to your pulpit, and use your talents for the good Lord's work."

MIKE LEFT THE COURTHOUSE. CLICKING OPEN HIS BRIEFCASE, he found the phone number for Brian Dressler's lawyer in Mobile. He held a moment before a young female voice answered.

"This is Beverly Dortch."

Mike introduced himself. "I'm calling about the subpoena served on Brian Dressler."

"He's not going to honor it," Dortch said before Mike could continue. "I've filed a motion to quash it in our local court."

"On what grounds? It was personally served on your client while he was in North Carolina."

"I'll present my argument to the court."

Mike conducted a quick debate whether to communicate any of the information he'd just obtained from Ken West.

"When is the hearing on your motion?" he asked.

"Wednesday afternoon at three o'clock. If you provide a fax number, I'll send you a copy of the notice."

"I don't have a fax machine."

"You don't have a fax machine? What kind of law firm do you operate?"

Mike bit his lip. "A small one."

"Do you have access to a computer with an Internet connection?"

"Yeah, they just ran cable lines to this part of North Carolina," Mike answered sarcastically, then gave her his e-mail address. "Send me the notice, but I won't attend the hearing. Your more serious challenge will be trying to fight an extradition order if Dressler's former employer and the local district attorney decide to file criminal charges against him for illegal money transfers."

"What are you talking about?" Dortch asked sharply.

"You'll find out when it's brought up in court."

Mike clicked off the phone. Lawyers like Dortch would make a return to the ministry, even with its challenges, a pleasant prospect.

HE CALLED DARIUS YORK AND BROKE THE NEWS TO HIM.

"Your work was a key," Mike said. "The mere threat of your appearance in court scared the assistant district attorney into dropping the charges."

"Right. Tell me what really happened."

Mike summarized his conversation with Ken West.

"What do you think?" Mike asked when he finished.

"I'm not sure it's a plausible scenario. I'm not up-to-date on bank security, but there are tamperproof safeguards that would catch someone manipulating accounts in the way you described."

"I may not be explaining it properly, but at this point it doesn't really matter to Sam Miller. Getting the charges against my client dismissed is the bottom line. It's not my job to police the rest of the world."

"Give my regards to Mr. Miller," York answered. "I appreciated his honesty and insight. Tell him that I'm already taking steps to correct at least one of my past sins."

Mike cringed in regret at his efforts to squelch Sam's comments to York.

"Okay, and I'll put the balance of your fee in the mail by the end of the week."

"Forget it," York responded. "Consider it my contribution to a worthy cause."

MIKE DROVE HOME SO HE COULD DELIVER THE GOOD NEWS TO Peg. He found her sitting on the couch in the great room with a book in her hand. She glanced up in surprise when he tapped lightly on the door frame.

"It was over before it began," he said.

Mike paced back and forth across the room while he talked. Peg wiped away a tear.

"Good tears?" he asked when he saw her rub her eye.

Peg nodded. "I'm so relieved for the Millers—and for you."

"I'm still trying to find a place to land."

Peg held out her hand. "Sit beside me and let me pull you back to earth."

Mike sat on the couch. Peg put her arm on his shoulder.

"You're a great lawyer who cares about his clients."

"It's easy when you only have one."

"Quiet. And I'm not saying that because I secretly want you to go back into law practice. Your three years in the ministry have changed you for the better. Even while working long hours on Sam's case, you spent time with God—and with me. I didn't feel shut out. I think God liked it, too."

"But now what?"

"That's for you to decide."

"Will you tell me what you think?"

"Yes."

"I'll be listening." Mike took her hand and kissed it. "We have a lot of time left on the sabbatical. I could get used to being with you on a perpetual vacation."

Later that afternoon they went for a walk in the backyard and checked on their flowers.

"What are you thinking about the church?" Peg asked.

"I'll have to face it soon. The real reason for my exile has ended. The elders will know what happened by nightfall. Bobby will make sure the word gets out."

"Or you could call Delores Killian right now with the news and ask her to keep it confidential."

Mike smiled. "I've missed her."

Peg put her hand on his forehead. "Uh-oh, you're delirious. Don't make any hasty decisions until your fever breaks. Wait for the elders to contact you."

"Milton Chesterfield and Barbara Harcourt aren't going to show up kneeling on our doorstep asking for forgiveness."

Peg brushed a stray strand of hair away from her face. "A simple apology would be a good place to start. You're totally vindicated by the DA's dismissal of the charges against Sam. That's a lot stronger than a not-guilty verdict because it proves Sam was innocent from the very beginning. A cynic could always claim a jury verdict of not guilty was the result of a tricky lawyer's manipulation of the facts. No one can say that now."

"If you see a tricky lawyer in the room, kiss him."

Peg gave him a peck on the cheek. "Do you want to return to the church if it takes a power play on your part to get back in?"

Mike turned his head so he could clearly see Peg's face.

"It's not much money, but the job at the church is our security."

"While you've been preparing for the trial, I've had plenty of time to get used to the idea of a different direction. We have enough in savings—"

"To buy a few diapers."

Peg's face fell, and Mike regretted his comment.

"I'm sorry," he said. "Maybe I need to ride to the top of Jefferson's Ridge and look into the future. At the moment, you have more faith than I do."

The phone rang. Peg answered it, then put her hand over the receiver.

"It's Braxton Hodges," she whispered.

Mike took the receiver.

"Can I buy you a victory hamburger to celebrate?" the reporter asked.

Mike looked at his watch. It was almost noon.

"I'll meet you there in thirty minutes."

"CALM DOWN," HATCHER SAID TO BUTCH NILES, MOTIONING for the nervous legislator to sit down on the other side of the bank president's desk. "It's about winning the war, not a single battle. Don't blow this setback out of proportion. It's a strategic retreat. Everything is under control. I have a plan."

Thirty

MIKE CHANGED INTO CASUAL CLOTHES AND RETURNED HIS DARK blue suit, like a coat of armor that hadn't suffered a scratch in battle, to its place in the closet.

"What are you going to tell Hodges?" Peg asked.

"With Braxton, I always listen more than I talk. Ken West didn't ask me to keep the information about Dressler confidential, but I'm not sure I want to unleash a reporter on a fact-finding mission." Mike slipped a ball cap on his head. "Do you want me to bring you back a couple of cheeseburgers and a large order of french fries?"

"No, thanks. I'll dip a few raw carrots and uncooked broccoli spears in ranch dressing."

Mike and Hodges arrived at Brooks at the same time and ordered their food. The long outside table was crowded with customers.

"Let's go to the park," Hodges suggested.

A few blocks from Brooks was a public park that contained a swing set, seesaw, and a couple of picnic tables. Both of the tables were vacant.

"How does it feel sitting here wearing a golf shirt and eating a burger with nothing to do?" Hodges asked after they were settled.

"Surreal."

"I came to the courthouse to watch a few minutes of jury selection, and you weren't there. I thought the world had ended, and you were snatched up to heaven, leaving the rest of us heathens to fend for ourselves."

"You have an overactive religious imagination."

"There was a break in the proceedings, and I asked Greg Freeman what happened in your case. He gave me the news that the charges against Sam Miller were dismissed. I tried to get a comment from Ms. Hall, but she brushed me off. I think she was more interested in getting ready to try her case than in talking with the media."

"It was her first felony trial. Maybe you should write about it."

Hodges shook his head. "I checked it out. The public isn't interested in a burglary case involving the employee of an auto parts store who came back after hours to steal the stuff he needed to fix up his 1957 Chevrolet. A picture of the car would be more interesting than an article about the trial. I want the inside story about the Miller case. Eat one more bite, then start at the beginning."

Mike took an extra long time to chew his food. Hodges ate two bites and looked at him impatiently.

"Come on. You can't hold out on me. Swallow your food, and open your mouth now that your lips aren't sealed by the attorney-client privilege."

"You're wrong. I can't reveal client information."

"I don't want to know what Miller told you," Hodges replied with frustration. "I want the scoop about Niles, Hatcher, the Cohulla Creek property, and the illegal payola. Don't worry. I'm not going to use your name in any article. You'll be the confidential unnamed source who refused to be identified."

"There's nothing sensational to tell. I uncovered a few bits of information, but my primary focus was proving that Sam had nothing to do with the two checks drawn on the Craig Valley church building fund account. I hired a handwriting expert, a former FBI agent, who was going to testify that the checks were typed on an old typewriter owned by the bank then signed using a signature stamp. Sam didn't own a signature stamp. The connection of the bank's typewriter to the checks broke the case open."

"That's not all," Hodges insisted. "Otherwise, you wouldn't have subpoenaed Linden, Bunt, and Dressler."

"I never nailed everything down. I wanted to expose the bank's motivation to discredit Sam, but the testimony of the others would have been based on innuendo that I'm not sure Judge Lancaster would have allowed. Judge Coberg knows about Sam's dreams and might have let me color outside the lines. Lancaster would have put a chain around my neck and forced me to try the case in a traditional manner."

"So you didn't uncover a smoking gun?"

"No. Dismissal of the charges had nothing to do with Cohulla Creek."

"That's a big letdown." Hodges sighed.

Mike sipped his drink. Hodges had helped him quite a bit with Dressler. He wanted to give him something in return.

"One thing I didn't mention to you," Mike said. "There is a memo of a meeting."

Hodges perked up as Mike summarized the contents of the memo Bobby slipped into the old deed book at the courthouse.

"Can you give me a copy of the memo?" the reporter asked. "I wouldn't use it unless I could substantiate its relationship to the overall scheme."

"Yes, I'll pass it along, but don't mention me as your source. The person who gave it to me could lose his job if my name is connected to it."

"Agreed. I found it blowing in the wind on a street corner."

DRIVING HOME, MIKE WONDERED IF HE SHOULD HAVE TOLD Hodges about his conversation with Ken West. If Dressler had framed Sam Miller, it would be a major news story, but in his gut, Mike didn't believe the former banker was the prime mover in the plot to destroy the old man. Dressler's lawyer in Mobile might be a jerk willing to file a groundless motion, but that didn't make her client guilty of anything but poor judgment in his choice of counsel.

When he arrived home, Mike turned on his computer to check his e-mail messages. Several items from the top, he spied a message line that caught his attention—"From Milton Chesterfield." Mike quickly clicked it open.

Congratulations on your successful representation of Sam Miller. The elders would like to meet with you and Mr. Miller this evening at 7:00 p.m. at the church. Unless I hear from you otherwise, we will see you then.

Mike printed the message and showed it to Peg in triumph. "Look at this! They're not only going to apologize to me, but also to Sam."

Peg took the sheet from him. "Where does it say that they're going to apologize?"

"Why else would they congratulate me and invite both of us to come?"

"It would be a major change of heart, but it's hard to imagine some of the elders humble enough to admit a mistake."

"I know, but will you let me be ridiculously optimistic for a few minutes?"

Peg smiled. "Okay. Did you call Sam?"

"Not yet. He's probably mowing a lawn."

Mike phoned Muriel, who promised to deliver Sam wearing clean clothes to the Andrewses' house in time for the two men to drive to the Little Creek Church by 7:00 p.m. Later in the afternoon, Mike received a call from Larry Fletchall, the chief deacon at the Craig Valley Gospel Tabernacle.

"I heard what happened in Sam's case," Fletchall said. "A lady from the district attorney's office called and told me charges should never have been filed. It was all a big mix-up. I can't tell you how relieved I am that Sam didn't do anything wrong."

"The system worked," Mike answered simply.

"And we'd like to celebrate. Could you be our guests at the church on Sunday?"

"Both of us?"

"Yes, along with your wives."

Mike hesitated. He didn't want to miss the opportunity for a triumphant return to Little Creek.

"Uh, not this week, but let's stay in touch. It would be an honor to attend a service."

SAM AND MURIEL ARRIVED AT 6:15 P.M. SAM'S FACE WAS SLIGHTLY RED.

"Forgot my hat and spent the whole afternoon working in the Blevinses' backyard," the old man said when Mike commented on his ruddy appearance. "They don't have a square foot of shade around that new swimming pool."

"How long do you think the meeting at the church will last?" Muriel asked.

"I'm not sure," Mike replied. "Normally, I prepare an agenda, but the only notice I received was an e-mail. If the elders want to talk about church business, I'll recommend that we do it another time. I don't want Sam waiting alone in the hallway for several hours."

Mike looked at his watch. "We don't need to leave for a few minutes. While we're together, I need to tell you why the charges against Sam were dismissed."

He related his conversation with Ken West.

"What do you think?" he asked Sam when he finished.

The old man shook his head. "I don't understand all that stuff about stocks and bank accounts. I saw darkness in Mr. Dressler's heart when we were with him and his wife at the hospital but thought it had to do with their relationship, not me."

"I know less than you do about Dressler's heart," Mike replied, "but I'm not convinced he wrote the checks and stamped them with your signature. When I called Darius York and told him what happened, he had his doubts, too."

"But are they going to leave Sam and me in peace?" Muriel asked.

"Yes," Mike said. "That's the one thing West told me we can count on. If he'd entertained thoughts of refiling criminal charges against Sam, he wouldn't have been so emphatic about why the charges were dismissed. It's over."

Muriel began to cry. Peg came over and put her arm around her. She, too, began to sniffle. Sam looked at Mike and smiled.

"We'll let you ladies be happy together," Mike said after a few moments. "We don't want to be late to church."

DRIVING OUT OF THE NEIGHBORHOOD, MIKE ASKED SAM, "WHY do you think the elders want to meet with us?"

"I don't know. I asked Papa about it during the ride over to your house, but I didn't hear anything."

They rode in silence down the hill and onto the valley road. Sam sat in the seat with his eyes closed. Several miles passed. Sam groaned slightly. A few moments later he groaned more loudly.

"Are you okay?" Mike asked.

Sam opened his eyes and grimaced. "My stomach aches. I think I put too much hot sauce on my collard greens."

"Do we need to go back to my house?"

Sam closed his eyes and didn't respond. Mike continued down the road. They neared the church.

"We're almost there," Mike said. "How do you feel?"

Sam opened his eyes and rubbed his abdomen. "My spirit is uneasy."

"I thought you ate too much hot sauce."

"No, this ache is coming from another place."

"We're here."

Mike turned into the church parking lot. The sun had just dipped below the hills in the west, but there was plenty of daylight to clearly see the property. So much had happened to Mike since he'd last been there that he saw it with fresh eyes. It felt right to return. The parking lot in front of the administration building was empty. Mike looked at his watch.

"We're only five minutes early," he said. "But it's not usual for people to be late. Come inside. I'll show you where we'll meet."

Sam moaned again as he unbuckled his seat belt.

"Can you do this?" Mike asked with concern.

"Yep, but I may hold you to your promise not to let the meeting go too long."

They entered the building and went into the conference room. Mike turned on the lights.

"I'll brew a pot of coffee. If you need to use the restroom, it's down the hall on the right."

Mike returned with the water and filled the coffeepot. As it dripped down, he checked his watch. Sam sat in one of the chairs with his eyes closed.

"I'll look outside and check the parking lot," Mike said.

Dusk had darkened when he opened the door and peered out. No one had arrived, and Mike began to wonder if he'd misinterpreted the message from Milton Chesterfield. He returned to the conference room.

"I'm calling Peg."

Peg answered on the second ring. "We're alone and it's ten minutes after seven," Mike said. "Did anyone phone to cancel the meeting?"

"No."

Mike thought a second. "I didn't bring the e-mail from Milton. It's on the table in the kitchen. Please read it to me."

Mike waited then listened to Peg repeat the words he already knew were on the paper.

"It couldn't be any clearer," Mike said. "What do you think happened?"

Sam raised his hand. "Mike, I need to leave. My stomach and left arm are really hurting."

"We're coming back to the house," Mike said to Peg. "Sam is sick."

Mike closed the phone, and Sam rose unsteadily to his feet. Mike turned off the coffeepot.

"Is it your heart?" Mike asked anxiously.

"I'm either going to faint or throw up."

"Should I call an ambulance?"

Sam shook his head. "No, let's go. Muriel can put a cool rag on my head. That always makes me feel better."

During the ride home, Mike kept glancing at Sam, who sat with his eyes closed and breathing irregularly. Each time Sam didn't take a breath, Mike worried it might be the sign of a heart attack. As they drew closer to the house, Sam sighed and stretched out his hands.

"It's passing," he said. "I could feel the snake turn loose of my belly."

"Snake?"

"That's the best way I can describe it. I was getting squeezed from front to back. Thanks for praying for me."

"I did more worrying than praying."

Sam managed a slight smile. "Papa can recognize compassion no matter how it's dressed."

They turned into the driveway. Sam exited the car without difficulty and walked beside Mike into the house.

"What's wrong?" Muriel asked as soon as they stepped into the kitchen.

"I'm not sure, but it was trying to kill me. My stomach, chest, and left arm were paining real bad."

"Should you go to the emergency room?" Peg asked.

"Nope. I'm okay now."

"How can you know?" Mike asked then turned to Muriel. "Has he had spells like this in the past?"

"Never exactly like this," Sam answered. "I guess it was one of those big snakes trying to smother the life out of me. What do they call them?"

"Pythons?"

"Yep. But it's slithered back into its hole."

Mike shuddered at the image. The phone rang. Peg answered it and held it out to Mike.

"It's Bobby Lambert."

"Good," Mike said. "Now, we'll find out why the session meeting was canceled."

He picked up the phone.

"Where are you?" Bobby asked in an excited voice.

"Standing in my kitchen. Check the number; you called my house."

"But where were you thirty minutes ago?"

"At the church waiting for you and the rest of the elders to show up for a meeting. What happened?"

"A dispatcher with the fire department just called me! The old sanctuary is on fire! There are two fire trucks on the scene, but they're not going to be able to save it!"

Mike almost dropped the phone. He slumped down in one of the kitchen chairs. Putting his hand over the receiver, he whispered intently to the little group in the kitchen.

"The old sanctuary at Little Creek is on fire!"

Muriel stopped close to Sam, who put his arm around her shoulders. Mike lifted his hand from the receiver.

"What caused it?"

"He didn't tell me. Explain again why you were at the church?"

Mike felt drops of sweat trickle down inside his shirt. He spoke slowly and deliberately.

"I received an e-mail this afternoon from Milton Chesterfield that the elders wanted to meet with Sam Miller and me at the church around seven o'clock. We went to the church and waited about twenty minutes, but no one showed up so we left. I turned on the coffeepot in the conference room, but we didn't go into the old sanctuary."

"I don't know anything about a session meeting. Milton Chesterfield has been in San Francisco on vacation with his wife and won't be back in town until tomorrow."

"I have the e-mail right here."

Mike read it to Bobby.

"Check the originating address for the e-mail," Bobby said. "Are you sure it came from Milton's computer?"

Mike glanced at the top of the message.

"It lists the sender as 'user@bcsd.com.'"

"I'm sitting at my computer, and that isn't the e-mail address I have for Milton. Did you say bcsd.com?"

"Yes."

Bobby was silent for a moment. "Barlow County School District. That e-mail was sent from one of the public schools. My daughter sends notes to me at the office with that return address."

Mike panicked. "Bobby, you know I didn't have anything to do with setting fire to the church."

"Of course not."

Mike continued speaking rapidly, "I'd come to terms with the reasons for the sabbatical and hoped we could work through any problems about my leadership now that the charges against Sam have been dismissed. That's why I went to the church. I believed it would be the first step toward my return as pastor."

"That was my goal, too. But we hadn't discussed when to meet with you or if Mr. Miller would be included."

"What are you going to do now?"

"Go to the church."

"I'll meet you there."

Mike clicked off the phone.

"The e-mail was sent from one of the schools," he said to the group. "But Milton is in California and won't be home until tomorrow."

Peg looked at him with sad eyes.

"Are you sure it's a good idea to go to the church?" she asked. "If someone is trying to make it look—" She stopped.

"It will look worse if the pastor of the church doesn't show up when a major building on the property is burning to the ground. Sam and I didn't do anything wrong, and no one can prove otherwise."

Peg appealed to Sam, "Tell him not to go."

The old man shook his head. "I'm not his master. It's up to him."

"Are you going with him?" Muriel asked Sam.

"Nope. I need to get home and ask Papa what He wants me to do."

After Sam and Muriel left, Peg turned to Mike.

"I'm not sure I can handle any more of this pressure. It was hard enough suffering alongside Muriel and Sam. If the police try to claim you had something to do with—"

"They'll be wrong. I'm gone. I've got to see what's happened."

As he drove to the church, the panic Mike had felt when Bobby first mentioned the fire changed into anger. He was mad. Setting fire to a church was an act of sacrilege. He sped down the road, passing several cars against the restrictions of the yellow line.

Close to the church, he had to stop as traffic slowed to a crawl. Mike impatiently tried to peer around the corner of the road. Trees along Little Creek hid the church, but there was no mistaking the orange glow in the sky. The ancient wood in the sanctuary would burn fast and hot. Noticing that no cars were coming from the opposite direction, Mike pulled to the left, zipped past the line of cars, and pulled off the road just past the creek. Two large fire trucks and several cars were on the church property. Firefighters were spraying water onto the rear of the old sanctuary. The front portion of the building was already a charred pile of black wood.

Mike got out of the car and saw a hose stretching from one of the trucks into Little Creek. A handful of spectators had parked their cars on the opposite side of the highway to watch the activity. A firefighter approached Mike.

"Sir, please move along."

"I'm Reverend Mike Andrews, the pastor of the church," he replied. "Is there a place I can stand so I won't be in the way?"

The man pointed. "Stay close by the creek. I'll let the captain know you're here."

Mike walked along the familiar path that ran alongside the creek. He stopped near the place where the spring bubbled up from beneath the earth. One of the crews was spraying water on the roof of the administration building. Fortunately, there was no sign of fire on the adjacent structures. No one else from the congregation was present. After a few minutes, a gray-haired man in firefighting gear walked toward him.

"I'm Captain Logan," he said.

Mike introduced himself.

"There was no chance to save it," Logan said. "As you know, it was a tinderbox covered with old paint."

"Are the other buildings going to be okay?"

"Yes, the fire is contained, and we're fortunate to have the creek close by."

"Who reported the fire?"

"I'm not sure, but I suspect a motorist saw the smoke and dialed 911. We were here in less than fifteen minutes, but there was nothing we could do except keep it from getting hotter or spreading to the other buildings."

"Do you know what caused it?"

"It's a clear night, so it's either electrical or arson. Did you have any space heaters or other electrical devices in the building?"

"Nothing except the lights. It had been converted to central heating and air-conditioning years ago. We didn't use it except for special occasions."

"I assume it's insured."

"Yes."

Logan left. Mike continued to watch. He saw Bobby Lambert's car turn into the parking lot. A firefighter pointed in Mike's direction. Bobby joined him. Neither man spoke. The remaining blaze at the rear of the old sanctuary was almost out. Without the light of the fire, the darkness of night crept in except where the lights of the firefighting equipment illuminated the figures moving around the destroyed building.

"What is happening here?" Mike asked.

Bobby ran his fingers through his hair. "I don't know. Did you talk to anyone?"

"The captain came over and told me it's either electric or a set fire. Is anyone else from the church coming?"

"It was on the radio news report while I was driving out here, so I suppose people will start coming soon."

"What are you going to tell them?" Mike asked.

Bobby continued to stare straight ahead. "Nothing. Absolutely nothing."

Thirty-one

It was almost 3:00 a.m. when Mike climbed wearily into bed. The smell of the burned building lingered in his nostrils. The responses of the church members who came to the scene and saw him beside the ruins of the old sanctuary had been heart-wrenching.

Delores Killian wept when she saw the church building of her childhood wiped off the earth. Mike put his arm around her shoulders and held her as she sobbed. He spoke to a firefighter, who retrieved a piece of the altar rail and gave it to her. Both ends of the carefully polished wood were charred black. Nathan Goode stayed by Mike's side for more than an hour. They didn't discuss Melissa Hall or Sam Miller. Most people stared at the devastation for several minutes, spoke briefly with Mike, then left. Around midnight, Bobby came over to him.

"Milton called from California. The neighbor who feeds his cat phoned him with the news. He was upset, not as seriously as Delores, but the old sanctuary was linked closely to his family."

"Did you mention the e-mail?"

"No. I told you I wouldn't bring it up."

Mike nudged the ground with the end of his shoe. "And thanks for meeting me in the deed room."

"Let's not mention that either."

"Okay."

The men stood beside each other in silence. Mike ached for the return of the lighthearted banter they had enjoyed for so many years. He turned toward Bobby.

"Will there ever be a Friday afternoon when we can play eighteen holes of golf without worrying about anything except avoiding the fairway bunkers?"

"I don't know when."

The next time Mike looked, Bobby's car wasn't there.

Mike stayed until the last firefighter left. He shook hands with every one of them and thanked them for their efforts. He drove home, sad about the destruction of the beautiful old building, apprehensive about questions he feared would come.

THE DOORBELL RANG THE FOLLOWING MORNING AT 6:30. MIKE, wearing his pajamas, stumbled downstairs. Through the sidelight of the door, he saw a couple of men he didn't recognize. He opened the door.

"Michael Andrews?" the younger of the two men asked.

"Yes."

"I'm Hank Perkins, a detective with the sheriff's department. This is Richard Shactner, a fire scene investigator who works with Barlow and four other counties. We'd like to ask you a few questions."

The officers' sober faces confirmed the seriousness of the visit. Mike's mind raced through his options. He could refuse to talk without the presence of an attorney, which was the advice he would have given any client who called him when faced with investigative interrogation. He could show them the e-mail and fully disclose every detail of his actions the previous evening. Or he could find out as much as he could while revealing as little as possible. Even the last approach held substantial risk.

Judge bounded out of the kitchen barking. Mike grabbed him by the collar. "I'll put him in the backyard. Come in and have a seat."

He held Judge's collar as the officers followed into the great room. Peg called from the top of the stairs.

"Who's here?"

"Two men who want to talk about the fire at the church. No need for you to come down."

Mike opened the back door for Judge. He motioned for Perkins and Shactner to sit on the couch.

"What can you tell me about the fire?" Mike asked. "I spoke briefly with Captain Logan, but he didn't have much information."

Shactner spoke. "I was at the scene first thing this morning. During my initial walk-through, I could identify an accelerant pattern that ran from the front door partway down the main aisle. The burn patterns were very distinct."

Perkins added, "And we found an empty gas can in the bushes behind the new sanctuary. Did a commercial company cut the grass at the church property?"

"Yes."

"Was it Miller Lawn Care?"

Mike's mouth went dry. "No. Did the gas can belong to Sam Miller?"

"It had his company name on it."

Mike licked his lips and unsuccessfully ordered his heart to stop pounding. "Mr. Miller cut the grass for us several weeks ago so he could submit a bid. We'd been using another service but thought he might be cheaper. He must have left the gas can when he was there."

"I know Mr. Miller was with you at the courthouse yesterday morning," Perkins continued. "Do you know what he did after he left?"

"Went to work. I believe at the Blevins residence."

"And after that?"

Mike stood up.

"Thank you for coming, but this conversation is over."

The two men remained seated. Perkins spoke. "Reverend Andrews, do you realize there will be consequences from your failure to cooperate with us?"

Mike's face flushed. "I'm not refusing to cooperate; however, you are aware that I represented Mr. Miller in a recent embezzlement case"—he paused and spoke with emphasis—"in which all charges were voluntarily dismissed by the district attorney's office. As his attorney, it would be improper for me to speculate about his activities, especially if he is the subject of a criminal investigation."

"This is part of an ongoing investigation that may or may not become criminal," Shactner said. "You're the pastor of the church, and we hoped you would assist us."

"Which I will, except to the extent that it violates the attorney-client relationship."

"Has Mr. Miller already retained you to represent him in this matter?" Perkins asked.

"The ongoing nature of the attorney-client relationship is privileged."

Perkins smiled crookedly. "Reverend Andrews. We're not just interested in Mr. Miller's activities yesterday. We also want to talk with you. Where did you go and what did you do after leaving the courthouse?"

Mike put his hands together. "That's all, gentlemen. It's time for you to leave."

Shactner stood and Perkins joined him. Mike started walking toward the door, then glanced over his shoulder to make sure they were following him. As the two men left the house, Perkins turned around on the landing and handed Mike his card.

"If you decide it's in your best interests to cooperate, please call me anytime. My cell number is on the back of the card."

Mike closed the front door and leaned against it. He looked up and saw Peg, her hair disheveled, at the top of the stairs.

"What is it?" she asked.

Mike crossed the foyer and quickly climbed to where she waited.

"The beginning of an inquisition that could make the previous charge against Sam seem like a traffic ticket. I may be implicated as well."

"What did they say?"

"Not much, except that they found one of Sam's gas cans in the bushes near the fire scene. I suggested he might have left it when he cut our grass, but I have doubts. The fake e-mail from Milton that lured us to the church; a gas can conveniently left in the bushes. I wouldn't be surprised if they don't produce an alleged witness who claims we ran from the building right before smoke started—"

Peg collapsed in Mike's arms and sobbed. He held her head close to his chest and gently rubbed her upper back while she shook in his arms. It was all he could do. Anticipating the next step of the people who wanted to destroy Sam, and now him, seemed impossible. After her body began to relax, he took a step back but still kept his hands on her upper arms.

"Will you lie down?"

Sniffling, she kept her gaze toward the floor. "I can't sleep."

"Just be still. Do you think we should contact Dr. Crawford and ask for a prescription that will help calm you down?"

"I'm not going back to bed, and there isn't a pill that can take away what I'm feeling!"

"Then come downstairs and lie on the couch. I need to phone Sam and warn him."

Mike let Judge into the house. The dog went straight to Peg and rested his head close to her hand so she could pet him without moving from the couch. Mike brought the cordless phone from the kitchen into the great room and dialed Sam's number. Muriel answered.

"I need to speak to Sam."

"It's too late. They already came and got him," Muriel said, her voice quivering. "He's been gone about ten minutes."

"Who came?"

"A deputy we didn't know took him to the jail."

"Did he ask Sam any questions?"

"No, he just told him to get in the police car."

"I'm on my way to the jail. I should be there in less than ten minutes."

Mike hung up the phone. Peg shook her head sadly.

"Is there a risk you'll be arrested, too?"

"Yes," Mike admitted.

Peg buried her face in her hands.

"I'm going to the jail to keep Sam from talking to any of the detectives. The last time he was arrested, he gave a statement that could have been interpreted as an admission of wrongdoing. I can't let that happen to him, or me."

Peg turned on her side so that she faced the back of the couch.

"Go," she said. "Leave the phone with me."

Mike touched her shoulder, which was stiff with tension. "I'll be back."

"When?"

"In a couple of hours."

Peg didn't respond. Mike stared at her back and searched for a reassuring word. None came. He turned and left.

THE EARLY MORNING TRAFFIC FLOWING INTO SHELTON SEEMED out of place. People shouldn't be getting up, drinking a cup of coffee, and slipping into the usual Tuesday morning routine. Mike parked in front of the jail. The familiar female deputy was on duty.

"I'd like to see Sam Miller," Mike said.

The woman hit a few keys on her computer. "He's in booking. I'll let you know when he'll be available."

Mike sat in the waiting area. The initial adrenaline rush produced by his encounter with Perkins and Shactner had faded, and he felt drained. He forced himself to begin analyzing Sam's plight, but so many possibilities rose to the surface that he couldn't begin to develop a cohesive plan. Fifteen minutes passed. He tapped on the glass. The deputy glanced up.

"Oh, you can go back now."

Mike stood in front of the metal door until he heard the click that signaled release of the lock. He pushed open the door and went to the second door where he waited again. When he passed through, he saw Sam dressed in regular clothes, sitting in a chair near the booking area. Detective Perkins approached Mike.

"I'm here to see Mr. Miller," Mike said to Perkins.

"That's fine. We just finished."

"Did you question him?" Mike asked, his voice getting louder. "I told you at my house that I was representing him!"

"That's not what he told us, and you didn't instruct me not to talk to him."

"Did he give you a statement?"

"After signing a Miranda waiver, he provided helpful details about both of your activities."

"Give me a copy of the statement."

"That will be handled by the district attorney's office. I'm sure Mr. Miller can tell you what he told me."

The detective turned and motioned for Sam to approach. Mike opened the door to the closest interview room and waited for Sam to enter.

"What did you tell him?" Mike asked as soon as the door clicked shut. "You know better than to talk to the police!"

"Nothing that they wouldn't have found out anyway," Sam replied. "We didn't do anything wrong."

"Haven't you learned anything?" Mike retorted in frustration. "Perception is as important as reality!"

Sam rubbed the top of his head. "I did plenty of sweating last night when I wrestled with the Enemy before I got the victory."

"Victory over what?"

"Fear," Sam answered simply. "It had me down, much worse than the sickness I felt when we went to the church last night. Right now, it's draped all over you."

Mike stopped. He couldn't deny the anxiety that gripped him.

"Are you saying I shouldn't be worried?"

"Ask the Master, not me."

"Please, don't lecture me."

"I'm trying to help you. Do you remember your dream about me sitting in the chair in this room? I thought about it as soon as they brought me in this morning. I think the dream was about now, not before. It's important for both of us that I stay at rest. It's easier for me since I've been through this jail once. This is your first time. That's always the hardest."

"I'm not in jail yet."

Sam looked directly in his eyes. "Do you believe they're going to let you go when we finish?"

Mike licked his lips. "I hope so."

"If they don't, what are you going to do?"

"Hire a good lawyer."

There was a knock on the interview room door. Mike opened it. Perkins stood there with a deputy beside him.

"Reverend Andrews, I'd like to see you before you leave."

"All right."

Mike shut the door. "It's too early in the morning to call a lawyer."

Sam bowed his head and began to pray. "Papa, You see inside this jail and into the hearts of all men. I don't believe Mike and I are in this place without a plan. Please show it to us so that we can do Your will. We forgive in advance the wicked men who are causing us this trouble, and help us in our time of need."

As the old man prayed, Mike began to calm down. When Sam said, "Amen," he opened his eyes.

"That helped," Mike admitted. "Except when I think about Peg. If I don't go home in a couple of hours, I'm not sure she can handle it."

Sam nodded. "Folks who are married and suffer for the Master endure four times the pain. The greatest fear I fought last night wore Muriel's face. I knew it wasn't her, but that didn't make it any easier to rebuke it. You may have to trust Papa to be there for Peg more than you will for yourself."

Mike slumped down in his chair. "How long do you think we should stay in here?"

"Until they break up our prayer meeting."

Mike looked at his watch. "Or it's time for me to call a lawyer. While we wait, tell me about your conversation with Detective Perkins."

"He asked what I did yesterday after I left the courthouse. I told him I worked at the Blevins house all afternoon then went with you to the church to meet with the elders, who didn't show up, so we left. Don't you think he would have found out about that kind of thing anyway?"

"Maybe, but they should get information on our terms, not theirs. Did you mention the e-mail from Milton Chesterfield?"

"Nope, I didn't remember his name."

"Did he tell you they found a gas can with your company's name on it near the scene of the fire?"

Sam raised his eyebrows. "I've been missing a can for a few days now. I thought I'd left it at a job in town."

"Are you sure you didn't leave it at the church when you cut the grass?"

"Nope. I've had it since then. It's only been gone since Friday or Saturday."

"Don't you see? Whoever set you up did so after realizing what I was going to bring out in your trial! That's why the embezzlement charge disappeared and a new one appeared. It's all the same."

"Same what?"

"Attempt to discredit you, and now, me. A man who would steal money from a church or burn one down shouldn't be believed if he tries to expose corruption by prominent men in the community. The only difference now is they'll try to bring me down, too. I figured out what they were doing while investigating your other case, which makes me a greater threat than you and your dreams."

There was another knock on the door immediately followed by someone opening it.

"Time's up!" a surly deputy announced. "Vacate this room."

"Is there a waiting list?" Mike asked.

Sam shook his head.

Mike followed Sam into the hallway and glanced apprehensively at the booking area.

Perkins came around the corner. "Mr. Miller, you are the subject of an ongoing investigation but may leave at this time."

"I'm not arrested?"

"No; however, you should not leave Barlow County without notifying the sheriff's office of your travel plans."

Normally, Mike would have objected to the notice requirement, but he was so glad Sam could leave that he kept his mouth shut.

The deputy grabbed Sam by the arm. "Come with me."

Mike started to follow, but Perkins stopped him.

"Reverend Andrews, please step into the booking area."

"Am I under arrest?"

"Not unless you want to confess to a crime."

Mike's eyes narrowed. "Your comments at my house made me believe you were going to try to charge me whether you had any evidence or not."

"That's not how we conduct law enforcement in Barlow County."

Mike followed the detective. The booking area contained two desks, several chairs, and a small side room for taking mug shot photos. Sitting beside one of the desks was Ken West.

"Have a seat, Mike," West said. "You got me up early this morning. Detective Perkins tells me you're reluctant to provide details of your activities after you left the courthouse yesterday."

"Those who know the system are cautious," Mike answered. "You'd be the same in my position."

"Probably right." West shifted in his chair. "However, it struck me as odd that Mr. Miller would walk away from an embezzlement charge and immediately burn down a church. Now, he tells Detective Perkins that he was with you during the relevant time period. Is that correct?"

"Yes, from approximately six-fifteen in the evening until we received a phone call at my house that the old sanctuary was on fire."

"Did the two of you go to the church?"

Mike hesitated.

"You don't have to tell me," West continued. "However, we received a 911 call from a witness who reported seeing you and Miller at the church."

"Who was the witness?"

"Didn't leave a name. The call was made from a pay phone at a convenience store about two miles from the church."

Mike leaned forward. "Ken, I'd rather not discuss what happened last night until I obtain legal counsel."

"Are you sure you want to go that far to protect Mr. Miller?"

"And myself."

West avoided Mike's eyes. "I've already begun the process of obtaining a warrant for your arrest; however, as a fellow attorney I didn't want to take that step before talking with you." He looked at Mike. "Will you provide fingerprint samples without the necessity of formal charges?"

"Why? My fingerprints would be all over Little Creek Church!"

"But not necessarily on the gas can found on the premises."

Mike couldn't remember if he'd touched one of Sam's gas cans, but he knew the sheriff's department could eventually obtain his fingerprints. If cooperation delayed an arrest and bought him a few more hours or days with Peg, it would be worth it.

"Okay," he replied.

Perkins summoned a female deputy, who expertly rolled Mike's fingerprints and pressed them on a card. While she did so, Mike glanced into the photo room and wondered how long it would be before the light flashed and his face appeared in the local paper with the caption "Local Pastor Charged with Burning Church."

Thirty-two

When he started his car, Mike entertained the wild thought of packing Peg and Judge in the car, emptying his shrinking bank account, and driving as far away from Barlow County as possible. He arrived home. Peg was sitting in the kitchen waiting.

"Thank God!" she said when he walked through the door.

They embraced. Mike held her a long time, memorizing the feel of her body pressed close to his.

"How was Sam?" she asked when he released her. "Muriel called. She's torn up."

"On his way home. But the wheels of injustice are turning. I'm not sure how long it will be before arrest warrants are issued."

"Warrants?"

"For both of us. I believe everything that's happened is connected. It's all designed to keep Sam, and now me, from ruining the Cohulla Creek land deal. There is a lot of money at risk."

"Money!" Peg raised her voice. "Call Mr. Forrest and promise to keep your mouth shut! We don't care whether someone builds a bunch of houses in the middle of the woods."

"The people behind this wouldn't trust me. And there may be corruption I don't know anything about. They're probably scared of going to jail themselves."

Mike told her about the encounter with Ken West. "If they claim my fingerprints are on the gas can, I'm sure I'll be arrested."

Peg bit her lower lip. "What will I do if that happens?"

"Get me out on bond. I'm going to hire Greg Freeman to represent me before I'm arrested. I have to do as much as possible while I still have my freedom."

"Do you think you should see Bobby?"

"Why?"

"I haven't been able to get him out of my mind. If he was on the bad side of this, he wouldn't have slipped you information at the courthouse."

"Okay, but what am I supposed to ask him now?"

"To help. I can't believe he would stand by and let this happen to us if he could stop it."

"He's not close to the center of power."

"No, but I'd like you to do it for me."

Mike shrugged. "Okay, it can't hurt."

He picked up the phone. It was still too early for the receptionist at the law office to be at work, so he dialed Bobby's cell phone. The familiar voice answered.

"Are you at the office?" Mike asked.

"Yes."

"Detective Perkins and an arson investigator came to see me early this morning. Sam Miller and I are under investigation for setting fire to the church."

"No! This is crazy!" Bobby responded with such feeling that Mike was encouraged to continue.

"I'd like to meet with you."

"When?"

"As soon as possible."

There was a brief pause. "The courthouse will be open in a few minutes. Be at the library."

Mike hung up and turned to Peg. "I'm not sure where this is going with Bobby, but I'm going to meet him at the courthouse. While I'm in town, I'll slip in and talk with Greg Freeman. He's trying a case in the main courtroom, but I can catch him during a break."

"Go ahead. I'm not feeling well," Peg replied. "I'm going to lie down."

"Should I take you to the doctor?"

"No, I'll be fine if I get off my feet."

Mike reluctantly left the house. He arrived at the courthouse and went to the library. Bobby was waiting for him. Mike had a sudden urge to ask Bobby if he was going to record the conversation.

"Is this off the record?" Mike asked.

"You're the one who wanted to talk."

"I'm jumpy. Who's behind this?"

"Delores phoned me late last night claiming Miller threatened to burn down the church several weeks ago. She was going to call the sheriff's department and report it. I guess that's what she did."

Mike groaned. "It was a dream. Sam had a dream in which he saw the church on fire. It wasn't literal; it had to do with the conflict that surfaced over my involvement in his criminal case. He never expressed any anger toward the church or its leaders, and I explained that to Delores at the time."

Bobby tapped his pen against a blank legal pad. "She remembered what she wanted to. Captain Logan also phoned and asked me about the company that maintained the church grounds. They found a gas can belonging to Miller in the bushes."

"I know. They want to dust it for my fingerprints, too."

"Did you touch it?"

"I remember talking to him when he came to cut the grass, but I don't know if I picked up any of his equipment. I could have helped him load or unload stuff at other locations when I went by to see him about his case. But there must be more behind this than Delores Killian and a gas can."

"You and Miller were the last people at the church. That doesn't prove anything, but it's circumstantial enough to make a detective start sniffing the air."

Mike stood up and started pacing.

"But are there any other reasons why this is happening?" he asked.

"Not that I'm aware of."

Mike stopped and stared hard at Bobby.

"Are you sure?"

"What are you driving at?"

Bobby seemed sincere. Mike didn't know how hard to push or what to reveal. He tried a different tack.

"Why was the embezzlement charge against Miller dropped?"

"Evidence surfaced that your client didn't have anything to do with the checks."

Mike put his hands on the conference table and leaned forward.

"Did this evidence involve Brian Dressler?"

"Yes, but I can't comment on the details."

"Was there another reason why the charges against Miller suddenly evaporated?"

"No."

"Did you and Mr. Forrest talk about the dismissal?"

"Of course, but you know he just brought me in to carry his briefcase and do some research. Mike, what are you driving at? You have more immediate problems than figuring out why you won the embezzlement case without firing a shot."

"I'm just wondering if the embezzlement and arson charges are related."

"How?"

"That's what I hoped you could tell me."

"I can't," Bobby replied with obvious frustration in his voice. "I'm your friend, not your enemy. I've tried to prove that over and over during the past weeks. What do you want me to do?"

"Peg asked me to talk to you, but I'm not sure why."

"Maybe because she knows you'll ride off to battle without thinking about the consequences. You need to hire a lawyer to protect you and Peg."

Mike sat down at the table. "Will you represent me?"

"Are you serious? I'm not a criminal defense lawyer. I'm comfortable with contracts, but I've never handled anything more complicated than a traffic ticket. You don't want me."

"What about Mr. Forrest?"

"He's furious with you for pestering the bank and dragging Bunt and Linden into town just to harass them for no reason. I could talk to him, but he needs a cooling-off period before he'd consider serving as your champion. You need help now."

"I'm going to talk to Greg Freeman. He's in the middle of a trial, but I'm going to catch him during a break."

"Good. Get to him as soon as you can."

"Will you let me know if you hear anything else about the fire?"

"Yes."

Mike hesitated. "One more thing. Why did Mr. Forrest believe I subpoenaed Bunt and Linden for harassment purposes only?"

Bobby put his pen in his pocket. "Because of their ownership in the bank, of course. In the past year, they've become the two largest stockholders."

"That's what he told you?"

"Yes."

Mike stood up. "I'm heading over to the courtroom. If you won't help me, I'm going to ask Greg Freeman."

Mike ignored the crestfallen expression on Bobby's face and left the library. He slipped in the back of the courtroom. Melissa Hall was questioning a sheriff's deputy who had identified Freeman's client as the man caught leaving the auto parts store through the back door late one Saturday night.

"Was he carrying anything in his arms?" Hall asked.

"No."

Hall looked flustered. "Wasn't he carrying property from the store?"

"Objection, leading," Freeman said.

"Sustained."

"Tell us what you saw," Hall tried again.

"I saw the defendant pushing a shopping cart piled high with a set of chrome reverse mag wheels, a CD player with six speakers, and a pair of sheepskin seat covers."

Hall relaxed. The questioning went smoothly from there. When she sat down, one of the jurors raised his hand. Judge Lancaster pointed to him.

"What is it?"

"Could we take a break? I'm not feeling well."

"Ten minutes," the judge barked.

Mike walked down the aisle. Both Freeman and Hall turned around as he approached.

"Greg, can I speak with you for a minute?" Mike asked.

Freeman came around the bar into the aisle. "This was your week to star in court."

"I almost wish I could have. There's more trouble brewing. Did you hear about the fire at my church?"

"No."

"The old sanctuary at Little Creek burned down last night. Sam Miller and I are under investigation for arson."

"What?" Freeman replied so loudly that Melissa Hall turned around and stared at them.

"Yes, and I want you to represent us."

"Is there a potential conflict of interest between Miller and you?"

"No."

Freeman jerked his head toward the man sitting morosely at the defense table. "I have to fly this plane into the side of a mountain first. My client claims his cousin broke into the store, but the police officer and an unbiased witness disagree."

"How long will the case last?"

"The prosecution should finish before lunch. I don't have any witnesses except my client. The cousin didn't want to come forward and confess. He's a repeat offender who would face a life sentence for a three-strike felony. The jury should have the case by late this afternoon. A verdict?" Freeman shrugged his shoulders.

"Okay."

"Has Miller been questioned?"

"Yes."

"What did he say?"

"I haven't seen the statement, but nothing that isn't common knowledge. I met him at the jail an hour ago and told him to keep quiet."

"Did they try to talk to you?"

"Perkins and an arson investigator named Shactner came to my house. Ken West was at the jail."

Freeman raised his eyebrows. "West came to the jail?"

"Professional courtesy. And they wanted my fingerprints to compare with those on a gas can found at the scene."

"Did you give them a card?"

"Yes, otherwise, I think I'd be calling your office from the phone outside the cell block."

"Call me late this afternoon. Unless the jury gets confused by the evidence, I should be out of here by five o'clock."

Mike left the courthouse. He wanted to be doing something, not simply waiting for the sheriff's department to act. However, he wasn't sure what to do. He drove home. Peg was in the great room lying on the couch.

"Better?" he asked.

She nodded in a way that didn't convince him. "I was nauseous right after you left. I guess it's better to face stress on an empty stomach. How did it go?"

"Nothing new from Bobby. He either doesn't know anything or is a good liar. After we met, I talked briefly with Greg Freeman and asked him to represent Sam, too."

Peg closed her eyes. Mike sat at her feet but stayed at the edge of the cushion.

"It's the inactivity I can't stand," he said. "There has to be something I can do to get to the bottom of this!"

"Maybe you're going to have to trust someone else to take care of it," Peg answered wearily. "Just like Sam did with you."

"That would be very hard for me to do."

They spent the rest of the morning at the house. Every time the phone rang, Mike jumped, but it was always a member of the church calling about the fire. No one mentioned the police investigation. Apparently, word of the day's earlier events hadn't leaked out into the community. Bobby had honored his word, and the sheriff's department hadn't issued a statement. Toward noon, the phone rang again. Mike answered it.

"Sorry to hear about the fire at your church," Braxton Hodges said. "Our photographer just showed me the pictures. Do you have a comment or two for the article?"

Mike hesitated. "Are you recording this conversation?"

"Yes, so I can quote you accurately."

"Turn off the machine. I want to come in and meet with you."

"Uh, okay, but this isn't a Brooks hamburger day. I have a two o'clock deadline to get this story into tomorrow's edition. Otherwise, it won't make it until Saturday."

"I'm on my way."

Peg lifted her head. "What are you going to tell him?" she asked. "I'm not sure it's wise to talk to a reporter."

"This is different. Trust me."

MIKE AND HODGES WENT INTO THE SPARTAN CONFERENCE ROOM where Mike met with Brian Dressler. Copies of the minutes of the Hatcher meeting and the e-mail from Milton Chesterfield were folded in Mike's pocket.

"This fire hit you hard, didn't it?" Hodges said as soon as they were alone.

"Worse than you know."

Hodges placed a blank pad on the table. "I'm listening."

"You can quote me—'*As pastor of the Little Creek Congregation, I'm saddened by the tragic loss of our historic sanctuary but believe the members of the church will pull together and go forward with the ministry God has given us to the community.'* How is that?"

"Typical. You could have given that to me over the telephone."

"From here on no notes. No recordings. This is between us and nobody else."

The reporter sat up straighter. "Mike, you have a trial lawyer's flair for the dramatic. I'm listening."

"I'm going to tell you the explanation Ken West gave for dismissal of the embezzlement charges against Sam."

Mike quickly laid out the story placing all the blame on the former banker.

"I don't believe it," Hodges responded when Mike finished. "It destroys my Pulitzer article."

Mike took out the memo of the Hatcher meeting. "Here's the memo I told you about."

The reporter read the sheet of paper then looked up. Mike continued, "At first, Dressler denied being in the meeting but last week told me Hatcher called him in to discuss Sam's embezzlement. That would have been difficult because the meeting was four days before the checks were written. Dressler either didn't remember correctly, or the plan to bring down Sam came out of the meeting. Take your pick."

"You know my preference."

"I confronted Dressler with the inconsistency when we talked on the phone. His reaction was reference to the Fifth Amendment. He's already hired a lawyer in Mobile."

Hodges leaned forward. "This is great! Hatcher must have found out that you'd gotten under their cover."

"I'm not sure. I never told anyone except Sam about the memo, but I believe the embezzlement charges went away because Hatcher didn't want me rooting around the courtroom. He may be afraid I know more than I do."

Hodges grunted. "Miller looked like an easy victim until you got involved."

Mike reached into his pocket, took out the e-mail, and placed it on the table. "It's not over. These people aren't giving up. In fact, it's worse."

When he summarized what had happened in the past twenty-four hours, Hodges's jaw dropped open.

"If you're arrested for arson, I'll have to report it," Hodges said when Mike finished.

"It will devastate Peg and ruin my career."

Hodges hesitated. "I can't stop—"

Mike interrupted. "I won't blame you for doing your job, and I'm not here to ask you to censor the news. Does anyone suspect that you're investigating Butch Niles and the Cohulla Creek development?"

"No, I haven't even mentioned it to our editor."

"Good, because you'd be at risk, too."

Hodges's eyes opened wider. "I hadn't thought about that."

"This is serious. Use caution. But don't quit. I'm already limited in what I can do."

"Do you have an estimate on the timing or any arrests?"

Mike shook his head. "No, but I was thankful when I left the jail this morning without having to call a bondsman. I'm going to hire Greg Freeman to represent me. I'll keep you in the loop of information. This fight may not be won in a courtroom."

Thirty-three

SATISFIED THAT HE'D TAKEN A POSITIVE STEP, MIKE DROVE AWAY from the newspaper office. When he arrived home, a sheriff's department car was sitting in his driveway. Taking a deep breath, Mike parked next to it and walked toward the house.

Chief Deputy Lamar Cochran, a cup of coffee in his hand, sat in the kitchen with Peg and Sam Miller. Puzzled, Mike greeted the officer.

"Hey, Lamar. Are you here to arrest me?"

"No. Sam asked me to come."

Sam spoke. "Pour yourself a cup of coffee."

"I don't really want—"

"Just do it," Peg said.

Mike obeyed and sat across from Cochran at the kitchen table.

"Now what?" Mike asked. "Are we going to play cards?"

"After I left the jail," Sam began, "I went home and lay down to rest for a few minutes. I didn't think I could sleep, but in no time I was out. I dreamed that you, me, and Lamar were sitting in your kitchen drinking coffee. We were having a nice conversation when a candle appeared over Lamar's head. That means he's going to get a good idea because we're together. I called the jail, and he agreed to meet us here."

Cochran took another sip of coffee. "I was relieved when the embezzlement charge against Sam was dismissed, and I don't believe he burned down the sanctuary at the Little Creek Church."

"He didn't," Mike responded. "We were together the whole evening. I wish you were in charge of the investigation."

"Show him the letter the elder sent you," Sam said.

Mike stared at Sam for a second. "I'm not sure that's a good idea until we talk it over with Greg Freeman. I've asked him to represent both of us, and he's agreed."

"I think we should share the letter with Lamar," Sam replied casually.

Sam made the e-mail sound as harmless as a cake recipe, and Mike could tell from the expression on her face that Peg wanted to walk out Sam's dream. He stifled his objections and went into the office and printed another copy.

"I thought it came from Milton Chesterfield," Mike said, handing it to Cochran, "but it was sent from one of the local schools. Milton was in California. Someone wanted to lure Sam and me to the church and place us on the premises close in time to the fire."

Cochran handed the e-mail back to Mike. "I know Mr. Chesterfield. My father used to work for his company. Anything else?"

"Not really."

"Tell him about your conversation with Ken West," Peg said.

Mike grudgingly obliged. When he reached the part about the 911 call from the convenience store, Cochran interrupted.

"Was it Carrington's One-Stop?"

"He didn't say, but that would be the right distance. The Burtons run a gas station two miles in the opposite direction."

"Yeah."

"There it is!" Sam said.

"What?" Mike asked.

"I saw a flash of light. I think it was coming from the candle."

"Did you see a candle?" Mike asked, not believing he was seriously asking the question.

"Nope, but what else would put out light like that?"

Mike turned to the chief deputy. "Can you tell us about your bright idea?"

Cochran shook his head. "No, but I'll keep thinking."

The radio on the deputy's belt squawked, and he pressed the Receive button.

"What's your 20?" a voice asked.

"East side of town on the ridge."

"Good. Do you know where Michael Andrews lives?"

Cochran looked at Mike as he answered, "Yes."

"Go to his house. If he's there, bring him in. The magistrate has issued a warrant for his arrest in the Little Creek Church fire."

Mike reached across the table and grasped Peg's hand.

"What about Sam Miller?" Cochran asked.

"We're sending Morris over to get him."

"No need. He's on this side of town, too."

"10-4."

"Can I have a minute with my wife?" Mike asked.

Cochran waved his hand. "Yes."

"And I need to call Muriel," Sam added.

Mike led Peg into the great room. His hand was sweating.

He spoke rapidly. "Greg Freeman is going to call as soon as he finishes his trial. Tell him I've been arrested. He'll know what to do about the bond. Ask him how much he needs as a retainer—"

Peg put her index finger on his lips and looked deeply into his eyes. "Do you love me?"

"Yes."

"That's the most important thing I need to know right now."

"Okay."

Peg continued looking directly into Mike's eyes. "Remember the look on my face if you start to worry about me." Placing his hand on her heart, she said, "And I keep hearing the same words over and over—fear not, fear not, fear not."

"Fear not."

"Right. I'll be here when you get out."

"It shouldn't be long—"

"It doesn't matter how long it is," Peg interrupted. "I'll be here."

As Mike followed Sam and Cochran from the house, Peg's words echoed in his mind and her face filled his vision. He and Sam got in the backseat of the patrol car.

"Peg's a fine woman," Sam said.

"Yes."

"And someday, what Papa has done in your marriage will be a bigger memory than the ride in this patrol car."

They rode in silence. Mike stared out the window. They passed landmarks known to him since childhood. Never before had they seemed so close, yet so far away. He could see a place but didn't have the freedom to stop the car and go there. Cochran drove to the rear of the jail where the prisoners entered through a secure entrance.

"I hope it's a short stay," Cochran said.

Mike felt a numb detachment as he returned to the booking area. Cochran left. Mike and Sam stood beside each other.

"We already have their prints," a male deputy barked. "Glamour shots only."

Mike stood on a line and stared, unsmiling, into the camera. A deputy handed him an orange jail uniform and a plastic bag for his regular clothes. Mike had left his wallet and watch at home. He changed clothes in a room no bigger than a closet. When he came out, Sam entered.

"Perkins wants them separated," the deputy said when Sam joined Mike in the open area. "Put Andrews in the holding cell and Miller in cell block A."

"Brinson, the guy who knocked the old man out the last time he was in here, is in A," a deputy said.

"Block B is two over limit."

"There's no need to put Mr. Miller in danger," Mike said, stepping in. "You could move Brinson into B."

"Your opinion about administration of the correctional facility isn't needed," the second deputy snarled.

Sam looked at Mike and shook his head. "It's okay. Papa is giving me a second chance."

The door to the holding cell closed behind Mike. He was alone. The small, dingy, white room smelled of antiseptic. There were no chairs or bed. A toilet without a seat stood in the corner. Mike sat on the floor and leaned against the wall. There was nothing he could do now but wait for others to help him. His dogged persistence and fighting spirit couldn't penetrate the walls that enclosed him. He was helpless. He closed his eyes.

And saw Peg's face.

She'd been right. The love and concern that filled her eyes were much more important than the practical information he'd frantically tried to download into her brain. He examined every detail: her slightly upturned nose, rosy cheeks, welcoming lips, and insightful eyes. Tears, not of sorrow but of gratitude for his wife's devotion, welled up and spilled down his cheeks.

Another scene from the past rose in his mind—a picnic along the Blue Ridge Parkway, not long after they married. Peg fell asleep with her head in his lap. Mike had watched her for a long time, alternating between her face and the hazy mountains in the distance. He'd always considered the picnic an idyllic time. Now, he knew it lacked depth. They'd not yet allowed God to lay the foundation upon which an enduring marriage could be built. Sam's words in the patrol car were true—the blessing on Mike and Peg's marriage was a greater reality than the other challenges they faced.

Mike normally considered enforced solitude maddening. However, instead of pacing back and forth like a caged animal, he relaxed and let his mind travel through pleasant memories. He went back to his childhood, reliving moments that bore the marks of God's grace: the Sunday school teacher who prayed with him when he was in second grade, a friend who would kneel on the ground and talk to God as if He were closer than the tree branches above their heads.

As a boy, Mike loved reading illustrated Bible stories in which he placed himself in the company of Israel's heroes. He remembered the vivid pictures and how the stories stirred him. During that formative time, a nescient faith entered his heart, a faith that matured into mountaintop experiences as an adult and altered the course of his life.

Mike didn't lodge an indictment against the Almighty. The goodness of God had been his lifelong companion. Unlike Job, he wouldn't blame heaven for the evils that marked the human condition. Other events from his life surfaced: the church retreat when he was in high school, a prayer session with Danny Brewster, a redemptive encounter with a homeless man, an afternoon when he preached with power at a food kitchen in Virginia. Time after time, hindsight revealed a plan its present concealed.

He stopped and wondered if he was losing his mind. Were these imaginary journeys the path to insanity? Like a man whose life flashes before him in the instant before death, Mike was watching an advance screening of his life's story. Why? As soon as he asked the question he knew the answer—so he could be thankful in the midst of suffering. The door to the cell opened.

"Supper time," a deputy said as he placed a tray on the floor.

"Thanks."

Mike didn't ask the time of day. He knew jail inmates ate early so the outside kitchen workers could go home. He left his food untouched. He didn't want to defile the memory of home-cooked meals until his stomach demanded it. More time passed. The deputy returned to take away the food tray.

"Could I have a Bible?" Mike asked.

The deputy didn't respond, but in a few moments the door opened and the officer placed a plain black Bible on the floor. Mike picked it up and started reading about others who had been wrongly imprisoned. Confinement, whether briefly or for years, was not an abnormal way station in the lives of saints. Old Testament prophets and New Testament apostles learned eternal lessons behind prison bars. Mike's jail had walls, not bars, but as he took time to carefully read about Joseph, Jeremiah, Daniel, Peter, Paul, and Jesus Himself, he entered into the exclusive fraternity of those who suffer imprisonment for doing good.

He put down the Bible. Ken West had called Mike a formidable adversary. Mike didn't feel formidable. The click of the electric lock on the holding cell door was an exclamation point of his personal frailty. But the recognition of his limitations enabled Mike to enter into the common denominator of those who suffer for righteousness—God's grace made perfect in human weakness. As he started reading again, liquid strength entered his spirit and hardened like concrete in the depths of his character. He looked up at the stark ceiling with gratitude. When he emerged from the cell, he had confidence that the change, no matter how small, would be permanent.

Hours passed. Mike dozed some but spent most of his time reading and thinking. He didn't try to characterize his thoughts as prayer, but nevertheless believed they were sanctified. The lights in the cell blinked on and off twice. The door opened.

A different deputy appeared. "Come out."

Mike stepped into the hallway. Even after such a short period of solitary confinement, the sight of people bustling around the booking and processing areas of the jail was a shock to his system.

"Can I keep this Bible?" he asked the deputy.

"Sure. We have stacks of them."

The deputy motioned toward the booking area.

"You can change into your street clothes. Your bail has been posted."

"What time is it?"

The deputy pointed to a clock on the wall of the booking area. It was 7:35.

"Is that evening or morning?" Mike asked.

"Morning. You're getting out too soon for breakfast. You'll have to handle that on your own."

Mike had spent almost twenty hours in the holding cell. He put on his clothes.

"What about Sam Miller?" he asked when he came out of the room.

"We're not authorized to release that information."

"I'm one of his lawyers."

The deputy stared at Mike in disbelief.

"He's right," said the female deputy who had been on duty in the waiting room when Mike came to visit Sam on previous occasions. "He's the lawyer who has been representing Miller."

"He's at the hospital. I don't know his current status."

"What happened to him?" Mike asked in alarm. "Did Brinson hit him?"

"I don't know his status."

Mike left the jail, then realized he didn't have a car parked out front waiting for him. He also didn't have a cell phone. He started walking down the street toward the Ashe Street Café where he knew he could make a call. A car pulled up beside him and slowed.

"Can I give you a ride?" a familiar voice asked.

It was Bobby Lambert. Mike got in the car. Bobby drove forward slowly.

"Do you know what happened?" Mike asked.

"Yes. I'm the one who posted your bond. I left the magistrate's office a few minutes ago to meet you, but they let you out before I arrived."

"Thanks. Did Peg call you?"

"Yes. I also talked to Greg Freeman."

"What about Sam Miller? He's at the hospital, either beat up or with heart problems."

Bobby shook his head. "I don't know anything about it. It took until morning to get everything straightened out for you. I was at the church late last night for an emergency session meeting."

Mike turned in his seat. "What happened?"

"You're out. Fired. I did my best to persuade them to wait for the truth to come out, but no one would listen to me. News of the arrest hit the street and swept you out of the church. I couldn't protect your sabbatical payments, either. I'm sorry. All ties are severed. It's over."

Mike took in the information as if listening to news about someone else.

"I know you tried," he said, facing forward. "Take me home. Then I need to go to the hospital."

As Bobby drove, Mike stared out the window at the same landscape he'd watched from the rear of Lamar Cochran's police cruiser. Things looked the same, yet different.

"Are you okay?" Bobby asked after several minutes of silence. "I mean, it's a stupid question, but you're not saying anything."

"Yeah. A night in jail can do a lot for your perspective on life."

Thirty-four

Mike stepped through the door and saw Peg waiting on the other side. In a split second, the love he'd carried in his heart to the jail cell was confirmed in her eyes. They embraced and held each other as if they'd been separated for years.

"You were right," Mike whispered into her ear before another wave of emotion washed over him. "I saw your face. It was glorious."

Peg pulled away and wiped her eyes with the back of her hand.

"No, it's not. I'm a mess."

Mike touched his heart and his head.

"Not in the places that matter."

Peg leaned against his chest. They held each other again.

"Do you know what's wrong with Sam?" Mike asked.

"Not exactly. Muriel phoned from the hospital. It's his heart. He's in a regular room hooked up to a monitor."

"Did he have a heart attack?"

"She wasn't sure. The doctors were still running tests."

"Let's go see them."

While Peg got ready, Mike held Judge's head in his hands and rubbed a spot behind the dog's ears for a few moments. Even his contact with the dog seemed more vibrant than the previous day. They got in the car.

"What happened at the jail?" Peg asked. "Were you in any danger?"

"Only from whatever is wrong in me. I was alone in a small holding cell the entire time. Your face—" Mike stopped. "I can't began to describe—"

"Don't. I'm satisfied now that we're together."

DURING THE DRIVE, MIKE BROKE THE NEWS ABOUT HIS TERMINATION from the church. Peg listened quietly.

"I don't want to go back," she said. "I let the answering machine screen calls while you were gone. Some of the people who left messages were almost obscene in their hatred."

"Who—?" Mike started then stopped. "I don't want to know."

They arrived at the hospital. The cardiac care rooms were on the second floor not far from where Marie Dressler died. Mike didn't have any problem identifying Sam's location—a deputy sheriff sat in the hallway. They approached the deputy, and Mike introduced himself.

"I'm one of Mr. Miller's attorneys."

"Go in. Chief Deputy Cochran told me you might be coming by."

Mike and Peg entered the room. Sam had the bed inclined to a seated position. The light blue hospital gown around his neck made his blue eyes sparkle. Muriel was sitting beside the bed. She rose and gave Peg a hug. Sam looked surprisingly normal.

"How are you feeling?" Mike asked him.

Sam patted his stomach. "My spirit is strong, but the doctor says my heart sent out an SOS. He and Deputy Morris want to keep me here and check me out."

"I thought you might have gotten beat up in a fight. Did you have any trouble with Brinson in the cell block?"

"Nope, but we have unfinished business to attend to. He showed me places on his arms where his stepfather used to put out his cigarettes. But the real burns are a lot deeper. The Enemy didn't want me sharing a revelation I got for the boy and sent my heart a-fluttering. I got dizzy, and the next thing I remember I was in an ambulance coming over here. They got me settled in, and I had a decent night's sleep that included a dream about you. Muriel, please hand me my notebook."

Sam held up one of his tattered notebooks. "See, Muriel brought it because you should always be prepared for Papa to speak to you."

"I'm listening to you right now. Does that count?"

"You know there's a big difference." Sam turned the pages. "But let's see. You were in a dark place that looked like a cave. You couldn't see anything so you were standing real still, waiting. A little light started shining in your right hand. I looked down, and you were holding an old black Bible. When you held up the Bible, the light increased so you could see your way out of the cave."

"That describes it pretty well, although I'm not sure about getting out of the cave for good. I may have to go back."

"Things happen fast in dreams. Working it out can take years."

Muriel spoke. "Mr. Freeman called us here early this morning. He sounded like a nice young man. He's going to try to get Sam's bond reduced. Right now, it's a lot more than our house and land are worth."

"He'll work on it today," Mike reassured her.

They spent the rest of the morning together in the hospital room. Mike brought in breakfast from Traci's for Peg, Muriel, and himself. Sam sampled the egg substitute on his hospital tray and pronounced it as edible as the wheat straw he spread over newly planted grass seed. Toward noon, a nurse arrived to prepare Sam for additional testing.

"We'll be back tomorrow," Mike said. "Will you be here?"

"Papa told me I was going home. It may be today; it may be tomorrow."

"Don't try to outrun Deputy Morris."

"When my time to go comes, he won't be able to catch me."

Mike stared hard at Sam for a second before the nurse came between them. Mike paused at the door and handed Morris his cell phone number.

"Would you call me if he takes a turn for the worse?"

"Yeah, but I go off duty at three o'clock."

"Please pass the number along to the man covering the next shift." Mike paused. "And try to spend a little time with Sam yourself. You won't regret it."

MIKE LOOKED AT THE BLINKING LIGHT ON THE ANSWERING machine in the kitchen.

"Do I want to check our messages?" he asked Peg.

"It's up to you."

"Go into the great room and rest. I'll listen to this batch."

Mike pressed the button. The first call was from a woman who'd recently started attending the church and promised, without a hint of condemnation in her voice, to pray for him. The second was from Greg Freeman.

"Mike. Call me at the office as soon as possible."

Mike phoned the lawyer's office.

"Mr. Freeman is at the courthouse but should be back shortly."

"Is his calendar clear?"

"Yes, and I know he wanted to talk with you."

"I'll be there in a few minutes."

Mike listened to three more messages: two slanderous, one supportive. He went into the great room.

"The messages are cleared. I'm going into town to meet with Greg Freeman."

"I put the checkbook for the money market account on the counter in the kitchen. He asked me for a retainer when I talked to him about your bond."

"Did he quote an amount?"

"Yes, $10,000 for you and $10,000 for Sam."

Mike swallowed. "It's not out of line for a felony arson charge. I've charged more than that myself, but it wouldn't leave us much in the bank if we have to front Sam's retainer, too. After Greg runs through that money, I'm not sure what we'll do."

"Maybe we can become one of Sam's miracle stories."

Mike tried to push away anxiety as he drove down the hill into town. Greg Freeman's office was located on the second floor of a small office building on the opposite side of the courthouse from Forrest, Lambert, and Arnold. Mike parked on the street and walked up a flight of stairs. Freeman's name and suite number were painted in black on a glass door. Mike stepped into a reception area about the same size as the cell he'd occupied at the jail. The retainer requested would go a long way toward paying the lawyer's overhead for the rest of the year. At the sound of the door opening, a young woman came around the corner.

"Mr. Andrews?"

"Yes."

"He's waiting for you."

Mike followed her down a short hall and stepped into a plain, rectangular office with a window overlooking the courthouse square. A picture of dark-haired Greg Freeman with his wife and baby daughter prominently occupied the corner of the desk. Freeman stood and shook Mike's hand. Mike took out his checkbook and placed it on the desk.

"Thanks for working with Bobby to get me out. I'm prepared to pay the retainer for myself and Sam. Since he's not doing well, I don't want to delay moving forward on his release."

"Hold on to your money for a few more minutes," Freeman replied. "We may need to renegotiate. I went over to the courthouse and met with Ken West and Melissa Hall, who, by the way, easily won her first case at my expense yesterday."

"Hopefully, Sam and I can give you more to work with."

"It wouldn't be hard. West and Hall tossed out a couple of facts that would hurt us. First, your prints were found on the gas can taken from the scene."

"I'm not surprised. I've been around Sam while he was working several times in the past weeks."

"And the church secretary claims Miller threatened to burn down the church after you were forced out for agreeing to represent him."

Mike shook his head. "It was a dream about the church, and she has her events out of sequence."

"We'll get the details on that later. But the main purpose of the meeting at the DA's office wasn't to browbeat me into submission. Do you know Lamar Cochran?"

"Of course, the chief deputy."

"He took the initiative to contact the convenience store where the 911 call was made connecting you and Miller to the fire scene."

"Carrington's One-Stop?"

Freeman glanced down at a legal pad on his desk. "That's the place. The store has an outside surveillance camera that runs on a twenty-four-hour cycle. Cochran reached the store owner before the tape recorded over the evening of the fire. Cochran reviewed the images. The pay phone is clearly visible, and only one person made a call close in time to the fire."

"Could he identify the caller?"

Freeman paused. "Yes, it was the brother of Rob Turner, the man I represented in court yesterday. The brother's name is Vann. Cochran picked him up, and Detective Kelso is interviewing him at the jail right now."

"Will he talk?" Mike asked excitedly.

"Probably not," Freeman said, shaking his head. "He's been arrested many times and knows keeping his mouth shut is the best way to stay out of jail."

"What else did West say?"

"Nothing except that he wants your opinion about who set the fire. He respects your ability as an investigator."

Mike spoke slowly. "I have definite ideas, but I don't think Ken West wants to hear them."

"Try them out on me. I'm your lawyer."

"I haven't paid you, and after I explain everything you may want to raise your retainer."

"It would be better for me to know all the facts before we go forward."

Mike adjusted his position in the chair.

"Okay."

Freeman made notes while Mike told what he'd learned representing Sam in the embezzlement case and the events surrounding the fire.

"Do you have the date and time of the e-mail purportedly from the elder at the church?"

"Yes."

"The schools have cameras. Maybe we can check with their security as well."

Mike also summarized his conversations with Braxton Hodges.

"Do you know what Hodges is going to do next?"

"No, except keep looking through Butch Niles's trash can."

When Mike finished, Freeman stared out the window for a moment.

"Write one check for $10,000," he said. "And I'll hold it in trust for a few days while we see what develops. In the meantime, it shouldn't be too hard to get Miller's bail reduced so he can go home from the hospital instead of back to the jail."

Mike left Freeman's office. It felt good letting someone share the weight of the knowledge he'd been carrying. When he arrived home, Peg handed him a packet delivered by a local courier service. Mike opened it and took out the paperwork formalizing his dismissal from the church. The termination letter was signed by Milton Chesterfield. Mike put the documents back in the packet.

"The pink-slip letter from the church. I'll save this for a day when I think my ego is getting out of hand," he said to Peg.

"That's my job, and I don't need any help."

"Do you want to go out and celebrate my release from jail?"

"We're broke. And I'd rather not see anybody. Let's lock the doors and turn out the lights."

"Are you serious?"

Peg touched him on the cheek. "I just want to be with you and hold your hand. If I squeeze tight enough, maybe no one will be able to take you away again."

So, they spent the evening together at home. Mike's appetite returned, and

Peg fixed a full meal. After supper, they sat on the couch together while Mike told Peg what happened in the holding cell at the jail. He made it through without tears until he showed her the Bible the guard gave him.

"Your face was my encouragement and this was my light," he said, holding it up. "I think the cave is behind me."

THE FOLLOWING DAY, FREEMAN PHONED WITH NEWS THAT SAM'S bail had been reduced to an amount that would allow a property bond secured by the Millers' property.

"I plagiarized your work in the embezzlement case," Freeman said. "It saved me a lot of time."

"Glad it helped. Does Sam know about the bond?" Mike asked.

"I tried to reach him at the hospital, but no one answered in his room."

"Is he okay?"

"I assume so. I dialed the room directly."

"I'll go over there and check," Mike responded quickly.

"The paperwork for his release is waiting at the magistrate's office."

Mike told Peg the good news about the bond but not his concern about Sam's health.

"I'm going to the hospital and help them get everything in order."

MIKE COULDN'T SHAKE A SENSE OF FOREBODING AS HE DROVE TO the hospital. Etched in his mind was the stark image of Marie Dressler's empty bed. He parked in one of the clergy spots near the entrance. The elders at Little Creek might take his pulpit, but they couldn't revoke his parking permit.

He walked rapidly through the lobby and waited for the interminable elevator to descend from the second floor. When it finally opened and took him to the second floor, Mike glanced toward Sam's room. There was no sign of a uniformed deputy. Mike started running down the hall. A nurse's aide looked up in surprise as he ran past. He reached Sam's room and burst inside. When he did, a deputy whirled around with his hand on the pistol holstered in his belt.

"Hold it!" Deputy Morris commanded.

Mike stopped and held his hands in the air. In the bed behind the deputy lay Sam, dressed in regular clothes. Muriel was sitting in a chair on the opposite side of the bed.

"I thought," Mike said, breathing heavily, "something had happened to Sam."

"Things are always happening with me," Sam replied with a smile. "If nothing is happening, it's a sure sign I've drifted from the Master's path. Vic and I were having a good talk. He told me about a dream his aunt had about him and his two brothers, and I was explaining it to him."

"Okay," Mike responded as his heart slowed. "I'll step outside so you can finish talking about the dream. But I wanted you to know that your bail has been lowered, and the paperwork is ready for signature on a property bond."

Sam looked at Muriel. "I told you we would be going home."

"What did the doctors say about your heart?" Mike asked.

"It's running on six cylinders instead of eight, which explains why it knocks and pings on me sometimes. Muriel was happy to hear that I've got to watch what I eat. The oil in fried foods doesn't lubricate my blood vessels as good as I hoped it did."

"Muriel can come with me while you finish talking with Deputy Morris," Mike said then turned to the deputy. "We'll bring back the order from the magistrate approving the bond."

"He'll still need to be processed at the jail," Morris replied. "The doctors have released him, but we're still waiting on the discharge instructions."

MIKE AND MURIEL LEFT THE ROOM AND WALKED DOWN THE hall toward the elevator.

"That gave me a scare," Mike said. "Is he really going to be okay?"

"The doctor talked pretty straight to him. Sam's stubborn, but I think he heard what he said. I'll make sure he doesn't forget."

"I'm sorry I interrupted his conversation with Deputy Morris."

"Don't worry. Sam will bring it around to the right place. He's a good talker."

They descended to the main level. As they crossed the lobby, Mike turned to Muriel.

"Do you remember how hard I tried to avoid representing Sam?"

"Yes."

"Just now, I panicked because I thought something bad had happened to him."

Muriel smiled one of her wrinkled smiles. "He has a way of pulling you in, doesn't he?"

Mike nodded. "When the Lord does call him home, it will leave a big hole in Barlow County."

Thirty-five

JACK HATCHER AND BUTCH NILES SAT AT THE SMALL CONFERENCE table in the corner of the bank president's office. Hatcher had locked the door and ordered his secretary not to disturb him under any circumstances.

"Let me do the talking," Hatcher said to Niles, checking his watch.

"This is your deal," Niles responded. "I've been serving the interests of the citizens of Barlow County who want to expand the local tax base through increased development of—"

"Shut up," Hatcher barked. "Save the campaign rhetoric. The amount of money flowing into your account and where it came from is enough to interest the U.S. attorney in Asheville. Being an elected official at this point is a liability, not an asset. The federal authorities would much rather take down a politician than a businessman."

"I'm not going to be threatened," Niles shot back. "Go ahead and phone Linden."

"Fine. We'll see what he has to say."

Hatcher punched in the number on the phone in the middle of the table. A male voice answered on the second ring.

"Troy Linden."

"It's me," Hatcher said. "Niles is with me."

"Give me some good news," Linden said.

"Andrews and Miller have been arrested and charged with arson."

"Are they in jail?"

"Andrews posted bond. Miller had a heart attack and is in the hospital."

"If he dies, that would be a simpler way to take care of him." Linden paused.

"I still think it would be cleaner to get rid of both of them permanently. One phone call and Andrews will have a biking accident, and the old man won't have another dream."

"No!" Hatcher responded. "That's not what we agreed to. We're simply working the system to our mutual advantage. Niles and I are businessmen."

"Who have accepted a lot of money from Bunt and me. We're giving you a chance to take care of this once and for all. If your way doesn't work, we'll step in."

"Be patient. The deal will close in two weeks. After that it won't matter what Andrews and Miller say."

"What is the status of the legislation?" Linden asked.

Hatcher nodded at Niles, who spoke. "Coming out of committee with a favorable recommendation by the end of the week. After that, approval on the floor of the legislature is automatic."

"Andrews snooping around put pressure on us to act sooner," Hatcher said. "It would have been a recipe for disaster if we'd let him cross-examine you."

"I could handle it. Bunt is the one who worried me."

"Everything will be fine," Hatcher said confidently. "But you need to transfer the money to exercise the options within a couple of days."

"And another $50,000 for me," Niles interjected.

Hatcher waved his hand angrily at Niles. There was silence on the other end of the line.

"Disregard Niles," Hatcher said. "Did you hear what I said about the options?"

"Yeah, but there has been a change in plans. Bunt has put the brakes on more money until he knows everything is going through."

"What about the options?" Hatcher replied. "We've got to complete the purchase of the privately held land or it won't matter what happens in the legislature."

"It's time for you to assume more of the risks," Linden replied.

"I don't have that kind of money!" Hatcher protested.

"You're president of the bank. Figure it out. Bunt and I are major shareholders. We won't object if you want to use bank money."

"But there are regulators who monitor—"

"We know what you have in your personal reserve," Linden interrupted. "There's enough to exercise the options."

Hatcher ran his fingers through his hair. "But that would wipe me out. I've worked thirty years to get where I am financially."

"And this is your chance to double up. Isn't that your goal?"

"Yes." Hatcher paused. "But I'll need you and Bunt to sign an amendment to our contracts."

"Send it up. Increase your percentage by the amount you're putting in. Do the math. You'll like what you see. Call me the first of next week."

Linden broke the connection. Hatcher looked at Niles.

"You're going to fund twenty-five percent of the purchase price for the land," Hatcher said.

"I'm broke! I need the $50,000 to remain solvent!"

"The bank will loan you the money and secure it by a second mortgage on your house along with your portion of the Cohulla Creek deal."

Niles glared at Hatcher.

"You're going to pay Turner," Niles said.

"He doesn't know I exist. You handled that contact."

"With a go-between to protect me. The other $25,000 has to be paid tomorrow if we want to keep him happy and quiet."

"You're not in a position to demand anything, but I'll make sure your second mortgage is approved first thing in the morning."

Niles swore. "I don't think that crazy old man's dream justified all this expense and hassle. He stopped me on the street the other day and started spouting off a bunch of stuff. Nobody would take him seriously."

"What did you say to him?" Hatcher asked sharply.

"Nothing."

"Good. Information is power. And remember, we're not just dealing with Miller. When Andrews got involved, everything went to another level. I didn't get to where I am without taking every threat seriously."

MIKE AND PEG SPENT A QUIET SUNDAY MORNING, BUT AFTER THE church service, the calls resumed. One of the first was from Bobby Lambert.

"The church was packed," Bobby said. "But it had the feel of an inquisition more than a church service. Milton explained the real reason for the sabbatical and apologized for not terminating the church's relationship with you at that time. All the elders except me stood behind him at the front of the church. Barbara also spoke. No questions were allowed. The final announcement was the formation of a pastor search committee as soon as possible."

"What did Dr. Mixon do?"

"Made it clear that he would serve as interim only until time to visit his daughter in Peru. He's a good man, not interested in getting wrapped up in the power loop. Some of the chatter after the service wasn't favorable to the elders. There will be a lot less people there next Sunday. I'm resigning from the session effective immediately. Elizabeth and I won't be back."

The thought of an exodus of people wounded by a church fiasco grieved Mike. Some might not only leave the church, but wander from the faith altogether. After Mike hung up the phone with Bobby, another caller urged him to start a new church once he was cleared of the arson charges. Mike deflected the suggestion.

"Larry McReynolds wants me to start a new congregation," he told Peg when he hung up the phone.

"You knew that would come up."

Mike shook his head. "I can't think about that now. Maybe never."

MONDAY AFTERNOON, MIKE RECEIVED A CALL FROM BRAXTON Hodges.

"I just talked with my cleaning lady," the reporter said. "That well has been as dry as the oil stock I bought on a tip from the guy over in classified ads." Hodges paused. "Until today. Guess what she found in the trash at Butch Niles's house?"

"A winning lottery ticket."

"Something better. A copy of the letter Sam Miller sent Jack Hatcher."

Mike gripped the phone tighter. "Do you have it?"

"Not yet. I told her to carefully check for anything with Sam's name on it, and she found it in the trash can in Niles's study."

"Where is it now?"

"I'm going to get it in half an hour then bring it to the paper."

"I'll be there waiting."

Mike told Peg about the find.

"How important is the letter now?" she asked.

"Not as much," Mike admitted. "But it's the pebble that started this avalanche. It might be helpful to Freeman, if he tries to do what I did with the embezzlement charge."

MIKE SAT IN THE PARKING LOT WAITING FOR HODGES TO RETURN. The reporter parked beside him. Mike got out and greeted him.

"Do you have it?"

Hodges, unsmiling, held up a rumpled sheet of paper. "Not exactly. It's notes Niles made about the letter."

Mike took the sheet from the reporter and smoothed it on the front of his car.

Hatcher believes the letter from Sam Miller (the yardman) connects Linden, Bunt, Hatcher, and me to the purchase of the Pasley tract at Cohulla Creek. Miller threatens to go public with his accusations that he calls "deeds of darkness." (A joke???) But Hatcher is paranoid.

The rest of the sheet contained three phone numbers, and the name *Dressler* underlined twice.

"It's not dated," Mike observed. "But the last sentence has a few whiffs of a smoking gun. A persistent lawyer could question Jack Hatcher for an hour about his paranoid tendencies and how he might act on them."

"It will go in my file."

"I'd like a copy for Greg Freeman. He's going to represent Sam and me."

They went inside the newspaper office. Hodges made a copy of the notes and handed it to Mike.

"How are you doing personally?" Hodges asked in a softer tone of voice. "I know it sounds strange coming from me, but I've been praying for you and Peg. Do you think God hears the prayers of a heathen like me?"

"Keep it up. God hears everything."

MIKE DROVE TO FREEMAN'S OFFICE. THE YOUNG LAWYER WAS eating an apple at his desk.

"No time for lunch today," Freeman said.

Mike handed him the copy of the notes.

"From Hodges's spy, the lady who works for Butch Niles."

"Niles is having a busy day," Freeman responded after he read the notes. "I saw him come into the sheriff's department when I was leaving the jail after meeting with a client."

"Had he been arrested?" Mike asked, leaning forward in his chair.

"No, he went directly into the sheriff's office. The sheriff may be hitting him up for a bigger allocation for county law enforcement from the state budget." Freeman took a final bite from his apple. "I'm glad you stopped by. I needed to talk to you anyway."

Mike settled into his chair. Freeman dropped the apple core into a trash can before continuing.

"I was meeting with Rob Turner, my car parts thief, at the jail this morning. He's due to be sentenced next week, and I'm working on a list of witnesses for the hearing. In the midst of the interview, I mentioned the video of his brother Vann and its connection to the fire at the church. Rob got quiet for a moment, then asked if providing information to the sheriff's department about Vann could reduce his sentence. I told him it depended on the type of information."

"He's willing to turn on his brother?"

"Apparently. He claimed Vann had a gas can that didn't belong to him in the back of his truck a few days ago."

"With Miller Lawn Care written on the side?"

"Yes. And Vann told Rob that he had connections in Raleigh who could get Rob's sentence reduced even if the jury found him guilty. When Rob asked his brother for help, Vann told him no and now won't talk to him. What do you think I should do?"

"Talk to West," Mike replied without hesitation. "You owe that to your client who's going to be sentenced. And it will let us know if West is serious about trying to find out who really set fire to the church."

"I'll call him now."

Thirty minutes later, Mike and Freeman were sitting in the conference room in the district attorney's office. West entered along with Melissa Hall.

"Ms. Hall is going to join us," West said.

Hall's eyes narrowed when she saw Mike at the table.

"Did Kelso get any information from Vann Turner?" Freeman asked.

"It's still under investigation," Hall said.

"I'll take that as a negative," Freeman replied. "I met with Rob Turner this morning, and he's willing to provide information about his brother Vann in return for a reduced sentence."

"What kind of information?" West said. "I've been interested in getting Vann Turner off the streets for years."

Freeman glanced at Mike before answering. "Rob saw a gas can that belonged to Sam Miller in his brother's truck a couple of days before the fire. We know Vann is the one who phoned 911 to report the fire."

West turned to Hall. "Get Kelso and Perkins in here."

After Hall left the room, West looked at Mike. "When are you going to tell me what's going on?"

Freeman spoke. "If you want to talk to Mike, there needs to be an understanding of his status."

"Our conversation might change his status," West replied, "but as of right now, he's an arson suspect out on bond."

Freeman turned to Mike. "What do you want to do?"

"Ask Ken a few questions," Mike replied.

"Go ahead," the district attorney answered.

"Do you believe Brian Dressler was behind the checks with Sam Miller's signature stamp on them?"

"I haven't performed my own investigation, but the bank is in the best position to uncover what took place."

"Dressler had a hand in the checks, but he was following orders from someone else."

"Who?"

Mike put his hands in front of him on the table. "Is there anyone in Barlow County you wouldn't be willing to prosecute?"

"Not if the evidence is there."

"Jack Hatcher?"

West stared at Mike and nodded.

"Butch Niles?"

"You believe Hatcher and Niles wanted to defraud their own bank of a hundred thousand dollars?" West shook his head. "That doesn't make sense."

"But would you prosecute Niles?"

"No one is above the law."

"Even if it results in political pressure against you?"

West shifted his massive frame in the chair, making it groan. "I've been district attorney of Barlow County for almost thirty years, and I'm fully vested in the retirement program. Fear of retaliation by a local politician isn't a big issue for me anymore. But before either of those men would be charged with spitting on the sidewalk, it would have to be a case with every corner buttoned down tight."

Mike relaxed. "I wouldn't expect anything else. Once the detectives get here, I'll lay it out."

There was a knock on the door, and Perkins and Kelso, a stocky, older detective with a ring of brown hair surrounding his bald head, entered the room. Once the detectives were seated, Mike put his briefcase on the table and clicked it open.

"It all began with a dream."

When Mike finished, Kelso looked at West. "It's no secret that Niles likes to hit the high-stakes tables in Atlantic City and Las Vegas."

West turned to Mike. "It would be foolish to build a case against a state legislator solely based on the testimony of a known criminal like Vann Turner. The key will be bringing pressure against one or more of the other individuals you mentioned and see if one of them turns against his coconspirators."

Mike handed Kelso a copy of the e-mail. "Do you want to check this out?"

"Yeah, we'll get our computer guy to work on it. He's good at tracking things down."

West shook his head. "I liked it better when the high-tech stuff involved identifying blood types."

MIKE AND FREEMAN WALKED TOGETHER FROM THE COURTHOUSE.

"How do you think it went?" Freeman asked.

"Too soon to guess. They were listening, but we need something a lot more important than a meeting at the DA's office. That was a huge risk, but I think it was worth it."

"Your story was even more convincing the second time," Freeman said. "You really thought outside the box in your investigation."

They crossed the street at traffic light four.

"By the way, how did you get the memo of the Hatcher, Bunt, and Linden meeting?" Freeman asked.

Mike stepped onto the sidewalk. "You're my lawyer, but that needs to stay confidential. I don't want to jeopardize a close personal relationship."

When they reached the other side of the street, Freeman spoke. "If we let Kelso dust it, I bet Bobby Lambert's fingerprints are on it."

"If I was as smart as you claim," Mike answered, staring straight ahead. "I'd keep my mouth more tightly shut."

AT HOME, MIKE PHONED SAM AND TOLD HIM WHAT HAD happened. Peg, who was sitting on the couch reading a book, listened.

"You should have seen their faces when I started off with your dream about the hatchet, nails, and tree," Mike said. "They probably thought Greg Freeman was going to claim that I was mentally incompetent, but when we left, they were already working on a plan to follow up, using my leads."

"I wrote a letter to the Brinson boy," Sam said. "What's the best way to get it to him at the jail?"

"Did you hear what I told you?" Mike asked. "The arson case against us is unraveling."

"Yep, but if I don't get the message to Brinson, I'll be in a kind of trouble no lawyer can get me out of. Papa has a call on that boy's life, and he needs to see the way to freedom so he can follow it."

Mike sighed. "You could send it by mail to the jail, but the quickest way would be to ask Lamar Cochran to deliver it in person."

"That's a good idea. I'll catch Lamar in town tomorrow. He likes to eat breakfast at Traci's."

"But don't tell him anything—"

Mike looked down at the receiver that had gone dead in his hand. He turned to Peg.

"When Sam claimed I was going to be like him," Mike said, "I thought he meant odd and hard to understand with a box of tattered notebooks on the floor of my closet. But it's really simple. He cares about other people and what God wants to do in their lives. That's a good example for anyone to follow."

Peg took a sip of water. "Pretty soon you'll be saying 'Papa' and rubbing your belly when you have a good idea."

Mike patted his stomach. "The only idea I have right now has to do with what we're going to eat for supper."

Thirty-six

THE FOLLOWING DAY, MIKE RECEIVED A CALL FROM GREG Freeman.

"I just got off the phone with Ken West. Things are happening fast. Kelso brought Vann Turner back in for questioning and confronted him with the gas can evidence, the convenience store video, and who knows what else that he made up. Vann got scared and started shifting blame to Butch Niles."

"What kind of blame?"

"That Niles used a third party to pass money to Turner as payment for making the 911 call. I suspect Turner, acting alone or with help, is the one who set the fire and then made the call blaming it on you and Sam, but, of course, he didn't admit that. After that, West came in and raised the specter of the recidivist statute. The thought of a life sentence without parole really loosened Vann's tongue, and he identified the go-between. That guy and Niles are being brought in for interrogation."

"Niles is the kind who will roll over on someone else."

"And West called the state attorney general to notify them of the investigation."

Mike's mental wheels were turning. "The federal authorities will also want a piece of Niles, especially when Linden and Bunt are mentioned. I'm sure there's more to them than I was able to uncover."

AFTER HE HUNG UP THE PHONE, MIKE WENT INTO THE ART ROOM where Peg was finishing her third watercolor for the baby's room. A chubby little girl holding a red ball lay on a beach towel in the shade of an umbrella.

"Does that umbrella block all the UV rays?" Mike asked.

"In my picture it does."

Mike sat on the bed and told her what he'd learned from Greg Freeman.

"It was strange—like hearing information about a case I was handling for someone else," he said. "But as soon as the call ended, I realized this is about me. West wouldn't have contacted Freeman if he still harbored doubts about what I told him."

Peg looked at him anxiously. "So, are the charges against you and Sam going to be dismissed?"

"That wasn't mentioned."

"Did you ask him?"

"No," Mike replied sheepishly. "I was too interested in what he was telling me about the ongoing investigation."

Peg held out a paintbrush toward him. "Call him back or I'll paint your nose redder than that ball in the picture!"

Freeman wasn't in the office, and Mike left a message.

THAT AFTERNOON'S EDITION OF THE LOCAL NEWSPAPER CARRIED a headline in the middle of the front page announcing "Legislator Niles Questioned."

Mike quickly scanned the article for new information. Braxton Hodges reported that Niles met with Detective Kelso but revealed nothing inflammatory. In fact, the big news was simply the fact of "an ongoing investigation." Mike finished the article and phoned the reporter.

"That was the teaser article," Hodges said. "Did you see the quote I got from Niles denying any wrongdoing?"

"Yes."

"That's the setup to make him look like a massive liar when the truth comes out. The second article will bring out his gambling habits. It's all designed to make readers anticipate the next revelation."

"Who's providing you information?"

"Not you," the reporter snapped.

"Don't be touchy. You didn't wait on me. Now that I'm the client, not the lawyer, I can talk if you promise not to use my information until confirmed."

"I confirm everything."

"Are you recording me?"

There was a brief silence. "Not now."

"Good. Don't let your finger slip over to the Record button by accident."

Mike told him what he knew about the investigation.

"This is what I suspected all along," Hodges said excitedly. "What about Maxwell Forrest and Bobby Lambert?"

"I hope they're not involved."

"Don't kid me. The lawyers in these kinds of deals always know enough to be indicted as coconspirators."

"Their names didn't come up."

"What about Brian Dressler?"

"He will probably end up as a material witness once he cuts a deal."

"When will this go public?"

"When the grand jury meets. After that, Ken West will have to issue at least a brief public statement."

"I need to be ahead of him. Do you have a contact at the Attorney General's Office in Raleigh?"

"No, my political connections are paper thin. Judge Coberg is the closest I come to the power structure."

Hodges was quiet for a second. "Never mind. I know who can give me some inside information."

AT FIVE O'CLOCK, GREG FREEMAN RETURNED MIKE'S CALL.

"I forgot to ask about the charges against Sam and me," Mike said. "What's going to happen?"

"I didn't know myself until a few minutes ago. Melissa Hall phoned and told me they want to leave everything status quo until indictments are handed down against Hatcher and his crowd. Dismissal of the charges would really tip off potential defendants that they are in the DA's sights."

"But the case against Sam and me is dead."

Freeman paused. "Yes. It's over."

MIKE HUNG UP THE PHONE AND TOOK A DEEP BREATH. HE'D grown so used to the crushing weight of his circumstances that he'd forgotten what a stress-free breath of air felt like. He went into the kitchen, found Peg, and told her the good news.

She cried. Mike held her and felt the tension draining from the muscles in her back.

"It's been worse for you than me," he said. "I'm sorry."

Peg wiped her eyes. "You don't need to apologize. I just want our lives back to normal."

"Once the charges are dismissed, we won't be back to normal," he said, stroking her hair with his hand, "but we'll be able to start looking for it."

Peg lifted her chin and gave him a quick kiss. "Normal is the love I have for you. That's where I want to live for the rest of my life."

LATER, MIKE COULD HEAR PEG SINGING SOFTLY. IT HAD BEEN A long time between melodies. Peg had hung the picture of the woman who looked like Muriel Miller in the kitchen. Mike looked at it while he phoned Sam.

"Yep. I thought this thing would work itself out," the old man responded. "What are you doing tomorrow?"

"Uh, I don't have any plans."

"I'd like to visit your mountain top. I had a dream about it last night."

"Is your heart strong enough for a climb?" Mike asked in surprise.

"I saw the doctor yesterday, and he told me to increase my exercise. I've been lying about the house too much. I need some fresh air."

"Do you mind if my dog comes along?"

"Nope."

"Okay. I'll pick you up around nine in the morning."

SAM GOT IN THE CAR AND PATTED JUDGE'S HEAD THAT DRAPED OVER the seat.

"Can we stop for a cup of coffee?" the old man asked. "Muriel likes it weak, and I haven't had a stout cup since Wednesday."

"Where do you like to go?"

"The place you passed on the way to the house is fine."

At the convenience store, Mike also purchased a few snacks for the hike. Sam eyed a rack of spicy beef jerky sticks, but Mike shook his head.

"I don't want us to get in trouble with Muriel. If she finds out you ate some of those, she won't let you come outside and play in the future."

"You're right, but I can't be cut off from treats. If that happens, I'll start dreaming about the foods I can't eat, and there won't be time for Papa to show me the important stuff."

Mike paid for the snacks and coffee.

"Tell me about the dream you had about me."

"There will be time for that later."

They arrived at the parking lot for Hank's Grocery. The weather had been warm all week, and the trees on the hillsides were full of fresh green leaves primed for a busy summer of photosynthesis. Clouds streaked the sky, but they were wispy and high up. The early morning breeze had died down by the time they parked near the trailhead.

"I always tell the man who owns the grocery that I'm here," Mike said when he turned off the car.

Mike and Sam entered the store. Judge stayed in the vehicle with the window cracked open and barked in anticipation of the hike. Buzz Carrier was behind the counter. He glanced up at Mike then awkwardly looked away.

"Buzz, I know what you've heard," Mike said. "But it's not true. Soon things will start coming out in the open. Keep reading the paper before you sell the last copy, and you'll find out."

"Sorry, Mike, it was a shock to our family. I didn't know what to think."

Sam looked around the store. "You sell about everything, don't you?"

"Yes, sir, but I can't compete with the big-box outfits. They sell most items for less than what I have to pay for them."

Sam pointed to an index card covered with faded pencil writing that was taped to the wall behind the cash register.

"Did your daddy write that card?"

Buzz turned. "Yeah. It's some Bible verses about running an honest business. Did you know him?"

"Nope." Sam rubbed the top of his head. "But I don't think your daddy would be upset if you decided to sell this place and open a motorcycle shop."

Buzz's mouth dropped open. He looked at Mike.

"Did you know that's what I've been thinking about doing?"

"No," Mike replied. "I saw your motorcycle parked out front last summer, but you never mentioned opening a shop to me."

Buzz kept talking to Sam as if he'd not heard Mike. "But I didn't want to go against the family heritage. We've run this place for three generations. I wanted to get my daddy's permission to sell it when he was sick in the hospital, but he died before I got the chance."

"You're a good man, and you honored him when he was alive," Sam said. "Now, it's time to go in the direction you believe is right."

Buzz nodded his head several times then stuck out his hand to Sam.

"Thanks, I really appreciate you talking to me. What's your name?"

Mike answered. "This is Sam Miller, the other man charged with setting fire to the Little Creek Church."

For the third time, Buzz looked perplexed. "Oh, sorry about that. You fellows have a good hike. And take your time. I'll keep an eye on the car."

Sam smiled. "When you open your motorcycle business, put that card behind the cash register."

Mike and Sam left the store and walked to the car. Mike opened the door, and Judge bounded out.

"Do you have any questions?" Sam asked as they moved toward the opening in the trees that marked the beginning of the old logging road.

"Let me answer it myself," Mike replied. "Papa told you what to say to Buzz because He loves him and wants to help him. What else should I ask?"

Sam chuckled. "I'm not used to you talking this way."

"Too confusing?" Mike asked.

"Yep. Let me ponder your question while we walk."

Mike carried a small backpack and set a slow pace, but Sam didn't seem to have any problem keeping up. As they walked along, the old man began identifying the trees and plants. Mike was amazed at Sam's knowledge.

"You must learn a lot working in lawn maintenance," Mike said after Sam identified a small fern sprouting from the middle of a moss patch.

"Papa has given us a beautiful world. I enjoy finding out as much about it as I can."

They took a couple of water breaks. Sam took sips from his water bottle. Mike took out the blue plastic bowl and served Judge. At the second stop, Sam took a deeper drink.

"I'm glad this part of the trial is going to be over soon," the old man said.

Mike propped his foot on a boulder and glanced up at the approaching ridgeline.

"You mean trail."

"No, this test you and I've been going through. It's not been easy. My business is down to nothing, and worry has put wrinkles on Muriel's face in places that will be hard for her to make happy with her best smile."

"Yeah. Peg is emotionally drained, and I've been—" Mike stopped and looked at Sam. "You know, I've been stressed out, but I'm more thankful than ever. God met me in that jail cell and put a peace in my heart unlike anything I imagined existed. It's crazy, but what makes me sad now is the news about what is going to happen to Jack Hatcher, Butch Niles, and the other people who tried so hard to destroy our lives."

Sam smiled. "Papa knew what He was doing when He told me to ask you for help. Do you know why it upsets you when you hear that someone is going to be caught and judged for their sins?"

"No."

"Because Papa wants to save people. These folks deserve to be punished, but if you'd never met Jack Hatcher and ran into him in a jail cell, would you tell him about the Master?"

"I hope so."

Sam patted Mike on the shoulder. "You would. Papa is letting you know what it means to love your enemies and pray for those who persecute you. I've been praying for those men since the day I had my dream. If I ever start hating them, I'd be in jail whether the sheriff's department puts me there or not. Now, even if they all go to prison, it won't be the end of our job. The Helper wants to help them get right with the Master."

They reached the crest of the hill. A pleasant breeze greeted them.

"Now, I want my dream," Mike demanded.

Sam took a few deep breaths. "Can't I enjoy the view of the promised land for a few minutes? Think about what I said. Judge wants to show me an interesting smell."

Mike watched the old man follow the dog around the meadow. Twice, Sam bent over as if sampling a scent himself. In a few minutes, he returned.

The two men stood near the rock where God called Mike into the ministry and gazed over the valleys and hills of Barlow County.

"You know," Sam said, "a mountain top isn't just a place on earth; it's a vision Papa puts in your heart. How big a ministry does the Master have for you?"

"I don't know. Right now, it's Peg."

Sam nodded. "That's a good answer—if you also include baby Isaac."

Mike laughed.

"See, even the mention of his name makes you laugh."

"Okay, tell me the dream."

Sam was silent. They continued to gaze at the scene. When Mike finally glanced at Sam, he saw a tear running down the old man's right cheek.

"What?" Mike asked. "Was it a bad dream?"

Sam shook his head. "Nope, but the goodness of it makes me cry. I've loved the people of Barlow County for a long time. It didn't matter what church they went to or whether they went to church at all. My job was to deliver Papa's message and pray it might open someone's heart to the Master. That's what I did with your friend Buzz. In my dream, you and I were standing on a mountain top."

Sam bent over and pulled up a blade of green grass. "What do you think I did?"

Mike was silent a moment. "You offered to pray for me."

"Yep."

Speaking more rapidly, Mike continued, "But I hesitated because I was afraid God might make me do something I didn't want to do. Then I realized the essence of obeying the Lord's call was doing His will, not mine. I knelt down, and you blessed me, just like they did in the Old Testament."

"That sounds right to me, only you use fancier words. What kind of blessing do you want?"

Mike stood so he faced the old man. "To carry on your work. We'll always be different, but we can both carry Jesus's love for the people of Barlow County in our hearts."

"Yep. And that's the part that makes me cry. There's no way a human heart can contain the Master's love. It always spills out."

Mike knelt in the grass at Sam's feet. The old man put his hands on Mike's head and prayed. The words weren't eloquent, the request simple. But Mike knew in his heart it was a prayer heard in heaven that would be answered on earth. When Sam finished, Mike stood and the two men embraced.

"Anything else?" Mike asked.

"Nothing, except the rest of our lives."

As they walked down the trail, Mike felt lighter and heavier at the same time. He asked Sam about it.

"His burden is easy, and His yoke is light. You feel the burden but also know the Master's strength."

They reached the parking lot.

"Do you have anything else to say to Buzz?" Mike asked.

"Nope, but when he opens his motorcycle shop, I hope Muriel will let me get one of those things. I hear they're real cheap on gas."

Thirty-seven

WITHIN THREE MONTHS, MULTIPLE INDICTMENTS BY STATE AND federal authorities were handed down against Niles, Hatcher, and their associates. Newspapers across the nation picked up Braxton Hodges's articles about the investigation. The criminal case against Mike and Sam disappeared. Hodges inserted a brief announcement about dismissal of the charges on the bottom of the front page of the Shelton paper, but Mike declined an interview for a feature article about his role in breaking open the scandal. To Mike's relief, neither Maxwell Forrest nor Bobby Lambert were indicted.

News of Mike's vindication prompted a flurry of phone calls from people in the community and members of the Little Creek congregation who congratulated him at the news. Apparently, no one really believed he was guilty in the first place. Mike referred questions about whether he might return to the church to the elders. When Delores called and tried to download a massive amount of church gossip, Mike politely stopped her. Nathan Goode asked if he could continue to meet with Mike on a weekly basis, and they set a time on Mondays in the choir room at the high school. Mike didn't hear a word from Milton Chesterfield, Barbara Harcourt, Libby Gorman, or any other remaining members of the session.

One Tuesday morning, Mike called Greg Freeman and Bobby Lambert and invited them to meet him for lunch at the Ashe Café. Mike and Greg arrived early and sipped sweet tea until Bobby, his tie askew, came through the door.

"Sorry I'm late," Bobby said. "It's been hectic. Jack Hatcher fired Mr. Forrest yesterday afternoon and hired some big guns from Atlanta. The board of directors of the bank are bringing in outside counsel in an effort to distance themselves from anyone in Shelton. All our bank files have to be boxed up for delivery to the new attorneys."

"How is Mr. Forrest doing?" Mike asked.

"He's aged five years in five weeks. It wouldn't surprise me if he retired by the end of the year and spent most of his time at his house on the beach."

Their waitress arrived, and the three men ordered their food.

"Did Mr. Forrest call you?" Bobby asked Mike after the waitress left.

"No."

"I told him he owed you an apology. He gave a grunt that I interpreted as agreement, but I could be wrong."

"I'm glad the authorities didn't try to drag you into the investigation," Mike replied.

Bobby gave Mike a grateful look. "I can't give details, but until you started your investigation, I didn't have a clue the Cohulla Creek development was anything except a business deal the parties wanted to keep confidential. You were way ahead of me on the underlying facts."

Mike sipped his tea. "I've been doing more investigation on a different piece of property. Did you know Bob Allen is going to sell his building near traffic light five?"

Greg shook his head. Bobby's face registered surprise.

"How did you hear about it?" Bobby asked. "I thought that was totally under wraps."

"A source."

"It's a nice piece of real estate," Greg said. "Do you know how much he wants for it?"

Mike squeezed a second lemon wedge into his tea.

"I had an interesting dream two nights ago," he said. "Do you want to hear it?"

The other two men nodded.

Mike stirred his tea. "In the dream, I was driving past the courthouse. When I came to the corner where Mr. Allen's building sits, I looked to the left and saw our three names written over the main entrance." Mike stopped and gave a sheepish grin. "Uh, that's it."

"We'd started a law firm?" Greg asked.

"I assume so. The sign said 'Attorneys at Law.'"

Greg turned to Bobby. "What do you think?"

"I'm not sure what to think," Bobby answered, glancing warily at Mike.

"It sounds like an interesting idea to me," Greg continued excitedly, "but Bobby is the one with the big-time practice. He would have the most to lose."

"True," Mike said, looking at Bobby. "If you strike out on your own, you'll miss the chance to take over Forrest, Lambert, and Arnold."

"That may not be an option," Bobby replied. "Mr. Forrest would want a lot of money for a buyout, and I'm not sure Arnold is going to hang around."

Greg turned to Mike. "But what about you? Aren't you going to find another job as pastor of a church?"

"I've found it," Mike answered.

"Where?" Bobby asked.

Mike swept his right hand across the table. "From one end of the county to the other. I may serve a congregation for a while, but as a lawyer, I can reach a lot of people who might never set foot in a church."

"Is Peg on board with this?" Bobby asked.

"Yes, we talked about it yesterday. After she and I talked, I made notes about organization of the firm that included a start-up budget." Mike took a sheet of paper from his pocket. "If the three of us join together, I'll help Greg develop as the primary litigator, and I could ease the demands of your business practice."

"You always worked efficiently," Bobby said, inspecting the numbers on the sheet of paper. "It's an intriguing idea. I'd like to think it over and discuss it with Elizabeth. She's fed up with what's happened at the office and would be happy if I left tomorrow."

"I'm tired of practicing alone," Greg said.

The waitress brought their food.

"In the dream, whose name appeared first?" Bobby asked after Mike prayed a blessing for the meal.

Mike laughed. "Do you really want to know?"

"Yeah, even though it sounds petty bringing it up after you've prayed."

"It was Lambert, Andrews, and Freeman. I don't want to create an image of primary responsibility for the firm, especially since I'll also be doing ministry work."

"That suits me," Greg said. "Since I'm still new to the law, it would feel strange with my name ahead of yours."

"And $300,000 is a fair price for that property," Mike said between bites. "It will probably require another $150,000 to equip it as a law office, but once that's done, it will be an appreciating asset."

"How did you know the price?" Bobby asked, putting down his fork. "I didn't even dictate a memo to the file about my discussion with Mr. Allen."

"It was in the dream."

Bobby shook his head. "From now on, I'm going to have to watch my thoughts around you."

Mike grinned. "Absolutely. My supervision of your soul will go to the next level."

IT WAS THE FIRST WEEK OF DECEMBER, AND SNOW BEGAN FALLING when Mike and Peg pulled into the driveway of their house. Peg rested her hand on her protruding abdomen. Sunday morning services at the Craig Valley Gospel Tabernacle didn't end until early afternoon. Mike had preached for more than an hour.

"I'm going to miss it," he said. "It's been a great four months, but I'm glad they found a permanent pastor."

"If you hadn't quit talking, I was worried I might have our baby in one of the pews."

"You know, it's difficult to stop when people keep yelling for you to keep preaching."

Peg winced. "Mike, let Judge out of the house for a minute while I get my suitcase. I think it's time to go to the hospital."

MIKE ROLLED A CLEAR PLASTIC BASSINETTE WITH A BLUE RIBBON taped to the top and "Andrews—Boy" written on a card into the hallway where Sam and Muriel waited. Muriel's smile lit up every crevice in her face. Mike proudly picked up the baby.

"He's beautiful," Muriel said, stroking the infant's cheek. "How's Peg?"

"Resting, but she wants to see you. I'll take the baby to the nursery."

Muriel slipped past the men into the hospital room. Sam stayed with Mike.

"What do you think we named him?" Mike asked the old man.

"Isaac."

"You're half right. His full name is Samuel Isaac Andrews."

Sam leaned over and gently kissed the top of Samuel Isaac's head. "Yep. That will work. I wrote something about him in my notebook last night. I'll show you later."

Reading Group Guide

1. What do you think about Sam's dreams? Do you believe that they were messages from God? Have you ever had such a dream?

2. What does God the Father mean to you? What is the significance of the name "Papa"?

3. In chapter 8 Sam says, "The right word in the wrong time is as bad as the wrong word in the right time." Do you agree?

4. Peg mentions that church members rarely reach out to help them. What needs might a pastor and his family have? Are there ways that you could minister to your church leaders and their families?

5. What contributed to the distance in Peg and Mike's marriage? What steps did each of them take that allowed them to reconnect?

6. Sam and Muriel take their roles as mentors to Mike and Peg very seriously. How do they care for them? Do you have a special person in your life who is a mentor to you?

7. How do you feel about the way Mike's church leaders handled their disagreements? Have you had an experience of conflict or distrust in the church? Compare and contrast how Mike's leaders conducted their meetings with Sam's church leaders.

8. Did Peg do the right thing when she told Mike about her past struggle with wanting to leave him?

9. Mike says, "The memory of a wrong isn't stronger than the grace to forgive and go on." Do you believe that is true?

10. Mike and Sam went to the hospital to talk to Dressler about Sam's case, but instead they ministered to him and his dying wife. Can you recall a time that you thought you were headed to do one thing, but God had different plans?

11. Have you ever written anyone a particularly special letter? Ever written a stranger? How would you respond if you received a letter like Sam's?

12. Which one of the dreams described had the most impact on you?

13. Which character did you identify with the most? Why?

14. The story deals with deeds done in darkness. Have you ever done something you knew was wrong and then God shed His light on it so you could repent and restore fellowship with Him?

15. What was the significance of the mountain top throughout the story? How did the author use the mountain top to develop the characters and their relationships with each other?

16. Did you relate to Mike's encounter with God during his night in jail? Do you agree with his conclusions about the role of suffering in a person's life?

17. In the end, Mike decides to return to practicing law. What do you think of that decision?

DEEPER WATER

To those who live to make the world a better place:

"Ye are the salt of the earth."

—Matthew 5:13

Prologue

MOSES JONES POLED HIS ALUMINUM JOHNBOAT THROUGH THE marshy waters where the Little Ogeechee River mingled with Green Island Sound. The snub-nosed boat rode on top of the water, a slight swirl marking its wake. A set of oars lay in the bow, but Moses preferred a long wooden pole. Quieter than oars, the smooth rod served double duty as a makeshift depth finder.

The old black man slipped the twenty-five-foot-long pole noiselessly into the water until it found the muddy bottom. He glided beneath the outstretched branches of a live oak tree draped in Spanish moss. Around the bend lay one of the best fishing holes on the brackish river. It was night, but the moon shone brightly, and his kerosene lantern sat unlit on the seat.

Moses lifted the pole from the water and balanced it across the front of the boat. He lifted his cap and scratched the top of his gray-fringed head. And listened. The only sounds were familiar night noises: the bullfrogs calling to each other across the channel, the plop of a fish breaking the surface of the water, the cries of crickets in the dark.

Sucking air through his few remaining teeth, Moses let out a long, low moan to let the faces in the water know he was entering their domain. The faces moved from place to place along the inlets and tributaries the old man frequented, from the Tybee River to Wassaw

Island. With the water as their grave, they weren't bound to one location. Their cemetery had no tombstones, no iron fences, no flower-edged borders. They could be anywhere.

Moses feared and respected the dead. One day, he knew, he would join them. Whether his face would be young or old, he didn't know.

He rounded the bend and measured the depth of the water. The pole didn't touch bottom. He quietly lowered the concrete block he used as an anchor and let the boat find its place. The slow current took him to the center of the hole. He could bait his hooks by moonlight without having to light the lantern and attract the curiosity of a thousand insects. He lowered his trotlines into the water. A five-gallon plastic bucket set in the bottom of the boat would serve as a makeshift live well. He waited.

Within an hour, he caught five fish that included three keepers. He put the three fish in the bucket. It would be a good night. He felt happy. The hole was teeming with life. He pulled up his lines and rebaited the hooks. The fish bumping against the side of the bucket joined the sounds of the night. When he leaned over to place the lines in the water, she floated up to the surface.

It was the little girl.

Moses squeezed his eyes shut. He wanted to scream, but his lips were clenched. He longed to cry, but his emotions were paralyzed. Memories that couldn't separate fact from fiction raced through his mind. What had he done that she would haunt him so?

He made himself breathe slowly. In and out, in and out. His heart pounded in his ears. Someday, the faces would grow strong arms and pull him into the water to join them. It would be justice. He continued to make himself breathe in rhythm. A bead of sweat escaped his cap and ran down his forehead. There was a jerk on the line he still held in his hand. Every muscle in his body tensed. Maybe tonight was the night of death.

He opened his eyes. All that remained was the dark water.

He wiped his forehead with the back of his hand and pulled in the fish. It was the nicest one yet, fat and lively. His breathing returned to normal. His heart stopped racing.

"Thank you, missy," he said softly.

He wasn't sure if the little girl sent the fish or could hear his voice, but it didn't hurt to be grateful, even to a ghost.

1

"TAMMY LYNN!" MAMA CALLED OUT. "YOU'D THINK A FANCY law firm in Savannah would know how to spell your name."

I left the pantry beneath the staircase and came into the kitchen. With lots of windows, the large kitchen protruded from our wood-frame house like Mama's abdomen a week before the twins were born.

"And is there a new law against calling an unmarried woman *Miss*?" Mama added as she opened a quart jar of yellow squash she'd put up the previous summer.

I deposited two yellow onions on the scratched countertop and picked up the envelope. It was addressed to Ms. Tami L. Taylor, 463 Beaver Ruin Road, Powell Station, Georgia. I'd thought long and hard about changing the spelling of my name to Tami on my résumé. First impressions are important, and I didn't want the hiring partner at a prestigious law firm to think I was a second-rate country singer who went to law school after she bombed out in Nashville.

T-a-m-i had a more sophisticated ring to it. It could even be short for Tamara. As long as I honored my parents in the important things, secretly changing the spelling of my first name for professional reasons wouldn't be a sin. Or so I hoped. I rubbed my finger across the address. I couldn't tell Mama the law firm made a mistake. That would be a violation of the ninth commandment. I kept quiet, trusting silence to keep me righteous in the sight of a holy God. Mama's voice rescued me.

"You're doing well in school, and I'm pleased with you," she continued. "But I'm afraid you wasted a lot of paper and stamps on those letters you sent out. You should have set your sights on working for Mr. Callahan. He might actually give you a job when you get out of school."

"Yes ma'am."

Mama wanted me working close to home, the only secure haven in the midst of a wicked world. Her disapproval that I'd mailed letters seeking a summer clerk position to one hundred law firms across the state wasn't a surprise. It helped a little when I reassured her I'd excluded Atlanta like the hole in the middle of a donut. To live in a place populated by millions of people after growing up surrounded by millions of trees wasn't a step I wanted to take either.

I took the letter into the front room. Our house didn't have a formal living room. The front room served as everything from homeschool classroom to temporary church sanctuary if the preacher stopped by for an impromptu prayer meeting. I plopped down on a sofa covered by a white chenille bedspread and closely examined the return address on the outside of the envelope. I was impressed. Braddock, Appleby, and Carpenter still used engraved envelopes. Most of the rejection letters I'd received arrived at my law school post office box in Athens fresh from a laser printer.

Mama was right. Trying to find a summer clerk job through unsolicited letters to law firms picked at random from a list in the placement office was not the best use of a first-class stamp. I'd already resigned myself to another summer working first shift with Daddy at the chicken plant. I opened the envelope.

Dear Ms. Taylor,

We received your résumé and appreciate your interest in a

summer clerkship with our firm. You have an outstanding record of academic and personal accomplishments. If you have not already obtained employment, please contact Ms. Gerry Patrick, our office administrator, to discuss one of the positions available at Braddock, Appleby, and Carpenter.

If you have taken another job or no longer have an interest in working for our firm, the courtesy of a prompt response notifying us accordingly would be appreciated.

Sincerely,
Joseph P. Carpenter

"Mama," I screamed. "I have a job!" I rushed into the kitchen and tried to hand her the letter. "Read this!"

"Calm down and wait a minute," she said, maintaining her grip on the large knife in her right hand. "I'm in the middle of chopping onions for the squash."

"I'll read it to you!"

I sat at the kitchen table, an oversize picnic table painted white, and in a breathless voice read the letter. Mama scraped the onions into the saucepan.

"Read it again," she said when I finished.

Mama sat across from me and wiped her hands with a dish towel. I read the letter more slowly.

"And here at the top it says the firm was founded by Mr. Benjamin Braddock in 1888."

"Are you sure it's a job offer? It sounds to me like they just want to talk to you about it."

"They wouldn't contact me this late in the school year if they didn't have a job. Maybe someone backed out and a spot opened for me."

Mama repositioned one of the hairpins that held her dark hair in a tight bun. She hadn't cut her hair in years, and when freed it fell to her waist. Mama and I shared the same hair color, brown eyes, tall, slender frame, and angular features. It always made her smile when someone mentioned how alike we looked. As a single woman, I was allowed to cut my hair, but it still fell past my shoulders. I only wore it in a bun on Sunday mornings.

"Why would they offer you a job?" she asked. "They haven't even met you."

"I laid my hands on the stack of letters and prayed before I mailed them. Then I thanked God for every rejection that came in. He saw my heart and came through at the last moment."

"Maybe, but I'm not comfortable with you claiming his approval so quickly. We need to talk about this. Savannah is on the other end of the state. How far away is it?"

"I don't know." I looked up at the clock on the wall beside the refrigerator. It was 5:10 p.m. "I should call right now and find out if this really is a job offer. That way we can talk it over with Daddy and not guess about anything."

Mama returned to the stove. I waited.

"Go ahead," she sighed. "You're at the edge of the river and need to know what's on the other side."

The only telephone in the house was in my parents' bedroom. When I stopped homeschooling in the ninth grade and went to public high school, Mama never had to worry about me having secret phone conversations late at night. She needn't have worried anyway. Most of my calls were about basketball practice and homework assignments.

I hit the numbers for the unfamiliar area code followed by the seven-digit phone number. The phone rang three times. Maybe the firm didn't answer calls after 5:00 p.m. Then, a silky voice spoke.

"Good afternoon, Braddock, Appleby, and Carpenter."

The sound made my mouth suddenly go dry.

"Ms. Gerry Patrick, please."

"May I tell her who is calling?"

"Tami Taylor. That's T-a-m-i."

I couldn't believe I'd spelled my first name. I stifled a giggle while the receptionist put me on hold and let me stew like Mama's squash and onions. I rehearsed my next lines to avoid another long-distance embarrassment. A more mature-sounding female voice came on the line.

"Gerry Patrick."

"Good afternoon, Ms. Patrick. This is Tami Taylor, a second-year law student at the University of Georgia. I received a letter from Mr. Carpenter about a summer clerk position. He told me to contact you."

There was a brief pause. "I have your résumé, but all summer job offers go through my office. I'd know if the firm sent you a letter."

My mouth went dry. "Could you check with Mr. Carpenter?"

"Yes, I want to get to the bottom of this myself."

A much longer pause followed. I counted the red tulips on the top border of the faded wallpaper in my parents' bedroom and prayed that Mr. Carpenter hadn't left for the day. Finally, Ms. Patrick spoke.

"It's fortunate for you that you called. I'd signed a stack of rejections this afternoon without knowing Mr. Carpenter made a copy of your résumé. Your turndown letter was in the mail room."

"Thank you." I swallowed. "Do you know why he offered me a job?"

"Not a clue. Mr. Carpenter isn't here, but his assistant confirmed the letter. Are you interested in the position?"

"Yes ma'am."

"I'll e-mail the details."

"Uh, I'm home on spring break, and we don't have a computer with an Internet connection."

I felt my face flush. The only computer in the house was an outdated one used for educational programs with the twins. Powell Station didn't boast a coffee shop with Wi-Fi.

"Do you have access to a fax machine?" Ms. Patrick asked.

I frantically racked my brain for a solution. "No ma'am. Would it be all right if I called you in the morning? By then I'll be able to track down a way for you to send the information."

"I'm usually here by nine o'clock. These jobs don't stay open for long."

"Yes ma'am."

I hung up the phone. Challenges raised by my family's lifestyle weren't new. Daddy always said obstacles were opportunities for personal character growth. However, that didn't keep routine problems from causing pain. I returned to the kitchen.

"I talked to Ms. Patrick, the office manager. It's a real job," I announced with reduced enthusiasm.

"What details did she give you?"

"She's going to send me information as soon as I figure out a way she can transmit it." I didn't mention the disdain I sensed in Ms. Patrick's voice.

"And that won't tell you anything about these people or their values, morals, beliefs, lifestyles."

I tried to sound casually optimistic. "No ma'am, but it's just a summer job at a law firm in Savannah. What could be wrong with that? I'll only be there for a few months, and it will give me an idea what to expect in a real law—"

"We'll talk it over with your father when he gets home," Mama interrupted.

I shut my mouth. When Mama invoked the title "father," it meant nothing could be discussed until he arrived.

We would be eating chicken and dumplings for supper. Thick noodles, chicken broth, and a few chunks of chicken went a long way toward feeding our large family. The slightly sweet smell of the dumplings competed with the pungent onions in the squash.

"Do you need help with supper?" I asked, leaning on the counter and sniffing.

"No, thanks. Everything is cooking. Why don't you check on the twins? I left them working on an essay."

I WAS ELEVEN YEARS OLD when Ellie and Emma were born, and we'd shared a bedroom since the first day they came home from the hospital. With preteen excitement about everything related to babies, I welcomed them into my world with open arms and a room decorated with balloons and a white poster board proudly announcing the girls' names in fancy script surrounded by flowers. My enthusiasm was instantly tested by a double dose of demands.

My first job was to change the girls' diapers and take them to Mama for the middle-of-the-night feeding. For months, I slept in fits and starts as I listened to the tiny infants sniffle and snort while I wondered whether they were hungry or feeling an uncomfortable gas bubble. If one cried, the sound immediately became stereo. But I didn't complain. Every child was a blessing from God.

Daddy put an old rocking chair in my bedroom, and my arms grew accustomed to holding the babies close to my heart. I kissed their heads enough to wear off the newborn fuzz. Later, when they were toddlers, they often ended up in my bed, especially on cold winter nights when the best warmth is found in closeness to a loved one.

Now, they welcomed me home with hand-drawn pictures and silly poems. The three of us couldn't fit in my bed, but we still enjoyed sitting in our pajamas on the circular rug on our bedroom floor and talking in the moonlight until the little girls' eyelids drooped.

I walked up the creaky stairs to the second floor of the house. No sounds came from the bedroom, a hopeful sign of serious educational activity. I peeked in the door. The twins were sitting across from each other at the small table beneath the room's wide, single window. My bed was to the right of the window. The twins slept in homemade bunk beds on the opposite wall. Both dark-haired heads were bent over sheets of paper.

"How's it going?" I asked.

Ellie looked up with blue eyes that could have made me jealous. "We're almost finished."

"Yeah," Emma echoed. "We wrote about different things so Mama wouldn't think we copied."

"Do you want me to check your papers when you finish?"

"Yes," both girls responded.

My side of the room was immaculate. The same couldn't be said for the twins'. Emma was the neater child, but without Ellie's cooperation, they both received blame for messiness. I straightened up their side of the room while they continued writing.

"Done!" Emma announced.

"I'm on my last paragraph," Ellie said.

"Keep working. I'll read Emma's paper."

Across the top, the older of the twins had written: "Deism and the Founders of Our Country."

For a woman who never went to college, Mama was an amazing teacher. Not many twelve-year-olds could spell *deism*, much less give a credible definition of the belief and explain in clear, simple terms how several signers of the Declaration of Independence viewed God as a cosmic clock-winder passively watching events unfold on the earth below. The twins would be prepared for public high school. Except for calculus and AP physics, I never made less than an A in high school.

"Show me your research," I said to Emma.

She handed me a stack of index cards, each one labeled with the reference. I checked the quotes in the paper against the information on the cards and corrected a handful of grammatical errors. While I worked, Ellie finished her paper and looked over my shoulder at her sister's work.

"You should have put a comma before the conjunction separating two independent clauses," Ellie said, pointing to one of my corrections. "Everybody knows that."

Emma pushed her away. "Wait until she reads your paper. It's full of mistakes."

"Stop it!" I commanded.

Emma and I sat on the bed and went over her paper. It was a very good first draft.

"How long have you been working on this?"

"About two weeks. Mama wants it finished by Friday."

Ellie's essay was titled "Thomas Jefferson's Bible." She focused on the rationalist beliefs of the primary author of the Declaration of Independence. There was overlapping research with her sister's paper, but also information unique to Jefferson, including a discussion of the founder's personal New Testament with all the references to miracles carefully cut out. Ellie was a better writer than her sister, but I was careful to make an equal number of corrections and suggestions.

"That's all for today," I said when we finished. "I'll tell Mama how well you're doing. Supper will be ready in a few minutes."

"I'll pray," Emma volunteered.

Our homeschool experience was saturated with prayer. Deism had no place in Mama's theology. God was omnipresent; a truth that both scared and comforted me.

We held hands while Emma prayed. I smiled when she included a heartfelt request for God's blessing upon Ellie.

"And thank you that Tammy Lynn will be home with us in a few weeks for the whole summer. In Jesus' name, amen."

I squeezed both small hands. To spend a summer in Savannah would require convincing more than my parents.

2

THE TWINS AND I WENT DOWNSTAIRS TO HELP MAMA SET THE table. From the kitchen I could see the dirt basketball court where I'd spent many hours practicing my three-point shot. While putting the forks in place, I glanced out one of the windows in time to see my eighteen-year-old brother, Kyle, leading a Hereford steer by a rope halter toward the feedlot on the opposite side of the family garden. A senior in high school, Kyle worked part-time for a local livestock broker. He'd already made enough money buying and selling beef cattle to buy an old pickup truck and a secondhand hauler. Trailing behind Kyle and the steer were our two dogs, Flip and Ginger. The dogs spent their lives outside and never entered the house. I would have loved a little indoor dog, but Mama and Daddy said our home wasn't Noah's ark.

Daddy always took a shower before he left the chicken plant, but I knew he carried the smell of fifty thousand chickens in his nostrils. As a line boss, he supervised a score of women who processed the naked, headless birds that a few weeks before had been tiny yellow chicks. For five summers I'd worked on Daddy's crew as an eviscerator, a fancy word for the person who cuts open the chicken and scoops out its internal organs. No part of a chicken was foreign to me.

My sixteen-year-old brother, Bobby, had finished his work in the garden and was sitting on the back steps quietly strumming his guitar. Bobby had been singing in church since he was a little boy; the guitar was a recent addition.

"He's writing his own songs," Ellie said as she took out a pack of paper napkins. "Bobby," she called through the screen door. "Make up a song for Tammy Lynn."

Bobby increased the tempo and volume. "Tammy Lynn! Tammy Lynn!" he called out. "Where have you gone? Why did you leave me here alone? I waited till dawn, but you never came home. Now, all I can do is moan."

I looked at Mama and rolled my eyes. "Are you going to let him do that?"

Mama smiled. "As long as he sings about his older sister, I'm not going to worry too much about it."

The dogs started barking and ran around the corner of the house to the front yard.

"Daddy's coming," Ellie said. "I'll set Tammy Lynn's place. I want her next to me."

"No, she's next to me," Emma protested.

"Put her in the middle," Mama said.

I heard the front door open, and the familiar sound of my father's uneven footsteps as he walked across the wooden floor. When Daddy was in the army, a drunken soldier shot him in the right foot. Two surgeries later, Daddy was left with a misshapen foot and a VA disability check that made the monthly payments on our house. He claimed the injury was a blessing in disguise, which sounded reasonable except for the pain on his face during cold weather. Daddy wore insulated rubber boots and two pairs of socks at work, but I think the foot still hurt because of the cool temperatures in the plant. When he came into the kitchen and saw me, he smiled.

A smile from Daddy after I'd been away from home for a few weeks at school could make me cry, so I lowered my gaze. I crossed the floor and gave him a quick hug.

"It was cloudy today until I saw you," he said, kissing the top of my head. "Did the girl from Dalton give you a ride home?"

"Yes sir. She didn't mind coming through the mountains."

"Did you give her gas money?"

"Yes sir."

Kyle and Bobby came inside and began discussing the status of the garden with Daddy. It was early spring, but our family used the entire growing season. In north Georgia, that meant early harvests of cabbage, leaf lettuce, and broccoli.

Unless company came for supper, Mama served meals from the stove. As soon as she called out, "Supper's ready," there would be a few minutes of chaos until all seven people were seated at the table. No one dared nibble a piece of corn bread until Daddy bowed his head and prayed a blessing. Then, conversation broke out on every side. Our family might be quiet around outsiders, but with one another we didn't hesitate to talk. Tonight, Daddy's focus was on me.

"Tell me about your classes," he said after his first bite of dumplings.

"This semester I'm taking secured transactions, introduction to labor law, municipal corporations, and civil procedure."

"Which class do you like best?"

"Municipal corporations. It's the study of city government law. The professor is a woman who worked for a firm in Seattle, Washington."

"How did she get to Georgia?" Mama asked in surprise.

"Lawyers move all over the place," I said, planting a tiny seed.

I ate a bite of squash and onions. Compared to Seattle, Savannah was next door. As supper continued, I brought Daddy up-to-date on my strictly regulated life—going to class, eating, studying, sleeping, reading the Bible, and praying.

"And I've been playing basketball. Several girls at the law school invited me to join a team that plays in a graduate school intramural league. We're undefeated in our first five games."

"Have you scored a basket?" Kyle asked mischievously.

"Of course," I replied.

In high school, I'd averaged fifteen points a game during my senior year.

"Ellie and I have been practicing every day since the weather warmed up," Emma said. "Will you play with us later?"

"Maybe tomorrow."

Mama had put extra effort into the meal because it was my first evening home. I complimented every dish individually and the entire meal collectively.

"Have you lost weight?" Daddy asked.

"Maybe a little. I do miss home cooking."

Mama smiled in appreciation.

"We'll have you home in a few weeks so we can take care of you," Daddy said. "When is your last exam?"

"I'm not sure about the exact date," I replied with a glance at Mama, who shook her head.

"The plant is running overtime," Daddy continued. "The company has taken on quite a few new growers, and production is way up. An experienced hand like you can really pile up the cash if you take all the available overtime."

"Is there a place for me?" Bobby asked.

"Next year when you're older would be a better time for you to get on as a temporary worker," Daddy replied.

"Could you ask?" Bobby persisted. "I'll still take care of my share of work in the garden. I want to save enough money to buy another guitar."

"What kind of guitar?" Mama asked sharply.

Bobby smiled. When he did, he looked like Daddy. "Don't worry, Mama. I want a better acoustic, not electric. Some of the best are made by a company called Taylor, so it would already look like it had my name engraved on it."

I wanted to yield my place on the eviscerating crew to Bobby right then. It didn't take long to master the art of cutting open a chicken with razor-sharp scissors and removing its entrails.

"I'll check with Mr. Waldrup," Daddy replied.

Mama surprised me with a lemon meringue pie for dessert. The peaks and valleys of white and light brown meringue were as pretty as a photograph of the Alps. I held the knife in my hand, almost hating to cut the pie.

"What are you waiting for?" Ellie asked impatiently.

I lowered the knife and destroyed perfection. Seven pieces later, the pie pan was empty.

"The twins and I will clean up," I said to Mama when we finished eating. "Sit on the porch with Daddy."

In spring and fall, Daddy liked to sit in the swing on the front porch after supper. It was his way of unwinding after the hectic activity at the chicken plant with its loud noises and fast pace. It was quiet at our house. Except for an occasional logging truck, we rarely heard vehicles passing by on Beaver Ruin Road. That left only the evening sounds of nature—in early spring a few katydids, in summer a more varied chorus. I especially enjoyed it when a great horned owl would issue a call. Daddy liked to hoot in return, drawing the bird into conversation. When I was a little girl, he would interpret the owl's hoots and make up stories about the owl's life. I loved owl stories.

After the twins and I finished cleaning the kitchen, I took my Savannah letter to the front porch. Daddy and Mama were sitting on the swing. The sun was down, but the sky still displayed a broad band of orange. Daddy had his arm draped over the back of the swing behind Mama's shoulders.

"Is now a good time to talk?" I asked Mama.

"Yes," she said.

Emma opened the front door and came outside.

"It's not a good time for you," Mama said to her. "Stay inside with Ellie."

Emma frowned but shut the door. I sat on the edge of the porch with my feet propped on the steps.

"Your mama says you got a job offer with a law firm in Savannah," Daddy said. "Tell me about it."

"Do you want to read the letter?"

"Yes."

I handed it to him.

"They misspelled your name."

"The spelling of my name isn't the important part," I replied with a twinge of guilt. "It's hard to get a summer clerkship like this one. The lady in the job placement office told me less than twenty-five percent of the second-year class is able to find a legal job with a law firm, fewer still with a law firm like this."

"What do you know about Braddock, Appleby, and Carpenter?" Daddy asked, reading the names slowly.

I told him about my conversation with Gerry Patrick, leaving out the intrafirm miscommunication concerning the offer.

"There's no harm in getting information about the job, is there?" I asked, trying not to sound whiny.

Daddy handed the letter back to me. "Not if you keep your heart right."

The condition of my heart was somewhat shaky, so I stuck to practical arguments.

"Bobby could take my place on the chicken line. And Savannah isn't as far away as Seattle."

"Did you apply for a job in Seattle?" Mama asked in alarm.

"No ma'am. I was just making a point about the relative closeness of Savannah."

Daddy pushed the swing back and forth a couple of times.

"I guess you could tell the lady in Savannah to send the information to Oscar Callahan's office. Didn't you list him as a reference on your résumé?"

"Yes sir, and if the Savannah job doesn't work out, I'll definitely talk to Mr. Callahan about working a few hours a week for him."

"Which is a much better idea than running off to a strange place to be with people you don't know anything about." Mama spoke rapidly. "Where would you live? How will you be able to afford the rent? What kind of cases does this law firm handle? You don't want to be representing criminals. Divorces would be just as bad. And the attorneys who manage a large law firm won't share your moral convictions."

These topics and many others had been discussed in great detail before I started law school, and I didn't want to revisit the debate. I remained silent. The band of orange had lost its hue. The sky was totally gray.

"I only have one question," Daddy said after a minute passed. "Will you honor your parents?"

I knew what he meant.

"Yes sir."

LATER THAT NIGHT I tiptoed into the darkened bedroom. Emma's voice from the top bunk startled me.

"Tammy Lynn."

"Quiet! You're supposed to be asleep."

"Exactly how old were you when we were born?"

I did a quick calculation. "Almost seven months younger than you are now."

"And you didn't mind sharing your room?"

"No, I was excited. But just like now, you were noisy when I wanted you to be quiet."

"I don't mind sharing the room with you when you come home."

"Thank you. I like being with you too."

I sat on the bed and slipped off my shoes and socks.

"When are you going to get married so I can have a baby to play with?"

"Don't be silly," I answered. "I've never even been kissed. Good night."

Emma sighed. Then sighed again.

"What is it?" I asked.

"Isn't Savannah the city founded by General James Oglethorpe for people in England who couldn't pay their bills?" she asked.

"Yes. Were you eavesdropping on my conversation with Mama and Daddy?"

"What's Savannah like now? We only studied about the 1700s."

"I've never been there, but it's very pretty with a lot of little parks and squares."

"How do you know that?"

"I read about it in a book that had pictures and information about historic places."

"If you take the job, does that mean we won't see you this summer?"

"I'll try to come home or maybe you can visit me."

"Would Ellie come too?"

"Of course, but it would be up to Mama and Daddy."

There was a moment of silence.

"I want you to be here with us. This is like you're moving away forever and never coming home."

I could hear a tremor in Emma's voice. I came over and stroked her hair. My eyes had adjusted to the dark, and I could see a forlorn expression on her face. I kissed her on the forehead.

"I love you wherever I am."

"But it's not the same if you're not where I can see and touch you."

I felt a pang of remorse. My focus had been totally selfish. There was great benefit in spending a summer at home. The love of family wasn't a daydream—it was the most enduring reality in my world.

I ALWAYS SLEPT BETTER in my own bed. I woke up when Chester, the family rooster, began to crow but managed to tune him out and sleep for another thirty minutes until a finger tapped me on the cheek. Through bleary eyes I couldn't tell if it was Emma or Ellie.

"Who is it?" I asked.

"Guess."

"Ellie?"

"That's right. Are you going to get the eggs?"

I pulled the sheet next to my chin. Not having to get up for class made the bed feel extra nice.

"Who's been doing it?" I mumbled.

"This is my week, but I wanted to help with the biscuits."

Too many thoughts were now in my head to allow another snooze. "Okay. I'll get the eggs."

I got up and pulled on a loose-fitting cotton dress. The women and girls in our family never wore pants, and we made most of our day-to-day clothes. Learning how to sew was part of our training. When I went to high school, Mama was nice enough to buy me some inexpensive skirts, dresses, and blouses at Wal-Mart. Store-bought clothes blunted the stigma of our private dress code, but I still stood out as a feminine island in an ocean of unisex apparel. Snide questions and critical stares were inevitable, but it helped that a few girls in the school came from families with similar rules. Those girls were my closest friends.

The high school basketball uniforms could have been an impossible fashion obstacle to overcome. Mama played basketball in high school and was willing to bend on the rules, so long as the coach ordered a uniform with extra-long shorts that reached to my knees and a shirt with sleeves that came close to my elbows. At first glance, it looked a couple of sizes too big, but no one paid attention to the length of my shorts or my baggy shirt after I hit a nice shot or made a crisp pass for an assist. People in the church criticized my parents for making an exception. Daddy told me not to worry about it.

I maintained the dresses-only rule through college and law school. I could always look Mama in the eye and answer truthfully when she asked me if I'd worn pants or blue jeans.

I SPLASHED WATER ON MY FACE, slipped my hair into a ponytail, and went downstairs. I grabbed the blue metal pail used to collect the eggs. The twins and I had decorated the pail with a chicken motif that included primitive portraits of some of our hens against a chicken coop landscape. I stepped outside into the cool morning air.

The wire enclosure where the chickens stayed was to the left of the basketball court. The birds stayed inside at night but were released to forage in the yard during the day. Flip and Ginger would bark at them, but our chickens' greatest enemies were possums.

Mama preferred white-shelled eggs, so we owned leghorns. We kept one rooster and four to six hens. Compact and muscular, our chickens bore little resemblance to the flaccid birds delivered to the processing plant in town. Daddy raised pullets to replace hens whose egg production declined. We never ate our hens. When they clucked their last cluck, the chickens received appropriate burial in the large pet cemetery at the edge of our property.

I went inside the pen. Chester charged in full-attack mode, but I ignored him. Top law students who could handle intense questioning by a tough professor would probably flee from Chester. The rooster came right up to my feet before giving a loud, self-satisfied squawk and strutting away.

I slowly entered the coop. Our hens were named after female characters in Shakespearean plays. Mama used an edited version of Shakespeare's works, with the bawdy jokes deleted, as part of her homeschool curriculum. Each bird's nesting box was marked with a carefully printed card: Juliet, Olivia, Viola, Cressida, Cleopatra, and Lady Macbeth. It was a noble company with Chester as their lord.

The hens knew what I intended to do and began protesting and pecking my hand as I slipped it into each box to pull out a warm egg. However, once the egg was gone, they abandoned the boxes and fluttered to the ground. Collecting eggs was the easy part of raising chickens. Cleaning the coop was the hard job. The coop needed cleaning. I hoped Mama had told one of the boys to do it. I carried the pail into the kitchen.

"Five for five," I announced.

"They're producing nicely," Mama replied. "There are more eggs in the refrigerator. Wash what you gathered this morning in vinegar and scramble up as many as you think we'll need."

Mama varied the breakfast menu. We often ate oatmeal or cereal with fruit, but once again she wanted to do something special in honor of my return. She knew I loved fluffy scrambled eggs with crisp bacon. The bacon was already beginning to sizzle in the skillet, and the biscuits were in the oven. I cracked open the eggs in a metal bowl and added salt and milk to make them lighter.

Kyle and Bobby didn't start spring vacation until the following week. They came into the kitchen dressed for school in slacks and short-sleeved collared shirts. My brothers blended in much easier than I did at their ages. Not only did women have to suffer the pain of childbirth, they also bore the reproach of nineteenth-century fashion in a twenty-first-century world. I beat the eggs harder to drive out my thoughts. Resentment led to the sin of bitterness.

The first bite of eggs after Daddy prayed was worth the early morning effort. Mama gave me two extra slices of bacon. Breakfast was a quiet meal. Everyone was thinking about the day ahead.

"I'll call Mr. Callahan's office," I said to Mama and Daddy. "I think his secretary gets there at eight thirty. I'd like to see him too, if he's available."

"Do you want me to go with you?" Mama asked.

"No ma'am," I answered a bit too quickly. "I mean, there's no need."

Daddy left for work, followed a few minutes later by my brothers, who rode to school in Kyle's truck. I cleaned up the kitchen while Mama and the twins began the school day. When I turned off the water, I could hear the sound of Mama's voice in the front room. She loved teaching. It would leave a big hole in her life when the twins reached high school age.

My homeschool years were pleasant memories. The yard, sky, woods, and the pond down the road were our science laboratory. I could identify many trees by leaf and bark. Math was incorporated into the practical functions of the household. Mama put a premium on being able to perform math mentally. Calculators weren't allowed; paper and pencil discouraged.

By age seven, I was reading the text in picture books and finished the entire Chronicles of Narnia a year later. Much of the day was spent reading. The county librarian, Mrs. Davis, would order anything Mama wanted through the state lending program. Twice a month, the old books went to town, and Mama returned with new ones. I'd read many of the classic works of literature required by my college English courses by the time I was in the ninth grade. Only the more controversial books didn't make Mama's list. When I finally read them, I usually understood why.

The twins were old enough that much of their study was self-directed. Mama guided them from the sidelines. She used a questioning format similar to my law school professors. After I started the dishwasher, I went into the front room. The twins were studying the Bible.

"Why do you think the apostle Paul thought he was serving God by persecuting the early Christians?" Mama asked.

"He was sinning," Ellie answered.

"But he didn't know it at the time. How is it possible for a person to believe he is obeying God when in fact he is doing the opposite?"

Emma knew what to say. "Where do we look for the answer?"

Mama gave references from three Pauline letters. "It's somewhere in those chapters. When you find the answer, write down the verses that apply. Then, I want you to think of at least one modern example of the same kind of mistake made by the apostle Paul."

The girls immediately opened their Bibles. Mama's question made me uncomfortable. I looked at the clock on the wall.

"I'm going to call Mr. Callahan's office."

3

Mrs. Betty Murphy answered the phone at Oscar Callahan's office. When I asked if I could talk to the lawyer, she put me on hold for a few seconds, then told me to come in anytime before noon.

"And can I have a fax sent to the office?" I asked. "It has to do with a job offer from a law firm in Savannah."

"Sure, honey. I'll be on the lookout for it."

I left a message on Ms. Patrick's voice mail and hoped she'd retrieve it in time to forward the information. Then I ran upstairs, showered, and dressed in a blue skirt and white blouse. I had a matching jacket that turned the outfit into a business suit but left it in the closet. I put on low black heels and slipped the letter from Savannah into a small black purse.

"May I borrow the car keys?" I asked Mama when I returned downstairs.

"You look fancy," Emma said.

"Like a woman preacher," Ellie added.

Our church allowed women to exhort the congregation. Mama rarely exercised the privilege, but when she did, her eyes blazed with the fire of God so that chills ran up and down my back.

"I'll tell Mr. Callahan to repent," I said, turning around in the center of the room. "I wore this outfit several times when I gave a presentation at school."

Mama reached over and touched the fabric of the skirt. "That's a nice blend."

"Is it modest enough?" I asked a bit anxiously.

"Yes. You look very professional."

"I'd hire you," Emma said. "And get you to sue Ellie for breaking the porcelain figurine that Aunt Jane brought back from her trip—"

"Emma," Mama interrupted. "Open to 1 Corinthians 6 and read what Paul wrote about Christians suing each another."

"I was joking," Emma protested. "I forgave her the next day."

"I know, but it's a good time to learn a lesson about lawsuits between Christians." She turned to me. "Take the van. Don't worry about putting any gas in it."

WITH A FAMILY OF SEVEN, a large passenger van was a necessity, not a luxury. Daddy selected the model, and Mama chose the color. She loved blue, and our vans were always somewhere between navy and azure. We didn't take long trips. Common destinations were town, church, and the homes of relatives. One of the boys washed the van on Saturday, but it couldn't stay spotless to the bottom of the dirt driveway. A light coat of red Georgia clay immediately coated the back bumper and created a film across the rear window.

I turned left onto Beaver Ruin Road and followed it a mile to a freshly paved two-lane highway. The highway zigzagged across the hills of north Georgia, making sure no crossroad was left out. I knew every curve and dip of the route well enough to navigate it in a driving thunderstorm. I reached the edge of town. Powell Station had a single main street with two red lights, a business district three blocks long, and a U.S. post office. For travelers, it was a forgotten slow spot in the road. To me, it was the hub of our lives.

Oscar Callahan was the only lawyer in town and jokingly claimed a monopoly on a business that didn't pay well. However, he'd made enough money to build a large home surrounded by a fifty-acre pasture where Angus cattle grazed in idyllic contentment. Kyle thought the lawyer's stock was the best of the breed in the area.

The basis for Mr. Callahan's success was his representation of workers injured in the small manufacturing plants, textile mills, and chicken processing facilities scattered across the region. If a worker sprained a knee, hurt a hand, or ruptured a lumbar disc, Mr. Callahan got the case. Insurance defense lawyers from Atlanta came north to litigate against him at their peril.

I first met Mr. Callahan when I was ten years old and Mama took me to his office for a field trip. He took an immediate interest in me, and that first field trip led to other visits during which we talked about everything from the U.S. Constitution to what it was like inside the county jail. When I graduated from high school, he sent me a check for a hundred dollars along with a note telling me I could become a lawyer if I wanted to.

Mr. Callahan's roots in Powell Station ran deep. His grandfather was one of the most famous preachers in the early days of our church. The lawyer and his wife attended a more traditional congregation, but he understood people like my parents and me.

I parked the van in front of a corner building at one of the two traffic lights. Mr. Callahan had remodeled the plain brick structure years before and installed nice wooden double doors with his name, "Oscar Callahan—Attorney at Law," in large brass letters across the top. The building was painted white. Even after the paint began to chip, it was a classy place. Everybody in town considered his office a landmark.

The inside of the building was cool on even the hottest days. It was the coolness of the interior that impressed me as a little girl. Our house didn't have air-conditioning, and we survived summer with fans that did little more than circulate the heat. The church sanctuary was air-conditioned, but people supplemented the anemic system with funeral home fans. Mr. Callahan didn't concern himself with what he had to pay the electric co-op. The oversized cooling unit behind the building never stopped humming.

Thick, deep carpet covered the floor beneath my feet. A leather sofa and eight chairs lined the wall. Neat rows of sporting, hunting, and women's interest magazines were displayed on a coffee table. Mrs. Murphy, a gray-haired woman, sat in the corner of the room behind a dark wooden desk. A man in overalls was talking to her. I stepped toward her desk but kept a respectful distance.

"Either Harriet or I will call you as soon as your settlement check comes in and set up a time for Mr. Callahan to meet with you," Mrs. Murphy said to the man.

"When do you think it will get here?" the man asked. "My wife's got her eye on a new double-wide, and we don't want it to get away."

"Within a couple of weeks."

"That might be too late."

"Who's selling the trailer to you?"

"Foothills Homes."

"I know Mr. Kilgo. Would you like me to call and let him know what's going on with your case?"

"Yes'm."

The client turned away, and Mrs. Murphy smiled at me.

"Here's your fax," she said, handing me a few sheets of paper. "He just got off the phone, and I'm sure he would like to see you. You look great, very professional."

"Thanks."

Beyond the reception area was a library that also served as a conference room. Opposite the library was Harriet Smith's office. In her early forties, the secretary had worked for Mr. Callahan over twenty years. Beyond the secretary's office were a file room and two smaller, unfinished offices, one of which Mama wanted me to occupy upon graduation from law school. Mr. Callahan had never brought up the subject during the short stints I'd worked at his office organizing files. However, he'd agreed to serve as a reference on my résumé.

The door to the lawyer's office was open, and I could see his feet propped up on the corner of his desk. A tall man, Oscar Callahan was sixty years old with a full head of white hair and intense, dark eyes. It was easy to imagine his grandfather as a fiery preacher. Mr. Callahan looked over his gold-rimmed reading glasses and rose to his feet.

"Welcome, Tammy Lynn," he boomed out. "It appears the transformation into sophisticated lawyer is well on its way."

Mr. Callahan motioned for me to take a seat. The lawyer had large hands that he used to emphasize points in conversation. He laid his glasses on his desk and pointed at the papers in my hand.

"Did you get your fax?"

"Yes sir."

"Is it from Savannah?"

"Yes sir," I answered in surprise.

Mr. Callahan nodded. "Joe Carpenter called me about you the other day. We were in law school together. He's a tight-lipped blue blood from the coast, and I'm the wild-eyed son of the red clay hills, but we've always gotten along fine. I've seen him at bar association meetings over the years. Did he offer you a summer job?"

I held up the papers. "Yes sir, I think so, but I haven't read the terms."

"Well, an offer is like bait on a hook. It doesn't count for anything unless a fish bites it. Look it over while I finish reviewing this medical report."

Mr. Callahan put on his glasses and resumed reading. I looked down at the three sheets of paper in my hand. Even the fax cover sheet had a classy look. I turned to the next page, titled "Summer Clerk—Offer Memorandum." My eyes opened wide at the amount of money I would be paid. The weekly salary would be greater than what I would make in two grueling weeks, including overtime, at the chicken plant.

The impact of a legal education on my economic future struck me like never before. If the law firm paid this much to a summer clerk, the compensation for first-year associates would be even more. I quickly calculated a likely annual salary in my head.

The rest of the memo was related to dates of employment, a prohibition against working anywhere else while employed by Braddock, Appleby, and Carpenter, an agreement that all my work product would belong to the firm as well as receipts from billings, and a confidentiality clause as to both terms of the offer and any proprietary information obtained during my employment. I wondered what in the world I might learn that would be valuable enough to sell. When I glanced up, Mr. Callahan was peering over his glasses at me.

"How does it look?" he asked.

I started to hand the fax to him, then stopped.

"I'd like your opinion, but I can't show it to you," I said. "It has a confidentiality clause."

The older lawyer laughed. "Consider me your personal attorney for a few minutes. A confidentiality clause doesn't prohibit consultation with a lawyer. I'll review it pro bono."

I sheepishly handed the offer sheet to him. He read it in a few seconds.

"The price of raw legal talent is going up," he said. "That beats hugging dead chickens, doesn't it?"

"Yes sir."

"And they're going to toss in a name change for free."

I didn't answer.

"Oh, don't worry about it," the lawyer said with a chuckle. "Everybody knows your mother as Lu; no one calls her Luella."

"Except my grandmother and Aunt Jane." I paused. "Mama and

Daddy think the different spelling of my name was a mistake by the law firm."

"Do you want to confess your sins to me?"

I remembered my comment about telling Mr. Callahan to repent.

"I can use it for the summer, then go back to the correct spelling."

"Don't worry about it. T-a-m-i has a nice look to it. I've never been fond of Oscar but couldn't come up with an alternative."

"You'll always be Mr. Callahan to me."

The lawyer laughed. "I'm sure I will."

"What else do you know about the firm?" I asked.

Mr. Callahan handed the fax back to me. "As you can see from the letterhead, the Braddock firm has been around for a hundred years. Samuel Braddock is a descendant of the founder. I don't know Nelson Appleby and told you about Joe Carpenter. How many lawyers are there? Sixteen or seventeen?"

I glanced down at the letterhead and counted. "Fifteen."

"I did a little research for you," Mr. Callahan said. "According to the firm website, less than half are partners. The rest are associates hoping they get invited to join. The firm's representative clients include a couple of shipping companies, several banks, blue-chip corporations, large foundations—the cream of the crop." Mr. Callahan smiled. "I doubt any of their lawyers would be interested in representing a man who rips the rotator cuff in his right shoulder while unloading a trailer in one-hundred-degree heat."

My face fell. "Do you think it would be a bad place to work?"

The lawyer held up his hand. "No, no. Don't let my bias on behalf of working folks taint you. I shouldn't have said that. There are many honorable places to land in the law. One of the best pieces of advice I ever received was to dabble in a number of areas, find what brings the most personal satisfaction, and become an expert in it."

Listening to Mr. Callahan's practical wisdom made me wish he would offer me a summer job. Even if he paid me chicken-plant wages it would be plenty of money for me, especially since I could live at home.

"It's a long way from Powell Station," I said, hoping my wistful comment might lead the conversation in that direction.

"You've gone a long way from here already. And I bet you've taken the best your family has to offer along with you. If you take the job in Savannah, folks are going to meet the kind of person who made this country great in the first place."

"What do you mean?"

Mr. Callahan looked past my right shoulder. He stared so long that I turned and followed his gaze to an old photograph of his grandfather on the wall. Preacher Callahan didn't look like he knew how to smile.

"You know exactly what I mean," the lawyer continued, his eyes returning to mine. "You're different, and it won't take long for anyone to find it out. Most people focus on the externals: the way you dress, the fact that you don't go to movies, the obedience to parents, the way you honor the Lord's Day by not doing anything on Sunday except go to church meetings. They don't realize that what makes you special is on the inside—your integrity and strength of character. That's rare, especially when joined with your intelligence."

Mr. Callahan's words made me uneasy. It sounded like an invitation to pride. I kept silent.

"Is it all right for me to share my opinion?" he asked.

"Yes sir. That's why I'm here."

The lawyer tapped his fingers on his desk. "Just the answer I expected, and although my ideas don't always line up with your beliefs, hear me out. When I look at you, I appreciate what my grandfather and those like him stood for. The strict ways don't work for everyone, but in your case they do. And I'm open-minded enough to acknowledge the good done by God's grace when I see it."

"Yes sir."

"So, what are you going to do about the job?" the lawyer continued.

"Could I work for you?" I blurted out.

Mr. Callahan smiled. "That's not the bait in the water. But to be honest, I thought about it after Joe Carpenter called me. I even prayed about it."

My eyes opened wider.

"Does that surprise you?" he asked.

"No sir. I mean, I guess it does a little bit."

"I believe in prayer," the lawyer said. "What does the Bible say? God blesses the children of the righteous to how many generations?"

"A thousand generations."

"Did they teach you that in law school along with the rule against perpetuities?"

"No sir. It's in Deuteronomy."

Mr. Callahan nodded and spoke thoughtfully. "Well, I'm only two generations removed from a very righteous man, and all my life I've felt the stirring of his influence in my soul. When I prayed about offering you a job, the Lord told me to 'ask for a continuance.' When does a lawyer request a continuance?"

"When he's not ready to try a case."

"Or when the case isn't ready for the lawyer to try."

I mulled over his words for a moment before responding. "Do you think I have to learn more before I'm ready to make a decision about coming back to Powell Station?"

"Maybe, but don't treat my opinion like someone standing up at the church and saying, 'Thus saith the Lord.' I don't claim infallibility or divine imprimatur. And it's not just about you. I need time to decide what I'm going to do over the next few years. Someday, I want to spend more time feeding my cattle than fighting with insurance companies. Unless I simply close the doors when I retire, I need to bring in a younger lawyer or two who can develop rapport with my clientele in preparation for taking over my practice."

I knew the meaning of patience. Instant gratification wasn't part of my upbringing.

"Yes sir. Can I share what you've told me with my parents?"

He leaned forward and clasped his hands together. "I'd expect you to. And if you need Internet access or use of the fax machine while you're home, come here."

"Thank you."

I stood up. Mr. Callahan spoke. "Don't let go of the good planted in you."

"Yes sir."

As I drove home, I couldn't shake a deep longing that, in spite of his comments, Mr. Callahan might offer me a job. It would be a gracious next step along the path to independence. As I rounded a familiar curve, I appealed the lawyer's decision to a higher judge.

"Lord, could you tell him a continuance isn't necessary?"

AFTER SUPPER THAT NIGHT, Daddy, Mama, and I returned to the front porch. After making sure neither of the twins was eavesdropping, I told them about my meeting in town. I left out the part about praying that Mr. Callahan might change his mind. Mama started to interrupt a few times, but Daddy put his hand on her arm.

"That's it," I said when I finished.

"So, the Spirit still moves on his heart," Daddy said. "Why would he wander from the fold?"

"His mother didn't like our ways," Mama replied. "And a family that isn't of one mind is a house divided. It will fall."

"But he's aware of his heritage," Daddy answered. "Do you think Pastor Vick and some of the elders should visit him?"

Mama was silent for a moment as they rocked back and forth. "It would be a glorious homecoming."

I stared across the darkening yard, not sure what my parents' interest in Oscar Callahan's spiritual pilgrimage meant to me. I needed them to make a decision. The Braddock, Appleby, and Carpenter job offer wouldn't remain outstanding indefinitely. If I didn't accept it, and Mr. Callahan didn't change his mind, my summer would be spent with thousands of dead chickens. I cleared my throat.

"What about Savannah?" I asked.

"We'll seek the Lord about it tonight," Daddy said. "And tell you in the morning."

Daddy's comment wasn't a religious put-off. He and Mama believed in praying until they received a definite answer. I'd seen the light shining beneath their bedroom door in the middle of the night when an issue of importance to the family required guidance from the Lord. People at our church would tarry at the altar as long as it took to find peace.

"I'll pray too," I answered.

"It's right that you should," Mama replied. "A cord of three strands isn't easily broken."

4

MOSES JONES LIVED IN A WATERFRONT SHACK ON AN UNNAMED tributary of the Little Ogeechee River. Years before he'd selected a place so marshy and uninhabitable that no one would have an interest in disturbing his privacy. No mobs of angry white men looking for a scapegoat threatened him.

It took several months to build his single-room dwelling with scrap lumber and plywood. When he finished, it rested on stilts four feet above the ground. Twice hurricanes damaged the house, but each time Moses scavenged enough lumber to rebuild.

It was a ten-minute walk through the woods to the lean-to where he kept his bicycle beside a narrow road. Every Monday morning, he pedaled into Savannah where he spent the day collecting aluminum cans to sell at the recycling center. He didn't pick up cans alongside the road. Moses had an arrangement with several bars and pubs that allowed him to haul away their beer and soft drink cans in return for cleaning around the back of their buildings. Included in his wages at one of the pubs was a free meal. The high point of Moses' week was sitting on a delivery dock savoring a plate piled high with spicy chicken wings.

After he sold the cans, Moses would buy a few fishhooks and fill up a plastic bag with free food from the community food pantry.

Clothes and shoes were castoffs that couldn't be sold at a local thrift store. He washed his clothes once a month at a Laundromat. People mistakenly considered him homeless. They didn't know about his shack in the woods. He never begged or panhandled.

The old man's most expensive regular purchase was the kerosene that powered his stove, heater, and lantern. He'd strap a five-gallon plastic container onto his bike rack and fill it with fuel at a hardware store. Five gallons of kerosene would last a long time in the warm summer months when he only used it for cooking, but in the winter he had to buy more. Winter was hard on animals and hard on Moses.

Fish and an occasional squirrel he caught in a metal trap were his sources of fresh protein. Moses liked fish coated in cornmeal and quick-fried; a gray squirrel grown fat on acorns from live oaks provided a different taste in meat. He drank water boiled in a large pot and poured into milk jugs. Alcohol hadn't passed his lips since he'd worked years before as a bolita runner for Tommy Lee Barnes.

Moses slept on eight pillows wrapped in an old sheet and laid on the floor. It was a lumpy mattress, but it was a lot easier hauling pillows through the woods than trying to carry a mattress. He had a folding table and two aluminum chairs, but he never had guests. It had been five years since his last visitor, a duck hunter who surprised him one morning. The hunter stopped for a brief chat then moved on. There weren't any ducks in the area, and the hunter didn't come back.

In good weather Moses cooked outside, which kept his shack from getting smoky or burning down. He kept the kerosene lantern for emergency use and rarely lit it. Except when he went night fishing, he lay down to sleep at dark and woke at dawn.

The old man kept his most prized possession, his johnboat, locked and chained to a tree. The key to the rusty lock hung on a leather strap around his neck. In winter Moses slept in the shack, but the rest of the year he liked to spend several nights a week on his boat. When he finished fishing, he'd tie up at a dock of one of the many houses that lined the waterway in every direction. He preferred the docks as moorings. Too many times, he'd tied up to a tree only to have a snake, spider, or an army of ants invade the boat in the middle of the night.

After he found a spot for the night, he'd remove one of the seats in the johnboat and roll out two rubber mats that he placed on top of each other in the bottom of the boat. He'd stretch out on the mats, drape mosquito netting over the edge of the boat, and watch the stars overhead while the boat gently rocked in the river. The faces in the water couldn't see over the edge of the boat, and after so many years, the memory of innocent blood running off his hands into the river rarely played across his mind. He felt at peace.

However, like a hidden log just beneath the surface of the water, Moses' habit of tying up at the river docks concealed an unknown danger.

AFTER PUTTING ON MY PAJAMAS, I took my Bible and journal downstairs to the front room. I turned on a small lamp and knelt in front of the sofa. God could speak quickly, or he might make me wait. To set a timetable for an answer would be disrespectful to his sovereignty. God was merciful, but prayer wasn't always meant to be a desperation plea by someone wanting a quick fix to a thorny problem.

Divine guidance about a summer legal clerkship with Braddock, Appleby, and Carpenter would have to come indirectly. Savannah, Georgia, didn't appear in the sixty-six books within the black leather cover, and the references to rabbinical lawyers, especially in the New Testament, weren't very complimentary. Any impression I received would be closely scrutinized by my parents.

I started by spending time thanking God for his past love and faithfulness. Although completely sufficient in himself, the Lord, like any parent, appreciated the thanks of a grateful child.

As I thought about God's goodness, I remembered a time in high school when I didn't have the money needed for a weeklong trip to Washington, D.C., and the deposit for the trip was due on a Monday. Without telling anyone except my parents, I prayed for the funds, and after church on Sunday morning a man in our church gave me a check for the exact amount I needed. Remembering how I felt at the time, a wave of emotion touched me, and I wiped a tear from the corner of my eye. More instances of God's goodness came to mind. I momentarily pushed aside the reason for my private prayer meeting.

I loved the Psalms and decided to quote Psalm 100 from memory, placing special emphasis on the verse about entering his gates with thanksgiving and his courts with praise. A civil courthouse was light-years from the place where David worshipped the Lord with all his might, but while meditating on the vast differences, a prayer welled up within me. I knew the next words from my mouth would be important.

"Lord, wherever I go, may I make the court of law a place of praise."

It was a beautiful thought. To find a place of holiness in the midst of a secular courtroom was something I'd never considered, and I marveled at a new facet of God's greatness. I might not shout "Hallelujah" in a judge's face, but my soul, like Mary's, could magnify the Lord, and my spirit could rejoice in God, my Savior. And the truth was even greater than that. Wherever I set my foot, not just a courtroom, could be a place of worship.

My mind raced ahead. The practice of law itself could be a place where I praised the Lord. I repeated, "Lord, wherever I go, may I make the court of law a place of praise," several times, pausing at different points for emphasis until each word was a brick laid on the solid foundation of faith. My tears returned. The prayer fit my life's journey. Since I was a little girl, I'd been called to live a holy life—every thought, word, and deed sanctified to the Lord. Now I could glimpse how this might be fulfilled in a new way in the future.

Lifting my hands in the air, I began to walk back and forth across the room. This was the time to tarry in secret. Not to rush. Praise offered in the night bears fruit in the day. I sat on the couch and made notes in my journal. When I finished, I peeked around the corner and saw the light shining underneath my parents' door. I didn't have an answer to my summer job question, but I was content. I'd received a greater good.

Before getting into bed, I stepped quietly over to the bunk bed, gently laid my hands on the twins, and asked that the grace poured out on me this night might also be theirs. Giving was always a part of receiving.

"GOOD MORNING," Mama said when I came into the kitchen with a half dozen fresh eggs. She stared at me. "What happened to you, Tammy Lynn? You're radiant with the joy of the Lord!"

"Yes ma'am. Last night—"

The twins came bursting into the room in the heat of an argument. Emma accused Ellie of switching a pair of good socks for a pair with holes in the toes.

"I know the good ones are mine!" Emma said. "I put them in the top drawer when I folded my clothes."

"We both have a good pair and a bad pair," Ellie responded. "She's gotten them mixed up."

Mama pointed upstairs. "Go back to your room and come back when you have this worked out."

The twins stomped out. Mama turned to me. "Wait till your daddy is here to tell me. He's going to stay a few minutes after breakfast so we can talk."

It was an oatmeal morning. Mama had fixed a huge pot that we dished out and garnished with fresh fruit, raisins, brown sugar, and nuts. Emma and Ellie returned after sorting out the sock controversy. Daddy and the boys joined us. I sat quietly and ate my breakfast.

Several times Mama glanced at me. Nothing excited her more than the move of the Spirit in a person's life, especially for one of her children. After breakfast, she shooed the twins from the room. Mama scooted close to Daddy and spoke.

"Walter, let her go first."

Daddy looked surprised. "Why?"

"Just listen."

I quietly told them what happened the previous night. At first Mama gave a slight nod or two, but by the time I finished, she'd gotten up from the bench and began walking back and forth across the kitchen, much as I'd done the previous night. When I finished, Daddy pointed at her and grinned.

"The twins are going to get some good preaching during Bible study this morning," he said.

"I can't sit still when the Spirit is moving like this," Mama said.

"So, you think it was the Lord?" I asked.

Mama looked to heaven and raised her hands in the air.

"That's a 'yes,'" Daddy answered, rising from the bench. "I'll get my Bible."

He returned with the tattered Bible he used at home.

"You know most of this by heart, but I want to read it," he said, turning the pages.

He began in Matthew 6, just before Jesus' reference to the lilies of the field. I loved listening to Daddy's voice. He read the Bible as if it was a letter from a loved one. He finished and looked at me.

"The most important thing is to seek first the kingdom. That's what you did last night. I told your mama that if your heart was fixed on the Lord, it would be the sign we needed." He paused and looked at her. She nodded. "You have our permission to take the job in Savannah if that's what you believe you're supposed to do."

It was a serious moment. I felt a shift in responsibility for my life to my own shoulders. A touch of fear gripped me.

"But what do *you* think I should do?"

"Exactly what you did last night," Mama answered. "Hear his voice and obey it."

"He didn't say anything about the job."

"What is in your heart to do?"

"My heart is desperately wicked," I began.

"Stop it!" Mama commanded. "Don't abandon your faith."

Daddy spoke more gently. "Have confidence in God's goodness. Isn't that what you felt last night?"

"Yes sir."

I looked at their faces. I knew they loved me. I knew Jesus loved me. I shut my eyes for a few seconds. No visions appeared behind my eyelids. I opened my eyes and looked at Mama.

"What does your heart tell you?" she insisted.

I tried to look past the darkness at the core of my being and spoke slowly. "I think God has opened a door for me to go to Savannah, even though I don't know what's on the other side."

"Then finish out the semester and go to Savannah with our blessing," Daddy said.

Mama hugged me. "You'll be back. I know it."

AFTER DADDY LEFT FOR WORK, I called Braddock, Appleby, and Carpenter. As the phone rang, I imagined what the firm's office might look like. With fifteen lawyers and support staff, it would be too large for a grand old house converted into a law office. Most likely, the firm was in a modern office building. The receptionist transferred me to Ms. Patrick.

"This is Tami Taylor in Powell Station," I began. "Thanks for faxing the information about the job."

"I hope you've made a decision. There are other deserving candidates."

I took a deep breath. Even with Daddy's permission, I felt tentative. "Yes ma'am."

There was an awkward moment of silence. "And?" Ms. Patrick asked.

"I'd like to accept," I responded quickly before fear jumped on my back.

"I'll notify Mr. Carpenter. Any questions about the terms of the offer?"

"No ma'am."

"Then sign it and mail it to my attention. Will you need help finding a place to stay?"

"Yes ma'am."

"Would you like to live alone or with a roommate?"

I hesitated. Alone would be expensive, and I needed to save as much money as possible. But a roommate could be risky. In college, I shared a dorm room with a teammate from my high school basketball team. We were different, but she respected my beliefs. She wore headphones while listening to her music and never brought a boy into the room while I was there. I kept the room immaculate and helped her pass freshman English and chemistry for nonscience majors.

"A roommate would be fine if we have a chance to talk before making a decision," I replied.

"One of the summer clerks is a girl from Atlanta. Do you want her name and number?"

"Yes ma'am." I grabbed a pen and a piece of paper from Mama's nightstand.

"Here it is," Ms. Patrick said in a few moments. "Julie Feldman. She's finishing her second year at Emory."

I swallowed. Feldman sounded Jewish. Our church believed the Jews were God's chosen people, but I'd never had to choose one myself. Ms. Patrick rattled off a phone number and e-mail address that I scribbled on the sheet of paper.

"Give Julie a call or send her an e-mail. She's already been down to look for a place to stay."

"Are there any other summer clerks?"

"Yes, a young man who grew up in Charleston. He's attending Yale."

My eyes opened wider. The thought that my neophyte legal work would be compared to that of an Ivy League law student was instantly intimidating.

"Okay. I'll get in touch with Julie."

Ms. Patrick spoke in a more pleasant tone of voice. "Call if you need help or have other questions. You'll have a great time in our program. Summer associates get to sample everything Savannah has to offer."

"Yes ma'am."

I hung up the phone. Ms. Patrick might be upbeat about everything Savannah had to offer, but it sounded ominous to me. Social pressures to conform were constant, but never welcome. I didn't relish the prospect of a future laden with the smorgasbord of sin. Not that I feared temptation. Doing the right thing was easy compared to defending my conduct to skeptics. I glanced at the slip of paper in my hand and decided not to contact Julie Feldman until I returned to school where I had constant Internet access. I'd made enough quick decisions about my future in the past twenty-four hours.

Mama and the twins were in the front room. I quietly watched them for a minute from the doorway. Emma and Ellie had their heads close together as they shared a science book. The sock dispute had vanished like the morning mist above the ground outside. Mama was sitting in a rocking chair reading a devotional book.

I'd loved my homeschool years with Mama. I wasn't naive about turning back the clock, but the refuge of home always seemed more precious when thinking about the hostile world at the end of the dirt driveway.

I spent the rest of the morning with Mama and the twins. The routine of the day restored my equilibrium. After helping fix bacon, lettuce, and tomato sandwiches for lunch, I mailed the summer clerkship agreement to Savannah. Turning toward the house, I absorbed every detail of the scene. I hoped my anchor in the hills of Powell Station was strong enough to hold me fast in the murky waters of Savannah.

LATE THAT AFTERNOON, I took two pillows to the front porch and positioned them on the swing so I could lie down comfortably.

The swing creaked as I shifted my weight. Flip and Ginger, hearing the sound of the swing, ambled around the corner of the house and took up their customary positions in the dirt beneath the porch.

I studied the massive poplar tree in our front yard. The new leaves showed no sign of the stress that would come with the onslaught of summer's heat. I wiggled my toes, which appeared as large as the trees on a distant hill. Before I realized it, Emma was tapping me on the shoulder.

"Wake up!"

I blinked. "Was I asleep?"

"Don't pretend you were praying," Emma said. "Is Mama going to let you live in Savannah this summer?"

Out of the corner of my eye I could see Ellie standing just inside the house.

"Ask her," I responded.

The twins ran toward the kitchen. I got out of the swing and followed.

Emma and Ellie were firing questions at Mama when I entered the kitchen. They knew that if they could persuade Mama to change her mind, it would negate my plans. Arguing with me would be a waste of time.

"Fix the spaghetti sauce for supper while I talk to your sisters," Mama said to me.

She took the girls onto the back steps. In a few seconds it was quiet. I opened two jars of canned tomatoes, added other ingredients from the spice pantry, and placed the pot of chunky sauce on the stove to simmer. Mama and the twins returned. She looked at me.

"Did you promise Ellie that she and Emma could visit you in Savannah this summer?"

"No ma'am," I said, and then continued quickly when I saw Ellie about to explode. "I told her a trip might be arranged if you and Daddy gave permission. I don't even know where I'm going to stay."

Mama turned to Ellie. "Is that what she said?"

"I'm not sure. I was sleepy."

"A trip to Savannah isn't like a drive for a picnic at the park. And I don't want to be like Jacob and have all my children leave and go down to Egypt. Unlike Canaan during the time of Joseph, there isn't a famine in Powell Station."

"But it meant the whole family got to be together," Emma said.

"Go upstairs and straighten up your room," Mama told the girls.

"I'm sorry if I caused a problem with my mention of a visit," I said when they left the room.

"It was a helpful diversion," she replied. "They love you so much the thought of your absence hurts. A trip to see you gives them something else to think about."

I stirred the sauce. "Do you think the whole family could visit? It would be a chance for the twins to see the ocean for the first time."

Mama lifted a huge pot of water for the noodles onto the stove. "Goodness. That would be a big undertaking. You know how busy summer is around here."

THE JOB IN SAVANNAH was the major topic of conversation at the supper table. My role in the decision didn't come out, but I saw Kyle and Bobby give each other a knowing look. It made me wonder what secret dreams they held about the future. A wave of fear washed over me that they might not be seeking God's will. It would crush me if a member of our family became a prodigal.

"I've sought the mind of the Lord about this," I said as a quick lesson to my siblings. "It's not an act of selfish independence or rebellion. Daddy and Mama are going to give me their blessing."

"And I'll be blessed if I can take your spot at the plant," Bobby added with a hopeful glance at Daddy.

"I'll mention it to Mr. Waldrup," Daddy said. "But are you sure you want to work inside on the line? I could try to find a place for you as a catcher."

The catchers went into the chicken houses, grabbed the birds, and crammed them into cages for transport to the processing plant. It was hot, nasty, physical labor.

"Did working on the line bother you?" Bobby asked me.

The days standing in the chill of the plant with razor-sharp scissors in one hand and chicken guts in the other were a numbing blur.

"The language of some of the women is bad," I replied. "But the chickens don't have much to say, and the smell is better than what you'd face as a catcher."

"What do the women say?" Emma asked.

Mama shook her head, and Emma plunged her fork into her spaghetti.

5

SUNDAY MORNING, OF COURSE, WE WENT TO CHURCH. I PUT MY hair in a tight bun and helped the twins get ready in their long dresses that reached to their ankles. Everyone in our van had assigned seats. I occupied the referee position between Ellie and Emma. It was about three miles to the church. The sanctuary was a large redbrick building with opaque white windows. Families similar to our own streamed into the parking lot. It was the one day during the week when normal looked like us. We took our usual seats about a third of the way from the front on the left side of the sanctuary.

Pastor Vick, a large man with a bald head and a booming voice, spoke with an eloquence that made my advocacy professor at the law school look like an oratorical amateur. This morning, he preached from Ezekiel 47. Daddy read the Bible with tender love; Pastor Vick could make the meekest verse echo with the thunder of Sinai. His text came from Ezekiel's vision of the river flowing from the temple in Jerusalem.

He measured a thousand cubits, and he brought me through the waters; the waters were to the ankles. Again he measured a thousand, and brought me through the waters; the waters were to the knees. Again he measured a thousand; and brought me through; the waters were to the loins. Afterward he measured a thousand;

and it was a river that I could not pass over: for the waters were risen, water to swim in, a river that could not be passed over.

Pastor Vick then described the apostate condition of the Israelites in a way that left no doubt as to the parallel for the present. That part of his sermon was always easy to hear. But then he turned his attention to the people sitting in the pews. Rhetorical questions were his most deadly bullets.

"That was their abominable condition, but what about you? Are you satisfied with dipping your toe into the river of God's glory and pretending you've sold out to Jesus? Is knee-deep water enough for you to play in and call yourself committed to the gospel? Do you believe you're righteous because the water laps around your waist?" Pastor Vick let his eyes scan the entire congregation. "Are any of you willing to cast yourself into the river of God where only Jesus can hold you up? Who will go into deeper water?"

My stomach quivered; a familiar feeling that meant an arrow shot from the pulpit had found its mark. I glanced sideways at Mama. Her attention was riveted on the front of the church. As Pastor Vick continued, my uneasiness increased. The river of God was both fearful and wonderful.

"The river is wide, the river is deep," Pastor Vick continued. "And only those whose eyes are fixed on Jesus can enter its waters. If that describes you this morning, the altar of God beckons you."

At the invitation, I was one of the first people to walk down the aisle and kneel in prayer. Being away at school for most of the year, I didn't have the option to hold back until another Sunday. I had to respond when the Spirit moved. One of the elders laid his hands on my head and prayed a long blessing. I rose to my feet encouraged. Outside the church, Mama gave me a hug.

"Watching you blesses me," she said simply.

It was the highest compliment I could imagine.

MID-AFTERNOON, THE FEMALE LAW STUDENT giving me a ride back to school picked me up. Everyone stood in a line in the front room for a hug. My suitcase waited beside the door.

"Let us know your exam schedule," Mama said. "So we can pray."

"We love you," Daddy added, his eyes sparkling with a mixture of happiness and sorrow. I could see him swallow after he spoke.

Kyle and Bobby gave me obligatory brother hugs. The twins grabbed me so tightly that I had trouble breathing.

I carried my suitcase to the car and put it in the trunk. I didn't look back until the last instant. Mama, Daddy, and the twins were standing on the front porch watching the car drive away, taking me back to the outside world.

I LIVED ALONE about a mile from the law school in Athens. My one-room apartment was a converted motel, but I'd joked to Daddy that it wasn't fully saved. It contained a stove, a compact refrigerator, a couple of cabinets, and a three-foot countertop with a sink. I brought in a twin bed, a small wooden table picked up at a garage sale, and a webbed lounge chair where I sat to read. My computer was on a desk in front of the single window that provided a view of the parking lot.

After the sun went down and the Sabbath was over, I turned on the computer and sent an e-mail to Julie Feldman, introducing myself and asking about her living arrangements for the summer. I closed my eyes and prayed before clicking the Send icon. I didn't want to be selfish or wasteful with money, but I liked the peace and quiet of living alone. It made life so much simpler.

None of my classmates at the law school knew the depth of my religious convictions, and their ignorance was my bliss. In Pastor Vick's terminology, I lived among the Babylonians without defiling myself with their idols or offending them with my differences. I didn't belong to either the Young Democrats or the Young Republicans;

both groups were far from the truth. I was simply the girl with long hair who wore skirts and dresses to class and baggy sweatpants when playing basketball or going out for a run.

When I unpacked my suitcase, I found letters from Emma, Ellie, and Mama. I'd left them notes hidden in places where they might not be found for a couple of days. Emma had drawn a picture of me with red hearts around the border. Ellie drew me as a scarecrow running away from a giant Chester the chicken. I saved Mama's letter for last. She expressed her thankfulness for my sensitivity to the Lord, passed on a few words of encouragement, and concluded by reassuring me that every thought of me brought her joy. Even though I'd just been home, the letters made me homesick.

I studied for a couple of hours and checked my computer. I had an e-mail from Julie Feldman. My heart went to my throat as I moved the cursor to open it. I immediately noticed there was an attachment with pictures.

Hi, Tami,

Got your e-mail. Look forward to a fun time with you this summer at B, A & C. Wish you'd called sooner. I just signed a lease for an apartment in an older home near Greene Square. I'd gone back and forth about taking a beautiful (but pricey) place overlooking the river that would have been great for two. The woman who owns it is going to be in Spain for the summer. Can you imagine that!

I'm sending pics and details of two other places I found and a photo of me taken a couple of months ago. Lynn Bynum is the leasing agent who helped me. Gerry Patrick at the firm knows her. The apartment on Price Street is not far from me. Call quick if you want to take one of these. There's a lot more about me on MySpace.com. See you in a few weeks.

Julie

I read the e-mail four times. I'd heard that some of the students at Emory could be snobby. Julie sounded nice enough, although her definition of fun was likely the same as Ms. Patrick's invitation to sample all Savannah had to offer. It was a relief not having to decide whether to room with someone for the summer.

I clicked on Julie's picture and watched it load from the top of the screen to the bottom. She had black hair that fell to her shoulders, a full figure, and wore glasses that made her look very smart. Her Jewish ethnicity was apparent in her face. Dressed casually in a blue sweater and jeans, she was sitting on a bench in front of a huge tree on the Emory campus. There was an open book in her hands that was the same civil procedure casebook we used at Georgia; however, Julie was holding the book upside down and staring at an unknown object in the distance. It was a posed shot, but the purpose of the photo with an upside-down book and faraway look in her eyes wasn't clear. I didn't try to access Julie's myspace.com page. I avoided the personal side of the Web because it was so full of lies and perversion.

I opened the photos of the places mentioned in the e-mail. There were multiple photos of the two apartments and a PDF file giving the specifications of each. The apartment near Julie's place was the second story of a detached garage, and the second location was an end unit of a block of townhomes. I was shocked to discover that one month's rent for the townhome equaled three months at my apartment. The garage apartment was even more expensive. I quickly closed the files. I would need to phone Ms. Patrick and find out about a cheaper place to live.

THE FOLLOWING MORNING at 5:30 a.m. I rolled over and opened my eyes. There were no chickens to tend, but I enjoyed getting up for an early morning run and loved breathing the fresh air of a new day. On even the coldest days of winter, I bundled up for a forty-five-minute jog that included a mile-long section alongside the Oconee River. While I ran, I rejoiced. It wasn't a time for intercession, and I didn't try to make it serious. I simply enjoyed the world God created and the physical strength he'd given me.

I covered the last half mile in a sprint that made my heart pound. When I finished, I walked across the parking lot, breathing heavily, with my hands on my hips. I drank two large glasses of water while I cooled off, showered, and dressed for the day. The runner's rush and the glasses of water curbed my morning appetite, and I didn't cook a complicated breakfast. Fruit, yogurt, and a hard-boiled egg were typical. While eating, I prepared for the day's classes. Information learned in the morning stayed with me better than what I studied at night. Most law students didn't crack a casebook in the morning and dragged themselves to class on a skid of strong coffee. I'd never finished a cup of coffee in my life.

After my first class, I went to the placement office and told the job placement director about the Savannah offer. She congratulated me and wrote down the information for her statistics. The placement office had rooms with phones and computers for students to use in job search activities. I closed the door and phoned Ms. Patrick.

"Your acceptance of the job arrived in the mail this morning," she said.

"Really?" It was amazing that an envelope could travel from Powell Station to Savannah in less than two days.

"Did you contact Julie Feldman?"

"Yes ma'am." I told her about my e-mail from the Emory student. "The places Julie sent me are not in my budget. I need to save as much money as possible."

"I'm looking at your résumé and see that you've worked with the elderly."

"Yes ma'am. I enjoyed it."

Starting in college, I'd found part-time work as a sitter for older women in nursing homes. Some were demanding; others docile. It was easy work that allowed time for study when my clients slept. One reference on my résumé was a woman whose mother I'd cared for.

"Would you be interested in staying with an elderly woman in Savannah?" Ms. Patrick asked. "Her daughter is a client of the firm and told me recently that her mother needs a live-in caregiver to spend the night. The mother is self-sufficient, but she's reached the age where it's better to have someone around the house on a regular basis. She lives in a beautiful old home a few blocks from our office. I don't know what the family would be willing to pay, but the daughter mentioned room and board if I could think of a woman to help."

A free place to stay within walking distance of the office sounded like a sign from heaven.

"Yes ma'am, but I don't want to violate my contract with the law firm. I promised to devote all my efforts to firm business."

Ms. Patrick laughed so loudly that I felt embarrassed. "I appreciate your integrity, but you're a summer clerk, not a first-year associate. Seventy-hour workweeks aren't part of the plan. This is your last opportunity to enjoy a law office without any responsibilities. When I talk to Christine Bartlett, I'll tell her what you'll be doing at the firm so she can take that into consideration."

"What's her mother's name?"

"I don't know her first name. I've always called her Mrs. Fairmont. She's an interesting woman."

Interesting could mean a lot of things, and staying with a woman in her own home would be a lot different from the controlled environment of a nursing facility. I immediately thought about the use of alcohol. I had no intention of becoming a dying alcoholic's barmaid.

"And I'm sure they would have a lot of questions for me." I paused. "I'd have a few too."

"Do you want me to pursue it?"

"Yes ma'am," I said quickly. "But I know from experience that compatibility is important. You can pass along Mrs. Frady as a reference. She's listed on my résumé."

I'd stayed several hours a week with Mrs. Frady's mother for over a year until the eighty-six-year-old woman died. I'd fought off bedsores, spooned chipped ice into her toothless mouth, brushed the old woman's hair, given simple manicures, decorated her room, and tried to make her last days on earth as pleasant as possible for a person trapped in a body that deteriorated before my eyes. So many people thanked me at the funeral that I was embarrassed. Any Christian should have done the same thing.

"She's kind. Her mother and I hit it off from the start."

"I'll call Christine and get back to you."

LATE THAT AFTERNOON I checked my e-mail at my apartment and immediately noticed a message from an unknown sender with the subject line "My Mother in Savannah."

It was from Christine Bartlett. She wanted to talk to me as soon as possible and left both an office and a home phone number. I didn't have a cell phone and made my phone calls through my computer connection. I looked at the clock. It was almost suppertime, the telemarketer time of day. I would eat and call later.

I ate in silence. The TV in the room wasn't plugged in; however, it was impossible to escape invading noise from the people living on either side of me. I used earplugs at night, but during the day, I sometimes tuned out distractions by daydreaming. Tonight I imagined that I was eating at home, sitting between the twins with Mama at one end of the table and Daddy at the other. Emma and Ellie were talking about our laying hens, and Bobby asked Daddy if he'd talked to Mr. Waldrup about a summer job. Mama had a slightly sad look on her face that I took to mean she was missing me. I missed her too.

I washed the dishes in the tiny sink. Compared to cleanup

following a meal at home, kitchen duty in my apartment couldn't be called work. After a few minutes, I returned to the computer and placed the call. Mrs. Bartlett answered on the third ring. She had the smooth accent of the coast.

"Is this a good time to talk?" I asked.

"Oh, yes, Ken and I are relaxing with a glass of wine on the veranda at our place on the marsh. Let me put you on the speaker-phone so he can hear as well."

I heard a click and some background noise.

"We're both here," Mrs. Bartlett said. "Gerry tells me you'll be moving to Savannah in a few weeks to work for Braddock, Appleby, and Carpenter."

"Yes ma'am."

"You'll love Samuel Braddock. He's one of the sweetest men in Savannah. He was Daddy's lawyer. He could have retired years ago but still works like a junior associate."

A male voice spoke. "He lets Joe Carpenter run the firm. Joe is a good lawyer, but I can't say he's one of the sweetest men in Savannah."

Mrs. Bartlett spoke. "Nonsense, I'm sure you'll love working there. Gerry told me all about you, and I took the liberty of calling Betty Lou Frady. We had the best talk."

"I enjoyed caring for her mother; however, she was in a nursing—"

"And she went on and on about you. Says you're tall and carry yourself like a New York model. So many young women these days slouch around and don't stand up straight enough to carry off a decent debut. Do you have a boyfriend?"

"No ma'am."

"I've got several young men I want to introduce you to while you're here this summer. My boys are grown and married, and we have two grandchildren, although I try not to look too much like an old granny. Stay out of the sun. I used to think a tan was a sign of good health. Now, I'm fighting the wrinkles."

"How is your mother's health?" I asked, trying to redirect the conversation.

"She was doing great until the first of the year. Living alone and walking to her volunteer job every day. Then they diagnosed her with, what is it, Ken? It's not Alzheimer's."

"Multi-infarct dementia."

"It sounds horrible, but she just has moments when things don't click right. My brother and I think it would be nice if someone stayed with her at night. The cleaning lady is at the house three or four times a week, and her gardener checks on her every time he comes by to water the flowers and take care of the bushes, but that doesn't cover the evening hours. She keeps one of those things around her neck at night in case she falls and can't get to the phone, but her problems are mental, not physical."

"Does she remember to check in with the monitoring service in the morning?"

"Half the time, I don't think she calls them. She's so fixated on getting that first cup of coffee that nothing and no one can stand in her way. We both drink it black and strong and love Jamaican blue. That's probably one reason her heart is acting up."

"What's wrong with her heart?"

"It races away every so often, but she's never had a heart attack. The biggest problem is her high blood pressure. That's the cause of the multiproblem thing."

"What medications is she taking?"

"Goodness, I don't know what they're all for. Of course, she takes something for high blood pressure, a pill to regulate her heart rate, and a blood thinner, but the doctors are always switching things around so much that I can't keep up with them. All that information is written on the door of the medicine cabinet in the kitchen. Gracie, the woman who cleans the house, fills up Mother's pillbox on Monday."

"How often do you see her?"

"I pick her up for lunch every week or so. For years she was so wrapped up in her own social circle that she didn't have time for mine. Recently, her friends have been dying off left and right. I've taken her to two funerals in the last six weeks. It's sad when the fabric of life begins to unravel. I never want to get to the place where I embarrass myself in public. Better to go with dignity."

"Christine," Mr. Bartlett interrupted. "Don't you think it would be a good idea to invite Ms. Taylor to meet your mother?"

"Absolutely," Mrs. Bartlett responded. "I've enjoyed this chat on the phone, but there's nothing like meeting in person. I realize you'll only be here for a short time this summer, but we still need to convince Mother that it's a good idea to have a live-in caregiver."

"You haven't asked her?"

"Not yet. I'm still planning my strategy. The last time she had a houseguest was when Nicholas Harrington moved in and tried to convince her to marry him. My brother had to fly in from Majorca to settle that problem and send him on his way. I can tell her she's doing you a favor by letting you spend the summer. That will keep her from suspecting the truth."

"I think it would be better—"

"Could you come this weekend?" Mrs. Bartlett continued. "Friday evening would be perfect. Ken and I will put you up at a bed-and-breakfast around the corner from Mother's house. We'll have a light snack at her place on Saturday morning, and after we all meet, you and I will slip away for a private chat in the kitchen. If everything is a go, you can ask Mother to let you spend the summer with her."

"I wouldn't feel comfortable inviting myself—"

"Don't worry. I'll set everything up. I know how to get her to do what I want." Mrs. Bartlett laughed. "She taught me how to get my way, so I learned from the mistress of manipulation. She doesn't even recognize her own tricks when I use them on her. Did Gerry give you the address for the house?"

"No ma'am. And I don't feel comfortable deceiving your mother about the reason for my interest in staying in her home."

"How sweet," Mrs. Bartlett responded. "Mrs. Frady told me you were a deeply religious girl. I think that's admirable. Mother has a lot of antiques and valuable artworks. Everything's insured, of course, but irreplaceable. Before we found Gracie there was a bit of petty thievery going on at the house."

"My concern—"

"And we're not deceiving Mother," Mrs. Bartlett continued. "Just creating a scenario that will work for her good. A circuitous route is often the best way to get from A to Z, and half an explanation cuts down on needless anxiety. Haven't you found that to be true when working with the elderly?"

"Yes. I guess so," I said, remembering my conversation with my parents.

"Don't worry. We'll do everything with integrity."

"Okay, but I'll need to arrange transportation."

"You're not flying, are you?"

"No ma'am. I don't have a car. I can try to find a ride to Savannah, but we're just back from spring break, and most students at the law school will be staying on campus this weekend."

I heard muffled voices; then Mr. Bartlett spoke. "Don't worry about it. I'll arrange for a rental car. What time are you finished with classes on Friday?"

"Two o'clock."

"And your address?"

I gave him the information.

"I'll have a car delivered to your place at three on Friday and e-mail you the information about the bed-and-breakfast," he said.

"And I'll be by to pick you up Saturday morning so we can go to Mother's house together," Mrs. Bartlett chimed in. "What's your cell phone number?"

"I don't have a cell phone."

"How in the world do you survive without a cell phone?" Mrs. Bartlett didn't try to conceal her shock.

"I'm sure Mrs. Frady told you I was punctual and reliable in my care for her mother. We worked out a satisfactory arrangement for communication."

"But no cell phone? Why would a young—"

"I look forward to meeting you," Mr. Bartlett cut in. "We'll get in touch with you at the bed-and-breakfast."

Mr. Bartlett ended the call.

I spent a few moments imagining the ongoing conversation between the couple before Mrs. Bartlett calmed down and took another sip of wine. If she thought the absence of a cell phone was an indicator of a radical lifestyle, she was in for a few more lessons once she got to know me better.

6

NOT MANY PEOPLE IN SAVANNAH REMEMBERED MOSES' FACE OR knew his name. Those who did were dying without anyone to take their places. Only a handful of longtime residents remembered the wiry young black man who always wore a gold Georgia Tech cap. That cap had been Moses' trademark when he was younger and earned him the nickname Buzz. Moses kept the pieces of that hat in a plastic bag at his shack on the river. It reminded him of happier days.

Unlike several of his cousins who spent hours and hours on the pedestrian walkways near the river, Moses never tried to pick up extra money playing sloppy jazz on a pawnshop saxophone or drumming the bottom of five-gallon plastic buckets. Around other people, he contented himself with the once-a-week rattle of a plastic bag full of empty aluminum cans.

Not that he wasn't musical.

Moses sang in church when his great-auntie took him as a boy. She had a fine voice, and Moses didn't hesitate to sing as loud as his ten-year-old vocal cords would let him. He could memorize most songs after hearing them once or twice. His rambunctious singing and outgoing personality attracted the attention of one of the deacons, who recruited him to work for Tommy Lee Barnes. Brother Kelso bragged that he gave ten percent of the money he earned from his take as a ward captain in the bolita racket to the church. It was enough money to earn him a seat of honor on the deacon board until a new pastor came to the church and kicked him out. Moses never tried to be a hypocrite; it took too much energy. His great-auntie died, and the church folks looked the other way when they saw Moses coming.

But a gift given is forever.

Sitting at the edge of a flickering fire on a spring evening, Moses could feel the blues rise up within him like the tidal surge in the nearby river. The first sounds came through his cracked lips with a soulful sigh and hum. Another sigh and longer hum would follow. And then emerged words in rhythm that gave substance to sorrow and turned it into a thing of bittersweet beauty. Moses used the blues to keep despair at bay. And they helped vanquish the sick feeling that came whenever he remembered the blood that once stained his hands.

However, melancholy songs in the night weren't an antidote for fear. Most people would have been afraid to live alone on a marshy, deserted stretch of a black-water river. Moses wasn't afraid of solitude. Fear kept Moses alone. It was a fickle companion that wore two faces. The panic he felt when the faces rose to the surface of the water caused adrenaline to course through his veins. Afterward he experienced the exhilaration of survival. And the satisfaction that once again, he'd cheated death.

But on those nights he didn't sing.

THE FOLLOWING AFTERNOON, I called Gerry Patrick to thank her for putting me in touch with Mrs. Bartlett and then told her about my upcoming visit.

"Did Christine talk your ear off?"

"Both of them. She had very nice things to say about Mr. Braddock."

"He's a true Southern gentleman. Will you arrive in time on Friday to visit the office?"

"I'm not sure. What time do you close?"

"Five thirty."

"No, it will be later than that when I get into town. Is the office open on Saturdays?"

"Most of the associates show up, but the doors are locked. I'd rather you come when I can give you a proper tour and introduction to the attorneys and staff."

"That makes sense." I paused before continuing. "If staying with Mrs. Fairmont doesn't work out, I'd like to look for another place to live while I'm in town."

"Of course. I'll send you contact information for Lynn Bynum, the location agent the firm uses. She knows what's available in any price range. Don't be bashful about asking for help. We send Lynn plenty of paying business."

Ms. Patrick seemed to have resolved her reservations about my receiving the job offer without her input. Perhaps she was a churchgoer.

"Julie Feldman mentioned Ms. Bynum in her e-mail." I said.

"Yes. We're in synagogue and Hadassah together."

My eyes opened wide.

"That's nice," I managed.

"Let me know if I can help in any way."

THAT EVENING I CALLED HOME and unleashed a torrent of information upon Mama about all that had happened with Mr. and Mrs. Bartlett.

"What do you think?" I asked when I finished and took a deep breath.

"You're bumping up against the world in a new way," Mama said calmly. "The daughter sounds like a person who's looking for someone to do for her mother what she ought to be doing herself."

"Yes ma'am."

Mama rarely missed a chance to point out an example of American self-centeredness. When we studied other cultures in homeschool, I was amazed by the differences in attitudes toward relatives that existed between civilized countries and those considered more backward. Mama said *sacrifice* was in the Bible and the dictionary but not in most people's hearts.

"A free place to stay would be a blessing," she continued, "but you've got to ask the Lord if he is sending you to help this woman. His will is all that matters. If he's in it, you'll find the grace to withstand the pressure."

"Yes ma'am."

"Daddy and I will pray about it and let you know if the Lord shows us anything."

"Thanks. Any other news from home?"

"Not much. Ellie was the last one to find her note from you. She thought you might have forgotten about her, which made it that much sweeter when she found it under the stuff piled on her nightstand."

"Maybe that will convince her to clean more often."

We talked about the routine things of life for several more minutes before saying good night. Talking to Mama always gave me strength. My mind had been racing too much about the uncertainties in Savannah. With the sound of her voice in my thoughts and earplugs lodged firmly in my ears, I slept peacefully through the night.

I HURRIED HOME FROM CLASS on Friday and opened the curtain all the way so I had a clear view of the parking lot. I packed my suitcase and put everything nice I owned into a garment bag. I didn't want to make the final decision about what to wear until I was in Savannah. Each time a car entered the parking lot, I went to the window to see if I recognized it. Most of my neighbors were either students without much money or young people working marginal jobs. A white van with a magnetic car rental company sign on its side pulled into the parking lot. It was an unusual choice, but I was used to driving a van. I grabbed my wallet and went outside.

"I'm Tami Taylor."

"We're here with your car," the rental company employee said.

A silver convertible with the top down came around the corner of the building and pulled into a spot beside the van.

"Is that the car?" I asked, my mouth dropping open.

"Yeah. I need to see your driver's license, and we have some paperwork for you to sign."

The car had a white leather interior. I had trouble focusing on the forms. I skimmed the fine print prepared by a lawyer in a faraway office and signed at the bottom.

"What kind of car is it?" I asked.

"A new Jaguar. We got it in this week. You're the first person to lease it."

I glanced over my shoulder and saw that one of my neighbors was standing in his doorway watching.

"It's a rental car," I said.

"Sweet," he responded with a nod of his head. "Let me know if you need company. It'll drive better with someone in each seat."

I finished signing the paperwork. The man driving the van handed me a card.

"Call this number when you want us to pick up the car on Monday. It's got a tank of gas, but there's no need to return it full. That's included in the rental."

"Sweet," the neighbor in the doorway echoed. "You can take the whole complex out for a joyride."

I smiled awkwardly. The men from the rental company got in the van and left.

"My name is Greg Overton," my neighbor said, stepping forward. "I don't think we've met."

"I've talked with your girlfriend a few times. Where is she?"

Greg opened his arms. "Working at the pizza parlor. She doesn't get off until ten o'clock tonight. We've got plenty of time to take that beauty out for a spin. We could even go by and see her if you want to."

I brushed past him and continued toward my door. "I'm leaving town in a few minutes."

"Don't be in such a—," I heard before I shut my door.

I leaned against the door for a few seconds to compose myself. I thought about the silver car and imagined myself behind the wheel. I put my hand to my mouth and began to giggle. In a few seconds, I was doubled over with laughter. The idea that I would be driving such an expensive automobile was so outlandish that I didn't know what to do but laugh.

I wished the twins were with me. They would scream with delight at the thought of riding in a convertible. The closest thing to a convertible they'd experienced was a quick trip around the yard in the back of Kyle's pickup truck.

I finished packing my suitcase. When I came outside with my suitcase and garment bag, there was a small crowd of people standing around the car.

"Are you the lawyer who lives here?" a teenage girl asked.

"I'm a law student."

"It looks like you've already won a big case," said an older man wearing a dirty T-shirt.

I pushed the button on the key that popped open the trunk. The trunk was large enough to swallow my luggage. I got in the car and started the engine.

"Buckle your seat belt," the girl called out.

I smiled at her. "Always."

I found the switch that raised the top and pressed it.

"No!" the girl yelled. "Drive with the top down."

The top closed over my head. After the expanse of the sky as my roof, the inside of the car seemed claustrophobic. I flipped the switch that returned the top to its boot. The boy waved when he saw me. I put the car in reverse.

When I stepped on the gas, the car rocketed out of the parking space. The crowd jumped back. I slammed on the brakes and jerked to a stop. Greg Overton laughed and pointed at me. I felt my face flush. I put the car in drive and drove gingerly across the parking lot.

As I crept along, the responsibility of operating such an expensive piece of machinery hit me. Even the slightest dent or ding would stand out like a broken leg. I stopped at the exit for the parking lot and waited until there wasn't a car in sight in either direction before pulling into the street.

The route out of town took me near the law school. I stopped at a light and heard someone call my name.

"Tammy Taylor! Is that you?"

It was one of the law students on my basketball team. She was standing on the sidewalk, waiting to cross the street. I waved nonchalantly.

"Hey, Donna."

"What a beautiful ride! When did you get it?"

"It's not mine. A man in Savannah rented it for me. I'm going down there for a weekend visit."

The girl's green eyes grew even bigger. "I didn't know you had a boyfriend."

"He's not a boyfriend. He's married."

The light turned green, and I had to pull away before providing a more complete answer. In the rearview mirror I could see Donna staring after me. Our next game wasn't until Tuesday, and she would have plenty of time to broadcast erroneous information to others before I could provide the facts. I debated turning around, but when I looked again in my mirror, she was gone.

As I drove along the city streets, people on the sidewalk and other drivers turned to stare. I was used to stares for dressing differently, but this was a new kind of stare. Two college-age boys yelled at me, and a balding man in a Corvette nodded my way when I pulled up next to him at a traffic light. It was a relief to leave the city behind.

The route south from Athens led me through the heart of middle Georgia. I'd tied my hair in a ponytail that swirled in the breeze. I passed through several small communities. The most picturesque was Madison, a town spared the torch by Gen. William Tecumseh Sherman during his march to the sea after the destruction of Atlanta. The restored antebellum homes lining the main street of town seemed grander from my seat in the convertible. And I looked at the houses in a new way. My car would fit in perfectly parked in front of one of the fine old homes.

I reached the outskirts of Milledgeville, the early capital of Georgia, and pulled into a convenience store to buy a bottle of drinking water. When I got out of the car, I could see my reflection in the plate-glass window of the store. With my collared, short-sleeved blouse, knee-length skirt, and plain sandals, I looked totally out of place beside the stylish sports car. I took my hair out of the ponytail and shook it. Through the strands in front of my face, I saw a man walk out of the store and glare at me with a hostile look that scared me. I sat back down in the car, flipped the switch to raise the top, and locked the vehicle before entering the store.

When I came outside, the man was putting gas in a blue van that looked a lot like the one parked in our front yard in Powell Station. In the front passenger seat I saw a middle-aged woman with her hair in a bun and behind her several children hanging out the windows. It could have been my own family a few years earlier. The man saw me and clearly broadcast a message of judgment against a frivolous, sinful girl who shouldn't be driving a fancy convertible and shaking out her hair in front of a convenience store. Daddy would never have looked at someone the same way, but there were men in our church who would.

In a more subdued mood, I drove away from the store and merged onto the interstate. The next fifteen miles I spent my time praying that the lure of wealth and the things it offered wouldn't ensnare me in sinful pride and compromise.

The interstate deposited me directly into the downtown area of Savannah. I stopped and lowered the top of the car. No one paid attention to me as I drove slowly into the historic district. I'd read about Savannah's twenty-one squares and the restored homes and buildings surrounding them. But as I drove along, the information and images were jumbled in my memory. There would be plenty of time later for leisurely exploring on foot.

My destination was a massive postbellum residence near the home of Juliette Gordon Low, the founder of the Girl Scouts. The bed-and-breakfast was built by a confederate blockade-runner who served as inspiration for Rhett Butler in *Gone with the Wind*. I slowed to a stop in front of the opulent three-story residence with iron railings in front of ornate windows. Carrying my own luggage, I entered the house where I was greeted by a stylishly dressed hostess.

"I'm Tami Taylor," I began. "I have a reservation."

"I'll have someone show you to your room. Mr. Bartlett made all the necessary arrangements"—the woman leaned forward—"including gratuities for the staff."

A porter who looked about the same age as my brother Kyle took my suitcase and garment bag. I followed him to the third floor where he opened the door to a very feminine room with high ceilings and a collection of antiques that surrounded a four-poster bed.

"The Mary Telfair room," he announced as he placed my suitcase on a stand. "It's decorated in Eastlake and named for the daughter of an early governor and plantation owner. The house is mostly vacant tonight, and I'll be glad to show you rooms appointed in Renaissance/Revival and French Empire, the architecture of the house itself. We also have a great wine selection."

Mama had taught me about art and classical music, and I could instantly recognize a Rembrandt and identify Beethoven within a few notes, but my knowledge about antiques and wine could be summarized on a 3 x 5 index card. Jesus made simple furniture and drank wine, but I'd never been around antiques, and no wine had ever touched my lips.

"You know a lot about antiques?" I asked.

He grinned. "I'm a senior at the Savannah School of Art and Design."

I reached for my purse. The young man held up his hand.

"No, it's taken care of. I'll be downstairs until eleven o'clock tonight if I can give you a tour or help in any way. What time would you like turndown service?"

"What?"

"Someone from housekeeping will prepare your bed."

"I'm a country girl from the mountains," I answered with a smile. "I've never been in a place like this in my life."

The boy leaned forward. He had nice eyes. "Most people who pretend to be experts about antiques and fine wine make fools of themselves. I've studied a lot to learn a little."

"Thanks. I guess I'd like turndown service about ten o'clock."

I peeked into the bathroom. It had a claw-foot tub. The twins would have so much fun in a room like this. I eyed the queen-size bed. The three of us could spend the night together, so long as I slept in the middle to prevent pushing and arguing.

After all the excitement of the day, I felt tired. I pulled back the covers, lay down, and stared at the ceiling. Every detail of the room was a work of craftsmanship.

I dozed off and woke with a start. It was almost 9:00 p.m. I hurriedly made the bed so it would be ready for turndown service.

The bathroom was stocked with four kinds of bubble bath and salts. None of them had been opened. I read the labels, debating whether to indulge. I turned on the water in the tub. The sight of water splashing against the bottom of the tub ended any debate. I'd taken bubble baths as a child, but the sensation of bath salts would be something new.

I lay exulting in the warm water until time to put on my pajamas in anticipation of the turndown service. For extra modesty, I slipped on the complimentary robe I found in the armoire and sat in a chair beside the bed. I didn't want to wrinkle the bedspread. Precisely at 10:00 p.m. there was a knock at my door. When I opened it, the young porter and a woman from housekeeping were there.

"Would you like a nightcap?" the porter asked as the woman brushed past me and walked to the bed.

I touched the top of my head. The robe was a nice extra, but I'd not slept with a cap on my head since I was a little girl on cold nights in the middle of winter. Some of the women in our church would wear a scarf as a head covering when they exhorted, but it wasn't mandatory. I could tell the porter was still trying not to laugh.

"I meant a hot drink, glass of milk, something like that," he managed.

"Oh, no thanks."

My face went red, and I turned away. The woman had finished folding down the comforter on the bed and placed a chocolate in a gold wrapper on one of the pillows. I didn't look back at the porter as the woman passed me on her way out of the room.

"Thank you," I mumbled.

The door closed, and I quickly locked it against a further faux pas. At least I knew the French words for a "social blunder."

7

I WOKE UP EARLY AND SNUGGLED DEEPER INTO THE COVERS FOR a few seconds before slipping out of bed to open the drapes. From the window, I could see the fountain in the middle of Lafayette Square and a white church with multiple spires pointing toward the morning sky. I wanted to jog around the borders of the historic district without worrying about traffic, and very early on Saturday morning seemed the perfect time. After dressing, I noticed an envelope slid underneath the door of my room.

My heart jumped. It was probably from the nice young porter telling me not to be embarrassed and offering to take me on a tour of the city. Turning down his invitation would only increase the awkwardness I felt. I bent over and picked up the envelope. It had the name of the inn on the outside. I opened the envelope and took out a sheet of paper.

I'd misjudged the porter. Mrs. Bartlett had left a phone message at the front desk asking me to meet her in the parlor at 10:00 a.m. I put the note on the nightstand beside the bed and went downstairs. The staff was setting up the dining room for breakfast. There was no sign of the porter.

It was a slightly muggy morning. After stretching, I ran south along Broughton Street to Forsyth Park, the largest patch of green in the downtown area. I explored the park and ran around a fountain with a statue of a Confederate soldier facing north on top. I left the park and ran south all the way to the Savannah River. Large container vessels slowly moved upriver to the port area. I ran along River Street, past Factor's Row and the Cotton Exchange. The streets were deserted. I felt the gates of the city had been opened just for me. As I jogged, I prayed that everywhere I set my feet would be a court of praise.

I crossed West Bay Street and reentered the historic district. After several wrong turns I finally stumbled upon Lafayette Square. There wasn't a place for a long, wide-open sprint, but I ran twice around the square at top speed before coasting to a stop.

When I returned to the B and B, preparations for breakfast were complete, a lavish spread of food that included everything from grits to quiche.

After taking a shower, I selected a bright dress that shared colors with the fruit platter downstairs. The dress reached to the midcalf of my leg. While I brushed my hair, I practiced standing up straight. Mrs. Bartlett was right about one thing. Good posture was always in style.

Downstairs, I sampled most of the items on the breakfast buffet. At home I ate a big breakfast because there was work to do that would burn up plenty of calories. Breakfast at the buffet was decadent—food for the sake of food. I bowed my head for a blessing before starting and kept a thankful attitude all the way to the final pastry.

After I finished, I returned to my room, brushed my teeth, and applied a very faint hint of lipstick not much darker than my natural color. Sunday mornings at home were makeup-free, but Mama said God ordained beauty to females in the human family and subtle enhancements were acceptable—as long as there was no intention to allure. The only times I saw Mama wearing makeup were rare occasions when Daddy took her out to dinner. She claimed her attractiveness to him was based on inner qualities, not her outward appearance. Daddy whispered to me and the twins that he thought

Mama was the most beautiful woman, inside and out, in the whole world.

I was blessed with naturally long eyelashes, and in college I'd experimented with a light touch of eye shadow. I liked the change, but I'd always quickly rubbed it off. Each time I put it on I thought it looked nice, but I'd never left the bathroom with it in place. This morning I gave it another try. Perhaps it was the fancy room or being in a new town, but this time I didn't remove it. Also, there was no chance of causing a man to sin since I would only be meeting with Mrs. Bartlett and her mother.

I sat in a comfortable chair in the corner of the narrow foyer that served as the lobby. The people coming and going seemed at ease with the sumptuous surroundings. Or perhaps they were pretending. A well-dressed woman in her fifties came in, and I nervously swallowed, but she wasn't Mrs. Bartlett. A grandfather clock chimed the hour. I thought about reading a magazine, but nothing on the coffee table looked interesting. At 10:15 a.m. a short, slightly overweight woman with reddish-blonde hair burst through the front door and scanned the room. I stood up.

"Mrs. Bartlett?"

"Yes, yes," she said. "You must be Tami."

I tried not to stare at Mrs. Bartlett's obviously dyed hair as she approached. It was accentuated with highlights that would require a lot of maintenance. She was wearing a blue silk blouse, black slacks, and sandals that revealed a pedicure as flawless as her hair color. I held out my hand, but Mrs. Bartlett ignored it and gave me a hug that included a European greeting. She had to rise up on her toes to deliver the peck on both my cheeks.

"You certainly are statuesque," Mrs. Bartlett continued.

"Yes ma'am. I played basketball in high school."

"An athlete? You'd never know it now, but I had a five handicap in golf until about ten years ago. I beat Ken all the time, although I never mention it in public. My putter can still work magic, but I have no distance off the tee."

"Please tell Mr. Bartlett I appreciate the car and thanks for providing such a beautiful place to stay," I said.

"You can tell him later. He's going to meet us this afternoon. Come on, the valet is holding my car at the curb."

Mrs. Bartlett took off.

"Do you ride in a cart or carry your bag when you play golf?" I asked as we rapidly descended the front steps.

"Carry my bag? That would be a plebeian thing to do. I get my exercise walking on the beach early in the morning."

"I ran down to the river and through the historic district this morning," I said. "I enjoyed looking at the houses."

"A runner? I thought you were old-fashioned. There are plenty of registered houses. And every one has a story with many chapters."

Mrs. Bartlett was driving a white Mercedes. She handed a twenty-dollar bill to the valet who opened the door for each of us.

"Mother's house is just a few blocks away on West Hull near Chippewa Square."

"Did you grow up there?"

"No, no. My father would never live in this part of town. She bought the house after he died about fifteen years ago. I grew up at Beaulieu on the Vernon River."

Mrs. Bartlett drove like she walked. Fast. Fortunately, the short streets didn't provide enough space between stop signs to give her the chance to do more than stomp the gas pedal then slam on the brakes. I couldn't imagine what it would be like to ride with her on the interstate. After several quick turns she came to a stop alongside the curb.

"Here we are. Built in 1860, just in time for the original owner to ride off to the war and get killed at Cold Harbor."

It was a square two-story brick structure with tall narrow windows on the first level and broad front steps. On the side of the house was an attached screened porch. Two large live oaks were planted between the house and the sidewalk. An iron railing extended from the steps down the street on either side, then turned toward the rear of the house.

"It's beautiful," I said.

"She wanted it and got it," Mrs. Bartlett responded crisply. "I thought it was a mistake at the time, but it's worth four times what she paid for it. Mother knows how to manage her money. Her father made a mint in real estate, and it rubbed off on her."

We walked up ten steps to the front door. I could see there was a basement with windows partly below street level. Mrs. Bartlett rang the door chime.

"I have a key, but she hates it when I walk in unannounced. It will make her happy to pretend we're here for a formal visit."

After a long wait, a white-haired woman shorter than Mrs. Bartlett but with a similar figure opened the door. She had bright blue eyes that narrowed slightly when she looked at me and made me feel like she was sizing me up in a split second. Mrs. Fairmont was wearing a carefully tailored yellow dress and white shoes with low heels. A string of pearls encircled her neck. Mrs. Bartlett kissed both her mother's cheeks.

"This is Miss Tami Taylor," Mrs. Bartlett said, "the young woman I told you about who is going to work for Samuel Braddock's firm this summer." She turned to me. "Samuel and Eloise Braddock have been here for cocktails many times before going to the opera."

Mrs. Fairmont took my hand in hers. She was wearing a large diamond ring accented with emeralds on her right hand.

"Good morning, child," she said in a slightly raspy voice steeped in a coastal accent.

"Pleased to meet you," I answered.

Mrs. Bartlett patted her mother on the shoulder and entered the house. Mrs. Fairmont still held on to my hand.

"The house has double parlors," Mrs. Bartlett called back from the interior. "It's not an uncommon design. Mother, was Gracie here yesterday? Everything looks so nice. I like the way she arranged these flowers. Where did she get them?"

Mrs. Fairmont stayed by the door, holding my hand. Her skin was wrinkled with age, and her knuckles revealed a touch of arthritis. She put her other hand on top of mine.

"You have nice hands," she said.

"Thank you."

"Enjoy them while you can."

"Yes ma'am."

"Don't block the door, Mother," Mrs. Bartlett called out. "Where do you want us to sit?"

Mrs. Fairmont looked up at me. "Do you prefer green or blue?"

"Blue is my favorite."

The house had two parlors separated by a foyer that faced the main stairway to the second floor. On the right was a pale green room; to the left one painted an ephemeral blue.

"That is the green room," Mrs. Fairmont said, gesturing with her bejeweled hand. "And this is the blue room."

Both rooms contained beautiful furniture, original paintings, and mirrors in gilt frames. I wondered how grandchildren and great-grandchildren fared in the house. A wrestling match between Kyle and Bobby could have caused thousands of dollars of damage. Mrs. Fairmont went into the blue room and sat in a side chair. Mrs. Bartlett motioned for me to join her on a cream sofa.

"You have a beautiful home," I said. "Mrs. Bartlett told me a little of its history."

"The couple who sold it to me did most of the restoration," Mrs. Fairmont said. "Before that, it was a rooming house. Can you believe it? Workmen and laborers renting rooms by the week." She leaned forward. "If I could understand the creaks in the night, I'm sure there are many stories to tell. Did you know our voices will echo in the universe until the end of time?"

"That's a silly notion," Mrs. Bartlett cut in. "A sound doesn't really exist if it can't be heard, like a tree falling in the forest when no one is around."

"What do you think?" Mrs. Fairmont turned her blue eyes toward me.

"Well, the Bible says God keeps a record of every word that's spoken and will judge us by what we've said."

Mrs. Fairmont nodded in satisfaction toward her daughter. "See, Christine, it's the same thing, only I didn't know God agreed with me."

"Let's not get into anything controversial," Mrs. Bartlett said. "I'd like to know more about Miss Taylor's background."

Controversial could be a synonym for my background, but I knew how to exercise discretion. As I talked, I emphasized my commitment to God and family without going into detail about the rules that guided my conduct. Mama said a question was an open doorway to proclamation of the truth, but I didn't want to come on too strong. Mrs. Fairmont seemed especially interested in our life in the country and asked questions about the garden and the chickens. Mrs. Bartlett interrupted when I described my homeschool experience.

"Your mother taught you Shakespeare?"

"Yes ma'am. I memorized long passages from several plays and quite a few sonnets."

Mrs. Bartlett shook her head. "Of course, I've heard about the homeschool movement, but I thought it an inferior model. Mother and I both attended private schools."

"It can be the best and the worst," I said. "The fact that I did well in high school, college, and now law school is proof it can provide the foundation for a successful academic career."

"Do you embroider?" Mrs. Fairmont asked, her eyes getting brighter.

"Please, Mother, Miss Taylor is obviously a traditional girl, but it's not fair to expect her to embroider."

"No ma'am. I can cross-stitch with a pattern, but I've never tried to create my own designs. I'd love to see some of your embroidery."

"It's in the bedrooms and upstairs along the hall," Mrs. Bartlett replied. "Mother doesn't allow anything in these rooms that isn't museum quality."

Mama proudly displayed my crude cross-stitch in the front room.

"I can't embroider anymore," Mrs. Fairmont sighed.

I saw a tear run down the older woman's cheek. I glanced at Mrs. Bartlett, who had picked up a ceramic figurine.

"Are you all right?" I asked the older woman.

Mrs. Fairmont wiped away the tear with a lace handkerchief she pulled from the side pocket of her dress.

"Please excuse me. It's not about the needlepoint. I've been crying for no apparent reason recently. It's one of the symptoms of a condition I have called multi-infarct dementia."

I couldn't hide my surprise.

"You're still smarter than I am," Mrs. Bartlett added with a nervous laugh. "And I'm not sure it's a good idea to study too much about medical things. That's why we have doctors. Talking about health problems can make anyone depressed. Did you tell me where Gracie bought the flowers?"

Mrs. Fairmont looked directly at me and spoke. "What do you think? Should I educate myself during lucid moments or try to ignore the fact that the blood vessels in my brain are slowing dying?"

"Please, Mother," Mrs. Bartlett spoke with agitation. "That's not a fair question to ask Miss Taylor. Do you have the coffee brewing?"

Mrs. Fairmont stared at me for a few seconds. Her face softened.

"Yes, of course," she said. "Let me serve you. I have decaf for me and regular for you and Miss Jackson."

Mrs. Fairmont used her arms to push herself from the chair. Mrs. Bartlett waited a few seconds then also rose from her seat.

"I'll help. Miss Taylor can relax here."

Standing very erect, Mrs. Fairmont slowly walked from the room. Mrs. Bartlett held back. When her mother was out of sight, she leaned over and whispered to me.

"I'm sorry she brought up her condition so abruptly. She's always been quick to offer her opinion about anything from politics to religion, but recently it's gotten worse. Did you see how quickly she forgot your name? A year ago she would never have made a social blunder like that. Most of the time, she can take care of herself. Still, I'd feel better if there was a watchful eye in the house every now and then. Any loving child would want the same thing. How do you want your coffee?"

"Uh, I'm not a coffee drinker. Does she have any tea?"

"Yes, but it might upset her if you don't drink coffee. I'll fix you a cup with cream and sugar, and you can pretend to sip it."

Mrs. Bartlett left, and I gave the parlor a closer inspection. Unlike my grandmother's home, the house didn't smell musty. The plantation shutters on the tall front windows were open and let in plenty of light. A compact but ornate glass chandelier hung overhead. The fresh flowers in a glass vase on a small round side table were an explosion of color. There was a fireplace in the parlor, and I peeked into the other room to see if it also contained one. Neither grate had been used in a long time. A well-preserved rug with ornate flower designs covered the floor.

My inspection was interrupted by the quick patter of tiny feet on the wooden floor and a sharp bark. Around the corner came a light brown Chihuahua. The dog stopped when it saw me and blinked its oversize eyes. I lowered the back of my hand to the floor as a sniff offering. The dog moved forward cautiously, stopped, and looked over its shoulder.

"Hello, little boy or girl," I said. "I bet you've never met anyone who worked in a chicken plant. I've washed my hands since then so you probably can't smell the chickens."

The dog inched forward and stretched out its head toward the back of my hand. I could hear a low growl in its throat. I kept still, aware that smaller breeds can be quicker to bite than larger ones. The Chihuahua took another step forward and sniffed my hand and fingers. The growl receded. I reached around and scratched the back of the dog's neck. The dog's eyes closed in satisfaction. I could see it was a male.

"What's your name, boy? I bet it's fancy. Sir Galahad would be nice. We have chickens at my house with unusual names."

The dog was wearing a narrow red collar decorated with rhinestones. Still scratching his neck, I repositioned the collar so I could see the dog's name tag. When I saw the engraving, I smiled.

"Flip. I have a dog named Flip, but he lives outside and sleeps in the dirt under the front porch in the summer. Have you ever slept in the dirt? Do you know what dirt looks like?"

I picked up Flip and held him in my lap as I continued to stroke him. I was careful not to let his tiny feet touch the sofa. Mrs. Bartlett and Mrs. Fairmont returned to the parlor. Mrs. Bartlett was carrying a silver coffee service. Her mother followed with a plate of miniature pastries.

"Careful!" Mrs. Bartlett cried out.

The dog launched himself from my lap. Barking ferociously, he skidded across the floor toward Mrs. Bartlett, who stuck out her left foot to keep him away. The tray tipped to the side. I jumped up and rushed toward her as the tray moved the other way and the coffeepot slid to the edge. Flip, his teeth bared, continued to bark and dance around her feet. Mrs. Fairmont stood motionless with her mouth slightly open.

"Stop it!" Mrs. Bartlett said. "Get away!"

Like a basketball player scrambling for a loose ball, I lunged to the floor and grabbed the wiggling animal with my right hand. But it was too late. Mrs. Bartlett lost control of the tray. The pot flew off, followed by three cups, saucers, the sugar container, and a cream pitcher. The sound of clattering metal and breaking china in the quiet house was deafening.

Mrs. Bartlett swore. The black coffee was pooling across the wooden floor toward the rug. Instinct took over. I grabbed the coffeepot, knelt on the floor, and positioned my dress between the coffee and the rug. I pressed down with my hands in an effort to block the progress of the coffee. The long length of my dress came in handy.

"Someone get a washrag or paper towels," I said.

Mrs. Bartlett hurried out of the room. Mrs. Fairmont stared at me and seemed stuck in the moment. I could feel the coffee against my free hand. In spite of my efforts, it was continuing to creep toward the rug. There was nothing else to do. I sat down on the floor between the coffee and the rug. I could feel the hot coffee on my thigh, but it wasn't warm enough to burn me. I looked up at Mrs. Fairmont. Flip calmed down, and I held him in my lap. The old woman put the pastry tray on a chair.

"Get up, child. It's not worth ruining your dress to clean up a spill."

"I couldn't let it ruin the rug. I can wash the dress, but I don't know how you would clean a rug like that."

Mrs. Bartlett returned from the kitchen with washcloths. Flip started barking again. Mrs. Bartlett handed the washcloths to me and quickly backed away. I slipped to my knees and tossed the cloths on the rest of the coffee. The rug was saved.

"I thought you were going to keep that dog in his room," Mrs. Bartlett said, turning toward her mother. "I called and reminded you this morning."

"He must have been in my bedroom," Mrs. Fairmont said apologetically. She looked down at me. "I'm so sorry about your dress."

Mrs. Bartlett turned to me as if just realizing what I'd done. "How courageous of you," she said. "To sacrifice your outfit."

"I'm not sure how courageous it was, Mrs. Bartlett. It was coffee, not a hand grenade."

I stood and moved one of the washcloths across the floor with my foot.

"It's that dog's fault," Mrs. Bartlett said, refocusing on Flip. "This isn't a house for a dog, no matter what you think. Especially a vicious one!"

Mrs. Fairmont, a dazed look in her eyes, stared at Mrs. Bartlett without saying a word. I picked up Flip and could feel a growl in his throat. I rubbed his back.

"Take him away!" Mrs. Bartlett said. "And lock him up in that dog palace you created for him."

Mrs. Fairmont seemed to reconnect with her surroundings.

"If Miss Taylor will carry him, we'll put him in his room."

"Yes ma'am."

I followed Mrs. Fairmont through the foyer.

"I'll call Gracie and have her come right over and clean up this mess," Mrs. Bartlett called after us. "She doesn't have a regular house to clean on Saturday, does she?"

"I can take care of it," I said over my shoulder. "Find the broom and a dustpan."

I patted Flip on the head and whispered in his ear. "I understand. You're just protecting your territory like your wolf ancestors."

8

"I HAVE A PLACE FOR FLIP IN THE BASEMENT," MRS. FAIRMONT SAID.

We walked down a short hallway past a paneled room that looked like a den or study. Bookshelves lined the walls on either side of a large television. Mrs. Fairmont turned and faced me.

"I keep Flip with me all the time," she said in a soft voice. "He even sleeps on my bed, although Christine doesn't know it. We'll take him downstairs, but it would be cruel to leave him there all the time. Does your family have a dog? Living on a farm like that, I'd expect you to have a dog."

"Yes ma'am. We have two dogs; one is named Flip."

"Really! What breed?"

"Mixed. Our Flip probably weighs about fifty pounds."

"My baby weighs six pounds, four ounces."

We went down to the basement. Light streamed in from the windows I'd seen from the front of the house. Mrs. Fairmont's home was three stories in the rear and opened onto a courtyard/garden. Windows lined the wall and let in light and the view. A wall ran down the center of the room. To the left was an open space used for storage. Mrs. Fairmont opened a door to the right, and we entered a suite with a kitchenette. A dog bed surrounded by chew toys lay in the middle of the floor. There wasn't any other furniture.

"Was this was one of the rooms for rent?"

"Yes. It's really a little apartment. No one has lived here since I bought the house. It's what they call a garden apartment."

"May I take a look?"

"Sure."

Still carrying Flip, I stepped across the living area into a bedroom with French double doors that opened onto a brick patio with a wrought-iron table. There was an old brass bed that looked like it hadn't been used in years.

"It has a nice view of the garden, but it sure doesn't look like a palace," I said without thinking.

"Christine is prone to exaggeration, as I'm sure you've noticed if you've been around her more than five minutes." Mrs. Fairmont sniffed. "She claims this house is worth three times what I paid for it."

I recalled Mrs. Bartlett's statement as "four times" but kept my mouth shut.

Mrs. Fairmont took Flip from my arms. The little dog licked her chin.

"Nice kisses," she said. "Now show us how you got your name."

She put the dog on the floor and made a circle with her right index finger. The Chihuahua stepped forward and did a backward somersault. It happened so fast that I didn't get a good look.

"Will he do it again?" I asked.

Mrs. Fairmont swirled her finger and Flip obliged. She leaned over and patted him on the head.

"I've never seen a dog do that," I said.

"He's a smart boy."

"What else can he do?"

"Love me," Mrs. Fairmont said, looking at me with her blue eyes. "When no one else does."

She gave Flip a treat and closed the door to the room. I listened for a moment but didn't hear any scratching or whining. We returned upstairs. The coffee on my dress now felt clammy against my legs. Mrs. Bartlett was in the hallway near the kitchen. She had a cordless phone in her hand.

"I can't get Gracie," she said, clicking off the phone.

"I said that I'd be glad to finish cleaning up," I said, trying not to sound disrespectful. "All I'll need are paper towels, a broom, and a dustpan."

"Gracie moved all the cleaning supplies to the closet near the porch," Mrs. Fairmont said.

I followed Mrs. Bartlett through a small formal dining room. Before reaching the porch, we came to a space designed as a coat closet. I grabbed what I needed, returned to the parlor, and began cleaning up the mess. Mrs. Fairmont sat down and rested her head against the back of the chair.

"All this commotion has taken away all my energy," she said. "I need to lie down for a few minutes."

"Not yet. We're not finished with our visit," Mrs. Bartlett replied. She pointed across the room. "Tami, I see a splatter of coffee all the way over there."

I went to the kitchen, moistened some of the paper towels, and while the two women watched, cleaned the floor, pushing the bits of glass into a single pile.

"You missed some glass beneath Mother's chair," Mrs. Bartlett said.

I turned on my knees so that my rear end was facing Mrs. Bartlett to hide the laughter threatening to explode. I didn't mind cleaning up the mess, but Mrs. Bartlett's bossiness was a comedy of the absurd.

"I need to moisten some more towels," I said as I stood and left the room.

I reached the kitchen, a compact room at the rear of the house, and let myself giggle for a few seconds.

From the kitchen sink I could see more of the small formal garden with its carefully manicured shrubbery and an array of spring flowers. A brick walkway wound through the garden that featured a fountain in the middle—a great place to read the Bible and pray. I turned off the water along with my daydream. I had no idea whether I should live in the house or not.

At the entrance to the parlor, I heard Mrs. Fairmont say, "What on earth gave her that idea? To presume after one visit that I would want her to live—"

"Oh, Tami," Mrs. Bartlett interrupted. "Thanks so much for helping us clean up this mess. You're a dear to do it and come to the aid of two helpless old women."

"You're welcome."

I resumed my work without any desire to laugh. I didn't mind being a servant, but Mrs. Bartlett's deception and supercilious statements about helplessness after she'd bragged about her golf game and long walks on the beach made me mad. I used the broom and dustpan to scoop up the broken pieces. Mrs. Fairmont didn't speak a word. A few more wipes of wet paper towel across the floor, and no sign of the morning's disaster remained. I looked up and saw Mrs. Bartlett mouthing words to her mother. I wanted to stuff a washcloth into Mrs. Bartlett's mouth.

"What should I do with the dirty cloths?" I asked icily.

"There's a clothes drop at the end of the hall," Mrs. Bartlett said. "Follow me."

As soon as we left the room, Mrs. Bartlett turned to me. "Give me a few minutes alone with Mother. She's ecstatic about the idea of you staying with her, but we need to work out the details in private."

"That's not what . . . ," I began, but Mrs. Bartlett was gone.

I found the dirty-clothes drop. Mrs. Bartlett's subterfuge was an out-and-out lie, and I had to set the record straight. If honesty destroyed the chance to stay rent-free in a beautiful house, then there had to be a low-rent apartment on a bus line somewhere in Savannah.

I returned to the parlor. The two women were sitting in silence. I could feel the tension. I moved to the edge of a cream sofa and started to sit down.

"Stop it!" Mrs. Bartlett cried out. "Don't sit down."

I jumped to my feet and looked around.

"Your dress is drenched in coffee," Mrs. Bartlett said. "It might bleed onto the sofa."

"Get a towel for her to sit on," Mrs. Fairmont said.

Mrs. Bartlett looked at her mother. "But I thought—"

"Get a towel from the upstairs linen closet," her mother insisted.

Mrs. Bartlett turned to me. "We won't be staying long. I'm sure you'd like to change out of that dress and into something clean."

Mrs. Bartlett left the room. As soon as her footsteps could be heard going up the stairs, I spoke rapidly.

"Mrs. Fairmont, I didn't come here to invite myself to live in your house. That's not the way I was raised. The office manager at the law firm gave my name to your daughter because I've helped take care of people with health problems in the past. I talked on the phone with Mrs. Bartlett, and she was kind enough to arrange my trip to Savannah. She even rented a car and put me up at the bed-and-breakfast on Abercorn Street last night. I completely understand if you don't want a houseguest for the—"

"Ken arranged for the car and lodging," Mrs. Fairmont interrupted. "If you ask me, he's a saint for putting up with Christine. Fortunately, the boys take after their father."

"Yes ma'am. But I want to be completely honest with you. This meeting was a setup."

Mrs. Fairmont eyed me as she had at the door upon my arrival.

"Do you like Flip?" she asked.

"Yes ma'am."

"More important," she said with emphasis, "he likes you. I've never seen him take to a stranger like he has to you."

"I'm used to being around animals. They know a lot more than we give them credit for."

"Yes, they do. How long will you be in Savannah this summer?"

I gave her the dates of my employment with the law firm.

"Would you be willing to stay in the downstairs apartment?"

"Yes ma'am," I said, startled.

Mrs. Fairmont leaned forward. "If you stay downstairs, it means Flip will have to sleep with me."

"Yes ma'am," I replied, smiling. "It would be a sacrifice on your part, but you would have no other reasonable option."

"And you're not wanting to be paid anything?"

"No ma'am. Although I'll be willing to help around the house."

"You've proven that this morning when you didn't have to."

Mrs. Bartlett returned with a peach-colored bath towel in her hand. "Will this one do? It was underneath the nice ones."

Mrs. Fairmont nodded. "Yes, and Miss Taylor and I have agreed that she will spend the summer with me."

Mrs. Bartlett's mouth dropped open. "But you were adamant—"

"Oh, that was the multi-infarct dementia speaking," Mrs. Fairmont replied lightly. "I'm in my right mind now. Miss Taylor, didn't you say your first name was Tami?"

"Yes ma'am."

"I can see how it will be positive for Tami and me if she spends evenings and nights here. I suggested the downstairs apartment, and she agreed."

"What about the dog?" Mrs. Bartlett asked.

"I'll find a comfortable place for him." Mrs. Fairmont winked at me.

I spread the towel on the sofa and sat down.

"Tell me more about your family, especially your twin sisters," Mrs. Fairmont said. "I went to school with twins, and we've been friends ever since."

FORTY-FIVE MINUTES LATER Mrs. Bartlett patted me on the arm as we left.

"Well, you're going to be a successful lawyer if you can manipulate people like you did my mother."

"I didn't manipulate her. I told her the truth."

"I'm sure. And nothing but the truth." Mrs. Bartlett sniffed. "Somehow, you got Mother to do what we wanted and made her think it was her idea. That's hard to do."

I didn't try to argue. We made a jerky trip back to the bed-and-breakfast. Mrs. Bartlett stopped the car in front of the inn and called her husband.

"Ken can't meet us," Mrs. Bartlett said after a brief conversation. "He's had something come up. But Mother already called him and told him that you were going to be her guest for the summer. Can you imagine her being that excited about it?"

"I'm looking forward to staying with her too."

"I'll be running on my way," Mrs. Bartlett said. "I wouldn't want to bore you with my activities of the day."

"From now on should I contact you or your mother?"

"Try Mother first; here's her number." Mrs. Bartlett took a card from her purse and wrote it down.

"Mother's first name is Margaret, but her close friends call her Maggie."

"I'm sure I'll be more comfortable with Mrs. Fairmont."

"Of course. She can be contrary at times, but after your performance this morning, I doubt you'll have any problems with her. The fact that you could handle that vicious dog of hers was very impressive."

I opened the door of the car and got out. "Please tell Mr. Bartlett how much I appreciate the arrangements you made for my trip."

With a wave of her hand, Mrs. Bartlett sped away from the curb. I went to my room, cleaned up, and changed into a long blue skirt, yellow short-sleeved blouse, and white tennis shoes. I packed my suitcase and garment bag and carried them downstairs.

"Do you know where the law offices of Braddock, Appleby, and Carpenter are located?" I asked the hostess on duty.

"It's on Montgomery Street." She drew a map. A different porter than the young man who'd helped me the previous evening carried my luggage to the car.

It took about five minutes to reach the law firm. A prominent, brick-framed white sign in front announced "Braddock, Appleby, and Carpenter—Attorneys at Law." I pulled into a parking lot covered with ornamental pavers. Several nice cars were in the lot, but none as fancy as my convertible.

The office was a two-story structure built of old brick with a slate roof and lots of windows framed by dark shutters. Two balconies were inset at either end of the second floor. The entrance was guarded by a set of small stone lions in front of large wooden double doors. Everything about the place spoke of prosperity and attention to detail. Mr. Callahan's chipped white office in Powell Station couldn't have served as a storage shed for this building. I wanted to peek inside, but I wasn't dressed for success and didn't want to give a wrong first impression.

The reality of what lay ahead hit me.

I wasn't admiring just another nice building. I was parked at the place where I would be working in a few weeks and, if God granted me favor and success, be employed for many years to come. I imagined myself walking into the office wearing the blue suit I'd worn to Mr. Callahan's office. But a blue suit wouldn't banish fear. Inside the beautiful office would be people smarter than me, more sophisticated than me, and better able to excel in the legal community than me. My mouth suddenly went dry.

I'd made a terrible mistake. I needed one more summer at the chicken plant before venturing into the world on my own.

I heard the sound of a motorcycle turning into the parking area. It was bright red with a fat rear tire. The rider crouched over the handlebars, circled in front of my car, then drove directly toward me. I reached over to start the engine, but the rider held up his hand. He was wearing a red helmet with white Mercury wings on either side. He turned off the motorcycle. I didn't want to get into a conversation with a member of a local motorcycle gang. The rider took off his helmet and approached. To my surprise, he was a nice-looking young man in his twenties with blue eyes and light brown hair bound in a very short ponytail. He was wearing blue jeans and black boots.

"I'm visiting and about to leave," I said.

"Who were you visiting?" he asked.

"No one. This is where I'm going to be working in a few weeks. I've got to go."

"Then I'll see you soon. I'm one of the lawyers."

"You're a lawyer?"

The man released the band that held his hair and ran his fingers through it.

"And a motorcycle rider," he replied. "Nice car."

"It's a rental."

"It's still a nice car." He stuck a tanned hand over the side of the car. "I'm Zach Mays, an associate with the firm."

I remembered his name on the letterhead. Zachary L. Mays. He was near the bottom of the list of attorneys. There was an asterisk beside his name and a reference indicating that he was also licensed to practice law in California.

"Tami Taylor, one of the summer clerks."

"I heard the firm was bringing in a clerk or two. What did you think of the offices?"

"I didn't go inside. I just wanted to know how to find it."

"I can give you a tour. One of my jobs as an associate is to make sure summer clerks have a positive experience with the firm."

"No, thanks. I'm sure you have a lot of work to do."

"There's always work to do. Come on." He pointed to the other cars. "None of the named partners are here. And there isn't anything on my desk that can't wait a few minutes."

I still wanted to drive off, but he reached out and opened the car door.

"No, Mr. Mays," I said. "I'd rather not."

He laughed. "Call me Zach. Save that title for the real bosses."

The young man didn't let go of the car door. I had no options. Self-conscious about my clothes and hoping my face wasn't red, I got out of the car.

"Okay, but I won't take much of your time. I don't want to impose."

"It's not an imposition. I know how tough it is to come from law school into an environment like this. It hasn't been that long since I was a summer clerk."

We walked across the parking lot. Beautiful flowers, bushes, and ornamental trees surrounded the building.

"Did you clerk here?" I asked.

"No, Los Angeles. I went to law school at Pepperdine and worked for a firm in the city with a big admiralty practice."

I'd heard of the law school but didn't know anything about it.

"I've been in Savannah for two years," he continued.

"How do you like it?"

"It's different from Los Angeles."

We passed the guardian lions. Zach swiped a card through a security device, and I heard the door click. He held it open for me.

We entered a high lobby open to the top of the building. The floors were covered in dark wood, and a curving staircase led to the second floor. Oriental rugs and ornate furniture were arranged throughout the area.

"This is amazing!" I exclaimed.

"And from what the partners tell me, it's paid for. Follow me. Downstairs is where the elite hang out."

Zach led me through the lower level that contained the partners' offices and two conference rooms. After seeing the lobby, I wasn't surprised at the opulence at every turn.

"Where is your office?" I asked.

"Upstairs. Do you want to take the elevator or the stairs?"

"I think the stairs are more elegant."

"Tell me about yourself," Zach said as we made our way back to the lobby.

"I'm a second-year student at Georgia and grew up in a rural area in the northern part of the state."

Zach glanced at me. "When you're asked that kind of question this summer you need to open up a lot more. People want to learn about you so they can decide whether you'll be a fit for the firm after you graduate."

"That makes sense."

The staircase was designed for a woman wearing a regal gown. However, the upstairs was a different world. In both directions there were open areas divided into small cubicles. It was like a beehive.

"This is where a lot of work takes place," Zach said. "Except for the partners' executive assistants, all the clerical, word processing, and bookkeeping is performed here." He pointed to an enclosed office. "That's where the office manager works."

"Ms. Patrick?"

"Right."

We came to a row of small, separate offices, each with its own window. Several of the doors were closed.

"These are for the associates and top paralegals. The closed doors mean someone is pretending to work on a Saturday."

"Why do you say pretending?"

Zach stopped, knocked on a closed door, and opened it before anyone inside could respond. A young woman dressed in casual clothes was sitting behind her desk with papers spread out in front of her and a dictation unit in her hand.

"This is Myra Dean, a paralegal in the litigation department," Zach said. "She is working, not pretending."

He introduced me.

"Sorry to interrupt," I said.

"No problem," she replied in a voice with a Midwestern accent. "Zach should have known I wouldn't be sitting here reading the sports page."

"Except in the fall when Ohio State is playing football."

The woman smiled. "On my own time."

Zach closed the door and continued down the hall.

"Myra was a bad choice to catch goofing off. She's in Joe Carpenter's group. If she wasn't a hard worker, she wouldn't have lasted a week."

He stopped at another closed door. "This is a sure bet."

He knocked and opened. A balding man was sitting with his feet propped up on his desk and holding a book about golf.

"Zach, knock and wait for an answer before barging in here!" he snapped before he saw me. "Oh, who's your lady friend?"

"Tami Taylor, one of our summer clerks. Just giving her a tour. This is Barry Conrad. He works in the transactions area."

Conrad held up the book. "And on my slice. Are you a golfer, Ms. Taylor? It's a great way to develop client relations."

"No, I play basketball."

Conrad looked at Zach. "Do we have any clients who play basketball?"

"I don't know. Who's paying for your golf study?"

"The firm. I'm billing it to professional development. Mr. Braddock wants me on the course at four o'clock this afternoon with the management team for Forester Shipping Lines. If I don't do something about my driver and hold up my end of our foursome, it could cost us thousands."

"Keep your shoulders square to the ball and don't rotate your hips too soon," Zach said, adopting a pretend golf stance.

"Get out of here."

We left the office, and Zach shut the door.

"Is Mr. Conrad a partner?"

"No, he's a permanent associate. He swallowed his pride when he wasn't asked to join the firm. It's not a bad life. The pay is good by Savannah standards, and there's no management responsibility."

"How long has he been here?"

"Maybe fifteen years." Zach added, "That's fifteen years averaging fifty to sixty hours a week working plus time spent in his office reading a golf manual or following his fantasy football team."

We stopped before an open door.

"This is my space," he said. "Come in and have a seat."

I hesitated. "I really need to be on my way."

Zach held up his right index finger and shook it. "What is lesson number one?"

"Open up and tell about myself when asked a question by one of the lawyers."

"Good. Rule number two. Don't miss an opportunity to talk to one of the lawyers when given the chance to do so. We're all busy and won't ask you to spend a few minutes with us unless we intend to use it efficiently."

"Yes sir."

"Don't call me sir or mister. My name is Zach."

"Okay."

"Come in."

He led the way into a small office. Directly in front of me was a window that overlooked the parking lot. I could see my car with Zach's motorcycle beside it. Two miniature motorcycles rested on the front of the lawyer's desk. In neat rows on the wall were framed diplomas and other certificates.

On the corner of his desk facing me was a picture of a very attractive young woman with a white flower in her blonde hair. Next to that picture was a photograph of an older couple I guessed to be his parents. The man in the picture had long hair that was gray around the edges, and the woman was wearing a dress that would have looked in style in the late 1970s. Zach picked up a legal pad and took a pen from the top drawer of his desk.

"Tell me about your spiritual journey," he said.

"My spiritual journey?" I asked in surprise.

"Yes, it's an allowable question under the antidiscrimination guidelines."

"Why do you think I have a spiritual journey?"

Zach held up three fingers. "Rule three about being a successful summer clerk. Never answer a question in a way that makes you seem evasive. It's easy to spot a phony. Better to be forthright and honest than beat around the bush and give what you think is a politically correct answer that will help you land a job upon graduation."

"I'd never do that."

"Good. Start by giving me a straight answer."

I sat up in my chair. A head-on challenge required fearlessness in the face of attack. Zach Mays probably didn't have the power to revoke the summer job offer, but even if he did, I wouldn't compromise.

"I've been a Christian since I prayed with my mother at the altar of our church when I was a little girl."

"Did your spiritual journey stop there?"

"No, it's a lifetime relationship with Jesus Christ that affects every aspect of life. I'm always trying to learn and grow."

"Do you believe there are other ways for sincere people to find God?"

"No, there is only one way."

"It's your way or the highway?"

I didn't like to be mocked, but it was part of the persecution of the righteous. At least I knew where I stood when an assault came.

"My beliefs aren't based on my opinions. The Bible says that Jesus is the way, the truth, and the life. No one can come to the Father except through him."

"Doesn't that sound narrow-minded?"

"It is narrow-minded. But truth doesn't depend on popular consensus or opinion polls. The Bible also says the road that leads to eternal life is narrow, and only a few find it. Pretending that someone who tries to live a good life or believes in the god of another religion will make it into heaven is a cruel deception."

"And you're convinced about your religious perspective?"

"Enough to tell you what I believe without beating around the bush." I looked directly into his eyes and took a deep breath. "If you had a wreck on your motorcycle later today and died on the side of the road, would you go to heaven?"

The corner of the lawyer's lips curled up. Whether in a smile or a sneer, I couldn't tell. He pointed to the picture of the beautiful woman on his desk.

"Who do you think that is?"

"I don't know."

"That's my older sister. She's a nurse at a clinic in Zambia."

I wasn't going to be easily deterred. "My question deserves an answer."

Zach ignored me. "She's a missionary in Africa."

"A Christian missionary?"

"Yes."

"Has she talked to you the same way I am?"

The lawyer shook his head. "No, actually, I'm the one who led her to faith in Jesus Christ. It happened at a summer camp for homeschoolers we attended in Oregon. One year she realized the faith of our parents had to become real for her."

I sat back in the chair. "You were homeschooled?"

"Since kindergarten. The first time I entered a public school classroom was to take a course at a local community college when I was sixteen. My high school graduation was sponsored by a homeschool association in Southern California."

I couldn't believe what I was hearing. I pointed to the picture of the older couple. "Your parents?"

"Yes. They were part of the Jesus movement and lived in a Christian commune for a number of years."

"A Christian commune?"

"Yep. Remember how the early believers in the book of Acts didn't claim any private property but held everything in common for the good of all?"

"Yes."

"That's what my parents and some of their friends did. Does your church believe that part of the Bible?"

"We believe every word of the Bible."

"Do you follow the part about sharing everything with other Christians?"

"Not exactly the same way, but we give to people in need. Members of the church have helped me financially even though they didn't have to."

"That's good, but it's not having all things in common. My parents held on to the ideal for years but gave up on group Christianity when I was about ten years old. After that, we lived in the same area as people in our fellowship, but every family had its own checkbook. It takes a zealous group of believers to be biblical in every aspect of their lifestyle."

I'd always considered myself and those like me the epitome of zeal, not in a prideful way, but in humble recognition of our responsibility to walk in the light given us. Suddenly, new biblical revelation I'd not considered loomed before me like a fog bank.

"What are you thinking?" the lawyer asked, interrupting my thoughts.

"Do I have to reveal my secret thoughts as part of the interview process?"

"No."

"And you haven't been taking notes."

The lawyer laughed. It was a pleasant sound.

"I won't be preparing a memo to Mr. Carpenter about the details of this conversation. It would require too much background information that he wouldn't understand."

"So why did you ask your spiritual journey question?"

Zach smiled. "I could tell that your beliefs dictated the way you dress. But your preferences could have been caused by a lot of things."

"It's not a preference; it's a conviction," I responded firmly. "We believe in modesty for women and that there should be a difference between the sexes in clothing. Women should wear skirts or dresses."

"You've never worn blue jeans?"

"Not one day in my life."

The lawyer started to speak, then closed his mouth. "I'll have time this summer to learn more about you," he said.

His comment made me feel like an insect under a microscope. I looked for an air of judgment or condemnation on his face but didn't detect it. As we walked out of the building, I told him we shared the common bond of a homeschool education.

"Until I attended the local high school," I said.

"And played basketball?"

"Yes. I'm on an intramural team now."

Outside, it was a pleasant day with a breeze blowing. The humidity of the previous afternoon had been swept away. Zach opened the car door for me. I hesitated.

"What brought you to Savannah?" I asked. "It's a long way from Southern California."

"We'll save that for later."

"But that violates rule number one."

Zach smiled. "Rules don't apply to me."

9

Moses Jones awoke to the sound of footsteps on the dock. He opened his eyes and peered through the mosquito netting. It was early morning with a heavy fog rising from the surface of the river. The fog covered the dock and kept him from seeing in the dim light. A different fear crawled over the gunwale of the boat.

"Who be there?" he called out, his voice trembling slightly. "That you, Mr. Floyd? I done told you, she ain't here!"

"Chatham County Sheriff's Department. What's your name?"

Moses sat up in the boat and pulled back the netting. Two sets of dark brown pants, khaki shirts, and shiny black shoes came into view. When he could make out faces, he saw two young deputies—one white, the other black. He took a deep breath and relaxed. These were flesh-and-blood men.

"Moses Jones, boss man."

The black deputy spoke. "Who gave you permission to tie up at this dock?"

Moses looked at the rope looped over the wooden piling. He couldn't deny his boat was connected to the dock. He quickly appealed to a broader reality.

"The river. It don't belong to nobody," he said.

"The river belongs to the State of Georgia," the same deputy responded. "And this dock belongs to the folks who live in that house over there."

Moses peered through the mist but couldn't see a house.

"Don't strain your eyes," the white deputy said. "There is a house there, and the people who live there built this dock, which is private property. You're trespassing."

"No sir. I didn't set one foot on this here dock. I've just been a-sleeping in my boat, not bothering nobody but myself."

"Do you have any identification?" the black deputy asked.

"I ain't got no driver's license. I don't own a car."

The deputy pointed to the white bucket in the front of the boat. "What's in that bucket?"

"Two little ol' fish that I'll cook for my dinner," Moses replied, then had an idea. "Would you gents like 'em? They're nice-size croakers, plenty of meat and plenty of bones."

"Are you trying to bribe us?" the white deputy asked.

"Uh, no sir, boss man. I'm just sharing my catch."

"We don't want your fish," the black deputy said. "Do you have a fishing license?"

"Yes sir. I sure do. I be totally legal."

Moses kept his fishing license in the bottom of his tackle box. He opened the box and rummaged around until he found it. He handed it up to the deputy, who inspected it.

"This expired two months ago."

Moses' face fell. "I guess the date slipped right past me. What are y'all going to do to me?"

The two deputies glanced at each other. The black one spoke.

"Mr. Jones, there are surveillance cameras on several docks up and down this stretch of the river. A man fitting your description has been illegally tying up his boat for months, and a lot of people have complained. We're going to have to take you to the jail."

"What about my boat?"

"It will be confiscated as evidence," the white deputy replied.

"What do that mean?"

The black deputy spoke. "It will go to the jail compound too. We'll keep it in the lot where we put stolen cars."

"But this boat ain't stole! It was give me by Jabo Nettles, the bartender who used to work at the Bayside Tavern. He got to where he couldn't use it 'cause of his sugar."

"Do you have a registration for it?"

"What's that?" Moses asked, bewildered.

"Mr. Jones, get out of the boat and come with us."

SUNDAY MORNINGS, I usually stayed at my apartment. There wasn't a church in the area similar to my church in Powell Station, and I preferred solitude with God to apostate religion. I had a drawer full of cassette tapes of sermons by Pastor Vick and guest preachers at our church. I'd listened to some of them so many times that I'd almost memorized the messages.

Two men from the rental car company came to pick up the convertible. I'd carefully checked the car to make sure it hadn't been scratched or dinged by another vehicle. It was a good lesson in the burden imposed by the objects of wealth. Watching after them was a hassle.

"How fast did you get it up to?" one of the men asked as he checked the mileage.

"Not above the speed limit."

The man looked at his coworker and rolled his eyes. "And I only had two beers last night. High-performance cars like this have to be pushed every so often to keep them running right. Use or lose it."

The other man eyed me. "Isn't that right, sweetheart?"

I set my jaw. "Do you want me to contact the district manager of your company and ask him why one of his employees called me 'sweetheart'?"

The man held out his hand. "I was only trying to be friendly."

"Professional would be a better goal." I put the car keys in his palm. "Thanks for picking up the car."

I peeked out the window of my apartment and could see the two men shaking their heads as they talked about me. Modest apparel helped keep males at bay, but it wasn't armor that prevented all attacks. The closest I'd come to physical harm happened in high school. One of the boys on the basketball team surprised me with a crude grab around the waist and attempted to kiss me on the lips while we walked in the dark from the gym to the bus. He received a stinging right hand to the cheek that knocked him back a couple of steps and left a mark I could see the following day at school.

After the men from the car rental company left, I spent the remainder of the afternoon reading a devotional book written by a sixteenth-century Puritan writer. The old saints had a better grasp of the demands of the gospel than contemporary Christians. In Oliver Cromwell's era, believers like my family would have found a welcome seat around the cultural campfire. Sometimes, I felt like I'd been born 350 years too late.

As soon as the sun set I called home. Mama held the phone so Daddy could listen. I told them about the rental car without the detail that it was a convertible and described the bed-and-breakfast simply as a clean place to stay. I provided a lot more information about my meeting with Mrs. Fairmont. Mama interrupted when I told about Flip and the use of my dress to save the rug.

"I never made you clean up a spill with your dress," she said.

"But you made me willing to do it. There's no telling what the rug on the floor was worth. I'm presoaking the dress in the sink right now. I think the stain will come out."

"And don't get any ideas about bringing a Chihuahua into our house," Daddy added. "I can tell you liked the little fellow, but if a dog can't scare possums away from the chicken coop or chase squirrels out of the cornfield, it won't find a place around our table."

"When was the last time Flip and Ginger ate in the kitchen?" I asked.

"You know what I mean," he replied.

I could picture the twinkle in his eyes.

"I won't bring home a pet without permission," I reassured him. "But a house dog might be just what you and Mama need after we're all grown and on our own."

"That's a ways off," Mama said. "Emma and Ellie seem slow to mature. Yesterday they got in an argument that would have shamed a pair of five-year-olds."

"The relationship between Mrs. Bartlett and her mother lacked maturity too," I said.

Mama and Daddy listened as I told them about my honesty with Mrs. Fairmont and her response.

"That cleared the way for her to ask me to live with her," I said. "What do you think?"

As soon as the question escaped my lips, I realized I'd made a terrible mistake. I'd accepted the invitation to live with Mrs. Fairmont without obtaining my parents' permission. It was an amazing lapse of protocol for an unmarried woman. Letting me make the decision to work in Savannah for the summer did not give me unfettered authority over my life. I could hear Daddy and Mama talking softly to each other on the other end of the line but couldn't make out what they were saying. If they rejected the arrangement, I would have no option but to call Mrs. Fairmont and Mrs. Bartlett and ask their forgiveness for prematurely acting without permission. Daddy spoke.

"Go ahead and stay with Mrs. Fairmont if you have peace about it. But don't be surprised if her daughter gives you trouble at some point."

"Yes sir," I said with relief. "I'll try to be a blessing to both of them, and it will help me save more money for the school year."

After my near miss on the Mrs. Fairmont issue, I decided not to mention my visit to the law firm. Mama would cross-examine me closely, and I wasn't prepared to discuss Zach Mays' comment concerning the communal lifestyle of Christians in the book of Acts or in Southern California in the 1970s and 1980s. It was a lot easier telling Mama and Daddy how much I loved them and ending the call.

RELIEVED THAT I'D FOUND A PLACE to live during the summer, I spent the final weeks of the school year in a sleep-deprived blur of academic activity. Second-year scores were very important because they would be part of a student's academic record during the fall hiring season. Post–law school job offers at firms like Braddock, Appleby, and Carpenter were often contingent on maintaining a certain level of academic achievement. I wanted to do well for several reasons, but especially because God's children, like the prophet Daniel in pagan Babylon, should excel.

Our basketball team finished the season undefeated. The other girls accepted my explanation about the convertible but gave me a nickname—Jaguar. I talked twice with Mrs. Fairmont, who agreed that the Friday before I started work on Monday would be a good time to arrive in Savannah. Daddy would help me move.

The night before Daddy was going to come help me, I began separating my belongings into two piles, one for Savannah, the other to be stored in Powell Station. Before unplugging my computer, I checked my e-mail. I had a message from Mrs. Bartlett.

Hi, Tami,

Change of plans. Another one of Mother's friends died today. Can you believe it! The poor woman dropped dead in the dining room at The Cloister. Her funeral is going to be in Brunswick late Saturday afternoon. Mother is going down there tomorrow to stay with the family and won't be back until Sunday. We'll be at the house by 2:00 p.m. See you then.

Christine Bartlett

I read the e-mail three times, trying to twist an alternate meaning from it. Mrs. Bartlett expected Daddy and me to haul my belongings to Savannah on the Sabbath. I didn't like putting my suitcase in a car on Sunday. I quickly wrote her back.

Dear Mrs. Bartlett,

My father is taking off work to help me move on Friday. Could arrangements be made to allow us into the house tomorrow? After unloading my things, I could stay in a motel until Sunday if you prefer. Please allow me to do this. It would be greatly appreciated.

Sincerely,
Tami Taylor

I prayed hard for fifteen seconds and sent the e-mail. I began packing my things in marked boxes but left my computer running. My anxiety level rose higher and higher. I checked the computer five times before a response came from Mrs. Bartlett. My heart pounded as I opened it.

Tami,

Got your message but it won't work. See you Sunday.

Christine Bartlett

I sat down on my bed too frustrated to cry. I couldn't handle something as simple as arranging the date of arrival for my summer job. I kicked myself for sending an e-mail instead of calling. I would have had a better chance of appeal on the phone. I had no option but to ask Mama and Daddy what to do. Daddy answered the phone.

"I'm looking forward to seeing you," he began as soon as he heard my voice. "I worked overtime earlier this week so I wouldn't have to take but two hours of vacation. I'll be on the road as soon as the sun rises."

"There's a problem," I said. "We can't go tomorrow. One of Mrs. Fairmont's friends died, and she'll be out of town. The house won't be open until Sunday afternoon."

"Sunday afternoon?"

"Yes sir."

There was silence on the other end of the line.

"What am I going to do?" I asked as tears now threatened to break to the surface.

"Have you talked to the law firm about starting work on Tuesday? I could try to change my schedule at the plant and ask off on Monday."

"I just found out tonight. I could call the law firm tomorrow. But what if they're not willing to be flexible?"

"Call anyway." Daddy paused. "I know you want to honor the Lord's Day and keep it holy."

"With all my heart. It's just hard when there are other people involved."

"Every test is an opportunity," he replied.

It was one of Daddy's sayings, a call to be optimistic about any problem. It always sounded more convincing in theory than in practice.

We agreed to talk in the morning. Daddy would delay going to work until I talked to someone at the law firm. After the call ended I didn't have the heart to continue packing but did so by faith. The Lord commanded the Israelites to prepare to leave Egypt even though the way to the Promised Land would be fraught with perils.

I spent most of my prayer time early the following morning asking for God's favor upon my call to the law firm. I debated whether to appeal directly to Joe Carpenter, but since I'd never talked to him I asked for Gerry Patrick instead. It was barely 8:01 a.m. Fortunately, Ms. Patrick was in.

"Good morning, Tami," she began in a chipper voice. "Christine Bartlett is thrilled that you're going to be staying with her mother. It sounds like you really impressed both of them."

"Yes ma'am, but there is a problem with my move from Athens to Savannah."

"What sort of problem?"

I explained the delay due to the death of Mrs. Fairmont's friend. "Would it be possible for me to start work on Tuesday?"

"When did you say Mrs. Fairmont will be home?"

I hadn't mentioned the day. I swallowed. "Sunday afternoon."

"Can't you move in on Sunday?"

"I'd rather do it on Monday."

"The firm has arranged a special catered luncheon for the summer clerks on Monday. All the partners and associates will be there, and with vacation schedules, it may be the only time this summer when everyone will be together," she continued with emphasis. "The one day you need to be here is Monday. A key part of the summer clerk program is the opportunity for the partners to get to know you."

I remembered Zach Mays' rules. "Yes ma'am. I'm aware of that. I want to meet people."

"Good. Then you'll be here?"

In desperation, an idea was born. "Ms. Patrick, are you Jewish?" I asked.

"Yes."

"Do you keep the Sabbath?"

"Not as strictly as my rabbi uncle in Fort Lauderdale would like me to," she said after a brief silence.

I took a deep breath. "I'm a Christian, and my family keeps Sunday as our Sabbath. We don't do any work on Sunday and spend the time after church services in rest and spiritual reflection. It would violate my religious convictions to move my furniture on Sunday."

"I'm not familiar with the New Testament teaching on the Sabbath."

It wasn't a question, and the inflection in Ms. Patrick's voice didn't sound like a request for a biblical explanation.

"Are you asking for a religious accommodation under the federal antidiscrimination laws?" she continued coldly.

"No ma'am," I answered hurriedly. "I'm not raising a legal issue or trying to put the firm in an awkward position. I'm appealing to you as a person. I've agonized over this ever since I received the news from Mrs. Bartlett last night."

"And I don't question your sincerity. But I'm not sure I can give you an answer. I'll need to check with Mr. Carpenter and let you know what he says."

My heart sank. No matter how well Ms. Patrick tried to explain my position, the reaction of one of the senior partners to my predicament was easy to imagine.

"Could you talk to Zach Mays instead?" I asked. "I realize he's an associate, but he understands something about my background."

"Zach Mays? How do you know him?"

I had no choice but to mention my brief visit to the office.

"Can you stay on the line while I see if he's in the office?" she asked.

"Yes ma'am."

While I waited on hold, I listened to classical music. It was a Bach organ concerto, composed to the glory of the God, whose laws the world now tried to ignore. It was a moment of musical irony. Ms. Patrick returned.

"I mentioned your dilemma to Zach. He thinks you should definitely be at the luncheon on Monday and offered to solve your religious objection by meeting you at Mrs. Fairmont's house on Sunday to unload the furniture for you. He also suggested that you read a verse from the New Testament about an ox falling in a ditch on the Sabbath and the owner pulling it out. I wrote down the reference—Luke 14:5."

"Is he also willing to load the truck in Athens?" I asked, chafing at the young lawyer's advice. "My ox is in two ditches at once."

"He didn't mention it. Do you want me to connect you to him?"

"No ma'am. I'm sorry. It's nice of him to offer to help."

"Zach is a fine young man and an excellent lawyer. There's no pretense with him."

"I'll call my father and get his advice. He's the one who will be helping me move. Oh, and please don't mention this to Mr. Carpenter. I wouldn't want to trouble him."

"I can't promise confidentiality," Ms. Patrick responded stiffly. "Everything related to personnel issues is an open topic for the partners. That's a part of my job."

"Yes ma'am. I understand. I'll call back later today."

I ended the call. People who didn't want to honor the Sabbath used Luke 14:5 as an excuse for just about any activity. I phoned home. Mama answered.

"Is Daddy still there?" I asked.

"Yes, I'll get him."

"We're both here," Mama said after a few moments.

I told them about my conversation with Ms. Patrick, leaving out Zach Mays. Daddy spoke.

"We prayed about the situation last night and this morning," he said. "Your mother and I both agree that this is a Luke 14:5 situation. The ox represents your livelihood, and now that you tell us about the Monday luncheon, it's clear you need to be there. If the only way to make sure that happens is for us to move your things on Sunday, then that's what we'll do. I'll be at your apartment by ten in the morning. Try to have all your boxes ready by sundown on Saturday."

"Yes sir," I mumbled.

"What?" Mama asked.

"Thank you," I said. "See you then."

10

WHEN DADDY ARRIVED, I THREW OPEN THE DOOR OF THE apartment and ran out to greet him before he turned off the motor. I threw my arms around his neck as soon as his feet touched the asphalt.

"Well, that's a nice welcome," he said.

"It's good to see you, Daddy," I said. "Sorry about what I'm putting you through."

He kissed the top of my head in the usual spot.

"Don't mention it again. Let's get your ox out of the ditch and load him on the truck."

All the stuff going to Powell Station was loaded in the front of the truck. To the rear was the furniture I would use in Mrs. Fairmont's basement apartment, my summer clothes, pots, pans, and dishes, toiletries, and books to occupy my free time in the evenings. Daddy's foot was bothering him, so I jumped in and out of the truck to arrange the load. When we finished, Daddy tied a blue tarp over the top of the pile and lashed it down.

"There's a chance of rain this afternoon as we get near the coast," he said.

WE LEFT TOWN and followed the same route I'd taken to Savannah. Being with Daddy, my spirits lifted. I liked riding with him in Kyle's truck ten times better than driving an expensive convertible with the top down. As we rolled along, I asked question after question about the family.

"Bobby starts at the chicken plant tomorrow," Daddy said.

"Is he going to be an eviscerator?"

"No, it wouldn't be good to throw him in with all those ladies. He's going to work on the loading dock."

"Coming in or going out?"

Dealing with frozen dead birds in cardboard cartons was much easier than the noise and stench of the live ones in wire-mesh crates.

"Coming in," Daddy replied.

Kyle's truck didn't have air-conditioning, and the late spring air blowing through the window was warm. I brushed a strand of hair from my face and returned it to the ponytail behind my head. I looked at Daddy. He was a relaxed driver, not stressed by the responsibilities of being on the road. Before he met Mama, he worked for a couple of years as a long-distance truck driver.

"What was it like driving across the country?" I asked.

"I liked it. But once I got married, I didn't want to be away from your mama for weeks at a time. Then when you came along, I had to come home every night and plant a new kiss on top of your head."

"What did you do about driving on Sunday?"

"My partner did it. He was a Seventh-Day Adventist. I drove on Saturday; he drove on Sunday. It worked out good for both of us."

"Did you ever go to California?"

"Los Angeles."

"What was it like?"

"Oh, the land out there is dry but green where they irrigate. It made me think about the verses in the Bible where the desert blooms like a rose. It's a fragile place. Unless people pipe in water, not much can live there. There are trees up in the mountains, but no forests on the flats."

"What about the city?"

He shrugged. "Every truck terminal is the same whether it's in Omaha or L.A. I couldn't tell you much about Los Angeles except that once it started it never seemed to stop. I never made it all the way to the Pacific. We'd drop a load, eat a steak at a truck stop, and head back."

I stared out the window. Trees had always been part of the landscape of my world. I wondered if there were trees where Zach Mays' family lived.

"One of the attorneys at the firm in Savannah is from Los Angeles," I said.

"How did he get to Georgia?"

"I'm not sure."

We stopped for gas.

"Do you want me to drive?" I asked.

Daddy stretched and rubbed the back of his neck. "That would be nice. I talk about being a long-distance truck driver, but those days are long gone."

The gears on Kyle's truck grated when I started off. Once I reached highway speed, Daddy leaned against the door frame and went to sleep. His ability to catch a nap at a moment's notice amazed me. He could stretch out on a blanket beneath the poplar tree in front of the house and doze off within seconds. Flip and Ginger would see him and curl up at his feet.

A small convoy of large trucks passed us, and I thought about Daddy driving across the country. I wondered what other dreams he'd sacrificed to be home at night to kiss me on the top of the head. Like Daddy's truck-driving career, my summer job at the law firm in Savannah might be no more than a detour through Los Angeles on the way to a greater good.

Daddy didn't wake up until we were close to the coast. He sat up and blinked his eyes as we passed a mileage marker.

"Did that say twenty miles to Savannah?" he asked.

"Yes sir. You must have been really tired."

"It's been a long week. Your mama got her money's worth out of me yesterday. I spent several hours in the crawl space underneath the house spreading tar paper on the ground and treating for termites. Do you want me to take over?"

"Yes sir, I'll pull off at the next exit. I don't trust myself shifting gears on the short streets of Savannah."

WE ENTERED the historic section of the city, and I gave directions.

"You already know your way around pretty good," he said as we made the third turn in four blocks.

"Yes sir. It's not far to her house."

The spring flowers I'd enjoyed during my first visit were giving way to summer's less-vibrant colors. Daddy had never been to Savannah.

"It doesn't remind me at all of Los Angeles," he said as we passed the James Oglethorpe statue in Chippewa Square.

"It's not Powell Station either," I said, wiping perspiration from my forehead. "There aren't any mountain breezes."

We made a final turn, and I pointed to the house.

"That's it, the one with the two large live oaks in front and ironwork up the steps. You can park at the curb."

"How is living in a fancy place like this going to affect you?" he asked as the truck rolled to a stop.

"Don't worry. I'll be living in the basement like a scullery maid."

Daddy didn't smile. "Don't underestimate the power of the world to pull you into its grip."

I pointed to my heart. "The truth you and Mama put in here is as alive as you are."

I led the way up the steps and pushed the doorbell. Mrs. Fairmont answered wearing an expensive blue dress with pearls around her neck and the same diamond rings on her fingers. I introduced her to Daddy. He shook her hand and bowed slightly.

"Hello, dear," she said to me. "Did you have car problems? I was expecting you yesterday."

My eyes opened wider. "No ma'am. I thought you were out of town at a friend's funeral. Mrs. Bartlett sent me an e-mail the other night telling me you wouldn't be home until this afternoon."

Mrs. Fairmont waved her hand in dismissal. "I told Christine about the change in plans. Didn't she get in touch with you? And it was a cousin who died, not a friend. The funeral was yesterday morning, and I came directly home. Sometimes Christine is worse about remembering than I am." The older woman's eyes brightened. "Today is a good day. I woke up feeling chipper this morning. How do you like my dress?"

"It's beautiful," I managed, still processing the information that Daddy and I could have driven to Savannah on Saturday.

"You have your father's eyes," Mrs. Fairmont said. "Come inside."

"But thankfully she mostly looks like her mother," Daddy said as we entered the foyer.

I turned to Daddy and mouthed an apology. He smiled and shook his head.

"Would you like to see Flip? I told him you were coming."

"Yes ma'am."

"Have a seat in the blue parlor while I get him. He's in the courtyard."

We went into the blue parlor. It was exactly the same except for a new arrangement of flowers. I heard the patter of little feet. Flip dashed into the room and began barking furiously. Daddy and I both lowered our hands in greeting. The little dog sniffed me briefly then spent more time examining the back of Daddy's hand. Daddy scratched the dog's neck.

"Another friend." Mrs. Fairmont beamed as she came into the room. "Your whole family must have a way with animals."

Mrs. Fairmont sat down, and Flip jumped into her lap.

"I never let him do that when Christine is here," she said. "Now, Mr. Taylor, I want to thank you for letting Tami stay with me this summer. Are there any instructions about her conduct you want to share with me? I've raised two children, imperfectly I must admit, but I'm willing to do what I can to help mold her character."

To my surprise, Daddy launched into a laundry list of guidelines, most of which would have been suitable for the twins. He included everything from cleaning my living area and helping with household chores to not staying out late at night and notifying Mrs. Fairmont when I wouldn't be home for supper. She nodded her head in agreement.

"That's very helpful," she replied when he finished. "I'll try, but you know how young people can be."

"Tammy is a fine young woman," Daddy replied. "All her mother and I ask is that you do the best you can. Now, we'd better unload her things from the truck."

Daddy got up from the chair and left the room. Slightly numb, I followed him outside.

"What was that all about?" I asked as soon as we reached the front steps. "Why mention all the rules to her? It sounded so juvenile."

Daddy put his hand on the side of the truck and faced me. "You'll do all those things and more, but it satisfied Mrs. Fairmont, didn't it?"

"Yes sir."

"It was for her benefit, not yours. She needs to see herself giving you more than a bed to sleep in at night."

We each carried a box into the house. Mrs. Fairmont was standing in the hallway with the door to the basement open.

"I'd better stay here," she said. "I don't want to chance my luck on the stairs."

Daddy followed me into the basement.

"It's a plain room," I whispered. "Mrs. Bartlett thinks the dog lives down here. It was rented out years ago when this was a boarding-house."

I pushed open the door and stopped in shock. The efficiency apartment had been completely redecorated with new carpeting and furniture. I peeked into the bedroom. Light streamed in onto a pretty twin bed. There was a white chest of drawers with matching night-stand. I opened the door to a bathroom that was sparkling clean.

"It's been totally redone," I marveled.

I bounded upstairs.

"Mrs. Fairmont, it's beautiful! You shouldn't have gone to so much trouble."

"Gracie and her nephews did all the work. It was fine as a hide-out for Flip when Christine came for a visit, but not fit for a young lady like you."

I leaned over and hugged her.

"Thank you," I said.

None of my secondhand furniture would look right in the garden apartment, so it only took thirty minutes to unload the truck. Everything else would spend the summer in Powell Station. It was work, but not as much as I'd expected. Mrs. Fairmont went into the den. Every time we passed the room on the way to the basement door, I could see her sitting in a chair, staring out the windows.

"I'll unpack the other things after the sun goes down," I said to Daddy after I hung my dresses up in a long, narrow closet in the bedroom.

We went upstairs. I knocked on the door frame of the den. "We're finished," I announced.

Mrs. Fairmont didn't respond. I couldn't see her face. I turned to Daddy, who gave me a questioning look. I walked softly across the room.

"Mrs. Fairmont? My father is leaving now. He'd like to say good-bye."

I reached the chair. Flip was curled up on the floor at Mrs. Fairmont's feet. The old woman continued staring. I reached down and gently touched her on the arm. She jerked so violently that I stepped back.

"I'm sorry," I said. "I didn't mean to startle you."

Mrs. Fairmont rubbed her temples. "I have a headache. Did you hear the bird flying around inside the house? We need to open all the doors and let it out. It came in through the veranda."

She pointed to a screened-in porch that overlooked the garden. I opened the door. All I saw was a set of beautiful wicker furniture and some green potted plants.

"Mrs. Fairmont," I said calmly, "there's not a bird in the house. The doors are all closed."

Mrs. Fairmont frowned and shook her head. "I heard it as plain as you talking right now. Be quiet and listen."

We were all silent. Mrs. Fairmont waited a few moments then sighed.

"It's gone." She looked up at me with sad eyes. "Or I had a hallucination. That can be part of my illness. What have I been doing?"

"Sitting in this chair and staring out the window while we brought in my things and put them in the basement."

"Gracie says I sit and stare at nothing. It's like my brain freezes up, and I don't know it. I'm so scared that I'll put something on the stove and won't watch it."

"Maybe I can cook for you," I said.

Mrs. Fairmont stared out the window in silence so long that I thought she'd had another brain freeze. She turned in her chair and saw Daddy. He stepped forward and gently took her hand in his.

"It was nice meeting you," he said. "I have to leave now. It's a long drive home."

"Yes, it is," she responded then continued staring.

Daddy and I quietly left the room.

"Her condition may be more serious than her daughter realizes," Daddy said as we walked down the front steps. "Keep a record of what happens for her family and the doctors. And pray there will be a chance to tell her about Jesus."

"Yes sir."

We reached the truck.

"Are you going to be okay on the drive?" I asked.

"Remember, I've hauled freight to California. The nap refilled my tank. I'll be in Powell Station by bedtime."

I longed to go with him. He hugged me and deposited a last kiss on the top of my head.

"Call us."

I nodded, not wanting to speak as emotion welled up in my heart. Daddy got in the truck and pulled away from the curb. I watched him leave, turned, and went inside the house.

Mrs. Fairmont was sitting in the den. She'd turned on the TV to an afternoon show. She muted the volume and motioned for me to come into the room.

"I'm better now," she said. "I drank a sip of water, and it washed away the cobwebs of my mind."

"That's good."

"But I know that water isn't the cure for what's wrong with me. Did I say anything stupid? I hate embarrassing myself."

"You were staring out the window," I answered slowly as I debated whether to mention the imaginary bird.

Mrs. Fairmont continued. "Your father is a good man. I can tell by the way he looks at you that he loves you very much."

"Yes ma'am. I'm blessed to have my family."

Mrs. Fairmont pointed at the TV. "This show is about children abandoned by fathers who turn up years later looking for a handout after the child becomes a financial success. What do you think about that?"

I watched the silent images of people pointing fingers and arguing with each other. The camera flashed to the studio audience, some of whom were on their feet yelling. It gave me a queasy feeling.

"That the producer of the TV show is more interested in entertainment than solutions. I wouldn't watch something like this."

Mrs. Fairmont glanced at me with a frown on her face. "You're probably right, but I want to hear what the host tells them to do. Why don't you go downstairs and finish unpacking your things."

I WENT DOWNSTAIRS but didn't unpack. My first action was to pray that God would spiritually cleanse the beautifully decorated apartment. I went into the bedroom and knelt beside the bed. I prayed for about thirty minutes, then turned my focus to Mrs. Fairmont.

The spiritual warfare to be fought for the elderly woman's eternal destiny was real, and I would need all the help heaven could muster. I asked God for grace and the ability to discern his voice directing my steps. A few seconds later, a deep male voice faintly called my name.

"Tami!"

I'd never heard the audible voice of God. My guidance had been less distinct, but nonetheless effective. I'd learned to trust the impressions that came to my spirit as divine communication, a birthright I enjoyed as one of God's children. Passages of Scripture about the experiences of Moses, Samuel, and Isaiah raced through my mind. I shut my eyes tighter and clenched my hands together. I quickly settled on the response of the boy Samuel when the Lord spoke to him in the middle of the night.

"Speak, Lord," I said under my breath. "Your servant is listening."

I waited. In a few seconds the voice spoke again, only louder.

"Tami Taylor!"

I kept my head bowed.

"Speak, Lord, for your servant is listening," I repeated.

I waited, but the voice didn't continue. The hair on the back of my neck stood up. I opened my eyes, but the narrow bedroom was empty. I heard a loud knock that made me jump.

"Are you in there?" the voice repeated. "It's Zach Mays from the law firm."

I looked toward heaven and saw nothing except the white ceiling. At least I now knew that God didn't talk like the young lawyer from California.

"Just a minute. I'll be right there," I called out.

I checked my appearance in the bathroom mirror. I certainly didn't look like I'd been to glory. After loading and unloading the truck, I resembled a chicken plant worker more than an aspiring lawyer. I quickly brushed my hair and splashed water on my face.

When I opened the door, Zach Mays was standing there wearing blue jeans and a white T-shirt with a big tomato on it. He had his hair pulled back in a short, tight ponytail. His motorcycle helmet was under his arm.

"I'm here to help you get your ox out of the ditch," he said with a smile. "Am I too late?"

"My ox turned out to be a kitten," I answered. "Since I visited a few weeks ago, Mrs. Fairmont has totally redone this place. I didn't need the furniture I brought from my apartment at school." I paused. "Does Mrs. Fairmont know you're here?"

"I sneaked in through the garden," he joked.

"I mean, she's not doing well mentally. She's confused and disoriented."

"No, I didn't notice anything unusual when she let me in."

At the mention of confusion, the absurdity of what I'd thought moments before hit me. Mrs. Fairmont imagined a bird flying around inside the house; I opted for the audible voice of God from the top of the stairs. Both of us were out of touch with reality. I started to chuckle, tried to stifle it, then burst out laughing. Zach stared at me in bewilderment.

"Mrs. Fairmont seems like a nice lady," he said. "I'm sorry she's having mental—"

I held up my hand. "No, no. It's what you said."

"What did I say?"

"My name," I managed. "Twice."

"And why is that so funny?"

I laughed again. Zach Mays probably thought I was certifiably crazy, but I couldn't stop. I motioned for him to come into the apartment. He eased onto the sofa and placed his helmet beside him. I plopped down in a chair and wiped away the tears streaming down my cheeks.

"I'm sorry," I said, taking a couple of deep breaths. "I was in the bedroom praying when you called my name from the top of the stairs. I thought it was the voice of God."

"You think I sound like God?"

I shook my head and stifled another wave of laughter. "I've never heard the voice of God, but under the circumstances, my imagination played a trick on me. I didn't know there was a man in the house, and when a male voice calling my name came out of nowhere, I assumed it must be a messenger from heaven. I guess I'm not making a very good second impression, but at least I'm not trying to hide anything."

"Good application of rule number three."

I remembered an older rule of hospitality.

"Would you like a warm bottle of water?" I asked. "I haven't been to the grocery store and don't have anything in the refrigerator."

"No, thanks."

"I need one."

I took a bottle from one of my boxes. It was tepid from the ride in the truck.

"I didn't see your convertible out front," Zach said.

"It was a rental. My daddy brought me and my belongings in a pickup truck this morning. We finished unloading a few minutes ago, and he's headed home." I pointed to the boxes on the floor. "All I have to do is unpack. There isn't much to do. I'll save most of the work until tomorrow."

Zach looked around. "The apartment is nice."

"Yes, and please understand I wasn't making fun of Mrs. Fairmont's mental condition. The reason I'm living here is to help take care of her."

"That's what Gerry Patrick told me."

I stared at Zach Mays. I'd never invited a man into my apartment at school. In my confusion about his voice, I'd allowed him across an invisible line without realizing it.

"We should go upstairs," I said quickly. "Mrs. Fairmont may be wondering what's going on."

I inwardly kicked myself at the wording of my last comment and stood up.

"Do you laugh a lot?" Zach asked.

"Only when something funny happens, usually to me."

"Are you going to let that side of you come out at the law firm?"

"I doubt it. And I can promise you one thing—I won't make the mistake of thinking Mr. Braddock paging me on the office intercom is the voice of God." I stepped toward the door. "We really should be joining Mrs. Fairmont. It's rude not to."

Zach's motorcycle riding boots clunked on the stairs. I peeked into the den. The elderly woman was sleeping in her chair with a black-and-white movie blaring from the TV. I touched my lips with my index finger and quietly entered the room. The remote control was on a stand beside Mrs. Fairmont's chair. Flip was curled up at her feet. When he saw me, he jumped up and growled, but I leaned over and scratched the back of his neck. With my other hand, I picked up the remote and turned off the television. Mrs. Fairmont stirred slightly then relaxed. I gently lifted her feet and placed them on an ottoman and positioned two pillows around her so that she wouldn't slip to the side. I gave Flip a final pat on the head and backed out of the room. I motioned for Zach to follow me into the foyer.

After we were safely out of earshot of the den, I said, "Thanks for stopping by. I'm sorry I acted like such a silly girl."

"No, it's okay. I'll see you tomorrow morning."

"Is that when all the other summer clerks begin?"

"The girl from Emory starts then. Vince Colbert has been here for a week."

"Is he the clerk from Yale?"

"Yes, and he seems like a nice guy. Very smart. He's a Christian too."

11

Moses Jones lay on his back on the bottom bunk and stared at the cheap mattress overhead. The man who'd slept above him since Moses was arrested had gone to trial and not come back. Moses didn't know if that meant his bunkmate had been released to go home or convicted and sent directly to the state penitentiary. He'd heard both stories from his cellmates. Rumors in the cell block were as plentiful as mosquitoes on the marshes of the Ogeechee in July.

Jail had changed a lot since Moses spent six months behind bars for hauling moonshine when he was in his early twenties. The old Chatham County jail had been torn down, replaced by a new one with air-conditioning, an indoor exercise facility, and completely integrated cell blocks. The deputies who arrested Moses drove him past the spot where blood once stained the curb. Moses turned his head and stared for a few seconds at the place that still refused to give up its secret.

In the new jail, prisoners with white, black, or brown skin lived close together. English and Spanish profanity shared equal airtime. There was tension between the three groups, but nothing as bad as the racial hatred Moses experienced in his younger years.

Moses' boss, Tommy Lee Barnes, couldn't have run his bolita racket without black runners, but they had to dodge beer bottles, curse words, and racist remarks to collect their fees. Eventually, Barnes was arrested for aggravated assault and spent two years at the Reidsville penitentiary in a ten-by-ten cell filled with men of different races. Moses heard that confinement with a black man caused the heart attack that ultimately killed the gambling kingpin.

Now, men of all races in the cell block shared one common physical characteristic—body art. The quality of images varied. A prisoner might have a flower worthy of Monet on his forearm and a tiger that resembled an anemic house cat on his shoulder. One man in the next bunk had a grim Reaper on his back that he'd asked a local tattoo artist to transform into a motorcycle rider. The result was a wreck that left no survivors. Moses was the only one in his cell block without adornment. The only marks on his wrinkled black skin were from long-forgotten fights and scrapes in the woods. Because of Moses' age, no one bothered him.

Soon after he arrived, Moses was given the task of emptying all the trash cans in the building. It took two hours, twice a day, to complete his rounds pushing a gray plastic buggy through the cell blocks, bathrooms, offices, and food service areas. He often hummed softly to himself while he worked. All the wasted food bothered him. When he cooked at his shack by the river, he never had any leftovers except skin and bones.

Moses dumped the trash into a large container behind the dining hall. When he went outside, he always peeked through the fence at his boat. It was in exactly the same place, chained to a light pole. The chain comforted him. It was a shiny new one, much stronger than the one he owned, and it would be hard for anyone to steal the boat. Some of the cars in the lot only stayed a night. Others had been there since the first time Moses peered through the fence.

Two days after his arrest, Moses talked to a young black detective for a long time. He told him about the faces in the water. The detective listened and wrote things down on a sheet of paper. He refused to tell Moses when he might be released to go home. Weeks passed. The old man felt as if he'd been dropped into a hole in the bank of the river and forgotten. His soul needed to sing, but there wasn't a solitary place to do it.

At least he had plenty to eat. The meat dishes weren't as tasty as fresh fish dipped in cornmeal and fried in a skillet over a kerosene fire, but institutional food kept away hunger. Dessert was the best part of the meals. Moses only had a few teeth left in his mouth, but he joked that all of them were sweet.

I WOKE UP EARLY and quietly left the house for a morning run. Included in my loop was a jog past Braddock, Appleby, and Carpenter. I slowed my pace as I passed the office. It was barely light outside, and there weren't any cars in the parking lot. I remembered my prayer a few weeks earlier in Powell Station.

"Make this a place of praise," I said.

I enjoyed a burst of energy as I ran around Forsyth Park and back to Mrs. Fairmont's house. There was no sign of Mrs. Fairmont. I drank two glasses of water and took a banana downstairs. I sat at the wrought-iron table outside my bedroom, ate the banana, and prayed.

After I showered, I put on my blue suit. The first day of work was a time to look my best. With my hair spilling past my shoulders, the only thing out of ordinary about my appearance was the absence of makeup. I applied just enough lipstick to slightly enhance the color of my lips.

When I went upstairs Mrs. Fairmont wasn't in the den or the kitchen. I approached the bottom of the stairs and looked up. It didn't feel right leaving the house for the day without telling her good-bye. I put my foot on the first step and debated whether to go upstairs. I didn't want to invade Mrs. Fairmont's privacy. Flip appeared at the top of the stairs and looked down at me.

"Is she awake?" I whispered.

I heard a door close.

"Mrs. Fairmont," I called out. "Good morning. It's Tami."

The elderly woman appeared, wearing an elegant green robe and slippers. Her hair looked like it hadn't been brushed. She blinked her eyes and peered down the stairs.

"Where's Gracie?" she asked. "Are you her helper?"

"No ma'am. I'm Tami Taylor. You're letting me live in the basement apartment this summer while I work for Mr. Braddock's law firm."

Mrs. Fairmont rubbed the side of her face. "My mind is foggy this morning."

"I'm leaving for work in a few minutes. Is there anything I can do for you?"

"Did you make the coffee?"

"No ma'am. Would you like some?"

"That would be nice. Cream and sugar."

Mrs. Fairmont shuffled away from the top of the stairs. Flip followed her. I went into the kitchen and started the coffeemaker. I checked the clock. I wanted to get to the office promptly at 8:00 a.m. and wasn't sure exactly how long it would take to get there on foot. I didn't want to be late, but I was living in the house to serve Mrs. Fairmont's needs. I watched the coffee begin to drip into the bottom of the pot. While I waited, I wrote a note that I left on the kitchen counter, thanking Gracie for renovating the downstairs apartment and telling her how much I looked forward to meeting her.

As soon as enough coffee dripped down, I poured a cup and added cream and sugar. I held the cup carefully while climbing the stairs. Halfway up, I thought about the spilled coffee incident in the blue parlor and had to fight off a giggle that threatened to cause the brown drink to slosh over the edge of the cup. I made it to the top of the stairs and knocked on the door frame of a room with the door cracked open. A bark from Flip confirmed that I'd found Mrs. Fairmont's bedroom. I slowly entered.

"It's Tami. I've brought your coffee," I announced. "With cream and sugar."

Mrs. Fairmont was sitting up in bed with pillows behind her. Like the rest of the house, the bedroom was filled with beautiful furniture. The bed had four massive posters and an ornate headboard. A tall bookcase filled with books stood against one wall. Against another wall was a long dresser with a large mirror above it. The top of the dresser was covered with family pictures. On the corner of the dresser was an old black-and-white photograph of a bride in a long elaborate gown and a groom wearing a tuxedo.

"Sorry, child. I was confused a minute ago," Mrs. Fairmont said. "I wasn't really awake. You're the young woman with twin sisters who have blue eyes."

"Yes ma'am," I replied, surprised at her recall of such a small detail. "Where should I put the coffee?"

"On the nightstand."

I set the cup in front of a picture of two girls in old-fashioned dresses.

"Who is that?" I asked.

Mrs. Fairmont turned her head. "That's Ellen Prescott and I at Forsyth Park. She came from a poor family but received a scholarship to my school. It was Ellen's little daughter who was murdered. She had blue eyes, just like your sisters. They never found the body."

I involuntarily shuddered. "How old was she when she died?"

"About ten or eleven. Ellen married late in life to a man with a lot of money and never had another child. She and her husband died in a car wreck a few years later."

Mrs. Fairmont reached over and raised the cup to her lips. Her right hand shook slightly, but she didn't spill a drop.

"That's good coffee for decaf," she sighed. "Thank you."

I moved away from the bed. "I'm leaving for my first day of work at Mr. Braddock's law firm. I'll see you this afternoon."

"Run along. With Flip's help, I'll try to hold on to my sanity."

I STOPPED FOR A LAST GLANCE at myself in the mirror in the green parlor. I looked appropriately professional and resolute. I practiced a quick smile that left me unsatisfied. People complimented me on my smile, even though the right corner of my lip curled up slightly higher than the left. I turned away from the mirror before a vain thought lodged in my brain.

The early morning sun served notice that it would be warm by the end of the day. I walked briskly down the steps and turned in the direction of the law office. My shoes didn't have high heels, but it was different from navigating the uneven sidewalks in running shoes. My feet crushed acorns left from the previous year's crop. I noticed details that had escaped me during my morning run. All of the houses were old, but there was remarkable variety in the use of brick or wood, the shape and placement of windows, the design of the front doors, and countless other nuances. I didn't try to take it all in at once. I knew that by the end of the summer, the walk to work would be as familiar to me as the woods on the west side of our house in Powell Station.

I passed a man walking his dog and two joggers running in the opposite direction. I crossed several intersections and reached Montgomery Street. The law office was several blocks from the Chatham County Courthouse, a modern structure uninfluenced by the beautiful area nearby. Traffic was busier on Montgomery Street, and when I reached Braddock, Appleby, and Carpenter, my heart began to pound in my chest. A few cars were in the parking lot.

"Make this a place of praise," I began to repeat under my breath.

I knew the prayer was right, but it didn't send peace to my heart.

I'd felt less nervous trying to make a crucial free throw at the end of a conference tournament basketball game. I took a deep breath when I reached the front door and opened it.

The receptionist sat to the right of the sweeping staircase. My low heels clicked on the wooden floor.

"May I help you?" she asked.

"I'm Tami Taylor, one of the summer clerks," I said, hoping my voice didn't shake. "I'm here to see Ms. Patrick."

The receptionist spoke to someone on the phone.

"Have a seat," she said to me. "She'll be down in a few minutes."

I sat in a wooden chair with curved arms and legs. The front door of the office opened, and a young woman entered. It was Julie Feldman, also dressed in a dark suit and white blouse. Without noticing me, she approached the receptionist. Julie was shorter than I'd imagined from the pictures sent via the Internet and a lot cuter. Her black hair was cut short. The receptionist pointed in my direction. Julie's eyes met mine, and she smiled. She sat down on a leather couch beside my chair and introduced herself.

"Are you nervous?" she asked.

"Yes."

"Me too. I've talked to two of my friends who have been working for a week at big law firms in Atlanta. They told me not to treat it like summer camp. Their firms don't want them to get bored, and the partner in charge of summer clerks has a bunch of activities planned to keep them entertained. I told them Atlanta may be different from Savannah."

Julie spoke rapidly, her dark eyes alert.

"All I know is that we're going to a luncheon today with the lawyers," I replied. "Ms. Patrick says it may be the only time all the partners are with us."

Julie nodded. "I've talked to her a bunch. Mr. Carpenter told me to meet with her this morning."

I wondered why I'd not received personal contact from the senior partner. Perhaps it was because I was a fill-in.

"What's he like?"

"Okay, I guess. He came to the law school for an interview day. I didn't think he liked me, but then I got the job offer. Did you find a place to live?"

I told her about Mrs. Fairmont's house.

"You're not far from my place near Greene Square. We'll have to go out together some at night."

My defenses flew up. "It depends on Mrs. Fairmont's condition. Staying at her house is actually a second job."

"What do you mean?"

"She has health issues," I replied, not wanting to give details that Mrs. Bartlett might want to remain private.

Julie lowered her voice. "Maybe you can sneak out after hours. I've already been to River Street twice. It's a lot of fun."

A middle-aged woman with dark hair and reading glasses on a chain around her neck came down the stairs and introduced herself. It was Gerry Patrick. Ms. Patrick was the same height as Julie. She gave Julie a quick hug and shook my hand.

"Did you move in yesterday?" she asked me crisply.

"Yes ma'am. Mrs. Fairmont completely renovated the downstairs apartment."

"That's good to hear. Let's go to a conference room. Vince Colbert is already here this morning. He's working on a project for Mr. Braddock."

When Ms. Patrick turned away, Julie leaned over and whispered, "Vince must be a gunner."

We went into one of the plush downstairs conference rooms Zach had shown me during my first visit. Ms. Patrick sat at the end of the table and offered us coffee or water. She then pushed the intercom button on the phone.

"Deborah, send Vince into conference room two."

I crossed my ankles under the shiny table. Opposite me was a massive oil painting of a harbor scene from the early nineteenth century. I could see bales of cotton piled on a wharf in front of a row of sailing ships. Scores of people filled the scene. The detail in the painting would have taken a long time to create.

"Is that Savannah?" I asked.

"Yes," Ms. Patrick said. "Mr. Braddock lets the art museum keep it for a year then brings it back to the office for twelve months."

The door to the conference room opened and a tall, lanky young man with wavy brown hair and dark eyes came into the room. He was wearing a dark blue sport coat, gray slacks, white shirt, and burgundy tie. He was carrying a very thin laptop computer in his right hand.

"Vince, meet Julie Feldman and Tami Taylor," Ms. Patrick said.

When I shook the male clerk's hand, I noticed a large, rectangular-shaped scar on it. The skin was oddly wrinkled and lacked pigment. I quickly glanced up. His eyes were on my face. He released his grip and sat on the opposite side of the table with his right hand out of sight.

"Vince already knows what I'm going to tell you," Ms. Patrick began. "But Mr. Carpenter wanted the three of you to have a sense of starting together."

She distributed cards that would give us access to the building twenty-four hours a day and rapidly outlined a lot of details about office procedures: names of support staff and their job duties, locations of copy machines and the codes to input when using them, Internet research policies, areas of specialty for each of the lawyers, and office schedules. Vince's fingers flew across the keyboard. Neither Julie nor I had anything to write on. Ms. Patrick didn't seem to notice.

"Will all this be included in an information packet or should I take notes?" I asked when she paused.

"You can copy my notes," Vince replied.

He slid the computer across the table. Julie and I leaned in and looked at the screen. He'd typed in almost every word on a template that made it look like a corporate flow chart.

"That works for me," Julie said.

"I don't own a laptop computer," I said, trying not to sound whiny. "Does the firm supply one?"

"Not for summer clerks," Ms. Patrick replied. "The younger lawyers bring one to meetings, but most partners don't. It's a generational difference."

I concentrated hard through the rest of the meeting. At least my memory, forged in the front room of the house in Powell Station, went with me everywhere. And it never needed rebooting.

"That's it," Ms. Patrick said in conclusion. "Any questions?"

I didn't know what to ask and kept my mouth shut. Julie spoke. "How will we circulate through the different sections of the firm?"

It was a good question, and I wished I'd thought to ask it.

"You'll find out at the luncheon. There isn't time during the summer for you to spend a lot of time with each partner. Anything else?"

"Is there a dress code?" I asked.

"This is a traditional firm with clients who expect a professional appearance at all times. We don't wear blue jeans on Friday."

"That's fine. I don't own a pair of jeans."

The other three people stared at me. I'd needlessly blurted out controversial information. I wanted to crawl under the table.

"Any other questions?" Ms. Patrick asked after an awkward pause.

I pressed my lips tightly together. The progress I'd made with Ms. Patrick after meeting with Christine Bartlett had been nullified by the events of the past few days.

"Very well," the office manager said. "Vince, you can return to your project with Mr. Braddock. Julie, Mr. Carpenter wants to meet with you in his office. Tami, wait here."

Left alone in the conference room, I had nothing to do but stare at the painting. Many of the figures on the wharf were slaves, toiling without pay in the burning heat as they loaded the heavy cotton bales onto the ships. I suspected the painter intended to portray normal life. However, normal in one era can be barbarian to the next. The slaves, a people oppressed for no reason except the color of their skin, illustrated that truth with a massive exclamation point. The painting was an indefensible snapshot of injustice. I sighed. Oppression took many forms, and often, the society of the day didn't recognize it.

Ms. Patrick returned to the conference room. I started to offer an apology but before I could start, she spoke.

"Come with me," she said from the doorway. "You're going to assist one of the paralegals this morning."

There was no denying my relegation to the bottom rank of the summer clerks. I recognized the large open work areas that were filling with people. We walked down a hall to an open door.

"Myra," Ms. Patrick began, "this is Tami Taylor."

The paralegal glanced up from a stack of papers on her desk. "Welcome, nice to see you again."

Ms. Patrick looked at me with raised eyebrows.

"Zach Mays introduced us when I came by the office on a Saturday a few weeks ago," I said.

Ms. Patrick waved her hand to the paralegal. "She's all yours until 11:30."

"Thank you," I said to Ms. Patrick's departing back.

Myra reached forward and picked up a thick envelope. "I'm in the middle of a project that has to be finished before the end of the day. Do you know where the county courthouse is located?"

"Yes ma'am."

The paralegal pulled back the envelope. "Unless you think I'm old, call me Myra."

"Okay."

She handed me the heavy envelope. "This is a response to a motion for preliminary injunction that needs to be filed this morning. Mr. Carpenter has a hearing in this case tomorrow, and the other side needs twenty-four hours' notice. We have electronic filing in federal court but not in the state courts. There are two copies. Have both of them stamped at the clerk's office, then take one to Judge Cannon's office. Bring the other back here, and I'll have a courier take it to the opposing counsel's office."

"I could take it," I offered.

"It's in Brunswick. It would be cutting it close for you to drive down and back before lunch."

"Oh, I don't have a car."

Myra stopped and stared at me. Stares had always been part of my life, but a new environment inevitably provoked a rash of them. Without further comment the paralegal turned her attention to the documents on her desk, and I backed out of the room.

My earlier confidence was gone. As I walked down Montgomery Street, the hopelessness of my situation washed over me. I had no business working in Savannah. My success was as unlikely as one of the slaves in the painting making the transition from dock laborer to cotton merchant.

I reached the courthouse and climbed the steps. After passing through security, I found the clerk's office where a helpful middle-aged woman date-stamped the response to the motion. But when I tried to pick up both copies, she held on to one of them

"One of these needs to go in the file. You can serve the other," she said.

"No, I need to take it to Judge Cannon's office. There's a hearing tomorrow afternoon."

The clerk pointed to a copy machine. "Then make another copy."

I panicked. "I didn't bring my purse and don't have any money."

An image of myself hot and sweaty, running back to the office, flashed through my mind.

"Which law firm do you work for?" the woman asked.

"Braddock, Appleby, and Carpenter."

"Use their copy code."

"I'm a summer clerk. It's my first day, and I don't have it with me."

The woman made a face that showed me I'd reached the end of her patience.

"Call and get it," she said.

"I don't have a cell phone."

The woman rubbed her hand across her forehead and through her hair. Without saying anything else, she reached under the counter and retrieved a black notebook. She flipped open the book and turned it so I could see the firm name with a number beside it.

"Thank you," I replied gratefully.

I made two copies in case I hit another unforeseen roadblock. I left the clerk's office and found Judge Cannon's chambers on the directory beside the elevator. It must have been a day for criminal court, because several of the people who joined me on the elevator looked like criminals. No one spoke, but two of the men stole sideways glances at me. I quickly stepped out when the door opened.

The judge's office had an anteroom where an older woman sat behind a scarred wooden desk. Public administration of justice didn't pay as well as the private practice of law. I identified myself and handed the envelope to the woman.

"The judge has something for you to deliver to Mr. Carpenter," the woman said in a raspy voice. "I was going to mail it, but you can deliver it in person."

"Yes ma'am. I'll be glad to."

She gave me a sealed envelope. Holding it tightly in my hand along with the service copies of the response to the motion, I retraced my steps to the law firm. It was hot, and I was doubly glad I'd not had to make an extra trip. By the time I reached the foyer of the law office, the cool air felt good on my hot face. I climbed the stairs to Myra's office. Her door was closed. I knocked.

"Come in," she said.

"Here it is," I announced. I laid the stamped copies on her desk. I held up the other envelope. "The judge's secretary gave me this to deliver to Mr. Carpenter."

"Take it downstairs to his office," she said without thanking me and resumed her work.

I didn't know where to go so I wandered the hallway looking for clues. I opened one door. An older man with a bald head and wearing glasses glanced up in obvious irritation.

"Sorry," I mumbled and quickly closed the door.

At that moment, Julie Feldman entered the hall.

"Where's Mr. Carpenter's office?" I asked in relief. "I have something to give him from a judge."

"He's on a conference call with a client, but his secretary is in there," she replied, pointing to a door next to the one I'd opened.

"What does he look like?" I asked in an anxious voice.

"Uh, he's tall with gray hair and a goatee. He reminds me of an actor whose name I can't remember. Some guy who used to be in old movies."

"Good," I said with relief. "What are you doing for him?"

Julie held up a thick file in her hand. "He gave me a research project, something about competing security interests in forklifts and other equipment at a big factory that's about to go into bankruptcy. There are claims by two banks and three companies that sold the equipment. I'm supposed to read all the documents and prepare a chart telling him which companies are secured as to each piece of property and for how much."

"That sounds interesting," I replied.

Julie gave me a strange look. "Are you kidding?" she asked.

"No."

Julie shook her head. "I'll see you at lunch. Until then, I'll have my head stuck in article nine of the uniform commercial code."

I entered the office, which was as fancy as the office at the courthouse had been plain. I introduced myself to a woman in her thirties and gave her the envelope from Judge Cannon.

"Have a seat," she said, motioning to one of two chairs in front of her desk. "Mr. Carpenter will want to meet you as soon as he finishes his conference call."

I sat down and waited. Fifteen minutes passed. The secretary ignored me. Both Julie and Vince Colbert were already busy on projects. I knew it was only the first day, but I already felt behind. Another fifteen minutes passed. In between phone calls, which she seemed to be able to handle without consulting Mr. Carpenter, the secretary's fingers flew across the keyboard. I wanted to be productive. But there was nothing to do except become intimately familiar with every detail of the room. More time passed. Finally, the secretary seemed to notice my existence again. She picked up the phone and told Mr. Carpenter that I was waiting to see him. The office door behind her opened, and a man matching Julie's description entered the room.

Mr. Carpenter had a slender build and extended his hand in a way that struck me as slightly effeminate. However, when I shook his hand, the grip was firm.

"Ms. Saylor," he said in a smooth voice.

"It's Taylor," I corrected, perhaps too abruptly.

"Sorry," he said. "Tami, right?"

"Yes sir."

We entered his office. It was about the same size as Mr. Callahan's office. Apparently, Mr. Carpenter liked boats, because the walls were covered with pictures of yachts.

"I've been on the phone with so many people this morning the names are running together."

He sat behind a large desk with a leather inlaid top and stared at me for several seconds without speaking. I shifted in my seat.

"You have a lovely office," I said.

His phone buzzed and he picked it up. "Put him through," he said after listening for a moment.

I started to get up, but he motioned for me to remain. The call involved a domestic relations case. Mr. Carpenter represented the husband who had filed for the divorce. I picked up that the man on the other end of the line was the lawyer for the wife. The main issue had to do with division of property.

"Our answers to your discovery set valuation of the marital estate at twenty-two million and change," Mr. Carpenter said. "I think we should be able to arrive at an amicable resolution. My letter of the fifteenth is a starting point, but there is room for discussion on several items."

Mr. Carpenter listened for a long time. I watched his jaw tighten and his lips turn downward.

"Bob, I don't think you want to go there," he said. "We can divide the pie, but if you try to throw it in my face, this will get messy."

It seemed like a silly comment, but the way Mr. Carpenter said it sounded ominous. He listened again, then spoke in a steely voice.

"If that's the way you want it, we'll litigate into the next decade. Have your paralegal call Myra Dean to set up the depositions." He paused. "And tell Mrs. Folsom my previous proposal is off the table. Our next offer will be less—a lot less."

He hung up the phone and looked at me.

"Welcome to Savannah," he said cheerily.

I gave him a startled look at his easy transition from threatening to friendly. "Thank you, sir. I appreciate the opportunity."

"Gerry tells me you're living with Margaret Fairmont. She's a gracious lady. Her husband was a great friend of Sam Braddock."

"Yes sir."

"And I have your résumé somewhere in here."

The lawyer leafed through a short stack of papers on the corner of his desk.

"Have you met Vince and Julie?" he asked as he continued to search.

"Yes sir."

"And you already know Zach Mays?"

"Not really. I met him a few weeks ago when I stopped by the office on a Saturday. He's been very helpful in helping me acclimate to the firm."

"Good, good. Zach is an earnest young man who isn't afraid to ask hard questions. Here it is," Mr. Carpenter announced, holding up a sheet of paper.

I watched while he skimmed the one-page summary of my life.

"That's right. You worked for Oscar Callahan. It's the reason I pulled your résumé out in the first place. Oscar gave you a glowing recommendation. If he'd stopped representing mill workers for petty injuries and crawled out of the mountains, he could have been one of the best litigators in the state."

"Yes sir," I said, not sure if agreeing with Mr. Carpenter would dishonor Mr. Callahan.

"His grandfather was a preacher, wasn't he?"

"Yes sir."

"If I recall, he was the leader of some kind of obscure religious sect that wanted to turn back the clock to the Dark Ages."

I swallowed, not sure if this was a time to defend the faith or accumulate more information.

"Is that what Mr. Callahan told you?"

"How else would I have picked up that bit of trivia?" Mr. Carpenter slapped his hands together. "Enough of that. Let's get down to business. Your summer at the firm will be a good mix of work and pleasure. I hope your experience will be intellectually stimulating. Law school prepares you to take tests, not practice law. We'll have plenty of projects that will involve research within your comfort zone, but there will also be practical opportunities to broaden your experience."

"Yes sir."

"I'm glad you had a chance to hear my side of the opening salvo in the Folsom divorce case. I don't handle many divorce cases, but our firm is deeply involved in J.K. Folsom's corporate dealings, and he doesn't want another law firm to know his business. J.K. pays our top hourly rate for representation. Using you to assist with research and deposition preparation, I can keep his bills lower."

My stomach went into a knot. I'd wanted to avoid domestic practice. Mr. Carpenter continued. "Have you taken a domestic relations course in law school?"

"No sir."

"That's not a problem. We'll see how fast you can get up to speed in an unfamiliar area. We have a couple of treatises in the law library. Read them to get a foundation and dive into the fray. Divorce work is exciting because the emotions of the parties run wild. It's key for the lawyer to keep her cool when others around her are losing theirs."

Even when talking to a summer associate, I could tell Mr. Carpenter utilized dramatic pauses.

"Sounds like Kipling," I managed, remembering a poem I'd memorized in homeschool.

Mr. Carpenter nodded approvingly. "Yes, it does."

He buzzed his secretary and gave her instructions about giving me access to the file. He stood up, signaling an end to our meeting.

"I'll see you at the luncheon. Until then, the library is your home."

The secretary spoke as I passed her desk. "I'll have a packet on the Folsom case ready for you by early afternoon," she said. "In the meantime, the case number is 207642."

"Thank you," I replied without much feeling. "Where is the firm library?"

"On this floor at the west end of the building."

Not being able to see the sun in the hallway, I wasn't sure which way to turn, but I guessed the opposite end from Mr. Braddock's office. I didn't want to walk unannounced into another lawyer's office. When I cracked open a wooden door and peeked inside I saw bookshelves. Sitting at a table with papers spread out before her was Julie Feldman.

"Are you alone?" I whispered.

"Not now."

I sat down on the opposite side of the table. Even with the advent of computer research, the firm still maintained an extensive library of books. Several computer terminals for online use were in a row along one wall.

"How's it going?"

"I'm shuffling papers and trying to understand what they say." She looked up. "I haven't taken a course in secured transactions. I know a few terms but none of the principles. I'm completely lost."

"I loved my secured transactions course. It was taught by one of the best professors at the law school, and I enjoyed figuring out the different rules. But Mr. Carpenter has assigned me to a big divorce case. I've not taken a domestic relations course, and the only thing I know about divorce is that God doesn't like it."

Julie's eyes opened wide. "That's unreal. I spent last semester doing research for one of the best divorce lawyers in Atlanta. She handles a lot of high-profile breakups and knows all the tricks of the trade. Reading her files was more interesting than most of the novels my mother keeps on the nightstand in her bedroom."

The irony of our predicament made me smile.

"Are you thinking what I'm thinking?" Julie asked.

"What? That we're both being pushed out of our comfort zones?"

"No. We should switch projects."

I shook my head. "Mr. Carpenter knows I haven't studied domestic relations. He wants to see how quickly I can learn a new area. It's part of the summer experience."

"But we could help each other."

Julie's suggestion surprised me. Law school was competitive, and a summer clerk opportunity raised the competition to a higher level because a job, not just a grade, was at stake. Even if we didn't talk about it, I'd expected jockeying for a permanent job to affect all my interaction with Julie Feldman and Vince Colbert.

"How would we do that?"

"Talk about stuff. You can help me with these documents, and I can give you pointers about the divorce case. Where is your file?"

"I won't have it until this afternoon. I'm supposed to be reading a treatise on divorce law in Georgia, but I'm not sure how many there are or which one is the best."

Julie looked at her watch. "Here's what we'll do. It will be just like my study group at school. Help me figure out what I'm supposed to do for an hour and a half. Then, I'll take you through a domestic relations treatise for an hour. I know which one to use. After lunch, we'll spend time identifying your specific issues. And we'll end the day in the guts of article nine of the uniform commercial code."

I felt a weight lift from my shoulders.

"Okay."

I took my chair around to Julie's side of the table. The next hour and a half flew by as I organized the documents, located the key language in each one, and showed Julie the important dates.

"Which company are we representing?" I asked when we took a break. "I've been treating this like an exam question to unravel, not a case to win."

"This one." Julie pointed to a stack of documents. "I didn't want to influence your opinion by letting you know in advance. Later, we can try to figure out how to make our case stronger."

"You're going to be a great lawyer. You have something law school can't teach."

"What's that?"

"Wisdom."

Julie rolled her eyes. "Whatever. I'll get the divorce book. Do we represent the husband or the wife?"

"Does it matter?"

"Not as much as it used to. Unless there are little kids, it's all about the money."

Julie went to the shelves and returned with a dark green volume. "You remind me of a rabbi," she said as she sat down.

"Why?"

"You think about stuff that rabbis care about. Clothes, what God thinks about divorce, wisdom, ethics."

"What do you care about?"

Julie looked at me and laughed. "See what I mean? That's a rabbi question if I ever heard one. You can't turn it off, can you?"

"No," I admitted with a small smile.

"That's okay. You're not going to offend me. My cousins in New York are ultraorthodox. They're always telling me what to do and think." Julie opened the treatise. "Do you know the divorce rate among Christians?"

"A few years ago, it was about thirty percent, the same as everyone else. But that doesn't mean all—"

"I think it's higher, now," Julie interrupted. "Closer to forty percent. Guess what the divorce rate is for ultraorthodox Jews?"

"I don't know."

"About three percent. Tell me, whose belief system is working? Of course, I'm not orthodox and don't want to be, so I won't have the benefit of those statistics." She opened the book and flipped over a few pages. "Let's see. Here's where we should start."

Julie launched into an efficient explanation of the divorce laws in

Georgia. I didn't like the subject matter, but it was much easier receiving it spoon-fed by a friendly face than groping along under the sharp questioning of a polemic professor. An hour later, the door opened. It was Vince Colbert, his laptop in his hand.

"Mr. Braddock sent me. It's time for the luncheon."

12

JULIE CHATTED WITH VINCE WHILE WE WALKED DOWN THE hall. I lagged behind. Her lack of antagonism to my beliefs was nice, but her casual attitude threw me off balance, as if she could trivialize the truth by rejecting it in a friendly way.

"Vince is our designated driver," she called over her shoulder. "He knows where to go."

Several lawyers were leaving the building at the same time. Introductions were made as we passed through the reception area and out to the parking lot. The bald lawyer I'd disturbed when I opened his door grunted when I offered an apology and returned to a conversation with one of his colleagues. Joe Carpenter wasn't in the initial group. Zach Mays was also missing. We reached Vince's car, a new BMW.

"Sit up front," Julie told me. "Your legs are longer than mine."

Vince looked at me as if evaluating the length of my legs. I blushed before opening the door and sliding into the passenger seat.

"Did you play sports in high school or college?" Julie asked me as soon as we were settled.

"Basketball in high school. Intramurals since."

"I played soccer in high school," she replied. "My father claims I'd have gone to Harvard or Yale if I'd not headed so many balls. What's Yale like?"

Vince backed out of the parking lot. "It's a law school. There are a lot of smart people."

Vince rested his hand on top of the steering wheel. The scar on the back of his hand was very visible. It made me wonder what would happen if it was unprotected against the sun.

"Did you play sports in high school?" I asked him.

"No."

"Are you going to take notes during lunch?" Julie asked.

"Yes."

"I wish you would transfer to Emory and join my study group," Julie said. "We need someone like you. But that would be a big comedown from Yale."

If I hadn't spent the morning with Julie, I would have considered it a sarcastic comment.

"She's serious," I added. "Julie would love having you in her study group. We accomplished a lot more this morning by working together."

"I'm not in a study group," Vince replied. He glanced at me. "Are you in a study group?"

"No, I'm a loner."

"Me too," he said.

I turned and saw Julie roll her eyes. The look caught me off guard and made me giggle. I put my hand over my mouth to suppress an outburst. Vince glanced sideways at me. The car swerved slightly.

"Are you okay?"

"Yes. Julie is trying to make me laugh."

"There are rabbis who laugh," she responded. "It's kosher."

Vince didn't say anything and stared straight ahead. I suspected he wanted to get out of the car and away from two crazy, immature women as soon as possible.

We turned into the parking lot of a plain-looking building on the outskirts of the historic district. A small sign beside the door identified it as "The Smith House—Private Parties Only." Gerry Patrick was standing beside the door.

"Have you been here before?" Julie asked Vince.

"For the rehearsal dinner before my sister's wedding," he said. "She was married in Savannah."

We got out of the car. One of the lawyers came over to Vince, and the two left us. Julie put her hand on my arm and stopped me.

"You'd better keep that laugh under control and out of sight," she said in a soft voice. "It may be kosher, but it's also unprofessional. I thought Vince might drive onto the curb and mess up the alignment on his car."

"It's your fault. Making fun of me because I'm a loner."

"Don't you think I know what it's like to be alone? I went to a college that didn't have enough Jewish students to fill a table for eight. I almost assimilated."

"What's that?"

Julie started walking toward the door. "Lost my distinctiveness in an effort to blend in."

"That's one type of pressure I understand."

Ms. Patrick greeted us. "How was your morning?"

Julie briefly told about our working together. I could tell Ms. Patrick was surprised.

"That's good," she said, looking at me. "Being part of a team is a good idea, especially on big projects. Go inside. Your places at the table are marked."

The inside of the building was dark, and it took my eyes a second to adjust to the change in light. The interior had the look and smell of tradition. The walls were paneled in dark wood and decorated with old English hunting scenes. There was a coat and hat room to the right of the front door and a bar area to the left. An older lawyer with an ample waistline, wispy white hair, and blue eyes was talking to Vince, but when we entered, he came up to us.

"Sam Braddock," he said, extending his hand.

Mr. Braddock began asking questions that made it clear he'd never seen our résumés. While Julie was summarizing her educational background, the door opened and Zach Mays came in, accompanied by a tall man who looked about the same age as Mr. Braddock but with ramrod-straight posture and assertive eyes. It was Nelson Appleby, the admiralty lawyer. When he shook my hand, I was surprised to notice that the veins on his stood out like those of a patient in a nursing home. His voice, however, was steady.

"Ms. Taylor, I think we're sitting next to each other at lunch," he said.

We moved into a large room with a table set up in the shape of a T. At the end of each table was a place for one of the named partners. Everyone stood around and talked for a few minutes until Mr. Carpenter arrived. A younger associate who looked frazzled came in with him.

My seat was to the left of Mr. Appleby with Zach Mays across the table from me. To my left was Barry Conrad, the lawyer I'd met when I first visited the firm. I started to ask him about his golf game, but he immediately began talking to the lawyer on his left. I heard the sound of a glass being tapped with a spoon and turned in my chair. It was Mr. Carpenter.

"Welcome to the firm luncheon in honor of our summer law clerks, Vince Colbert, Julie Feldman, and Tami Taylor. Before we begin the meal, I'd like each of them to tell us why they decided to spend the summer at our firm and an interesting or unusual fact about themselves. Tami, please go first."

I'd not known an introductory speech was part of the program. Going first made it worse. My stomach suddenly felt queasy and my mouth went dry. I took a quick sip of water and stood up. Everyone was looking at me. I licked my lips. Julie, who was sitting beside Mr. Carpenter, gave the same eye roll she'd delivered in the car.

"It's an honor working here this summer," I began. "I'm here because Mr. Carpenter sent me a letter offering me a job."

There was a smattering of laughter.

"And after praying about it and discussing the job with my parents, I decided to accept it."

The smiles were replaced by a few puzzled expressions.

"I look forward to working with as many of you as possible. I want to learn, and I'm willing to work hard." I paused and glanced at Zach. "There are many unusual facts about my life, but one that I share with Zach Mays is a homeschool education. Thank you."

I sat down. No one clapped or said anything. Vince was next. He was from Charleston and mentioned his family's longtime personal connection to Mr. Appleby as the reason for his interest in working for the firm. As an interesting fact, he described his Eagle Scout service project, in which he created a training program to teach and implement household safety in lower-income areas and a database of needy families to receive help. The program was adopted in Charleston County as part of a United Way initiative. There was polite applause when he finished.

Julie stood up. "I'm here because Savannah has always been my favorite city on the coast." She hesitated and then spoke with feeling. "I wouldn't trade two Charlestons and three Wilmingtons for one Savannah."

Several lawyers pounded the table in agreement.

"I'm as excited about being here as I was spending two months last summer sailing across the Caribbean with my father. We visited over a dozen ports including the Caymans and the Virgin Islands. I didn't think about law for eight weeks and spent most of my time working on my tan."

"You can come on my boat!" one of the younger lawyers called out.

"Mine's newer and bigger!" another lawyer countered.

"And you're married," Mr. Carpenter said, pointing to the second lawyer. "Thank you, clerks. Enjoy lunch."

I looked across the table at Zach. He avoided my eyes.

"What's this about a homeschool?" Mr. Appleby asked the young associate. "You never mentioned that before."

"Who taught it? Your mother?" Conrad added.

Zach looked at Conrad with a steely expression. "Yes. All the way through high school. She was an excellent teacher."

Having caused this problem, I wasn't going to abandon Zach and sit on the sidelines.

"The tutorial system was the preferred method for educating European royalty for hundreds of years," I said. "And several modern studies have proven it works well today, even if the parents aren't college educated."

Mr. Appleby spoke. "My brother and I had a private tutor when our family lived in Nigeria. My mother taught grammar and literature; the tutor handled math and science. I've always thought those were the best years of my education. I was way ahead of my peers when we moved back to Baltimore."

I saw Conrad turn in his chair and begin talking to the person next to him.

"Tell me more about your educational background," Mr. Appleby said to me.

I started to give a two-sentence answer, then remembered Zach's advice about taking the opportunity to talk when asked a question by one of the partners.

"I'd be glad to."

It was an easy subject. I'd defended homeschooling against all comers for years. Mr. Appleby asked several insightful questions, and I talked steadily through the salad course up to arrival of our entrée, a seafood dish as rich as anything I'd ever eaten. Once, I looked at Zach and silently offered to pass the ball to him, but he gave a slight shake of his head. This was my chance to impress Mr. Appleby. So, I continued talking.

"And do you believe this type of education makes you a better law student?" Mr. Appleby asked.

"Yes sir. I didn't wait until law school to learn how to analyze an issue and evaluate possible solutions."

Mr. Appleby turned his attention to Zach, and they began to discuss a case involving a Norwegian shipping company. I couldn't follow the unfamiliar admiralty terms. Learning the law of Georgia was challenging enough; the prospect of applying U.S., Norwegian, and international law to a legal problem was overwhelming. As a waiter took away our plates, Mr. Appleby looked at his watch.

"It will be too late to call Oslo when we get back to the office," he said. "Send Bergen an e-mail outlining our position so he can read it in the morning. If he wants to continue to do business with our client in the port of Savannah, there will have to be concessions on the container surcharge and agreement on the arbitration language."

Dessert was a custard dish that dissolved on my tongue and sent shivers down my spine. I wanted to ask for the recipe so I could make it for my family, but I didn't want to draw attention to myself. Julie didn't seem to have that problem. I could hear her laughing loudly at the other end of the table.

Mr. Carpenter stood and tapped his glass again. The room became quiet.

"I hope you've enjoyed this luncheon. Every time we do this, it makes me wish we spent more time together as a firm."

I heard Conrad clear his throat. Mr. Carpenter continued.

"We don't have any prizes to give away, but there is a drawing of sorts for our summer clerks."

I sat up straighter.

"Judge Cannon has agreed to allow our summer clerks to handle minor misdemeanor cases under appropriate supervision. These are pro bono matters. The clerks won't be providing as important a contribution to the community as Vince did with his Eagle Scout project, but every citizen of the land deserves legal representation. Ms. Taylor picked up an order authorizing this work at the courthouse this morning. The judge is authorizing the firm to delegate the cases; however, I think it would be appropriate for the clerks to have a hand in the selection process."

He paused. I suspected his last comment was meant to be a play on words, but no one laughed. He held up three folders.

"Each of these folders contains a brief description of a case and an order from Judge Cannon specially authorizing you to make an appearance on behalf of the defendant."

One of the younger lawyers called out, "When I was a summer clerk I had to represent a man caught playing video poker!"

Mr. Carpenter spoke. "And as I recall you gambled with his future, and he spent ninety days in jail."

"Bob lost a hundred dollars playing the machines while investigating that case," another lawyer said.

"If our clerks will step forward," Mr. Carpenter said, "I'll let them choose their fate."

Julie stood beside Mr. Carpenter. Vince and I joined her. Mr. Carpenter held out the three folders.

"Ms. Feldman," he said.

Julie chose the one in the middle and opened it.

"*State v. Ferguson,*" she said. "I think he's charged with impersonating a public official—a water-meter reader."

"Say that fast three times in front of the judge," one of the lawyers said.

"Why would someone do that?" Julie asked Mr. Carpenter.

"Allegedly," Mr. Carpenter corrected. "Meet with your client and investigate the facts; then we'll talk about a theory of the case." The senior partner pointed to the lawyer named Ned. "Mr. Danforth, I want you to supervise Ms. Feldman's efforts on behalf of the defendant."

"Can we do it on my boat?" the lawyer asked.

"Not without appropriate adult supervision," another lawyer responded.

The flirting banter in the room made me uncomfortable. I glanced at Julie, who didn't seem upset by the innuendos. Mr. Carpenter turned to Vince.

"Your turn."

Vince selected the file on the left and opened it.

"*State v. Brown*," he said. "Operation of a motor vehicle at excessive speed while racing and improper muffler."

"A racer!" one of the lawyers called out. "Where was he arrested?"

"At 10746 Abercorn Street."

"That's near the new mall," the lawyer replied. "He and his buddies were probably dragging between stoplights."

Mr. Carpenter spoke. "Russell, since you're such an expert on street racing in Chatham County, I want you to work with Vince."

"Do I get to drive his BMW?" the lawyer asked.

"Only with proper adult supervision," Mr. Carpenter replied.

Several people laughed. Mr. Carpenter looked at me.

"That leaves you, Ms. Taylor."

"Without a choice or a chance!" one lawyer called out.

I took the file from the managing partner and opened it. There were multiple sheets of paper filled with charges. The number of counts was overwhelming. At first, I suspected that I'd gotten some kind of serial criminal by mistake. But as I read the charges, I realized each count was identical except as to location of the offense.

"*State v. Jones*," I said, quickly turning the pages until I reached the final one. "Twenty-four counts of trespassing. Mr. Jones illegally tied up his boat for the night at twenty-four private docks."

"Allegedly," Mr. Carpenter said. "Not necessarily illegally."

"Yes sir," I replied, although it seemed hard to imagine twenty-four instances of honest mistake or sudden emergency.

"Who would be a suitable mentor?" Mr. Carpenter asked as he looked around the room. No one raised his hand. I glanced at Zach, whose eyes were lowered like a schoolboy trying to avoid the teacher's gaze.

"Sounds like a first cousin to an admiralty case," Mr. Carpenter said. "A lower-level type of piracy on the high seas. Mr. Mays, I want you to help Ms. Taylor."

Zach raised his head, and I studied his reaction. He had a fixed expression that appeared to be a cross between a forced smile and a grimace. I returned to my seat. General conversation resumed in the room.

"Thanks for helping," I said to Zach.

"I'm a man under authority," he replied.

Mr. Appleby left the table. I leaned forward. "Are you upset with me for mentioning your homeschool background?" I asked in a whisper. "I didn't mean to embarrass you."

Zach shook his head. "No, there's just a lot of pressure with my workload. I didn't need another project on my desk."

"I'm sorry. I won't ask for much help."

I left the table and went to the restroom. No one else was there. I stood in front of the mirror. Challenges surfaced by the minute at the law firm. I wasn't convinced that I hadn't embarrassed Zach Mays. I washed my hands and lightly touched a wet paper towel to my cheeks and forehead.

When I returned to the dining room, everyone was getting ready to leave. Zach and Mr. Appleby were near the door. I started to go to them, but heard Julie call my name.

"Tami!"

I turned around as she came up to me.

"Your case sounds like a lot of work," she said. "Do you think you'll have to interview the owners of every dock where your client tied up his boat?"

"I haven't thought about it," I replied.

"I'd subpoena every one of them," Julie said. "Rich folks don't want to show up in court, and if they don't testify it will knock out a count."

I held up the folder in my hand. "I suspect at least a few of these people would make an appearance, and the punishment for two counts probably wouldn't be much different than for twenty-four."

"But you may be able to wear down the prosecutor and get your client a good deal."

I wasn't interested in a strategy session, but when I looked back to the door Mr. Appleby and Zach were gone.

"Ned says we may raise a Halloween defense for my client," Julie continued. "We could claim he was delusional and believed every day is Halloween. The water-meter outfit was his costume of the day."

"You haven't talked to the client yet."

Julie laughed. "I'm kidding. I wouldn't ask him to lie, but Ned has a great sense of humor. This firm isn't nearly as stuffy as I thought it would be."

Several more lawyers came over and introduced themselves. Julie received most of the attention.

"Is there a firm directory?" Julie asked as the crowd thinned. "I won't be able to remember everyone's name."

Vince patted his laptop. "I have that information in a file."

Julie put her arm in his. "We've only been here half a day, and already I don't know what I'd do without you."

Ms. Patrick joined us. "That went nicely," she said. "I'm glad you were all able to be here."

"Yes ma'am," I replied.

On the return trip to the office, Julie talked nonstop from the backseat while Vince and I sat in silence. She repeated several stories told by the lawyers at her table.

"Did you hear anything interesting?" she asked as we pulled into the firm parking lot.

"Just a few comments from Mr. Braddock about the project I'm working on," Vince said. "Nothing that would interest you."

"Tami?" Julie asked.

"Mr. Appleby wanted to talk about homeschool education," I said as Vince parked the car.

"Yeah, it took courage to mention that," Julie said. "It was way outside the box. What was his reaction?"

"Positive. His family had a private tutor when he lived in Africa as a boy."

"Cool."

Julie got out of the car and walked rapidly toward the office. Vince lagged behind, and out of courtesy I stayed with him.

"Did you have offers from other law firms?" he asked as we walked across the parking lot.

"No, I was surprised when I got the letter from Mr. Carpenter."

"What were you going to do?"

"Work as an eviscerator in a chicken plant."

"Cutting open the chickens?"

"Yes. How did you know?"

"The Latin root of the word."

I laughed. "Do you type in Latin?"

Vince smiled slightly. "No, but I'd like to learn more about homeschooling from someone who went through it and became academically successful."

"Why?"

We reached the front of the office. He opened the door for me.

"I like to learn, especially from a person with strong convictions. Maybe we could go to lunch?"

"I'm sure they will have other events on the schedule."

We reached the hallway. Vince turned toward Mr. Braddock's office suite.

"Thanks for the ride," I said.

"You're welcome."

I stopped by Mr. Carpenter's office. His secretary had made copies of the documents in the Folsom divorce file. Even at this early stage of the proceedings, it was thick enough to require a large, expandable folder. Carrying it with both hands, I returned to the library. Julie glanced up when I entered.

"Did Vince ask you out?" she asked.

13

I GAVE HER A STARTLED LOOK.

"Don't act so innocent," she responded. "Anyone with half a brain could tell he was interested in you."

"How?"

"Did he ask you out?" she repeated.

"He mentioned lunch, but I didn't commit."

"Yeah." Julie nodded with satisfaction. "He's nerdy but nice, and tall enough for you. The chemistry is explosive when two loners get together. I wondered about the scar on his hand. Do you think his whole body is scarred? Usually something like that is the result of a childhood burn. It may explain why he didn't play any sports."

"I'll let you ask him personal questions."

"Oh, he'll tell you when he's ready. Guys like him are waiting for a sympathetic ear to pour out their innermost thoughts and feelings."

"How can you be so sure?"

Julie sniffed. "My family spends a lot of time psychoanalyzing our relatives and friends. All the best psychiatrists are Jewish. It's part of our cultural DNA. Some study Freud and get a fancy diploma and charge hundreds of dollars an hour for what the rest of us do for free."

"Then why aren't you in medical school?"

"Organic chemistry, and I'm more of a talker than a listener. At least once a week, I want you to tell me to shut up."

"I don't tell people to shut up."

"You will if you want to help me become a better person. Plus, I'm bound to get on your nerves. We'll both need to regularly vent and clear the air." Julie pointed at the folder in my hand. "That looks heavy. Drop it on the table and let's see what's going on in the dirty corners of the Folsom household."

We spent the rest of the afternoon dividing our time between Julie's project and mine. The selfishness and sin that had brought the Folsom family to the place of breakup was depressing. I focused on the financial data. Julie read the file like it was a cheap romance novel.

"I can't believe what he did to her ownership in this company," I said as I reviewed the minutes from a corporate meeting. "He bought back her shares at a fraction of their fair market value."

"Shares that he gave her in the first place," Julie responded. "Folsom transferred the stock to his wife so she could put it up for collateral against a construction loan for the North Carolina mountain house titled in her name. Then, he let his mother-in-law stay in the house every summer for five years. Mr. Folsom is a prince who should be protected from his gold-digging wife."

A few minutes later I handed Julie a memo attached to a financial statement. "A wicked prince with a harem. He's paying five thousand dollars a month in child support for a little boy his wife doesn't know about."

Julie read the memo. "What a jerk! I guess it's better than dodging his responsibilities, but I'm not sure how Mr. Carpenter intends to camouflage those payments. The accountant labeled it 'Miscellaneous Benevolence,' but that won't get Folsom through a deposition."

Mid-afternoon we switched to Julie's project. After an hour of online research, I helped her draft a memo about the competing parties' interests in the collateral. I located a Georgia Court of Appeals decision that really helped our position. No one else came into the library. Late in the day, Julie stood up and stretched.

"This is a good place to take a nap."

"Shut up and get back to work," I said from my place at the worktable.

Julie looked surprised.

"I wanted to get it out of the way," I said with a smile. "It's been hanging over me all afternoon."

Julie shook her finger at me. "That's not the way it works. It has to be said with feeling in the right context. I won't cater to your Protestant guilt trip."

"I've never told anyone to shut up in my life."

"There's a lot you've probably never done. This summer is going to be a space trip into the unknown."

I sat back in my chair. "Can I ask you something serious?"

"Yes, but only because you found the Paxton case."

I waited. Julie sat down across from me.

"Okay," she said. "I'm listening."

I put my hands against the edge of the table. "People are always trying to pressure me to do things that violate my Christian beliefs. When that happens it creates stress and awkwardness. Problems build my character, but I'd like to be able to relax around you and not have to defend myself all the time. Would you let me be who I am without trying to change me?"

Julie was silent for a moment. "Would you let me be who I am without trying to change me?"

I was caught. It was my privilege and duty to tell Julie about Jesus. My inner conflict couldn't be hidden from my face. Julie continued.

"Several Christians have tried to prove to me that Jesus is the Messiah and get me to pray to him. But it never made much sense to me. Jews don't try to convince everyone to agree with them. We rarely agree ourselves. It's the way life is lived, not the words spoken, that is important."

"That last part is the truth," I said.

"Okay. Do we have a deal? Neither of us tries to change the other."

I thought about my parents and what they would say. "No. I can't do that."

Julie stared at me for a second, then reached across the table and patted my hand. "Good. We'll have more fun if nothing is off-limits. I'll try to corrupt you, and you can try to convert me."

Ms. Patrick came into the library. "Mr. Carpenter left the office for a meeting earlier this afternoon and asked me to check on you at the end of the day."

Julie told her what we'd done, giving me extensive credit for helping her.

"That's good," Ms. Patrick replied. "I told Mr. Carpenter you were working together, and he gave his permission. However, the lawyers will also want to see how you handle assignments on your own." She looked at her watch. "You can leave anytime after five o'clock. It's five thirty now, so be on your way."

"Can we leave our work in here?" I asked.

"Yes. We're in the process of creating a cubicle space for both of you on the second floor if you want it, but this is a better research environment."

Ms. Patrick left. Julie and I put everything back in our files. It seemed like I'd been at the firm a week, not a day.

"Do you want to grab a beer?" Julie asked when we finished. "There are several nice pubs along the river. I'll buy the first round."

"No, thanks," I replied nonchalantly.

"That would have been a good place to say shut up," Julie responded. "You'll catch on."

We reached the reception area. Julie headed toward the door. I hesitated at the base of the stairs. Julie turned around.

"Aren't you leaving?"

"In a minute. I need to talk to Zach Mays about my criminal case."

"It can wait."

I glanced up the stairs, then followed Julie out the door. It was sticky hot.

"Can I give you a ride?" Julie asked. "Not to get you drunk along the river, but to the house where you're staying."

I didn't relish a hot walk in my business clothes. "Thanks."

Julie drove a new compact car. She had a yellow plastic flower taped to her dashboard. A scent wafted from it.

"It's an air freshener," Julie said when I reached out and touched it.

"Reminds me of the mountains."

"Your new boyfriend is still working," Julie said as we passed Vince's car. "If the firm is only going to hire one new associate, you and I should probably consider this a summer vacation. Vince is a lock."

"That's a lot more likely than the boyfriend part."

"How many serious boyfriends have you had?" Julie asked as she turned onto Montgomery Street.

"Less than you."

That's all it took. During the short ride to Mrs. Fairmont's house, Julie told me more than I'd wanted to hear about her love life. She'd even been engaged for two months when she was a senior in college.

"But I caught him with one of my sorority sisters when he thought I was out of town for the weekend. That's when I decided to go to law school."

"Here it is," I said, pointing to the curb.

"Cool," Julie said, peering through the windshield. "I'm in a garage apartment. You're in the mansion."

"My apartment is in the basement," I said. "But it's very nice."

Julie stopped the car. "Call me if you change your mind about grabbing a beer."

I got out without responding and walked up the brick steps. I could hear Flip barking inside. Unlocking the door, I stepped into the foyer.

"Mrs. Fairmont. It's Tami! I'm home."

Saying the word *home* touched me in a soft place. This place wasn't home, but the English language didn't provide an alternative that fit. There was no response from Mrs. Fairmont. I checked both parlors then walked down the hall, past the kitchen, and to the den. The elderly woman was sitting in her chair, her eyes closed.

"Mrs. Fairmont," I repeated.

She stirred in her chair and slowly opened her eyes. She appeared disoriented.

"I'm Tami Taylor," I said. "I'm living in the basement apartment."

"I know that," Mrs. Fairmont replied, touching a tissue to her nose. "And you just finished your first day as a summer law clerk working for Sam Braddock's firm. Gracie has fixed a nice supper for us, and while we eat, I want you to tell me all about it."

There was a small pot roast with carrots and potatoes in the oven. It was still warm. A simple tossed salad was in a metal bowl in the refrigerator. I took out the food and fixed two plates while Mrs. Fairmont set the table in the dining room.

"What kind of dressing do you want on your salad?" I called out.

"French," she responded.

I carried the food into the dining room. Mrs. Fairmont was already sitting in her seat with Flip on the floor beside her.

"What would you like to drink?" I asked reluctantly.

"Water with lemon would be nice."

I brought two waters and joined her at the table.

"This has been a good day," she said. "After Gracie finished straightening up the house, we spent the afternoon organizing some of my papers and memorabilia. Christine may throw everything away when I die, but at least she'll know what she has. But all the work made me so tired that I fell asleep and didn't hear you come in."

"I didn't want to startle you."

"Don't worry about it. Let's eat."

"Could we pray first?" I asked.

Mrs. Fairmont returned her fork to its place. "Go ahead."

I prayed a simple prayer of thanks for what we'd been able to accomplish and a blessing on Gracie for fixing our supper. The pot roast was fork tender and very juicy.

"Gracie was in a singing mood," Mrs. Fairmont said as she nibbled a piece of carrot.

"What kind of songs?"

"Anything you want to hear. She knows show tunes from way before you were born, songs from her church, the blues. I accuse her of making up her own songs, but she won't admit it. Flip follows her around the house when she's singing. He doesn't want to miss a note."

The normalcy of Mrs. Fairmont's thoughts and speech made me want to squeeze in as much conversation as possible. She had other ideas.

"But my life is dull and almost over. I want to hear about your day."

She listened attentively. When I mentioned the luncheon at the Smith House, she interrupted me.

"My husband owned that building years ago and rented it to a printing company. The printing company moved to a bigger location, and Harry sold it to the people who redid the interior. The last time I was there was for a wedding reception."

"Was it for the Colbert family? Vince Colbert is one of the other summer clerks. He's from Charleston, but his sister had a reception at the place where we ate lunch."

"Do you know who married his sister?"

"No ma'am."

While I talked, Mrs. Fairmont ate a good supper. I nibbled in between sentences and ate faster when she left the table for a few minutes. We carried our plates into the kitchen.

"You'll have to invite Julie over for supper," she said. "Let me know, and I'll ask Gracie to do something special. She cooks a very nice pork loin topped with a cranberry sauce."

"That might not be the best choice. Julie is Jewish, but I'm not sure she follows any dietary laws."

Mrs. Fairmont raised her eyebrows. "Gracie doesn't know much about kosher cooking."

I fixed Mrs. Fairmont a cup of decaf coffee.

"Let's sit in the blue parlor," she said. "I promise not to spill a drop."

It was pleasant in the peace of the parlor. More than any other time since my arrival in Savannah, it reminded me of Powell Station. Mrs. Fairmont sat in a chair contentedly looking at interior decorating and antique magazines. From time to time, she would mark a page with a Post-It note. I curled up in a corner of the sofa and read my book about the Puritans. Flip hopped onto the sofa and let me scratch his neck.

"I'd like to call my parents before it gets late," I said after time had passed.

"Go ahead."

I used the phone in the kitchen. Mama answered then let me talk to the twins before they got ready for bed. After I finished with them, Mama held the phone so she and Daddy could both listen while I told them about my day. They were very interested in the conversation with Mr. Appleby about the merits of a tutorial education and Zach Mays' homeschool background. I felt a twinge of guilt in revealing Zach's history as new information. I didn't give details about my work projects, focusing on the people instead. As I talked, I realized the anxiety I'd felt in the morning when I arrived at the office had subsided. It was a new world, but at least I'd established a beachhead.

"It sounds like you're off to a good start," Daddy said. "Take it each day at a time."

"Yes sir."

"Can you tell us more about the cases you're working on?" Mama asked.

"No ma'am. The confidentiality rules are strict. But as a clerk I won't have much contact with clients. I think most of the day will be spent doing research and getting to know the lawyers in the firm."

"Don't compromise your convictions," Daddy said.

"Yes sir."

"And we'll be praying for the Jewish girl," Mama added. "They're the vine; we're the branch."

"Yes ma'am. I'm going to read Romans 9–11 before I go to sleep."

I hung up the phone and returned to the parlor. Mrs. Fairmont was still sitting in her chair, but her head was tilted forward, her eyes half-closed. She yawned when I entered.

"I'm not much of a hostess," she said. "Especially for a young woman like you."

"No, this has been a great evening, just what I needed after all the pressure of my first day at work. I'm ready to go downstairs and read. But we should test the intercom connection between the basement and your room."

"I don't think I'll ever use it."

Mrs. Fairmont stood up and told Flip to go outside.

"Can we check it anyway?" I asked.

"Suit yourself."

I followed Mrs. Fairmont as she slowly climbed the stairs. Flip rejoined us and scampered past.

"He seems happy that it's bedtime," I said.

"He's always happy. That's one reason I'm glad he's with me."

We entered the bedroom. A sudden urge to hug the older woman came over me. I leaned over and gave her a quick embrace. She remained stiff.

The intercom was on a bureau covered with personal items expected of an elderly woman like Mrs. Fairmont, who was meticulous about her appearance. On the corner of the bureau was the intercom unit. I found an outlet, plugged it in, and set it to "A."

"I'll run downstairs and call you," I said.

I went to the basement and checked the white box beside my bed. I set it on the same channel and pressed the Call button. I heard it beep, but there wasn't any answer. I pressed the Talk button and spoke.

"Mrs. Fairmont, press the Talk button and say something if you can hear me."

I heard Flip barking.

"I'm here," she said.

"Now press the Call button," I said.

I waited a second, then heard the double beep signaling a call. I pressed the Talk button. "Hello."

"Hello," Mrs. Fairmont responded.

"We're connected." I hesitated a moment. "Could I say a good-night prayer? My family does it every night when I'm at home."

There was a scratchy silence, and I wondered if I'd gone too far too fast.

"Are you praying?" Mrs. Fairmont said. "I can't hear you."

"No ma'am. If it's okay, I'll start now."

I said a simple prayer of thanksgiving and blessing.

"Good night," I said when I finished.

There was no response. The static of the intercom continued for a few seconds, then stopped.

I put on my pajamas, read Romans, and prayed. It had been a long time since my prayer list had grown so much in a single day. When I laid my head on the pillow the creaks and pops of the old house didn't disturb my sleep.

14

I LOVED ROUTINE, AND MY EARLY MORNING RUN PROVIDED A comfortable beginning point for the day. Savannah's historic district offered many interesting places to see, and I didn't want to settle into the same route. So, I included a longer loop along the river before climbing a set of ancient uneven steps to the plateau on which the city was built. I ran down Bay Street to Bull Street and turned into the heart of the town's old section. I went around some unfamiliar squares before winding my way back to Mrs. Fairmont's house.

Flip greeted me inside the door, but Mrs. Fairmont didn't make an appearance before I left for the office. I brewed coffee and left her a good morning note. My route to the office wouldn't vary. Shortest was best. I wore a casual khaki skirt, a blue blouse, and white sandals. The sandals were much more comfortable than the low heels I'd worn the previous day. I passed the same people walking their dogs and arrived at the office a few minutes before 8:00 a.m. The door was locked, and I slid my card to open it.

I went to the library, but Julie wasn't there. I picked up the folder for *State v. Jones.* The door opened. I glanced up, expecting Julie, but it was Vince Colbert.

"Good morning," he said. "Ready for another day?"

"Yes."

He handed me several sheets of paper. "My notes from the meeting with Gerry Patrick and a pictorial directory of the firm I put together from the website."

He'd cut and pasted every partner and associate's picture along with a brief personal summary and description of practice areas.

"Thanks, this is great. Do you have a copy for Julie?"

"I only did it for you, but I'll run another for Julie. Where is she?"

"Not here yet."

Vince glanced down at the floor. "Do you have lunch plans?"

It wasn't even 8:15 a.m.

"No, but don't you think we should be flexible in case one of the lawyers asks us out?"

"I'm flexible," he said, looking up. "Just let me know if you can't make it. I'll be working on a project for Mr. Appleby in the main conference room."

"Okay."

Vince left, and I went upstairs. The clerical staff was milling around, and I saw more coffee mugs than computer screens switched on. The door to Zach's office was closed. I knocked.

"Come in," a voice answered.

Zach, his tie loosened around his neck, was facing his computer. He was wearing the same clothes from the previous day.

"Have you been here all night?" I asked in surprise.

He stretched and rubbed his eyes. Strands of light brown hair had escaped from his ponytail. His eyes looked tired.

"Yeah. Sit down. I had to catch the Norwegians first thing Oslo time. One of their ships was scheduled to leave Gdansk in a few hours bound for New York or here. We just wrapped up a deal memo a few minutes ago to keep the business."

"Did Mr. Appleby stay up too?"

Zach smiled. "No, he talked to our client yesterday afternoon and gave me the guidelines I had to work within. The rest was left up to me."

It was a lot of responsibility. I looked at the young associate with new respect.

"Are you going home now?" I asked.

"For a few hours. Then I'll come back and draft the long form agreement. The deal memo is solid, but I'll feel better when everything is tied up."

"Did they agree to the right kind of arbitration clause?"

"You remembered. Yeah, any disagreements will be resolved through a dispute resolution firm of maritime experts based in London."

I started to leave.

"No, wait," he said. "Why did you come to see me?"

"I won't bother you. I wanted to talk to you about the case assigned to me yesterday at the luncheon, but it can wait."

"Let me see the file," he said.

I handed it to him. He read the charges.

"Moses Jones," he said. "Drawn out of the water by the local police and thrown in the pharaoh's prison. How many counts of trespassing?"

"Twenty-four."

Zach handed the file back to me.

"Should I file a motion for bond?" I asked.

"No, go to the jail and talk to Mr. Jones. They usually set bond in cases like this when the person is arrested. Advise him not to give a statement to the police." Zach yawned. "I could give more help if he'd been abducted from a Portuguese freighter in the Malaysian Straits. We have a firm that knows the exact amount of ransom to offer. I just don't have time to do much with you until I catch a break in my caseload. Until then, you're on your own."

I left Zach's office hurt and confused. When I returned to the library, Vince was giving Julie her copy of the materials he'd prepared for me. Julie was wearing black slacks and a tight-fitting top. She smiled when I entered.

"You should have gone with me last night," she said. "There was a great blues band at one of the clubs along the river."

She turned to Vince. "Vinny, does blues music make you happy or sad? I think it can go either way. For me, hearing about someone else's problems puts my own in perspective. But it makes one of my friends sadder."

Vince glanced down at his laptop and didn't answer.

"Isn't it the same with Southern gospel music?" Julie asked me. "You know, lyrics describing life as a peach pit until Jesus spits it out so that it can grow into a tree that reaches to heaven."

I wanted to tell Julie to shut up, but before I spoke, I saw a spark in her eyes that let me know she was baiting me.

"That's the worst idea for a song I've ever heard," I responded. "And you're confusing the Gospel of Matthew with 'Jack and the Beanstalk.' I'm not a big fan of Southern gospel music, but it's nothing like the blues. In Southern gospel, hardships are real, but sorrow is not the final destination."

"That's poetic," Vince said.

"I need to get to work," Julie said, rolling her eyes. "You can continue the music theory discussion without me."

"I'll check with you about eleven thirty," Vince said, moving toward the door.

After he left, Julie turned to me. "Sounds like a lunch date. Did he call you last night and ask you to go out with him today?"

"No, first thing this morning."

"I may be wrong about gospel music, but I know men. All the world's greatest matchmakers are Jewish."

"That's why I'm praying to Jesus and asking him to find the right husband for me. You know Jesus is Jewish, don't you?"

"Yeah, a lot of Jews have a touch of the messiah complex in them," she replied. "Let's work on *Folsom v. Folsom*. A dose of divorce will keep you balanced as you go forward with Vinny."

We spent most of the morning sorting through financial documents and memos to and from Mr. Carpenter and J. K. Folsom. The business dealings were as confusing as a shell game at the county fair, but one thing became clear—Mr. Folsom didn't want his estranged wife looking in every place he'd hidden money. Julie contacted the law firm she'd worked for in Atlanta, and a paralegal e-mailed research and pleadings Julie had prepared in two other cases.

"Are you sure this is okay?" I asked. "The agreement I signed with the firm said it owned my work product."

"I didn't sign anything in Atlanta." Julie shrugged. "Beth is a friend who wouldn't do anything wrong. It's mainly research and sample questions, not facts about an identified client."

I had to admit that the information was very helpful. Julie had done a good job.

"Did you make up all these interrogatory and deposition questions?" I asked.

"No. Most of them were pulled from other files and transcripts. I organized them and made them fit our case, just like you'll do for Folsom."

"I wish I had something like this for my criminal case," I said. "I talked to Zach Mays for a few minutes early this morning, but he stayed up all night working for Mr. Appleby and doesn't have time to help."

Julie looked at her watch. "Uh-oh, that reminds me. I'm late for a meeting with Ned about our bogus water-meter reader."

She grabbed her file, a legal pad, and rushed to the door. "Have a good lunch with Vinny," she said. "Maybe you can hold hands under the table."

After she left, I worked steadily on a long list of questions for Mr.

Carpenter to ask Marie Folsom during her deposition and didn't check my watch until the library door opened. It was Vince.

"Sorry," he said with a sad face. "Mr. Appleby asked me to have lunch with him. I'm in the middle of a big project, and the general counsel for our client is coming into town from Birmingham. It may be the only face-to-face contact I have with the client all summer, so I can't miss it."

"Sure," I replied. "We'll do it some other time."

"How about tomorrow?"

"Maybe," I replied noncommittally.

Vince left. I stood and stretched. I'd reached a good stopping place in my work and wasn't sure what to do next. I picked up the thin folder labeled *State v. Jones.* There was no use delaying. One lesson I'd learned from Mama was that if I didn't begin a project, it wouldn't get done. I went to the reception area.

"Where is the jail?" I asked an older woman on duty after I introduced myself. "Is it near the courthouse?"

"Used to be, but they moved it to the new complex with the sheriff's department." She gave me an address and told me it was several miles away.

"Does the bus line run there?" I asked.

She gave me an odd look. "Why would you want to take a bus?"

"I don't own a car."

"Is your visit to the jail personal or business?"

"Business."

"Then ask Gerry to let you use the firm car."

"The law firm has a car?"

"Of course. The runners use it, and it's available to the lawyers if one of them needs a vehicle." She smiled. "I understand the air conditioner works. That and a motor is all you'll need in Savannah."

I went upstairs to Ms. Patrick's office. She was eating a salad at her desk.

"May I use the firm car so I can visit a client at the jail?" I asked somewhat breathlessly.

"Probably, unless it's checked out."

"Who keeps that record?"

"The receptionist on duty."

I returned downstairs. The woman saw me coming and spoke before I asked a question.

"Yes, it's here, and no one has reserved it until later this afternoon. I should have told you."

I turned around and climbed the stairs. Ms. Patrick made a photocopy of my driver's license, and I signed several sheets of paper without reading them.

"The receptionist can give you directions and the keys."

"Thanks," I said, then stopped. "Oh, and I had a wonderful evening with Mrs. Fairmont last night. She's a very gracious lady. We talked a long time at dinner and spent a time together in the parlor. She was completely lucid. I appreciate you putting me in touch with her daughter."

"I hope things continue to go well," Ms. Patrick said, returning to her salad.

I stepped outside into the heat, which made me doubly thankful I wouldn't have to stand on a street corner, waiting for a bus or ride in a smelly cab. I found the car. It had just been returned, and the air conditioner began to cool the interior by the time I left the parking lot. Several minutes later I parked in front of the Chatham County Correctional Center. The size of the sheriff's department complex surprised me. It was larger than I suspected.

I didn't feel very confident. I'd gritted my teeth all the way through criminal law and procedure, and the law school course trained us to argue a case before the Supreme Court, not figure out the best way to dispose of a petty criminal offense. I wasn't even sure how to conduct an effective interview.

I presented the order from Judge Cannon to a female deputy in the lobby area of the jail. She left with the order. Beyond the lobby was a large open room with chairs and phones on either side of clear glass. It wasn't visiting hours, and the room was empty. To my surprise, the jail smelled as clean as a hospital. The woman returned and handed the order to me.

"Wait here until someone brings the prisoner from lockup," she said. "Jones is a trusty so they may have to track him down."

I didn't know what "trusty" meant, but it made me feel better about meeting a man who lived behind bars. A door behind the woman opened and a male deputy appeared.

"Tami Taylor?" he asked.

"Yes sir," I answered before realizing it probably wasn't necessary to be so formal.

The deputy grinned. "Follow me."

The door clicked shut with a thud behind me. We walked down a short hallway to another door that opened when the deputy pushed a series of buttons. I could see surveillance cameras mounted on the wall. If the twins had been with me they would probably have waved to the cameras.

We entered another room with several numbered doors around an open space. None of the doors had windows in them. A deputy sat behind a desk at one end of the room.

"He's in room 5," the deputy said.

"Do I go in alone?" I asked.

"I don't think Jones is a security risk," the deputy answered. "If you have a concern, you can leave the door open. Deputy Jenkins and I will be on the other side of the room."

"All right." I nodded grimly.

I approached the door and pushed it open. It contained a small table and four plastic chairs. Standing by the table was an old black man with graying hair.

"I'm Tami Taylor," I said. "Are you Mr. Jones?"

"Yes, missy. But you can call me Moses."

The man extended his hand. It felt like old leather. His fingernails were cracked and yellowed with age. I let the door close. The deputy was right. Moses didn't look like a serious threat to my personal safety.

"You be my lawyer?"

"Sort of," I said, then quickly added, "I'm a law student working for a law firm in Savannah this summer. One of the firm's lawyers will be supervising what I do for you."

I put a blank legal pad on the table. We both sat down. I clicked open my pen. I wanted to be professional and efficient.

"First, I need some background information. Your full name, Social Security number, and date of birth."

Moses turned his head to the side and made a sucking noise as he drew air into his mouth. I couldn't see more than a couple of teeth.

"Moses Jones is all I go by. My mama, she give me another name, Tobias, but I don't never use it. I lost my Social Security card. The boss man, he pays me cash under the table. What else you want to know?"

"Date of birth."

"I was born on June 5."

"What year?"

"I'm seventy-one years old," he said, "if that helps you figure it."

I wrote down the date and other information on the legal pad.

"And your address?"

"I ain't got none."

"You're homeless?"

"No!" he said with more force than I expected. "I got me a place down on the river, but it ain't on no road or nothing."

"Are you married?"

"No, missy. I ain't had a woman in my life for a long time."

"Any children?"

"I had one, a boy, but he be dead."

"I'm sorry."

Moses leaned forward and his eyes became more animated. "I never seen his face in the water. If'n I did, I don't think I could stand it."

"What water?" I asked.

"The black water. In the night. That's when the faces come up to look around. They don't say nothing, but I can read their thoughts. They know that I know. They be calling out to me."

I wrote down his words. When I saw them on the legal pad, it made me feel creepy. I looked up. The old man was staring past my shoulder. I quickly turned around. All I saw was the blank concrete wall.

"Do you see something in this room?" I asked hesitantly.

"No, missy. But the faces ain't never far from me. You from Savannah?"

"No."

Moses Jones was obviously delusional and had mental problems much more serious than twenty-four counts of misdemeanor trespassing in his boat. He needed professional help. No one in our church ever admitted going to a psychologist or psychiatrist, but it made sense to me, at least until God came in to straighten out a person's life.

"Well, you may need to talk to someone about that later," I said.

"I told the detective all about it. He asked me a lot more questions than you."

"Which detective?"

"I don't know his name. He be young and black."

"Did he question you about tying your boat up to docks where you didn't have permission?"

Moses nodded his head. "Yeah, but I told him the river, it belong to God who made it. How can anyone own a river? It always be moving and changing. You can't hold on to water like you can a piece of dirty ground."

I was startled by his logic. In a way, it made sense.

"But when a person builds a dock on the river, that's private property," I answered. "That's why you were arrested, because you tied up your boat where you didn't have permission."

"Who'm I going to ask? Will a man be happy and hug my neck if'n I come up on his house in the dark, beat on his door, and say, 'I want to tie up for the rest of the night. I won't hurt a thing. My rope, it don't leave a mark. And I'll be slipping away at dawn light?'"

"The law says you have to get permission."

"You be the lawyer. Make the law right so I can leave this jailhouse with my boat."

"Where is your boat?"

"In amongst the cars behind that tall fence. I can see it, but I can't touch it. I don't know if it be leaky or not."

"It's here at the jail?"

Moses nodded.

"I'll check into that for you. Have they set your bond?"

"I reckon, but I ain't got money for no bondsman. My boat ain't worth nothing to nobody but me."

"Have you had a court hearing of any kind?"

"I ain't been before no judge, if'n that's what you mean."

"So they'll leave you in here indefinitely for trespassing?" I asked, expressing my private thoughts.

"That be your job, missy. Most of the time, the lawyer be the one to get a man out of this jail."

"Okay."

I opened the folder and looked again at the twenty-four counts. The scenario seemed clear. I spoke slowly.

"You would fish at night and tie up at a private dock for a few hours of sleep until the sun came up."

"Yes, missy. That part be true. I never took nothing that weren't mine." He looked away. "Except for some other stuff."

"What other stuff?"

"At the taverns where I cleaned up. I'd grab cooked food, a knife, a fork. Not every week, only when I was extra hungry or needed it."

All theft is wrong, but these newly admitted offenses weren't part of the case I had to resolve, and I wasn't a prosecutor. I sat back in my chair.

"So what is our defense to the charges against you? They've listed twenty-four counts of trespassing when you tied up without permission at private docks. I agree with you that the river belongs to God, but the docks are private property."

Moses looked at me and blinked his dark eyes. "I want my boat back and to get out of this jailhouse so I can go to the river and catch fish. I won't bother nobody else. Never again."

"Will you stop tying up at private docks?"

He rubbed his hand across the top of his head. "I been on that river before there be docks. I reckon I can say to myself they ain't there no more."

"Does that mean you won't tie up there?"

"Yes, missy. That be exactly what that mean."

15

I WATCHED DEPUTY JENKINS ESCORT MOSES OUT OF THE INTERview area. I wasn't sure I'd conducted an adequate first interview or not. I glanced down at my single page of notes. There didn't seem to be any benefit in asking the old man about each count. I'm sure the story was the same. I considered my options.

I could remind the judge that God, as the Creator of all things, owned all the rivers of the world and looked favorably on baby Moses when his basket trespassed onto waters reserved for Pharaoh's daughter. Such an argument, while creative, wouldn't make me look like a competent lawyer-in-training. I could follow Julie's advice to subpoena the twenty-four dock owners to trial and hope none of them showed up. While trying the case would give me courtroom experience, it would also drag Zach Mays away from his more important work at the firm.

The best course of action was obvious. Moses Jones ought to plead guilty to the charges with a promise not to trespass in the future. After receiving a stern lecture from the judge, he could be placed on a short period of probation. I reached the lobby.

"Could I find out the name of the detective who interviewed my client, Moses Jones?" I asked the woman deputy on duty.

"Give me the case number."

I handed her the file. She opened it and returned my notes. "You might want to keep this."

"Thanks."

"Wait here."

She left for several minutes. While I waited a deputy brought in a woman in handcuffs accompanied by two small girls. She stood forlornly with the little girls holding on to her legs while the officer spoke on a walkie-talkie to someone in another section of the jail. I stared, unable to pull my gaze away from the tragedy. The woman looked at me with eyes that pleaded for help. I took a step forward, then stopped. I had no right to intrude. The deputy took the woman by the arm and led her into the lockup area with the children trailing along behind.

The woman officer returned.

"It's Detective Branson. He's on his way up to see you."

"He's willing to talk to me?"

"I showed him the order from the judge."

A different door than the one I'd taken to the interview area opened, and a black man in his thirties wearing a casual shirt and dark pants entered.

"I'm Sylvester Branson," he said.

"Tami Taylor."

"Come with me."

I followed him through the door into a suite of small offices.

"Have a seat," the detective said.

On the detective's desk was a picture of a woman and two girls about the same ages as the ones I'd seen a few minutes before.

"You're working for Braddock, Appleby, and Carpenter?"

"Yes sir."

"Mr. Carpenter represented my father and his brothers in a civil case several years ago. He's a great trial lawyer, one of the best cross-examiners in this part of the state."

"That's what I've been told. I hope to see him in the courtroom while I'm here."

"Did he send you down here to represent Moses Jones?"

"In a way. He asked Judge Cannon to appoint summer clerks to work on misdemeanor cases so long as another lawyer in the firm supervised our work."

The detective didn't say anything. I shifted in my chair, not sure about the proper way to proceed.

"When I met with Mr. Jones, he mentioned that he had been interviewed by a detective," I said.

"That's right. I talked to him."

"Could you tell me what he told you?"

Branson tapped a folder on his desk. It was much thicker than mine.

"After waiving his Miranda rights, he talked freely about the charges."

"Did he sign a statement?"

"Yes, but I won't give it to you now. You can obtain a copy once you file the proper request with the court."

"I'm going to have to research how to do that." I bit my lower lip and tried to think of something else to ask. I decided to broach the ultimate issue. "If Mr. Jones wants to enter a plea, could I talk to you about that?"

"No, the district attorney's office will have the case assigned to a prosecutor. All plea negotiations are handled by the prosecutor."

"Who has the case?"

"I'm not sure. No one has contacted me."

I ran down my mental checklist. "Is there a bond set in Mr. Jones' case?"

"Yes, it's five thousand dollars."

"I don't think he has much money."

"That's why he's still in jail and represented by an appointed lawyer."

"I'm sorry. That was a stupid question."

The detective smiled. "No need to apologize. There are a lot of lawyers in Savannah who ask stupid questions. They could use a dose of your honesty."

"Have you talked to any of the people who claim he tied up his boat at their dock?"

"One of my assistants and a deputy verified the information contained in every count listed in the accusation. The complainants are from the same homeowners association."

"Can you give me the name of the association?"

The detective opened the file and read a name.

"Was there any physical damage to the docks?" I asked.

"Is there any mention of criminal damage to property in the charges?"

"No."

"Then it's not part of the case at this time."

"Good. Do you think the complainants would oppose probation for Mr. Jones if he promised to stay away from their docks?"

"That wasn't discussed. Their primary goal is to put a stop to your client's trespassing. This area is only partially developed, and there is still a lot of marshy wilderness. It's disturbing when a stranger comes around a private residence. Break-ins have occurred."

"But nothing linked to Mr. Jones?"

"Not at this time."

I looked at a certificate on the wall of the detective's office. It had something to do with proficiency in the use of a weapon I'd never heard of.

"Is there anything else?" the detective asked.

"Yes, I think Mr. Jones may need treatment from a mental health professional."

"That's already started. He's meeting with a counselor who, I believe, placed him on medication."

"Thanks."

I got up to leave but then sat back down. "I appreciate your patience, but there is one other thing I don't understand. Did Mr. Jones talk to you about seeing faces in the water?"

"That's the reason for the referral to mental health."

"He said he talked to you about the faces in the water for a long time."

The detective didn't respond.

"Is that right?" I asked.

The detective closed his file. "Any conversation with Mr. Jones is difficult. Your client has a tendency to talk about what he wants to."

"Thanks for taking time to meet with me. I'm just learning what to do and really appreciate it."

"I'll walk you out. Give my regards to Mr. Carpenter."

When we reached the entrance area, I remembered the woman with the two children.

"Oh, a woman in handcuffs was brought in a few minutes ago," I said to the detective. "She had two little girls with her. Can you tell me what she did wrong?"

"Running a meth lab in her kitchen. One of the other detectives is talking to her now."

"What will happen to the children?"

"Probably stay with a family member if someone is suitable. Otherwise, they'll be placed in foster care."

"It's a sad situation."

"Would you like to represent her too?"

"No," I said quickly. "I don't think I'm going to be a criminal defense lawyer."

DURING THE RETURN TRIP to the office, my mind went back and forth between Moses Jones and the woman with the little girls. My first encounters with people in jail had left me thinking more about their tragic circumstances than the punishment they deserved.

Back at the office I returned the keys to the receptionist.

"Did you fill it up with gas?" she asked.

"I didn't think about it. Should I—"

"I'm kidding," she interrupted. "Did you have trouble finding the jail?"

"No ma'am."

I went to the library. It was empty, and everything looked the same as when I'd left for the jail. I worked alone on the Folsom case for over an hour before taking a break. It was quiet in the library, which helped me concentrate, but I had to admit that I missed Julie. The door opened, and I looked up, expecting to see her. Instead, it was Zach Mays. He'd changed clothes and shaved.

"Gerry told me you were working in here," he said. "Can I interrupt?"

"Sure."

He sat across the table from me. "I feel better after sleeping for a few hours. Do you ever stay up all night studying?"

"Never, I always plan ahead. Not that I'm saying you don't organize your time," I added quickly. "In law school there aren't negotiations with businessmen in Norway. All our classes are on eastern standard time."

Zach's long hair still looked slightly damp.

"I shouldn't have told you that I was too busy to help you," he said. "I was tired."

"That's okay. I understand."

"And I want to apologize."

My attitude toward the young lawyer rotated 180 degrees. Confession was one of the most trustworthy signs of genuine faith.

"Thank you," I said as sincerely as I could.

Zach smiled. "And to prove my repentance, I'll take you to the jail so we can talk to our mutual client. What's his name? Mr. James?"

"Moses Jones, and it's too late. I've already interviewed him, along with the detective who questioned him about the charges."

Zach sat up straighter in his chair. "What did you find out?"

I gave him a detailed account of my initial investigation. He listened without comment until I finished.

"I'll do a conflict of interest check on the homeowners association," he said. "We may represent it. Ned Danforth does a lot of that type of work for Mr. Braddock's clients."

"Would that disqualify us from the case?"

"No, but it might give us an advantage in talking to the homeowners. What about Jones' prior criminal record? If he's had multiple convictions, it would impact a plea agreement."

"I didn't ask."

"And the detective didn't mention it?"

"No."

"Search the state and county websites."

"Do you know the links?"

"No, you track them down. Also, contact the administrator at the district attorney's office and find out the prosecutor assigned to the case. We can meet with that person together." Zach pointed to my folder. "Make a copy of everything in the file for me."

"Okay."

"Jones sounds like an alcoholic who's pickled his brain and sees dead people floating around in the jar with him. Did you ask him if he recognized the faces in the water?"

"No, it was weird, something that should be explored by a mental health worker, not me."

Zach rubbed his chin. "You're probably right, but I'm curious. Next time, I'll ask him."

After Zach left, I went to the downstairs copy room, and after one false start, navigated my way through the codes and buttons to make the copies. I organized Zach's folder exactly the same as my own and took it to his office. He wasn't there so I left it on his desk. On the corner near the photograph of his parents was a light blue envelope with Zach's first name written in a woman's hand across the front.

I used one of the computer terminals in the library to research Moses' background. There were countless defendants named Jones, but only one with the first name Moses. I found a felony conviction for illegal transport of moonshine whiskey that corroborated Zach's suspicion that Moses' brain had been damaged by alcohol. I didn't know much about bootleg liquor, but I'd read that a bad batch could cause blindness, brain damage, or death. The county database didn't reveal any other convictions or subsequent arrests.

It was close to 5:00 p.m. when I called the district attorney's office. After waiting on hold for several minutes, the woman who answered the phone told me the case had been assigned to an assistant DA named Margaret Smith.

"May I speak to her?" I asked.

After another long wait a female voice came on the line. "This is Maggie Smith."

I identified myself and the purpose for my call.

"My first taste of the criminal justice system came when I was a summer clerk for the Braddock firm," she said. "I'll never forget it. My client was charged with simple battery of his fifteen-year-old stepson. I wanted to see my client behind bars, not set free. That case, and the fact that Braddock, Appleby, and Carpenter has never hired a female attorney, are two big reasons why I decided to be a prosecutor."

"How many other female summer clerks have worked at the firm?"

"Several, but no women have ever made it onto the letterhead. Don't get me wrong, it's a nice place to spend the summer and looks decent on your résumé, but unless things have changed, there won't be an opportunity for employment after law school. The history of male bias at the firm is conclusive, and everyone in town knows it." Smith paused. "Hold on while I pull the Jones file. I don't recall seeing it come across my desk."

While I waited, I wondered why God would miraculously open a door of opportunity with a brick wall behind it.

"I have it," the assistant district attorney said.

"When did you work here?" I asked, still thinking about her comments.

"Five years ago. Try to forget what I said. I guess I'm still bitter at the double standard. You might be the one to break the gender barrier."

"There's another girl at the firm this summer."

"Really? I was the only female clerk my year."

"Did they hire an associate?"

"Yeah, Ned Danforth, but he never clerked. Let's see now, twenty-four counts of simple trespass. Can't your client read a No Trespassing sign?"

"Actually, I'm not sure he can read. Were there signs posted on the docks?"

"I don't know. It's not a legal requirement to post private property. Look, I know Joe Carpenter wants you to gain experience by making my life miserable with motions and frivolous hearings, but I don't have time to play games. There are a lot of serious cases on my docket. Do your investigation; talk to everyone who lives on the Little Ogeechee River if you like; then make me a plea offer. If it's reasonable, I'll recommend it. On a case like this, I doubt Judge Cannon will give us a problem, and your client can get on with his life."

"Okay."

I wondered if I would sound as confident and forceful as Maggie Smith after I'd been practicing law for five years.

"And best of luck to you and the other girl working at the firm.

There's always a first time for everything. If you get a job offer, I'll buy you a double of your drink of preference."

"That would be sweet tea for me."

"Whatever. Get back to me with your proposal."

A few minutes after I hung up the phone, Julie returned, looking frazzled.

"Do you like dogs?" she asked.

"Yes."

"Then I wish Mr. Carpenter had given you my case. Ned and I got a list of the State's witnesses to interview. We drove through several run-down neighborhoods trying to track down people and ask them what they'd seen. I've never run into so many dogs in my life. Ned is allergic to dogs so he sent me to knock on doors." Julie pointed to her right leg. "Can you see the dog slobber on my pants?"

I leaned forward. There was a distinct shiny streak from mid-thigh to below her knee.

"I got that from the biggest, hairiest dog I've ever seen. A dog like that has no business living in Savannah. He should be in the northern tip of Maine."

"At least he didn't bite."

"I was afraid it was a preliminary lick before he chomped down. I ran out of there as fast as I could go."

"Were these nice neighborhoods?"

"No, the owners spend all their money on dog food. There was one house with two pit bulls. I refused to go inside the gate. A man heard the dogs snarling and came to the door. I yelled questions to him across the yard."

"What did you find out?"

"We didn't talk to everyone, but a few people remembered Ferguson because he wandered around after pretending to look at the water meter. I think I've figured out what he was doing."

"You've given up on the Halloween costume defense?"

"Yeah," Julie answered. "I'm serious. I think Mr. Ferguson was scoping out houses to rob."

"But you said the neighborhoods weren't upper class."

"Exactly. Poor people prey on other poor people. There were houses with burglar bars on the windows that I wouldn't want to go inside if the door was left wide open."

"And dogs in the yards."

"Yeah, the people bought those brutes as an alternative to a sophisticated security system."

"Is your client linked to any of the robberies?"

"I hope not, but if he's charged with burglary, it would be a felony and take the case out of my basket."

"When are you going to the jail to talk to him?"

"He's not in jail. He's out on bond working his real job."

"What does he do for a living?"

"Get this. He works for the city's animal control department. That's probably how he got access to a meter reader's uniform."

"And explains why he isn't afraid of dogs."

Julie rubbed her arm across her forehead. "Are you ready to leave? I haven't needed a shower so badly since I played soccer on a muddy field in middle school."

"I'm not trying to make you stay."

"Let's go together. I'm giving you a ride home. I want every detail about your lunch date with Vinny. Did he ask you out to dinner? Did he talk about his last girlfriend and why they broke up?"

"I didn't go to lunch with Vince. He had to meet with Mr. Appleby and a client."

"What did you do?"

"I went to the jail and interviewed my client."

"Then tell me about that. At least you didn't have to worry about getting mauled by a pack of dogs."

After meeting with Tami, Moses finished his first trash run of the day. Then the deputy in charge of the dining hall ordered him to clean the tables. Each stainless-steel table was surrounded by four metal stools bolted onto strips of metal that extended like spokes from a central post. Fights during mealtime were rare at the jail, but if an inmate did lose his temper, a chair couldn't be used as a large blunt object.

Moses carried a plastic bucket of water in each hand. One bucket contained warm, soapy water; the other, clean rinse water. After wiping off each table and chair, he dipped a rag in the rinse water and removed the soapy residue. Moses didn't just clean the surface of the tables; he also scrubbed under the rims. The deputy gave him a screwdriver to dislodge fossilized pieces of chewing gum. Moses worked slowly. Getting done in a hurry wouldn't earn him any reward except an earlier return to his cell where he had nothing to do but lie on his bed.

The tall girl who talked to him said she wasn't a lawyer but then acted like one. It didn't make sense. She reminded Moses of the young woman with blonde hair who'd met with him a few days earlier. She said she wasn't a doctor but then acted like one. The blonde-haired woman asked questions about his health, wrote notes on paper, listened to everything he told her, and told the jail nurse to give him a green pill every morning. Moses dutifully swallowed the pill, but he knew getting back to his life along the river was the only medicine he really needed.

As he cleaned the tables he thought about the tall, dark-haired girl who wasn't a real lawyer. She looked familiar. That's why he asked if she lived in Savannah. Moses knew a lot of people by face if not by name. He'd met hundreds of people when he worked for Tommy Lee Barnes as a bolita runner and could remember faces for years and years.

A bolita runner collected money from the players of the simple betting game and handed out slips of paper that served as proof of the numbers chosen. Beginning early in the morning, Moses went all over the city calling on regular players and trying to attract new ones. At precisely 6:00 p.m., five winning numbers between 1 and 100 were announced by randomly selecting five numbered Ping-Pong balls from a large bag. Prior to the drawing, Moses and one of the other runners tabulated the most popular numbers of the day, and Tommy Lee would remove those numbers from the sack to avoid a big loss.

Tommy Lee made the daily drawing exciting. He had a preacher's voice and always asked a pretty girl to stick her hand in the bag and draw out the Ping-Pong balls. Runners notified winners the following day and delivered their winnings. Moses liked counting out the greasy dollar bills to a winner. Even with payouts, Tommy Lee would make a couple of hundred dollars a day. Each Friday, Moses would take envelopes of cash to the police officers who let the game operate. Mr. Floyd, Tommy Lee's boss, paid the mayor's office directly.

The tall girl who wasn't a real lawyer reminded Moses of a girl he'd known during the time he worked for Tommy Lee Barnes. She didn't play bolita, but the old woman who owned the big house where the girl lived guessed ten numbers every Wednesday. When the girl saw Moses on the sidewalk outside the house, she would tell him to go away. Moses would nod respectfully and sneak around the corner where he would wait for the old woman to come out to meet him. If she had a winning number, Moses would pick up the ticket and redeem it for her.

Moses wasn't sure what had happened to the girl. She would be an old woman herself by now. Once or twice, he thought he'd seen her face in the water, but it didn't make sense that she would be there.

16

BY THE END OF THE FIRST WEEK, I HAD BEGUN TO DOUBT MS. Patrick's promise that a summer clerk job at Braddock, Appleby, and Carpenter would be more fun than toil. Mr. Carpenter added two more projects to my workload and three more to Julie's stack. She and I worked together on the Folsom case, and I revised her memo on the secured transaction issue, but we had to go our separate ways on the new projects. She worked directly with Mr. Carpenter. I found myself reporting more and more to Robert Kettleson, a senior associate who confidently informed me that he was next in line for partner.

Kettleson, a tall, skinny man, communicated with me via e-mails that he typed at all hours of the day and night. He wanted my responses in writing so there would be no doubt about my opinion. The process bothered me, but I had to admit it forced me to be very careful in my research.

I had no time to work on the Jones case. When I asked Zach about it, he pointed to the files on the corner of his desk and told me justice for indigent defendants like Moses Jones would have to wait another week. At least the old man had food to eat and a roof over his head.

Late Friday afternoon, Julie returned to the library and plopped down on the other side of the table.

"Are you coming to work tomorrow?" she asked. "Please say no because I don't want to be the only clerk who abandons the office to spend a few hours at Tybee Island beach. Why don't you come with me? We're both pale as white bread, but we could lather up with sun-screen and pretend we're from Nova Scotia."

"Nova Scotia?"

"If that's not exotic enough, you can be Norwegian and I'll be Lebanese."

"I don't own a swimsuit."

"You're kidding."

Apparently my face told her the truth.

"Don't worry about it," she continued. "I'll buy one for you and put it on my credit card. You can pay me back when we get our pay-checks next week."

"Do your orthodox cousins in New York go to the beach?" I asked.

"Yeah, there are places where they can go and be among the faith-ful on certain days of the week, but they don't wear—" Julie stopped. "Rabbi, are you that conservative?"

"Yes."

"Wow. You are hard-core."

Her words stung, but I stayed calm. "I have strong convictions about modesty," I replied quietly.

"Okay. Suit yourself, or rather don't if it offends your morals. My parents want me to walk on eggshells around my cousins, which is one reason I don't like to visit them. But I still want to know if you're going to spend the day at the office. If you do, it will make me and Vinny look bad."

"You already talked to Vince?"

"He agreed to take the day off. I didn't say anything to him about the beach, but if it was okay with you, I wanted to invite him to join us. Two girls and one guy would be irresistible odds."

"The two of you can go."

"And steal him from you? He's not my type."

"I'm not sure he's my type."

"What is your type?"

"I'm not sure. I haven't met him."

"Don't be so dense," Julie snapped. "You have to meet men to find out who you're compatible with. I'm trying to help you, but you're not making it easy. You'll never find out the truth about other people or yourself with your nose stuck in a Bible or a prayer book."

"I don't use a prayer book, and I didn't ask for help."

"But you need help. Lots of it. I'm sure glad we're not sharing an apartment. I don't think I could stand your self-righteous attitude 24/7. You're so uptight I'm surprised your eyes open in the morning!"

My uptight eyes suddenly stung with tears I vainly tried to blink away. Most people didn't keep attacking after I made my convictions clear. Julie saw that I was upset and swore.

"I'm sorry," she said.

I quickly wiped my eyes. "Everything you say makes sense except that I believe God controls my future. I can't abandon my confidence in him. To do that would be to deny who I am as a person." I pulled a tissue from my purse and blew my nose. "Does that make any sense to you?"

Julie shrugged. "You fanatic religious types are all alike."

"People judge me because of the things I do and don't do. But I'm not a mixed-up mess of legalistic rules and regulations. I'm a child of God who wants to live in the freedom from sin Jesus provides through his death on the cross."

"Okay, okay," Julie said. "You can step down from your pulpit. My efforts to corrupt you are over for the week."

This time I didn't cry. I pressed my lips tightly together before I spoke. "I guess I'll walk home."

"No need to get hot and sweaty. I'll give you a ride. I said I was sorry."

Partway home, Julie broke the silence. "You've never had a boyfriend?"

"No."

"My Jewish intuition tells me that's about to change."

We reached Mrs. Fairmont's house. Julie stopped the car.

"So, are you going to the office tomorrow?" she asked.

"No. I wouldn't do anything to try to gain an advantage."

"Good. I'll call Vinny. This summer is our last chance to have fun before we have to enter the real world of work."

I opened the door. "If you go to the beach, use plenty of sunblock."

"You won't recognize me on Monday. I may not look Lebanese, but in a couple of days I'll be able to pass for an Israeli."

I COULD HEAR THE TV BLARING when I entered the house. I peeked into the den. The TV might be on, but that didn't mean she was watching it. Mrs. Fairmont's eyes were closed. She tried to maintain a schedule, but I'd learned that even though she went to bed early, her sleep patterns were irregular. Twice when I'd come upstairs to the kitchen in the night, she had been awake watching TV. Flip didn't seem to mind. He matched his sleep schedule to hers. The little dog barked and came over to me for a welcoming scratch behind the ears.

"Mrs. Fairmont," I announced.

She stirred. Her eyes fluttered open and glanced in my direction.

"Who is it?" she asked with alarm in her voice.

"Tami Taylor. I'm staying with you this summer."

The older woman's lapses of short-term memory made my heart ache. I picked up Flip, who licked my chin.

"Flip knows me," I said as I let the tiny dog lick my chin. "I'm staying in the basement apartment and working for Mr. Braddock's law firm."

Mrs. Fairmont stared at me. Generally, it only took a few comments to tether her mind in reality.

"Where's Gracie?" she asked.

"Gone for the day."

"Did she let you in the house?"

"No ma'am." I held up a key. "Your daughter, Mrs. Bartlett, gave me a key."

Mrs. Fairmont pushed herself up from the chair. "I'm going to call Christine this minute. She has no right giving out keys to strangers!"

I deposited Flip on the floor. This was the most serious spell of confusion I'd witnessed.

"What do you want me to do while you call her?"

"Wait on the front steps would be the polite thing to do," she answered curtly as she walked unsteadily toward the kitchen. "Proper young women don't barge into a house uninvited."

"Yes ma'am."

Keeping the key in my hand in case she locked the door behind me, I retreated toward the front of the house, but I positioned myself by the hallway door in the green parlor so I could hear the conversation in the kitchen. I wasn't sure whether Mrs. Fairmont would remember Mrs. Bartlett's phone number. There was silence for several seconds, then I heard Mrs. Fairmont begin talking to someone about her house key. After a couple of sentences she stopped talking.

"Yes, I took my medicine," she said. "Gracie always gives it to me."

A longer period of silence followed.

"Are you sure?" she asked. "Samuel Braddock?"

After a shorter silence, she said, "No, I can take care of myself."

I heard her hang up the phone. I quickly moved through the foyer and outside to the front steps. I waited, praying that Mrs. Fairmont had regained connection with reality. The front door opened. She stared at me again.

"Christine says you're staying here so you might as well come inside, but I don't want you telling me what to do."

"I'm here to help."

Mrs. Fairmont turned and walked away. I stood in the foyer and watched her climb the stairs to the second floor without looking back. Flip followed her. I went into the kitchen and hit the Redial button on the phone. Mrs. Bartlett answered.

"What is it now?" she asked.

"It's Tami Taylor. I overheard your mother's phone call. She thought I'd gone outside, but I was listening from the parlor. I came in from work a few minutes ago, and she didn't recognize me. Usually, her confusion goes away after we talk for a minute or so, but this time it didn't. It's the worst spell she's had since I've been here."

"Where is she now?"

"Upstairs."

"No, I'm not!" a voice screamed behind me.

The sound startled me so violently that I dropped the phone. It hit the floor with a sharp crack. Flip barked and ran around the kitchen.

"Who are you talking to?" Mrs. Fairmont demanded with fire in her eyes.

"Your daughter, Christine," I managed.

I picked up the phone and handed it to her. "Here. Talk to her yourself."

Watching me with suspicious eyes, she put the phone to her ear. "Who is this?" she demanded.

I couldn't hear the other side of the conversation, but the expression on Mrs. Fairmont's face slowly changed. I stepped backward to the far side of the kitchen and waited. Mrs. Fairmont closed her eyes several times as she listened. I inched closer, fearing she might faint.

"Yes, yes," she said, followed by, "No, no."

She handed the phone to me. "Talk to her."

"Hello," I said.

"Has she calmed down?" Mrs. Bartlett asked.

"I think so."

"I can't drive into town tonight. Ken and I have a dinner engagement that has been on the books for months. She'll be all right in a few minutes. These things pass. It's even happened with Gracie."

"But what do I—"

"Call my cell phone or 911 if there is a true emergency, although if you're patient she'll be fine. You can take care of this. That's why I hired you. Good night."

The phone clicked off. Mrs. Fairmont was leaning against the counter with her eyes closed and her hand resting against the right side of her face. It was such a sad sight that the remaining tears I'd bottled up at the office when Julie attacked me gushed out in compassion. Mrs. Fairmont opened her eyes. The fire was gone. She looked tired.

"Why are you crying?" she asked.

"Because I care about you. I'm here to help you. The last thing I want to do is upset you."

"I don't feel well," she said.

"May I help you upstairs?"

She started shuffling toward the door. I followed behind her. Flip stayed out of the way but close to her feet. When she reached the steps, Mrs. Fairmont grasped the railing tightly as she climbed. Halfway up, she wavered, and I reached out my hand to steady her. She reached the landing at the top of the stairs, then walked slowly to her room. I followed.

"Here's the intercom, if you need me," I said, making sure it was still turned on. "I have one in the basement. Press the Call or Talk button, and I'll be here as soon as I can."

She sat on the edge of the bed. "What's happening to me?" she asked.

"You were confused."

She rubbed her temples. I noticed she was wearing shoes that didn't match.

"Why don't you lie down and rest?" I suggested.

She leaned back on the bed and closed her eyes. I gently removed her shoes and positioned a pillow under her head. The air-conditioning was on so I put a lightweight cotton throw over her legs and feet. I picked up Flip and put him on the bed. He curled up near her feet.

"I'll be back in a little while to check on you," I said, turning toward the door.

"You can sing a song now," she said softly.

I came closer to the bed. "What kind of song?"

"You know, the kind you sing every night before I go to sleep."

I thought back to some of the songs Mama sang to me when I was small. All of them had biblical themes.

"All right," I answered softly.

My brother Bobby was the best singer in our family, but I could carry a tune. I decided humming might be a good way to start. I leaned close to Mrs. Fairmont's head and began to hum a melody whose roots lay in the spirits of early Christian pioneers. Mrs. Fairmont's facial muscles relaxed. When I switched to words, she took a deep breath. In a few seconds, she was asleep.

I didn't stop.

I finished that song and started another. Mrs. Fairmont was unconscious, but I wasn't singing to her mind—the lyrics were intended for her spirit. I knelt on the floor beside her bed, continued through three songs, then tapered off to another hum. I finished by praying in a soft voice for healing, salvation, and blessing. When I lifted my head, Flip was watching me through a single, drooping eye. I slipped quietly from the room.

Several hours later, I came upstairs in my pajamas for a drink of cold water before going to bed. Mrs. Fairmont was sitting in the den watching the late-night news. I peeked in at her. An empty dinner plate was on a table beside her chair.

"Hello, Tami," she said when she heard me. "Did you have a good day at work?"

"It was challenging," I answered.

"You must have worked late. I had a long nap and feel much better. Gracie left supper, but your plate is still in the refrigerator."

I'd been so upset by the events earlier in the evening that my appetite had disappeared. "I may eat it tomorrow."

"That's fine. I'm going to bed after the news is over. Good night."

"Good night."

SATURDAY MORNING, Mrs. Fairmont was back to normal. I brewed her coffee and fixed a light breakfast that we ate at a table on the veranda that opened into the den. She didn't mention the chaos of the previous night, and I didn't see any benefit in bringing it up. While I watched her carefully spread orange marmalade to the edges of an English muffin, I thought about her irrational anxiety and felt a lump in my throat. Aging was part of life, but I wished people could leave earth in a blaze of glory like Elijah, not spiral down into pathetic incompetence.

"Are you all right?" Mrs. Fairmont interrupted my thoughts.

"Yes ma'am. Would you like another cup of coffee?"

"That would be nice."

I went to the kitchen. The doorbell chimed. Flip charged in from the veranda to warn the possible intruder of the dog's fierce presence. I followed him into the foyer and opened the door. It was Zach Mays with his motorcycle helmet under his right arm.

"I hope I'm not too early," he said.

"What are you doing here?"

"It's a nice neighborhood. May I come in? Did you just wake up?"

"No, I've already run four miles that included a quick trip by the office. The parking lot was empty at six thirty."

The young lawyer stepped into the foyer. "I'll be there later today but wanted to go for a ride before it gets too hot."

"Mrs. Fairmont is on the veranda. I'm getting her a fresh cup of coffee."

Flip, continuing to growl, circled Zach's feet.

"Will he bite?" Zach asked.

"I'm not sure. It's probably a good thing you're wearing boots."

Zach followed me into the kitchen. Together, we went to the veranda.

"Mrs. Fairmont, do you remember Zach Mays?"

The old woman extended her hand. "No, but it's good to see you again. Please sit down."

For the next thirty minutes, we enjoyed a pleasant conversation. Mrs. Fairmont asked Zach questions. She was mostly interested in people he'd met whom she knew. I didn't try to sort out the cast of characters. The intricacies of Savannah society seemed as complicated as Chinese history. At a pause in the discussion, Zach looked at me.

"Are you ready to go?" he asked.

"I'm not working today."

"I'm not talking about the office. I meant for a ride."

"On your motorcycle?"

"Make sure you wear a good helmet," Mrs. Fairmont said.

"I have an extra with me," Zach replied. "It's strapped to the bike."

"But I've never ridden a motorcycle." I paused. "And I don't have any jeans. I wouldn't feel comfortable behind you on the seat."

"You don't have to put your arms around my waist, and you can wear anything you like," Zach replied. "I have a sidecar. It's not much different than the fancy convertible you were driving, just a little bit closer to the ground."

"It sounds like fun," Mrs. Fairmont said. "Ferguson Caldwell used to own a motorcycle. He took me for a ride."

"I'm not sure," I said.

Zach held up his hand as if taking an oath. "I promise not to go any faster than you like. If you feel uncomfortable, we'll just go around the block, and I'll drop you off by the front door."

I was wearing a loose-fitting blue skirt and a white short-sleeved blouse. "I need to do the breakfast dishes," I said.

"I'll help," Zach volunteered.

"Go ahead, I'll be fine," Mrs. Fairmont added. "It's so pleasant out here this morning."

In the kitchen I studied Zach's face. "Why are you asking me to go for a ride?" I asked.

"I'll tell you later," he replied. "I promise."

There wasn't time to call my parents and get their counsel. I had to decide myself. My mind leaned toward no, but my mouth must have been connected to another part of me.

"Okay, but not long."

It only took a few minutes to clean up the kitchen. Zach loaded the dishwasher exactly the same way I did. I went downstairs, brushed my teeth, and tied my hair in a ponytail. I threw some things in a casual handbag. Zach and Mrs. Fairmont were on the veranda, continuing their conversation about Savannah.

"I'm ready," I announced.

"Have fun," Mrs. Fairmont said.

I followed Zach outside. Parked alongside the curb was a big black motorcycle with a sidecar attached to it.

"I thought you had a red motorcycle," I said.

"I do. This one belonged to my parents. It's twenty years old. I used to ride in the sidecar when I was a kid. That's when I fell in love with motorcycles. My father was going to sell it last year, so I bought it from him. I couldn't stand the thought of it leaving the family."

The passenger carrier had orange flames flickering along the side.

"You make it sound like a family heirloom."

"In a way, it is." He handed me a black helmet also decorated with the orange flame motif. "This is my mother's helmet. It should fit."

I pulled the helmet over my head. It rested snugly against my ears. A plastic shield covered my face.

"It feels claustrophobic," I said, speaking extra loud so I could be heard.

"You'll be glad the first time a june bug crashes into your face at fifty miles an hour." Zach slipped on his helmet. "And you don't have to yell," he said in a voice that echoed inside the chamber. "There is a microphone connection embedded near the right corner of your mouth. It helps with the guided-tour portion of our ride."

"Testing, one, two, three," I said.

He tapped the side of his helmet and nodded. "I'll help you get settled in the sidecar."

He held out his hand, but I ignored it and stepped in. As I sat down, I quickly slid my legs forward, making sure my knees remained covered. My feet barely reached the nose of the narrow car.

"It has plenty of legroom, doesn't it?" Zach asked.

"Like a limo." I reached down with my hands. "Where's the seat belt?"

Zach threw his right leg over the motorcycle seat. "There isn't one. If a motorcycle wrecks, staying attached to it isn't always the safest thing."

He started the motor and revved the engine. It caused the sidecar to vibrate. I couldn't believe I'd left the peace and safety of Mrs. Fairmont's veranda to sit a few inches off the ground beside a motorcycle operated by a man I barely knew.

"Ready?" Zach spoke in stereo into my ears.

I nodded grimly.

He looked over his shoulder at the street and pulled away from the curb. The first thing I noticed was the immediate sensation of speed. The street seemed to fly past.

"How fast are we going?" I shouted.

"About thirty. You don't have to yell. It might make me wreck."

Some of the streets in the historic district were in need of repair, and we bumped along for several blocks. The helmet limited my view so I turned my head from side to side. Everyone we passed stopped to stare. If the twins had been on the sidewalk and saw me ride past attached to a motorcycle and wearing a black helmet with orange flames on the side, they would have fainted.

"Where are we going?" I asked.

"To a smoother road."

We left the historic district and turned onto President Street Extension, a broader, four-lane highway. The motorcycle picked up speed, and I could feel the wind rushing past my arms and neck. Even though it felt fast, I noticed that Zach stayed in the slow lane, letting most of the cars pass us.

"How do you like it?" Zach asked.

"Better than the back of a pickup truck," I admitted.

We left the city behind, but both sides of the road were still marked by commercial development. We stopped at a light, and I looked at the street sign.

"Are we going to Tybee Island?"

"Yes. Have you been there?"

"No."

"Is that okay?"

"Sure."

I doubted Julie and the rest of the bikini crowd would be out this early. Without the presence of girls, the half-dressed men wouldn't be seen either. And there was no reason why I couldn't take a quick look at the ocean. My promise to Julie had been to stay away from the office. As we drove along, I relaxed and enjoyed the ride. I thought about Zach's mother sitting in the sidecar.

"Did your parents ever take long trips like this?" I asked.

"Maybe a couple of hundred miles or so in a day. There are roads in California unlike anyplace else. The views are incredible."

"Do you miss it?"

"Yes."

We popped over a bump that made me hit my knees against the top of the sidecar.

"Sorry," Zach said. "That one snuck up on me."

We came to Tybee Creek, an indistinct waterway that meandered through the landward side of a large marsh. The tops of the marsh grass rippled slightly in the breeze. A few white egrets stood motionless in the water. The tide was going out, exposing mussel beds at the edges of the watery channels. Expensive-looking homes lined the edge of the marsh on both the island and the mainland. We crossed a bridge onto Tybee Island.

"We'll stop near the main pier," Zach said.

We passed through residential areas with sandy driveways guarded by dune grass and into an aging business district. Several people on the sidewalks pointed in our direction as we passed. It made me feel special. We turned down a narrow street and parked in front of a meter. Zach turned off the engine. I climbed as gracefully as I could from the sidecar and removed my helmet. My skirt was wrinkled.

"That was fun," I said before Zach asked me. "You're a good driver."

"Thanks, but you drive a car; you ride a motorcycle."

Zach put on a pair of dark sunglasses. He locked the helmets to the motorcycle with a thin steel cable.

"You don't need any money," he said. "Bring your bag or I can lock it in the sidecar."

"Lock it up. All I want is my hat."

There was a cover that slid over the sidecar, turning it into a storage compartment. Without the helmet over my face, I could smell a tinge of salt in the air. The morning breeze was coming in from the ocean. I put on my hat.

"Ocean views, this way," Zach said, retying his hair in a tight ponytail.

Two- and three-story frame houses with rooms to rent crowded against the sidewalk. There weren't many people on the street.

"It will be crowded here by noon," Zach said.

After a couple of blocks the street made a turn to the left, and I could see the blue glint of ocean in the distance. There were seagulls riding the air currents. Sand scattered the sidewalk. The street ended at a modest sand dune. Looking to the right, I could see the pier stretching its thick finger past the surf into deeper water. Tiny figures of fishermen stood at the end of the pier. I took a deep breath, enjoyed the sensation for a few seconds, and exhaled.

The pier was thirty feet above the water and wide enough for two cars to drive side by side. We passed fishermen using long, sturdy poles. Coolers of bait shrimp and fish rested beside the poles. Most of the fishermen were shirtless, tanned, and smoking cigarettes. I kept my eyes directed toward the water.

"What are they fishing for?" I asked Zach.

"Fish."

"What kinds?"

"Saltwater varieties. I'm not an expert about pier fishing."

We passed several black men with poles in the water. "Moses could tell me what kind of fish live in these waters," I said.

"Who?"

"Moses Jones. Our client charged with trespassing."

"Maybe, but as I remember he also sees faces in the water."

We reached the end of the pier. Here were the serious fishermen, each with multiple poles. I watched one man bait four hooks on a single line and fling it into the air. It plopped into the water far below. Nobody seemed to be catching any fish. Gulls cried out as they swooped down, landing on the pier to scoop up bits of discarded baitfish and shrimp.

The pier gave a panoramic view of the beach. When I was eighteen, I'd traveled to the east coast of Florida for a mission outreach sponsored by our church and waded briefly in the Atlantic early one morning before the sunbathers wearing nothing more than brightly colored underwear made their appearance. Even that brief contact with the sea intrigued me. Like a mountain panorama, the ocean revealed the expanse of creation—a vista so big and unfathomable that only an omnipotent God could have fashioned it. With the tide going out the strand was broad, the waves small. Zach and I found an empty spot along the north side of the pier to watch.

"Are there many shells on this beach?" I asked. I couldn't see anyone stooping over.

"No. It's sand, sun, and water."

"The one other time I was at the ocean, I loved collecting shells," I said. "I have a jarful on a shelf in my bedroom at home. Most are broken, but there is still beauty in them."

Zach nodded his head. "People are like that too."

I turned toward him. "Are you teasing me?"

"No."

More people streamed from the oceanfront motels toward the water. Included were the beginnings of the bathing suit crowd. Seeing the bikini-clad women made me wonder where Julie would spend the day.

"I'll help you with the Jones case this week," Zach said, breaking the silence.

"Okay. Just let me know."

We stood beside each other without speaking for a long time. A crazy thought raced through my mind that Zach wanted to throw me off the pier. I gauged the distance to shallow water. If I survived the fall it would be an easy swim. Zach touched my arm, and I jumped.

"Are you ready to go back to the motorcycle?" he asked.

"Yes."

As we walked off the pier, the fear of harm at Zach's hands didn't leave me. It would be easy for him to ram the sidecar into a tree, endangering my life.

"Why did you invite me on the motorcycle ride?" I asked.

"I'll tell you at our next stop."

"How far is that?"

"It's on the island."

I put on my helmet and stepped into the sidecar. I wanted to return to Mrs. Fairmont's house as soon as possible. Zach backed the motorcycle away from the curb with his feet and started the engine. We retraced our route onto the island. Before crossing the bridge at the marsh, Zach abruptly took a side road.

"Where are we going?" I asked, my anxiety rising.

"You'll see."

After a few hundred yards, the paving gave way to sand. There were a few houses hidden among the trees. Zach turned down a driveway with no house at the end of it and stopped the motorcycle. It was a lonely spot. My heart was pounding in my chest. I sat in the sidecar, not moving.

"Get out here," he said.

"I'm ready to go back to Mrs. Fairmont's house," I said, trying to keep my voice calm.

"And I need to spend several hours at the office. We'll only be here a few minutes."

I licked my lips and climbed out. Zach didn't bother to lock up the helmets.

"It's a short path," he said, heading off into the underbrush.

I didn't know whether to refuse and stay by the motorcycle or run down the road for help. I reluctantly followed. After about twenty yards we came into a clearing. There was the foundation of a destroyed house and a rickety pier with a lot of the boards missing. Zach pointed at the outline of the house.

"The house burned down shortly before I moved to Savannah. Mr. Appleby represented the owners who had to sue the insurance company on the policy."

"Why?"

"The company alleged arson. There was no question it was a set fire, but the evidence connecting our clients was sketchy. They used the insurance money to pay off business debts and avoid bankruptcy instead of rebuilding the house."

The strip of land extended out and provided a nice view up and down Tybee Creek. In the distance I could see cars crossing over the bridge.

"It's a pretty spot," I said. "Can we go now?"

"You can see better from here," Zach said, walking toward the water.

I followed him to a gazebo near the edge of the water. It didn't take many months for wood to weather in the salt air. Only a few flecks of white paint remained. The vines planted at the edge of the structure were in summer green. Zach didn't enter the gazebo but sat on the front steps. I stood beside him. He was right about the view.

"I like to come here and pray," he said. "I've been in every season of the year."

I looked at him in surprise. I'd been thinking about him in such a negative way that his comment caught me off guard.

"Why here?" I managed.

"It reminds me of a place I liked to go in California. It wasn't near the ocean, but it felt the same."

"What sort of place?"

"Up in the mountains near an abandoned cabin that had fallen in on itself. That's where the Lord told me to come to Savannah."

I sat down on the far end of the steps, leaving a healthy distance between us. "How did that happen? You promised to tell me."

"I know." Zach smiled and took off his sunglasses. "And I try to always keep my promises."

It was such a sweet smile that I blushed in embarrassment at my fears of a few moments before.

"Mr. Appleby read an admiralty case note I wrote for the *Pepperdine Law Review* and contacted me. I'd never visited this part of the country and agreed to fly out for a visit. I already had three offers from law firms on the West Coast but thought it wouldn't hurt to check out Savannah. I met with Mr. Appleby, and he offered me a job before I left town. The money didn't compare with the other firms' offers, but the cost of living is so much lower here that it was worth considering. Of course, like you, the most important consideration for me was God's will."

"Did you ask your parents?"

"We discussed it. They wanted me closer to home but tried not to let their emotions get in the way. In the end, they left it up to me. That's probably easier to do with a son than a daughter."

"My parents allowed me to make my choice this summer."

"Good for them. Anyway, I rode the black motorcycle into the mountains so I could spend time praying about the decision. I took a tent and sleeping bag so I could spend the night."

"Alone?"

"Except for the bears and mountain lions. The old cabin was built on land purchased by the state to include in a park. It was okay to camp there, but I couldn't build a fire. Just before the sunset I was reading in Acts about the fellowship the early Christians enjoyed in Jerusalem."

"When they had all things in common?" I interrupted.

"Yes, only the part that touched my heart was the phrase 'fellowship of believers.' In my family, relationship with other Christians stood at the center of everything. I knew if I took one of the other jobs, I might make more money, but that the fellowship of believers waited for me in Savannah."

"Where are these people?" I asked, feeling excitement rise up inside me. "I could go to church with you tomorrow."

Zach shook his head. "I'm not sure I've met them. I'm part of a church that meets in a house on the north side of the city. It's a great group, but as I've continued to pray about the verse, I think it may be more personal than corporate."

"I don't understand."

"The best fellowship often happens one-on-one with another person, not in a crowd of people."

I swallowed. "Are you talking about male/female fellowship?" I asked.

Zach laughed. "With everything shared in common. You're already good at cross-examination."

"Why are you telling me this? You're not talking to me as you would a summer clerk."

"That's right. You're the type of girl who deserves the truth, the whole truth, and nothing but the truth. I want to be completely up front with you. I'm interested in getting to know you better, but only with your permission. If you say no, I won't bring it up again, and there won't be any hard feelings on my part."

It was the most flattering, pure-hearted invitation I'd ever received from a male.

"I'll need to talk to my parents about it."

"Sure. You can talk to Joe Carpenter if you like. I'm not suggesting we date or agree to anything beyond getting to know each other in a transparent way." Zach gestured with his hand across the expanse of the marsh. "Without the distractions of phony barriers."

I stared at the marsh for a few moments. My heart beat a little faster. "I've never had anyone approach me like this," I said.

Zach pulled on his ponytail. "And I'd bet you've never met a Christian lawyer from California with long hair who owns two motorcycles."

17

DURING THE RETURN TRIP TO MRS. FAIRMONT'S HOUSE, THE SUN climbed higher in the sky. The artificial breeze created by the speed of the motorcycle kept me outwardly cool, but inside I felt flushed.

I barely knew the young lawyer, but he'd already shown the ability to get behind my defenses. No one, not even the boys at church who'd known me all their lives and shared the same religious convictions, ever came close to relating to me as a person. The novelty of the ride in the sidecar couldn't compete with the new thoughts racing through my head. I spoke into the microphone.

"How long have you been thinking about what you said to me on the island?"

Zach glanced sideways. "Is this a good time to talk about that question?"

"Yes."

"Since the first time we met."

"Was it the homeschool connection?"

"It was everything. Put yourself in my shoes. How hard is it to meet people whose main goal in life is to love and obey God?"

We stopped in front of Mrs. Fairmont's house. I handed him the helmet. "Do you want to come in for a few minutes?" I asked.

"No, I'm going to the office."

"Thanks for the ride."

As I reached the front door, I heard Zach pull away from the curb. I couldn't resist stopping to watch him ride down the street until he was out of sight.

Flip greeted me at the door. Mrs. Fairmont was sitting in the den with a book in her lap. Her eyes were closed. I quietly walked over to her chair. The book in her lap was a biography of Abigail Adams, wife of John Adams. I wondered how many pages she'd read before falling asleep or losing the ability to concentrate. She stirred and opened her eyes.

"It's Tami Taylor," I said quickly.

She rubbed her eyes. "I know who you are, but thanks for reminding me. Did you have a good time?"

"Yes ma'am. We rode out to Tybee Island."

"When I was a little girl one of the highlights of the summer was the train ride to Tybee."

"A motorcycle was exciting for me."

Mrs. Fairmont nodded and pointed a frail finger at the book in her lap. "Life has to be lived while you can. You only have one chance."

IT WAS NO USE TRYING to call home. I knew Mama and Daddy would be working all day Saturday. So, I cleaned and scrubbed my apartment for several hours, then offered to take Flip on a walk through the neighborhood. As soon as he saw the red leash, Flip ran to the front door and began jumping up and down. I fastened the lead to his collar and headed out the door. The leash seemed unnecessary. The little dog stayed by my side with his head held high in the air. We walked all the way to Forsyth Park where I let him drink from a special water fountain just for dogs. When we returned to the house, Mrs.

Fairmont held him in her lap and made me repeat in detail everything that had happened. The two of them took a long nap in the den.

Late in the afternoon Mrs. Fairmont woke up and started watching TV. I slipped into the kitchen to phone home. One of the twins answered. It sounded like Ellie.

"It's Tami. Is this Ellie?"

"Do I sound like Ellie?"

"Yes, I need to talk to Mama and Daddy."

"Are you in trouble?"

"No."

"Then why are you in such a hurry to talk to them? Don't you want to know what Emma and I have been doing today?"

I realized that I'd sounded curt. "Sure. Did you clean the chicken coop?"

To my surprise, the girls hadn't worked much at all. After they cleaned their room, Mama took them to a basketball scrimmage for girls their age at the high school.

"We each wore one of your old uniforms," she said. "It was funny because we looked alike and had the same number."

I'd purchased my high school uniforms because no one else would want to wear extra-long shorts and baggy shirts.

"Who had the most assists?" I asked.

"They didn't keep up with that, only points and rebounds. I had four more points than Emma."

"What about rebounds?"

"She got some lucky bounces."

"And then threw the ball to you while you were running down the court. If you scored on her pass that would be an assist."

"Yeah, that happened a couple of times. Anyway, the new coach for the middle school team was there watching. She talked to Mama after the scrimmage about us being on the team."

"But you won't be enrolled at the school."

Ellie spoke with excitement in her voice. "The coach says the school board has adopted a new policy for homeschoolers that lets them play sports. I'm not sure how it works, but Mama and Daddy are going to pray about it. Would you pray too? The other girls were nice to us and had fun trying to tell us apart."

It would be much easier for Ellie and Emma to face the world together than it had been for me going it alone.

"Two are better than one," I said, quoting part of a verse from Ecclesiastes.

"Yeah, but I also sank some free throws," Ellie said. "It's only one point, but most of the girls didn't come close. Emma and I only missed two each."

I didn't try to correct her. "Now, will you let Mama and Daddy know that I'm on the phone?"

"I love you," Ellie said.

"I love you too."

I could hear the television in the den. It sounded like Mrs. Fairmont was watching a war movie. Mama came on the line.

"I'm here," she said. "Ellie said it was urgent. Are you all right?"

"Yes ma'am. It couldn't be too urgent. I listened to Ellie talk for ten minutes about the basketball scrimmage. Are they going to play on the middle school team next year?"

"We're praying about it."

"Is Daddy there?"

"He's gone with Kyle to look at a few head of cattle. I think Kyle has them sold for a profit before he buys them. That boy is going to be a success. I just hope it doesn't become too important to him and draw him away from the Lord." Mama paused. "But tell me everything about your week."

I'd already thought out an efficient way to summarize my activities. When I mentioned interviewing Moses Jones, Mama interrupted me. "You met with a criminal alone?"

"Yes ma'am. But it took place in an interview room at the jail with deputies everywhere."

"That part of being a lawyer has always worried me. Be careful."

"Yes ma'am." I took a deep breath. "And I've enjoyed getting to know most of the people I'm working with. One of the associate lawyers is a serious Christian. He's supervising my work in the criminal case."

"Then he should be with you when you meet with this man. Don't be shy in insisting that he come along."

"I won't. He's already told me that he wants to be there at the next meeting with the client."

"Good. How is Mrs. Fairmont's health? Your father and I have been praying for her."

I told Mama about the rough night and how God helped me. When I described the time of singing and prayer, she interrupted. "Amen! The Spirit is all over what you're doing at that house. To me, it's a thousand times more important than any work at a law firm. I'll mention it in our Sunday school class. Once Gladys McFarland hears about the need, you know she'll pray."

"Yes ma'am."

"Are you going to a church in the morning?"

"No. The Christian lawyer mentioned a home group he attends. I may visit, but not tomorrow."

"Be careful, but you've learned how to discern truth and error."

"Yes ma'am. And the lawyer also asked permission to get to know me better."

I stopped. The news was out. I waited.

"Did you say something?" Mama asked. "The phone went dead."

"Yes ma'am. The Christian lawyer wants to get to know me better."

"Isn't that why they offered you a summer job in the first place? That shouldn't be too hard if you're working on a case together."

I spoke rapidly. "Yes ma'am, but he meant on a personal level. He has a homeschool background all the way through high school. We have a lot in common."

There was silence. This time, I knew why.

"How old is he?" Mama asked in a measured tone of voice.

"I'm not sure, but he's only been practicing law for three years. He's probably twenty-seven or twenty-eight."

"So you don't know much about him."

"He's from California and very polite. He's smart and a hard worker. The senior partner he works for has a lot of confidence in him. This week he was working on an important case involving a company in Norway."

Mama ignored the data. "Tell me exactly what he said to you."

"That he would like to get to know me on a personal level. I told him I would need to talk to you and Daddy, and he thought that was a great idea. I've never met anyone like him. He understands my convictions and doesn't criticize me."

"How could he know that much about your beliefs? You've only been in Savannah a few days."

"It seems longer than that to me. Zach and I have discussed things at work and spent time together." I stopped. Mention of the motorcycle ride to Tybee Island at this point would kill all prospects. "We talked this morning. He came by the house, and we sat on the back porch with Mrs. Fairmont and had a great time."

Slightly breathless, I stopped and waited.

Mama spoke calmly yet firmly. "I'm sure your father and I would want to meet this young man before agreeing to anything. If he's as spiritually mature as you say, he shouldn't have any problem with that approach."

It was a predictable response. But as I'd presented my brief case, I'd realized how badly I wanted Mama to give me the okay. Parental approval of a budding romance was a safeguard against the anguish and heartache caused by aborted attempts to find the right soul mate. Mama said the serial dating practiced by most girls was often nothing more than preparation for multiple divorces.

"Yes ma'am. Talk to Daddy, and I'll keep my interaction with Zach strictly business."

"And remember that our home is open if you want to bring him here for a visit. You're mature enough to get married. It's just a question of letting God find your mate."

I raised my eyebrows. "You really think I'm ready for marriage?"

"Yes, but the timing should be in the Lord's hands. How many times have we prayed for your husband without knowing his name?"

"Hundreds, ever since I was a little girl."

"We want you to have your own home and family. I'm not the perfect wife and mother, but I hope I've given you a good example."

"Yes ma'am."

"I miss you most as a daughter, but also as a worker." Mama chuckled. "You'd think I would get twice the help from Emma and Ellie, but I think, with them, the help is divided rather than multiplied."

Mama's lighthearted comments encouraged me.

"Tell me about your week," I said.

Listening to Mama felt good and bad. It was good to hear about home, bad to face again the ache of separation from my family.

"Tammy Lynn," she said when the conversation was coming to an end, "thanks so much for telling me about your conversation with Zach."

Hearing Mama speak his name startled me.

"We trust you," she continued. "Which is one of the greatest gifts a child can give to a parent."

I felt a stab of guilt because I'd not told the whole truth. I quickly searched my heart for a way to provide additional information.

"We love you," Mama said. "Bye."

The call ended. I stared for a few seconds at the phone receiver in my hand. Even if I didn't tell Mama the whole truth, I could still honor her wishes.

MONDAY MORNING, I arrived early at the office and went directly to the library. I already felt more comfortable in my surroundings. A few minutes later, Julie and Vince, their faces reflecting the red of a glorious sunset, came in together.

"I don't have as much Middle Eastern blood in my veins as I thought," Julie said. "And Vinny is a pure Caucasian."

"Did you go to Tybee Island?" I asked.

"No," Vince replied. "Ned Danforth invited Julie to spend the day on his boat, and she brought me along."

"As my bodyguard," Julie added. "I could tell Ned was miffed when we drove up to the marina together, but I pointed out that it was an opportunity to get to know both of us at the same time. Ned and Vinny ended up spending a lot of the time fiddling with the navigation system while I served as a hood ornament."

"I think you were a bow ornament," Vince corrected. "We were on a boat."

Julie looked at Vince in surprise. "Did the sun shining on your head give you a sense of humor? Either way, you ignored me by asking question after question about Tami."

Vince's expression changed, but he was so sunburned that I couldn't tell if Julie's comment embarrassed him or not. She continued. "Summer clerks have to stick together, and you two should go to lunch today and satisfy your mutual curiosity."

Before I could deny curiosity, Vince gave me a hopeful look that stopped my words in their tracks.

"I'd like that," he said. "Are you available?"

"I'm not sure," I answered. "I haven't checked with Mr. Carpenter."

"Be here at noon," Julie said to Vince.

After Vince left, Julie sat across the table from me. "I owe you an apology," she said.

"Why?"

"For giving you such a hard time about not putting on a bathing suit so you could meet men. Friday night I get a predatory call from Ned Danforth. At least, I could tell what he had in mind and convinced Vinny to ruin the party. You might not have been savvy enough to see it coming. Anyway, after we spent four pleasant hours sailing along the coastline, I thought I might have been paranoid. But then while Vinny was below deck with his nose stuck in an onboard software program, Ned came up to the bow and made a comment I couldn't ignore. I had to put him in his place like a ninth grader. It was awkward for both of us. He immediately turned the boat around. The sail back to port seemed twice as long as the ride out. Ned spent the rest of the trip hanging out with Vinny, and I got cooked because I didn't want to join them. Fraternization between associates and summer clerks is so unprofessional." Julie looked down at the paperwork in front of her. "What did you do this weekend besides read the Bible and pray?"

"Fraternized with one of the male associates."

Julie's mouth dropped open. "Get out."

"Yeah, one of the attorneys and I went to Tybee Island."

"Who?"

"Zach Mays, but don't get the wrong idea," I added. "It was nothing like your boat cruise with Ned. He had me back to Mrs. Fairmont's house before noon so he could come to the office and work."

"I didn't peg you as a pathological liar, but that makes no sense. Tell me straight what happened."

I pointed to the books open on the table in front of me. "Don't you think we should get to work?"

"No!"

Julie sat back in her chair and folded her arms across her chest. It took twice as long as it should have to tell her about the motorcycle ride because she constantly interrupted.

"I'm just trying to make sure you're not holding back. So when did he talk to you about the homeschooling thing?"

"Weeks ago."

"How is that possible if you didn't interview in person for a summer job?"

"Let me finish telling you about Saturday before you drag up another example of fraternization."

Julie shook her head. "Maybe you're not as uptight as I thought."

"No, I'm more uptight than you can imagine, but it feels right to me." I finished as quickly as I could. I left out the entire discussion about asking my parents' permission to get to know Zach on a personal level.

"I had no idea the two of you had something brewing so fast," Julie said thoughtfully. "He doesn't look religious, and the motorcycle deal doesn't fit the stereotype. I just hope he didn't come up with a strategy to seduce you after the first meeting."

It was such a brusque comment that it shocked me.

"He's not a Ned Danforth. I would be able to see through that in a second."

"Maybe." Julie paused. "But where does this leave poor Vinny? I had him all psyched up about what a great girl you are."

"I thought he asked you question after question."

"Maybe one, but I felt so rotten about the way I talked to you on Friday that I tried to make it up by praising you to him. Now, he's going to find out that he's a lap down before the race even starts."

I studied Julie carefully for a moment. "Did you make him think I was interested in him?"

"Uh, no. Except that like a good Christian you love all people equally, no matter their age, race, gender, or hair color."

"That's how you put it? It sounds like a sentence from the federal antidiscrimination laws."

"In so many words or less."

"Maybe I'll get the truth from Vince at lunch."

Julie held up her hands. "Just leave me out of it. I need a social director more than you do."

18

Midmorning, Myra Dean came into the library and summoned Julie to a meeting with a prospective client in the main conference room.

"Bring a blank legal pad and a pen," Myra said. "You won't say anything. Mr. Carpenter wants you to take notes while he conducts the interview. It's a new client who is the money guy behind a huge real-estate deal that is heading toward litigation. He's checking us out, and Mr. Carpenter will be putting on a full-court press to get the business. Rich clients like to know they have a bigger army of lawyers and staff than the people on the other side."

"Will I be the only person taking notes?" Julie asked. "Vince is so quick on the computer. I might miss something important."

"No," Myra replied. "I'll be there too. You're my backup."

After they left the library I stood up to stretch and take a break. Julie's tough exterior was showing cracks. While in college, I'd led several girls to faith in Christ. Some of them came from religious backgrounds. Others were crying out for help from a pit of sinful despair. But I'd never had the chance to pray with a Jewish person. There was a buzz on the phone extension located in the library and a female voice spoke into the room.

"Tami Taylor, please pick up on line 127."

I pushed the three buttons. "Hello," I said.

"It's Zach. Can you take a break?"

"That's what I'm doing right now."

"Good. Come to my office."

The phone clicked off without giving me a chance to reply. Zach was definitely more abrupt in his conversations at the office during the week than on Saturday at the beach.

Upstairs, people were walking back and forth carrying papers, folders, and documents. Everyone was busy and no one paid any attention to me. I walked down the hallway to Zach's door and knocked.

"Come in," he called out.

I opened the door and peeked in. Zach was on the phone with his hand over the mouthpiece. He motioned for me to sit down.

"I understand," he said, removing his hand, "but I haven't had a chance to talk to our client. The judge isn't going to make me go to trial a couple of weeks after he assigned the case to our firm."

Zach listened for a moment. "Just because the jail log shows that Tami was there early last week doesn't constitute effective assistance of counsel. We haven't filed the standard pretrial motions or learned the names and addresses of any of your witnesses."

There was another pause.

"Yes, it will help if you open your file and allow us to review everything you have, but that's just the beginning. We'll need to do our own investigation." Zach turned toward his computer. "Yes, I'm available tomorrow afternoon, but I need to check with Tami to confirm her schedule. The main reason Judge Cannon assigned the case to our office is so she could gain courtroom experience, even if it's limited to preliminary matters."

Zach pushed a button and changed the computer screen from a calendar to his mailbox.

"Right," he said. "I appreciate the pressure you're under. We'll consider the offer and discuss it with Mr. Jones."

Zach hung up the phone. "Good morning," he said.

"I'm not sure," I replied. "That conversation didn't sound like a good way to start the day or the week."

"Don't worry; we'll sort through it in a minute. Did you talk to your parents?"

"Uh, just my mother." I tried to put a hopeful look on my face. "I told her how nice you've been to me and that we had a lot in common. I mentioned your homeschool background and that you're well respected in the firm." I stopped. "It's very awkward repeating this to you."

"I'm not trying to embarrass you. I respect you."

"I told her that too." I sighed. "She's going to talk to my father, but she thinks we shouldn't take any steps toward a personal relationship until they have a chance to meet you."

"Did you make it sound more serious than I intended?"

I stared at Zach for a second, not sure whether to cry or run out of the room. My face must have revealed my feelings.

"No, that was wrong," he added. "Can you forget that last sentence and back up to the part about me respecting you?"

"I'll try."

"Thanks. Would it be okay for me to talk to them?"

"I wondered about that," I admitted. "But not until I hear from my father. I don't want to manipulate them."

"Of course, they taught you to appeal to authority, not rebel against it."

"Exactly," I replied in surprise.

"It's good training for becoming a lawyer. Including the case of *State v. Moses Jones*," Zach replied, tapping a folder on his desk. "That was Ms. Smith, the assistant DA. Her call was routed to me instead of you. The bottom line is that she wants to fast-track *State v. Jones* and bump it up the trial calendar. Several of the complaining homeowners are going to leave town for the summer and don't want to be held hostage as witnesses for a trial. I guess they have homes in the mountains so they can escape the malaria on the coast."

"Malaria? Are you serious?"

"A hundred years ago, it was a big problem."

"Whether a few people are here or not shouldn't matter," I said. "There are twenty-four counts. It would still be a minority."

Zach flipped open the folder on his desk. "How closely did you read the charges?"

"What did I miss?"

Zach ran his finger down the sheets of paper in front of him while I fidgeted.

"There are twenty-four counts but only five different physical locations," he said after a minute. "Think about it. Jones was looking for a convenient hookup for his boat, not a change in scenery. He wouldn't have sought out a different dock every night."

"I missed that."

"And I'm no criminal law expert, but the first rule of an admiralty case is to carefully read the documents. It's the same for any area of the law. Check out the paperwork."

"I'm sorry."

"Just learn the lesson."

"What did Ms. Smith say about a plea bargain?"

"I'm getting to that. A few of the rich folks on the river want Jones removed from polite society. Each count carries a sentence of up to twelve months plus a one-thousand-dollar fine. If you laid those end to end, Moses Jones could be in jail the rest of his life."

My jaw dropped.

"But no judge would lock him up and throw away the key," Zach added. "The DA's initial offer is six months in jail followed by three years on probation with no monetary fine."

I thought about Moses sitting in the interview room breathing through his few remaining teeth. In spite of my mother's fears, he didn't seem to be a huge threat to society.

"That sounds harsh. I mean, he didn't steal or damage anything."

"And that's her first offer. You can make a counterproposal."

"Me?"

"Remember, it's your case. I'll help, just like I promised. However, we need to meet with him as soon as possible. The case is set for Judge Cannon's arraignment calendar tomorrow afternoon. If we work out a deal, it could all be taken care of at that time."

I took a deep breath. "That sounds great."

Zach glanced at a clock on the corner of his desk. "We can run over to the jail, discuss options with the client, and grab a late lunch on the way back. All in the context of business."

"Could we go to the jail later today? I promised Vince that I'd have lunch with him. We tried to get together several times last week, and it kept getting pushed back. I don't want to hurt his feelings."

"Hurt his feelings? What kind of lunch is it?"

"What do you mean?"

"Did you talk to your mother about Vince Colbert?" Zach asked.

I felt my face flush. "No. He didn't ask me to."

Zach looked up at the ceiling for a few seconds before lowering his eyes and meeting my gaze. "For a laid-back California guy, I'm not doing very well," he said. "Have a good lunch with Vince; then check with me. I'll carve out at least two hours for a trip to the jail to meet Mr. Jones."

In the hall outside Zach's office I ran into Gerry Patrick.

"Hope your first week wasn't too dull," she said cheerily. "We have some events planned that will liven things up."

"No ma'am. It's been very stimulating," I replied. "Much more than I'd guessed."

"Good. I'm here if you have any questions."

I returned downstairs to finish a memo for Bob Kettleson. In double-checking my research, I discovered that one of the cases I relied on had been seriously criticized in a recent appellate court opinion. After offering a quick prayer of thanks, I pointed out the potential pitfall in an extra two paragraphs of the memo before sending it to the senior associate. No one came into the library until Vince, the ubiquitous notebook computer in his hand, arrived at precisely 11:50 a.m.

"Are you still available?" he asked.

"Yes."

I noted my time on a log and closed the folders.

"Julie is in a big meeting with several of the partners and associates," Vince said as we checked out at the reception desk.

"I was there when Myra Dean asked her to come."

We walked outside into the hot sun. The slight coolness I enjoyed during my early morning runs didn't last past the point most people in the city were sipping their first cup of coffee.

"How does Savannah compare to Charleston?" I asked.

"Same and different."

We walked in silence. A lunch with Vince might be similar to my morning quiet time. He unlocked the passenger door and held it open for me. Before he reached the driver's side, the car's engine started and the air conditioner started blowing warm air.

"I've never been to Charleston," I said. "Does your family live near the Battery?"

Vince smiled. It was a nice smile without a hint of mockery.

"No. I have a great-aunt that lives south of Broad Street, but I grew up in a newer area. My father is a chemistry professor at the College of Charleston. He also holds several patents in the plastics industry."

I thought about my daddy working at the chicken plant in Powell Station. He was more into biology than chemistry.

"Would you like to go to a café I found before you and Julie arrived?" Vince asked.

"Sure."

Without Julie around to interrupt, I found Vince capable of holding up his end of a conversation. During the drive, I learned that he had two older sisters: the one who was married in Savannah and another who lived in Boston.

"Did you think about going to Harvard?" I asked, expecting him to say that he'd not been accepted for admission at the older institution.

"Yes, it was a tough choice," he replied. "Both Yale and Harvard are good schools."

I stifled a laugh. He glanced over at me.

"What's so funny?"

"Oh, you know, the dilemma of having to pick between two of the finest law schools in the country. At least you didn't have to worry about Virginia, Michigan, and Stanford."

"Virginia and Michigan accepted me, but I didn't apply to Stanford. I didn't want to be on the West Coast."

I looked out the car window. Vince parked on the street.

"The café is a block north," he said. "I hope you'll like it."

The restaurant was in the downstairs of an older home near Greene Square. A hostess wearing a black skirt and white blouse placed us at a table for two where we could look through a window into a garden much more elaborate than the one at Mrs. Fairmont's house. Everything about the place, from wall decorations to furniture, had a French flavor.

"This is really nice," I said after I'd had a chance to look around.

"The food is good too."

I opened the menu and didn't recognize a single entrée by name. Only when I read the ingredients could I partially decipher what was offered.

"It really is a French place, isn't it?" I said.

"The chef is from Marseille."

"How do you know?"

Before he answered, a short waiter wearing rimless glasses came to our table. Vince spoke to him in French, and the man left.

"Is he from Marseille too?" I asked, dumbfounded.

"No, he's from a little town in Provence. He'll send out the chef so we can find out what he recommends."

"You speak French?"

"Enough to get by."

I took a sip of water. The more I learned about Vince, the less confident I felt in his presence. The waiter returned accompanied by a rotund man wearing an apron and a tall white chef's hat. Vince continued to speak exclusively in French. The chef bowed toward me. Vince held out the menu while the three men had a rapid-fire conversation. Most of the other patrons in the restaurant turned to watch. I pressed tightly into my seat, not even trying to pretend I could understand. The chef and waiter left.

"How did it go?" I asked.

"He's going to put together something special that isn't on the menu."

"The menu didn't have any good options?"

"Yes, but he wants to make the lunch memorable."

"It's already that. I've never been in the middle of a French conversation before."

"What foreign language did you take in college?"

"Spanish, but I've only used it in public with a few of the workers at the chicken plant."

As soon as I mentioned the chicken plant, I wanted to cram my napkin in my mouth. This was not the time or place for another discussion about my previous experience as an eviscerator. Vince looked across the room.

"Do you see that painting?" he asked, nodding toward the far wall. "The one above the fireplace."

I turned my head and saw a pastoral scene with vibrant colors. "Yes."

"It's an original. Twentieth-century but in an earlier style. What do you think?"

"I like it."

When I looked back, Vince was staring at me.

"Tell me more about you," he said. "Where you're from, something about your family, your travels."

"Well, I've lived my whole life in rural north Georgia with my parents, two brothers, and twin sisters. I didn't apply to any law schools except Georgia because I can't afford out-of-state tuition. Yesterday, I saw the ocean for the second time in my life. My conversational Spanish doesn't function past basic communication. I can't compete with you in any area of life or experience."

"Life isn't primarily about competition, is it?"

"No, it's about glorifying God," I said.

Vince nodded. "Gerry Patrick told me you were a serious Christian. Your faith made an impression on her, and I wanted to find out why."

"I'm not sure it was a good impression."

"She seemed positive, but the Bible says we shouldn't be surprised by persecution and misunderstanding."

I couldn't believe my ears. "Are you persecuted?"

Vince shrugged. "Imagine how people at the law school react when they find out I believe the Bible is true and Jesus Christ is the only way of salvation. The only acceptable belief is no belief, and the greatest foolishness is commitment to truth."

"How did you come to believe?" I asked.

Vince rubbed the back of his scarred right hand. "In high school I suffered a serious chemical burn to my right hand and arm when a lab partner caused a minor explosion during an experiment. The corrosive activity of the chemicals didn't stop until they took me into surgery."

I winced.

"I spent almost a week in the hospital and have had multiple skin grafts. I usually don't tell people this, but as I suffered, I thought about hell, where the fire never stops and the pain never ceases."

The waiter brought two cups of chilled soup.

"This is an asparagus-based soup," he said. "It sounds weird, but give it a try."

I touched a tiny spoonful to my lips. It was a puree with a much lighter flavor than I expected. I ate a larger spoonful.

"It's good," I said.

Vince ate several bites without speaking. I waited for him to continue. He kept eating, occasionally glancing around the restaurant.

"Are you going to leave me wondering why you decided not to go to hell?" I asked. "That would be stranger than this soup. Which is delicious," I quickly added.

Vince put down his spoon. "Sorry, I have a tendency to focus on one thing at a time. I'm not the best multitasker."

"Then eat your soup before you tell me more."

Vince efficiently reached the bottom of the cup.

"I'm listening," I said when I saw he'd finished. "Why did you think about hell at all? Not many preachers ever mention it."

"In a literature class I'd read Dante's *Inferno* and Jonathan Edwards' 'Sinners in the Hands of an Angry God.' I had a cultural knowledge of the Bible and was familiar with the concept of eternal punishment. But until the accident, everything was theoretical. Afterward pain dominated my life. In between morphine injections I suffered horribly. The pain would ease, but I knew it would return and my mind couldn't escape the thought of suffering at an even more extreme level—forever."

"That's terrible."

"Do you want to change the subject?"

"No, no. Our church believes in hell, but I don't like to think about it. I'm more interested in learning how to obey the Lord in my day-to-day life."

The waiter brought our meal. The food looked like a picture from one of the magazines at Mrs. Fairmont's house.

"What is it?" I asked.

"*Blanquette de veau.* It's a veal dish."

I took a bite. There were unusual flavors with a hint of onion.

"Can you keep talking?" I asked. "In between bites?"

Vince nodded. "Hell wasn't the only thing I thought about in the hospital. Of course, I thought about my lab partner. He should have been the one suffering, not me. Many times I imagined the chemicals spewing onto his hand and arm instead of mine. Then I read what Paul wrote about forgiving people who have sinned against us. It made logical sense. If I wanted God to forgive me so that I wouldn't go to hell, I needed to forgive the student who sinned against me. I talked to my parents about it. My father listened, but my mother thought I was delusional."

"What did she say?"

"That my mind was too precious a gift to throw away on Judeo-Christian mythology. She's a strict humanist. My father sees the order in science and that makes him doubt random chance as the explanation for the universe."

"Discussions around your supper table must be interesting."

"Anyway, after I got out of the hospital, I started reading the Bible and started attending an Episcopal church not far from our house. The thoughts of hell went away, and the love of God filled my heart."

Vince's description of his conversion left me with doubts. It didn't sound like he'd prayed it through.

"What about your lab partner? Did you forgive him?"

"Yes, and when I told him what happened to me, he prayed to receive Christ too. Now, he's in a postgraduate chemistry program at Rutgers."

We ate in silence for a minute.

"But how do you know God's love is in your heart?" I asked.

Vince smiled. "Oh, when it happens, you'll know."

During the remainder of the meal, he plied me with questions. I had to fight the sense of being interviewed by an anthropologist studying a primitive religious sect. Several times he appeared puzzled, but there was no hint of criticism. I finally decided everything I told him was going into an internal computer file to be processed later.

Dessert, custard topped with fresh blueberries, arrived. The custard was the creamiest substance I'd ever put in my mouth.

The chef returned at the conclusion of the meal. I smiled as sweetly as I could while Vince complimented him on the meal.

"Why did you take a summer job with Braddock, Appleby, and Carpenter?" I asked him during the drive back to the office. "With your academic background, you could have worked anywhere."

"One, it's close to home without being there. I'll spend next weekend in Charleston."

Vince turned onto Montgomery Street. I waited for other reasons. None came.

19

After I thanked Vince for lunch, I grabbed the Jones file from the library and rushed upstairs to Zach's office. His door was open. Fast-food paper wrappers from lunch were strewn across his desk.

"Are you ready to go?" I asked.

Zach looked at his watch. "I worked until one o'clock, then went out for a burger. Mr. Appleby doesn't take a two-hour lunch unless there is going to be a twenty-thousand-dollar fee on the line."

"Vince took me to a French café near Greene Square. The food was good, but the service was on European time."

Zach wadded up the food wrappers and threw them across the room into a round trash can.

"Nice shot," I said.

"When did you go to Europe?" he asked, standing up.

"I haven't. Vince told me the French take a lot of time with their meals. Eating is more of a social event with them than it is for us."

"Let's socialize with Mr. Jones at the jail," Zach said. "While you were leisurely dining, I stopped by the courthouse and copied the district attorney's file."

"What did you find?"

"I'll let you look it over in the car."

I'd never seen Zach's car. He owned a white Japanese compact. The engine didn't start until he turned the key in the ignition. He handed me the file.

"See what you think," he said.

I opened the folder. There was a one-page arrest record, and the names of the five property owners mentioned in the criminal charges. Beside each name were several dates and the words "video surveillance."

"Do you think the police were watching Moses for several weeks and videotaped him each time he tied up at one of the docks?" I asked.

"No. Video surveillance refers to images from security cameras. That's how they knew which night Moses was at each location. Each count has a specific date. While I was waiting for you, I called three of the five homeowners. They were nice enough to talk to me. That's how I found out about the surveillance cameras. The homeowners association has a contract with a security agency that services everybody."

"What else did you find out?"

"That Moses Jones did not have permission to trespass. One woman said she was terrified that Jones was going to assault her and burglarize her house. She saw his boat floating at the end of her dock early one morning and called the police. He was gone by the time they arrived, but that's when the investigation started."

"Did she talk to Moses?"

"None of them did. The two other owners I reached didn't know he'd been there until the security company checked the recordings for all the houses on the river. Jones was arrested at the dock of a homeowner who didn't answer the phone."

I turned to the next page in the folder and found the statement Moses gave to Detective Branson.

"Moses doesn't talk anything like this," I said after quickly scanning the four-paragraph statement with my client's crude signature at the bottom. "These are the detective's words put into Moses' mouth."

"Stylistic objections aside, what is your opinion of the statement?"

"Moses admits tying his boat up at the docks. I know he's guilty, but the way the detective crafted the statement bothers me."

Zach glanced sideways at me. "Are you turning into a left-wing criminal defense lawyer before my eyes?"

"No, I don't want to miss anything else. I didn't pay enough attention to the charges."

"Should we file a motion to suppress the confession?"

"I don't know if there are legal grounds."

"Research it before we appear in front of Judge Cannon tomorrow afternoon."

We arrived at the jail complex. I pointed to a parking area.

"That's near the entrance for the cell block where he's kept. Didn't you handle a criminal case when you clerked for the firm?"

"Remember, I didn't clerk in Savannah."

I felt embarrassed. Zach had told me he had clerked in Los Angeles, not Savannah, but I hadn't paid attention to the details. I started to apologize, but that would have only reinforced my blunder. We entered the waiting area. A different female deputy was on duty. I showed her the order from Judge Cannon, and a deputy took us to the interview area.

"I'll have the prisoner brought up," the deputy said.

In a few minutes the door to the cell block opened and Moses came in. He saw me and smiled. I couldn't help feeling some compassion for the old man.

"Mr. Jones, this is Zach Mays," I said. "He's a lawyer who is going to help you."

"Call me Moses," the old man said. "No one calls me Mr. Jones unless they be wanting my money, which I ain't got none."

We entered the interview room.

"What you do about my boat, missy?" Moses asked before we were seated. "It be in the same place as before."

I'd forgotten my promise to check on the status of his boat.

"Uh, that's not been decided. We'll talk to the district attorney about it and include return of the boat as part of the plea bargain in your case. Mr. Mays has been working hard on your case and has some things to tell you."

Zach told Moses about his interviews with the homeowners and Ms. Smith's plea offer. When the subject of jail time came up, Moses looked puzzled.

"She want me in this here jailhouse for six months more? I done been here 'bout two months."

"Which is long enough," Zach said. "I think they should let you out for time already served and put you on probation for less than three years."

"Oh, yeah. Plenty boys get prohibition. But the policemans, they turn that into hard time if they be wanting to. This ought to be over and done with."

"That may not be possible," Zach said. "Some probation, or 'prohibition' as you call it, will be included in your sentence. Do I have your permission to talk to the district attorney about a deal? You would have to be willing to plead guilty to at least some of the trespassing charges and agree not to do it again."

"I told missy here, I be tying up to an old tree from here on." The old man's eyes watered. "I just be needing a place of peace where they can't find me."

"Who?" Zach asked.

Moses looked at me. "The faces. I ain't on the river, but that little girl, she found me last night. I dream 'bout the river an' there she be. How she do that? In my dream, miles from the river edge?"

"What is the girl's name?" Zach asked. "Do you know her?"

"It's not relevant to the case," I said to Zach. "We don't need to ask about this. Please leave it alone."

"What's her name?" Zach persisted, leaning forward in his chair.

Moses licked his lips. "It be Prescott. She a pretty little thing. No more than ten or eleven year old. I don't do nothing bad. So, why she bother me all these years?"

I remembered the photograph in Mrs. Fairmont's room. The blood rushed from my head, and I felt slightly dizzy.

"Did you say Prescott?" I asked in a voice that trembled slightly.

"That be right, missy."

"What color eyes and hair does she have?"

"She be yellow-haired with eyes like the blue sky. Even in the dark, dark water, that hair, it still glows, those eyes, they see right through my soul."

"Is she the girl who was murdered?"

Moses stared at me and blinked.

"What are you talking about?" Zach asked me sharply.

I bolted from the room and let the door slam behind me. I leaned against the wall and took several deep breaths. The deputy on duty in the room started walking toward me. Zach came out of the interview room and joined me.

"Are you okay?" the deputy asked.

I held up my hand. "I just needed to leave the room for a minute. I'm okay."

"Are you sure?"

"Yes sir."

The deputy backed away.

"What's going on?" Zach asked as soon as the deputy was on the other side of the room. "Who is the Prescott girl?"

I didn't answer. Zach put his hands on my shoulders and came close to my face. "Talk to me!"

I pushed away his hands. "That's not necessary," I said. "Give me a second."

He backed away.

In a shaky voice I told him about the old photograph and Mrs. Fairmont's story.

"A terrible crime like that would have been the talk of the town for months," Zach said matter-of-factly. "Everyone else in Savannah would have known all about it. The girl's picture would have been on the front page of the paper every time it ran an article."

"But that doesn't explain why Moses sees her face in the water. You heard him. He wanted to make sure we didn't think he'd done anything wrong."

"Which proves?"

My frustration with Zach flew to the surface. "That you don't understand we may be representing a man who should be charged with murder, not trespassing!"

"Keep your voice down," Zach whispered as he glanced across the room toward the deputy. "We're here to talk to Moses Jones about a misdemeanor trespassing case."

"Then why did you keep going on about the girl in the water after I asked you to stop? This isn't my fault!"

"I'm not blaming you," Zach answered. "But we can't leave Jones alone while we argue. I'm going back in. We need to finish meeting with him about the trespassing case before thinking about anything else."

We returned to the interview room.

"Sorry to leave you like that," Zach said to Moses.

I stared at the old man's hands. They were arthritic now, but when he was younger they could have been lethal weapons.

"How did the Prescott girl die?" I blurted out. "Was she strangled and drowned?"

"No, Tami," Zach said. "Leave it alone."

Moses didn't pay attention to Zach. "People, they know. I not be telling the policemans. How could I?"

Zach spoke. "Mr. Jones, you don't have to talk about this if you don't want to." Moses blinked his eyes and began to cry softly.

"Tami, do you have a tissue?" Zach asked.

I reluctantly took one from my purse and handed it to Moses. The old man wiped his eyes and put his head in his hands. There was nothing to do but watch. Moses' shoulders shook slightly from the sobs. He sniffled several times.

"Mr. Jones, maybe we should come back later," Zach said.

Moses raised his face. His eyes were bloodshot.

"I be tired," he said. "I been rowing this boat way too long. Time to pull it up on the bank and lighten my load."

"What do you mean?" Zach asked.

Moses turned to me. "Do you believe I done hurt that little girl, missy?"

The old man's face didn't look sinister, but how could I trust my eyes?

"I don't know."

"Row my boat," he replied softly. "All I done, is row my boat. That be the whole truth. He give me a shiny silver dollar, but I throwed it in the river."

"Who?" Zach asked.

"He gave me that dollar, and talk about that little girl," Moses said with a faraway look in his eyes. "But it make me scared."

"Who gave it to you?" Zach persisted.

Moses refocused his eyes on Zach. "Ol' Mr Carpenter, the big boss man, he give it to me. He be toting a wicked-looking gun."

I looked at Zach. "Joe Carpenter?"

Moses turned to me and shook his head. "No, missy. Ol' Mr. Carpenter, he be dead and in the water hisself."

Zach pushed his chair away from the table. "Okay, that's enough. Mr. Jones, I need to apologize to you. I let my curiosity get the best of me and asked you questions that don't have anything to do with your trespassing case. Ms. Taylor and I are here to discuss the hearing in front of Judge Cannon tomorrow. You'll have to plead guilty or not guilty. I need your permission to work out a plea bargain with the district attorney's office. If I can get you out of jail for time served followed by a reasonable period of probation and the return of your boat, does that interest you?"

"I be listening," Moses replied. "You be the lawyers."

Zach looked at me before he answered. "I'll interpret that as your agreement for us to negotiate a better plea bargain; however, you'll make the final decision tomorrow."

Moses stared at me for a few seconds. I waited for him to speak.

"Yes, missy," he said. "You be thinking about all Moses done told you. That other tall girl. She listen, but I think you be knowing more than she do. Taking a green pill, that don't change the past."

Zach rose to his feet. "We'll see you in the courtroom tomorrow," he said to the old man.

I watched the deputy return Moses to the cell block.

"Who is the 'other tall girl'?" Zach asked when Moses was gone.

"Probably a mental health worker who prescribed medication. Detective Branson knew Moses needed professional help."

A deputy led us back to the main entrance.

"Should we talk to Mr. Carpenter about this?" I asked as we left the building.

"And ask why his family name was linked by an insane old man to the death of the Prescott girl?" Zach replied. "That kind of conversation might shorten your stay as a summer clerk."

"No, I want to ask his opinion of whether it's right to get Moses out of jail on probation when he may be guilty of murder."

WE PHONED MAGGIE SMITH from Zach's office. The assistant district attorney wouldn't be available until the morning.

"What do we do in the meantime?" I asked.

Zach pulled on his ponytail. "Wait."

"I know what I'm going to do," I said. "Find out more about the Prescott girl's death."

"Are you sure that's smart? Our job is to represent him in a trespassing case. The rest of it is probably a fantasy of random information swirled together in his mind. We don't even know there was a murder investigation."

"Mrs. Fairmont wasn't confused when she mentioned it."

"And could be remembering a rumor. On something like this, it's best to be skeptical. I'm not sure I'm going to let you—"

"Investigate it at all?" I interrupted sharply.

"Calm down," Zach answered.

I imagined steam coming out of my ears. After a few moments, Zach spoke. "We'll get on the phone to the district attorney's office first thing in the morning about a plea bargain on the trespassing case. After that's taken care of, you can decide if you want to talk some more with Moses about the faces in the water or let him slip back into the marsh. If you still want to check it out, I won't stop you."

WHEN I RETURNED TO THE LIBRARY, Julie was sitting hunched over one of the research terminals. She turned around when I entered and held up her right hand. It was clenched in the shape of a claw.

"See my misshapen hand?" she asked. "That's what two and a half hours of nonstop note-taking will do to otherwise healthy fingers. While you were laughing it up with Vinny, I barely had time to take a sip of water."

"Is it an interesting case?"

"If you think sorting through fourteen shell companies, some registered overseas, others with dummy boards, is more fun than the Sunday crossword puzzle, this client will be a blast. At one point, I think Mr. Carpenter was having second thoughts about trying to get the business, but when the main guy agreed without argument to the amount of the retainer, all reservations flew out of the room. Now, I'm researching information about the other side. They seem as devious as our client." Julie pushed her chair away from the computer. "So, what about Vinny? Did you tell him you have a crush on Zach Mays?"

"No and no."

"What do you mean? You have to tell me!"

"Why? So you can make fun of me?"

Julie held up her claw hand. "Don't make me use the claw on you. Your arms are longer than mine, but I'm tough in a catfight."

"I'm not scared, but there is a lot more to Vince than either of us realized." I paused. "And I don't have a crush on Zach Mays."

"More," Julie commanded.

I gave her a quick summary of lunch.

"Vinny is a genius," Julie sighed. "If they only make an offer to one clerk, there's no way you or I will land a permanent job with the firm. We may as well goof off the rest of the summer."

"They're paying us to work."

"Oh, don't bring that up." Julie turned back toward the computer screen. I decided not to tell her anything else about Moses Jones. The old man might be delusional, but I wanted to keep his strange comments confidential. I opened one of the Folsom files and began working. Shortly after 5:00 p.m., Julie announced it was time to go home.

"I need to ask Ms. Patrick a question," I replied.

"Don't be long. I have a headache."

I ran upstairs to the administrator's office. Her door was open, and I knocked on the frame.

"Come in," she said. "How are you?"

"Fine. I'm going home now but may want to come back tonight and do some research. Do I need to be concerned about a security system?"

"Not until eleven o'clock. After that, a code has to be entered."

"I won't be that late."

I started to leave.

"Tami, are you respecting the opinions and beliefs of others?" Ms. Patrick asked.

I turned around. "I think so. Have there been any complaints?"

"No, but misplaced zeal can be unprofessional."

"And I hope strong convictions aren't squelched," I responded.

Ms. Patrick had caught me off guard, and the words popped out before I scrutinized them. I inwardly cringed.

"Use restraint," she answered curtly. "I think that is a universal virtue."

"Yes ma'am." I returned more slowly down the stairs. Julie was waiting for me in the reception area. We stepped into the oppressive late-afternoon heat.

"If I'm not offered an associate job at Braddock, Appleby, and Carpenter, I don't think it will be because of Vince," I said.

"Why?"

"It's hard to get a job when you're competing against yourself."

Julie rubbed her left temple. "I'm not feeling well enough to figure that out."

She dropped me off in front of Mrs. Fairmont's house.

"I'll pray that you feel better," I said.

"And I'll take an extra painkiller in case that doesn't work. See you tomorrow."

MRS. FAIRMONT WAS DOZING in her chair in the den. Flip barked when I entered and ran across the floor to greet me. Mrs. Fairmont stirred in her chair. I waited, hoping she was lucid. Her eyes opened and focused on me.

"Good afternoon, Tami," she said. "Have you been home long?"

"No ma'am. I just walked in the door. How are you feeling?"

"A little groggy. Gracie fixed supper. It's in the oven and needs to be warmed up."

"Are you ready to eat?"

Flip barked loudly.

"I know you're hungry," I said to the little dog.

Mrs. Fairmont pushed herself up from the chair. Even on days when she didn't leave the house, she wore nice clothes. When I'd asked her about it, she told me that unexpected company could arrive at any moment.

"Let's feed Flip and turn on the oven," she said.

I knew where Mrs. Fairmont kept the dog food, but taking care of Flip was one of the things she enjoyed most. She carefully measured a scoop of food and poured it into the dog's dish. He immediately began munching the multicolored food with gusto. Gracie had left a note on the oven door with cooking instructions.

"It's a chicken dish," Mrs. Fairmont said. "I think there's garlic in it. I could smell it in the den when she put a clove in the crusher."

"That's fine so long as we both eat it," I replied.

"And the vegetables are in the refrigerator."

The vegetables, succotash and new potatoes in butter, were in pots. I put them on the stove. Without Gracie's help, Mrs. Fairmont wouldn't be able to stay in her house.

Flip finished his dinner and ran out the doggie door. Mrs. Fairmont slowly leaned over, picked up his water dish, and filled it with fresh water. It was time to ask the question that had been in the forefront of my mind since I walked through the front door.

"Do you remember showing me the picture of your friend, Mrs. Prescott, the woman whose daughter died?"

Mrs. Fairmont straightened up. "Yes."

"You and Mrs. Prescott were really good friends?"

"Yes. That's why I have her picture beside my bed. We were really close all through school and beyond. We had a lot of pleasant times before Lisa's death."

"Lisa Prescott," I said softly.

"It's a pretty name, isn't it?"

"Yes ma'am."

I stirred the succotash and checked the potatoes. "Mrs. Fairmont, I don't want to bring up any painful memories, but how much do you know about Lisa's death? Are they sure it was murder? Was anyone ever arrested and charged with a crime?"

"They never caught whoever killed her. I saved all the newspaper clippings."

"May I read them?"

"I think they're in a box downstairs, but I'm not sure where."

"Could I try to find it?"

Mrs. Fairmont shrugged. "Better let me help. Even as young as you are, you could spend the rest of your life going through the junk I've saved. Christine will probably send it all to the dump, but a lot of it meant something to me."

I checked the clock. The chicken would be ready in ten minutes. The vegetables were on simmer.

"Could we look now?" I asked.

"No, child," Mrs. Fairmont said. "I can't go right to it."

"After supper? It's important."

Mrs. Fairmont gave me the same look I'd seen when she first inspected me at the front door.

"Why are you so interested in Lisa Prescott's death?" she asked.

I avoided her eyes. "I can't tell you, except something happened at work today that made me want to find out."

"Christine probably remembers more than I do," Mrs. Fairmont replied. "Let's give her a call."

"No!" I said more strongly than I intended. "Uh, there may not be anything to my curiosity. At this point, I'd rather keep this between us."

"Christine is a blabbermouth," Mrs. Fairmont said, nodding her head. "I don't tell her anything that I don't want spread all over Savannah."

Mrs. Fairmont was quiet during supper. I'd enjoyed the fancy lunch with Vince, but preferred the chicken and nicely seasoned vegetables prepared by Gracie. Mrs. Fairmont yawned several times. I talked, trying to keep her alert enough to lead an expedition into her basement archives after supper.

"Bring the sliced cantaloupe from the refrigerator," Mrs. Fairmont said when we finished eating. "Let's have some for dessert."

I brought the cantaloupe to the table. Mrs. Fairmont ate the fruit with maddeningly slow deliberation.

"This is perfect," she said. "I love it when it's firm and sweet."

"Yes ma'am," I answered as I tried to will her to eat faster. "My family grows very good cantaloupes and watermelons."

She finished the meal with a final large yawn. "Excuse me," she said. "That is so rude, but I can't help it."

She pushed her chair away from the table.

"Have a good evening," she said. "I wish Flip could carry me upstairs to bed. I'll sleep for a while and probably be wide awake in the middle of the night. That's how it is with my condition."

"Yes ma'am," I answered. "Do you think you could put off going to bed for a few minutes so we can locate the newspaper clippings you saved about Lisa Prescott?"

"I forgot," she said with another yawn. "It all happened so long ago, it's hard to imagine it being terribly urgent."

"It is," I said bluntly. "I need to have the information by the morning."

"Very well. But you'd better hold my arm while we go downstairs. I don't want to break my neck."

It was a horrible image—Mrs. Fairmont lying in a twisted heap at the bottom of the stairs. I'd been hired to protect the elderly woman, not to place her in harm's way.

"Maybe we should wait until you wake up in the night," I said. "I can adapt to your schedule."

"No, no. That cantaloupe was sweet enough to give me a few more minutes of energy."

"Are you sure?"

She didn't answer but started walking toward the basement. Flip and I followed. I firmly held her arm, and we made it to the bottom of the stairs without mishap. I turned on the bare lightbulbs that illuminated the open area opposite my apartment. Large cardboard boxes were stacked on top of one another. Furniture not in use was covered by white bedsheets. Shelves affixed to two of the walls contained scores of smaller boxes. I wouldn't have known where to begin. Mrs. Fairmont stood at the bottom of the stairs and stared at a lifetime of accumulation.

"I think I keep the older records over here," she said, moving down a row of the large boxes.

I followed. Most of the boxes were labeled. We passed dishes, extra china, and souvenirs from travel. Mrs. Fairmont stopped and pointed.

"Could you lift that one out?" she asked.

"Yes ma'am." I sprang into action.

It was marked "Of Interest." I placed the lightweight box at Mrs. Fairmont's feet and removed the top. It was filled with yellowed newspapers.

"This is it!" I exclaimed.

"Maybe," she said.

I reached in and grabbed a newspaper that promptly crumbled in my hands. "Oops," I said.

"Don't worry. I'd never have seen it again if you hadn't asked me about Ellen's daughter."

I carefully retrieved what was left and held it up to the light. It was a Savannah paper almost seventy years old. Mrs. Fairmont leaned close to my shoulder.

"That's from my school days," she said. "My mother probably saved it because it contained news about me and my classmates."

I stared at the other papers in the box. "Would everything in this box be that old?"

"At least," she said. "Put it back. I don't want to read it."

I returned the box to its place. Mrs. Fairmont pointed to another box. This one was labeled "Newsworthy Items." I put it on the floor and removed the top. Inside were stacks of manila folders grown discolored with age.

"That's Christine's handwriting," Mrs. Fairmont said, pointing to the tab on the top folder. "These will be more recent."

One by one I took the folders from the box. They contained everything from Christmas punch recipes to information about horses.

"Christine loved to ride jumpers when she was younger. She wasn't afraid of anything."

I remembered my brief ride in the car with Mrs. Bartlett. I thought she might try to jump the curb in her Mercedes. Toward the bottom of the box, I saw a folder with the name "Lisa" on it and opened it. My eyes fell on the front page of the Savannah paper and a grainy picture of a little girl. I showed it to Mrs. Fairmont. She stared at it for a second.

"It's Lisa," she said in a sad voice. "That picture brings back a lot of memories. Lisa loved dressing up and sitting in a parlor chair with her feet dangling in the air. Ellen brought her over several times for afternoon tea."

While Mrs. Fairmont talked, I quickly scanned the article. On a Tuesday afternoon, the ten-year-old girl vanished following a piano lesson. The piano teacher, a woman named Miss Broadmore, was questioned by police and reported that Lisa left the teacher's house at precisely 4:30 p.m. for the five-minute walk home along familiar streets. Lisa never made it. Within an hour the police were notified.

Requests for assistance were broadcast on the local radio stations. Anyone seeing her was urged to come forward.

"It was a sad time," Mrs. Fairmont continued. "The whole city was touched by the Prescotts' loss. I think Christine saved all the articles she could. Most of my news came directly from Ellen."

There were other articles in the folder. All of them featured the same photograph. Even in a black-and-white image, Lisa fit Moses Jones' description.

"Do you remember anything else Ellen told you?"

Mrs. Fairmont shook her head. "There are lots of things jumbled up in my head. Trying to sort them out would be an unhappy way to end the day."

"Yes ma'am. I understand. Thanks for helping me."

I assisted Mrs. Fairmont up the stairs to the main floor and then to her bedroom. I examined the picture of Ellen Prescott on the nightstand more closely. Lisa looked a lot like her mother.

"How old were you and Ellen in that picture?" I asked.

"About seven or eight. Young enough that a trip to the park with a friend was a special treat."

I turned to go downstairs. I was anxious to read the rest of the newspaper articles.

"Tami?" Mrs. Fairmont asked.

"Yes ma'am."

"I like having you in the house. It makes me feel safe."

"Thank you."

I took the box into my apartment and carefully removed the newspapers. They weren't as brittle as the very old ones. Beginning with the first account of Lisa's disappearance, I read the unfolding story more slowly.

There wasn't much to tell.

One day Lisa was a bright, vivacious girl. The next she vanished without a trace. The second article was the longest and featured a map with Lisa's most likely route from Miss Broadmore's house to the Prescott home on East McDonough Street. Close to the Prescott home was the Colonial Park Cemetery.

Several follow-up articles included quotes from people claiming to have seen Lisa during her walk home. Unfortunately, the claims were inconsistent and would have required Lisa to walk several blocks out of her way instead of following the most direct route. The police chief offered cryptic comments without substance to the newspaper reporters. One fact seemed clear. No one saw the little girl after she neared the cemetery. The police focused their investigation on that area and scoured it for physical evidence. Not a piece of sheet music or bit of clothing was discovered. No ransom note was delivered. The possibility of a kidnapping faded.

After a week of daily articles, there was a two-day gap followed by a brief update without any new information. A week went by before another article repeated familiar facts with the conclusion that the police suspected "foul play" but had no suspects. Two months later there was a notice on page two of "Memorial Service for Girl Presumed Dead." It was a harsh headline. More than eight hundred people attended the service at a local church. I returned the newspapers to the box. I looked over my notes and decided I hadn't uncovered anything that warranted a nighttime walk to the office.

And, even though Lisa Prescott's unexplained disappearance occurred decades earlier, I didn't want to go out after dark.

20

THE WORLD APPEARED LESS MENACING IN THE MORNING WHEN I went for my run. I modified my route to include Lisa's likely course home from her music teacher's house. It wasn't far. And in a simpler time, when children played outside without constant supervision, the brief walk would probably have been considered good exercise. I did a slow loop around Colonial Park Cemetery. The graveyard had many old headstones and looked like it had been closed for business for many years. It probably hadn't changed much since Lisa Prescott saw it.

Returning to the house, I was surprised to find Mrs. Fairmont, wearing a green silk robe with flowers embroidered on it, standing in the kitchen. Coffee was filling the pot.

"Good morning," I said, pouring myself a glass of water from a jug in the refrigerator.

"Good morning. Did you read the newspaper articles about Lisa?" she asked.

"Yes ma'am. They never mentioned murder, but there wasn't another explanation."

"We hoped for a while that it was a kidnapping. Money wouldn't have been a problem."

"But no ransom note came."

"Right." Mrs. Fairmont nodded. "You know, the Prescotts had a funeral for Lisa. Ellen didn't want to do it, but her husband and the rest of the family insisted. It was a pathetic affair, no casket, all the unanswered questions. Ellen maintained hope Lisa would return. I grieved when Ellen died, but I also thought at least she was with Lisa again."

It was a poignant thought. I poured Mrs. Fairmont a cup of coffee. The elderly woman seemed particularly lucid.

"What can you tell me about the criminal investigation?" I asked.

"Ellen and her husband met with the police several times, and she told me what was said. The detectives had ideas." Mrs. Fairmont stared across the room.

"Do you remember?" I asked.

"There was the blood on the curb at Colonial Park Cemetery. They didn't have all the fancy tests they do now. At first, the police thought it was from an animal hit by a car because they found a dead dog nearby, but later they figured out it was human blood."

"That wasn't in any of the newspaper articles. Was it Lisa's blood type?"

"They weren't sure. The tests back then weren't very accurate. Ellen and I went to the curb before rain washed away the stain. Even though she wasn't positive the blood came from Lisa, Ellen stared at the spot for a long time and cried. I didn't know what to say." Mrs. Fairmont looked directly at me. "What would you have told her?"

"I don't know. I've never lost a close family member. I hope God would give me a special grace for that time. Just loving her was probably the best thing you could do as her friend."

Mrs. Fairmont placed her coffee cup on the counter. "Do you think God will give me a special grace for the time I'm going through?"

"That you will get better?"

She nodded.

It was a difficult question, and I didn't want to give a casual answer. I believed with my whole heart in divine healing. Some people in our church had been healed of serious diseases; others died.

"I know God loves you," I said slowly. "Asking for his help is up to you."

Mrs. Fairmont smiled. "You sound like Gracie, only she puts a lot more feeling behind it. God brought her into my life to help me years ago, and it looks like he's added you for reinforcement."

"Yes ma'am. I want to help."

"I know. Run along and get ready for work."

I turned to leave.

"And promise you'll tell me as soon as you can why you're interested in Lisa Prescott's disappearance," Mrs. Fairmont said. "That's an old wound, and it's not right to open it up without a reason."

"Yes ma'am."

I returned the newspaper clippings to the folder so I could copy them at work. When I came upstairs, I saw the back of Mrs. Fairmont's head above the top of a chair in the den.

"I'm leaving for work," I said.

"Christine?" she called out without turning around.

"No ma'am. It's Tami." I stepped into the older woman's line of sight. "Do you want to call her?"

Mrs. Fairmont stared intently at me. "No, no. I thought you were Christine. What were we talking about earlier? My brain has gotten fuzzy."

"I asked you about Lisa Prescott."

Mrs. Fairmont shook her head with a sad expression on her face. "You know, they never did find her body."

"Yes ma'am, I know. Don't worry about that today."

All the way to work, I prayed for Mrs. Fairmont.

I WENT STRAIGHT TO ZACH'S OFFICE. His door was open, and papers were stacked on his desk. His tie was loosened around his neck. He was taking a sip of coffee when I entered.

"I didn't know you drank coffee."

"I'm a backslider," he replied.

"No, I didn't mean it that way."

"I'm not offended. I needed a boost since I came in to work a couple of hours ago. Getting a head start on this project for Mr. Appleby is the only way I can create enough time in my schedule for the Moses Jones case this afternoon."

"Could I go alone?"

"No." Zach smiled. "You'll do all the talking, but Judge Cannon wouldn't appreciate a law student showing up in his courtroom without a supervising attorney."

"I did some research about the little girl, but the most interesting information came from Mrs. Fairmont."

I handed him the initial article and waited for him to read it.

"What did Mrs. Fairmont say?"

Zach listened without taking notes while I talked. He took another sip of coffee before he spoke.

"It's obvious. Moses Jones was hired by a man named Floyd Carpenter to dispose of Lisa Prescott's body and was paid a shiny, silver dollar to do it. He dumped her in the Ogeechee River, and the little girl's face has haunted him ever since."

Hearing Zach succinctly state my fears made me shudder. "That's awful."

"Yes, if there's a shred of truth to it."

"But it makes sense. Why else would Moses say the things he does?"

"Because he may be in a permanent mental fog. Did you research our obligation to suggest half-baked theories implicating our client in a forty-year-old missing child case to the district attorney while trying to convince her to release him on probation on a trespassing charge?"

"No."

"And you don't have to." Zach pushed his chair away from his desk. "Before I began my other work this morning, I spent time praying about the Jones case. Once my head cleared of the misguided curiosity that dominated our interview session with him yesterday, I realized we shouldn't be pretending to be a cold-case investigation team. We're not actors on a TV show. Moses Jones is a real person who trusts us to help him with an immediate problem."

"But what about Lisa Prescott?"

"Her disappearance was a tragedy. But why should we try to solve what police officers and detectives close in time to the events couldn't figure out?"

I took a deep breath to avoid getting angry. "I believe everything happens for a reason," I said deliberately. "It wasn't an accident that I saw the picture of Ellen Prescott on Mrs. Fairmont's nightstand and asked about it. It wasn't a coincidence that Moses mentioned the Prescott girl to me. And this morning, Mrs. Fairmont tells me information known only to the police and Prescott family."

"So God sovereignly brought all this together?"

"Maybe."

"Which still doesn't get you off the hook about making a choice. I've made my choice, and so should you. I think you should focus on what Judge Cannon appointed you to do—represent Moses in the trespassing case."

I scrunched my eyes together but held my tongue.

"Make a face if you like," Zach said, "but I'm trying to teach you to be a professional. It's my job. Come back at nine o'clock, and we'll call Maggie Smith."

He looked down at some papers on his desk. Steaming mad, I left his office and walked down the stairs to the first floor. My shoes clipped against the wooden floor. One choice was easy. My interest in getting to know Zach Mays better on a personal level was gone. Julie was in the library when I arrived.

"Good morning," Julie announced brightly. "My headache is gone. A bad one can hang around for a couple of days, but I'm feeling super."

"That's great," I managed.

"Uh-oh," Julie responded. "It's too early in the day to be depressed. Is the pressure of maintaining two boyfriends getting to you?"

"Shut up," I said.

Julie's jaw dropped.

"I did it," I said softly.

Tears rushed into my eyes, and I stumbled out of the room.

Right into the arms of Mr. Carpenter.

The older lawyer steadied me for a moment, then let go. Julie opened the door, saw Mr. Carpenter, and quickly closed it.

"What's going on here?" Mr. Carpenter asked.

I sniffled. "It's been a rough morning," I said.

"That's obvious. Come to my office."

"Now?"

"Yes."

As I walked down the hall I glanced back and saw the library door close again. My tears receded, but my eyes were still red as we passed the secretary's desk. She didn't pay any attention to me.

"Sit down," Mr. Carpenter said.

I sat in a blue leather chair.

"Answer me directly," the lawyer continued. "Why were you crying in the office hallway at eight thirty in the morning?"

"It's a combination of things."

"Tell me every one. As managing partner, I'm responsible for this office and the people who work here. It's better to address problems as soon as they surface instead of letting them fester."

"I don't want to get Julie in trouble."

"I appreciate your sentiment, but I don't know what took place. You might be the one in trouble."

I hadn't considered that possibility. Confessing sin, even if I wasn't the primary guilty party, happened all the time in my family and wasn't a new concept to me.

"I told her to shut up," I said. "And I'm sorry. I'll apologize as soon as I can."

Mr. Carpenter tilted his head to the side. "Much worse things than that have been said in our partnership meetings. Why did you tell her to shut up?"

I realized Mr. Carpenter was going to ferret out every piece of information hidden in my brain, so, in a methodical manner, I told him about Julie's challenge. He listened without interruption.

"Anything else at the office upset you this morning?" he asked.

"Yes sir, I'm struggling with the best way to represent Mr. Moses Jones, my client in the misdemeanor criminal case. Zach Mays and I don't agree on the best way to proceed."

"What did you say was the client's name?"

"Moses Jones."

"Tell me about the client."

"He's an African-American man in his early seventies. He had a prior criminal conviction many years ago, something to do with moonshine whiskey."

"Been in Savannah a long time?"

"I think his whole life."

Mr. Carpenter touched his fingers together in front of his chin. The phone on his desk buzzed. He picked it up.

"Tell Bob Groves that I'll be there in a couple of minutes. I'm almost finished with Ms. Taylor."

I waited, not sure whether the next few minutes would be my last on the job. If I left, it would be with a clear conscience. Mr. Carpenter hung up the phone.

"I've received good reports from several sources about the way you and Ms. Feldman have been working together," the lawyer said. "The incident this morning is an opportunity for growth. Julie is probably scared that you're telling me a boatload of bad things about her. That may be punishment enough for baiting you. When you go back, I expect you to confront her actions in a gracious yet professional manner."

"Yes sir."

"I'll meet with her later today." Mr. Carpenter paused. "And keep me posted via weekly memos on the Jones case."

"Yes sir."

I left Mr. Carpenter's office. I still had a job. I looked at my watch. It was past time for the phone call to Maggie Smith at the district attorney's office. I turned to go upstairs, then remembered my obligation to Julie. I walked quickly to the library and opened the door. Julie looked up from a casebook.

"I'm sorry," she said hurriedly. "What's he going to do?"

"Mr. Carpenter thought you'd be worried."

"Worried? I've been frantic! Trying to figure out how I was going to break the news to my parents if I lost this job."

"He wants to talk to you later."

"Am I going to get in trouble? What's he going to do to me?"

"Probably tell you to act more professional," I said. "That's what he said to me. He knows we've been working well together. He realizes this was a temporary blowup."

"Are you sure?"

"Yes."

"Okay. Anything else?"

I looked directly in her eyes. "I'm sorry I told you to shut up. We can joke around but shouldn't be cruel."

Julie looked down at the table. "Sure, like I said, I'm sorry too."

I WENT UPSTAIRS TO ZACH'S OFFICE, determined to act professional. The stack of papers on his desk was higher than before.

"Sorry I'm late. Mr. Carpenter called me into his office," I said.

"You didn't miss anything. I just got off the phone with the DA's office. Smith won't want to commit to any modification of her plea offer without the judge getting involved. It's an extreme position for a misdemeanor case, but she wouldn't budge. We won't know anything else until we go to court this afternoon."

"Okay."

"Why were you talking to Mr. Carpenter?"

"He had some questions for me."

Zach stared at me for a few seconds. I remained silent.

"Fine," he said. "We'll leave for the courthouse thirty minutes before the calendar call. The order of cases isn't released in advance. We could be first; we could be last."

I nodded and left.

Julie wasn't in the library when I returned. On my side of the desk was a memo from Bob Kettleson. He wanted me to research a complicated municipal corporation issue before the end of the day. I read the memo again, thankful that I'd completed the course in law school and received an A.

Shortly before noon, the library door opened. I looked up, expecting to see Julie. It was Vince.

"Lunch plans?" he asked.

I smiled. "Thanks, but I don't have time for a long meal. Bob Kettleson needs an answer to a question, and I have a hearing in my criminal case this afternoon."

"My appointed case is on the calendar too," he said. "The client is going to pay a speeding fine and replace his muffler in return for dismissal of the racing charge."

"I wish my case was so simple," I sighed.

"What's the problem?"

I eyed Vince for a moment. He was smart and less likely than Zach to try to impose his will on me in a condescending way. His input might be helpful.

"I'll tell you if we can grab a quick sandwich."

"I know a place," he replied.

While notifying the receptionist that we were leaving for lunch, I glanced up the staircase and saw Zach looking down at us. He quickly walked away.

It was hot outside, and Vince started his car with his remote as soon as we left the building.

"It won't do much good," he said, opening the car door for me. "But it's a nice thought."

He drove a few blocks to a deli near the river. There was a parking place directly in front on the curb.

"Do you ever pray for parking spots?" he asked.

"No, I don't own a car."

"That will change once you graduate and get a job," Vince said.

"I wonder where I'll be."

"Why not here?"

There was no tactful way to mention what Julie and I knew—Vince would be the summer clerk offered an associate attorney job.

"We'll see," I said.

The deli featured a dizzying selection of meats, cheeses, and breads. Vince waited while I looked at the menu.

"Could I order for you?" he asked.

"Sure. You did fine with lunch yesterday."

"Is there anything you don't like?"

"Chicken livers. My mother has cooked them every way possible, but I always have trouble convincing my mouth to send one down my throat."

Vince placed the order, and I watched a man behind the counter slice two types of meat, three kinds of cheese, and add an assortment of unknown condiments to a piece of dark bread. We took our food and drinks to a booth for two next to a window. I could see the river glinting between two buildings. Vince prayed. I took a bite of the sandwich.

"This isn't dull at all," I said after I'd chewed and swallowed a bite. "I'm not used to a sandwich like this having much flavor."

"Okay. Do you want to tell me about your case?"

I had the sandwich halfway up to my mouth. I stopped. "Not until I eat."

Vince made a few comments while we ate. He seemed more relaxed than the previous day, and I realized he might have been nervous during our lunch. The thought that a man would be nervous around me suddenly hit me as funny, and I laughed.

"What is it?" Vince asked, quickly touching a napkin to his mouth. "Is there sauce dripping off my chin?"

"No." I sipped my drink. "You're fine. It was a private thought about me."

I ate most of the sandwich and wished I could give what remained to the twins. They would have turned up their noses until coaxed into trying a bite.

"Now, tell me about *State v. Jones*," Vince said.

"You remember the name of my case?"

"Your client is charged with multiple counts of trespassing, and Julie's client, Mr. Ferguson, was allegedly impersonating a water-meter reader."

"Why am I surprised?" I shrugged.

I began with the first interview. As I talked, I had the impression Vince would remember more about the case than I would.

"Did Jones say anything else about the man named Carpenter?"

"No."

"Have you done any research at the courthouse or on the Internet?"

"No."

Vince looked at his watch. "We need to get back to the office. Let me think about it."

With Vince, I knew the statement wasn't a put-off.

I was able to deliver a memo to Kettleson with fifteen minutes to spare before leaving for the courthouse. I opened my *State v. Jones* folder and reviewed my notes. I knew if a plea bargain wasn't reached with the district attorney, Moses would be expected to plead not guilty to the charges. I ran over in my mind Moses' argument that he couldn't be convicted of trespassing because the river belonged to God. If that was true, the posts put there by man were the real trespassers. Even a summer clerk couldn't make that argument to a jury of sane adults. I went upstairs to Zach's office. He was pulling his tie tighter around his neck.

"I'm ready," I said.

"Really? Did you contact the homeowners I hadn't interviewed?"

"No."

"I did. One of them will be in the courtroom."

Zach picked up his briefcase. "I'll fill you in on the way over there."

As I followed Zach to the first floor of the office, two thoughts crossed my mind. Both Zach and Vince were smarter than I was; however, Vince didn't go out of his way to remind me.

21

"YOU'RE KIDDING," I SAID, STANDING BESIDE ZACH'S BLACK motorcycle with the sidecar attached.

Zach handed me the helmet I'd worn on Saturday. "Ride or walk. It's not very far. I didn't unhook the sidecar after our ride to Tybee Island."

"But you knew we had the arraignment calendar today. You could have driven your car."

"Maybe I forgot," he said with a grin.

I debated whether to go back inside and request use of the law firm car, but when I looked around the lot it wasn't there. I took the helmet.

"This isn't funny," I said, slipping it over my head.

Zach put on his helmet and spoke into the microphone. "We'll be able to park close to the entrance. There are special spaces reserved for motorcycles."

I didn't answer. Refusing his offer of a hand to steady me, I got into the sidecar as gracefully as I could. Zach turned on the motor and backed up. As he did, a car passed behind us as it entered the lot. I turned my head and saw Julie, her mouth gaping open, staring at me from the passenger seat.

"Do you want to know what the homeowner told me?" Zach asked.

"Tell me after we get there."

The pleasure I'd felt toward the end of the motorcycle ride on Saturday didn't return during the short, bumpy trip to the courthouse. I clutched the Jones file in my lap and looked straight ahead. I didn't have to wonder if every pedestrian or the people in other vehicles were staring at me. Zach turned into the courthouse parking lot and stopped next to a green motorcycle.

"That's a nice bike, made in Italy," he said as we took off the helmets.

I pushed myself up with my hands and got out of the sidecar. "I'm not wearing motorcycle clothes. Did your father take your mother to church in a motorcycle sidecar?"

"Sometimes. But you have to remember, my parents were living near L.A."

Zach locked up the helmets.

"Which courtroom?" he asked as we climbed the steps.

"I'm not sure."

"Follow me."

I held back for a second, but it looked silly for me to walk two steps behind him. We entered the building together.

"What about the homeowner?" I asked.

"After I told Mr. Fussleman about Moses' life on the river, he said it reminded him of Huck and Jim. He's willing to ask the judge for a lenient sentence."

"What about the other dock owners?"

"I hope they won't be here. Moses used Mr. Fussleman's dock more than any of the others, so you can argue he's the party who suffered the most damage." Zach glanced sideways at me as we waited for an elevator. "Have you written out your argument for the judge?"

"No."

"You'll have a few minutes after we talk to Mr. Fussleman, and maybe our case won't be the first one called."

"Vince has a case—" I stopped. I could have ridden with Vince and avoided the sidecar.

We got off the elevator and turned left down a broad hallway. A cluster of people were milling around.

"I hope all these people aren't on our calendar," Zach said.

He opened the door to the courtroom. It was a large room with bench seating. At least a hundred people were already present. The thought of making my unprepared argument to Judge Cannon in front of a big crowd made my hands sweat. Zach walked to the front of the courtroom. I followed. He turned around and spoke in a loud voice.

"Is Mr. Fussleman here?"

All the conversations ceased, and everyone looked around to see if Mr. Fussleman identified himself. No one raised his hand or came forward. There was a row of chairs in front of a railing that separated the crowd from the area in front of the bench and the jury box on the right-hand side of the room. Zach sat down and motioned for me to join him.

"What is Mr. Fussleman going to say?" I asked.

"Fussleman grew up here and knows men like Moses who roam up and down the river. I want him to meet Moses before the calendar call. Once Fussleman sees how harmless he is, he may ask the judge to let Moses go free without any more jailtime and even allow Moses to use his dock as long as he doesn't do anything except tie up for the night. That would take care of two problems at once."

It was a much better plan of action than the nonexistent one I'd come up with.

"That's great," I said.

Zach glanced sideways at me. "I promised to help."

I felt ashamed. I'd been petty and prideful. I pressed my lips together and silently asked God to forgive me. Zach stood up again. An apology to him would have to wait.

"Is Mr. Fussleman here?" he called out again.

An older man with gray hair and wearing a business suit raised his hand in the air.

"Come on," Zach said to me.

We walked to the rear of the courtroom. Zach extended his hand and introduced himself. "Thanks so much for coming," he said. "I know it's inconvenient."

Zach introduced me to Mr. Fussleman, who smiled.

"Mr. Mays told me this was your first case," he said. "One of my daughters is a young lawyer in Washington, D.C. When I thought about her, I had to see what I could do to help you sort this out."

"Thank you," I said gratefully.

"Let's step into the hallway," Zach suggested.

More people were entering the courtroom. We found a quiet spot. Mr. Fussleman looked at me expectantly. I knew my job—to tell him Moses Jones was a harmless old man who wouldn't hurt anything except the fish he caught for supper. I did my best, but I kept thinking about the newspaper photograph of Lisa Prescott and her face that continued to accuse Moses from a watery grave. Mr. Fussleman listened thoughtfully. The few times I glanced at Zach, I couldn't decipher his expression. Vince walked past us and into the courtroom.

"What do you want me to do?" Mr. Fussleman asked when I finished.

"Tell Judge Cannon that as one of the dock owners, you support releasing Mr. Jones for time already served in jail, and in the future would allow him to tie up for the night at your dock so long as he didn't interfere with your use of the facilities or cause any damage to your property."

"I want to meet Mr. Jones before I agree to anything, but I don't think I have any objection to releasing him from jail." He hesitated a moment before continuing, "But I can't agree to let him use my dock."

My face fell.

"Unless he checks with me first," he finished.

"It may be late at night," I replied.

"I'm usually up past eleven. If it's later than that, he will have to pole his boat back down the river."

His proposal was more than fair.

"Can we meet with Moses?" I asked Zach.

"Let's try."

We returned to the courtroom.

"There's Maggie Smith," Zach said.

There were three female members of the district attorney's staff stacking up files at one of the tables used by the lawyers.

"Which one?"

"The shorter one with brown hair."

Zach ushered Mr. Fussleman to a seat directly behind the railing. We approached Ms. Smith. Zach extended his hand.

"We met at a young lawyers section meeting last year," he said. "You may not remember me—"

"It's hard not to notice a male lawyer in Savannah with long hair who rides a motorcycle."

I glanced down. Ms. Smith wasn't wearing a wedding ring.

"One of the dock owners, a Mr. Fussleman, is here," Zach said. "He'd like to meet our client."

"Why?"

Zach turned to me, and I explained our purpose. Smith shrugged.

"Okay. If none of the other dock owners show up, I won't oppose a guilty plea for time served as long as there is a period of probation. I don't want Jones claiming ownership of a dock by adverse possession."

"Will you support the plea?" Zach asked.

Smith looked at Zach and smiled. "No, but I'll be very clear that I don't oppose it."

"Thanks," he said.

We returned to the area where the lawyers were sitting. Vince and Russell Hopkins, his supervising attorney, were at the opposite end of our row. A side door opened, and a long line of prisoners wearing jail uniforms entered. Toward the end of the line I saw Moses. None of the men in his group were shackled. A smaller group in leg irons and handcuffs followed.

"Why are some of them wearing handcuffs?" I asked Zach.

"Probably felony cases. Moses and the others are the misdemeanor, nonviolent cases."

Moses saw me and smiled. It made me feel creepy.

"Let's talk to the deputy," Zach said.

Zach went up to one of the deputies I recognized from my visits to the jail and told him about Mr. Fussleman. The deputy motioned to Moses.

"You can talk to him at the end of the row," the deputy said. "But you'd better make it quick. The judge will be here in a minute, and he'll want everyone in their places."

"Get Fussleman," Zach told me. "I'll tell Moses what we're trying to do."

I brought Mr. Fussleman over. Zach was whispering into Moses' ear.

"What dock be yours?" Moses asked Fussleman.

"The one with the blue and white boat."

Moses nodded. "Yes sir. That's a mighty nice piece of boat."

"Thank you."

"Moses, are you sorry that you used Mr. Fussleman's dock without permission?" Zach asked the old man.

Moses looked at Zach then Mr. Fussleman. "I didn't use nobody's dock except as a place to put a piece of cotton rope. I'm sorry that the policemans put me in jail and lock me and my boat up. That's what makes my heart cry in the night."

"Moses doesn't believe the river belongs to anyone," I said, "but he's agreed not to tie up at private docks without permission in the future, right?"

I held my breath for a second, hoping Moses wouldn't back down on his promise.

"That be right, missy."

"And Mr. Fussleman might be willing to let you tie up if you ask his permission in advance before eleven o'clock at night," I added.

Moses looked at Mr. Fussleman. "That's mighty nice of you, boss man. You let Moses know, and I'll clean that blue and white boat for free and scrub your dock. And you know that yellow line at the edge, the one that be going away fast? I paint it for you."

Mr. Fussleman shook Moses' hand. "Come by when you get out of jail, and we'll talk about it." The dock owner turned to me. "This man doesn't need to be locked up. I'll testify if you need me."

"All rise!" announced one of the bailiffs on duty. "The Superior Court of Chatham County is now in session, the Honorable Clifton Cannon presiding."

The judge, an older, white-haired man, sat down without looking in the direction of the lawyers.

"Be seated!" the bailiff called out.

The judge turned toward the DA's table. "Ms. Smith, are you ready?"

"Yes, Your Honor."

"Let's hear pleas first, reserving the motion to suppress in *State v. Robinson* to the end of the calendar."

"Yes sir, we have twenty-six cases here for arraignment. Based on the discussions with counsel, several of those intend to plead guilty."

I licked my lips. There was less than a five percent chance that Moses' case would be the first one called. I desperately wanted to watch a few experienced lawyers navigate the waters before I was thrown in. I leaned close to Zach.

"What if we're first?"

"Then I'll be back to the office in time to get some work done."

It was an unsympathetic answer. Ms. Smith picked up a file from her stack.

"*State v. Jones*," she called out.

Zach stood up. I was so shocked that I didn't move.

"Come on," Zach said.

I got to my feet and stepped into the open area in front of the judge. A deputy culled Moses from the rest of the prisoners and brought him to stand beside me.

"Your Honor, I'm Zach Mays, and this is Ms. Tami Taylor, a summer clerk with our firm," Zach said. "You appointed Ms. Taylor to represent Mr. Jones, and the firm asked me to supervise her work on the case."

Judge Cannon had bushy white eyebrows. He brought them together and glared at me. Ms. Smith spoke.

"Mr. Jones is charged with twenty-five counts of trespassing by tying up his boat at private docks on the Little Ogeechee River."

"I believe it's twenty-four counts," I corrected.

"A difference without a distinction," the judge grunted. "How does he plead?"

I looked at Zach.

"Mr. Mays is not your client," the judge barked at me.

"Uh, Your Honor, Mr. Jones has been in jail for over two months, and we would like to enter a guilty plea as long as he is released for time served followed by a one-year period of supervised probation."

Moses' voice startled me. "My boat, missy. Don't be forgetting."

"Yes sir. His boat was seized, and he would like it back."

"Ms. Taylor, you do not enter into plea negotiations with me while I'm sitting on the bench trying to work my way through a crowded calendar."

"Yes sir. We talked to Ms. Smith," I responded quickly. "She has no objection to my proposal."

"Is that right?" the judge asked the assistant DA.

"We will leave the sentence to Your Honor's discretion but do not oppose defense counsel's suggestion."

"Was there any physical damage to property warranting restitution?" the judge asked.

"No sir," I replied. "And one of the dock owners, Mr. William Fussleman, is present and willing to testify in favor of the proposed plea."

I pointed in the direction of Mr. Fussleman, who stood up.

"That won't be necessary," the judge said. "Mr. Jones?"

Moses looked up.

"Are you Moses Jones?" the judge repeated.

"That be me."

"Are you aware of the charges against you?"

"Yes sir."

The judge looked down at the papers before him. "Did you illegally tie up your boat at these docks without permission of the owners?"

"I just be stopping by for a while to get some sleep. I don't hurt no one or nothing."

"Counsel, will you agree your client's statement is the equivalent of an affirmative answer?" the judge asked me.

"Yes sir."

"Mr. Jones, do you realize that I do not have to accept your lawyer's suggestion about releasing you from jail and could sentence you to twenty-four one-year sentences to run consecutively, said sentences to be served in the Georgia State Penitentiary?"

Moses stared at the judge without a hint of understanding in his eyes.

"Your Honor," I began. "I explained—"

"I wish I had more time for you to practice being a lawyer, Ms. Taylor, but I don't. I'm not going to accept your recommendation for sentence. Mr. Jones has demonstrated a repeated and callous disregard for the property of others, and I have no confidence he will modify his conduct in the future. If he wants to plead guilty, I will refer him for a presentence investigation, then sentence him in a way I deem appropriate. If that is acceptable we'll proceed. Otherwise, you may withdraw your offer of a guilty plea."

I turned to Zach in panic and whispered, "What do I do?"

Zach spoke. "Your Honor, we withdraw the plea."

"Very well. Have him enter his not-guilty plea on the accusation."

Ms. Smith pushed a piece of paper in front of me and pointed to a place beneath the words "Not Guilty." Moses scrawled his name in the space provided. It was the same signature I'd seen at the bottom of the confession. The deputy led Moses back to the group of prisoners. When I turned away, Vince, a look of genuine sympathy on his face, caught my eye.

"*State v. Brown*," Ms. Smith called out.

Vince and Russell stood. Zach and I passed them as we walked down the aisle. Mr. Fussleman joined us. The three of us returned to the hallway.

"Was that a surprise?" Fussleman asked.

"Yes," Zach answered. "There is no guaranteed result in front of a judge, but they often look to the prosecutor for recommendations on sentencing. Otherwise, the system totally bogs down."

"We're bogged down," I said. "What do we do next?"

"Get ready to try the case," Zach said, his jaw firm.

MOSES WATCHED THE TALL GIRL who wasn't a real lawyer and the young lawyer helping her leave the courtroom. The man sitting next to him nudged his arm.

"They gave you a couple of practice lawyers?" the man asked in a low voice.

Moses grunted.

"Judge Cannon," the man continued. "They named him right. He'll blow you up into a million pieces. I saw what he did to you. One of my cousins pleaded guilty to writing a few bad checks and got sent to a work camp for a year and a half."

"I couldn't handle no work camp," Moses said.

"Oh, they wouldn't do that to you," the man reassured him. "At your age you've got nothing to worry about. They have a special prison over in Telfair County that's like a nursing home. They bring three meals a day on a tray to your room and change your bedsheets three times a week."

Moses glanced sideways at the man to see if he was telling the truth. A faint smile at the corners of the man's mouth betrayed the lie. Another prisoner was called forward. Moses watched and listened. The man was charged with destroying the front of a convenience store by ramming it with his truck when the clerk inside wouldn't sell him any beer. The man's lawyer wore a fancy suit and smiled when he spoke to the judge. The prisoner received probation and was ordered to pay for the damage. He returned to the group with a grin on his face. Moses heard him speak to the deputy.

"General, once I get my civilian clothes, you won't be seeing me anymore."

"You'll be back as soon as you get your hands on a fifth," the deputy replied impassively. "We'll save a spot for you."

Moses rubbed his head. He hadn't put a scratch on anyone's dock. Why couldn't he be set free? The next defendant was represented by a different lawyer. He also received probation. The man sitting next to Moses was called forward. He had a long history of drunk driving. The lawyer with the fancy suit represented him too. Moses expected the judge to give the man probation, but instead he sentenced him to three years in prison. When the man returned to the other prisoners, the smile at the corners of his mouth was gone.

As the afternoon dragged on, a deep ache was churned in Moses' gut. He would be returning to the jail and didn't know how long he'd be there. Locked behind the thick walls with the high, narrow windows was little better than living in a casket. He closed his eyes and found himself in the dark on the river. The pain in his stomach was joined by a black sadness in his mind. *Hope* hadn't been in the vocabulary of his heart for many years, but at least he'd been a survivor. Now, he wasn't sure he wanted to live. The ache in the darkness increased. He saw the little girl's face. Her golden hair, like wispy cords of death, reached out for him.

22

NEITHER ZACH NOR I SPOKE INTO THE HELMET MICROPHONES during the return trip to the office. I was sorry that he would have to find time in his busy schedule to help me, and I felt bad that I would have to defend a man who was guilty of trespassing—and probably much worse. Zach parked the motorcycle. I climbed out, handed him the helmet, and tucked my folder under my arm.

"The case will have to be placed on a trial calendar this summer," Zach said as we walked up the sidewalk. "Otherwise, you'll be in school."

"How soon?"

"That's up to the DA's office. I don't know much about the criminal court schedule. Call the court administrator and find out possible dates, then let me know so I can enter them on my calendar. You'll need to get ready."

Zach held the door open for me. Usually, the cool interior of the office refreshed me. This afternoon, I didn't notice. We stood in the reception area at the base of the staircase. I faced Zach.

"How do I prepare to try a case for a man who signed a confession and whose only defense is based on an argument that God, who created the rivers and oceans, is the only one who can complain about trespassing on waterways in the state of Georgia?"

"You said the confession doesn't sound like Jones."

"I know, but would that be grounds to suppress it?"

"No, but it can be argued to a jury." Zach stopped at the bottom of the stairs. "Look, I'm not a criminal law expert. I'm doing the best I can."

"I'm not criticizing you," I responded quickly. "It was a great idea to ask Mr. Fussleman to come to the hearing. I wouldn't have had the courage to ask him for help."

"You saw how that worked out."

"Yes, but I owe you an apology. You took care of me when I wasn't looking out for myself or the client. I'm learning as fast as I can."

Zach put his hand on the stair railing. "And you're about to learn a lot more."

JULIE WAS IN THE LIBRARY when I opened the door. I placed the Moses Jones folder on the worktable and sighed. Julie put down her pen.

"You look upset, but I'm not going to say anything stupid about Zach or Vinny," she said. "Mr. Carpenter assured me that you didn't try to get me in trouble, which I really, really appreciate. He told me to apologize, put the incident behind me, and be more professional."

I waited.

"What?" she asked.

"Is that your idea of an apology?"

"Oh, I'm sorry."

It was such a lame effort that I had to smile.

"Hey, great," she said. "I heard you and Vinny got rid of your criminal cases today."

"Vince's case may be over, but mine is getting more serious."

"What happened?"

In telling Julie, the magnitude of the disaster grew.

"Wow," she said. "That stinks."

I touched one of the Folsom divorce files with my right hand.

"Divorces and criminal law," I said. "I think my mother knew this was going to happen and tried to warn me before I came here."

"How did she want you to spend your summer?"

I thought about endless rows of dead chickens. Surely, that wasn't Mama's desire for my future.

"She left it up to me," I replied. "Now, as my father would say, I have a chance to grow in the midst of difficulty."

The family platitude sounded hollow in the moment. I sat down at one of the computer workstations and began typing a memo to Mr. Carpenter about the status of *State v. Jones*.

By the end of the day, Julie had returned to her chipper self. We worked together on the Folsom case, but Moses and Lisa Prescott stayed at the edge of my mind. I expected Vince to stop by and offer his condolences on my courtroom fiasco, but he didn't appear. Julie dropped me off at Mrs. Fairmont's house.

"Are you sure you don't want a ride in the morning?" she asked.

"No thanks. I enjoy the walk when it's still cool."

"Okay, but remember to call me if it ever rains."

Mrs. Bartlett's car was parked at the curb in front of her mother's house. I could hear her voice as soon as I entered the foyer.

"It's Tami," I called out.

"We're in the den," Mrs. Bartlett responded.

Mrs. Fairmont was in her favorite chair facing the television. Mrs. Bartlett was on a leather sofa to her right with a cup of coffee beside her. I sat in the remaining chair.

"How are you feeling?" I asked Mrs. Fairmont.

"Well enough to listen to Christine talk nonstop for an hour."

"Don't be ridiculous," Mrs. Bartlett replied. "You've held up your end of the conversation very well."

"Did you have a good day at work?" Mrs. Fairmont asked me.

"It was difficult," I replied.

"Mother tells me you're snooping around looking for information about the Lisa Prescott case."

"Yes ma'am." I couldn't blame Mrs. Fairmont for forgetting to keep our conversation secret.

"If you solve the mystery, it would be a great story to tell on one of those television shows where they go back in time and figure out what really happened. Only, I'd prefer not to have a TV crew filming inside Mother's house. With all the antiques and valuables around here, it makes no sense giving a thief an inventory of what he might find."

"I'll remember that when the producer calls."

"Ellen Prescott was one of Mother's dearest friends," Mrs. Bartlett continued. "Lisa was a bit of a brat. I know it sounds harsh to say, but it's true. I took care of her a few times when our parents went out for the evening. Lisa was sharp as a tack and had a mind of her own." She turned to Mrs. Fairmont. "Do you remember the time she unlocked the front door of their house and ran out to the sidewalk to hitchhike a ride to the ice-cream shop? I don't know where she got the idea that a young girl could ask a stranger for a ride. I ran out and grabbed her, of course. Later, when I heard that she didn't come home one afternoon, the first thought in my mind was about her running to the sidewalk and sticking out her thumb like a homeless person."

"How long before she vanished did that happen?" I asked.

"Oh, I don't know. It couldn't have been more than a year or so."

"Do you remember anything else?"

"There were all kinds of wild rumors."

"What kind of rumors?" I asked.

"Some I wouldn't want to repeat, but we almost had a race riot when some vigilantes marched into the black district and started searching houses."

"Why did they do that?"

"It was a sign of the times. Anytime a white girl disappeared, there were people who immediately blamed the black population. When the police didn't come up with a suspect, low-class trouble-makers would take to the streets and try to find a scapegoat."

"The Ku Klux Klan?"

"No, they didn't try to cover their faces. The KKK wasn't around much when I was a child."

"Did they have a particular person in mind?"

Mrs. Bartlett rolled her eyes. "Don't expect me to remember details like that. It was a mob. My father locked the doors and turned out the lights when they came by our house. My bedroom was upstairs. I peeked outside and saw that some of the men were carrying guns. I'm surprised you didn't see an article about it in the newspaper. Do you remember that night, Mother?"

"Yes. It was scary."

"And there wasn't a particular black man who was a suspect?" I asked.

Mrs. Bartlett studied me for a moment. "Do you have a name? Mother and I have lived here all our lives. Between us, we've known a lot of people of every color under the sun."

"I can't say."

"Attorney/client privilege?"

"I can't answer that either."

"Do you hear this, Mother?" Mrs. Bartlett said. "Tami has found out something about Lisa Prescott after all these years. Does the newspaper know you're conducting an investigation?"

"No!" I said. "And please don't mention this to anyone."

"I'm not subject to any rules of confidentiality." Mrs. Bartlett sniffed. "This is hot news for anyone who has been in Savannah for a long time."

I gave Mrs. Fairmont an imploring look.

"Don't give the girl a heart attack," Mrs. Fairmont said. "If you spread this around town, she could get in trouble."

"That's right," I added. "I could lose my job."

Mrs. Bartlett appeared skeptical. "Okay, but I have to mention it to Ken. I'm sure he remembers the Lisa Prescott mystery."

"Will you ask him not to say anything?" I asked.

"Of course. Don't panic. Anyway, hasn't the statute of limitations run out on that case?"

I didn't respond.

"Well?" she repeated.

I looked directly in her eyes. "There is no statute of limitations for murder."

MRS. BARTLETT DIDN'T STAY for supper. After she left, Mrs. Fairmont joined me in the kitchen while I warmed up leftovers from Gracie's Sunday dinner.

"Do you think Mrs. Bartlett will keep quiet about my interest in the Prescott case?" I asked as I stirred the black-eyed peas.

"I never could bridle Christine's tongue," the older woman said. "I'd be surprised if you have any success either."

After we ate, Mrs. Fairmont returned to the den to read magazines. She would read the same ones over and over. She'd tell about articles that piqued her interest, not realizing that she'd mentioned the same piece a few days before. After listening for the third time in a week to new ideas for Savannah-area flower gardens, I excused myself to call home. Mama answered the phone.

"It's me," I began.

"What's wrong?" she asked immediately.

"How do you know something is wrong?" I asked.

"I'm your mother. I could tell what was the matter by the way you cried as a baby."

The thought of cuddling up in Mama's arms held a lot of appeal to me.

"Mostly work matters that I can't discuss. Is Daddy there?"

"No, he and Kyle are out again checking on some cows. I think Kyle is going to make enough money to get a new truck by the end of the summer."

"Maybe his cattle business will get big enough that he'll need a corporate attorney."

"I told Daddy about the young lawyer who wants to get to know you better."

"That's not an—"

Mama kept talking. "He agrees with me that you should keep your distance until we can meet him. However, we talked it over, and you can bring him home for the July Fourth holiday if he can give you a ride home."

The thought of a five-hour ride in the sidecar followed by the shock on my parents' faces when Zach parked the motorcycle beneath the poplar tree in our front yard made me smile. Of course, Zach owned a car, but in my mind he was inextricably linked to the motorcycle.

"That's sweet of you, Mama, but I'm not sure I want to invite him." I paused. "However, there is someone else, one of the summer clerks who's a Christian and very nice. He lives in Charleston, so I don't know what he's doing for the holiday, and I may have to stay here to prepare a court case. If I can get away, and Vince wants to drive me home for a visit, would that be okay?"

"Who is Vince?" Mama sounded slightly bewildered.

I told her a little more about him. As I talked I realized that compared to Zach Mays, I had little to hide about the brilliant law student.

"And he maintains his Christian witness at Yale?" Mama asked.

"Yes ma'am. He's had to face challenges and overcome them, just like me."

"I'll mention it to your daddy."

"Thanks. Now, tell me about the twins, the garden, Bobby, church, the chickens, the dogs, anything about home."

LATER THAT NIGHT in my apartment, I read the old newspapers, seeking more information about the mob described by Mrs. Bartlett. Two-thirds of the way through the stack, I found a second-page article. Scant on details, it was obviously a major event that should have received front-page coverage. A group of fifty men invaded the black district in response to "unfounded rumors" related to Lisa Prescott's disappearance. Rocks were thrown, windows broken, and a fire started in the front yard of one residence. The mob was confronted by a squad of police officers that included several on horseback. Five men were arrested for disorderly conduct, and the rest dispersed. The incident wasn't mentioned again.

THE FOLLOWING MORNING, the receptionist stopped me when I arrived at the office.

"Vince Colbert wants to see you," she said. "He's in the small conference room near Mr. Braddock's office."

Puzzled, I went to the opposite end of the building from the library. The conference room door was shut. I knocked.

"Come in," Vince called out.

Vince, his laptop open before him, was sitting at one end of the shiny table. He always wore a suit, tie, and starched shirt. This morning he'd taken off his jacket and hung it on the back of a chair.

"What's going on?" I asked.

"Sorry about court yesterday."

"It was a blow. What happened in your case?"

"No problems. My client will be on the road in his quieter car by the weekend. But I spent time last night doing some research that I wanted to tell you about."

"You came back to the office last night?"

"Yes, there is a code needed after eleven o'clock. I can give it to you—"

"I know," I interrupted. "What were you looking into?"

"Please shut the door and sit down."

I closed the conference room door and sat in a chair beside him.

"Careful with the jacket," he said. "I have a meeting in an hour with Mr. Braddock and one of his clients."

"Sorry." I moved the jacket to the back of another chair.

"I've been doing some research to update the firm website. This firm has been in existence since 1888," Vince began. "The founding partners were Mr. Braddock's great-grandfather and an attorney named Vernon Fletchall. After Mr. Fletchall died, the firm was simply known as the Braddock firm until Mr. Braddock brought in another partner in the early 1900s. Mr. Braddock's son joined the firm, and about thirty years later his grandson, the current Mr. Braddock's father, a man named Lawrence, who graduated from Vanderbilt after World War II, started practicing in Savannah. In the meantime, the founding Mr. Braddock died and not long after that, his son also died."

"I'm not taking notes. Is there going to be a test?"

"No, but learning more about the history of the firm gave me an idea."

"Okay," I answered, mystified.

"Mr. Samuel Braddock and his father practiced law together for a long time. Lawrence died about ten years ago, although he'd been retired for many years. Mr. Appleby is originally from Norfolk and joined the firm when the father was still practicing." Vince paused. "Mr. Carpenter did too. Mr. Carpenter's family—"

Realizing another long genealogical recitation was coming, I couldn't stifle the giggle that bubbled up within me.

"What did I say?" Vince asked.

"I'm sorry. I don't know where you're going with this, but your attention to detail is incredible. Are you the same way with your Bible study?"

"I try to be."

"How many books of the Bible have you memorized?"

Vince shook his head. "I'm not answering that. Are you going to let me finish? It's going to be hard to find time later today."

"All right. You were starting Mr. Carpenter's genealogy."

"Mr. Carpenter's family is from Savannah too, but his family history isn't documented except for the names of his parents. When I saw his father's name, I remembered our conversation the other day at the deli."

"Floyd Carpenter?" I asked in shock, putting my hand to my mouth.

Vince nodded. "Yes."

"I never really thought—" I stopped.

"Did you mention that to Mr. Carpenter?" Vince asked.

"No. I thought it would sound foolish."

"That was probably very wise." Vince moved the cursor on his laptop. "At that point, I stopped working on the website and started searching the closed file records."

"Looking for what?"

"References to the significant names: Prescott and Carpenter as clients of the firm."

"What did you find?" I asked.

"Not much. Floyd Carpenter died not long after Mr. Braddock's father passed away."

My heart sank.

"However, the old files haven't been destroyed," Vince continued. "The State Bar Rules would allow it, but the firm is proud of its history and put its records on microfilm in the 1980s. They're stored off-site. I'm just not sure how to get access."

"Mr. Carpenter obviously isn't an option."

"Why don't you ask Zach?"

I shrugged. "I'm not sure he'll help. He thinks I need to concentrate totally on helping Moses with the trespassing case and forget about Lisa Prescott."

"You can do both." Vince closed his laptop. "There may be nothing to it, but access to privileged information is a unique opportunity, something the police didn't have when they were investigating Lisa's disappearance."

Everything Vince said made sense.

"How long did it take you to do this?"

Vince smiled. "Less time than it took to memorize the first two chapters of Ephesians. I'll check with you this afternoon."

I LEFT THE CONFERENCE ROOM. When I passed Mr. Carpenter's office suite, his secretary stopped me.

"Tami, hold on. I was about to come looking for you. I'll let Mr. Carpenter know you're here."

"Could it wait?" I asked, trying to think of a good reason to postpone a meeting.

The secretary already had the phone receiver in her hand. She shook her head. I had no choice but to wait. I offered up a rapid prayer for help. Mr. Carpenter opened the door to his office.

"Good morning, Tami," he said. "Come in."

I entered the office and sat down. He didn't go behind his desk but sat across from me in a leather side chair. Sitting so close to him increased my anxiety.

"I hope I'm not in trouble," I said lamely.

"Of course not," Mr. Carpenter answered lightly. "I read your memo about the Jones case with great interest. Clifton Cannon can be hard to deal with, especially if his sciatica is acting up."

"I don't know, but it must have been bad yesterday. It's disturbing that the judge's back condition might affect how many years a man or woman spends in prison."

"The practice of law is filled with intangibles that law school doesn't prepare you for."

"Yes sir."

"What are you going to do next on the case?"

"Uh, get ready to try it. I have to phone the courthouse and find out the dates for criminal trial calendars this summer."

"Zach will guide you. He's a bright young man. If both of you get in over your heads, call on me."

"Yes sir."

Mr. Carpenter stood. "Keep those memos coming. You're a good writer. Written and verbal communication skills are the main keys to success for an attorney."

23

I WENT TO THE LIBRARY AND PICKED UP MY FOLDER CONTAINING the old newspaper clippings. Julie wasn't there, but I needed a place to think without interruption. I'd not told Julie anything about Lisa Prescott and didn't want to start now.

I went upstairs to Gerry Patrick's office. The firm administrator's door was open. She was on the phone but motioned me to come inside. I stood in front of her desk and waited until she finished the call.

"How can I help you?" she asked.

"You'd mentioned the possibility of a cubicle where I could work. Is that still available?"

"Did you and Julie have another problem?" Ms. Patrick asked with an edge to her voice.

The fact that the previous day's incident was common knowledge in the hierarchy of the firm worried me, but I knew interoffice communication only required a few computer keystrokes and the click of a mouse.

"No ma'am. Each of us met with Mr. Carpenter, and our relationship is better than ever. But I need to do some research without any distractions. Julie and I work well together, but we still take a few minutes here and there to talk."

"What are you working on that requires that level of privacy? Julie is also an employee of the law firm."

It was an insightful question that rendered me temporarily speechless.

"You're right," I said after an awkward pause. "There's no good reason for me to set up in a second workstation."

Ms. Patrick looked down at her desk. "Good. Have a nice day."

I MADE COPIES of all the newspaper articles and put them in a separate folder. I had no option but to talk to Zach. His door was closed. I knocked lightly and opened it a crack before he answered. He was staring at his computer screen and tugging on his ponytail.

"Hey," he said. "Did you get the dates for the trial calendars?"

"Not yet, but I will. Do you have a few minutes?"

"Yeah."

I sat down next to the now familiar picture of Zach's sister. "Do you promise not to get upset at me if I ask for some advice?"

Zach gave me a puzzled look. "Have I been that hard to work with? My only goal is to help you mature as a lawyer as quickly as possible. The best way for that to happen isn't to coddle you, but to challenge you and keep you focused."

"You're not mad at me?"

"No. I've told my parents all about you."

"What did you say?" I asked in surprise.

"The truth as best I know it." Zach smiled. "They know how unusual it is to meet a woman with your faith and convictions. I'd like to meet your family."

"Really?"

"Of course. How can we make that happen?"

"I'm still working on it," I answered, perplexed. "But this case is all I can think about right now. I need your help. How can someone access the firm microfilm records?"

"Through Gerry Patrick. She has a key to the storage facility. It's on Abercorn Road near the mall."

"Would you mind asking her? Ms. Patrick doesn't like me."

"Why?"

"For some of the same reasons you think I'm a woman of faith and conviction. We've had misunderstandings that make her suspicious of anything I say."

It was Zach's turn to give me a puzzled look. "That makes no sense. Just tell her the name of the case, and the supervising attorney. She shouldn't give you any problem."

I grimaced. "You're the supervising attorney. It has to do with *State v. Jones.*"

Zach sat up straighter in his chair. "Start talking."

Thirty minutes later, I finished. Zach read a couple of the articles while I nervously fidgeted in my chair.

"Is that all?" he asked, looking up from the newspaper clippings.

"Pretty much. I don't think I left out any important details."

"And Mr. Carpenter isn't aware of your suspicions?"

"I don't think so."

"He's a smart man."

"I know."

"Do the partners know Vince is helping you?"

"No. I think he worked after hours."

Zach frowned. "Have you thought this through to its logical conclusion?"

"What do you mean?"

"We've had this discussion before—Moses, a man named Floyd Carpenter, the shiny dollar, and Lisa Prescott's body in the Ogeechee River. What changed?"

"Additional information makes it seem more plausible."

"Which still doesn't address the ultimate issue. What is the significance of solving a missing person case after everyone except our client is dead? Lisa was an only child, and her parents are deceased, right?"

"Yes."

"And Floyd Carpenter is dead?"

"Yes."

"Which leaves Moses, an old man, alive." Zach spoke with emphasis, "And our client."

"But the truth needs to be known."

Zach picked up a pen and twirled it around with his fingers. I steeled myself, determined not to back down.

"What are you going to do if you search the firm archives and find out that Floyd Carpenter consulted with Mr. Braddock or his father about the disappearance of the Prescott girl? What if there are incriminating notes, even a written confession? What if Moses Jones is mentioned by name as an accessory or principal in the commission of a crime? Are you going to violate your ethical duty and turn the information over to Maggie Smith? Would you run to the newspaper and humiliate the Carpenter family in a massive exposé? What would be helped by that except a reporter's career? If you contact the newspaper, make sure you suggest a headline that includes the verse about the sins of the fathers being visited on their children to the fourth generation."

With each question, my resolve weakened. "But don't you want to know what happened to Lisa?"

"Of course I'm curious. But a lawyer has to consider the consequences. It's a boring analogy, but I leave out favorable contract provisions if I think they might trigger a response from the other side that could cause greater harm to my client's primary interests. Your decision is much more important because of the impact on Moses' freedom."

Zach's last comment gave me an idea. "If Moses isn't guilty and can shed light on what really happened to Lisa Prescott, it could help his trespassing case."

I could tell from the look on Zach's face that for once, I'd brought out a point he hadn't considered.

"That's far-fetched," he said.

"It would enable the police and district attorney's office to solve a crime and close a file even if it's decades too late to bring someone to justice."

Zach still looked skeptical.

"And I'm not ignoring all the good points you made about not humiliating Mr. Carpenter and his family, but I can't get away from the belief that I'm supposed to dig as far to the bottom of this as I can. I need to get over pretending to be a crusader and go forward only to the extent I should as a lawyer—"

"Law student."

"Who is acting in a professional, ethical manner. I'm working at the firm with at least a small hope of landing a job after graduation. Throwing that away for no reason would be stupid. I don't want newspaper publicity for myself and don't want to hurt someone else's reputation. I've been persecuted enough to know how it feels."

"But once you release information, you can't control where it goes. We should try to lessen interest in Moses so he can slip back into the river marsh and live out his life in peace, not make him an unwilling celebrity."

"That sounds nice," I said, "but you're wrong. Moses Jones is not at peace."

"And you're not his pastor." Zach glanced at his watch. "Look, I have a meeting with Mr. Appleby and a client in five minutes. Do you still want the key to the storage facility?"

"Yes."

"I'll okay it, but tell me what you find out. I can't escape the responsibility that will fall on me if you get out of line."

I'd not considered the possible risk to Zach's job.

"Yes. And I've listened to what you said."

Zach leaned forward and spoke with intensity. "But have you heard?"

I bit my lower lip and nodded.

Zach left to get the key from Gerry Patrick. In at least one way, this morning's conversation had been a success. I'd avoided an emotional meltdown when Zach Mays challenged me. Returning, he handed me the key.

"It's checked out in my name, so let me return it to her. Are you going to use the firm car?"

"Unless you give me the keys to your motorcycle."

Zach managed a slight smile. "This is a more explosive situation than you realize. A getaway on a motorcycle might be your best means of escape."

"And I'm not going to be reckless, on or off a motorcycle." I stepped toward the door. "I'll talk to you before doing anything else. I promise."

THE FIRM CAR had been checked out by the runner going to the federal courthouse. She wouldn't be returning for an hour and a half.

Bob Kettleson's paralegal had left me a note on the library door. I went to her cubicle where she handed me a memo instructing me to research the relative priorities of eminent domain for a parcel of riverfront property claimed by a private utility and the city, state, and federal governments. When I returned to the library, Julie was there.

"Oversleep?" she asked.

"No, I've already talked to Vince, Mr. Carpenter, and Zach this morning."

"Not all at once, I hope."

"No, although that could happen."

"Yeah, if Mr. Carpenter served as mediator. Vinny has come by twice looking for you. I think he used a bathroom excuse to get out of a big important meeting with Mr. Braddock and a rich client."

"What did he want?"

"I don't know. I asked him if it had to do with lunch, and he shook his head. Have you hurt his feelings?"

"No."

"You know how confident he always looks with that laptop under his arm, but he seemed worried about something. I offered to be a sounding board for him if he gets lovesick and needs a friendly ear."

"No, you didn't."

"But I thought about it. I've helped more couples work through issues than a marriage counselor. My mother still wishes I'd become a psychologist."

"Vince doesn't need psychotherapy. He's more stable than the hard drive of his computer."

"That's not bad," Julie said approvingly. "I'm rubbing off on you."

I BEGAN WORKING on the eminent domain project but kept a careful eye on the clock. Vince didn't return, and Julie was engrossed in her own research. As soon as an hour and a half passed, I went to the receptionist desk. The car was available until noon, and directions to the storage facility in hand, I drove across town to a modern, three-story building with a reflective glass exterior. Microfilm can't be kept in a miniwarehouse without climate control, and the storage company shared the space with two insurance companies, an investment adviser group, and a CPA firm. I took the elevator to a top-floor office. A nice-looking man about my age with dark hair and dressed in blue jeans and a casual shirt sat behind a tall desk. He wore a name tag with "Eddie" on it. The area was filled with rows of lockable file cabinets in the middle and small rooms around the edges.

"I'm from Braddock, Appleby, and Carpenter. I need access to their microfilm records."

"Sign in," Eddie said, sliding a logbook in front of me. "Have you been here before?"

"No. I'm a summer clerk."

"Where are you in law school?"

"University of Georgia."

While I wrote my name, Eddie typed on his computer. "There is a reader set up in their site," he said. "If you want hard copies, it also serves as a printer. It's a lot like the machines you find in a modern deed room."

I'd not been in enough modern or old-fashioned deed rooms to know what he meant. I followed him to one of the enclosed rooms.

"This is it."

I put the key in the door and opened it.

"Make sure you sign out at the front when you leave," he said.

I hesitated.

"Do you know how to use the reader?" he asked.

"No."

We stepped inside. The walls were lined with lateral filing cabinets that had numbers on the front. The reader looked a lot like a computer.

"Slip the film in here," he said, "then turn this knob until you reach the file you want. If you want to make a copy, press the Print button."

The button was clearly marked.

"How do I find a particular file in the cabinets?"

He pointed to two cassettes lying beside the reader. "You can scroll through the index of files alphabetically and locate the numbers for the cassettes in the cabinets."

It seemed easy enough. I sat down in a chair in front of the reader. "Thanks," I said.

Eddie didn't leave. "If you need specific help, I'll be here," he said. "I'm going to start applying to law schools after the first of the year. How do you like it?"

"It's hard but a great education."

"Do you have a business card?" he asked.

The fact that I was alone in the facility with a man I didn't know made me feel suddenly uneasy. I turned in my chair and cleared my throat so I wouldn't sound nervous.

"No, they don't give those to summer clerks."

"How about your home number or e-mail address?" he asked. "I'd like to chat sometime. You know, get your opinion about schools."

"I don't give out personal information to people I don't know," I said, trying to sound professional.

He pointed to his name tag. "My name is Eddie Anderson."

"Eddie, if you'll excuse me, I have work to do."

He left. I took a few deep breaths and made sure the door to the tiny room locked behind him. However, I suspected the custodian of the records probably had a master key for the whole facility. I offered up a prayer for protection. The thought of looking through old files that might hold clues to Lisa Prescott's disappearance was creepy enough without adding the young man to the mix.

I checked the index for files with Carpenter in the heading and wrote down the locations. Before I had a chance to pull any of the cassettes, a knock at the door made me jump. I didn't want to open it, but couldn't think of a way to avoid it. I stood and planted my right foot firmly in place to prevent him from easily forcing his way into the room. I cracked open the door.

"Yes?" I asked tensely.

"Someone from your office called when he couldn't get you on your cell."

I quickly decided not to inform him that I didn't own a cell phone. "Is there a message?"

"Call Vince Colbert."

"Do you have a phone I can use?"

"Sorry, but it's not allowed. And you took my request a few minutes ago the wrong way. It wasn't a lame pickup line. I'm trying to find out information about law schools from people who actually go there. I took a tour through the admissions office at Georgia, but I'm sure part of it was propaganda—"

"I'm not the best person to give you a broad view," I interrupted. "I live off campus and keep to myself, but I'll take a minute to talk before I leave. Where is the nearest phone?"

Eddie glanced past me.

"In your purse?" he asked, gesturing toward the place where I'd put it on the table beside the reader.

"No."

"Then you can use my cell. It's at the sign-in desk."

"Thanks."

As we returned to the entrance area, I felt slightly ashamed at my harsh reaction. Eddie reached under the desk and handed me a phone.

"Reception is best in that part of the room," he said, pointing to a place near a window.

"Thanks."

I went to the window, called the office, and asked for Vince. While I waited on hold, I tried to imagine why he'd made the effort to track me down at the storage facility. He picked up the phone.

"What are you doing?" he asked.

"Trying to solve the mystery of Lisa Prescott's disappearance. Is there a problem?"

"Interest in what you're doing has gone up the ladder at the firm. I went into Mr. Braddock's office to get a file for a meeting and saw a memo on his desk from Mr. Carpenter. The subject line included your name."

"What did it say?"

"Both Mr. Carpenter and Mr. Braddock are very familiar with the Prescott case. Mr. Carpenter attached copies of your memos about Moses Jones and mentioned that it was time 'for us to find a way to finish what our fathers started.'"

"What does that mean?"

"I'm not sure, and I don't know how or why, but Mr. Braddock is also involved. Both of them are very interested in Moses."

"Why?"

"Think about it. For some reason, Moses is a threat that could damage the reputation of their families in Savannah. Can you imagine the impact on the law firm and its business? A lot of money flows through this office. If they think the threat is real, their goal may be to silence him. You could be hurt too."

My stomach turned over. "I can't believe that."

"I don't think they would physically harm you, but there are ways to destroy your future or credibility. I hope I'm wrong, but there's no need to take any chances. Maybe you should put a halt to this."

"How? I don't have enough information to go to Maggie Smith at the DA's office and implicate Floyd Carpenter and Mr. Braddock's father in an unsolved murder."

"That's not what I meant. Maybe you should ask to be taken off the case. You could claim your religious beliefs prohibit representation of someone who is factually guilty."

It was a plausible argument—one that my mother would agree with. But at that moment, a different kind of religious conviction rose up within me. My faith was a foundation, not a crutch. I'd spent my whole life fighting pressure to compromise my convictions, and in every serious situation I'd passed the test. This was a different type of challenge, but I felt the same resolve and didn't want to yield to what my conscience told me was evil pressure.

"I don't know," I answered slowly. "That's not necessarily true. I'll have to think about it." I paused. "And hear what God says."

24

I CLOSED THE COVER ON THE CELL PHONE AND WAITED FOR A still, small voice to tell me what to do, but nothing came. I stared out the window. No angel with a drawn sword appeared in the sky over Savannah and called me to battle.

I returned the phone to the young man.

"Thanks," I said.

"Are you finished?"

"No," I answered slowly. "I'm just getting started."

I returned to the archive room and began checking the actual records. There were many files involving Floyd Carpenter and the Braddock law firm. The professional relationship between Lawrence Braddock and Floyd Carpenter spanned many years. As I worked my way through the files, a familiarity appeared in the correspondence that revealed a growing friendship.

One thing became quickly apparent. Floyd Carpenter had considerable problems with the Internal Revenue Service. His written comments to Lawrence Braddock about the federal revenue agents sounded like field reports of a Confederate officer. At one point, massive tax liens were filed against Floyd.

My heart beat faster and my mouth got dry as I scrolled to the next file. The title of the file grabbed my attention: "Floyd Carpenter re Lisa Prescott." I clicked to the next screen that contained a single typed entry: "The contents of this file were not archived."

I stared at the screen for several seconds. I pushed the button to advance the page, which revealed an intake sheet for a divorce case between a couple named William and Lynn Mitchell. I checked the index and found the next folder listing Floyd Carpenter in the subject matter.

It was dated a year after Lisa Prescott's disappearance and confirmed payment of several hundred thousand dollars to satisfy the federal tax liens filed against Floyd Carpenter and several businesses apparently controlled by him. The Braddock firm was paid over fifty thousand dollars for legal services. The next file involved formation of a real estate investment trust four years after Lisa's disappearance. As I moved through the years, my hope of finding anything relevant faded. One routine business transaction followed another. The last file was the probate of Floyd's will. Joe Carpenter served as executor.

With a sigh, I leaned back in the chair. I'd stared at the screen so intently that I'd gotten a headache. I looked at my watch. It was midafternoon. I suddenly realized that I'd gone way over the time period allotted for my use of the firm car. I turned off the reader and hurriedly returned all the cassettes to their proper places. Locking the door, I walked rapidly toward the exit. The young man was sitting at the entrance.

"I skipped my lunch break so we could talk," he said.

"Sorry, but I'm late getting back to the office," I replied. "Call me at Braddock, Appleby, and Carpenter."

"And your name?"

"Tami Taylor. It's on the sheet I signed when I checked in."

"Right."

I almost never exceeded the speed limit, but during the drive to the office I kept pace with the fastest traffic on the road without looking at the car's speedometer. I parked next to Zach's red motorcycle.

"Did I mess up someone's schedule?" I asked when I returned the keys to the afternoon receptionist.

"Mr. Kettleson's car is in for service. I think he ended up borrowing a car from one of the other lawyers."

"Was he upset?"

The woman leaned forward. "I've been working here for five years, and I'm not sure I've ever seen him smile."

I laid the keys on the counter. It was another nail in the coffin of my legal career. However, if I didn't get a job offer or even a good recommendation from Braddock, Appleby, and Carpenter, it wouldn't be the end of the world. A legal career in Savannah wasn't the dream job of a lifetime. I could always return to Powell Station and beg Oscar Callahan to hire me.

Julie wasn't in the library. Trying to ignore my headache, I began working on the eminent domain memo. Delivering an opinion as soon as possible might soften Bob Kettleson's reaction to my tardiness in returning the car. The library door opened. It was Zach. He quickly glanced around the room.

"I'm alone," I said.

"Did you check out the old files?"

I handed him the key. "Would you return this to Ms. Patrick? I have a headache and a complicated memo to research for Bob Kettleson."

Zach ignored my problems. "Any smoking guns?"

"Smoke but no gun."

He sat down across the table from me, and I told him about the empty folder, leaving out what I'd learned from Vince about the memo from Mr. Carpenter to Mr. Braddock and his advice that I consider quitting the case. Zach seemed to relax as I talked.

"Do you feel you've reached the end?" he asked.

"Not really."

"What else can you do except show Moses the newspaper articles and ask him if they help him remember anything? If he says something about Floyd Carpenter, what does that prove? Without corroboration, any information from Moses is unreliable because of his mental status."

"What about your mental status?"

Zach's eyes narrowed.

"I'm sorry," I continued. "It's just that all you seem to care about is getting me to drop the whole thing. It's frustrating knowing that something is there but not being able to figure it out."

"Welcome to the practice of law. I had no idea Floyd Carpenter was a shady character, but that shouldn't cast a shadow on his son. My big concern is that you're going to hurt people who don't deserve it and put a client at risk in violation of your ethical duty to him. You're a disciplined person; transfer that to your professional life and focus on what you're supposed to be doing."

"Don't you get tired of preaching the same message?"

Zach stood up. "Not if I believe it's the truth. You'd do the same thing."

After Zach left, I pressed my fingers against my temples. The pressure felt good as long as I didn't move my hands. After a minute, I released them and continued working on the eminent domain project. I made slow progress but hadn't started to type anything when Julie returned at 5:00 p.m.

"I have a headache," she said. "Are you ready to leave?"

"I have the same problem. What caused yours?"

"Ned and I met with the client in my criminal case and then went round and round about the best way to handle it. Ned is pressuring me to take it to trial in front of a six-person jury for the experience. I think the best thing is to work out a plea agreement that will get my client out of jail and on with his life. Don't you think I should put the client's interests first, not what might be more beneficial or interesting to me?"

"I'm ready to leave," I answered.

THAT EVENING, Mrs. Fairmont was in a mild fog. She didn't speak much during supper except to ask me three times if I'd turned off the television before we sat down to eat. My headache eased as we ate, and I realized it was probably caused by lack of food combined with eyestrain.

"Is there anything you would like to do this evening?" I asked as we finished supper.

Mrs. Fairmont blinked her eyes a few times and stared past my left shoulder. "I miss my friends," she said sadly. "So many of them are gone."

I reached across the edge of the table and put my hand on hers. "I'm sure you had many good friends."

Mrs. Fairmont's eyes brightened. "Would you like to look at my picture albums?"

"You have albums?"

"Yes. They're in the small dresser in my show closet. Would you bring one or two to the green parlor?"

I remembered seeing the small white piece of furniture. "Yes ma'am. Are there any particular ones you want to see?"

"No, surprise me."

I cleaned up the supper dishes while Mrs. Fairmont went into the parlor. Upstairs, I discovered that every drawer in the dresser contained photo albums. I grabbed one from each drawer and returned downstairs. We sat beside each other on a firm sofa. I placed an album in her lap, and she opened it.

It was from Christine's early years.

"What was Mrs. Bartlett like at this age?" I asked, pointing at a photo of the family and several other young girls at the beach in front of a huge sand castle.

"Christine has always been social. She recruited those other girls and got them to haul buckets and buckets of sand to build that castle while she bossed them around." Mrs. Fairmont stared at the picture. "I knew she would have to marry someone with plenty of money because she wouldn't lift a finger to do any work herself. What do you think made her that way?"

I didn't try to answer. Mrs. Fairmont turned the page. The faded images seemed to bring a spark of life back to her. We finished one album. I handed her another.

"Aren't you bored?" she asked.

"No ma'am."

I'd picked an album of pictures from before Christine was born. It was filled with black-and-white photos of Mr. and Mrs. Fairmont. Mrs. Fairmont spent time inspecting each picture, especially the ones with her friends. She couldn't remember every name, but when she identified one, it was like discovering the missing piece of a jigsaw puzzle. One picture was a group scene from a fancy outdoor party in the spring. I could see the flowers but not the colors in the black-and-white photo. Mrs. Fairmont touched it with her slightly gnarled index finger.

"That was a big soiree. A lot of our social set was there."

The women were wearing fancy dresses and the men stood around in suits and ties. Several servants could be seen in the photo.

"There's Ellen Prescott," Mrs. Fairmont said, pointing to a statuesque woman beside a tall man. "Of course, this was a long time before Lisa was born."

"Is that her husband?" I asked.

"No, it's her older brother Floyd. The party was at his home."

"Her brother was named Floyd?"

"Yes, Ellen was a Carpenter before she married. Their father worked as a clerk in a shoe store. Ellen was so sweet and married Webster Prescott, who had inherited a lot of railroad stock. Floyd was the black sheep of the family, but he made a lot of money and that has a way of making people forget the past."

My eyes opened wider as I stared at the photo. "Why was he a black sheep?"

"Oh, I never heard anything but rumors."

Mrs. Fairmont reached out to turn the page, but I held it firm.

"What's wrong?" she asked.

"I'm still looking at that picture. What did Floyd Carpenter think about Lisa?"

Mrs. Fairmont gave me a strange look. "I don't know, but I'm sure everyone considered Lisa the little princess. Her blonde curls stood out in any crowd. Christine claims Lisa misbehaved, but I think Christine was probably looking at herself in the mirror."

While Mrs. Fairmont talked, I tried to come up with an innocent way to frame my next question. "Did Floyd's name come up in conversations after Lisa disappeared?" I asked nonchalantly.

Mrs. Fairmont's eyebrows arched downward. "What an odd question. I'm not sure what you mean."

"I'm just curious about Floyd and Lisa and their families."

"Floyd had a son named Joe, who is a lawyer."

"He's my boss."

"Of course, he works with Sam Braddock. Joe and Lisa were the only children in the two families. After Lisa was murdered, the Prescott line ended when Webster and Ellen died."

"But no one is sure Lisa was murdered."

Mrs. Fairmont pushed my hand away from its grip on the page. "If Lisa had gotten lost, someone would have found her. She was either kidnapped or killed. I'm sure there are other interesting photographs in this album."

Mrs. Fairmont turned the page and continued reminiscing about old friends. I barely paid attention and hoped a polite "Yes ma'am" and "No ma'am" would give the impression of interest. There weren't any other pictures of Floyd, and the album ended before Lisa's birth. Mrs. Fairmont's enjoyment returned. I took the book from her hands.

"There's nothing like family and close friends," I said.

"This has been like therapy for me. Would you like to do it again?"

"Yes ma'am."

Flip opened his tiny jaws in an amazingly expansive yawn.

"My baby is ready for a nap and so am I," Mrs. Fairmont said.

"I'll carry the albums upstairs," I said.

I led the way and returned the books to their respective drawers across from the shoe racks. I wanted to take out the other albums and discover if one of them held clues, but without Mrs. Fairmont as a guide, the photos wouldn't have any more significance than a magazine spread.

"I'd like to call my parents before it gets too late," I said as I leaned over to give Flip one last scratch in his favorite place.

"Of course," Mrs. Fairmont replied. "Seeing those pictures probably made you homesick."

I returned to the kitchen. I didn't feel homesick. I was frustrated at my inability to penetrate the deepening mist surrounding Floyd Carpenter and Lisa Prescott.

DADDY ANSWERED THE PHONE. I could almost hear his smile when he realized it was me. I touched the top of my head where he liked to kiss me. We talked for a few minutes about the weather and the garden.

"Are you changing, Tammy Lynn?" he asked.

I pondered his words a moment. "That's a good question. I've been too busy to take inventory."

"Being too busy can happen to anyone. It doesn't matter whether you're working in a chicken plant or a law firm. Ask the Lord to search your heart and give you a readout."

"Yes sir."

"That's what Oscar Callahan has been doing," Daddy continued. "Did your mama tell you about his heart attack?"

"No sir."

"It happened a few days after you left for Savannah. We didn't get much information about it at first because they transported him to the intensive-care unit at a hospital in Atlanta. Pastor Vick and one of the elders drove down to pray for him. He let them anoint him with oil and pray the prayer of faith."

"Is he going to be okay?"

"We're praying. The whole church came together at the end of the service last week and spent time at the altar."

"That's good."

"He's been home for a week or so. I spent some time with him yesterday because Kyle is taking care of his cattle. I think he's going to give Kyle a fine-looking calf as payment."

"Good."

"And he felt well enough to tell me a few stories from the old days and asked me to pray for him. He's tender toward the Lord. Talking to him gave me a lot of hope that he'll get right before his time comes. "

"What about his clients?"

"He's already brought in an experienced lawyer from Dalton who does the same kind of work. I can't place his name, but he's going to take over the practice. I think he brought along an associate too."

In a split second my safety net had evaporated.

"And he asked about you, of course," Daddy continued. "I told him you were getting along fine."

"Yes sir," I managed. "I guess he had to find someone to help his clients immediately."

Daddy didn't notice the strained tone in my voice.

"I suppose you mainly called to talk about the young man you want to bring home for a visit."

"Which one?" I blurted out, then coughed into the receiver as a diversion. "Excuse me," I said after clearing my throat. "I'd like to put that topic on hold for a while. I need to concentrate on my work without being distracted."

"Good girl," Daddy replied. "That sounds like a wise decision."

"I hope so."

"Continue to seek his will, and he'll take care of helping you find your life partner. Do you want to talk to Mama? She's upstairs with the twins. They had a spat this afternoon and need to do some repenting."

"No sir. Tell her I love her."

That night I lay in bed and tried to come to terms with what had happened to Oscar Callahan. I felt guilty about dwelling on the effect his heart attack had on my future and tried to force myself to pray for the lawyer's recovery. I could concentrate for several minutes before my thoughts drifted back to the air-conditioned white office on the corner now occupied by lawyers who wouldn't need an inexperienced female associate to drive up overhead costs. After tossing and turning for an hour, I turned on the light and wrote a long prayer for Mr. Callahan in my journal. The discipline of writing helped me focus. I wrote "Amen," then started another prayer for the Moses Jones case. It was good seeing the names of the people involved in the sentences requesting God's help. It put them, and the situation, in a better perspective. When I turned out the lights the second time, I quickly fell asleep.

25

After the monotony of days, weeks, and months of unchanging jailhouse routine, the smells and sounds of waking up in his shack by the river began to fade from Moses' memory. The air-conditioned environment of the jail didn't vary more than a couple of degrees, but Moses would have traded confined comfort for the hottest heat of the summer or the coldest rain of the winter along the Little Ogeechee.

Each day, he wondered if the tall girl who wasn't a real lawyer would visit and reveal his future. Twice a day, he pushed his gray buggy down the halls and collected trash. At the dump bin, he always spent a few seconds peering through the fence at his boat, which remained chained to a pole in the stolen-car impound. But as time passed, the boat looked more like a piece of dented aluminum waiting for the scrap heap than a river vessel that became a graceful extension of himself when floating on the water.

He passed from depression to despair. He'd rarely talked to the other prisoners before, but now he was sure some of the newcomers wondered if he could speak at all. The old man had become a familiar part of the jailhouse scene. Years, he'd waited for death. He'd always thought it would come suddenly when the pain that occasionally moved from his chest down his left arm would double back and explode his heart while he was leaning over the edge of his boat, trying to haul in a big fish. The thrill of the moment would trigger the end, and he would tumble easily into the water to join the mystery of the dark beyond.

He now feared that he would pick up a heavy bag of trash one afternoon, collapse in a heap on the concrete floor, and be hauled out by his replacement, in the gray buggy, to the dump bin.

WHEN I ARRIVED at the office in the morning, there was a note on the table in the library asking me to come to Mr. Carpenter's office as soon as I arrived. I read the note twice, hoping it said something different the second time. I'd never been a quitter, but my resolve of the previous day had faded, and for a few seconds I entertained the notion of leaving the building, never to return. I had no idea what Mr. Carpenter had discovered about my activities, but it was naive to think he didn't know what I was doing. I marched as resolutely as my legs allowed down the hallway.

"Mr. Carpenter is expecting you," his secretary said. "Go on in."

I tentatively opened the door. The managing partner was sitting at his desk with a stack of papers near his right hand. He looked up. "What have you been doing?" he asked.

"Mr. Carpenter," I began in the most respectful voice I could muster.

"I thought you were going to have a memo about the status of the Gallagher Corporation holdings in the Folsom case ready for me before you left the office yesterday. I have a deposition scheduled in an hour and a half and want to be able to sort out how Mrs. Folsom finagled her way into a majority position."

My mouth dropped open. "Uh, I left the memo on your secretary's desk two days ago."

Mr. Carpenter picked up the phone. "Sharon! Do you have a memo about Gallagher Corporation from Tami Taylor on your desk?"

The lawyer glared past me at the door, which opened in a few seconds. The secretary entered and walked gingerly past me. She handed Mr. Carpenter the memo without looking at me.

"Here it is. It was placed in another file by mistake."

Mr. Carpenter didn't say anything but grabbed it and began reading it. He grunted several times. I sat still.

"Where is the documentation supporting your opinion?" he asked.

"In the file in the library."

"Get it," he said.

I fled from the office and returned to the library. Julie was there.

"What's going on?" she asked when she saw my face. "Is it Vinny or Zach?"

"Neither. Mr. Carpenter's secretary misplaced that memo I wrote about Gallagher Corporation. She found it, but he wants the documents and research." I riffled through the folders looking for the correct one. "Is being a lawyer worth the stress?"

"Oh, yes. Of course, I don't have a clue myself, but if I believed differently, I would be on my way to the beach this morning."

I grabbed the folder and returned to Mr. Carpenter's office. Sharon didn't look up as I passed her desk.

"Here it is," I said, handing it to him. "I'm sorry for the mix-up."

"It's not your fault," he said with a wave of his hand. "How are the documents organized in the file?"

"Reverse chronological. I flagged the ones that are particularly helpful with red tabs."

Mr. Carpenter flipped through the file and grunted again. "Good work," he said. "Next week I'll have another case for you to work on. It has similar issues."

"Yes sir."

I left his office. It wasn't even 8:30 a.m., yet I felt drained. When I returned to the library, Julie was talking to Vince.

"He wants to see you," she said when I entered the room. "I'm doing the best I can to entertain him, but I can tell he's getting bored."

Vince looked at me. "Are you available for lunch today?"

"I'm not sure. I've been putting out a fire with Mr. Carpenter."

"What kind of fire?" Vince asked a bit too loudly.

"It's not that," I responded quickly. "It has to do with a divorce case."

"What?" Julie interjected. "Are you working on something together?"

I looked at Vince and shook my head.

"Out with it," Julie said, sitting up straighter in her chair. "We're all equal here, except that you're ten times smarter than the rabbi and me put together."

"It's controversial," Vince replied.

I wanted to reach out and put my hand over Vince's mouth.

"And unverified," he added.

"Julie," I said, "I'm not going to discuss this with you." I looked at Vince. "And neither is he. End of the discussion."

"Is it about Moses Jones and the Prescott girl who was murdered?" Julie asked.

I stared at her in shock.

"You left the folder in here a few days ago." She shrugged. "I couldn't help glancing through it, reading the newspaper articles, deciphering your notes."

"That's wrong! You had no business—"

"We're in the same firm," Julie said, shrugging again. "Secrets don't exist."

Before I could respond, the library door opened. It was Zach. Everyone turned and stared at him. He stopped in his tracks.

"What's going on in here?" he asked.

"Tami and her investigation into Moses Jones' involvement in the Prescott murder," Julie said. "I busted her, and she's acting immature about it. Did she try to hide it from you as her supervising attorney?"

Zach surveyed the room. "Tami and Vince, let me talk to Julie for a few minutes," he said.

Vince and I stepped into the hallway.

"What's he going to do?" I asked.

"Not much. She's right."

"What?" I blurted out. "How can you say that? I thought you were on my side."

"I am, but client confidentiality doesn't restrict the flow of communication among employees of the firm. There is no basis for hiding information from one another."

I couldn't believe Vince's position.

"So, you think I should summon Mr. Carpenter and Mr. Braddock to the conference room and confront them with the facts I've uncovered?"

"No, but there's no legal reason why they couldn't order you to disclose your research. Everything you've done originated as work product for a client of the firm. When I came into work this morning, the sign in front of the building read 'Braddock, Appleby, and Carpenter.' This is their law firm, and in our employment contract we agreed that the work we performed this summer belonged to them. That's one reason I urged you to reconsider the scope of your investigation."

I stepped back against the wall. "I might as well quit and go back to north Georgia for the rest of the summer. There's no way I'm going to ever think like a lawyer."

"I disagree," Vince responded in a matter-of-fact voice. "You know how to focus on the most important aspect of any legal matter."

"Which is?"

"The determination of the truth. If you try the Jones case in front of Judge Cannon, that's one of the first instructions he'll give the jury. It's the practical effects of what you're doing outside the scope of the case that are spinning out of control."

"Thanks a lot . . ." I began.

Before I could continue, the library door opened, and Zach motioned for us to come inside. "I think we're on the same page," he said as soon as we returned.

I waited for a more complete explanation.

"You should have asked for my help," Julie said. "We've worked well together on our other projects."

Vince didn't say anything. I looked at the other three people in the room. "Is that a solution?" I asked.

"Yes," Zach replied. "You don't have to ask Julie to help, but she's available. As your supervising attorney, I'll leave that decision up to you. Did you check the criminal court schedule for the rest of the summer?"

"No, but I'll do it right now."

"Let me know."

Zach left with Vince right behind him. I sat down across from Julie.

"What did Zach say to you?" I asked.

"That it was unprofessional to snoop in your file. Why didn't you tell me the connection between Moses Jones and the disappearance of the Prescott girl?"

"I didn't want you to get all worked up about it."

"And start running my mouth?"

"Yes."

"I wouldn't do anything to prejudice our client. The rules of ethics—"

"I know. Zach has given me more than one refresher course."

"Okay, I won't repeat it. What are you going to do now?"

"Call the courthouse."

After several transfers from one clerk to another, I found out that there were three weeks of criminal court scheduled during the rest of the summer. Two of those weeks were assigned to Judge Cannon, and the judge for the third week was a woman named Linda Howell. I called Maggie Smith, and her assistant informed me the Jones case had not yet been placed on a specific calendar. I sent Zach an e-mail with the dates. He immediately responded with a request that I come to his office. I trudged up the winding staircase that no longer reminded me of a plantation mansion.

"Is there a problem with the dates?" I asked.

"One week in front of Judge Cannon is out because I'll be on vacation in California. I'll let the DA's office know. The other two weeks will depend on my schedule, but I've already let Mr. Appleby know what's going on."

"Okay." I moved away from the door.

"No, come in and sit down," Zach said.

"I don't need another lecture this morning," I replied wearily. "The fruit of patience in my life may not be as mature as I'd hoped, and I don't want to get upset."

"We need to set a day and time to talk to Moses Jones and discuss trial strategy. It will also be a chance for you to show him the newspaper articles if you want to."

"Okay."

Zach studied me for a few seconds. "What else have you found out?"

"Do you care?"

"You can tell me now or later."

I took a deep breath. "I'm not finished in the microfilm records. I want to uncover the connections between Floyd Carpenter and this firm." I paused. "Especially regarding Floyd and his relationship with his sister and niece."

"Who?"

"Ellen and Lisa Prescott. Mrs. Fairmont told me about the

Prescott-Carpenter connection while we were looking at old photos last night."

I could tell Zach was surprised by my latest information. He pulled twice on his ponytail. If the lawyer ever cut his hair, he would have to find something else to do with his hands during moments of intense mental activity.

"How does this fit?" he asked.

"I don't know until I do more research. Should I ask Julie to do it?" I asked sarcastically then immediately felt guilty.

Zach ignored my dig. "No, you're so far ahead of her that it would be inefficient. Wait here while I get the key from Gerry so you can finish your research. We can meet with Moses later today."

While Zach talked to Ms. Patrick, I checked on the firm car. It was scheduled to return in a few minutes and I reserved it for a couple of hours. I went to Zach's office where he handed me the key.

"Gerry started asking questions," he said. "I simply thanked her and left."

"But she's an employee of the firm. According to your logic . . ." I began then stopped. "Will you pray that God will put a rein on my tongue? It's been out of control since I got to the office this morning."

"No man can tame the tongue," Zach said. "Does that include women?"

"Yes." I turned the key over in my hand. "And thanks for confronting me when you think I'm out of line. My mother does a good job of correcting me, but I thought I'd be without that kind of help this summer."

"Sure, but I don't want to be a surrogate mother or father. Did you find out a date and time when I can meet them?"

"Not yet. When will you be in California?"

Zach gave me the dates and eyed me closely. "Is there a reason why you wouldn't want me to meet your parents?"

"Let's not talk about it now. I have too much to think about."

"If there is something—"

"We'll talk soon," I said. "I promise."

I GOT OFF THE ELEVATOR and opened the door to the archive facility. Eddie, the young man who wanted to go to law school, looked up and smiled.

"Welcome back," he said.

I signed in. Only two people had visited the facility since I'd been in the day before. Apparently, business was slow for dead records. I put down the pen, and Eddie started to walk toward the storage room.

"I know the way," I said.

Eddie stopped. "Okay. Let me know if you need to use my phone."

I turned on the microfilm reader and used the index to locate the earliest Prescott file. I found the proper cassette and inserted it into the reader. It was toward the end of the roll, and I scrolled through pages of documents typed with the font of an old typewriter. The letterhead for the Braddock Law Firm still listed the date of birth and death for Vernon Fletchall. When I reached the beginning page it contained records for the purchase of a house near Colonial Cemetery. Nothing relevant.

The next file was on a different cassette and related to a business deal. It contained several pages of handwritten notes by Lawrence Braddock. The lawyer wrote in a tall, yet tightly compacted script and fully utilized a sheet of paper. Once I got used to his style, it wasn't hard to read. On a third cassette, I found a copy of a Last Will and Testament prepared for the Prescotts when Lisa was about three years old. It was a lengthy document. My hand stopped advancing the pages when I reached Item XXI, a catchall provision that designated the beneficiary of the will upon the deaths of Webster and

Ellen if Lisa predeceased her parents and there were no other surviving children.

If that event occurred, the sole beneficiary of the will was Ellen's "beloved brother," Floyd Carpenter. I bit my lower lip in disbelief. I pressed the Print button.

I'd found the smoking gun. And it contained three bullets, not one.

The page inched out of the printer. I held it in my hand and read it again. In crafting a plan for wealthy individuals, estate lawyers have to consider remote possibilities that no one expects to happen. Unless, of course, human intervention makes the unlikely certain. Lisa's disappearance and death, followed by the deaths of her parents, was a simple matter of economics and federal tax liens.

It was hard to imagine the evil that could murder an entire family for money. I thought about the grainy picture of Lisa in the newspaper and the picture of Margaret Fairmont and Ellen Prescott as little girls standing on tiptoe to get a drink of water. Tears came to my eyes. I took a tissue from my purse.

After the tears passed, I returned without enthusiasm to the index. I found several more Prescott files. Righteous indignation rose up in me when I found notes from a consultation Webster and Ellen had with Lawrence Braddock a few days after Lisa's disappearance. The Prescotts, upset over the lack of progress with the police investigation, met with the lawyer to discuss the case. In his notes, the lawyer promised to make "appropriate contacts" with state law enforcement officers in Atlanta who could assist in the investigation. However, the last line of Mr. Braddock's notes was the most incriminating. "Call F.C."

I printed the notes. The next file was the probate of the Prescotts' will after the car wreck. Mrs. Fairmont was wrong. The couple lived only slightly over a year after Lisa's death, just long enough to provide a buffer against any suspicion. The circumstances surrounding their car plunging into a tidewater canal weren't mentioned—they were simply listed as the "decedents."

The file contained pages of inventory about stocks, bonds, bank accounts, antiques, art objects, and real estate. I slowed when I came to a petition asking the court to judicially declare Lisa deceased even though no body had been found. Several law enforcement officials were listed as witnesses, and three weeks after the petition was filed, the probate judge signed an order granting Lawrence Braddock's request.

The provisions of the will didn't require an accounting to the probate court identifying the total value of the estate, but I found a handwritten memo from Mr. Braddock to Floyd Carpenter listing a summary of all tangible and intangible assets—the Prescotts left their child's killer slightly under two million dollars, a huge sum at the time, and more than enough to satisfy Floyd Carpenter's tax liens.

I printed out the entire probate file. While I waited for the pages to inch from the printer, I prayed for God's guidance. But I was numb with shock. I returned all the film cassettes to their proper places and put the documents in a file folder. This time, I wouldn't leave the information lying around where Julie could find it. Zach and Vince's claim that no secrets existed among employees of Braddock, Appleby, and Carpenter didn't apply to what I'd uncovered. After forty years, it still bore the stink of death.

"Find everything okay?" Eddie Anderson asked as I wrote down the time on the entry and exit log.

I looked up at him, not sure how to answer. He quickly glanced away.

I drove back to the office and pulled into the parking lot but didn't get out. I didn't know what to do next. I couldn't talk to my parents. Oscar Callahan was at home recovering from a heart attack and, although a lawyer, had no more right to privileged information than the courier I watched walk up the sidewalk to the front door of the office. My confidence in Zach and Vince as reliable counselors had been seriously weakened. And if Mr. Carpenter summoned me into his office again, I wouldn't be able to look him in the eyes and find a way to dodge his probing questions. For the second time, I considered fleeing Savannah like the Confederate army that faced Sherman. I closed my eyes and let the coolness from the air-conditioning vent blow over my face. A knock on the car window made me jump. It was Zach. I pushed the button to lower the window.

"This isn't the place to take a nap," he said.

"I'm not in a joking mood."

"What did you find in the microfilm records?"

"I'm not ready to talk about it."

"Why not?"

I shook my head. "Don't pressure me."

Zach leaned closer to the open widow. "Tami, when a lawyer isolates herself on a case, there's a much greater chance of a mistake."

"I'm not a lawyer yet, as you so gently reminded me the other day. And I'm debating whether I ever want to be!"

I opened the door and pushed Zach out of the way. He backed up as I marched past him and met the courier leaving the firm. I returned the car keys to the receptionist.

"Did you see Mr. Mays?" she asked. "He was looking for you."

"Yes."

It was close to lunchtime, and I desperately hoped Julie wouldn't be in the library. I opened the door and peeked inside. The table where we usually sat was empty. On one of the bookshelves I found a set of out-of-date tax treatises no one would likely use and hid the folder behind them. As I repositioned the books, the library door opened. It was Vince. He looked around the room.

"Are you alone?" he asked.

"Yes."

"I owe you an apology," he said. "Can we talk?"

Given how vulnerable I felt, I didn't want to be around anyone.

"I accept your apology, but let's not talk," I answered.

"I'm sorry, but it can't wait."

Vince shifted on his feet. He was unbelievably persistent about spending time with me.

"All right," I sighed. "But I'm only going to listen. Don't expect me to respond."

26

"Is the sandwich shop near the river okay?" Vince asked as we passed through the reception area.

"I don't care. I'm not hungry."

We rode in silence. Vince had to park a block away from the deli. As we walked on the uneven cobblestones, the sights and sounds of the people along the waterfront seemed out of touch with reality. The deli was crowded. Vince ordered a ham sandwich. I picked up a bottle of water.

"Thanks for coming," Vince said as we sat down. "Where did you go after we talked this morning?"

"That's a question, not an apology."

"I'll get right to it. You were right that your investigation into Lisa Prescott's disappearance shouldn't be common knowledge at the firm."

Vince paused as a waitress brought his sandwich. I took a sip of water.

"At ten thirty I was supposed to go over a research memo with Mr. Braddock in the conference room. He wasn't there so I went to his office but had to wait because he was in a meeting with Mr. Carpenter. The office door was cracked open. I couldn't hear Mr. Braddock's voice because he's so soft-spoken, but I caught some of Mr. Carpenter's side of the conversation. He told Mr. Braddock that you had sent him a memo on Tuesday to update him on the Jones matter and he should be hearing from you again soon. Then he said 'stronger pressure should have been applied to Moses Jones a long time ago.'"

"What does that mean?" I asked.

"I don't know exactly, but it doesn't sound good. Mr. Braddock must have talked for a while; then Mr. Carpenter said, 'As soon as Ms. Taylor is out of the picture, we'll get to him before it's too late.' It was quiet while Mr. Braddock talked, and then Mr. Carpenter came barreling out of the office. I almost fell out of the chair."

"Did he realize you were eavesdropping?"

"I hope not. He was in such a hurry to leave the office that I don't think he paid any attention to me."

Vince took a bite from his sandwich. I glanced past his shoulder at the people lined up at the counter. Two women were pointing at items in the display case as they discussed what to eat. My decision was much more serious—how much to tell Vince about my morning discovery.

"Your intuition or discernment or whatever you want to call it was correct," Vince said between bites. "I thought about going back to Julie and warning her to keep her mouth shut, but that would probably make her more likely to talk."

"Yes."

Vince pushed his plate away from him and covered his sandwich with a paper napkin.

"I'm not hungry either," he said. "It was so bizarre hearing two respected attorneys talk like gangsters that I didn't know what to think."

Vince's dilemma mirrored my own. "I completely understand," I said slowly. "Only this morning I was reading about a forty-year-old conversation between two different men named Carpenter and Braddock."

Vince listened to my story, then spoke. "If I hadn't read the memo and overheard today's conversation, I wouldn't think that the current Mr. Carpenter and Mr. Braddock had done anything wrong," he said. "Now, I don't know. Mr. Braddock was just beginning to practice law with his father when all this happened, and Joe Carpenter was in high school or about to enter college. Maybe they were pulled in somehow."

"I'm not sure I want to know. The immediate crisis is what to do about Moses Jones. Even if he did something wrong a long time ago, he should only be punished by the proper authorities. Do I have a greater obligation to protect him from 'stronger pressure,' or should I just keep quiet and represent him in the trespassing case? Would it be unethical to tell the assistant district attorney that he needs to be kept in jail for his own safety?" My voice trembled slightly. "What if he gets out of jail and something bad happens to him?"

"What does Zach think? Have you talked to him?"

"No! From the beginning, he's been reluctant to help and argues with me about everything. I think it's time to draw a circle around us and agree that we're the only ones who need to know what's going on."

Vince leaned back in his chair. "Okay. But while you're thinking about Zach and Mr. Jones, you need to decide what you're going to tell Mr. Carpenter. He's expecting to hear from you."

"I know, but I think it all leads to the same place. First, I have to talk to Moses. This is his case, his life."

We returned to the office. The firm car was checked out and would be gone for the rest of the afternoon. I was stranded.

"You can borrow mine," Vince offered.

"Are you sure?"

He handed me the keys. "Of course. You're only driving across town."

"Thanks." I walked rapidly to the library. I didn't want to run into Zach or Mr. Carpenter. All I needed was the folder containing copies of the newspaper clippings. It was time to find out whether Moses' memory, like Mrs. Fairmont's, could be unlocked by a picture. I opened the library door. Julie was sitting at the table.

"Any success?" she asked.

"Not yet," I answered quickly. "I'm going to the jail to talk to Moses Jones. The date of trial hasn't been set, but I've got to start getting ready."

"Are you going to ask more questions about the Prescott girl?"

"Maybe."

Julie placed a book on top of the papers stacked in front of her.

"I'm going with you. You'll need a witness of what he tells you."

"That's unnecessary," I answered, trying to stay calm. "You should be working on your own cases."

"Not if I need to help you. Besides, we can take my car."

"Vince is loaning me his car."

Julie's eyes widened. "When are you going to move into his apartment?"

I felt a flash of heat across my entire body and an overwhelming urge to yell at her. I closed my eyes to fight it off.

"Okay, I'm sorry," Julie said. "I keep forgetting that you don't share my sense of humor."

"And I don't need your help."

Julie held up her hands. "Don't be so touchy. But you can't trust your judgment when you're so upset about everything."

"I'm not upset about everything. Just your crude comment."

"You're wrong about that." Julie held up her right hand and pointed at her fingers. "You're upset with Mr. Carpenter because his questions scare you, mad at Zach because he doesn't agree with you all the time, and tired of me teasing you. I don't know for sure, but I also suspect Gerry Patrick and Bob Kettleson have gotten under your skin. To top it all off, you're frustrated by everything that's been happening in the Jones case. Judge Cannon and the assistant DA are blocking you at every turn, and you don't see a way out. If it weren't for your iron will, you'd be close to cracking."

Julie sat back in her chair with a self-satisfied look on her face. My mother couldn't have done a better job of dissecting my struggles.

"Maybe you should have gotten a PhD in psychology," I replied as evenly as I could, "but I still don't want you to go to the jail with me."

"Suit yourself. But I'm here if you need me."

I picked up my folder and left. The midday heat had driven out the effects of the air-conditioning left from our drive to lunch. I turned the fan motor on high. Backing out of the parking space, I heard the sound of a horn and slammed on the brakes. Turning my head, I saw Mr. Braddock behind me in his silver Mercedes. He shook his head and smiled. I said a quick prayer of thanks that I'd not hit his car, but all the way to the jail couldn't get the look on his face out of my mind. How could a man with such deep-seated evil living within his soul smile and wave? The Old Testament prophet was right when he wrote that the heart of man was deceitfully wicked above all else, who can fathom it?

Arriving at the jail, I identified myself to the female deputy on duty and asked to see Moses. I waited in the open area outside the interview rooms until he appeared, escorted by a corrections officer who looked as young as my brother Kyle. We went into an interview room.

"Hello, Mr. Jones," I said as the door closed with a low thud.

"Yes, missy," he replied as we sat down across from each other. "I be worrying that you forgot about Moses and going to leave him in this place to die."

"No sir, I've been working hard. Your case will be coming up for trial sometime in the next few weeks. I don't know the exact date, but as soon as I do, I'll be here to let you know. There's a chance we will have a different judge."

"That may be help." The old black man nodded. "But I not know what I'm going to say."

"We'll practice going over your testimony until you know everything I'm going to ask you," I replied with more confidence than I felt. "You can't deny tying up your boat at private docks for the night, but we'll let the jury know that you didn't realize it was private property."

"That river, it belong to God who made it."

"Yes, I understand and agree, but that's not our best argument. An innocent mistake on your part will be easier to explain, and we'll also be sure to produce evidence that you didn't damage anyone's property or scare the landowners. Ignorance of the law isn't usually a legal excuse, but the jury can find you not guilty if they think you had an honest misunderstanding. Does that make sense?"

Moses shook his head. "No, missy. You be talking and talking."

"That's okay for now. We'll go over everything and break it down so you can follow."

I laid the folder with the newspaper clippings on the table. When I did, I felt my heart beat a little faster. I cleared my throat. Moses ran his tongue across the most prominent tooth in the front of his mouth.

"Moses, I have something else to show you." I opened the folder and took out the initial article about Lisa Prescott's disappearance. It contained the largest version of the photograph that ran in all the subsequent articles. I slid the sheet across the table and turned it so Moses could see it.

"Do you recognize this girl?" I asked.

He lowered his head closer to the table and tilted it to the side. "She be dead," he said in a soft voice after a few moments. "Where you get this?"

"It's a copy of an old newspaper article. Is this the girl whose face you see in the water?"

Still staring down, he nodded. I leaned forward. "Why do you see her face in the water?" I asked.

Moses let out a long sigh that slightly whistled as it passed through his teeth. "'Cause that's where she be," he said softly.

"How did she get there?" I asked, trying to stay calm.

"There weren't nothing else I could do."

I sat back in my chair. Moses looked at me and blinked his eyes. The old man was about to cry. I'd seen many confessions with tears at the altar of the church in Powell Station, but none that involved a murder.

"Do you want to tell me?"

He put his weathered hands on the table and closed his eyes. "I go fishing. Not in that boat chained to the pole out back, but in an old wooden thing that leaked termite-bad. I be minding my own self when I heared the sound on the bank. I thought it must be a hurt critter and rowed over to see for myself. It be getting dark, but I seen a piece of yellow scrap that caught my eye. I touched the bank and hopped onto the ground. I heard another sound. The bushes were thick, and I got cut bad getting to her."

He opened his eyes and pointed to a two-inch scar on his forehead. "I be bleeding bad my own self by the time I got to her. She was a-hurtin' and bleeding here and here."

The old man pointed to his mouth and ears. "Her eyes be open, but not seeing nothing."

He stopped and bowed his head. I could tell he was slipping completely into silent memory and pulled him back.

"Was she alive?" I asked.

He looked up. "She be breathing. I run up the bank to an old dirty road, but no one there 'cause it way out in the country. I yell and holler. No help be coming. I go back and pick up that girl. She not much heavier than an old blanket. I put her in my boat. We both bleeding together. I row down the river as fast as I could go. It be getting darker and darker. I get to the big water so I can get her to the bridge for the hardscape road to town. Cars be there for sure. I put down my ear to listen." He shook his head. "And she be gone."

"She fell into the water?"

"No, missy. She be dead."

"Did you take the body to town?"

Moses shook his head. "I be black; she be white. We both be bleeding. What happen to me if'n I carry her to town? That night I be hanging by my neck from a tree with nobody asking no more questions."

It made perfect sense.

"What did you do with the body?"

"I take her to the place on the river where I be staying. I don't know what to do. I stay up all night a-crying and walking round in circles. Before the sun comes arising, I tie a rope about her little feet and then onto a big rock. I push off into a deep spot, say a prayer, and that's it. She be there today."

"Did you ever tell anyone what happened?"

"My brother, he knew. And my auntie that helped raise me."

"Are they alive?"

"They be long dead."

"What about Mr. Floyd Carpenter? Did he know you found Lisa Prescott?"

"People talk, maybe my brother, and Mr. Tommy Lee bring me into his office and make me see Mr. Floyd."

"Who is Mr. Tommy Lee?"

"My boss man when I run bolita. Mr. Floyd, he be the big boss man."

"What is bolita?"

"The numbers."

I gave Moses a puzzled look. He held out his hand and rubbed it. "You tell me two numbers and give me a dime. If they be right, I give you five dollars the next day."

"Gambling?"

"Yes, missy. But I never did sell bootleg. I drink it way back then, but I don't haul it. That be my brother. Only ways I go to jail for half a year instead of him."

Moses' connection with the sale of untaxed alcohol wouldn't help me find out what I wanted to know.

"Why did Floyd Carpenter want to talk to you about Lisa Prescott?"

"I be thinking they call me a thief, but I turn in all my money. But all the talk is about the little girl, asking me what I saw, where I been. I be scared and say nothing. Mr. Tommy Lee, he holler at me and lift up his fist, but he don't mean it. Next day, I on the street running numbers, just like before."

"Did Floyd Carpenter suspect you found her on the riverbank?"

Moses shook his head. "I don't be knowing, only I see his face to this day."

"Where?"

"In the water. Why do you think that be so?"

It was an unanswerable question.

"Didn't you tell me Floyd Carpenter gave you a dollar that you threw in the river?"

"Later, he come all the way down on the river where I be staying. I was eating my breakfast when he walk out of the woods with a long rifle on his shoulder. 'Bout scared me half to death. But he talk soft. Give me a shiny silver dollar."

"Why did he give you the money?"

"He say if I be telling the truth, that dollar will make me a rich man. If I be lying, then I won't never have nothing. I be poor my whole life except I got my boat."

"Telling the truth about what?"

Moses pointed to the picture in the paper. "That girl with the yellow hair and blue eyes."

"Did you tell him then that you found her on the bank and tried to save her?"

"No, the voice in my head tells me something ain't right. I just shake my head and act dumb, but I be scared if'n he don't believe me. So I start sleeping more on the river, but he find me there."

"He came to see you in a boat?"

"No, missy. Ain't you listening? His face. It don't need no boat." He pointed again at the newspaper article. "He be like her."

I sat back in my chair and studied Moses Jones in a different way. The old man had lived most of his life haunted by people he'd never harmed.

"I'm sorry this happened to you," I said after a few moments passed. "All of it."

He looked at me and bowed his head slightly. I started to offer another consoling word, but the horrid, unjustified malice directed against Moses by Mr. Carpenter and Mr. Braddock hit me.

"Moses, did you know Mr. Floyd Carpenter had a son?"

"Yeah. He be a big-shot lawyer."

"He's my boss. And he wants to know everything you've been telling me."

Moses gave me a puzzled look. "Why he care about me after all these years done flowed by?"

"Because of Lisa Prescott. He and another lawyer named Samuel Braddock believe there is a connection between you and the little girl. They see you as a threat."

"What you mean?"

"You were scared of Mr. Floyd and his gun. They're scared of you and what you know."

"Why? I be sitting in this jail and can't hurt nobody."

"That's true. But they think you can harm them by changing the way people in Savannah think about them. The guilt of past generations is chasing them. And that guilt doesn't ever get tired." I paused. "Floyd Carpenter was the person responsible for Lisa Prescott's death."

Moses' face revealed his shock. "Why he do that? She not be more than a little thing."

I rubbed my hand as he had earlier. "For a lot more than a chance at five dollars."

27

Moses shook his head after I spent almost an hour explaining as best I could what I'd uncovered.

"That be too much old thoughts for my brain to hold."

"I know it's complicated, but what I really need is your permission to talk to the district attorney's office about the possible danger to you. The DA's office could call in the police to investigate, and you could tell Detective Branson what happened that evening on the river. He seems like a good man."

"You be a nice'un, but out there"—Moses gestured with his arm—"ain't nobody gonna believe me. Nowadays I may not be strung up on a tree limb, but I never get out of this jail. No, missy, you best keep this to me and you."

"Don't you understand? You could be in real danger."

"For sure, every way be a rocky path. But the less folks that knows the way I go, the better off I be."

I searched for another approach to convince him. "Please, think about it. It would be awful if something bad happened to you."

Moses gave me a slightly crooked smile. "That be a kind word. I not hear talk like that since I was a small boy at my auntie's house."

"I misjudged you, and I'm sorry."

Moses didn't answer. I looked down at my legal pad. It was blank.

I'd been so engrossed in what Moses had told me that I hadn't taken a note. Perhaps no notes about our conversation would be better.

"I'll be back to see you soon," I promised.

"And don't be forgetting about my boat. If'n I get out of here on prohibition, I want that boat going with me. It ain't done nothing wrong."

THE DRIVE BACK to the office didn't give me enough time to figure out what to do next. Investigating Lisa Prescott's disappearance had been theoretical. The danger to Moses was immediate and certain.

Vince was working in the conference room adjacent to Mr. Braddock's office. Two paralegals were at the other end of the table organizing documents. I placed the keys on the table and leaned close to his ear.

"Thanks," I said. "Do you have time to talk?"

Vince motioned toward the other end of the table.

"They're up against a deadline, and I need to pull off some data from the Internet for Mr. Appleby."

"You're working for Mr. Appleby?"

"Yes. The information is in French and no one else can translate it. I should be finished within an hour. Where will you be?"

"In the library."

To my relief, Julie wasn't in the library. I logged on to one of the terminals and checked my office e-mail. There was a message from Mr. Carpenter asking for an update on the Moses Jones case. I skipped to the next item. It was from Zach.

Tami,

I talked with Maggie Smith. She agreed to place Moses Jones' case on Judge Howell's trial calendar. She also brought up the possibility of running the plea bargain past Judge Howell. If the judge goes along with the deal, Jones could be released in a few days. Thought you might want this good news as soon as possible. Follow up with me upon your return to the office.

Zach

A few hours before, this would have been welcome news. Now, it doubled the pressure I felt. I noticed that Zach had also sent it to Mr. Carpenter. My mouth went dry, and the pressure doubled again. I glanced at the ceiling and offered up a prayer for help.

I tried to work on the Folsom divorce case while I waited for Vince to finish, but it was trivial compared to the threats facing Moses. I checked my watch every five minutes. Shortly, before the hour was up, the library door opened. I looked up in relief.

It was Zach.

"Did you read my e-mail?" he asked.

"Yes."

"And?" he asked, raising his eyebrows.

"It sounds hopeful, but I'm not sure Moses is ready to get out of jail. You heard what he said when we explained the terms of probation to him. He'll violate the terms of release and go back to jail without any chance of getting out for a long time."

"He's a grown man. As long as he understands what's expected of him, compliance is his responsibility. Do you think he wants to stay locked up? We don't have the right to keep him in jail if there is a reasonable chance to get him out."

"We might get a not-guilty verdict at trial," I responded. "Then he wouldn't have to worry about probation. I met with him this afternoon and explained our trial strategy. As we talked it made more and more sense. I mean, jurors are regular people who can appreciate an honest mistake, especially when no property damage has occurred."

"I don't want to hurt your feelings, but I can't believe what I'm hearing. The case is exactly where we want it to be, and you think the best course of action is for our client to go to trial? What's really going on? This has to do with Lisa Prescott, doesn't it?"

I pressed my lips tightly together.

"What did you find in the microfilm records?" Zach continued. "Even if you uncovered incriminating information about Moses Jones, it doesn't give you the right to be judge and jury, sentencing him to jail."

The door opened, and Vince stepped in. He saw Zach and started backing out of the room. "Sorry to interrupt," he said. "I'll check with you later."

"Hold it," Zach said.

"What?" Vince asked.

Zach stared at Vince, then turned toward me. "Because you two are working on the Jones case together doesn't mean you can withhold information from me. Tami was supposed to take me with her and conveniently forgot to let me know."

"Oh," I said, stung, "I got caught up and—"

Zach interrupted. "I want to hear what's happened since we met this morning."

The three of us sat around the table, with Zach at one end and Vince and I across from each other.

"Out with it," Zach said.

I looked at Vince, who seemed nervous. Zach hesitated for a moment, then spoke. "I'm only an associate. Do you want me to bring in one of the partners to help sort this out? I don't know who's here this afternoon, but Mr. Carpenter is the most familiar—"

"No!" I blurted out. "That would be cruel."

"No more than the accusations you've made against him," Zach shot back.

"Not cruel to me," I replied testily. "Leave me out of this. I've never had a realistic chance of working here, and based on what I know now, I wouldn't accept a permanent job if Mr. Carpenter offered me one. This is all about Moses Jones. You have no idea what you're about to do to him."

Zach's neck was slightly red. "Then tell me. I'm listening."

I looked at Vince.

"Go ahead," he said.

I faced Zach. "First, I need to ask you a question. Is your primary loyalty to Moses Jones as a client or to this law firm?"

"Is there a conflict between them?"

"Yes. And if I don't tell you the details, then you won't have to make a choice."

I saw Zach hesitate. I knew he liked his job working for Mr. Appleby. I turned to Vince.

"And everyone knows you're a lock as the next associate of the firm. You warned me the other day, but have you thought about the negative impact this could have on your future? Are you helping me because God has called you or because it gives us a chance to be together?"

The slightly embarrassed look on Vince's face told me what I needed to know.

"I'm trying not to be cruel to either one of you or anybody else," I continued in a calmer tone of voice. "I came to the conclusion this afternoon that what happens to me doesn't matter as much as taking care of my client." I stood up. "From now on, I'm not going to discuss this with either one of you. I'm exhausted and ready to go home."

I left Zach and Vince together in the library. I didn't know where Julie might be, but I wasn't going to stick around. I found her coming out of Ned's office.

"Are you ready to leave for the day?" I asked.

She looked at her watch. "Yeah, it's later than I thought. I have a few things to grab from the library."

"I'll wait for you at the car."

"It's blazing hot outside."

“Then you’ll hurry, okay?”

Julie glanced questioningly over her shoulder. I hoped the thought of me roasting in the late-afternoon heat would keep her from having a long conversation with Zach and Vince. I walked slowly along the sidewalk in the shade cast by the building. I reached the car and watched the front door. In less than a minute Julie joined me.

“Was anyone in the library?” I asked.

“No, why?”

“Just curious. I’d finished a meeting with Zach and Vince, and they stayed after I left.”

“About the Jones case?”

I knew I had to answer, and partial information was much more likely to satisfy Julie’s curiosity so we could change subjects.

“Yeah, I met with him this afternoon at the jail,” I said casually. “One of the things we discussed was trial strategy. I think my chances of getting a not-guilty verdict are greater than you might think, but Zach and Vince are unconvinced.”

“Your client admits the crime. I can’t imagine a credible defense.”

I stretched out my explanation until Julie stopped in front of Mrs. Fairmont’s house.

“You’re dreaming,” Julie said. “The best you could hope for would be a hung jury if you convince a couple of people to feel sorry for him.”

“And a hung jury might be as good as an acquittal. How many times do you think the district attorney’s office wants to take up the court’s time trying a misdemeanor trespassing case?”

“You have a point,” Julie admitted with a nod of her head. “Once again, I underestimated you. I didn’t think you had the guts to force a trial.”

As Julie drove away, I wasn’t sure I had more guts than an eight-pound chicken.

INSIDE THE HOUSE, I greeted Flip, whose excitement at my arrival seemed to increase each afternoon. Mrs. Fairmont was asleep in her chair with the television blaring. I gently touched her on the shoulder. She didn't respond. I shook her harder. To my relief she stirred and opened her eyes.

"How do you feel?" I asked.

"Who are you?" she asked as she glanced up at me with bleary eyes.

"Tami Taylor. I'm staying at your house this summer while I work for Samuel Braddock's law firm."

"Samuel Braddock?"

"Yes ma'am."

It was the first time Mrs. Fairmont's memory for people she'd known for years was fuzzy.

"Are you hungry?" I asked. "I'd be happy to fix your supper."

Mrs. Fairmont closed her eyes for a few seconds, then opened them. "Yes, that would be nice."

Gracie hadn't come that day, but there were leftovers in the refrigerator. I quickly prepared two plates of food and began warming one up in the microwave. After the stress that threatened to crush me at the office, the normalcy of fixing supper was therapeutic.

I returned to the den and found Mrs. Fairmont sitting in the chair with her eyes closed. It was a sad sight that made me ache over the ravages of aging. I heated up the other plate of food and placed them on the dining room table. Flip, smelling the meal, took up his position beside Mrs. Fairmont's chair. I returned to the den and roused her again. At first I thought I might have to assist her to the table, but once on her feet, she walked without any problems to the dining room.

Mrs. Fairmont seemed to enjoy her supper but didn't respond to my attempts at conversation beyond a single word or two. I was just getting to know her and didn't want to see her slip away permanently into a pit of mental confusion.

"Lord, please don't let this be the time," I prayed softly.

Mrs. Fairmont glanced over and gave me a sweet smile. "You're a nice young woman," she said. "Would you like to stay for a cup of after-dinner coffee?"

"Yes ma'am. I'll fix it for you."

I brought coffee to the table along with a cup of tea for myself. We drank in silence. Mrs. Fairmont touched a napkin to her lips.

"I should invite Samuel and Eloise Braddock over for dinner," she said. "They are such a gracious couple, and we have many good memories together."

"It would be best if I'm not here that evening," I said.

"Why?"

"So you can discuss good memories."

I LAY AWAKE THAT NIGHT. Most of the challenges I'd faced in my life seemed theoretical compared to the sober reality facing Moses Jones. My responsibility to the old man rested on my chest like a great weight and reduced me to one of the simplest prayers.

"Help me," I prayed over and over and over.

I finally drifted off to sleep with the words lingering on my lips.

I AWOKE IN THE MORNING and enjoyed a five-second stretch before reality returned. I sighed and reluctantly resumed my burden. During my morning run, I took a new route away from the historic district into the modern part of the city. I needed new scenery.

Mrs. Fairmont wasn't downstairs when I returned, but she responded when I pressed the Call button on the intercom.

"How are you feeling this morning?" I asked.

"Fine. I'm going to call Christine and tell her to take me to lunch. Have a nice day."

I walked as resolutely as I could to the office and went directly to the library. Julie hadn't arrived, and there weren't any notes from Zach or Vince. One of my main goals for the day was to avoid contact with either one of them. I checked my law firm e-mail account. I'd received another project from Bob Kettleson. I grimaced. One consequence of my leaving the firm would be increased work for the senior associate. Julie burst through the door.

"Wow, what a night," she said. "I met the most awesome guy. He lives on my street, and we met while he was walking his dog, a cute little thing with pointy white ears. Joel graduated a few years ago from the design school here and opened his own studio. He's a photographer, and some of his shots were the most amazing things I've ever seen. He asked me out to dinner on the spot and took me to the neatest French restaurant in a house on West Oglethorpe Street."

"I know the place," I said.

"He lived in Paris for a year after graduation. And get this, he's Jewish without being over the top about it. Just like me. We had so much fun. I haven't laughed so hard in months. His work is so good that I've got to get my father to buy a few prints for my mother. He invited me to synagogue Friday night, then to the beach on Saturday. My mother will flip when she finds out. Maybe we can do something clean and wholesome one evening with you and either Vinny or Zach."

Julie stopped and laughed. "That sounds strange, doesn't it?"

"Yes."

The library phone buzzed, and I picked it up. It was the front desk receptionist.

"This is Tami."

"You have a call from Ms. Smith at the district attorney's office. She asked for Zach, but he's not here."

"I'll take it," I said after a moment's hesitation.

Maggie Smith wasted no time on pleasantries once I took the call. "I spoke with Zach yesterday, and I was able to reassign the Jones case to Judge Howell's docket. I ran the plea bargain past the judge, and she's fine with it—release Jones for time served and a year on probation with no monetary fine. It's specially set on her calendar this afternoon at two o'clock. I sent Zach an e-mail confirmation."

"I'm not sure my client—" I began, and then stopped.

Moses had not withdrawn his agreement to the plea, and I couldn't tell her otherwise.

"What about your client?" Smith asked.

"I need to let him know about the hearing."

"Fine, but the prisoner request list went over to the jail first thing this morning. He'll be there and released in time for a cornbread supper. See you this afternoon."

I hung up the phone.

"Good or bad news?" Julie asked.

"It depends. We're going in front of another judge with the plea bargain in the Jones case. The assistant DA thinks it will go through."

There was no avoiding Zach now. No matter how cooperative Judge Howell might be, she wouldn't allow me to appear in court without a supervising attorney. I buzzed back to the receptionist.

"Please let me know when Zach Mays arrives."

"He walked in the door right after I transferred the phone call."

There was no use putting off the inevitable. I slowly set the phone receiver back in the cradle.

"Does Joel have any photos of the river marshes?" I asked Julie.

"Yeah, at all times of the day. They're gorgeous."

"If you want to buy me a going-away present, that would be a good choice."

I left Julie with a puzzled expression on her face and went upstairs to Zach's office. He turned around when I entered.

"Maggie Smith called," I said. "The case—"

"Is on for two o'clock this afternoon. I read her e-mail."

I turned to leave.

"One other thing," Zach said. "Mr. Carpenter is going to be there."

I spun around. "Who invited him?"

"Nobody. He's been keeping up with the case independently of your information."

"What does that tell you?"

"That he's more interested than I knew. But you're not sharing information with anyone, and I don't want to speculate about his motives."

"*Motive* is a good word." I stopped and took a deep breath. "And I know I'm doing the right thing keeping you and Vince out of this."

28

SOMEHOW, I NEEDED TO CONVINCE MOSES TO REJECT THE plea bargain and remain in the relative safety of the jail. All paths might be rocky, but not all held the danger of a fatal rock slide. I needed time to figure out the best way to safety.

I checked on the availability of the law firm car. It was checked out for the entire day. I wouldn't suffer the indignity of riding in the motorcycle sidecar or in the same vehicle with Mr. Carpenter and didn't want to ask Vince to let me borrow his car. That left Julie. I returned to the library.

And came face-to-face with Bob Kettleson.

"Let's go," he said. "We have a meeting with the developer on the eminent domain issue you researched."

"Why do you need me? Everything I know is in the memo, and there is a hearing on my appointed criminal case this afternoon. I have to get ready."

"It's a plea bargain," Julie said. "And you told me the assistant DA is recommending it to the judge."

"What time is the hearing?" Kettleson asked.

"Two o'clock."

"We'll be back in plenty of time. The main reason for the invitation is that I've been pleased with your work and wanted to get to know you better. It's a forty-five-minute drive to the client's business, and I hate wasting the time."

I'd long since abandoned Zach Mays' rules for summer associates. I silently appealed to Julie. All she gave me was a smirk.

I picked up the folder that contained my memo and followed Kettleson out of the office. Because the client developed real estate up and down the coast, its main office was located between Savannah and Brunswick. We left the city and drove south. Kettleson spent the first thirty minutes of the trip talking about himself and didn't direct a single question toward me. Finally, he asked me to list every course I'd taken during my second year of law school, the professor who taught the class, and the grade received.

"Your municipal corporations background shows in your analysis. I wish you could have had Professor Sentell. He was the best."

"He gave a few guest lectures."

I spent the rest of the trip listening to Kettleson tell me about his experiences in law school where he'd been selected for the law review. I was tempted to ask him to list all his second-year classes and the grades he'd received, but I kept my mouth shut and tried to organize my thoughts about the Jones case. Kettleson's nasally voice didn't help me concentrate.

The meeting with the client included an architectural presentation of the plans for the disputed property and legal analysis by Kettleson in which he read my memo without giving me credit for the research.

"Joe Carpenter, our top litigator, will be the lead lawyer if a lawsuit has to be filed," Kettleson said in conclusion. "But I hope litigation won't be necessary after our senior partner, Mr. Braddock, makes his calls to the politicians. No one is better connected in Chatham County, and he has well-placed friends in Atlanta and Washington."

The client catered lunch. I anxiously looked at my watch.

"Mr. Kettleson, don't forget I have to be back for my hearing," I said.

"Don't worry. We won't stay long."

He was wrong. We stayed until the company's managers began to drift back to work. On the ride back to Savannah, I kept looking at my watch and taking a peek at the speedometer. Kettleson stayed quiet, and I didn't try to interrupt his thoughts. We pulled into the law firm parking lot at 1:50 p.m. If I'd brought the Jones file with me, Kettleson could have dropped me off at the courthouse.

"It's only a couple of minutes to the courthouse," the senior associate said as he turned off the car.

"Except I don't know how I'm going to get there." I rushed into the building. Vince was sitting in the reception area.

"Here's your file," he said. "I'll drive you to the courthouse."

We passed Kettleson on the way out of the building.

"That worked out great," the senior associate said. "Look for another project from me when you get back."

We reached Vince's car.

"How did you know about the hearing?" I asked.

"Julie told me."

"For once, I'm glad she has a big mouth."

It was only a few blocks to the courthouse.

"Did you see Zach or Mr. Carpenter leave?" I asked.

"No. Why is Mr. Carpenter going to be there?"

"You know he's probably been shadowing everything I've done. I wouldn't be surprised if he knows I've been snooping around the microfilm records."

"Are you going to tell me more?"

"No."

We stopped and waited for a light to turn green.

"I want to help," Vince said, moving forward.

"You're helping right now. Trust me, this is for the best."

"I'll let you out and find a place to park."

Opening the car door, I climbed the steps two at a time. Fortunately, there wasn't a line at the security check, and an elevator was waiting with the door open. It was 1:58 p.m. when I opened the back door to the courtroom. It was much smaller than the one used by Judge Cannon. Zach and Mr. Carpenter were sitting in the area reserved for the lawyers. Moses and a single deputy were in the prisoner dock. There was no sign of Maggie Smith or the judge. I walked breathlessly down the aisle. The two lawyers turned toward me as I approached.

And I had a sinking feeling in the pit of my stomach that Zach and Mr. Carpenter had been working together all along.

"Glad you could make it," Mr. Carpenter said.

"Bob Kettleson—" I began.

"We know," Zach said. "I checked on you a couple of hours ago."

I couldn't bear to look Zach in the face. "I need to talk to Mr. Jones," I said.

Zach stood up.

"No!" I said so loudly that it filled the courtroom. "Alone."

Zach looked at Mr. Carpenter, who shrugged.

"Okay," Zach said.

I went to Moses. The deputy moved several feet away. I positioned my body so Zach and Mr. Carpenter couldn't see. Up close, the old man's face was as wrinkled as a crumpled-up newspaper. His eyes were slightly yellow around the edges.

"That's Floyd Carpenter's son," I whispered.

"I see that, missy. They favor each other."

"I don't know exactly why he's here, but it can't be anything good. Until I can figure out a way to protect you, I think you should stay in jail. It's the safest place you can be."

"I done told you I ain't gonna die in no jailhouse." Moses spoke louder and gestured toward the deputy. "He brung all my stuff in those two pokes. I be thinking about going home. Is that right?"

"If the judge accepts the plea bargain. But what I'm trying to tell you is that it won't be safe for you on the street."

"I be going straight to the river. Only who gonna tote my boat for me?"

The old man's concern about his boat gave me an idea.

"We'll ask the judge to let you stay in the jail until arrangements can be made to transport you and your boat at the same time. It would be a shame for you to get out and then have the boat sent for scrap."

"It ain't no big beer can—"

Before Moses could finish, a side door to the courtroom opened. Ms. Smith and a slender, dark-haired woman wearing a judicial robe entered the courtroom.

"All rise!" the deputy called out.

"Be seated," the judge said. "Ms. Smith, call your case."

"*State v. Jones.*"

Moses and I stepped into the open area in front of the bench. Zach joined us. I stood between him and Moses. Mr. Carpenter remained in his seat. Vince sat behind him.

"This is Ms. Tami Taylor, a rising third-year law student at the University of Georgia," Zach said in a syrupy voice that made me want to slap him. "She's a summer clerk with our firm. Judge Cannon appointed her to represent Mr. Jones in this matter."

"Welcome to Savannah, Ms. Taylor," the judge said. "I hope you're having a pleasant summer."

I was barely able to muster a crooked smile. The judge nodded toward Ms. Smith.

"Proceed."

Maggie Smith handed a file to the judge. "As you know, opposing counsel gave me permission to discuss a potential plea bargain in this case ex parte with you—"

"I didn't agree to any ex parte—" I interrupted.

"I did, Your Honor," Zach cut me off. "I'm the supervising attorney. Under the circumstances, it was the most efficient way to dispose of the case."

"What circumstances?" I asked.

"Ms. Taylor," the judge said, "we're not in a rush here, but you and Mr. Mays can discuss a better method of interoffice communication at a later time. If you'll be patient, I'd like to hear from Ms. Smith."

"Yes ma'am."

Smith spoke. "The defendant is charged with twenty-four counts of trespassing by tying up his boat at private docks. No property damage occurred, and one of the complainants, Mr. Bill Fussleman, sent a letter to my office offering to accommodate the defendant's boat at his dock upon reasonable notice in the future. We are recommending that the defendant be sentenced to time served of eighty-two days, plus one year probation."

"What 'bout my boat?" Moses spoke up.

Smith continued. "The defendant's boat was confiscated when he was arrested. It's in the impoundment lot at the jail and can be released simultaneously with the defendant."

"So, he should remain in jail until arrangements can be made for the transport of his boat," I said.

The judge gave me a puzzled look. "Is that what your client wants to do?"

I swallowed. "We were discussing that when you called the case."

Moses, Maggie Smith, Zach, and I all stared at one another.

"Our firm will make arrangements for the boat to be removed and delivered to Mr. Jones," Zach said, breaking the stalemate.

"Very well," the judge said. "Are we ready to proceed with the plea?"

"Yes ma'am," Zach responded.

I frantically searched for another delay tactic but came up empty. Zach's duplicity was infuriating.

I listened numbly as Judge Howell went through the constitutional litany required when a defendant enters a guilty plea. Most of the phrases had been the subject of intense scrutiny in cases that made their way to the Supreme Court. Today, it sounded like meaningless gibberish.

"Is your client prepared to enter a plea of guilty to the charges?" the judge asked.

"If that's what he wants to do," I answered resignedly.

The judge looked from me to Moses. "Do you want to plead guilty, Mr. Jones?"

"Yes'm, so long as I get to go home."

"All right, I'll accept your plea and sentence you to time served of eighty-two days, plus one year supervised probation. The defendant is released on his own recognizance. Mr. Jones, your attorneys can assist you in setting up the initial schedule with your probation officer. After that, make sure the officer knows how to get in touch with you and keep all scheduled appointments. I don't want to see you in court again. Anything else?"

"Yes'm. My boat."

Judge Howell smiled. "Of course. Your boat is released from impoundment without payment of any storage fees. Remove it from the lot within seven days."

Judge Howell rose and left the room. Ms. Smith turned to Zach and me. "I'm glad we could work this out. Trying cases like this gives the public the impression we don't have anything important to do."

"Thanks for your cooperation," Zach said.

Smith shook Zach's hand and smiled sweetly. "I know you don't do criminal work, but I hope to see you around."

The assistant DA left the room. The deputy handed Moses two plastic bags.

"Keep catching those big croakers," he said. "You've been the best worker we've had on trash detail for a long time, but I hope we don't see you again."

"Thank you, boss man," Moses answered.

I took Moses by the arm to guide him out of the courtroom behind the deputy.

"Tami!" Mr. Carpenter called out. "Just a minute."

Moses and I kept moving toward the side door of the courtroom. The senior partner walked over and blocked our way. He faced Moses.

"My name is Joe Carpenter."

"I know who you be," Moses said, staring at the floor.

"And Mr. Jones is leaving now," I said, trying to keep my voice steady. "I'll see you when I get back to the office."

Mr. Carpenter didn't budge. "It's not you I want to talk to," he answered. "I have business with Mr. Jones."

I knew there was no use appealing to Zach. I frantically looked to Vince for help. He stepped back and didn't say anything.

"Sit down on that bench," Mr. Carpenter commanded Moses.

The old man complied. Mr. Carpenter turned to me. "Ms. Taylor, your business here is finished. Go back to the office. I'll meet with you later this afternoon before you leave."

"I'm not going anywhere," I responded, planting my feet as if guarding a basketball goal.

Mr. Carpenter's head jerked back. "What did you say?"

"I'm staying here with my client," I said more bravely than I felt.

Mr. Carpenter's eyes narrowed. "What I have to discuss with Mr. Jones has nothing to do with you."

I nodded my head toward Moses. "That's for him to decide. Moses, do you want me to stay with you?"

"Yes, missy."

I looked Mr. Carpenter in the eyes. "And that's what I'm going to do."

"I'm going to ask this man some—"

"Mr. Jones doesn't have to talk to you or answer any questions," I interrupted.

Mr. Carpenter turned toward Zach and Vince. "Go!"

The two young men stared at each other for a second.

"I want them to stay," I said.

"Why?" Mr. Carpenter asked, his face getting red. "They have no more business here."

"So they can witness what you're about to do."

"What I'm about to do is fire you and tell you to get out of my sight," Mr. Carpenter exploded. "Now move aside!"

Zach and Vince stepped back at the sound of Mr. Carpenter's voice. I held my ground. The river had been crossed. All that mattered was protecting Moses.

"Do whatever you want to do about my job, but I'm not going to abandon my client."

Mr. Carpenter turned to Moses. "Mr. Jones, has Ms. Taylor told you she's a lawyer?"

"No sir, she always be saying she's not a real lawyer, but she sure enough got the grit to be one."

"I'd say she has grit where she should have brains," Mr. Carpenter replied sarcastically.

"You can insult me, Mr. Carpenter," I replied, my own eyes flashing. "And you can fire me. But Judge Cannon signed an order authorizing me to represent Mr. Jones, and that's what I intend to do."

Mr. Carpenter glared hard at me for several seconds until a sneer turned up the corners of his mouth. "Ms. Taylor, I want to be totally clear about this situation. Are you refusing to let Mr. Jones talk to me unless you are present?"

"Yes sir. And I'm telling him that he doesn't have to talk to you at all if he doesn't want to." I looked down at Moses. "In fact, I'm advising him not to answer any questions or provide information about recent or past events now or at any time in the future."

"That's quite comprehensive," Mr. Carpenter replied.

"Yes sir. That's what I intend."

Mr. Carpenter nodded his head. "Very well, I have a few things to say to you."

I stood up straight. I had no intention of slouching in the face of the firing squad.

"First, Oscar Callahan told me you were a young woman of exceptional conviction and personal courage. Nice sentiments, but I had no idea how firmly rooted those qualities are in your character. Fearlessness in the face of intense pressure can't be taught; it is forged in the trials of life. Second, I never dreamed that a summer clerk would take representation of a client so seriously that she would risk losing a job and damaging her entire career to maintain zealous though misplaced advocacy. I have no doubt that you will someday be an outstanding lawyer. Third, you have earned the right to know why I want to talk to Mr. Jones."

"It doesn't matter what you say—" I began, aware I was being manipulated.

"Tami! Let him finish," Zach interrupted.

"And I don't mind Zach and Vince staying if those are the terms you set for me. Why don't we all sit down?"

Without waiting for an answer, Mr. Carpenter pulled up a chair and sat across from Moses. My mind reeling, I sat on the bench beside Moses. Mr. Carpenter gestured with his hand, and Zach and Vince sat down. The older lawyer looked at Moses.

"Mr. Jones, I'm going to tell you some things, but I don't want you to say anything to me without Ms. Taylor's permission." He looked at me. "Is that agreeable?"

Mr. Carpenter was a cagey man seeking a way to gain control of the situation through flattery and deceit.

"No sir. Talk to me first."

Mr. Carpenter's jaw tightened, but he kept his composure. "Very well. My father was a businessman here in Savannah. People described him as 'colorful,' which is a euphemism for a criminal who has enough money to buy his way into respectability."

The senior partner's candor shocked me.

"Many years ago while I was in college, his niece, a little girl named Lisa Prescott, disappeared and was never found. Our family always suspected foul play, but the police never found her body or identified a suspect. Through some of his criminal connections, my father heard a rumor that Mr. Jones knew something about Lisa's disappearance. According to information in a file kept by my father, Mr. Jones was questioned at least once but denied knowing anything. Now you know why I took such an interest in this case. Moses Jones isn't a name easily forgotten, and when Sam Braddock and I pulled out the old records, we realized the connection. We didn't even know if Mr. Jones was still alive." He looked directly at Moses. "We're all getting older, and once and for all, I want to know the truth."

Moses turned to me. "What you be thinking, missy?"

Mr. Carpenter's matter-of-fact recitation of the facts threw me completely off guard. His approach bore none of the threatened pressure.

"What are you going to do if Moses doesn't want to talk to you?" I asked, stalling for time.

"Keep working on what my father started. That's more important than anything he could tell me."

"What do you mean?"

"Not only did we lose Lisa; her parents died a year later in an automobile accident. The double tragedy was the catalyst for change in my father's life. He stopped being 'colorful' and moved into legitimate business activities in which he made a lot more money than he ever did on the shady side of the law. Lawrence Braddock helped him go straight. Together, they set up the Lisa Prescott Foundation."

"Foundation?" I asked in a subdued voice.

"Yes. Lisa's mother, Ellen, was my father's baby sister. Her husband didn't have any surviving family, and everything passed to my father under their wills. He didn't touch a penny of the money, but established a charitable foundation that has given away millions to children's causes in Georgia and South Carolina. Sam Braddock and I have served on the board of the foundation for more than thirty years."

"Why didn't you tell me anything about this?"

Mr. Carpenter raised his eyebrows. "Why should I? You were representing Mr. Jones in a trespassing case."

"But why did you want to talk to Mr. Jones alone?"

"I wanted to push him hard for the truth." Mr. Carpenter rubbed his hands together. "However, that won't happen since his attorney has demonstrated a tenacious ability to frustrate my efforts at communication."

"Do you believe Mr. Jones was responsible for Lisa's disappearance?"

"I don't know; the notes in the file mention a rumor that Mr. Jones found her body. The rest is a mystery I'd like to solve. Will you allow me to question him?"

I looked at Zach and Vince. Neither one spoke. I turned to Mr. Carpenter. "Only if it is considered an ongoing part of the attorney/client relationship between Mr. Jones and Braddock, Appleby, and Carpenter."

Mr. Carpenter hesitated. "So that I will be bound by the attorney/client privilege and couldn't disclose the information obtained to the police. That's finesse."

"Agreed?" I asked, ignoring the compliment.

Mr. Carpenter nodded. "Yes."

"And I'll ask the questions first," I continued. "It will go a lot smoother that way; then you can follow up."

"But you don't know what to ask," the older lawyer protested.

"Just listen. You can evaluate my effort."

FOR THE NEXT THIRTY MINUTES, I guided Moses through his story. When he described Lisa's injuries after he discovered her on the riverbank, I glanced at Mr. Carpenter, whose eyes were red and moist. The lawyer wiped away tears when Moses told about the simple burial in a watery grave. For the first time since Mr. Carpenter blocked our exit from the courtroom, I allowed myself to relax. The tension flowed out of my shoulders.

Moses concluded with the two times Floyd Carpenter tried to talk to him, and the reason he kept his mouth shut. Mr. Carpenter pulled out his handkerchief and wiped his eyes for at least the third time.

"I'm sorry," Moses said. "But I be too scared to say nothing to your daddy."

"I understand," Mr. Carpenter replied.

I spoke. "Is there anything else you remember about what happened to Lisa?"

"No, missy. That be it."

"Mr. Carpenter, do you have any questions?"

The lawyer bowed his head for a moment. "Do you know the place where you laid her in the water?"

"Yes sir."

"I know she's not there, but could you show it to me sometime?"

"Yes, boss man."

"And did you ever hear any rumors or stories of why she was left on the riverbank or how she got there that evening?"

Moses pressed his lips together. I held my breath.

"I be thinking something myself. That little girl been hit in the head a lot worse than if she'd been in a bare-knuckle fight. Something hard done that. And there be small pieces of glass caught up in her dress. I saved a few of them in a tin can for a long time, but they be lost now."

"A hit-and-run driver," Mr. Carpenter said, turning to me. "Who didn't leave her lying in the road or call an ambulance, but thought she was dead and dumped her off in a secluded place. The police found blood on a curb along the route Lisa would have taken home from a music lesson on the day she disappeared. The first test was inconclusive, but the second came back as a blood-type match. Of course, there wasn't DNA testing back then, and the blood type was one of the more common ones."

"Why wouldn't someone who hit her call for help?" I asked.

"The driver could have been drinking, on drugs, driving a stolen vehicle, or simply panicked. We'll probably never know. People don't always think things through in the heat of the moment."

I could certainly identify with that type of mistake.

Mr. Carpenter continued. "Every car taken in for repair to the front grille or bumper during the next few months after Lisa disappeared was inspected by police, but nothing turned up. If it was a hit-and-run driver, he laid low long enough to avoid being identified. My father hired a private detective firm that continued seeking clues after the police shut down the active file. Nothing turned up."

Mr. Carpenter stood and extended his hand to Moses. They shook hands. I watched in disbelief.

"Mr. Jones, thank you for trying to help Lisa," Mr. Carpenter said. "Knowing someone tried to save her means so much to me." He choked up again. "And hearing your story gives me hope that she may not have suffered as much as, or in ways, we'd always feared."

"No sir, she never woke up until she passed."

Mr. Carpenter nodded. "How can I get in touch with you about going to her burial place on the river?"

"Through Bill Fussleman," Zach offered. "He's the homeowner who is going to let Mr. Jones tie up his boat for the night at his dock. Fussleman's address and phone number are in the file."

"That be fine, boss man," Moses said. "I be looking out for you."

"Can I take you someplace?" Mr. Carpenter asked Moses. "I'll drop you off anywhere you like."

"No sir. I be walking. It gonna feel good breathing free air and stretching out my own two legs."

"And you?" Mr. Carpenter asked me. "Are you going back to the office? You still have a job."

"Yes, and thanks, but I think I'll walk. Free air sounds good to me too."

29

THE THREE MEN LEFT THE COURTROOM. I STAYED BEHIND with Moses and watched the door close behind them. The courtroom became totally quiet. *State v. Jones* was over. I collapsed on the bench, put my head in my hands, and began to weep.

"What be bothering you, missy?"

The crushing pressure of the past weeks demanded an emotional release. My weeping turned to sobs. I felt the old man lightly place his hand on my back. Several minutes passed before I regained my composure. Thankfully, no one disturbed us. I lifted my head and sniffled loudly. Moses was sitting beside me. I cleared my throat.

"I've been sharing your burden for a few weeks. You've been carrying it for forty years. I don't know how you've done it."

Moses nodded. "That be right, missy. I be toting a very heavy load. Just like the big rock that dragged that poor little girl's body to the muddy bottom."

I took a tissue from my purse and blew my nose. I looked at the old man's weathered face. Pure love for him rose up in my heart. I touched him lightly on the arm.

"And it's time you stopped carrying that load, along with the other loads dragging you down all your life."

"What you mean?"

I turned sideways so I could look directly into his face. "Jesus gave his life so you wouldn't have to carry the burdens of the past, no matter where they came from. His burden is easy and light. Give what's left of your life to him."

The old man blinked his eyes. "You sound like my ol' auntie. I know that be true for young folk, but not for an old broke-down fellow like me. Too much done gone by for me to catch up." Moses looked across the room. "The faces in the water, they be talking to me. They tell me the end of my days."

"No," I answered with feeling. "Listen to Jesus. God wants you to look up, not down."

Moses slowly tilted back his head. After a few moments, there was a puzzled expression on his face. "That be a sweet sound," he said.

I didn't hear anything, but my heart understood. "That's what happens in a court of praise."

And in a gentle, natural way, the Lord used me to guide Moses Jones to a place of freedom and peace. Our tears, young and old, flowed together as he received the love of Jesus with childlike wonder. The spillover blessed me from the top of my head to the tips of my toes. Mama would have shouted in victory. Our celebration, though quieter, was no less triumphant.

"Are you ready to go?" I asked after the last prayer ended.

"I never be more ready." Moses paused. "And you know what, missy?"

"What?"

"I think you be a lot more than a real lawyer."

WE LEFT THE COURTROOM and went in opposite directions. It was hot outside, but the heat had lost its power to oppress me. I walked at a leisurely pace. Wisdom adapts to things that cannot be changed, so I took my time returning to the office. The thanksgiving that had bubbled up in my heart while the Lord touched Moses returned. God was good. My mistakes and foolishness hadn't stymied his purposes.

I arrived back at the office ready to confess my sins to Zach. But he wasn't in his office, and the attractive secretary who worked for him informed me that he and Mr. Appleby had left for an emergency weekend meeting in Mobile with representatives of a Chinese shipping company. The Chinese company was going to increase its business on the East Coast and the Gulf of Mexico and wanted a single law firm to coordinate their activities in the United States.

I was a bit ashamed as I admitted to myself that I was relieved he was not in. I dreaded rehashing my embarrassing miscalculation of Mr. Carpenter's interest in Moses Jones and Lisa Prescott.

"Zach will be making trips to Shanghai if this deal goes through," the young woman said. "I told him I'd like to stow away, carry his suitcase, do anything to see that part of the world."

"What did he say to that?"

"Oh, you know how he is," she gushed. "He pulled on that cute ponytail and smiled."

"DID YOU GET THE CASE TAKEN CARE OF?" Julie asked lightly when I entered the library a few minutes later. "Joel is going to the cocktail reception at Mr. Carpenter's house tonight. I want you to meet him, but promise you won't say anything goofy. I told him you were super-religious—kind of like my cousins in New York—so he won't be totally shocked."

"Has he told you to shut up yet?" I asked.

"No, don't be silly. He's a great conversationalist, especially for a guy. He said more in thirty minutes than Vinny has all summer. Not that I'm trying to dump on Vinny, but you know what I mean. What happened in your case?"

"Judge Howell accepted the plea agreement. Moses is free."

"Awesome. I know that's a relief. What about the little girl? What did you find out?"

"That he didn't do anything criminal. He tried to help her."

"How sweet. Oh, I almost forgot." Julie pointed to a fresh folder on my side of the table. "Bob Kettleson's secretary left that for you. She says he wants an answer Monday morning."

I sat down and flipped open the folder. Fortunately, the problem was in an area of civil procedure familiar to me. I spent the next forty-five minutes documenting what I knew to be true. The memo could be typed first thing Monday morning.

Julie looked at her watch. "Listen, do you think we could sneak away early? I'd like some extra time to get ready for the party."

"Why don't you go ahead. I'd like to get a head start on this memo. I can just walk to Mrs. Fairmont's." I didn't want to get into a big discussion with Julie about it, but I really didn't plan on attending the party.

The door opened, and I looked up to see Vince entering the library. Julie greeted him first.

"Tell me everything that happened in court today. Tami made it sound so vanilla that I know she's holding out on me. She is absolutely the worst liar on the planet."

Vince looked at me.

"I didn't lie," I answered.

"But I didn't get the truth, the whole truth, and nothing but the truth," Julie responded.

"I don't have time now," Vince replied. "I broke away from a meeting for a couple of minutes. Maybe we can talk tonight at Mr. Carpenter's house."

"That won't work. I'll be with Joel at the party, and he's not within the attorney/client relationship."

"We'll get alone for a few minutes and make him jealous," Vince answered.

"Where did that come from?" Julie asked. "But it's a great idea."

Vince looked at me. "Would you like me to pick you up?"

"I'm not sure that I'm going to make—"

"You'll be there," Julie interrupted. "I'm sure there will be fancy flavors of water for the nondrinkers in the crowd. You might even have time to witness to Ned before he tosses down too many martinis. If anyone needs to repent, he's it."

"I wish you would go, Tami," Vince added. "I'd really like to talk to you about something."

"If I go, it's only a few blocks from Mrs. Fairmont's house. I can walk."

"Pick her up at seven thirty," Julie cut in. "Cinderella never walks to the ball; she always arrives in a coach."

Vince held out his hands, palms up.

"Okay," I replied with a smile. "I'll see you at seven thirty. Do you know where I'm staying?"

"Of course he does," Julie answered. "He's been stalking you since day one."

"I know the house," Vince said.

After Vince left, Julie turned to me. "What are you going to wear? This is a dressy occasion."

"Maybe the blue suit I wore the first day of work."

Julie rolled her eyes. "I'm not saying you need to buy a strapless cocktail dress, but please don't wear something frumpy. I'd offer to go shopping with you, but that would destroy our friendship."

After a moment of rare silence, Julie asked, "So, is Vince the front-runner?"

"I'm not sure if either he or Zach is a runner."

Shaking her head, Julie expelled an exaggerated sigh.

I WENT UPSTAIRS to see Gerry Patrick and knocked on the door frame.

"Come in," she said, looking up from her desk.

"I need to buy a dress for the party tonight at Mr. Carpenter's house. Any suggestions?"

"Waiting till the last minute, aren't you?"

"Yes ma'am."

The office manager tapped her pen against a legal pad, then began writing. She tore out the sheet and handed it to me.

"Use the firm car. You can just bring it back on Monday. Tell Marie I sent you. She knows how to make modest Jewish girls look classy; she can do the same for you."

An hour later, I left the shop with a beautiful pale green dress that, while not hugging my figure too closely, didn't deny the fact that I was a woman. Mama wasn't there to judge it. I was on my own.

CHRISTINE BARTLETT'S CAR was parked along the curb when I arrived at Mrs. Fairmont's house.

Flip didn't greet me in the foyer. With Mrs. Bartlett present, I suspected the little dog had been banished to the basement. I found the two women in the kitchen. Mrs. Bartlett had fixed a late-afternoon pot of coffee. Mrs. Fairmont was sipping from a cup as I entered.

"It's decaf," Mrs. Fairmont said. "Guaranteed not to give me a brain freeze."

"Mother and I have had a great afternoon," Mrs. Bartlett chimed in. "It's been like old times. We went to a cute place for a mid-afternoon snack but wanted home-brewed coffee. Did you have a nice day at work?"

I smiled. "That wouldn't be the word I'd use to sum it up, but all's well that ends well."

"That's somewhere in the Bible, isn't it?" Mrs. Bartlett asked.

"No ma'am. It's John Heywood. He lived in England a generation before Shakespeare."

"Did your mother teach you that at home?" Mrs. Bartlett asked, her eyes slightly buggy.

"Yes ma'am, and a lot more."

"Amazing."

I poured a drink of water and leaned against the counter. "Have either of you heard of the Lisa Prescott Foundation?" I asked.

"Of course," Mrs. Bartlett replied. "It made a big gift toward the new pediatric wing of the hospital a few years ago. I think it only supports projects that will benefit children. Mother, who runs that foundation?"

"Sam Braddock and Floyd Carpenter's son are involved," Mrs. Fairmont answered. "Which makes sense given the family connections. Was it mentioned in the newspaper articles you found in the box downstairs?"

"No ma'am, but I wish it had been."

Mrs. Bartlett stepped closer and lowered her voice. "What else have you found out about Lisa? Mother says you promised to fill her in on the details of a new investigation into her death as soon as possible."

"I'm not the person who can answer that question. My role in the case is over without anything to report."

"Drat," Mrs. Bartlett said. "It's not often I have a chance for a scoop guaranteed to be ahead of everyone else in the city. The whole mystery came up Monday at my bridge club, and I promised to get back to everyone."

"Tell them about the foundation," I suggested.

"That's old news, but I'll come up with something." Mrs. Bartlett placed her coffee cup on the kitchen counter. "Mother is going to eat dinner with Ken and me tomorrow evening. Will you join us?"

It was a nice gesture and made me feel less like the hired help. "Thank you, but this has been a long week, and I'm going to rest up this weekend. I'll stay here and take care of Flip. Is he downstairs now?"

"Yes," Mrs. Fairmont answered, giving her daughter a resentful look. "We'll set him free when Christine leaves."

A few minutes later as Mrs. Fairmont walked out on the front porch to bid her daughter good-bye, I liberated Flip. He rewarded me with a backward somersault that I rated ten out of a possible ten.

I DIDN'T SAY ANYTHING to Mrs. Fairmont about the party at supper, but when she saw me come upstairs wearing the dress, she immediately insisted I wear a necklace.

"And it will look better if you put your hair up," she added. "How long will it take you to do that?"

"Five minutes."

I returned with my hair caught up behind my head.

"No," she said after making me turn around several times. "I was wrong. Leave it down until your wedding."

I brushed out my hair. At seven thirty the doorbell chimed, and Flip raced into the foyer. I picked up the dog and opened the door.

"This is Flip," I said. "Can he join us?"

Vince stared at me.

"Come in and meet Mrs. Fairmont," I said after an awkward pause.

Mrs. Fairmont and Vince chatted about Charleston for a few minutes. Vince held the door open for me as I got into the car.

"We'll be there in a couple of minutes, so I have to talk fast," Vince said as he pulled away from the curb. "I totally messed up the Moses Jones case and led you astray. I meant well, but that's no excuse. Will you forgive me?"

"What?"

"You trusted me, and I let you down. It's as simple as that. When I saw that Mr. Carpenter was about to fire you, I should have jumped in and taken the blame, but I froze. It was a cowardly thing to do."

"But what did you do wrong?" I asked, mystified.

Vince glanced sideways at me. "You're nice to say that. And you look great too. If I hadn't fed you wrong ideas about the reason behind the memo from Mr. Carpenter to Mr. Braddock and sent you off to the microfilm records operating under a false assumption as to their motivations, none of this confusion would have gotten past first base. When you toss in the spin put on the conversation I overheard outside Mr. Braddock's office, there's no wonder you were confused."

Vince turned onto Congress Street. "Here we are," he said, turning sideways in the seat. "Before I let you out near the front door, I need to know you forgive me."

"Of course."

"Thanks. That takes a tremendous load off my mind."

"And park the car. We'll walk together."

He found an empty space around the corner from the large home. I'd bought new shoes at the dress shop, and the narrow heels made me wobble on the cobblestones. Vince put his hand on my elbow to steady me. I instinctively pulled away.

"I need to ask your forgiveness too," I said. "I dragged you into the Jones case in the first place. You were only trying to help me."

"I knew you would say that, but most of the blame flows my way."

We reached the house simultaneously with Bob Kettleson and a very thin woman whom he introduced as his wife, Lynn.

"Bob has enjoyed mentoring you," Lynn said. "He says you're a quick learner."

"Thanks. He's quite a teacher."

We entered the house, which was as lavishly furnished as I'd expected. Mr. and Mrs. Carpenter were standing on a silk rug in the foyer greeting their guests. Vince was immediately ushered into the living room by one of the younger partners.

"Welcome, tiger," Mr. Carpenter said, shaking my hand.

"Actually, I already have a nickname."

"What is it?"

"Jaguar."

Mr. Carpenter nodded. "Did you know they are the most unpredictable of the big cats?"

"No sir."

Mr. Carpenter turned to his wife, a tall, stately woman with silver hair. "Maryanne, this is the summer clerk I told you about. I've never seen anyone take the duty to zealously represent a client so seriously." He lowered his voice and leaned closer to me. "And coax open a rusty old memory that might have remained closed to a heavy hand. Come, I want to show you something."

"But your guests—"

"Won't miss me for a few minutes. Besides, I'm the boss."

I followed the senior partner down a hallway and into a paneled study. He pointed to a bookshelf that held a row of pictures—all of Lisa Prescott.

Placed in chronological order, they began with a baby photograph in a lacy bassinet and continued, one per year, to a pose similar to the picture in the newspaper. I spent a few moments with each one, imagining what the little girl was like, comparing her to Ellie and Emma. I reached the end and sighed.

"Thank you," I said. "It's sad, but it helps me to see more of her life."

"None of us knows the number of our days," Mr. Carpenter replied.

I glanced sideways, wondering if the lawyer knew his words were lifted from a Bible verse.

"And over here is a picture of the first board of the foundation," Mr. Carpenter continued.

On the wall was a picture of five men in dark suits. It was easy to spot Floyd Carpenter. None of the others looked familiar.

"Which one is Lawrence Braddock?"

"There he is," he said, pointing to a slender, balding man. "Sam

Braddock favors his mother's family and their much higher cholesterol count."

When we returned to the foyer, Julie and a dark-haired young man were talking to Maryanne Carpenter. Julie was wearing a revealing black dress that made me blush. She saw me and waved.

"This is Joel," she announced proudly.

The young man was wearing clothes that hinted at his artistic bent.

"Julie has told me a lot about you," he said.

"All positive," Julie cut in. "Let's get something to eat. I'm starving."

There was a rich selection of hors d'oeuvres laid out in the dining room. I could have skipped supper with Mrs. Fairmont. I collected a small sample of cheeses, fruit, and a pair of chicken wings that might have come from the processing line in Powell Station. Thankfully, Mr. and Mrs. Carpenter included a nonalcoholic punch option. Taking my plate into the living room, I encountered Mr. Braddock.

"You've been at the firm for weeks, and we haven't had a chance to talk," the portly lawyer said. "Although we did have a close call the other day in the parking lot."

"Yes sir. I'm thankful I didn't hit you. I was driving Vince's car. He was kind enough to loan it to me."

"Vince is quite remarkable, isn't he?"

"Yes sir."

"He's so much smarter than I am that it's intimidating," the lawyer added.

"I've felt that way too," I answered in surprise.

Mr. Braddock smiled. "But practicing law isn't just brainpower. Learning how to read people and discern their real motives and interests is often more important than the black-letter rules of statutes and analyzing judicial precedent."

"I have a long way to go in that department too."

"Really? That's not what Joe Carpenter tells me. I can't remember when he was as impressed with the way a summer clerk or associate handled a pressure situation. He says you pushed him so hard he cracked." Mr. Braddock laughed. "There is a boatload of lawyers in this city who would love to make that boast."

"The truth is—"

"That you're also very humble," Mr. Braddock interrupted. He pointed toward Bob Kettleson. "And don't think I'm unaware what you're contributing without getting credit for it. Keep up the good work, and we may be talking about a longer-term relationship."

The senior partner moved away. Vince came over to me.

"Did you impress Mr. Braddock without even trying?" he asked.

"Who knows? I feel more out of my league than I did as a ninth grader on the basketball court."

"That's not what everyone else thinks, especially me."

30

I WOKE UP SATURDAY MORNING, STRETCHED, AND RELAXED FOR a few extra minutes as I enjoyed again the release of Moses' burden. My burden, too, was lighter. As I lay in bed, I also reflected on the validation I'd received the previous evening at the cocktail party. It felt good, but I knew the praise of men was a hollow substitute for the approval of God.

After my morning run, I showered and brewed a pot of coffee. I tiptoed up the stairs and peeked into Mrs. Fairmont's bedroom. Flip, who was curled up near her feet, barked in greeting. Mrs. Fairmont opened her eyes.

"Can I bring you a fresh cup of coffee?" I asked.

The old woman scooted up in bed and repositioned her pillows. "That would be nice, and you can tell me all about the party while I drink it."

I'd just about finished my account of the previous evening when the doorbell chimed.

"Who could that be so early?" Mrs. Fairmont asked.

I bounded down the stairs and glanced through the sidelight. Standing outside with his black motorcycle helmet under his arm was Zach. I opened the door with a puzzled look on my face. "What are you doing here? I thought you and Mr. Appleby had a meeting in Mobile today."

"We were supposed to, but the representatives of the shipping company had to reschedule the meeting, and we ended up returning just late enough last night to miss the party." Zach looked at me and smiled. "Am I too late this morning to invite you for a ride?" he asked. "I know you like to get an early start on the day."

Parked at the curb in front of the house was the motorcycle with sidecar attached.

"I don't know," I answered. "Riding in the sidecar was a once-in-a-lifetime event, and I've already done it twice. Why don't you ask your secretary or Maggie Smith?"

Zach pointed to his watch. "What female besides you is up at this time on a Saturday morning having already run ten miles?"

"It was four miles."

"At least you're wide-awake." Zach stepped toward the door. "Do I have to enlist Mrs. Fairmont's help to convince you to come out and play?"

"She's still in bed, sipping her first cup of coffee."

"Then you've finished your morning chores. I promise to have you back before the sun gets hot."

"Can it wait until Monday?"

Zach pointed up at the blue sky peeking through the trees. "This is the day which the Lord has made; we will rejoice and be glad in it. Let's go or we'll miss a great opportunity."

"I know we need to talk—"

"And we will." Zach tapped the helmet. "Microphones."

Zach's charm, when he turned it on high, was a worthy opponent for my willpower.

"Okay, I'll tell Mrs. Fairmont. Where are we going?"

"To familiar places."

I returned with my bag packed, and Mrs. Fairmont's words to

have fun chasing after me. I slipped into the sidecar and positioned the helmet without assistance. Zach drove slowly through the historic district, providing tour-guide commentary.

"How did you learn all these facts?" I asked into the microphone.

"Until you started working at the firm, Tammy Lynn, I had nothing to do in my free time except study local history."

"Why did you call me Tammy Lynn?" I asked in surprise.

Zach turned his head sideways. I could see him smiling. "I'm not the only one who can research old records," he said.

We turned onto the highway to Tybee Island. As we increased speed, I let myself enjoy the ride. We reached the marsh, crossed the bridge, and turned down the sandy road where I'd been so afraid. Zach pulled into the driveway of the burned-out house and stopped the motorcycle. We took off our helmets.

"The marsh looks different early in the morning," I said.

"The tide is in; it's deeper water."

I smiled. We walked down the path to the gazebo. Zach sat on the steps; I stood between him and the marsh.

Zach reached down and pulled up a few straggly strands of grass. "I thought a lot about the Moses Jones case while we were traveling yesterday," he said. "Did you talk to Vince and Mr. Carpenter?"

I nodded. "Vince apologized to me, which was crazy but sweet. He barely let me get in a word of remorse. Mr. Carpenter showed me pictures of Lisa in his study at home last night and has no idea what I thought he was doing. He thinks I'm a tiger or a jaguar."

"Jaguar?"

"They're the most unpredictable of the big cats."

"And Moses? How did you leave it with him? I know you stayed behind after we left the courthouse."

I looked out over the marsh. Somewhere in the backwaters of the coastal rivers, I prayed, an old, almost toothless man was having a pleasant morning. Tears came to my eyes.

"It was wonderful," I said simply.

"Can you tell me?"

I sat down on the steps, and in a soft voice I told Zach what had happened in Moses' heart and soul, the unforeseen fulfillment of a promise birthed in my heart in Powell Station. He listened quietly. When I finished, we left the gazebo and walked to the edge of the water. The marsh grass looked more vibrant than I'd remembered.

"It's your turn," I said. "What is your evaluation of *State v. Jones*?"

Zach leaned back against a post. "There's so much you did wrong I don't know where to begin. But you hung in there with Moses past the point anyone else would have bailed out, and in the end earned Mr. Carpenter's respect."

I waited. Zach's eyes revealed more thoughts.

"What else?" I asked.

He leaned closer to me. "My opinion doesn't matter. Heaven only sees what you did right."

LATER THAT EVENING I called home. Mama answered.

"I finished the criminal case I mentioned," I said. "My client pled guilty and received probation."

"Thank goodness for that. It worried me that you would help someone who is guilty try to escape justice."

"He got justice and mercy."

I expected Mama to ask for details, but she wanted to move on. "Now that the case is over, are you going to be coming home for a long weekend?" she asked. "We really miss you."

"Yes ma'am. And I'd like to bring someone. Is that still okay with you and Daddy?"

After a brief moment of silence, she said, "Yes. Who is it?"

I'd known this important question was coming and had given it prayerful consideration. I'd imagined Zach Mays and his ponytail sitting at the kitchen table explaining to my parents why his family, like the early Christians, spent years in a commune sharing everything; and I'd wondered what would happen if Vince Colbert, his BMW coated with red clay, sat on the edge of the sofa in the front room and told my daddy and mama how he'd become a Christian in the Episcopal church.

I took a deep breath.

IT WAS PITCH DARK when Moses woke from his nap and untied his boat from Mr. Fussleman's dock. A neatly lettered sign on the gray post read "Reserved for Mr. Moses Jones—Trespassers Will Be Prosecuted." He quietly slipped the long pole into the murky water and pushed the boat downstream. Twenty minutes later, he let it drift closer to the bank. When he reached the right spot, he lowered the cement-block anchor and waited for the ripples to fade. Dawn was still a hope away, and he wanted to catch something fresh for breakfast. He hummed a note or two—with a smile on his face.

Moses wasn't far from the spot where he'd taken Mr. Carpenter. One Sunday morning the lawyer met him near the base of the new highway bridge and sat in the front of the boat while Moses took him to the burial place. Neither man spoke as the boat, like a funeral barge, passed noiselessly through the water. Trees along the shore had grown tall, died, and fallen into the water since Moses laid the little blonde-haired girl to rest, but he knew when he reached the right spot.

"This be it," he said, halting the forward progress of the boat.

Mr. Carpenter bowed his head for a moment, then placed a bouquet of fresh-cut flowers on the water. An invisible eddy caused the flowers to swirl slowly in a circle before the main current captured them and carried the memorial toward the ocean. The two men watched until the bouquet disappeared from view.

"She be gone for good," Moses said.

"Yes, Mr. Jones. And it's good that I finally know where she's gone."

"You ready to get home?"

Mr. Carpenter nodded. Moses pushed against the slow current toward the bridge. After a few minutes, he spoke. "That tall girl who isn't a real lawyer. She help me more than you be knowing."

"How is that?"

"She show me where to lay my burdens down and not be picking them back up again. That day at the big court, it change me forever and forever."

"Tell me what you mean."

And for the next few minutes a man with little formal education taught a man with multiple advanced degrees.

When they reached the bridge, Moses skillfully held the boat steady while Mr. Carpenter stepped onto the bank.

"Thank you, Mr. Jones," he said. "For everything."

"You be more than welcome. And if'n you need my help, I be here for you."

MOSES DEPOSITED TWO FAT FISH into the white five-gallon bucket. Breakfast was secure. Dinner still swam beneath him. He baited a hook and lowered it into the water. There was a slight effervescence to the fishing line that caused it to shimmer in his fingers as he played it out. He waited. A fish broke the surface. It was a top feeder. Moses leaned over the edge of the boat and peered into the dark water.

No images rose to terrify him. The faces had fled. Fear no longer held his future.

The water stilled and became a mirror to the few remaining stars. Moses looked up and tilted his head to the side. Sometimes, if he listened closely, he could hear a whisper of an invitation.

One day, he would rise to accept it.

Acknowledgments

Writing a novel is both a solitary and collaborative process. I greatly appreciate my wife, Kathy, who safeguards my creative solitude. During the collaborative stage, Allen Arnold and Natalie Hanemann at Thomas Nelson Publishing, along with Traci DePree (tracidepree.com) and Deborah Wiseman, provided invaluable input.

Reading Group Guide

1. In the Bible, a name change bears notable relationship to a life transformation (e.g., Saul to Paul, Abram to Abraham). What significance does Tammy Lynn's name change to "Tami" bear?

2. Compare and contrast life in Powell Station for Tammy Lynn with life in Savannah for Tami. What are her support systems in each? How are those lives different from her life at school at the University of Georgia in Athens. Where is she most alone?

3. Are all the standards of Tami's family faith as hard and fast as she believes? Discuss times when her parents were more flexible than she had thought they'd be. Discuss instances in which Tami makes allowances in her beliefs. Is this hypocritical or part of maturing as a believer?

4. Is Tami judgmental? Does her character evolve?

5. In what ways does Zach's shared background and beliefs comfort Tami? Likewise, how do their dissimilarities challenge or frighten Tami?

6. How do Vince's and Zach's differences with one another affect Tami? Which character holds the stronger possibility of courtship with Tami?

7. What accounts for Tami's relaxing the rules where Vince is concerned while she passes all considerations regarding Zach through her parents?

8. There are several biblical references in this book ("Joseph and Maryanne Carpenter," "Moses" in the river, etc.). Is there a "Christ figure" (traditional redemptive character)? If so, who is it?

9. How has Tammy Lynn's upbringing, background, and birth order prepared her to be a caretaker for Mrs. Fairmont?

10. Shakespeare frequently raises the theme of mental instability in characters vital to the storytelling process. This creates issues of doubt and trust with the reader. How does the question of Moses' and Mrs. Fairmont's states of mind affect this narrative? Are the most factually reliable characters necessarily the most trustworthy?

11. For all of her endeavors to do the right thing, how does Tami misstep? Recall instances of her not revealing the whole truth. How does her selective editing strike you? Is this an oversight or a calculation?

12. Who do you believe Tami brings home to visit her parents?

13. Deeper water can be more challenging to ford or more buoyant. It can reveal spots teeming with fish to delight fishermen or conceal corpses and frustrate lawmen. In what ways did this book lead you to deeper waters?

About the Author

ROBERT WHITLOW is the best-selling author of legal thrillers set in the South and winner of the prestigious Christy Award for Contemporary Fiction. A Fuman University graduate, Whitlow received his J.D. with honors from the University of Georgia School of Law where he served on the staff of the Georgia Law Review. Whitlow and his wife, Kathy, have four children. They make their home in North Carolina.